THE SENSATIONAL NEW VOICE IN EPIC FANTASY

"Excellent technique and a fine use of bountiful imagination. Even the minor characters come alive for the reader, and one must know what will happen to them. THE BARBED COIL is a book to be reread."

—**Andre Norton**

"Jones is one of the few writers [who] can take basic fantasy concepts and combine them with her own incredible imagination to create something truly original. . . . Everything about it is just wonderful, from the original plot to the engrossing characters to the speed at which you move along. Do yourself a favor and read THE BARBED COIL."

—*Explorations*

"J. V. Jones has proved that she is a writer to be reckoned with."

—*The Plot Thickens*

"Fascinating. . . . With the clean writing and crisp dialogue . . . Jones keeps events moving and the plot elements fresh."

—*The Magazine of Fantasy and Science Fiction*

"A superb novel, sculpted from colorful vocabulary and fantastic clarity [by] a brilliant storyteller sure to continue her dazzling career. . . . Read it, or regret it later . . . a triumph."

—*SFX*

RAVES FOR J. V. JONES, AUTHOR OF THE BOOK OF WORDS

"A highly successful, popular fantasy epic. . . . A substantial cast and a vivid, colorful landscape. . . . A remarkable epic."

—*Dragon* magazine

J.V. JONES

THE BARBED COIL

WARNER BOOKS

A Time Warner Company

WARNER BOOKS EDITION

Copyright © 1997 by J.V. Jones
All rights reserved.

Cover design by Don Puckey
Cover illustration by Mike Posen

Aspect® is a registered trademark of Warner Books, Inc.

Warner Books, Inc.
1271 Avenue of the Americas
New York, NY 10020

Visit our Web site at
www.warnerbooks.com

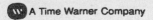 A Time Warner Company

Printed in the United States of America

Originally published in hardcover by Warner Books
First international Paperback Printing: October: 1998
First U.S. Paperback Printing: April, 1999

10 9 8 7 6 5 4 3 2 1

FOR BETSY

ACKNOWLEDGMENTS

I owe thanks and appreciation to Betsy Mitchell for her invaluable help and advice, to Colin Murray, Wayne D. Chang, Russell Galen and Danny Baror, Mari C. Okuda, Sona Vogel, and Daniel R. Horne. On matters of illuminated manuscripts, their painting and preparation, I am indebted to works by Michelle P. Brown and Janet Backhouse (though I must admit to inventing a few of the nastier preparations such as ground glass suspended in a binding mineral pitch myself!). And, as always, thanks to Richard . . .

THE BARBED COIL

he one who would soon be king ran naked through the woods. Night birds, night creatures, and night insects traveled with him through the vein-dark maze. Smells were sharp, the air was thin. The moon was a blade meant for cutting.

Tree roots thrust like fists through the soil. Tree branches cracked like whips as he passed. Everything—the faraway stars, the night-tainted clouds, the rain-moistened earth, and the beasts in the shadows—were his for the taking this night.

Five weeks before kingship. Five weeks before the start. Five weeks to prepare himself to do what must be done.

So much power in the number five, so much ancient and terrible magic.

The one who would soon be king turned his gaze to the west. The Vorce Mountains were spikes in his mind's eye. The last vestiges of snow on their peaks were a virgin's colors meant to taunt him. He would enjoy bloodying the mountain passes; thrusting through the time-worn gorges to the fertile land beyond.

Garizon had been too long without a saltwater port, too long without a shore to call its own. But then it had been too long without so much more as well. Crushed, defeated, subjugated, then forgotten, Garizon had survived on blood and dirt and bile.

Fifty years had passed since it last had a king. More than enough time for those to the west to die, or forget, or lose their minds to syphilis. More than enough time for Garizon to be styled "our grainfield in the east" and "our friend in times of need."

Garizon would soon be no one's friend in need. Garizon had needs of its own now. Pride had to be restored. Land had

to be reclaimed. A king had to be crowned with the Barbed
Coil of gold.

Fifty years of subjugation versus five hundred years of
conflict. The one who would soon be king smiled to himself
as he ran through the trees. The west had a short memory,
and those who failed to remember were destined to a fate far
worse than repeating their mistakes.

San Diego Union-Tribune, March 28

THWARTED BANK ROBBERS MAKE OFF
WITH SECURITY DEPOSIT BOXES

By Jeff Welz
Special to the Union-Tribune

A security officer was shot in the chest and approximately three hundred safety deposit boxes were stolen in
a break-in on Tuesday night at the La Havra National
Bank in Chula Vista.

Samuel Ossaco, 46, is listed in critical condition at
Scripps Memorial Hospital. He was able to alert the police approximately forty minutes after the robbers left the
scene by setting off a manual alarm. All telephone lines
appear to have been cut before the break-in.

The robbers attempted to gain access to the main
holding safe by using a mini-incendiary device. Police
speculate they broke into the security deposit vault after
this attempt failed. As yet there are no leads.

"This is a very professional job," said Lt. Jamie Per-
alla of the Special Investigation Division. "These men
knew what they were doing. They knew which lines to
cut, they knew where all the alarm devices were situated.
They came fully equipped."

George Bonnaheim, president of the bank, has offered a $10,000 reward for tips leading to the recovery of
the security deposit boxes. "These thieves have stolen
fragments of people's lives," he said. "There's no telling
what is in those boxes." (See BOXES on Page A-3)

$\mathscr{S}$ettling down to enjoy her breakfast, Tessa McCamfrey skimmed over the first few pages of the *Union-Tribune*. Headlines, photo captions, and advertisements were the only things she stopped for. She could see and read the smaller type of the articles and editorials, but she didn't like to concentrate on the characters for very long. Their size made her nervous.

Leaning over her white, laminated desk, Tessa grabbed her bacon sandwich from its place by the phone. As always before she bit into the toasted English muffin, she took a peek inside, checking that everything was just right. She liked to see the grain of the meat.

Satisfied, she took a bite of the sandwich, then flicked the paper to the next page. "Hmm," she mumbled to herself as her gaze flicked across the headline STILL NO SIGN OF THE MISSING BOXES. How long had it been now? A month? Six weeks? They'd probably never turn up again.

Just as Tessa threw the paper on the desk, the phone rang. Her body stiffened for the briefest moment. Three more rings, and then the brand spanking new Sony Deluxe Home Answering System clicked into action. Cassette wheels turned, appropriate lights blinked, then a voice that was not Tessa's own advised the caller, "Our family isn't at home right now. Please leave a message after the tone and we will call you back."

Tessa grimaced. *Our family.* She really should replace the prerecorded message with one of her own. Even as the thought occurred to her, she knew she'd never change it. She never could bring herself to do anything that needed to be done.

An efficient beep sounded and was quickly replaced by a soft male voice. "Tessa? . . . Tessa? Are you there?" A pause followed, and when the voice came again it had lost some of its softness to frustration. "Look, I know you're there. I'm coming over. We need to talk."

Tessa was out of her chair and pulling on her shoes before the last sentence started. The bacon sandwich was discarded, car keys located, pocketbook checked for, and wool sweater pulled over her cotton shirt. It was time to go for a walk.

Tessa hated those end-of-relationship talks. She hated the look in the man's eyes, hated herself for failing again. All her relationships had ended the same way, with the same phone call and the same recriminations and guilt. How could she tell the men she felt nothing for them yet couldn't understand why?

There *was* no way to tell them, which was why she spent her money on a series of successively better answering machines. She couldn't tell them, so she'd screen them out instead. And if, like Mike Hollister, they threatened to come round and confront her in person, she'd simply take off to the woods.

The southern California sun was brighter than Tessa liked. Despite the fact that it was now May and the temperature was in the low seventies, Tessa didn't discard her sweater. She always felt too exposed with just a single layer of fabric between her and the outside world.

Her yellow Honda Civic was a good friend. Unlike those faithless cars in movies that always stalled when the heroine needed to get away, the Civic purred into action the moment the key was turned.

Where to go? Tessa wanted to see some green. Not the chemically enhanced green of land graded and ready for building, or the clipped and cultured green of the Mission Gorge golf course. She wanted some real green. Some living green.

Turning the car onto Texas Street, Tessa headed north from University Heights and east on Highway 8, past lines of hotels, shopping malls, bowling alleys, and driving ranges. It was early Saturday morning, so the freeway was a breeze.

The sky was southern California blue: pale, cloudless, hazy. The sunlight filtering through the driver's side window was warm on Tessa's hands and face.

In some deep and secret part of herself, Tessa was glad to be on the run. It seemed the only times she was really happy in her life were when she was on her way somewhere. If she was lucky, there were minutes, even hours, when the anticipation of arrival was so overpowering that she forgot about everything except the journey itself. Without exception, when she finally reached her destination she was always vaguely disappointed. She never seemed to get just where she wanted to go.

As Tessa drove she was aware of a mild ringing sensation in her temples. *Shsssssh,* like fingernails scraped across a chalkboard. Tessa's heart slowly sank in her chest. Not now. Not today. She'd gone so long without feeling it, she'd secretly hoped it had gone. Pushing her foot down on the accelerator, Tessa tried to put some distance between herself and the noise. From experience she knew the longer and faster she drove, the less her tinnitus would bother her.

Tinnitus: a buzzing or ringing sound in the ear. Tessa had first been diagnosed with it when she was five years old, just before her family had left England for America. She clearly remembered sitting in the square stretch of grass that passed for their front garden in those days, pushing her fists into her ears and asking her mother when the "pinging noise would stop." It felt as if a tiny bell had been struck inside her head.

The noise went on and on. After a week the family doctor was called. Dr. Bodesill was a large, red-nosed man who smelled of port and had a peculiar fondness for wearing brightly knitted waistcoats. After much highly impressive "umming" and "aahing," he advised Tessa's mother that Tessa needed to go to London to see a specialist. Ten days later Tessa was bundled up in a thick winter coat in defiance of the heat, her hair was pulled back and her socks were pulled high, and she was dragged along to the station, protesting all the way.

Tessa liked the train. The rhythmic *thug, thug* of the metal wheels skimming over the track and the multipitched sound of the engine masked her tinnitus completely during the two-hour journey. So completely, in fact, that by the time they arrived in London Tessa was sure the ringing in her ears had gone. Just as they coasted into Euston Station, Tessa turned to her mother and said, "Mummy, the noise has stopped."

Tessa's mother had looked genuinely distressed at this statement: all the way to London, a specialist waiting to see them, and now her unruly and ungrateful daughter had taken it into her head to pronounce herself cured! Tessa's mother was saved the anxiety of facing the London specialist with a miraculously and most selfishly cured child by the approach of a porter with a loud whistle.

In all her life, Tessa would never forget the sound of that whistle. The train window had been rolled down since Stoke, and it was still down when the porter walked along Platform 4 and, picking a position less than three feet away from Tessa's left ear, blew sharply on his professional stationmaster's whistle.

The sound razored through Tessa's left ear, slicing nerves and tissue and membranes, setting her whole brain, her whole being, ringing with a dense clamor of noise. It sounded like a great metal machine clanging away inside her skull. Tessa remembered screaming hysterically and begging her mother to make it stop. Hours later she learned that the sound of her own screams had aggravated her condition further.

By the time they reached Harley Street, Tessa's mother had tied her daughter's hands behind her back with her yellow nylon scarf. It was the only way to stop Tessa from beating the noise from her temples.

The specialist, an otolaryngologist named Dr. Hemsch, gave Tessa a sedative, a glass of lemonade, and a teddy bear to hold during the examination. Over the course of the following hour, Tessa's ears were probed with light and cold metal instruments, her hearing was tested by exposure to a series of low- and high-pitched sounds, and urine and blood samples were taken by a plump nurse with cool hands.

Dr. Hemsch explained his conclusions separately to mother and daughter. Tessa would be forever grateful to him that he spoke to her first. "Tessa," he said, leaning forward and taking off his glasses, revealing blue and kindly eyes beneath, "you have what we call tinnitus. Now what that means is that you hear buzzing noises in your ears. There will be times—just like today when the porter blew his whistle in the station—when the noises will sound louder than normal. And other times when you'll hardly hear anything at all."

The doctor touched Tessa on her shoulder. "You and I, Tessa, are going to be a team. We've got to make sure that you stay well away from loud noises like the porter's whistle, because although we don't know what causes tinnitus, we know that loud noises make it worse."

"Can you make the noises go away?" Tessa asked, emboldened by the exciting thought of her and Dr. Hemsch being a team.

Dr. Hemsch looked her straight in the eyes. "I can't do anything to make the noises go away. I *can* do things to lessen their effects, and if the tinnitus doesn't get better on its own account, we will have to look into those alternatives together."

Tessa smiled, a little sadly, as she overtook a black pickup truck in the left-hand lane. She and Dr. Hemsch never did get chance to be a team. Shortly after that first visit, she and her parents had moved to New York. The tinnitus stopped sometime during the nine-hour flight and didn't reappear until seven years later, relegating the blue-eyed doctor and his cool-handed nurse to fond memories in the past.

The driver of the pickup truck hit the accelerator and roared past Tessa in the inside lane. As the pickup pulled ahead, Tessa noticed the bumper sticker I DON'T TAKE IT—I CREATE IT spelled out in bold, black script on the back bumper. Instinctively she eased off the accelerator.

She knew she drove too fast. She couldn't help herself. During the summer she learned to drive, her tinnitus reappeared, and she quickly discovered that the farther down her foot was on the accelerator, the more noise the car engine made. The best way to deal with tinnitus was to mask it: to offset the high-pitched sound in the ears with an equally loud but low-pitched external noise. The theory was that the two sounds canceled each other out. Which wasn't entirely true, but it did help. Sometimes more than others.

Spotting the turnoff for the I-15 North, Tessa guided the yellow Honda onto the left lane, slipping directly behind the black pickup. The brake lights on the pickup flashed the moment her car was in lane. Tessa's foot found the brake pedal. The freeway was clear, yet the pickup's lights flashed twice more in rapid succession, forcing Tessa to slow down.

The I-15 junction was a third of a mile ahead, according to the California Transit sign. As Tessa's gaze dropped from the sign back to the pickup, the noise in her ears sharpened. The brake lights flashed red again. Tessa slammed her foot on the brake. She felt the force of the seat belt pushing her back in her seat. The driver of the pickup smiled into his rearview mirror. He had a dark mustache, a double chin, and a small mouth crammed with teeth. Anger flared hot in Tessa's sights. She wanted to ram the back of his truck, ram it, then cut in front and slam on her brakes.

Old words came to her ears, though. Words of caution well worn from twenty-one years of use: "Calm down, Tessa. Calm down. The doctor said you were never to get excited—it might make the noises come back."

A lifetime of self-control exerted itself over Tessa and she pumped the brake, forcing the Honda to fall back to fifty-five. The pickup shot ahead toward the turnoff. Tessa was shaking. Gray noise ground through her temples. Suddenly she didn't want to take the I-15 North. She didn't want to meekly follow the pickup truck, defeated. Palms damp upon the wheel, Tessa pulled out of the exit lane and slipped back onto the 8 East.

Angry at herself now, she felt the tinnitus growing worse. It was always this way: She wasn't supposed to get excited, yet the very act of not getting excited agitated her even more.

The Honda sped eastward along the 8, past clinics and strip malls, DIY warehouses, and apartment complexes promising "Free Move-in and Cable" on worn pastel signs. Back up to seventy now, Tessa tried to relax and let the engine noise soothe her worn nerves. She no longer knew where she was going. Mission Trails, with its old oaks and pines and its hiking tracks leading through shaded valleys and over sandy hills, had been her intended destination. Now she was simply driving east.

The incident with the pickup had left her shaken. Tessa tried to put it behind her, but the tinnitus—the ringing in her ears that appeared and then disappeared in sharp bursts throughout her life—was getting worse.

"Soothing music," her last doctor had said, "will help whenever the noises start." Dr. Eagleman had handed Tessa a cassette of something entitled *The Healing Ocean*, for which he had billed her $99 one month later. The cassette turned out to be a mix of waves lapping against the shore, threaded through with some tinny New Age music that would have sounded right at home in a small-town airport lobby.

Fumbling in the driver's door pocket, Tessa's hand closed around *The Healing Ocean*. She brought it up to the dashboard, took the cassette from its striped blue box, and yanked on the length of exposed tape. Streams of shiny brown ribbon raced through the spools and into the air. Holding the cassette firmly against the steering wheel, Tessa pulled and pulled on the tape until there was nothing left of it in the cassette.

The sight of the tape spaghettied on her lap made Tessa grin. Dr. Eagleman's *Healing Ocean did* have therapeutic properties after all—it had just taken her a while to find them. For good measure she tossed the empty cassette onto the backseat. Yes, she definitely felt better now.

The Honda Civic sped eastward past La Mesa and the sprawling expanse of El Cajon. Tessa, her nerves eased by the small act of destroying the cassette, risked turning up the radio. Something classical was playing—Bach, she guessed. If her father had been with her, he would have known for sure. Easing back into her seat, Tessa settled down to enjoy the drive. Hospitals, gyms, and furniture stores gave way to self-storage units, gun shops, and For Sale signs. The freeway narrowed to two lanes and began to climb up toward Alpine Heights.

Despite the fact that the Honda was speeding along at seventy, the shrill, metal ringing increased. The sound was close to the surface now. Tessa could almost feel it straining to break free of her skin. She turned Bach up a notch and deliberately shifted her thoughts away from the noise.

Mike Hollister would be arriving at her door right about now. Always polite, he would knock softly—even after he realized that she had run away on him. Tessa felt bad about that. She liked Mike a lot. He was a kind man, a good father to his four-year-old daughter, and he shared Tessa's interest in illuminated manuscripts. That was how they had first met—at an exhibition of medieval books of hours given by the San Diego Museum of Art. Mike was the curator. When Tessa reached out to touch one of the tiny, leather-bound prayer books, Mike had been the one to tell her touching wasn't allowed. The penalty was dinner with him and his daughter.

Tessa smiled as she guided the Honda around the twists and bends in the road. She couldn't understand why she felt such a great need to break up with him.

By turns the freeway wound then sliced through the hillside, offering dizzying views downward one minute and high walls of jagged rock the next. The way ahead was steep, and Tessa slipped into third. The gears screeched as they moved into place. Tessa winced. The noise in her ears sharpened to a high buzz. It sounded like someone screaming.

Why was it getting worse? She'd done nothing to bring it on. Since moving to San Diego seven years ago, the only time she had experienced the sensation was when she attempted to do anything that required great concentration, like filling out her IRS forms or attempting to copy a pattern that caught her eye.

Patterns fascinated her: Celtic jewelry, Oriental rugs, Victorian tilework, Roman mosaics—anything where shapes and forms repeated themselves to form a design. Whenever she came across a complicated pattern she tried to copy it. At some point during the process, though—when she became so involved that she began to perceive the strategy behind the lines and the grid beneath the forms, catching a whiff of the artist's intent—the ringing in her ears would softly start. Gentle as a pulse felt by hand, but a warning nonetheless. Tessa had long since given up trying to do anything too ambitious. She allowed herself only to admire patterns now or trace them idly with little thought.

Tessa yanked the steering wheel left. Her concentration had been slipping and the Honda had begun to drift to the right. A drop of sheer shadows had torn chunks from the roadside, narrowing down her lane and exposing a dark pine-wooded valley like a bed of nails below.

The buzz in Tessa's ears extended outward, forming a band of noise across her forehead. A needling migraine of a noise, a thousand times worse than any headache. Tessa bit her lip. Her eyes never left the freeway for an instant.

She was surrounded by a world of green now. Hills and valleys bristled with pines. Bushes and shrubs crowded close around the road. She hadn't been this far east on the 8 for nearly a decade. If she remembered correctly, the freeway led through the center of the Cleveland National Forest. By the looks of all these trees she must be getting close.

A sign on the left of the road welcomed Tessa to Alpine. The population was offered beneath, but Tessa couldn't take in the numbers. The tinnitus was a serrated blade cutting through her thoughts.

Something flashed red in her lap. Glancing down at the ribbons of cassette tape still coiled there, Tessa saw a drop of blood soaking into the fabric of her jeans. Quickly she wiped her chin with the back of her hand. The skin came back bloody. She had bit right through her lip.

She knew she should stop. Pull into one of the quaint wayside restaurants with wooden eaves and old-world signs promising fresh pies and hot coffee, and rest. Take a couple of Tylenol, massage her aching temples, close her eyes, and wait until the noises subsided.

Tessa didn't stop, though. The distance between knowing what was best and *doing* what was best was growing longer with every second. The ringing in her ears was no longer an irritant, it was a crowbar driving a wedge between reason and action.

The Honda sped through Alpine and into the wooded hills beyond.

Tessa felt as if the tinnitus were driving the car for her. Bends were taken sharply, motor homes were passed with rallylike precision. Accelerate, brake, turn. Tessa had little experience driving on mountain slopes, yet her hands shifted gears with the skill of an old-timer. When a turnoff came, she took it without question. With her thoughts ripped to shreds by screaming sirens, questions were the last thing on her mind.

She drove and drove. No longer on the freeway, Tessa wound inward toward the heart of the forest. The paved road gave way to a dirt road and then deteriorated to a hunting track.

Tall gangling pines formed armies to either side of the path, blocking out light and barricading all exits. Tessa had no choice but to move forward. When she glanced in the rearview mirror, the very forest itself seemed to have closed in across the road.

Noises hammered through Tessa's temples. Tears swelled in her eyes. What was happening to her? The noises had never been so bad before.

A grove of oaks and willows appeared ahead. The wide and sloppy trees looked liked a haven amid the disciplined pines, and Tessa, spying a fork in the path, steered the Honda toward them.

The temperature in the car cooled the moment she turned the wheel. Once in the shade, the light level dropped farther and midday took on the look of twilight. Tessa shivered. The dirt track flared out to form a semicircle and came to an end. Bringing the Honda to a halt, Tessa rubbed her throbbing temples. Blood drummed fast and hard against her fingers. She had to get out of the car.

The Honda door squealed as she opened it—another sharp ribbon of noise that bound the tinnitus tighter. The sound in her ears was unbearable now. Hardly aware of what she was doing or where she was going, she stumbled through the trees. The canopy of oaks and willows blocked out the midday sky. To Tessa's tear-glazed eyes they seemed unnaturally close to each other. On and on she walked, finding a path then losing a path, through brush and grass and trees.

The pain in her head was like a wire that pulled her forward. Her feet took steps that her mind had no part in, and her eyes discerned forms she was no longer able to name.

The terrible, unbearable noise defined Tessa McCamfrey. She was no longer a twenty-six-year-old woman with a job at Clairemont Telesales and an apartment short of furniture and attention; she was a child seeking comfort. And when she topped a small rise and came upon a cleared glade, she found what she was looking for.

Lying amid the yellow grass and long-dried-out bushes,

nestling in a collection of positions and angles, like playing blocks scattered over a nursery floor, were hundreds of dull gray boxes. All open. Their contents in small piles, flapping gently as their weight permitted.

The minute Tessa saw them the noises in her head stopped.

everic, counselor to kings, scholar of the ancient texts and master of the old patterns, slumped against his scribing desk, clutching his chest. A trickle of dark blood ran from his nose. Following the lines of his much creased face, the droplet slid down to his chin and then splashed against the illumination that lay beneath his left hand. Blood spattered both manuscript and skin. Even now Deveric was more than wise enough to know a message when he saw one. This would be the last pattern he ever scripted. His last and his best.

Five days and five nights he had worked on it, his old eyes squinting, his shaking hands stilled first by drugs and then by his assistant. Every pattern Deveric knew was encompassed in the illumination. Every rule had been adhered to, every interlacing of animal and plant life properly separated by the correct set of lines. Everything—the symmetry, the repetition of shape and color, and the mirroring of motif and symbol—had been perfectly rendered down to the last line and curve.

Great power had been drawn into the illumination. Enough power to tear through the magic of the Shedding. In that deeply creviced place, where the debris shed from all worlds accumulated as silently and inevitably as dust above a mantel, something stirred. Deveric had felt it building as he worked; each turn of his quill was a summoning, every scratch of the nib drew forth something extra with the ink. Patterns so intricate they defied the eye, paired with symbols of such weight that even to paint them seemed a kind of sacrilege, combined to make the illumination shine. Not with light, as the word suggested, but with truth and meaning and might.

The pattern, with its elaborate filigree of loops, shapes,

and colors, was a work of sorcery as much as art. Creating it had taken everything Deveric had inside him. His heart, his mind, his very soul, were now lost within the lines.

It was only fitting that his blood was now upon it too.

"My lord?" came a soft, hesitant voice. "My lord, are you all right?"

Deveric heard the words, understood the meaning, but was powerless to reply. His very old heart had beaten for the last time. The second the final curve was drawn, the instant the pattern was complete, his heart had broken in two.

He had done his job, drawn forth a chance for hope. The world of warm sunlight and cool evenings was lost to him now. It was a good life he had lived, with children and grandchildren and a wife who loved him dearly. If his sons had only been kinder, he could have asked for nothing more.

"My lord. Wake up! Please, *wake up!*"

Deveric smiled. Emith, the gentle man who was his assistant, whose love and loyalty could be heard on every breath and whose life for the past twenty-two years had been dedicated to serving his master, had no idea of the power that had just been drawn. The tanglings of the pattern—the strands that twined and retwined across the parchment, the shapes that chased each other around the borders, and the threads that brushed quill close yet never met—were the key to its drawing. Yet to Emith they were little more than lines.

Pain cleaved through the collapsed muscle that was now Deveric's heart. He would miss his old assistant very much.

All he could hope for now was that this final pattern, which in itself formed part of a larger pattern that he had worked on for the last twenty-one years, would do what it was scribed for: bring together those who could set a monstrous wrong to right.

Today a man would crown himself king of a country that lay east beyond the mountains. Garizon had been fifty long years without a sovereign—and with good reason. The ruling house of Garizon consumed land with all the mindless greed of a firestorm.

Even now, before the Barbed Coil had been placed upon his head, the one who would be king was looking to the west.

Deveric knew what he wanted. He knew the nature of the man.

Glancing down, Deveric counted the specks of blood that had splashed from his chin. Five: three on the parchment, two on his hand.

As the world faded away, as his assistant fussed and pleaded and physicians and family were called for, Deveric did the last thing he would ever do. Turning his wrist so that his palm was facing upward, he smeared the two drops of still-wet blood on the back of his hand onto the parchment.

There.

Five drops of blood on the illumination. Five drops of blood on a pattern colored crown gold, sea blue, forest green.

House deeds, wills, stocks and bonds, war medals, marriage certificates, naturalization certificates, employee of the month certificates, high school and college diplomas, address books, love letters, hate letters, children's drawings, hair clippings, faded ribbons, photos, videos, and greeting cards. Tessa sat in the yellow grass surrounded by a spiked railing of pine trees and sorted through the contents of the security deposit boxes.

The papers and photos on the tops of the piles were fading with the sun. Those on the bottom, lying upon the ground, were damp and covered in blue-black mold. Tessa knew what they were the instant she had spotted them: the stolen security boxes from La Havra National Bank. Already she had seen enough to know that anything of value had been removed. There were no family heirlooms, no jewelry or currency. No cash, coins, bearer bonds, or gold.

The only things remaining were papers, books, and photographs.

Tessa was beginning to know the people who owned these boxes. The Sanchez family's box was a testament to their good-natured pride; all five of them smiled up at Tessa from photos of family reunions, engagement parties, high school sports galas, and Disney World vacations. A handsome family with wide brows and square shoulders. Their father had taken out a second mortgage on their house.

Lilly Rhodes' box smelled of violets. A newspaper clipping proclaimed her "Deb of the Season" for winter 1938. A second clipping told of how her fighter pilot husband was shot down over the English Channel in 1944. It showed the couple on their wedding day; Charles' and Lilly's shoulders touching as they leaned forward to slice the cake. Lilly looked like Rita Hayworth.

Gary Ubois was dead. His box contained a photocopy of his death certificate. He had been an athlete. Dozens of photographs showed him limbering up before races, crouching for his mark, running across finish lines, and holding up trophies to small but enthusiastic crowds. Neatly lining the bottom of his box was a single row of birthday cake candles. Nineteen. One for each year he'd lived.

Tessa felt like an interloper. Prying, reading, searching, then discarding, she rifled through everything within reach. She couldn't stop herself. She knew it was wrong, yet the sight of one more folded document, or a faded report card, or a last will and testament, was enough to send her into a frenzy of *wanting to know*.

These were her people now. She knew their legal status, their financial standing, their college grades, and their secrets.

Hours passed. The sun sent shadows circling around the glade. Tessa was blind to everything except the latest fragment in hand. By turns she was a detective hunting for clues and then a child scrambling for prizes. One married couple had their own separate boxes: The man had kept all his wife's love letters tied together with a satin bow. The wife kept Polaroids of herself nude with another man.

Almost in a trance, Tessa knelt forward and reached for the last pile. Fat with envelopes, legal pads, greeting cards, and computer printouts, it looked much the same as the others. Tessa had only one rule: If an envelope was sealed, she wouldn't open it. She knew it was a hypocrite's law but kept to it all the same. If someone wanted to keep something so secret that locking it away wasn't nearly enough, she felt bound to honor their wishes.

The robbers had opened most envelopes anyway. Certainly the larger ones that may have contained jewelry or cash had been torn apart, their contents thickened by shuffling hands, their once gummed flaps now paper curls on the breeze.

Take this last pile: almost everything had been opened and searched. Tessa sorted through the various envelopes. A company sales report, an adoption certificate and all the attending legal papers, a collection of fishing flies taped to bright yellow cards, and a series of old girlie magazines featuring fifties starlets in swimsuits and ostrich feathers. It was funny what people considered valuable.

In the whole lot there was only one envelope that did not appear to be opened. A long manila envelope that had somehow got wedged between the fishing fly cards and the adoption papers. Instinctively Tessa knew it belonged to neither pile. The envelope was too frail, too delicately colored, to fit in with the rest of the papers.

Glancing around, she checked the boxes nearest to where the pile had been. It was impossible to tell which document had come from which box.

Turning back to the envelope, Tessa spotted a thumbprint smudged upon the top right-hand corner—just where a stamp would be. She knew the mark well by now. She had seen it before on Lilly Rhodes' newspaper clippings and the Sanchez family portraits. It was the mark of a thief. The man who had pried open these boxes and sifted through their contents like a prospector panning for gold had picked up traces of ink along the way. His fingers bore the vestiges of all the documents he had touched. Greed-driven sweat had ensured the ink was stamped from deed to deed.

Tessa's own hands were cool and dry.

As she flipped over the letter, a gust of wind cut across the glade. The flap of the envelope lifted up from the gummed line. Something small shifted in Tessa's chest. The letter *had* been opened. The flap was merely resting against the seal.

Grasping the envelope by its top corner, she shook it open. Nothing fell out. Disappointed, she pried her fingers into the slit and looked inside. The shaded manila interior revealed no contents to the eye.

Something wasn't right. Tessa weighed the envelope in her palm: the subtlest of pressures was weighing down the bottom corner.

Excitement fluttered from Tessa's chest to her stomach. Grasping the envelope in both hands, she tore it in two. The paper ripped with an oddly musical sound, like the skitter of beads in a jar. Discarding the top part with the flap and the seal, Tessa turned to the bottom half and pulled it open. The late afternoon sun thinned to a buttery line and shone straight down upon the dark inner folds.

First glance revealed the usual creases and lines. Second glance revealed that the main fold running down the center of the envelope was oddly distended. Something was jammed behind it.

Tessa's heart was beating fast now. She tore the envelope a second time—right down the center. A spark of golden light flashed in the air, and then something very small yet heavy landed in her lap.

It was a ring. A golden ring made up of thread upon thread of precious metal, wound in an intricate design. Trapped behind the seams of the envelope, it had gone unnoticed by the thieves.

Tessa picked it up. Closer inspection revealed the threads had thorns. The ring was a miniature coil of barbed wire. As tangled as a pit of smoke-drowsed snakes, the gold didn't reflect light, it *sprayed* it. Tessa blinked three times in quick succession: it was difficult to focus too long upon the design. When a chill draft blew east across the glade, Tessa was braced and ready. For some reason she had been expecting it.

There was something here, something locked within the coils of the ring, and if she could only stop blinking and concentrate for a while, she would surely uncover it.

A faint buzz sounded in her ears. Unlike earlier, when the noise was high and jarring, this time it was a mellow rush: a seashell held to her ear.

Tessa turned the ring in her hand. The gold writhed in circles with neither beginning nor end. It was ancient—that much she knew—but the period and style eluded her. The basic design had a Middle Eastern feel, yet the interlacing of the threads was almost Celtic. The goldwork itself was so exquisitely wrought, it could only have been created by a master craftsman.

Tessa wondered how it would look on her hand. She wondered if it would fit her.

With the sound of a distant sea sifting softly through her

ears, and the last shaving of sunlight slicing light from the glade, Tessa chose to put on the ring. In the fifth hour past noon, on the fifth day of the month, in the fifth month of the year, Tessa McCamfrey opened her fingers wide and slipped on the golden band.

She didn't feel the barbs until the moment the ring was in place. The gold slid upon her hand like a cool-fingered caress. Down it went over knuckle and nail to the broad base of the joint. Only then did it show its teeth. Tessa felt a tiny pin-prick near the back of her finger. Then another, then another, then another after that. Within seconds her finger was circled by a ring of biting thorns. Somehow the barbs on the outside had turned in.

The pain was like nothing she had felt before. It was shocking, like warm feet on cold tile, or hands thrust under a scalding tap, but there was something more as well. She was reminded of medieval texts that spoke of exquisite, enlightening pain. She felt breathless, exhilarated, close to the core. She felt the old world moving away.

The sound of the sea grew louder, the light wavered once, then died. Blood formed a lacework upon pumice-pale flesh, as five golden barbs etched their secrets upon the bone.

Ravis couldn't understand why he'd missed his ship to Mizerico. He was not a man to overstay his welcome. And he never needed much sleep. Why, then, had he overslept, waking a full two hours past the crack of dawn? And, more important, why had *Clover's Fourth* seen fit to sail without him? Biting down on the scarred flesh of his lip, Ravis switched his gaze from the empty dock out to sea. He had to leave this city today.

After a moment scanning the sparkling blue water of the Bay of Plenty, Ravis spied a dark thumbprint about to disappear over the horizon. *Clover's Fourth*. It was the last he would ever see of his ship.

"Aye, my lord Ravis," said a dockhand, breaking into his thoughts, "they must have thought you were already aboard. 'Tis an easy mistake to make."

Two things struck Ravis about the man. First, if the ship had sailed an hour ago, why was he still on the dock? And second, how did he come to know the name Ravis? Raising his teeth from his scar, Ravis forced himself to speak calmly. "Did you happen to see the good captain this morning?"

The dockhand beamed, his teeth offering an eye-catching collection of texture, color, and gaps. "Aye, that I did, my lord. But you know Captain Crivit—never one to speak with the likes of me."

Ravis *did* know Crivit, and although he would indeed prefer not to speak with the likes of the man before him, he wasn't above paying for their silence. The dockhand smelled of fine berriac and the mountain-pressed, oak-aged liqueur sold in the dockside taverns for ten pieces a glass. The dockhand would be lucky if he earned half of that in a week.

Ravis took a coin from his scored-leather tunic, looked at it, then tossed it into the sea. The silver piece flashed once and then disappeared into the dark blue waters of the harbor. Satisfied by the sight, he repeated the action. The dockhand watched him with growing disbelief. By the time the third piece sank, the dockhand spoke up:

"My lord Ravis, if it's money you're wishing to throw away, why not toss it toward a family man rather than straight out to sea?"

A family man? Ravis sucked at his lip. Suppressing his impatience, he tossed a fourth coin into the water and said, "I'm looking for the truth, my friend, and I'm hoping the old woman of the sea will help me find it."

Comprehension dawned on the dockhand's pitted face. "The old woman of the sea had the tides to turn this morning, my lord. I doubt if she saw a thing."

Another coin in the water. "Ah. Then perhaps you watched the bay on her behalf?"

"That I did, my lord."

Ravis threw the next coin toward the dockhand, who caught it like a lizard snagging flies. For a man who stank of wine, his reflexes were remarkably good. "So, my friend, what did you really hear this morning?"

The dockhand bit on the coin before he spoke. "Captain knew you weren't aboard."

"And?" prompted Ravis, tossing another coin the man's way.

"No one knew where you'd got to. Captain ordered the ship to be searched, and when there was no sign of you, he upped anchor and set sail."

Things were becoming clearer now. Crivit *had* searched for him. So the good captain had genuinely not known where he was, which ruled out foul play such as sleeping drafts in wine but still left open the possibility of profiteering from a fortunate happenstance.

"Did *Clover's Fourth* set sail on time?"

"To the minute."

Ravis made a small hard sound in his throat. All his worldly goods—all his weapons, his possessions, and his profits from the last three years—had sailed off into the sunrise with that ship. By sticking meticulously to his sailing schedule, Crivit had secured himself quite a stash.

"Did anyone suggest they hold sail until I arrived, or send men into the city to look for me?" Ravis threw the dockhand a third coin.

Catching it, the dockhand shook his head. "First mate wanted to send someone into the taverns, but Captain said they didn't have time. Said the tides would likely turn at any minute and the ship would be stuck in the harbor for another full day."

Ravis drew a thin breath. The tides were a captain's best friend and his most often used excuse. Crivit had executed a perfectly legitimate robbery. Ravis knew he would never see his possessions again; they would be lost at sea, stolen by pirates, ruined by salt water, or eaten by marauding sharks. Any half-plausible excuse the captain could come up with.

Ravis kicked at the rotten, bird-limed timbers of the gangway. How had this happened? He never overslept. He had been drugged often enough to rule out that possibility— his head and stomach were feeling altogether too settled for that—yet there was no other explanation. He had not been knocked out, bound up, or seduced to the point of passionate abandon. Nothing to unduly tire or hold him. Yet here he was, an hour late for the ship that would finally have taken him a safe distance from this place.

Glancing over his shoulder, back toward the hazy blue-gray mass of the city, Ravis found himself shaking his head. Bay'Zell was about to run out of time.

"My lord," said the dockhand, idly reeling in the last of the mooring rope, "if you be needing a place to stay until the next ship south ups anchor, you're welcome to stop with me."

Ravis waved him away. "I doubt very much I could afford your rates, my friend. Anyone who drinks fine berriac for breakfast is bound to charge too much for me." After bowing to the man, Ravis made his way back up the gangplank to the quay. Truth was, his finances were now stretched to the point of breaking. He didn't need to weigh his purse to know that it held a good deal more silver than gold. And even that was scarcer following his stunt of throwing coins out to sea.

Well. That would teach him. Impressing dockhands with shows of nonchalance was a lot more expensive than it was amusing. Now he had some real problems to deal with.

He was stranded in a city that would see him hanged if they discovered who he was and what he had done. He had barely enough money to buy silence from a gatekeeper. And one hundred and fifty leagues southwest of here, somewhere in the jasmine-scented south-facing hillsides of Mizerico, a certain beautiful lady would be counting the days to his arrival. Doubtless she would have to count a few extra now. And she was exactly the sort of woman who hated to count and wait.

All in all there was little amusing about it. Later today, on the far side of the Vorce Mountains, Izgard of Garizon would crown himself a king. Now the people of Bay'Zell, the finest port and northernmost city in Rhaize, might think this no concern of theirs. Yet they were about as wrong as it was possible to be. Izgard had spent the last ten years planning the taking of just two things: the Barbed Coil and all the land that lay between Garizon and the sea.

Things were going to get very difficult for the people of Bay'Zell, and Ravis had no intention of being here when they did.

Walking along the harbor front, Ravis tried to ignore the fishwives pulling backbones from herrings and drunks drying out in the shade. The everyday sights of Bay'Zell made him uncomfortable. When the wind tugged stray hairs from its binding, he shoved them behind him like buzzing flies.

What by all four gods was he going to do now?

"Aagh!" A high-pitched scream ripped through the spring clear air.

Automatically Ravis turned his head in the direction it came from: an alleyway nestled between two inns. He knew the place well; prostitutes took their one-silver clients there. Two-silver clients were treated to a bed.

"Get away from me!"

Ravis had just decided to carry on walking—he was in enough trouble already without venturing into the notoriously dangerous world of pimps and their charges—when the second cry sounded. He was struck by the foreignness of the woman's voice. She might be a whore, but she wasn't a homegrown one. He had never heard an accent quite like hers before—husky, rhythmic, and oddly compelling—and try as he might he couldn't place it.

A small, hysterical gasp came from the alleyway.

Hearing it, Ravis glanced out to sea. It was turning out to be quite a day: for the first time in his life he had overslept and missed his passage, and right now, when he should be contacting the one man in the city who could help him, he was about to do something very rash instead.

He changed his path. Cutting across the cobbled road toward the inns and the alleyway, he felt for his knife. The movement was smooth, fluid, almost a reflex action. For seven years he had entered no taverns, brothels, private homes, or palaces without first feeling for his blade. Hard lessons had been learned the day his bottom lip was sliced in two.

Ravis stepped into the alley. Shadows fell on his back. His eyes took a moment to grow accustomed to the dark, but his body moved ahead of his sights. Out came his knife. The blade—sharpened every morning before he shaved or splashed water on his face—was pointing up. The pattern-welded edge was as dark as acid could make it.

Three figures formed a triangle at the alleyway's end. Two large bulky men and a woman, back pressed to the wall. Thrusting his body forward, Ravis drew zagging lines with his blade. The steel skin whistled as it cut the air. The largest of the two men moved forward to meet him. He was carrying the tanged, cross-guarded blade of an Istanian mercenary.

Ravis feinted to the left—a simple move designed to test the speed of his opponent's reflexes. As he pivoted his weight onto his left knee, Ravis caught a sharp whiff of the tanner's yard. Falling back into the space he had just vacated, Ravis took his opponent by surprise. His blade sailed toward the man's exposed right flank.

Even as the fabric of the Istanian's tunic parted, Ravis assessed the threat from the larger man closest to the wall. Lashing out with his right foot, he kicked the first man to the ground. Mud sliding beneath his boots, he swung toward the wall. The second man had bloody scratch marks on his cheek. Someone with very sharp nails had just raked through a portion of flaking, scrofulous skin.

Ravis toyed with the idea of marking the other cheek in a similar way with his blade. Toyed and then discarded it: far better to go for his throat.

Ravis worked swiftly. Moves were shaped by his body with only a passing bow to his brain. Keeping the injured man down with a series of hard kicks to his wounded flank, he struck out at the second man, sticking arm and shoulder flesh with his knife. Falling into the cadence of a well-rehearsed dance, Ravis did what was required of him, nothing more. No plays were wasted, no thrusts failed to bite. Everything was executed with hard-learned thrift.

Oh, he had been party to showier fights, but down a dark alleyway set well back from Bay'Zell's northern harbor, with two men attacking him and an audience of merely one, show had little meaning. Ravis could see no benefit in wasting his talents on the dark.

When finally he pulled his knife from the brittle bone of the second man's shoulder, he was out of breath and shaking. A gob of skin and muscle tissue slid down the wax-stewed leather of his tunic. As he turned around to face the third figure, whose presence he had barely registered during the fight, he worked hard to control his ragged breaths. Even in the dark he preferred to keep his weaknesses concealed.

"Are you injured, my lady?" The honorific was probably more than the woman deserved, but Ravis had known enough prostitutes in his time to realize that many had better manners than the finest court-bred maidens.

The woman pressed her slight form against the wall. She said nothing. Judging from the play of shadows on her body, she appeared to be dressed most strangely. By the gods! She was wearing men's britches.

Ravis disguised a deep breath beneath a mocking appraisal. "You're either a little too early for carnival, my lady, or your last client had a fancy for a boy."

"Where am I?"

Ravis was surprised by the anger in the young woman's voice. Most prostitutes were skilled masters at parrying insults. And then there was that accent again: soft, raspy, rounded. He tried once more. "Did someone drug you and bring you to this place?"

"What *is* this place?" The woman all but screamed out the words. In her frustration she stepped forward into the sliver of light that marked the alley's center.

Ravis bit on his scar. Hair the color of dark honey caught the light. Eyes spindled in black and gold flashed in anger.

"If you are not willing to tell me where I am, then you leave me no choice but to find someone who will." She stepped over the second man's body. "Thank you for saving my life, by the way."

Ravis almost laughed, but didn't. As every second passed he was less sure of who the woman was. She looked, acted, and spoke like no prostitute he knew. Someone must have brought her here either blindfolded or unconscious. Catching hold of the woman's arm, he said, "You are near the harbor front."

The woman pulled away. "What harbor front? What city? Why are you dressed like a man from a film? And why do you sound like a"—she struggled for words—"like a pirate?"

Ravis did laugh then. Long and heartily, his chest pumping hard against the lacings on his tunic. The woman looked at him with barely concealed malice. She didn't move away, though, he noticed. After a moment he calmed himself.

"I have been called many things, my lady, in many different cities, but I have yet to stoop to piracy. I would need a ship for that, and following a rather regrettable set of circumstances this morning, a ship is the one thing I definitely don't have."

Ignoring this statement, the woman said, "Please, just tell me where I am." She sounded tired now.

Ravis noticed a trickle of blood dripping down her right middle finger. The source of the cut was hidden by a ring of many-stranded gold. There was something vaguely familiar about the interlacings of the threads. Ravis felt a pulse of unease beat deep within his heart. "You are in Bay'Zell, in the kingdom of Rhaize."

"Bay'Zell? What language is that?"

"My lady, Bay'Zell is an ancient city. Its name goes back further than I care to recount at this moment." Ravis glanced at the body of the second man. "We must go now."

"Why?"

"Why? Because I have just killed two men this day. And I don't know about where you are from, but I assure you that here in Bay'Zell they skin men for less."

Ravis took the woman's arm once more, and when she resisted him this time, he didn't allow her to pull away. Marching her out of the alleyway, he checked the harbor front for likely witnesses. Everyone—the fishwives, the drunks, the passersby, and the dockworkers—were all looking ostentatiously out to sea. Which meant everything was worse than he thought. They all knew what had gone down in the alley and were trying, very badly, to pretend that they didn't. The good citizenry of Bay'Zell were famous for many things, but the ability to hold their tongues wasn't one of them.

"Keep your head down," he hissed to the woman, positioning himself so that his body was between her and the people on the street. There was little point in hiding his own identity now, but there was still a chance the woman might go unnamed.

"Where are you taking me?" she demanded.

"Lady, for someone on the run you ask far too many questions." Normally Ravis would find pleasure in issuing such a tidy reply, but the truth was he had no idea where he was headed. He just knew he had to get away.

The woman struggled to free herself as they raced down

the street. Ravis pressed his fingers deep within her flesh. She was going nowhere. He hadn't saved her just to let her get away. A foreign accent, a lack of basic geography, and a ring whose golden strands defied the eye were just a few of the things that intrigued him.

Ravis marched the woman on a course back toward the main docks. With rows of tall ships, mazes of rigging, and a fleet full of street girls and merchant seamen on the move, it was the perfect place to fall in with the crowd. Of course it didn't help matters that the woman was dressed like a boy. Ravis shrugged. The port city of Bay'Zell had seen stranger things in its day.

As he drew level with the gangway that had been so recently vacated by *Clover's Fourth*, Ravis spied the dockhand he had spoken to earlier. The man was sitting on the dock, legs swinging out above the water, an unstoppered flask in his hand.

"Hey! You!" Ravis cried.

The dockhand looked up, squinted, and then laid a palm on his chest. "Me?"

"Yes, you." Ravis beckoned him over.

Draining the last drop from his flask, the dockhand scrambled to his feet. He was dressed in flamboyant rags, like an actor playing the part of a beggar. His green linen britches flapped about his ankles, and his flour-sacking tunic was tied and belted with string. He scuttled forward quickly, walking with his shoulders hunched and back bent in the manner of a man twice his age. When he spotted the woman standing behind Ravis, he touched his forelock with exaggerated respect. "Good day to you, miss," he said, his gaze dropping swiftly to her legwear.

The woman opened her mouth to reply, but Ravis silenced her by scoring his fingernails into her shoulder.

A thin cry sounded in the distance. Other cries followed quickly. Ravis guessed the two bodies had been found. There was no time to waste. Turning to the dockhand, he said, "Earlier you mentioned you had a place where I could stay until the next ship sailed south. Take me there now."

The dockhand lifted his chin in the direction the cries had come from. "Matter of some urgency, is it?"

Ravis was losing his patience. Reaching forward, he grabbed the strings of the man's tunic. "Take me there now or I'll slit your belly where you stand and leave your innards for the gulls."

The woman gasped.

The dockhand nodded. "Aye," he said calmly. "If that's the way it is, my lord, you'd better come with me."

THREE

Camron finished the letter and then leaned back in his chair. His head ached and his thoughts didn't seem as clear as they had earlier. Clenching his fist, he beat down on the letter and the table beneath. There was no way to get around it: his father was going to be hurt.

Berick of Thorn was a great and noble man—everyone said it. Yet sometimes Camron thought his father was too great, too noble. It was hard to argue with a legend. Camron took a deep breath, then unclenched his fist. He had to believe that what he was doing was right.

He could leave right now, with no warning, retreating into the darkness like a smuggler rowing out against the tide. That wasn't his way, though. Disagreements were one thing, deception another. Camron smiled gently, but not without bitterness. Perhaps he had more of his father in him than he knew.

Uncomfortable with that thought, Camron stood and made his way across the room. Flinging back the shutters, he looked outside, searching for something, *anything,* to distract him. The lights of Bay'Zell sparkled to the west and Camron focused upon them with almost mad intent. He didn't notice the quill still nestled in his hand. He didn't feel its tip jab hard against his leg.

The letter was all but done now—it waited upon a signature, nothing more. Camron could imagine his father reading it, the parchment held only as close as his fierce pride would allow, the tendons on his wrists taut with the strain of steadying his grip. Only Camron knew just how hard his father worked to prevent his hands from shaking.

It was then, thinking about his father's courage—the terrible strength of his will now pitted almost exclusively against the slow wasting of his limbs—that Camron knew he had to deliver the letter himself. He owed his father that.

Back at the oakwood desk, he brought the quill to the ink. A drop of his blood gleamed upon the tip. Camron shrugged, dipping the nib into the silver pot and replacing the red bead with black. With a heavy hand he signed his name. Camron of Thorn. It was a formal signature, but then it was a formal letter: a notice of leavetaking and a declaration of intent.

Harsh words had been said earlier. Words that even now, hours later, brought heat to Camron's face. He loved his father, but things had been said and ultimatums had been given, and now there was no going back.

Camron shaved a portion of sealing wax from the block and held it in a spoon above the flame. Tinted by a complex mixture of sulfates and vegetable dyes, the wax had an unmistakable purple cast. It was the color of veins stretched over bone. Besides Camron and his father, only one other person on the continent sealed his letters with that hue.

When the wax smoked and turned to liquid amethyst, Camron let it spill upon the page. He stamped it with a seal that he kept inside a box, and then, just as the wax began to harden and bloom, he scored a *C* upon it with his nail. The sight of the crude initial made Camron frown. He hadn't sealed a letter that way for years. When he was just a boy, before he had been allowed to use the family emblem or colors, he had sealed all his letters with a *C*. His father had insisted upon it, saying he always wanted to be sure of reading his son's letters first.

Camron tugged his hands through his hair. Closing his eyes for a moment, he tried hard to find some peace.

There was none to be found. He and his father had moved too far apart, their differences were too many. Berick refused to move against the Garizon king. He wanted to watch and wait and *see*. Camron respected his father's judgment in all things, but he was wrong about this. You didn't watch a man like Izgard of Garizon, you destroyed him before he destroyed you.

Camron heard a faint sound in the distance. Smashing

pottery. One of the servants must have dropped a tray. The noise prompted him to action. Slipping the letter inside his oxblood tunic, Camron made his way down to his father's apartments.

Castle Bess was situated on the coast southeast of Bay'Zell. Like a crab, it nestled amid the rocks and tidal pools: dark, secretive, shielded. It was not an elegant structure like the manor house at Runzy. There were no gardens, or fountains, or dainty facades, no courtyards or shaded arbors or palisades. There were stone walls cut ten paces deep and foundations that bored straight down to hell. It was a Garizon-built castle in the heart of Rhaize, and there were a score of others like it along the coast.

Garizon had twice conquered and occupied Rhaize. Once five centuries ago in the dark, chaos-filled days following the breakup of the Istanian empire, and then again three hundred years later during the time of the plague. Fifty years ago they had tried again.

And Berick of Thorn, Camron's father and the person he was about to leave to his life of nursing stick-thin bones and muslin-thin skin, was the man who had smashed the Garizon forces at Mount Creed. Nineteen, Berick was. Nineteen, commanding a force of twenty thousand men. The Garizons had not been expecting opposition. The Sire and his forces had traveled to the lower south for the Shrine Wars, and Berick had been forced to raise an army single-handed. The Battle of Mount Creed was one of the bloodiest in history. Forty thousand men died over two days and a night. Berick had won a hard-fought victory, coming down from the mountain with less than fifteen hundred men.

Camron pressed his lips into a hard line. That victory had lain heavily on his father's mind for half a century. Only hours earlier, in the heat of their fight, when Camron had blasted his father for refusing to take action against the Garizon king, Berick had cried:

"What value is victory when all a nation's sons are dead?"

That was at the heart of the matter: his father's conscience. Berick lived every day with regret. Every night he dreamed of forty thousand corpses laid out upon the northern face of Mount Creed.

At nineteen Berick of Thorn had been a general. At twenty he was a diplomat, a politician, a man of peace.

Slowly Camron shook his head. Peace was a fool's policy now that Izgard was king.

Footfalls sounded in the distance. Camron tensed for the briefest of moments, then relaxed. It was the nightwatch taking their positions for dusk. A little later than usual, but then everyone in the castle knew that Hurin's normal punctuality was currently waylaid by lust. The captain of the guards was attempting to bed the plump, beautiful, and famously cool-shouldered Catilyn of Benquis.

More footsteps padded softly below. The tiniest of warnings pulsed high in Camron's cheek. The castle guards were not known for stepping lightly. Hurin insisted that all his men wear stiff, boiled leather boots.

Camron stopped for a moment and listened. Nothing. The only sound came from cooling beams shifting in their couchings. He hurried downward: something wasn't right.

He saw the blood before he saw the body. At first he thought it was a cloak—a wide flare of crimson spread over the bottom three steps—then he spied a pale hand trailing in the pool of silk. Camron's gaze traced the line of an arm up through the shadows to a torso of raw meat. The guard, a young nephew of Hurin new to his post this past winter, had been sliced open from throat to groin in a series of clean butcher's cuts. The skin and soft tissue beneath had been pared from the rib cage, then pulled back to expose the heart.

A ritual slaying.

Camron's stomach clenched shut like a trap.

Father.

The pulse in his cheek became a sharp, rapping pain. The world sloughed away to a single, desperate line. The distance separating Camron from his father's study was the one thing that mattered in the black pit that had become the night.

Camron moved with the savage intent of a madman. He saw, heard, and felt nothing unless it was directly in his path. His life was reduced to a series of doorways and passages. He had no weapon, no plan, no thought for himself: everything that counted lay dead ahead.

Distances were measured in heartbeats. Seconds passed

like jabbing needles through his heart. The sound of his feet slapping against the stone was the only thing he heard as he ran. Camron raced across the main hall and into the solarium beyond, down through the south wing and up to his father's apartments.

Two guards lay dead at the entrance. Camron's throat tightened. His gaze flicked from one body to the other. No ritual slaying for these men: crossbolts fired at close distance. Dimly Camron was aware of what that meant, but his hands were on the door and his mind was bent on reaching his father, and anything that had no bearing on those things didn't count.

"Father!"

Camron burst into the room screaming. A rancid animal smell, like bones left to rot in a lair, filled his lungs on his first breath. The blaze in the great hearth dazzled him. Dark forms moved around it like witches about a cauldron. A seam of blind terror shot through Camron's temples, sharp as a metal spike. He felt sick with fear. The room was crowded with light. The air itself was heavy as a blanket. Camron had to push his way through it like a diver through water. He had a knife in his hand—though he had no memory of where it came from—and he brought the blade forward to slice his way through.

A low, cackling laugh sounded to his left, and Camron whipped his head round. A face emerged from the light. Teeth bared, nostrils quivering, it was barely recognizable as a man. Even as a fresh wave of terror crackled down Camron's spine, anger rose up to meet it. This was his *home*.

Throwing his arms against the light, he beat his way toward the cackling face. The dark forms by the fire made no move to intercept him. Only bodies blocked his path. Camron stepped over men he had broken his fast with at dawn: Hurin; his second, Mallech; and his father's old servant, Bethney. Limbs were torn from bodies, entrails seeped from wounds. Drying blood sucked at the soles of Camron's shoes.

He reached the cackling figure. The light began to dim. Shadows and shadings began to reshape the room. Camron found himself close to a bookcase. The figure in front of him grew silent; now that recognizable forms were emerging from the brightness, he was beginning to look more like a man. Was it a trick of the light that had turned him into a monster?

All questions slipped from Camron's mind as he spied the body at the man's feet. The green robe, the gray hair, the worn leather sandals: it was his father.

Camron's throat closed. Breath turned to ice in his chest.

He fell upon the body. Tearing away his father's tunic, he clamped his fist against the open wound. Blood pooled around his fingers as his hand sank into the unresisting muscle below. Scared, Camron pulled away and began pumping at his father's chest, striking the rib cage with increasing force until one of the old bones snapped beneath his fist. Biting back a cry, Camron picked up the body and hugged it fast against his chest, smothering, shaking, then cradling—determined not to let his father go.

The figures by the fire began to move toward the door—heads bowed, their bloodied swords bounced light across their faces. Camron knew they wouldn't touch him. The ritual slaying by the stairs had been meant as a marker. Someone wanted him to bear witness to this carnage. Someone had exacted revenge and issued a warning and left one man standing to tell the tale.

The armed figures filed out of the room. Just men now. Just a room.

The one who had laughed walked away. When he reached the door he threw something down upon the rug. By the time the object landed the man was gone.

Camron held his father's head in his lap. With a small movement, he brushed the hair from his face. Such fine gray locks. Silver almost. Funny how he had never noticed just how bright his father's hair was. Camron swallowed hard. Closing his eyes for a moment, he reached for his father's hand. A childhood's worth of memories pressed against his thoughts, and for one brief moment he expected his father to meet him halfway.

The body in his arms was unresponsive. A tight band of pain ringed Camron's chest. The letter was a lead plate against his heart. "Dear father," it read, "I am leaving Bay'Zell tonight. I can no longer honor your wish for peace. I must take action of my own against the Garizon king."

Camron opened his eyes and saw a room sprayed red. He scanned the bodies of the three men he had known and respected before his gaze came home to his father. For the first time he noticed a knife in his father's right hand. Bone-thin fingers were curled around a blade tipped with blood.

Seeing it, Camron clenched his fists so hard they shook. Berick of Thorn had gone down fighting. This great man, who had fought wars in his youth and long-held beliefs in his prime, had taken up a knife and defended himself against his attackers. He was almost seventy years old.

Camron nestled close to his father's body, trying to press back the heat; he couldn't bear the thought of him growing cold. Only hours earlier, in this same room, with the afternoon sun slanting obliquely through the rosewood shutters, Camron of Thorn had called his father a coward.

"So where are you from, then, miss?" The woman, who had introduced herself as Widow Furbish, sister to the dockhand named Swigg, reached forward and touched the fabric of Tessa's blouse. "Must have come from somewhere fancy, with linen as smooth as that."

Tessa opened her mouth to say that the fabric was in fact cotton, not linen, then held her peace instead. She wasn't sure if the woman would know what cotton was.

"You must be a mite cold with such a thin stretch of cloth on." Widow Furbish walked over to the shutters and opened them wide. "Are you sure you wouldn't like to change into something warmer?"

A cool breeze cut through the room. Tessa shivered. She had been fine until the shutter was opened. "Do you have a shawl I could borrow?"

Widow Furbish shook her head emphatically. She was older and heavier than her brother. When Tessa had first met her, she was wearing an elaborately embroidered eyepatch over her left eye. Now the eyepatch was pushed up to her forehead, revealing a perfectly fine, if rather beady, eye beneath. "No shawl, miss. No. But I do have a warm woolen dress I could give you." As she spoke, she opened the second set of shutters.

The smell of decaying vegetables, rotten meat, and urine wafted up from the river below. Tessa took shallow breaths. How could people live with such a stench?

"Of course, I'd need something of yours in return." Widow Furbish waggled a fat finger. "Favor for a favor, as they say."

Tessa frowned. She had figured out some time earlier that the woman wanted her blouse. Sky blue with white buttons and a single breast pocket, it really wasn't much of a prize. "Very well," she said. "You can have my clothes in exchange for a dress."

Both of Widow Furbish's eyes narrowed, though the one that had been under the patch shrank the most. "All of them?"

"Yes, all of them. But I want to see the dress first."

Widow Furbish looked set to protest—her cheeks puffed out, her finger came up, and her lips shrunk ready for spitting—but after a moment she swallowed hard, made an odd pecking motion with her head, and left the room.

Tessa drew a huge sigh of relief. Alone at last.

She stood up and walked across the rush-strewn floor to the first of the windows. Her hands crisscrossed her body with every step: scratching, swatting, flicking. Mosquitoes buzzed past her collar and cuffs, and an acrobatic flea was busy hopping down the length of her arm. The place was crawling with vermin. Other creatures crawled up Tessa's back and inside her jeans, their touch as light as dangling thread. Tessa slapped at her legs and shoulders, flattening. She hated bugs.

As she pulled her left hand off her blouse, she heard the fabric rip. Damn. It was the ring. Its barbed edges had caught on the shoulder seam. She had completely forgotten she was wearing it. Carefully she freed the ring from the cotton fibers, working the fabric over the gold until she could pull her hand free. Her palm was still caked with blood, but apart from a faint itching sensation at the base of her middle finger, she felt no pain.

The light in the room came from a smoking brass lantern, and Tessa moved toward it to better see the ring. Sulfurous fumes caught in her throat as the dim mustard flame cast its glow upon the gold. What would happen if she took it off? Would she return to the glade?

And if she could, did she want to?

The last thing Tessa remembered of the forest was the smell of dry grass. She remembered it clearly because it stayed with her through the journey—or whatever it was that had brought her here. The sound of the ocean and the smell of dry grass.

There was pain and darkness, then light. There were separate instances like dots upon a page: pain, anticipation, and fear. Tessa remembered moving through each state—stomach hollowing, rib cage pressing lung against lung, eyelids like heavy coins against her face. She remembered the exact instant when the stench of the alleyway replaced the smell of dry grass. And then the very sun itself changed angles.

From west to east it moved. Not in one quick shift, but in a gradual turn. Tessa felt the sunlight pass from her right cheek to her left in a continuous, slow-moving arc. In all her life she had never experienced anything like it. Her body, her soul, and most of all her skin reeled with the sheer force of the shock. The sun never moved that way. *Never.*

Then, as the sun settled into place and new sounds slipped in with the sea, she opened her eyes.

Everything had changed. Seagulls shrieked above her head. Dogs barked, pigs squealed, geese honked. The smell of the place was overpowering. The sweet, sickly odor of rotting vegetation vied with the smell of the sea. Sunlight blazed across her face and the wind ragged along her body, pushing her blouse against her chest. Rats scuttled and bluebottles hummed. Tessa's head spun with all the new sensations. Her feet slipped in something that she hoped very much was mud, and as she tried to right herself two men approached. Seeing them, Tessa realized that everything hadn't changed after all. Men were still men. And strangers were still dangerous.

She stepped from the sunlight running down the center of the alley into the shade of the wall. The two men—one large and fleshy and one just large—stepped with her. Tessa shivered. The shade was colder than she expected. Keeping her eye on the two men, she moved back, using her ankles to feel the way.

When her left ankle smashed into a wall she knew she was in trouble. Spinning around, she came face-to-face with a dead end. Even as she turned back, she heard the first man shout:

"*Let's have her.*"

Tessa saw them coming for her. She saw them draw their knives. A fist of pure fear slammed down her spine, and in that instant she did something she hadn't done for twenty-one years.

She screamed.

A note high and clear came from her lips. It rose like a battle cry, cutting through rival sounds as if it were a blade. With it came memories of warnings long given and well heeded. *Tessa, remember the porter's whistle. . . . Don't get excited. . . . Stay clear of loud noises . . . and never, ever, scream.*

The two men stopped in their tracks. Finished, Tessa pressed her lips together. She held her breath. Waiting. It took her a moment to realize what she was waiting for: the ringing to begin in her head. Seconds passed. The noise didn't come. The only sound from inside was the rap of her heart. Something deep within her relaxed. There was no metal rasping. No punishment. There was silence where there should have been noise.

When the two men stepped closer, she screamed again. Words this time, loud and clear: "*Get away from me!*" There was power in her voice —she could feel it. Once again the two men hesitated. The fleshy man glanced sideways at his accomplice, waiting for a nod to carry on. Tessa had her eye on his knife, and when it swung toward her in a wavering curve, a short gasp of horror escaped from her lips. And then she scratched the knife-man's face.

After that things moved too quickly to track. A stranger appeared out of nowhere and attacked both men. Wasting nothing of himself as he fought, the stranger took no breath that wasn't needed, landed no blow that didn't count. Tessa remembered feeling blood spray across her face as the stranger flicked his knife clean between stabbings. She heard his teeth grind together as he moved in for the kill. It took him less than two minutes to dispose of both men. Tessa didn't want to remember the soft hiss of their flesh and last breaths.

When it was over and his knife was back at his waist, the stranger turned to her. His face was yet another surprise in a day brim full with them. Dark hair, dark eyes, and a full bottom lip with a scar cutting through to the left. He had the richest voice she had ever heard; low and soft, it seemed to come from the space directly behind his scar. Tessa had been about to tell him he sounded like an actor when she chose the word *pirate* instead. He sounded far more dangerous than any man on a stage.

A fact that was proven true only five minutes later when he threatened to kill the dockhand Swigg if his orders weren't obeyed.

The hour that followed was the strangest one of her life. Swigg took them on a journey through the heart of the city and into the fringes beyond. Up until that point, Tessa hadn't given any thought to her surroundings—fear liked a clean slate to work with—but as she walked down lanes piled high with refuse, pushing past small-eyed, angry hens and dogs nursing crusted wounds, the truth began to sink in.

She was somewhere else entirely.

Not in a different land, or a different time, but an altogether different *place*.

Bay'Zell, the man who called himself Ravis had said. Northernmost city in the kingdom of Rhaize, greatest port upon the Mettle Sea. Tessa thought at first she knew these names—they were oddly familiar and sounded right upon the tongue—yet when she tried to place them, her mind came up blank.

The city itself was a dense, narrow-streeted maze of buckled buildings. White and gray stone structures, sinking beneath their own weight, were propped up by huge black timbers that wept turpentine under the strain. Strings of mist escaped from covered wells, and piles of refuse smoked as they decomposed. High lichen-corroded walls cut down the light, and brightly painted doorways and shopfronts shone out of the dimness like lit signs.

Tessa was overwhelmed. She couldn't take it all in. As Swigg led them through a series of increasingly busy streets, noises assaulted her senses. The jarring sound of metal hammered against metal rang in one street, the sound of sawing timber in the next, a huge market square was filled with the flapping and cawing of birds in bamboo cages, and on every other street corner young women wearing black lace hoods called out to passing men.

Nothing had any effect on Tessa's hearing. She frowned. Here, in this strange city filled with a carnival of noises, she had finally found some peace.

Turning to Ravis, she had said, "Tell me about Bay'Zell."

Ravis gave her a hard look. After glancing ahead at Swigg, he leaned close and murmured, "Bay'Zell is a beast marked for the kill."

Tessa shivered. Ravis' voice was cold. There was a glint of something hidden in his eyes. Unnerved, she pulled away. He made no move to stop her, and they walked the rest of the way in silence, feet apart.

Swigg led them down to the riverbank. Swarms of darting mayflies formed squalls across their path, while dragonflies and mosquitoes stalked beggars in the shade. The smell became unbearable. Even to Tessa's untrained eye, the district seemed to have taken a turn for the worse. Houses squatted close to the ground, shutters rotting on the hinge, walls crumbling to dust.

The river itself was more mud than water. Banks of gray-brown silt flared wide to either side. A stone bridge arched across its width, and Swigg guided them toward it.

Buildings crowded along the bridge's length, some leaning out over the river on stilts and others meeting in the middle to form tunnels. Swigg came to an abrupt stop by a door boasting the sign WIDOW FURBISH—FORTUNE-TELLER TO THE MERCHANT CLASSES AND SEAMSTRESS TO THE HOLY LEAGUE.

Widow Furbish promptly manifested her powers of foretelling by opening the door before them.

Tessa's first instinct was to step back. The woman was large and heavy, with a network of broken veins across her nose and a gold, embroidered eyepatch over her left eye.

"You're late," she said to Swigg. "And you've been drinking." Her voice was flatter than the floorboards she stood on.

Swigg shrugged magnificently, his shoulders reaching up to his ears. His gaze circled the sky like a vulture in mid-flight before coming to land on Ravis. "I have visitors, my little herring."

Catching sight of Ravis, Widow Furbish underwent something close to a metamorphosis. Her thin lips fattened to cushions and her eyebrows parted like gates. After a quick scan around to ensure no one was looking, she pushed the eyepatch away from her eye. "Aah, guests. Come! Come! Swigg, hurry inside and pour some arlo for our friends."

"The two-year?" asked Swigg.

Tessa, fearing the sight of slack eye sockets or sewn-up eyelids, had closed her eyes the moment the widow's patch went up. When she opened them again, she not only saw that Widow Furbish did in fact have two perfectly good eyes, but also that both of them were now trained on Ravis' kid-leather tunic.

Gaze rising from Ravis' tunic to the gold medallion at his throat, the widow said, "Let's open the seven-year flask."

Just before Tessa walked over the threshold, Ravis caught hold of her arm. "Tell these people nothing about yourself," he hissed.

Arlo tasted vaguely of apples, and burned going down. Until she took a mouthful, Tessa hadn't realized how much she needed a drink. Without a doubt it had been the strangest day of her life. Funny, but not once during the whole day had she thought she was imagining it all. Bay'Zell was real, Ravis was real, and arlo was so strong and biting that it could never have existed in a dream.

"My lady friend and I need shelter for a night or two,

madam. And your worthy brother was good enough to offer us refuge." Ravis bowed from brother to sister as he spoke.

They were sitting in Widow Furbish's parlor, a gloomy room with many cupboards. Widow Furbish filled Ravis' glass. Tessa's was also empty, but the good lady chose to ignore that fact. "Swigg takes after our dear papa," she said, fat fingers toying with the strings of her patch. "Hospitality nestles in the bosom of our family."

"You are both very kind."

Widow Furbish nodded with satisfaction, as if receiving the exact cue she had hoped for. "Just as you are generous."

Ravis showed his teeth. "Madam, I have already given your brother my last gold crown as a deposit. Would you demand the rest up front like a bathkeeper or a bawd?"

Widow Furbish slapped a large hand to her chest. "Sir, I am seamstress to the Bay'Zell Holy League. My reputation is second to none."

Tessa looked at Widow Furbish's big-knuckled hands. *Seamstress?*

"Madam," Ravis said smoothly, "I meant no offense. You are obviously a good woman who keeps a highly reputable house. Now, if you will excuse me, I must take my leave for a short while. I trust you will keep my companion entertained in my absence." With that he rose and walked toward the door. "Think of her as a further deposit."

As soon as Ravis left, the flask containing the seven-year-old arlo was returned to one of the many cupboards. Swigg mumbled something about seeing to his vats and scuttled out of the room before his sister had chance to object. Widow Furbish snorted but made no attempt to stop him. Having collected and counted all four arlo glasses and flicked an offending speck of dust from her sleeve, she turned her attention to Tessa.

"How long have you known Lord Ravis?" she asked, pulling up a high stool and sitting barely a foot away from Tessa's knees.

"Oh, it seems as if we've known each other forever," Tessa said with a dismissive wave of her hand. Dodging questions was a way of life for her—she had never felt comfortable talking about herself. There was so little to say.

The next hour passed with Widow Furbish questioning Tessa's accent, her marital status, her occupation, her relationship with Ravis, and her age. When the good lady failed to get the answers she required, she moved on to the subject of Tessa's clothing. For some reason she seemed especially interested in the blouse, and when she offered to swap one of her dresses for it, Tessa quickly accepted. She knew that if she was going to stay in this place, she needed to look like everyone else.

Which brought her straight back to the question of the ring. Tessa glanced at the gold strands glowing in the lamplight. Was she going to stay here? Did she want to? And, when it finally came down to it, did she have a choice?

Widow Furbish could be heard rummaging through chests in the next room, looking for a dress that would fit. Tessa had a feeling that the one she chose would be ugly, shapeless, and dull. Widow Furbish was not a woman's woman.

Frowning, Tessa crossed to the window. She wasn't sure what she felt about being here. Everything had happened so fast, she hadn't had time to form opinions. Bay'Zell wasn't some magical fairyland where everything was peaceful and pretty. It was a real place, with real people and real dangers. In the space of one day she had been attacked, rescued, marched through a city, and then left in a lodging house in lieu of a deposit. Events moved swiftly here, and Tessa had a feeling that she had somehow been thrown into the middle of them.

There seemed little for her to return home for. Her parents loved but didn't need her. Living close to a golf course in Arizona, they were just settling down to enjoy their retirement. Whenever Tessa called they always seemed to be on their way out to play bridge or a round of golf or to visit with friends. Tessa was glad they were happy, secure in the knowledge they were safe.

She had no friends to worry about, she never had. There was always a distance between herself and other people. She found them hard to judge, got wary when they drew too close. People called her shy, but Tessa didn't feel shy, just *reserved*. She had never felt free to make commitments.

Her possessions had never amounted to much. Her rented

apartment contained only the barest amount of furniture. Her wardrobe contained just a minimum of clothes. Even her car was over ten years old. There was nothing and no one to draw her home.

Nothing and no one.

Tessa felt a prickling sensation at the back of her neck. Against her will, she remembered the journey through the forest. She remembered thinking how she never seemed to get where she wanted to go. She glanced through the window to the city beyond. Had she finally got here at last?

Slowly, very slowly, Tessa's hand came up to grasp the ring. The outer barbs had lost their bite and her fingertips could press against them without fear of piercing the skin. Grasping the ring between thumb and index finger, she began to pull it off. Pain stung her bone as she twisted the band up toward the knuckle. Then, as the inner barbs broke free of the skin and the ring slid along her finger, Tessa felt a shearing sensation pass along her body. Noises, light as feathers, skimmed past her ears and a warm breath of air glided across her face.

As soon as the ring was free of her finger everything stopped. Tensed, ready for something she could neither name nor imagine, Tessa felt only relief when she found nothing had changed.

She was still in Widow Furbish's parlor. Mosquitoes still pestered and the oil lamp still smoked.

Drops of dried blood were set within the latticework of the ring like jewels. Their presence changed the pattern, making it easier to follow with the eye. The gold threads now had markers.

"Here we are! Found the dress. The color's a little wanting, but the quality of the fabric is second to none." Widow Furbish burst in the room, brandishing something that looked like a horse blanket. "Here," she said, thrusting the shapeless cloth into Tessa's hands. "Feel the quality."

Tessa closed her fist around the ring. Widow Furbish's sharp eyes caught the movement. "Very nice," said Tessa, speaking to distract her. "Very . . . er . . . durable."

"Durable! Durable! Why, this is fine Taire wool. Worth more than any fancy linen blouse from overseas." Widow

Furbish looked pointedly at Tessa's fist. "Worth over two gold crowns at market."

"A deal is a deal, Widow Furbish. The dress in exchange for my clothes. Nothing more."

Widow Furbish's mouth hovered like a wasp contemplating a sting. Her left hand plucked at the strings of her eyepatch.

"However," Tessa said, surprising herself with the shift of her thoughts, "if you can get me something to draw with and a clean sheet of paper, you can have one of these." Reaching up, Tessa unclipped a gold earring from her ear. She held it out toward Widow Furbish.

"Paper?"

Tessa thought for a moment. "Parchment, slate—anything will do."

"I've got a length of charcoal and a smoothed hide." Widow Furbish took the earring. "Though the hide alone is worth the pair."

Nodding, Tessa unclipped the second earring. "Bring them now while I try on the dress."

As soon as the woman left the room, Tessa opened her fist. She didn't know why, but all of a sudden she had a strong desire to try to copy the separate threads in the ring. It was the blood, she supposed. It gave the gold depth by adding contrast, made the whole thing easier to *see.* Tessa felt as if she could trace the lines to their source and discover the design behind the curves.

Quickly she shrugged off her clothes. With the shutters open the parlor was cold and she wasted no time pulling the dress over her head. The fabric was rough, but her skin had already been assaulted by fleas and dive-bombed by mosquitoes, so a little coarse wool was merely one irritation more. The dress didn't come even close to fitting. It was made for a woman shorter, plumper, and—Tessa judged—more thick-skinned than she. Briefly it occurred to her to ask Widow Furbish to take it in, but she rejected that idea. Despite the sign outside the door, the lady of the house couldn't look less like a seamstress.

"Charcoal. Bleached cow's hide." Widow Furbish reentered the room and handed over the items. Looking Tessa up and down, she sniffed with satisfaction. "Decent at last, I see."

Tessa ran her fingers over the hide: it was very rough. "Is there anywhere I can be alone?"

"There's the stock room—but I'm not lighting a fire, and I can only give you tallow, not a lamp."

Not really sure what tallow was, Tessa nodded. "Sounds fine. I just want somewhere quiet to work."

"Quiet? Why on earth would you want anywhere quiet?" Widow Furbish looked genuinely perplexed. She shrugged. "Ah well. Follow me."

The stock room was filled with bolts of clothes, pincushions, reels of thread, and ribbons. As soon as Widow Furbish left—mumbling warnings about touching the wares and pilfering the trim—Tessa placed the hide on a chest and knelt beside it. Tallow turned out to be some kind of candle, only smokier, and she brought the flame forward to better inspect the ring.

Knees resting on floorboards covered in hay, eyes squinting from the smoke, and palms damp with sweat, Tessa began to draw. The charcoal was brittle and inclined to break. The hide was rough and knotted; odd hairs from the cow still clung to the underside, and the flesh side was creased with lines. Nothing mattered. Tessa sketched on and on. Tracing and retracing, studying, smudging, judging angles and curves: trying to copy the ring.

She drew for hours. At first she was tense, waiting for the first telltale signs of tinnitus to reappear, but after a while, when the only sounds reaching her ears were the distant hoot of an owl and the creaking of cooling wood, she began to relax, letting her newfound freedom work its way onto the page.

FOUR

Are both men dead?" Izgard of Garizon shrugged off his crown of gold. Some kings, it was said, had bled to death after wearing the Coil. Izgard's skin wasn't even broken.

The scribe Ederius looked tired and ill. The moment he hesitated, Izgard knew something was wrong. "Tell me, my friend," Izgard said, bringing a hand up to rest on Ederius' shoulder, "what happened?"

Ederius was old and thin and silver haired. His flesh shook beneath Izgard's palm. "Sire, something went wrong—a miscalculation, a mistiming, a curve gone awry."

Izgard's fingers idled along the scribe's collarbone. "You wouldn't tell me they are both still alive."

"No, sire," Ederius said quickly, his whole body shrinking from the touch of his king. "One is dead. The raid on Castle Bess went as planned."

"And the son?"

"The son was left alive."

Izgard nodded, once. "Good."

They were in Ederius' makeshift scriptorium. Pots of powders, dyes, inks, and brushes huddled on trestle tables, scenting the air with a chemical tang. The largest windows in the fortress, cut barely a month ago to Ederius' exact requirements, were shuttered for the night, and three custom-made candelabras blazed in place of the sun.

"It was the first killing that didn't go as planned," Ederius said, his feet scraping softly against the bare stone floor. Rushes were seldom spread in a scriptorium—the vermin they harbored could distract a scribe during a vital penstroke, causing a break in concentration that might take hours to rebuild.

"I thought everything was in place," Ederius continued. "I was sure I'd done my part."

"What went wrong?"

"Sire, I do not know. The harras turned up as planned, but the man wasn't there."

"You were supposed to ensure he *was* there." Izgard's voice was soft enough to soothe a fretful baby. His fingers continued drumming along the scribe's left collarbone.

"I made the illumination . . . I felt it working. I thought all was going well." Ederius attempted to shrug, but Izgard pressed hard on his bone and wouldn't let him. "I was weary, and I had to draw a second illumination to strengthen the harras—we had to be sure they would defeat the guards at Castle Bess."

"So you rushed the first illumination?"

"No, sire. No." Ederius actually managed to sound indignant. "The pattern was a simple one. There was no need to rush it."

Izgard took a thin breath and said, "Let me understand this: you are telling me that you did your part and the harras did theirs? So how then did our old friend escape?"

"I do not think escape is the right word, sire. Just as I began the second pattern I felt something—what I can't be sure—but someone or something intervened on his behalf."

"Why then did you not take measures to stop it?" Izgard's voice was a whisper now. His fingers pitter-pattered along the scribe's shoulder.

"At the time I wasn't sure, I—"

Izgard slammed the heel of his hand into Ederius' collar. The bone split as easily as rotten timber, and it made the same damp, muffled crack. The scribe screamed. His hand shot up to his collar. Fingertips black with ink grasped at the knot of bone. Pigment pots rolled along the desk, some smashing to the floor.

Izgard drew his fist to his chest and held it there. He wanted to strike Ederius again. The desire was strong— stronger than the times before—and for a moment his whole body shook as he fought it.

The scribe collapsed downward in his chair, shuddering and crying softly. Watching him, Izgard was struck by the way the light from the candles shone upon the old man's skin. Ederius looked like a painting by one of the great Veizach masters. This observation calmed Izgard, and after a moment he trusted himself enough to reach out and touch the scribe. "Ssh, Ederius. Ssh."

The bone was broken. A jagged point pressed against the coarse wool of Ederius' tunic. Even as the scribe's eyes filled with tears, he let himself be calmed by his king, nuzzling his cheek against Izgard's palm and pressing his lips together to hold back cries of pain.

Izgard fought back a stab of regret, reminding himself that the man had deserved the blow. "The pain will pass," he said after a moment, touching Ederius' jaw to force him to look up. "You should know enough about my position by now to realize that I cannot afford to let anyone who fails me go unpunished." He waited for Ederius to nod. "Good. I will send the surgeon to you at once."

Izgard ran his finger down Ederius' throat, pausing to smooth a flap of loose skin that hung from the scribe's jaw like a yellowing leaf, and then walked across the room. The man's muffled whimpering accompanied him to the door. "By the way," Izgard said, spinning around upon the threshold, "I expect you to be back at your scribing desk by dawn."

He didn't bother to wait upon an answer. His point was made.

Izgard took a deep breath as soon as the door clicked shut. He was surprised to find himself trembling. When he first struck the scribe there had been a moment when he felt out of control. Something inside of him had not wanted to stop.

Letting the air roll out of his lungs, Izgard forced himself to shrug. His anger *had* been justified. Ederius needed to realize that things were different now. They were no longer friends. The time when the Barbed Coil drove them closer had passed. All those years spent planning, struggling, and fighting had finally paid off. They had both got what they wanted: Ederius had exclusive rights to study the Coil; and *he* had exclusive rights to wear it. Whatever happened in the months to come, neither could claim the other had stepped forward blindly.

Not liking where his thoughts were heading, Izgard swept them away with a snap of his wrist. He was king now. And kings had no friends, only servants.

Besides, Ederius would recover soon enough. Izgard had made sure of that: he seldom struck a blow that wasn't planned. A broken collarbone was painful in the extreme, but it wasn't seriously debilitating. In choosing the left side, Izgard had ensured the scribe would still be able to use his right hand to lean on and scribe as normal. The pain might bother him. Drugs were out of the question; they might slow his mind and impair his work, endangering long-term plans and sudden strikes.

Walking through the low, barreled passages of Sern Fortress, Izgard turned his thoughts to his coronation. It had been a simple affair: no processions, no fanfares, no show. Only those whose presence was absolutely necessary had attended. Lecturs, warlords, counselors, and enemies: everyone who held power was kept close. The ceremony itself was brief. The choir sung their prayers over the rumble of supply carts, the clerics chanted their blessings to the hammering of nails. Even the sacred oil had been anointed with haste.

Until ten days ago everyone had thought the coronation would take place in Veizach. The capital was the usual site for such stately affairs. Not this time, though. Matters of war took precedence over pomp.

Sern was a mountain castle. Hard as rock, plain as stone, impenetrable as the very mountain it clung to. Its walls had been standing for over five hundred years, and not once in that time had an invading force managed to breach them. The fortress itself had been hewn from the face of Mount Iviss. The ramparts had been known to sheet with ice in midwinter, but the north wind always passed them right by. No one could build a fortress like a Garizon.

Izgard permitted himself a small, satisfied smile. Useful though Sern's defenses were, it was its position at the foot of the Vorce Mountains that had lured him here for his kingmaking. Half a day's march from the Rhaize border, two days' march to Mount Creed: it was the perfect position from which to mount an attack.

It wasn't enough to be crowned king of Garizon—one

had to spill the blood of one's enemy to keep the throne. The thorns on the Barbed Coil bit outward as well as in.

And Ederius, old man and mystic, illuminator and scribe, was the one who would ensure each barb dealt only mortal blows.

"My lord," came a high, breathless voice from behind.

Izgard tensed. He was not in the mood for tears and childish tantrums tonight. He had meetings to attend, battle plans to finalize: war and the Garizon crown walked hand in hand. Without looking around, he said, "Go to your chamber, Angeline."

Light footsteps tapped a path to his heels. "Can't I come with you?"

Izgard felt a hand grasping for his. Pulling his own hand away, he hissed, "I want to be alone tonight."

"But, Izgard, Gerta said—"

"I don't care what that old maid of yours said. Leave me now." Izgard spun around to face his wife. Her pale child's mouth was trembling. Her pale blue eyes were already filling with tears. She was as exquisite and transparent as a jewel, and without her he could not have taken the throne.

Angeline of Halmac owned a third of Garizon land. This past year her family had been hounded by tragedy, and now only the womenfolk were left.

Last summer her father, the great land baron Willem of Halmac, had burned to death. Like many foolish men who spent their youths in the lower south fighting the Shrine Wars, Halmac suffered from periodic bouts of wet fever. During a particularly bad attack, his physician had ordered that Halmac be closely bound in brandy-soaked cloth to encourage sweating. Every night a cleric came and bound him, sewing the linen strips around his torso and his limbs. One night the poor man drew his candle too close and a lick of flame caught the cloth. The bandages ignited and Willem of Halmac was engulfed by flames. As the cleric tore off the bindings, Halmac's skin came with it.

Both men perished that night. Halmac died screaming in agony, while the cleric wisely killed himself, jumping off old Banas Bridge into the cold black water of the Veize.

Most said he got off lightly. In this country, where the

forests ran like rivers and the pastures curved more gently than a thousand open palms, land barons were second only to God.

Angeline's brother had died two months later. Blind, stinking drunk, he'd choked on his own vomit in a tavern in Veizach's Arlish Quarter.

The physicians called it a terrible tragedy.

Izgard called it fate.

A soft sob escaped Angeline's lips, stirring Izgard from his memories. She held out a plump hand, hesitant, like a child touching something she thought might bite. "Don't send me away," she said. "I get so lonely here on my own."

Despite everything, Izgard felt himself weakening. Sickened, he pushed her from him. Angeline's bottom lip trembled as she tried, very hard, not to cry.

Shadows flickered in the far corridor. People were heading toward them. Izgard's gaze shot from the shadows to his wife. He had no choice but to play the part of a loving husband. Even here, a hundred leagues west of Veizach and its ever-vigilant court, in a mountain fortress designed to let in neither enemies nor light, certain appearances had to be maintained.

"Come, my love," Izgard murmured, offering Angeline his arm. "Let us share a cup of wine before we retire." The words burned as they slid down his throat. He could no longer understand what he had once seen in his wife. What at one time he had admired as childlike innocence, he now realized was plain simple-mindedness, nothing more. Gaining possession of the Coil had helped him see that more clearly.

Izgard marched Angeline to his chambers, his fingers bearing down upon her arm. They crossed paths with two lords who knelt before them, yet Izgard spared them not a passing glance. Anger beat at the pulse points in his jaw as his eyes focused directly ahead.

Today he had been crowned a king, yet his queen was no more than a childish little girl. He wished he could be rid of her, but a suspicious death too soon after a marriage might result in the loss of both the Halmac lands and his crown. And he had worked far too long and hard bringing his country together to let one small act of personal satisfaction get in his way. Only when old scores were settled and new victories were won could he safely turn a dagger to her throat.

"You have to kiss me, Izgard," Angeline murmured as they approached the entrance to his chamber. "Gerta says we don't kiss nearly as much as we used to." Her breath plumed hot on his cheek and her breasts pushed hard against his side. Izgard felt his body respond to her touch and was powerless to stop it. Briefly he found himself thinking back to their betrothment. Had there actually been a time when he'd wanted her as much as her land?

Although the two sentries who guarded the door looked away, Izgard did not prevent his wife's tongue from curling down his neck.

By the time they were in his chamber, Izgard's anger was mixed with desire—Angeline still had that over him. Her hands cupped and caressed, assuming countless subtle forms. Her neck arched backward and her chest came up, and all the while, as her body twined around his like a vine around a tree, she whispered words of encouragement in her soft, little girl's voice.

When finally she drew him to the bed, her skirts up around her waist, her tongue darting across his throat, he was torn between the desire to crush the life right out of her and begging her never to stop.

"I'm sorry to keep you waiting, Ravis," Marcel said. "But I had some business to attend to in Fale."

Ravis raised an eyebrow. "Fale? Last time you left Bay'Zell was when the Great Fire razed the entire banking quarter to the ground. And even then you stayed within sight of the walls." Although Ravis had been waiting in Marcel's town house for over two hours, he kept his tone light. "Tell me, what business could possibly be pressing enough to drag you away from the city?"

The Bay'Zell banker filled two small glasses with berriac. Judging from the way the pale coppery fluid clung to the side of the glass, it was at least an eighteen-year-vintage. Well fed, well dressed, and well heeled, Marcel liked his creature comforts.

Just how much he liked those comforts could be seen in the furnishings of his study. Glossy bookcases and richly colored tapestries lined the walls, silver oil lamps shone from satinwood chests, and hide-bound benches strained under the weight of enameled boxes, gold-bound primers, and ivory figurines. It was well after midnight now, but even so Marcel traveled around the oak-paneled room, systematically checking that all the shutters were closed and bolted. He was a man who valued safety and privacy in equal measure.

"An old friend of mine died this morning."

"You have no old friends, Marcel. Only clients."

Marcel's mouth tightened only for the briefest instant. "Then we have a lot in common, you and I."

Ravis laughed: he wanted something from this man. "So, my friend, who died?"

Once, in a bout of maudlin brought on by the aftermath of heavy drinking, Marcel had confessed that he had yearned to be an actor in his youth, and watching him now, Ravis could well believe him. The banker put on a fine show of bankerly reticence, shaking his head slowly as he sucked in his breath.

"It might be a little indelicate for me to say."

So it was someone important. Ravis knew better than to betray his interest—Marcel would work himself round to a revelation soon enough. As long as his own plump neck wasn't in danger, of course. In matters of personal safety or enrichment, no one could be as discreet as Marcel of Vailing.

"Well," Marcel said, stretching the word into a dramatic introduction, "you know that old scribe who used to be the late sire's chief counselor before he fell out of grace?"

"Deveric?"

Marcel nodded. "He had a seizure at dawn. Terrible tragedy. He died right at his scribing desk. No one was expecting it—his wife said he had been in excellent health prior to the attack." The banker took a sip of berriac. "Of course the first thing his eldest son did was send a messenger into the city to fetch me."

"You hold his will?" The question was merely cursory. If you were a man of substance in Bay'Zell or its surrounding towns, you banked and litigated via Marcel of Vailing.

"Yes. He left his estate in a terrible mess," Marcel said. "Sentimental men always write the most preposterous wills. They make the mistake of trying to be *fair*, of leaving everyone something of value. Of course all that happens is that everybody begins to resent everybody else. One son gets a south-facing meadow, while another is stuck with a field that won't drain. The Holy League is bequeathed the family home, while the widow retains the contents. Squabbles start over land and property, and then, before one knows it, grown men are busy fighting over belt buckles and spoons." Marcel shuddered in mock distaste. "And it's all so unnecessary. A man should leave his property to one person and one person alone. Family fortunes can flourish only as long as they remain undivided."

Ravis clipped the base of his glass against the table. The words were too true for his liking. "So," he said, working to change the subject as smoothly as he could. "What did you bring back from your trip?" He indicated the square-shaped wooden frame that Marcel had been carrying as he'd entered the room.

The banker reached over his desk and patted the object. "Illuminations. The press prevents the parchment from being damaged."

Something half-forgotten turned over in Ravis' brain. He leaned forward, suddenly interested. "Illuminations, you say?"

"Yes. Deveric's assistant—Emith is his name—slipped them to me as I left. Apparently Deveric left them to him in his will and he wanted to be sure they were kept safe."

"Can I take a look at them?"

As a rule Marcel was hard to surprise, yet Ravis could tell from the subtle narrowing of his eyes that the banker had been caught off guard. "I don't believe you came here to admire works of art, Ravis. In fact, now I come to think of it you shouldn't be here at all. Wasn't your ship due to sail this morning?"

Some people might make the mistake of falling for Marcel's faltering memory act. Ravis knew the Bay'Zell banker never forgot a thing. He had over three hundred clients, and at any given time he could tell you the exact financial standing of all of them.

Ravis strolled over to the desk. Taking the wooden press in his hands, he said, "May I?"

Marcel shrugged. "Go ahead. See what you think. I intend to commission an appraisal of them as soon as possible. I have a feeling they may be worth something."

Ravis began twisting the copper pins from the press. A labyrinth of spiraling snakes and birds was carved upon the heavily waxed frame.

"Did you decide to sail at a later date?" Marcel asked, pouring them both a second glass of berriac. "Or has something come up to keep you here?"

One by one the pins came out. "Something came up."

"Business?" Marcel breathed a perfect mix of greed and fear into the word.

"No. I missed my ship."

A short laugh escaped Marcel's lips before he realized that Ravis wasn't joking.

Ignoring him, Ravis removed the last pin from the press and pried apart the two wooden layers. The acrid smell of fresh pigment rose up from the parchment. Straight away, Ravis could see it was the finest calfskin, stripped from the newborn before the flesh was marred by age. Lightly colored to begin with, the vellum had been further whitened with chalk. It was smooth to the touch, so perfectly scraped that Ravis couldn't tell whether he was looking at the flesh side or the hair side.

He flipped over the first leaf and looked upon the face of the illumination.

"In this day and age, Ravis, no one misses their ship. Why, the damn shrine bells alone are enough to wake the dead. Not to mention the cockerels."

To Ravis, Marcel's words were like so many buzzing flies. He was looking at something so complex, so exquisitely detailed, that his eyes couldn't take it all in. Ribbons of color spread across the parchment, forming a skin of shape and light. Animals with grotesquely long tongues and tails twined around each other in an endless variety of ways.

Threads of gold and blue and green wove through the pattern likes arteries and veins.

Ravis ran his tongue over the scar on his lip. He had seen patterns like this once before. Over two years ago now, in a certain well-built castle in the east.

"Very pretty," Marcel said, taking the leaf from him. "Done in the old Anointed style if I'm not mistaken. Of course there's little market for this sort of thing today. Nowadays collectors want to see people, not patterns."

Just as Marcel took the vellum from him, Ravis spotted several dark drops on the bottom left-hand corner of the pattern. It looked like blood. Something cold, like a freezing splinter, worked its way down Ravis' spine. Unsettled, he pushed away the rest of the illuminations, unseen.

Ravis decided it was time to state why he'd come here—he no longer had the stomach for small talk and games. He took a deep draft of berriac and then said, "Marcel, I need your help."

A smile so quick Ravis would have missed it if he'd blinked flitted across Marcel's face. The banker let the illumination fall onto the desk. "What can I do for you?"

Hearing those words, Ravis suddenly wished he were anywhere but here. "I need cash," he said. "A lot of it. *Clover's Fourth* set sail with all my gold on board."

Marcel nodded like a doctor listening to symptoms. "I see."

"Until I catch up with Crivit and force him to repay me, I have nothing to my name."

"Most unfortunate." Marcel's smooth finger rimmed the berriac glass. "However, it was a little naive of you to take the gold straight to the ship."

"No more so than if I'd taken it to the place where I chose to spend the night." Ravis abandoned all attempts at good humor. "I need no lessons in asset management from you, Marcel. I just need a loan."

"Yes. A loan." Marcel sat back in his chair. "What collateral can you give me?"

"I have just told you I have nothing." Ravis' voice was very low now. His hands sought out the manuscript press.

"What about Mizerico? Surely you must have another contract awaiting you there?"

Ravis shook his head.

"Friends? Lady friends? Savings?"

In one fluid movement, Ravis slammed the wooden press onto the desk. It landed just short of the banker's plump fingers. "Look, Marcel, I need cash, and either you're going to loan it to me or not. Now which is it going to be?"

Marcel's eyes hardened, but his voice remained calm. "How much are you looking for?"

"A hundred crowns."

Shaking his head, Marcel pushed away the wooden press. "Can't be done."

"I think it can." Ravis ran his tongue over his scar. The thick knot of skin burned cold in the warmth of the chamber. "You owe me, Marcel."

"*Owe?* I owe you nothing, my friend. I received and banked your payments while you worked in the city this past year, and that's as far as our relationship goes."

"I don't think the city fathers of Bay'Zell would excuse our relationship so lightly. They'd see your part as treason."

Marcel stood up. He walked over to the door and opened it. "I don't think either of us would benefit from the truth coming to light."

Ravis showed his teeth. "How many locks do you need to turn before you rest easy at night, Marcel?"

His words had the desired effect. The banker looked him straight in the eye, and although he tried to hide it, Ravis could tell he was afraid. It was obvious what Marcel was thinking: he was weighing up his risks, deciding whether or not he could trust Ravis to keep his silence. Moments passed, and then finally he said, "You have no future contracts, you say?"

"No."

"So I can presume you are looking for employment?" Marcel looked to Ravis for an answer. When one didn't come he said, "Of course, I could always initiate inquiries on your behalf, contact certain associates, make appropriate overtures—"

"You are not my pimp, Marcel."

"You can hardly expect me to loan you money without

surety. I must have some sort of undertaking from you that the amount will be repaid."

Ravis decided it was time to move toward the door. "You will get your hundred crowns back before the year is out."

Marcel made a hard sound in his throat. "If you live that long."

Reaching forward, Ravis flicked a stray hair from Marcel's tunic. As he moved, he had the satisfaction of seeing the banker flinch. "If you need to worry about anyone's neck, Marcel, I'd suggest you worry about your own."

Marcel's throat quivered as he swallowed. The door was already open, but he forced it even wider. "I think you should leave now. I'll see what I can do. Contact me in the morning."

Ravis nodded. It was never a good idea to push a man too far. "Until the morning, then," he said, stepping past Marcel and over the threshold. "I know your conscience won't stop you from getting a good night's rest."

Marcel opened his mouth to issue a reply, but a servant appeared in the hallway, so he kept his peace instead.

Ravis bowed and walked away.

There was not a corridor or wall in Marcel's house that wasn't lined with silk, and as Ravis made his way down to street level, his feet barely made a noise. Approaching the main hallway, Ravis heard voices: a servant girl asking a visitor if he'd like a drop of brandy to warm his blood and then the visitor's low-spoken reply.

Uneasy for many different reasons, Ravis checked for his knife.

He need not have bothered. As he took the last steps and the two people came into view, the stranger turned his face to the wall. Ravis had slipped in and out of Marcel's town house enough times to recognize the behavior of a genuine client when he saw one. Marcel was well-known for receiving attention-shy midnight guests.

Ravis waved away the maid and let himself out of the door. He was eager to be gone. Deep in thought, he made his way back to the river. His every instinct warned him not to trust Marcel, but he didn't really have a choice.

essa first became aware of an itch on her right leg. She ignored it successfully until it began to *move*. Her eyes snapped open and her head sprang up. Throwing off the blanket, she slapped at her thigh. Something black and shiny was crawling up her leg. Horrified, she sent it flying toward the wall.

A soft laugh caused her to whip her head around. Ravis stood in the corner of the room, his face half-covered by shadow. He gestured to her thigh. "You'd make a fine pikesman with reflexes like that."

Tessa drew the blanket over her leg. Her mind was still heavy from sleep, and the right half of her face was numb from being pressed against a floorboard all night. Blinking hard wake-up blinks, she tried to think of something scathing to say. Nothing clever came to mind, so she settled on an indignant snort instead. A bell began to toll at exactly the same instant as she made the noise, robbing it of any impact she'd intended.

Church bells. Her thoughts skipped from Ravis and how he came to be standing over her, to the stark reality of where she was: in a oak-timbered house built on a bridge that spanned a muddy river, in a city named Bay'Zell.

Tessa rubbed the sleep from her eyes, half expecting when she opened them again to find herself back in her bedroom at home. Instead she found herself looking at Ravis once more. Her stomach fluttered. It felt as light and hollow as a paper bag. All that had happened yesterday came back to her: the tinnitus attack, the safety deposit boxes, the alleyway, the fight . . . the *ring*. Tessa brought her left hand up to her face. The ring wasn't there. Panicking, she looked around the room. What had she done with it? Where had she worn it last?

"Is this what you're looking for?" asked Ravis, uncurling his fist to reveal the jagged golden band. One of the barbs had cut into the meat of his palm, and a fat bead of blood rolled between his fingers.

Tessa's jaw snapped shut. Hardly aware of what she was doing, she flew off the bench and snatched the ring from Ravis' hand. It was *hers*. No one else had a right to handle it. No one's blood should be upon it, only her own.

As soon as the ring was in her possession, its weight reassuringly familiar in her hand, Tessa began to feel foolish. Her breathing was accelerated and her cheeks were flushed. What had she been thinking? Embarrassed, she stole a quick glance at Ravis.

He caught her gaze and smiled, the scar on his lip growing taut and pale. "That's a very interesting trinket you have there. You caught its likeness well."

Likeness? Tessa was confused until she saw what Ravis held in his other hand. It was the sketch she had worked on last night. The patterns within the ring. For a moment she was overcome with the desire to snatch the sketch away from him too. Scared by an impulse she didn't understand, she forced herself to hold back. The act of holding back, of restraining herself, was so ingrained within Tessa that it was almost a reflex action. *Don't scream. . . . Don't get excited. . . . Always think before you act.*

Taking a deep breath to calm herself, Tessa dropped both hands to her side. What had she been thinking? What difference did it make if Ravis saw the sketch or held the ring? She was acting irrationally.

"There's something about this drawing that reminds me . . ." Ravis' words trailed away as he raised the sketch into the band of sunlight cutting into the room.

"Of what?" Tessa asked, taking the opportunity to smooth her dress and hair while Ravis' attention was elsewhere.

"Of something I saw last night." Ravis looked at her sharply. After a moment of silent scrutiny, he turned, rolled up the sketch in his fist, and handed it to Tessa with a bow.

"Make yourself ready. You're coming with me this morning. I'll wait for you outside on the bridge."

Tessa opened her mouth to object, but Ravis was already at the door.

"Don't be long," he said. "I have neither the time nor patience to wait upon a woman preening." With that he stepped smartly out of the room, letting the door bang shut behind him.

Annoyed at being ordered around in such a manner, Tessa glared at the door. No one had spoken to her that way in years, and she didn't like it one bit. What could she do about it, though? Besides Widow Furbish and Swigg, Ravis was the only person she knew in this place. He was certainly the only one who would help her. And at the end of the day, she *did* need help. She had to find out more about the city, discover where she was, how she had got here, and if there was any reason behind it. She needed Ravis for that.

As she thought, Tessa toyed with the ring, turning it in her hand and tracing her fingertips over the barbs. Although taking it off last night hadn't changed anything, it was still her sole contact with home. She couldn't let anyone else handle or even see it. She had to keep it safe. That decided, Tessa looked around the room for a suitable piece of ribbon or string. The best thing she could do would be to keep it tied around her neck, out of sight.

She had spent the night in the stock room, among all of Widow Furbish's embroidery paraphernalia, falling asleep on the floor amid a nest of rough blankets and thinly stuffed cushions. The blankets smelled vaguely of camphor and old dried goods, and the entire room had the dry, woody feel of an attic. Shelves crammed with all manner of materials lined the walls: bolts of cloth, reels of thread, wooden frames, and other odd-shaped things that Tessa had no name for.

Spying what looked to be a loose length of ribbon hanging down from a work top, Tessa yanked on the end, attempting to pull it out from the papers that were piled high on top of it.

The moment she pulled, Tessa knew she had made a mistake. The layers of boards, cloth, and parchment that lay on top of the ribbon slid off the table and went crashing to the floor. Black dust, lots of it, wafted up from the odd stack of materials, billowing over her dress and catching in her nose and her throat.

"Damn," she hissed, eyes closed, hands fanning the dust cloud away from her face. What was this stuff? *Mister* Furbish's remains?

"The pounces!"

Tessa spun round in time to see Widow Furbish burst into the room. Ignoring Tessa, the woman dashed over to the pile of papers on the floor, knelt, and began dusting them off. "You stupid girl!" she hissed, gathering a pile of the papers in her arms. "Don't you know better than to upset the powder?" Knees cracking, she stood upright and began laying the boards and parchment on the table. She shook her head savagely. "It will cost you, you know. I'll have to bring Bernice in to spread them again, not to mention the originals—looks like one of them's been cracked to me."

"What are you talking about?" Tessa brushed down her dress with venom. She was beginning to get tired of being ordered around and scolded.

Widow Furbish snorted. "The pounces, girl. For copying the embroidery patterns. Some of these originals are years old—cost the late Mister Furbish a fortune, they did."

Tessa, still unclear about what the widow was talking about, went to touch one of the thickly painted patterns. The widow slapped her away. "Get out!" she cried. "Get out before you do any more damage."

As a reflex action, Tessa raised her own hand to retaliate, but she willed herself to stop before returning the blow. Slapping the woman back would only make everything worse. "I'm sorry," she said, teeth grated. "I'll be on my way."

"You just be sure to tell Lord Ravis that he'll be paying for the damage." Widow Furbish shook her head some more. "The gods only know what replacing an original will cost."

Despite everything, Tessa could not resist issuing a huff of disbelief as she walked toward the door. Widow Furbish was just the type to exaggerate the cost of any damage. She was probably cracking the originals herself right now—whatever that meant. Just as she stepped from the room, Tessa remembered the sketch. For some reason she didn't want to leave it where Widow Furbish might find it. Bending, she scooped up the scrap of parchment, folded it in half, and tucked it away down her bodice. If Widow Furbish saw the action, she didn't say a word.

As Tessa crossed into the main room, she was forced to dodge Swigg to get the door. The man smelled of booze, and his eyes were watering. The vats he'd seen to last night were obviously something to do with brewing. And from the look of him, he'd been sampling his wares. Either that or he'd fallen into them headfirst.

As she went to raise the latch on the door, Tessa realized she still had the ribbon in her hand. Turning her back on Swigg, she threaded the ribbon through the ring and tied it around her neck, slipping the slack beneath her bodice. It was getting quite crowded down there. Feeling rather pleased with herself, she stepped onto the bridge.

The early morning sun dazzled her, and it took her eyes a moment to adjust. Blinking, she focused on a dark form moving toward her.

"Well, I must say you're the first woman I've ever met who looks worse after freshening herself up." Smiling, Ravis took her arm. "Tell me, is black dust on one's face considered a beauty enhancement where you are from?"

The powder! Tessa rubbed a hand against her face: it came back black. Seeing her look of horror, Ravis laughed. Tessa felt herself blushing. She must look terrible.

"Here," Ravis said, handing her a silk square pulled smoothly from his tunic. "Use this."

Tessa took it, turned her head away, spit on it, then scoured her face. Ravis had the decency to look out over the bridge while she cleaned herself up.

"Did the widow give you that dress?" Ravis asked as they came to the section of the bridge that curved down to the bank.

"No, I exchanged it for my clothes."

"Aah."

The skeptical syllable turned Tessa's head. "What do you mean, *aah*?"

"I mean you struck a poor deal." They reached the end of

the bridge and took a path down a narrow street. Ravis carried on talking as normal, but his eyes flicked in all directions, as if he were expecting trouble or worse. Tessa suddenly felt nervous. She became aware of a bitter taste in her mouth: the powder from the pounces.

Ravis continued speaking, his light tone and manner in direct contrast with his bearing. "The dye used to color your undershirt is the most precious to be had on the continent. Women spend years saving up just to buy a stretch of cloth that shade of blue."

Tessa's eyes narrowed. So that was why Widow Furbish was so eager to get her hands on the blouse. But sky blue? "Surely gold or purple or some other royal color would be more precious?"

Ravis shook his head. "No. Light blue dyes are made from lapis lazuli, which is mined from the foothills beyond the Azhensas. It takes a full year for the raw stone to reach Rhaize by cart." As he spoke, Ravis guided Tessa down a wide street and into the shade cast by west-facing buildings.

"Azhensas?"

Ravis gave her a hard look. "They are a range of mountains far to the east."

Tessa looked quickly away. From Ravis' tone she guessed she'd just made a glaring error. For all she knew the Azhensas were as well-known here as the Himalayas were at home. To cover her mistake, she said quickly, "Have you ever seen them?"

"I have been to many places and seen many things, none of which are fitting discourse for daylight hours in Bay'Zell."

The hairs on Tessa's arms stood up. Ravis' voice was cold, hard, and unpleasant. What had she said to change his mood so quickly? Breathless from the pace Ravis was setting, and shaking from his tone of voice, Tessa stopped in her tracks. She didn't care for Ravis' company anymore.

Ravis pulled at her arm. "Come," he hissed. "We can't be caught idling on the streets."

"You mean you can't," Tessa said very precisely. "I can idle all I want. In fact, that's exactly what I'm going to do." With that she snatched her arm from Ravis' hold and set back in the direction they'd just come from.

Ravis was upon her in an instant. "You fool!" he hissed, his fingers biting into the flesh of her upper arm. "You won't last till midday on your own in this city."

"You don't know me. You don't know what I'm capable of." Again, Tessa went to walk away.

"I know you're not from here." Ravis made no move to stop her this time. He stood his ground. His voice was very low as he spoke, but it carried well all the same. "You're not from this city or this kingdom or even this continent. Any child on the street knows more about the world than you do."

Tessa stopped in midstep. Spinning around, she looked at Ravis. How much did he know or guess about how she had come to be here?

Ravis' smile gave nothing away. "And you may have forgotten, but when I found you yesterday morning you were in no fit state to look after yourself." He shrugged. "Then again, I may have misinterpreted the whole situation: those two men I found you with may have been about to *proposition*, not murder you. I've killed men before now for more foolish mistakes than that."

Even though Tessa hated his sarcasm, she knew he was right. She was in no position to go storming off on her own. Where would she go? Back to Widow Furbish's parlor? She glanced down at her dust-covered dress. She would hardly be welcome there at the moment.

The truth was she was alone in a city she didn't know. A foreign city with narrow-shuttered buildings harboring lots of shade and thin streets winding past dark doorways, crumbling arches, and dead ends. She already knew the alleys were dangerous. And judging from the look on Ravis' face, wide-open streets like this one were too.

No. Going off on her own wasn't a good idea. Yet, she thought, gaze dropping from Ravis' face to his white-knuckled hands, there were advantages to be gained by pretending she was still considering stalking off. Ravis ill liked standing here in the street where anyone could see him. The desire to move on was so strong, it could be seen as a palpable force in his face. His teeth scored away at his scar.

Looking at Ravis, seeing his gaze darting from an old man pulling a cart, to two stout-hipped women balancing a tray laden with pies between them, to a young man standing in a shop doorway doing nothing at all, Tessa guessed he could be persuaded to make a concession or two.

Toe tracing a figure eight in the dirt, she said, "I'll come with you only if you agree to answer some questions."

"What questions?"

Gaze carefully on the ground, Tessa tried to think of some questions she needed answered. She didn't want Ravis guessing she had none ready to ask. "Very well, tell me where you're taking me. And why."

Ravis bit at his lip. "Walk with me, and I will answer your questions."

Hearing the tone of his voice, Tessa could tell he was running out of patience, so she let herself be led along the street. There was little to be gained from pushing him further. Besides, Ravis' nervousness was catching, and Tessa found herself eyeing everyone who crossed her path with the same suspicious glances.

The street they were on was lined with shops. Tables laden with carved boxes, bolts of cloth, wheels of cheese, pyramids of fruit, and bundles of spices jutted out onto the road. Shopkeepers stood guard by their wares; some carried brass scales, others pewter scoops, bone spoons, lead weights, or coiled wire. All had a club or stick tucked in their belts.

Morning was passing, and the shade provided by the buildings slimmed to a dark line. Seagulls shrieked overhead and a sharp breeze sent shop signs creaking back and forth. Tessa's hair blew in her face.

"You were about to tell me where we are going?" she prompted as they turned into another, less populated street.

"I'm taking you to a frie—" Ravis caught himself. "A business associate of mine. I expect him to loan me some money so I can leave Rhaize."

"So why take me?"

Ravis raised an eyebrow but didn't deign to look Tessa's way. "You are here purely so I can keep an eye on you."

The arrogance of this statement annoyed Tessa, yet she said nothing, preferring to ask more questions before Ravis grew tired of the game. "Why are you so anxious to leave Rhaize? It seems like a perfectly fine place to me."

Ravis turned on her. "By all the gods, woman! I will not

be questioned like a prisoner dog-hooked to a wall. My private affairs are just that: private." Having reached a fork in the road, he cut sharply to the left, his fingers bearing down on her arm much harder than was necessary. "This way."

Tessa felt a flutter of fear. At five feet three and a hundred and twelve pounds, she couldn't put up much of a fight if things came to it. Certainly not enough to overpower this tall and powerful man at her side. She'd have to settle for a swift kick to his shins, followed by an even quicker retreat. Tessa smiled despite herself. The idea of kicking Ravis appealed to her.

The district was gradually changing. The farther away they got from the river, the better the buildings and the people looked. Dirt roads gave way to cobbled streets, and the smell of baking bread and woodsmoke mixed with, then overpowered, the stench of rotting waste. Tessa's stomach rumbled. For the first time in over twenty-four hours she thought of food. Breakfast: bacon, eggs—not scrambled—mushrooms, tomatoes, and toast. Tessa's stomach rumbled again. Plenty of hot buttered toast.

To stop her mind from torturing her stomach, she asked the first question that popped into her head. "You said 'by all the gods' before. Does that mean you have more than one god here in Rhaize?"

Ravis made no move to answer the question, didn't even acknowledge hearing it, so Tessa followed his gaze to see what was distracting him. His attention was focused on a group of young men blocking the pathway ahead. "Keep your eyes down," he ordered.

Tessa felt her face coloring. "But I was just looking—"

"Women don't just look in Rhaize. Women hold their peace and know their place and open their legs when needed. Now be quiet and do as I say." Ravis pulled her arm to the right. "Follow me." He steered her to the far side of the street, away from the group of men.

Even though Tessa was looking down, she saw Ravis' free hand stray to the knife at his belt. She smelled his sweat.

A second later one of the men called out. "Hey, mate! Fancy sharing your good fortune? She looks more than woman enough for two."

One of his companions, a stocky man with a broken

nose, cried out in agreement. Another man whispered something that Tessa couldn't quite catch, and then all five men laughed at once.

Tessa felt Ravis tense. "Ignore them," he told her quietly, fingers closing around the hilt of his knife.

Tessa felt her heart pumping in her chest. Despite Ravis' warning, she risked another glance at the men. "Are you going to fight them?"

Ravis made a hard sound in his throat. "For both our sakes I hope not. Odds of five to one are a little too high for my liking."

Tessa shuddered. Why did he have to sound so brutal? Out of the corner of her eye, she saw two of the men moving toward them. A third man, the tallest, held his position against the wall, a fourth was slapping a club into the palm of his hand, and a fifth was making crude gestures with his hips.

Ravis didn't take his eyes off them. Looking at the expression on his face, Tessa felt her stomach clench. A hot flush of panic rolled up her chest. Things were getting too much. Ravis' brutal words jarred in her thoughts. The fourth man slapped the club loudly. The fifth man shouted an obscenity. Tessa felt herself becoming stiff. She knew from experience that tinnitus would soon follow. There were too many noises, too many things happening all at once.

The sun slipped behind a bank of clouds, plunging the street into shade. The sound of wood cracking against wood filled the air as a street full of vendors decided that now was exactly the right time to close shop. People scuttled into doorways or took the fastest, shortest turnoff they could find.

"On my word run back the way we came. Don't stop until you get to Parso Bridge." Ravis spoke between clenched teeth. His scar was white.

Tessa was rigid. She could barely move her legs. The pulse points around her temples began to throb. Any minute now the ringing would start.

"Did you hear what I said?" Ravis' voice was harsh.

Dazed, Tessa nodded. "Run back the way we came."

The two men were feet away now. The other three were on the move, gravitating inward to form a wall across the path. The man who had first shouted out drew a knife. His companion rolled up his sleeves.

Tessa swallowed, looked down.

"Come on, bitch. Show us what you've got."

"Get rid of the foreign bastard, and we'll show you what real men can do."

The words were addressed to Tessa, but she could tell they were really meant for Ravis. This wasn't about her now.

Blood rushed through Tessa's ears. This place wasn't safe. Two days. Two attacks. She wanted to go home. Without thinking, she brought her hand up to finger the ring. Even through the rough fabric of her dress, the barbs bit into her finger. Strangely, the pain helped her relax. Without realizing it, she had been holding her breath: waiting for the tinnitus to start. The sun appeared from behind the clouds, shining directly on her face.

In a movement so swift, Tessa's sun-dazzled eyes couldn't follow it, Ravis drew his knife. With one mighty thrust he pushed her away.

"Run!"

Tessa felt herself falling back. As she struggled to keep her footing, three of the men rushed toward Ravis. The man with the club raised his weapon above his head. Tessa flung out her right arm to steady herself. As she brought up her left arm to shield her face, she felt something wet on her lips. Just as she realized it was blood drawn by the ring, a voice rang out in the street.

"Everyone stay where you are." A cold voice. A deadly voice.

Automatically Tessa found herself responding to it. Her footing regained, she looked up in time to see the man with the club slowly fall forward onto his face. There was something comical about the sight of him keeling over, and Tessa was struck with a mad desire to laugh. Something that might have been his nose or jaw cracked as he hit the ground. Then she saw the arrow shaft quivering in his back. He had been shot.

Suddenly Tessa didn't feel like laughing anymore.

Everyone, including Ravis, stood still.

Tessa's gaze followed the line of the arrow back in the direction it had come from. A man stepped out from the splinter of shade remaining on the west side of the street. He was hooded, the fabric forming a dark eyelet around an even darker face. His left arm was extended, the bar of a crossbow resting on the crook. His free hand was on the trigger.

Out of the corner of her eye, Tessa saw more men step forward into the street. She counted three. There might have been others. All had crossbows.

Ravis' knuckles formed a bracelet of bone around the hilt of his blade. The only thing that moved were his eyelids. They dropped slowly, reducing his eyes to black-and-white strips.

The hooded man made a minute gesture with the crossbow. His head turned toward Ravis. "Walk on, sir," he said, his voice softer but infinitely more compelling than before. "Go about your business with your lady. I will see these men bother you no more."

Tessa didn't doubt him for an instant. His fingers slid over the trigger.

Ravis remained where he stood. Minutes passed. The two men faced each other; one with his features hooded by shadow, the other with his eyes hooded by flesh. Finally Ravis moved. Tessa released a pent-up breath as his shoulders relaxed and his back curved into a softly mocking bow.

"It would seem that I am in your debt, stranger," he said, rising to his full height. "Show yourself so I may know the face of my creditor."

The crossbow shifted in the hooded man's hands. It was now pointed directly at Ravis. "You owe me nothing, my friend. I saved you purely for my own ends. Now begone before I change my mind and shoot you in cold blood instead."

Tessa shuddered. The stranger's voice had an edge of madness to it.

Suddenly one of the four men in the middle let out a cry and dropped to his knees by the corpse. Even as Tessa's gaze sped back to the hooded man, she heard the soft *thuc* of the bolt.

The kneeling man screamed.

Tessa closed her eyes. Her stomach turned to liquid. The urge to retch was overpowering. She couldn't understand why she felt so sick: one man had already died within her sights today.

Ravis seized her arm. He grabbed her so hard, the ground seemed to fall from under her feet. Off balance, gorge rising, she was dragged away like a naughty child. They flew past the three remaining assailants and then past two men with crossbows. Although Ravis had his eyes on the hooded man, his feet never misstepped. He knew exactly where he wanted to go. In the whole street they were the only things that moved. No shutters rattled, no gulls swooped, no dogs fought over scraps.

A sickening burn rose up Tessa's throat. Her saliva tasted sharp and sweet, like milk gone slowly sour. Jabbing her tongue against the roof of her mouth, she swallowed as hard as she could. For some insane reason that she couldn't begin to fathom, she began to count as fast as she could. *One two three four five six seven eight nine . . . one two three four five six seven eight nine.* Over and over again, under her breath.

It seemed to work. By the time Ravis spun her round the corner, her stomach was settling down. She didn't risk unclenching her jaw, though; despite the counting, her mind was still replaying the dying man's scream.

Once they turned onto a new street, Tessa expected Ravis to slow down. He didn't. His grip didn't let up, either. He seemed full of fury. The scar on his lip was white and knotted like a fossil. His heavy-lidded eyes carried a look just short of murderous.

After marching to the end of the street, taking a quick turn, and then another one, they came to a halt by a well-kept three-story building. White stone steps led up to a gleaming black door. Without a word, Ravis rapped against the wood. Fewer than five seconds passed before the door swung open. Ravis went to walk in first, then stopped himself at the last minute. With a sharp bow, he indicated that Tessa should go ahead of him.

Only as Tessa walked into the cool, dark interior of the house did she remember about her tinnitus. The attack hadn't started after all.

"Pear liqueur," said the man named Marcel as his eyes flicked from the glass to Tessa's breasts. "I find it most . . . *invigorating* when one has had a minor upset."

Tessa took the proffered drink, intending to down it in one. Something stopped her, though. Perhaps the look that passed between Marcel and Ravis as they watched the glass pivot upward to her lips. So she took a cat lick instead, letting the thick and perfumed liquid merely scald along her tongue. From the taste of it, it was a close relation of arlo. And from the look of the flask it came in, not a poor one at that.

Tessa liked Marcel's house. She liked the silk rugs, the fragrant woods, the cushions stuffed to bursting, and the shiny, bony, grainy, artifacts that were scattered from room to room. She didn't like Marcel, but he *had* given her refuge, and she was so relieved because her tinnitus hadn't reappeared that she was inclined to treat him benignly.

Ravis leaned against the broad white-stoned fireplace, drink in hand, lips curved to half a smile, eyes firmly on Marcel. In the six paces it had taken him to mount the steps and walk through the man's door, Ravis had changed entirely. The angry look, the flashing eyes, the crisscrossed brow: all gone. Even his scar had receded. Watching him shrug off his mood as casually as others shrugged their shoulders made Tessa uneasy. She made a mental note not to forget it.

A soft knock came upon the door, and a beautiful dark-haired girl entered the room. "Sir," she said gently, gaze cast down to the floor, "may I have a word?" Marcel nodded once and left the room. He closed the door behind him.

"Are you feeling better now?" Ravis asked, turning his lazy smile upon Tessa. "Your color has certainly improved."

"My color didn't improve as quickly as your mood." Tessa was beginning to feel in control of her day at last. From the very instant she awoke she had been ordered around, shouted at, dragged about. She wasn't used to such treatment, and somewhere along the line, instead of taking a stand and protesting, she had simply given in to it. This might be a new place, but she was still Tessa McCamfrey.

Or was she?

Tessa's hand flitted to her temple. Two days she had been here. Two instances where she was sure the tinnitus would come on. Loud noises and extreme stress were the main precursors to an attack. In the past forty-eight she had been subject to both of them, yet nothing had happened. The first time didn't mean anything—it was a fluke. But today . . . Tessa shook her head. Today she had been sick with fear and still nothing had happened.

It didn't make any sense, but then neither did anything that had happened since yesterday morning. No sense at all.

Tessa stood up. She needed to make sense of everything; find the design behind seemingly arbitrary events. She knew from years of studying patterns that if you looked at them too closely, you saw nothing but so many lines and curves. You had to stand back to see the whole.

Which meant she had to find out all she could about this place called Rhaize. "You never answered my question from earlier," she said to Ravis. "How many gods do you worship here?"

To her disappointment, Ravis' face didn't register even a flicker of surprise at being asked such an abrupt and arbitrary question. "Only one," he said with a small shrug. "A thousand years ago we used to worship the four old gods, but counting the devil himself, that added up to five." He smiled. "So now we just have the one."

Nodding, Tessa tried to understand what Ravis said: four gods and one devil? "What's wrong with having five gods?" There was little point in pretending she knew any of this now. Establishing the background detail of the pattern was more important than keeping up lies. Besides, Ravis had already guessed that she wasn't what she seemed.

Ravis took a sip from his glass. "Old superstition. Many people believe that five was the first number ever named. They say there were no sorrows in the world until the one true God had his fifth son and the child's mother died upon the birthing. Now all sorrows, deaths, and misfortunes are counted in fives. Pregnant women once cut their growing babies from their wombs rather than risk giving birth in the fifth month of the year, and fathers smothered their fifth-born children, lest they bring bad fortune upon the families who raised them. Even today, scholars still hold that more calamities occur on dates with the number five in them, and that more wars are won and lost."

"But none of this is true?"

Ravis made a hard sound in his throat. "Tell that to the men who fought the Shrine Wars—they spent most of their lives in the lower south destroying all the temples and shrines built to honor the old gods. Tell that also to Izgard of Garizon. He likes to plan his military campaigns in fives: five battalions, five warlords, five of anything he can think of." A tooth scored over his scar. "He believes there's power in it. A lot of people do."

Struggling to keep up, Tessa said, "So the devil was the fifth god?"

"That's what the Holy League came to believe, anyway, so they forbade all worship of the old gods and made everyone worship the one true God instead." Ravis drained his glass. "They sought to rob the devil of his due."

Tessa plucked at the rough fabric of her skirt. Her own world seemed very far away. "And who is Izgard of Garizon?"

"Izgard of Garizon is a man who takes what he wants."

Ravis' voice was so cold when he spoke, Tessa felt the words on her cheek like ice smoke. "Where is Garizon?"

Just then the door swung open. Marcel walked into the room. The elegantly dressed banker looked slightly rumpled. A lock of his hair had fallen onto his face, and there was a red mark circling his wrist.

Ravis shot Tessa a warning glance. "When next we see a map, my love, I'll be sure to point it out."

"Map?" echoed Marcel.

Ravis yawned. "Yes. Our lovely Tessa here is developing quite an interest in the lapis mines in Azhenestan."

Marcel smiled at Tessa. His gaze alighted on her breasts, then quickly shifted away. "Beauty and a thirst for knowledge. Ravis is a lucky man indeed." He bowed. "Now if you will excuse us, my dear lady, Ravis and I have business to discuss." And then to Ravis: "I have a new case of berriac in the cellar. Would you care to step down and take a look?"

While Marcel was speaking, Ravis rubbed a bony knuckle over the pink flesh of his scar. When the banker had finished, he turned to Tessa and smiled. It was a mischievous smile, and the first one she had seen that actually reached his eyes.

"Marcel," he said, "Tessa has lived in Taire for the past

five years—and there's no need to tell you just how uncivilized that sheep dip of a town is. I'd wager my last silver that she'd like to join us for a sip."

Hearing him speak, Tessa couldn't help but return his smile. This was a new and charming side of Ravis, and a rather crafty one as well. How could Marcel refuse such a genial request?

He didn't. "Very well, Ravis, if you insist." A long glance was exchanged between the two men. Marcel was the first to look away. "Follow me."

Marcel led them down a narrow flight of stairs. Tessa descended three steps behind him, eyes firmly on his bald patch, nose inhaling his soft bookish scent. The temperature dropped with the light. Wooden panels gave way to flaking plaster, which in turn gave way to naked stone. Tessa shivered. She was suddenly very aware that her stomach was empty, though she didn't feel hungry at all. Behind her, Ravis' steps sounded as light and weightless as leaves rustling against a window in a breeze.

Marcel was carrying a lamp that burned with a steady, almost smokeless flame. Reaching the bottom of the stairs, he handed it to Tessa as he patted his waistcoat for the key. The key went in the lock, and it rattled against the barrel, but Tessa had her eye on Marcel's red-wealed wrist, and she saw neither bone nor tendon turn.

"Here we are," he said, swinging open the door. "My personal little treasure trove. The heart of my humble abode."

Tessa glanced at Ravis. Surely he could see that something wasn't right? Ravis inclined his head slightly, an indication that she move forward straight away.

Marcel disappeared quickly, taking the light with him and leaving Tessa and Ravis in the dark. A moment later a large wall lantern came to life, flooding the cellar with light. Tessa looked around. Row upon row of crossed shelves dissected the room into squares. The shelves were cut into V's and small casks, bottles, and earthenware jars were piled at varying heights within the slats. The floor was formed from diamond-cut stone that didn't quite match the lines of the shelves. The disparity jarred in Tessa's sights: the cellar was a pattern with a noticeable flaw.

True to his word, Marcel tapped a barrel and filled three wooden cups to the brim. In an unspoken agreement, neither Tessa nor Ravis drank until the tendons in Marcel's throat pulsed, indicating liquid had been swallowed. Tessa took a sip of her berriac. Ravis emptied his cup.

"So," he said, handing the cup to the banker to be refilled. "Have you had any thoughts on our conversation of last night?"

Marcel's gaze flicked to Tessa. Raising her cup so that it rested against her chin, Tessa attempted to cover her breasts. She needn't have bothered. Marcel was already looking away, his pale eyes focused firmly on Ravis. It was just the same as earlier in the street: she no longer mattered. Slowly Tessa backed away from the two men, putting a hand out behind her to feel for a shelf she could lean against.

"I have given our conversation my deepest consideration, Ravis," Marcel said. "Nothing else has been on my mind since."

"Nothing?" Ravis' tone was light. Did he glance at Marcel's wrist? Tessa couldn't tell from where she stood. "So, will you make the loan?"

"Yes." Marcel's voice was a tapering line.

"Hand it over."

"It's not as easy as that. I—"

"You what, Marcel?" Ravis' tongue lashed against his scar like a whip.

"I need surety." Marcel's eyes flicked to his left. Tessa followed his gaze. A tall block of shelves that might, or might not, have been resting against the back wall. "I need to be sure I won't be cheated."

Ravis took a step toward Marcel. "And what do you have in mind?"

The banker looked frightened. Just as he opened his mouth to reply, a voice echoed through the cellar:

"I will act as underwriter to your loan."

Tessa gasped. She had heard that voice before. This morning. On the street.

A man stepped out from behind the far shelf. He was wearing a hood, and as he stepped into the lantern's halo, he drew it back to reveal his face.

S I X

R avis, let me present Camron of Thorn."
Marcel's words hung in the room like smoke. No one moved. Tessa glanced at the newcomer: his face was hard, gaunt. His eyes looked artificially bright.

Ravis' face was no more than a dark backdrop for his scar. A jagged line marring perfectly formed lips.

The two men looked at each other. Tessa felt the hairs on her arm prickle. If she was an outsider this time, she was not alone: neither man spared an eyeblink for Marcel.

An overhead beam creaked and a rat scuttled along the floor, its little pink feet following the cracks in the stone. Time was impossible to gauge. Every muscle in Tessa's body ached with the strain of holding herself steady. She knew she had no business moving first.

Ravis sucked in air, then exploded into motion, covering the distance to the door in just three steps. He turned on the threshold and faced the room. A hand shot out toward Tessa, but his eyes found and settled on Camron of Thorn. "As you pointed out this morning, I am not in your debt. And I think it better for all concerned that we leave matters that way. Good day." He bowed and turned to Tessa. "Come, my love, it is time we broke our fast."

"Leave now and my men will cut you down before your boots skim the dirt on the road."

Tessa froze. The stranger's voice was utterly cold. His eyes held a spark of insanity.

Marcel raised his hand to speak, but Ravis snapped out his forearm, warning him to stay silent. "If you would be so good as to see Tessa home for me . . ." Ravis waited for Marcel to nod his assent before turning to look at the stranger.

"All things considered," he said, looking directly into Camron of Thorn's gray eyes, "I think I'll take my chances with your men."

With that he sent a regretful smile to Tessa and took his first step out the door.

"Would you also take your chances against Izgard of Garizon?"

The softly spoken words stopped Ravis in midstep.

Tessa felt a feather of icicles drift along her spine. The cellar, with its jarring, mismatched angles and its lines that ran in all directions, suddenly seemed like a cage. Tessa wanted to leave. She didn't understand anything, not what had happened earlier in the street nor what was happening now. The only thing that kept her from speaking out was the curious feeling she was watching a scene from a play.

"What would you know about Izgard of Garizon?" Ravis forced his voice low to mask his anger. His hand sought and found the hilt of his knife.

The man called Camron shrugged. "I know he tried to murder you one morning ago as you slept in your bed."

Ravis ran his tooth along his scar until his smile pushed it out of reach. He laughed, waited until the arrogant curve slackened from Camron's cheek, then stopped. The silence in the cellar was his now. One step upon the diamond-cut stone and the space was his as well.

"Murder is a strong word, my friend. You should be sure of your facts before you say it." As he spoke, Ravis took his first real look at the man. Camron was angry, yes, but there was something more. Something that showed itself in mercury flashes as he blinked. Something that Ravis knew all too well.

"Facts, Ravis of Burano?" Camron said, running his hand through his dark, golden hair. "Here are the facts: At midmorning yesterday four of Izgard's harras burst into the brothe"—a quick look at Tessa—"tavern you stayed at, and sliced the bed you slept in into ribbons. For some reason they obviously expected you to be there at that hour."

Ravis went to bite his scar, then didn't. After he'd missed *Clover's Fourth* he hadn't returned to the brothel. Which meant that what Camron said could be true. After all, it was only a matter of time before Izgard made his move. There were a world of reasons why the Garizon king wanted him dead. And now that the contract was over between them there was much to be lost, and nothing to be gained, from letting his former hired hand walk away.

A small part of Ravis' scar ran on the inside of his lip, and he trailed his tongue across it as he considered all that Camron had said.

Ravis of Burano. No one in the city besides Marcel knew his full name—all those he had been acquainted with this past year called him Ravis. So if Marcel had told Camron that secret, what else had he disclosed? And why?

Then there was the timing of the assassination. Ever since yesterday, Ravis had assumed he had overslept and missed his ship. Now, if Camron's words were to be believed, it sounded as if he had *underslept* instead. Ravis knew Izgard. He knew that Izgard would not send his assassins out to kill a man without first being sure that everything was in place.

The harras had probably traveled overland from Veizach and may not have reached Bay'Zell until after first light. Izgard wouldn't have wanted to run the risk of his intended victim sailing to Mizerico before his assassins had a chance to do their job, so he would have taken action to ensure Ravis missed his ship.

Ravis made slow fists with his hands. Izgard had arranged for something—sorcery, alchemy, drugs—to make him sleep. His assassins had burst into the brothel *expecting* him to be there. Only he wasn't. For some reason he had awoken earlier than he was supposed to.

The memory of serpents and ribbons coiling across a page flashed in Ravis' mind. Intricate patterns burned into the vellum like tattoos on naked flesh.

Illuminations.

Three times now he had seen designs like that: once in Veizach when he had interrupted Izgard in a meeting with his scribe, late last night in Marcel's study, and then again this morning when by chance he overturned a sketch drawn by the woman whose life he had saved yesterday by the docks.

Ravis didn't believe in coincidences. He didn't believe in anything except himself.

Quickly he glanced at Camron. Looking at his gold-streaked hair and the deep shadows under his eyes, Ravis suddenly realized Camron was the man he had passed in Marcel's hallway late last night. The man who had gone up to see Marcel after he left. The revelation didn't make anything clearer, it was merely one more morsel to digest.

What did this man want with him? The Thorn family was one of the oldest and wealthiest in Rhaize. Known as Thoren on the far side of the Vorce Mountains, they had a well-documented claim upon the Garizon throne. Indeed, the very castle they now occupied on the outskirts of Bay'Zell had once belonged to the first Garizon king.

Ravis smiled. He'd finally caught a whiff of the main course. "Tell me, my friend," he said to Camron, "why are you so willing to act as underwriter to my loan?"

Marcel sucked in air for speaking, but it was Camron who spoke first. "I have need of your services."

"Not only will he guarantee the loan, he'll pay you extra as well."

Ravis quieted Marcel with a single piercing look. Marcel's neat banker's hands twisted into knots. It was obvious why he had arranged this meeting: Marcel didn't want to loan any of his precious gold without surety. Camron's father was one of the five richest men in the country: Berick of Thorn could provide surety enough for a lifetime's worth of loans. The only question that mattered now was how much Marcel had told Camron.

"My services?" Ravis raised an eyebrow. "I'm afraid I have no services to offer; I roll dice tolerably well, dance the tarella with only limited grace, and although I *have* been known to write love sonnets, no maiden has yet succumbed to their charms."

Camron shot forward. His arm swung up and his fist barreled toward Ravis. Pivoting sideways to throw Camron off balance, Ravis swung back at the last instant and caught his wrist. Camron was younger and stronger than him, but Ravis knew a few tricks of his own. Twisting Camron's wrist back toward his body, Ravis forced the young nobleman to his knees.

"Gentlemen! Please!" Marcel came rushing forward. "There is a lady present."

Lady? Ravis almost laughed. Marcel had no interest in protecting Tessa. He had stepped forward only when it looked as though Camron might lose the fight. Wealth and wealthy people were the only things that mattered to Marcel of Vailing.

Ravis released his grip. Camron straightened up. Gray eyes nail hard with hatred never left Ravis for an instant. Again Ravis got the sense that there was something raw and hurting inside the man.

Rubbing his wrist against his cheek, Camron said, "I know who you worked for and what you did. Don't insult me with petty tales and foolish jibes."

Ravis shot a glance at Marcel. The banker wouldn't meet his eye.

Camron continued speaking. "One year you've been in Bay'Zell: watching the ports, hand-picking men. Recruiting an army for Izgard of Garizon. Maribane archers, Istanian cavalry, Balgedis engineers—any man who came through this port looking for a fortune or a fight, you picked, you paid, and you sent overland to Veizach." Camron managed a bitter laugh. "What better place than this? The very city that Izgard covets most. More men come through Bay'Zell than any other port in the west: mercenaries, fortune hunters, knights, heretics, and fools. You had your eye on them all. You chose them as carefully as Marcel chooses his vintage wines, and you bought them at the same premium rate."

Camron's voice was low and filled with loathing. "It would have been forgivable if you were a Garizon yourself—that I could understand and respect. But no, you're nothing more than a Drokho bastard. A mercenary recruiting mercenaries for a fiend."

Ravis tasted copper in his mouth. He had bit right through his scar. Swilling the blood over his tongue, he willed himself to stay calm. "I am nobody's bastard, Thorn."

Camron's lips twisted to a smile. "No. You were just treated like one by your brother."

"Gentlemen! Gentlemen!" Marcel filled the space between them, moving as fast as a man could move when his assets were in danger. "Please! Let us have some civility! We are here to talk of business, not of lineage."

Ravis barely heard what Marcel said. Blood pumped in his ears, his temples, his cheeks. He imagined killing the man before him in a hundred torturous ways. He wanted to kill both of them: Camron *and* Marcel. He knew he shouldn't be surprised that the banker had betrayed him—betrayal had been a dog at his heels all his life—but even now, after fourteen years of relying only on himself, in believing solely in himself, the treachery of a friend still made him sick.

Friend. Ravis smiled at his only folly. Marcel had never been his friend. Marcel had but one friend, name of gold. That was why he had arranged this meeting today. It was what had brought them together in the first place.

When Izgard had needed a banker to carry out certain transactions on his behalf in Bay'Zell, most particularly the transfer of funds to cover the costs of mercenaries and supplies, he had naturally turned to the most discreet and flexible source of money in the west: Marcel of Vailing. Marcel hadn't dared turn down Izgard's offer to do business. What if Izgard's invasion was successful? What would happen if Bay'Zell was overrun with Garizon militia, Garizon merchants close behind, ready to take over and exploit? Marcel would be the first to lose his holdings. He thought that by acting as Izgard's banker in Bay'Zell, he was protecting himself against just such a catastrophe. And as long as he kept it quiet, no one in Rhaize would ever know.

Marcel was hedging his bets. After all, he would argue, a banker's first duty was to ensure the security of his assets at any cost.

Ravis shrugged. What could one expect from a banker besides bankerly greed?

Marcel coughed his professional cough, forcing attention to himself, drawing the room to order. "Gentlemen . . . If we may get down to business?" He looked first to Camron and then to Ravis. Undiscouraged by the dark looks and balled fists, he continued speaking. "Let us start with the facts, shall we? Ravis, you need cash. You have no immediate prospects and no future commitments and are free to sign any contract you choose—"

"I *choose* to sign no contracts in Bay'Zell." Ravis didn't spare a glance for the deal maker. His eyes were fixed firmly on Thorn.

"Traitors always have limited choices," Camron said, sauntering forward like the nobleman he was. "They either take what is offered or knot themselves a noose."

Ravis' scar burned into his lip, his bone, his jaw. "And what exactly is being offered?"

"I want you to give me all the information and assistance I need to assassinate Izgard of Garizon."

Ravis' first reaction was to laugh. Camron of Thorn was either a raving witless madman or an idealistic fool. Assassinate Izgard! No one would ever get near enough, or be cunning enough, to take a shot at the king. Something stopped him from laughing, though, something to do with the way the light shifted in Camron's eyes, revealing so many subtle shades of gray.

"What makes you think I can help you? After all, I am just a mercenary." Ravis tried hard to say the word lightly, but somehow the syllables stuck in his throat, and he ended up sounding bitter instead.

"I wouldn't call the man who spent two years in Garizon training Izgard's army and instructing his warlords on warfare *just* a mercenary."

To distract himself from all the terrible, damning emotions Camron's words evoked, Ravis looked straight at Marcel. And kept on looking until the banker was forced to give way and meet his eye. If he had been looking for small satisfaction, he would have found it shining in Marcel's eyes—there was fear and even a degree of shame—but Ravis wanted nothing except a reason to stay angry.

The Bay'Zell banker had told Camron not only about their business together in the city, but also about what Ravis had done before. Secrets that were not his to tell. Agreements struck in private between a soulless Drokho nobleman and a man who would be king. Marcel had not been privy to the deal. He had not even been in the same country when it was sealed with hot wax, darting glances, and dry palms. It was purely between Izgard and himself.

Two years Ravis had spent working for Izgard in Garizon, then another year here in Bay'Zell. Three years in all, where every day he sold himself anew. Everything he had learned in the east—all the knowledge he had garnered while his body moved around a continent and his heart stayed dead in one place—he had itemized, tallied, and sold to the Garizon king.

Oh, it wasn't the first time he had sold his skills. He had been back from the east for seven years now, and there had been many men willing to pay for his insight and his instinct. In the small hallowed circles where such things mattered, his name was whispered with awe. *Ravis of Burano*, they said, *he turned round Alvech's forces in less than half a year. He took the Chaniz Palace guards and made a killing force out of a laughingstock, and after fourteen months consulting with Mallangaro of Endez, that much beleaguered duke won a war.*

Ravis sucked at the dried blood on his scar. He had not been idle since returning from the east.

Every commission he took, he learned more. The eastern barbarians fought differently from those of the west. They had no knowledge or interest in plate armor, no desire to be caged up like birds. They laughed at the west's knights, thinking them top-heavy and slow, puzzling at their reliance on defense. The east respected tactical planning, brutality, and speed. Not for them the delicious code of honor of the knights. They attacked whenever they could regardless of the civilities of war. Foot soldiers were used effectively and respected, infantry were deliberately kept light to allow free and quick movement on the field. The east wasn't mired down in five hundred years of tradition; they saw what was effective and used it wherever they could.

Not that they knew all the answers. In the past seven years Ravis had come to realize that many countries had valuable practices, techniques, or weapons, and the secret was to take the best of all of them—Maribane archers, northern Drokho pikesmen, Istanian cavalry, and eastern attack strategies—and form a single, cohesive, fighting force.

Ravis crossed the room and stood next to Tessa. At some point during the proceedings, she had tapped herself a cup of Marcel's vintage berriac, and when she saw Ravis coming toward her, she held out what little was left. Ravis was grateful for it. He suddenly felt very tired. This meeting was going on far too long.

As he raised the cup to his face, he was aware that Tessa

was watching him. What was she thinking, this woman who did not belong here? Where had she come from? And why was she here?

The berriac was an angel on Ravis' tongue. Warmed by Tessa's palms, it released fifteen years of stillness in one volatilized sip. It sung to his nose and the back of his tongue and reminded him of all that was good in Rhaize. As he swallowed the golden liqueur it tantalized him with images of high vineyards, lime-rich soil, and sheer limestone cliffs.

Ravis' gaze settled on Camron. He wouldn't be surprised if Berick of Thorn owned the very vineyard that this wine had come from. It was well known that the Thorn family owned huge tracks of land flanking the Vorce and Boral Mountains.

Perhaps thinking the same thing, Camron said, "I can and will pay you well for your services."

Ravis smiled—oak-aged berriac had that effect on him. "I am no assassin's mate, Thorn. I may have assembled Izgard's army, but I am not party to his plans. What he does and where he goes are his concern, not mine. I cannot help you. I have neither the information nor skills you need."

"You are lying. You spent two years with him. You know his security arrangements, you helped train his personal guard. Don't stand there and expect me to believe you know nothing about Izgard of Garizon when"—in his anger, Camron struggled for words—"you spent the last thirty-six months in his pay."

Ravis let out a thin breath. There had been the brief moment when he'd thought Camron was about to say something else entirely. Something even Marcel, with his watchful banker's eye and his clutching banker's hands, didn't know.

Relaxed from both the effects of the liqueur and the relief of knowing he still had one secret left, Ravis said, "Assassinating Izgard is out of the question. No outsider will ever be able to get close enough. He has men who will willingly throw themselves in the line of an arrow or a blade aimed his way. He has more food testers than most kings have kitchen staff, his fortresses and defenses are impossible to penetrate, and the harras are loyal to him alone."

Ravis' mind flashed back to the one time he had interrupted Izgard with his scribe:

"I am worried about the troops. The harras are loyal, but the men we bring in from Istania and the north will need to be monitored closely."

Izgard's gaze flicking over his scribe's shoulder. Patterns. Patterns on the scribe's desk, snaking red and blue and gold. Matching glints of color reflecting off Izgard's pupils as he spoke his reply. *"Your job is merely to train the men, Ravis. My job is to inspire loyalty."*

"I don't accept there is no way to defeat Izgard." Camron spoke over Ravis' thoughts, breaking his link with the past.

"Defeat?" Ravis replied softly. "I don't believe I said there was no way to defeat Izgard. I said it would be impossible to assassinate him."

"Defeat! Assassinate! Don't mince words with me, Ravis of Burano. I want Izgard off the Garizon throne. I want to see him dead."

"The two things are not one and the same. I tell you now, Thorn, it would be easier to defeat Izgard's army here, on Rhaize soil, than try to assassinate the man himself in Garizon."

Camron punched the wall with the heel of his hand. Pottery clinked and chimed. A solitary bottle rolled off the shelf and went smashing to the floor. "I don't give a damn what you think. Izgard will rot in hell before this year is through."

"Why?" Ravis cried, stirred by something he heard in Camron's voice. "Why does Izgard's death mean so much to you?"

Marcel stepped forward. "Ravis——"

"Hold your peace, banker. This story is not yours to tell." Camron looked straight into Ravis' eyes. Liquid metal shifted through his irises. A muscle at the corner of his mouth began to quiver. "After the harras left the brothel yesterday morning they headed out to Castle Bess. They laid low amidst the rocks until nightfall, and then entered the castle via the garderobe shaft. We believe there were less than a dozen men in total, yet they still managed to butcher the entire nightwatch. When I finally caught up with them they had just slaughtered my father."

Tessa gasped.

Ravis closed his eyes. He felt Camron's pain as if it were

his own. He knew what it took to speak calmly, rationally, about the death of a loved one. He knew the cost inside. "Camron, I—"

Camron had turned his back on them. His fist beat a warning against his thigh as he shook his head at the wall. "Don't you dare say you're sorry. Don't say it. Don't think it. Don't even *feel* it. Your pity means nothing to me."

The words stung Ravis. They shouldn't have—after all, he had heard worse in his time, a lot worse—but they did. Flicking away at the strings on his tunic, he feigned a nonchalance he did not feel.

"Here." Tessa's strange lilting voice broke the silence. She handed Camron a cup of berriac. "Drink this. It will make you feel better."

Ravis noticed the way Camron looked at Tessa, as if he were seeing her for the first time. His eyes were very bright, and despite the dark shadows and deep lines on his face, he suddenly looked very young. They both did.

Abruptly, Ravis spoke. "You say the men were Izgard's harras. How can you be sure?"

Camron drained the cup of berriac. Without looking at Tessa, he held out the empty cup for her to take. For some reason this annoyed Ravis.

"They weren't wearing Izgard's colors, if that's what you mean," Camron said. "They had knowledge of the garderobe shaft and the layout of the castle—Izgard could have access to that. His ancestors built the fortress. It once belonged to King Hierac himself. The plans are probably still in Veizach."

Ravis nodded. It would be just like Izgard to use any advantage he could. "What did these men look like?"

"Look like?" Camron spat out the words. "They looked like animals. *Animals.* Teeth bared, shoulders hunched." He shuddered. "It was as if they weren't human."

Tessa flashed a cautionary glance Ravis' way, warning him not to push Camron any further. Ravis was inclined to ignore her. "I never trained the harras to be animals. I trained them how to best use their minds and their weapons, how to overcome greater forces and constantly think on their feet." He moved forward as he spoke. Slivers of broken glass crunched under his boots. "The harras are Izgard's elite troop, hand-picked for their weapon skills and their loyalty. It doesn't sound to me as if you were attacked by them at all, more like a pack of rabid dogs."

"Would a dog slice open a man's torso?" Camron's voice was sharp, almost hysterical. "Would he pull back the skin to show the heart?"

Ravis bit on his scar. The practice of pulling back the skin to reveal the heart of the corpse had been carried out in Garizon for centuries, and he knew from experience that Izgard had a special fondness for that old and bloody tradition. During his two years in Veizach, Ravis had seen several corpses prepared in such a manner, serving their purpose as warning, marker, or threat. He had even seen a man who was still alive laid out that way. Heart still pumping. More than anyone else on the continent, Izgard understood the importance of fear.

Running his hand over his tunic, fingers tracing the leather above his heart, Ravis tried to make sense of all Camron had said. Animals? Less than a dozen men defeating a full watch? And then there was the business at the brothel. An empty bed sliced to ribbons? No man *he* trained would waste time destroying furnishings during daylight hours in a hostile city, where any moment they might be caught.

What sort of evil was Izgard dealing with now?

"Before your father was murdered, were you planning to leave Bay'Zell?" It was Tessa, asking Camron a question that wasn't important. Ravis cursed her under his breath. He had forgotten why he had even brought her.

Camron took a deep breath and, for the first time in Ravis' hearing, spoke in a gentle voice. "Yes, I had planned to leave the city. Today."

Tessa nodded. She didn't say anything more.

Silence cut the room. Camron's hands, which had been balled into fists during most of the meeting, fell slack at his side. Muscles worked in his throat. Ravis almost reached out and touched his shoulder. But he didn't.

Marcel leapt into the pause. "Well, I think we all know why Berick was murdered."

"We do?" Ravis said softly.

"Why, yes." Marcel looked quickly at Camron, perhaps

expecting to be interrupted. Camron was silent, head tilted to the floor, eyes down, so Marcel carried on. "Izgard was exacting revenge for the defeat at Mount Creed. If it wasn't for Berick of Thorn, Rhaize might be part of Garizon today."

Ravis watched Camron closely as Marcel spoke, looking for any reaction. There was none, so he decided to let the matter rest with Marcel's explanation. If there was more to the murder, it was not his place to say.

"So, Ravis," Marcel said. "Will you take the commission? I can arrange to advance you fifty crowns today."

Camron swung around to face Ravis full on. His eyes were very bright and his lips were pressed to a line. Ravis was glad he didn't say anything.

There was little choice here. Camron's crossbowsmen would shoot him the instant he left Marcel's house, and even if by some miracle they missed, the whole city would be after him by dark. All Camron had to do was go to the authorities and tell them what he had learned from Marcel—minus Marcel's involvement, of course. Some deal must have been struck between them last night. Camron had probably begun the bargaining by threatening to take his newly inherited assets elsewhere for management. The banker would agree to anything under financial duress. Marcel of Vailing had sold his own country for gold.

Ravis ran his hand over his lip. He *had* no country: Drokho had been lost to him for fourteen years. He couldn't set foot upon its rich, red clay soil without fear of being killed.

He had nothing. No family, no country, no gold.

Izgard had tried to assassinate him once and would certainly try again. The Garizon king couldn't risk Ravis' expertise and insider knowledge being used against him in the coming war. Ravis' fingers found his scar. At the end of the day, though, as good as that sounded, it wasn't the real reason why Izgard wanted him dead. Not the real one at all.

Ravis looked at Marcel. The banker was timing his blinks, anxious to appear unanxious, deliberately looking calm. Watching him, Ravis felt nothing but loathing. The man had no sense or understanding of loyalty—he didn't even have the decency to keep up a pretense. Whatever was best for him, he did. No questions, no moral uncertainty, no doubt.

And Izgard was the same, only worse.

Ravis traced the line of his scar with his fingertip. The flesh was cold and rough. A ghost's worth of pain shimmered along its length, reminding him of the time and the place his lip was sliced in two.

Ravis shivered.

So few people in his life. So much pain and disloyalty.

He made his decision.

"I will take the commission," he said, looking straight at Camron of Thorn. "I will help you bring the Garizon king to his knees."

S E V E N

Tessa popped a slice of herring in her mouth and then quickly washed it down with a large swig of arlo. Funny, but the little fish wasn't nearly as bad as she had expected. In fact, it tasted quite delicious. What on earth was it stuffed with? Briefly she considered asking Ravis, then decided against it. There were some things it was better not to know.

They were sitting in a small, low-ceilinged tavern close to the fire. Rushlights on the walls sent charcoal shadows slanting downward, and bursts of light and steam from the kitchen occasionally lit up, then dampened, the room. The tavern-keeper, a mournful, long-jowled man named Stade, was busy filling every spare inch of the table in front of them with food: terrines of steaming soup and fragrant mussels, platters of pale white fish in even paler cream sauce, grill-scorched sausages, wafer-thin sliced duck, hard-boiled eggs, and fresh fruit tarts. And cheese. Everywhere there was cheese: soft, hard, crumbly, running, colored red and yellow and white. Tessa didn't know where to start.

Ravis sat beside her in silence. They had left Marcel's house shortly after he agreed to work for Camron of Thorn. A few private words had been exchanged between the two, a second meeting had been arranged, and then Marcel had seen them to the door. Although Tessa hadn't seen the banker slip Ravis any money, Ravis' tunic now boasted an extra bulge above his heart.

"My lord Ravis," said Stade, hovering around the table like a guest at a funeral, "you are not eating. Is there something wrong with the food?"

"No, Stade. The food looks and smells delicious."

Stade ran a shiny hand down his brilliantly white apron. "Then there is another problem?"

"Perhaps."

"Aah." Stade nodded his head dolefully. "A woman, then?"

Ravis sent Tessa a gentle smile and then nodded. "You know me so well, Stade."

Stade smiled with a sort of tragic satisfaction. "Women and food." He shook his head with feeling. "What else is there?" After sending Tessa a reproachful look and fussing with various sprigs of mint around the platters, he walked solemnly away.

Tessa continued eating. This was her first meal in two days, and nothing was going to spoil it. After finishing off the herring, she moved on to the duck, trailing slices in the apple-glaze sauce, then slapping them over bread rolls. While she ate, she watched Ravis out of the corner of her eye. Stade was right: Ravis wasn't eating. He did drink, though. Cup after brimful cup.

The meeting in Marcel's cellar had left him looking haggard, older. Even with the firelight glancing off his face, his eyes still looked dim.

After eating for a while longer but drinking no more, Tessa decided to speak. Something had been on her mind for some time now: a slender thread seized upon while Ravis and Camron were speaking in the cellar. "When we first arrived at Marcel's house you mentioned something about your ship. You said you missed it. And then later, Camron said that if it wasn't for his father's death, he would have left the city last night."

"Yes." Ravis' gazed into the fire. "What is your point?"

"All three of us, you, me, and Camron, were waylaid yesterday. None of us had planned to be in Bay'Zell today—especially not me. Yet here we are." Seeing little interest in Ravis' face, Tessa struggled to make her point clearer. "It's almost as if we've been drawn together, like lines in a pattern."

"A pattern," echoed Ravis.

Tessa thought she had lost him, but a moment later he leaned forward. "Last night I saw some illuminations in Marcel's study. They were the most exquisite and complex things

I had ever seen in my life. The man who painted them died yesterday morning."

Excited, Tessa pulled on the ribbon round her neck, exposing the golden ring. "I found this yesterday morning. You missed your ship."

Ravis reached toward the ring but didn't touch it. "And Izgard sent his men out to kill me," he said softly, his gaze not leaving the gold.

Stade picked that moment to reclaim the empty platters. He shook his head morosely at all the fish and cheese that was left. "Women. Food." He sighed as he walked away.

Ravis waited until he was out of earshot before saying, "What made you sketch the ring last night?"

"I don't know. There was something about the way the gold weaved around itself . . . and then when I saw where my blood had caught in the thread, I just wanted to try to copy it."

Ravis looked at the ring a long moment and then stood. "Come on. Wrap some of that cheese and bread in a cloth. We're going to visit a dead man's assistant in Fale."

Widow Furbish shined the gold coin against her sleeve, then bit on it. Nothing tasted quite as good as gold. This was pure, too. No copper or silver to tarnish the palate. No lead or brass at the heart.

Yes, thought Widow Furbish as she flung open the shutter to search for signs of her good-for-nothing brother Swigg, Lord Ravis and his strange little miss were turning into quite a find. The late Mister Furbish, had there ever been one, would be smiling in his grave.

Imsipia Rodrina Mullet, more lately known as Widow Furbish, had learned very early on in life that it didn't do to be a single woman in this day and age. Most especially a clever, ambitious one. Her father, a man who moved, looked, and reeked like the very fish he spent all his days catching, had moved early to marry her off.

A fisherman himself, he'd naturally assumed that a fellow fisherman would be the perfect catch. Having grown up scaling, gutting, boning, and *hating* fish, Imsipia Rodrina did not agree. A terrible row followed, where terrible fishermen's curses were sworn and dire fishermen's threats spoken: "Either marry him, or leave this house now with nothing but the dress on your back and the remains of yesterday's catch in your basket."

Imsipia Rodrina had taken the fish and run.

She'd soon realized that being an unattached woman alone in a large city marked you as either a prostitute or a sister of God. Not having any great fondness for God, the color black, or wimples, Imsipia Rodrina had reluctantly taken to the streets. Being a naturally sharp-tempered and sarcastic person, she hadn't done particularly well as a prostitute and had no regular customers to speak of. Indeed, it had taken her six years to save just one gold crown.

Once she had the gold crown, though, there was no stopping her. She'd promptly paid a year's lease on a building, purchased a crystal ball, scrying bowl, and eyepatch, virtually kidnapped her younger brother from her father's fishy clutches, and bribed the local parson into scribing details of a fictitious marriage ceremony into the parish nuptials register. One week later Widow Furbish, fortune-teller to the masses, set up shop. The seamstress line came later.

She hadn't looked back since. As a widow she was respected, admired, and sometimes pitied. She could go where she wanted, when she wanted, and as long as she had the *appearance* of male guidance in her life—Swigg, as a supportive brother figure served nicely—no one could find anything to criticize.

Everything was proceeding to plan. There may not have been as much money to be made in fortune-telling or seamstressing as she had hoped, but a clever woman never relied on trade alone.

Widow Furbish hung her fleshy frame out of the window. Where was Swigg? He'd been gone for nearly four hours. He must have found those foreigners by now.

Just after Lord Ravis and his oddly spoken strumpet had left this morning, Bernice, Widow Furbish's housemaid, cook, and embroideress, had turned up full of tales about two mysterious foreigners looking for a man who had killed two people down a dark alley yesterday morning. There were rewards, she said. The men spoke like Garizons and were as easy with their gold as dockside wenches were with their favors.

Widow Furbish had promptly sent Swigg out to look for them. Lord Ravis might have a pouch full of silver coins in his tunic, but Widow Furbish seriously doubted that she'd be seeing any more of them. And she did so much want to move away from the river. She was tired of the mud, stench, and flies.

Just then Widow Furbish spied her brother walking across the bridge. Two tall, dark-cloaked men were steps behind him. Spying his sister, Swigg waved enthusiastically, rubbing his hands together and waggling his thumbs in the direction of the men behind his back.

Widow Furbish smiled. At times like these she was almost fond of her younger brother.

Springing into action, the widow tidied the room, closing all shutters except those that angled light onto her walnut cupboards and the silk tapestry that hung above the hearth. There. No one would find Widow Furbish's house wanting in luxury.

Pulling the eyepatch over her left eye, Widow Furbish waited by the door until she heard three pairs of feet pounding up her steps.

"Welcome, gentlemen. Welcome." Widow Furbish flung open the door.

Swigg smiled up at her.

A crunchy, sucking noise came from close behind his back. His smile froze. His eyes widened in confusion and then a soft hiss escaped his lips. Staggering forward, he collapsed over the threshold.

Widow Furbish caught him, firm hands slapping on his back to hold him steady. At the exact same instant she felt something wet trickle between her fingers, she saw one of the black-cloaked men held a knife.

The blade was red with blood.

She screamed.

The knife-man lunged forward. The skin was pulled tight across the bridge of his nose and his lips were pulled back, revealing wet, pink gums. A strong, feral scent of earth and blood and animal fur caught in Widow Furbish's nostrils. She let Swigg drop to the floor. Still screaming, she backed into the room, arms up to shield her face.

The door slammed shut.

The second man kicked Swigg in the soft flesh between rib cage and hips. Swigg didn't respond.

As Widow Furbish's gaze shifted from her brother back to the knife-man, she felt a soft swish of air skim her face. Pain exploded in her jaw. Her teeth slammed together, severing the tip of her tongue. Her mouth filled with blood. A white-hot razor of pain tore along her tongue. Tears flooded her exposed right eye. She couldn't *see*.

A series of dull, thumping noises came from close to the door. Widow Furbish blinked furiously, clearing her vision enough to see a shadowy form bending over Swigg. She couldn't tell what was happening, but something blunt like a club or chunk of wood was moving so fast it was only a blur.

Widow Furbish tried to call her brother's name. Blood gushed from her mouth, but words wouldn't come. A knife jabbed at her throat. She sucked in air. Her tongue rang with pain. Kicking out with her left leg, she tried to distance herself from whatever was at her throat. She was no longer sure it was a man. A hand clawed at her arm. The fleshy, animal smell was suddenly overpowering.

Panicking, Widow Furbish lashed out with her free hand. A fist punched at her stomach and she collapsed onto the floor. A dark form moved into her line of vision, slowly leaning over her body. Something wet dripped onto her hand. Thinking it was blood, she went to wipe it away. The liquid was clear—like saliva.

Widow Furbish let out a small, desperate breath as the shadow moved in for the kill.

A glint of teeth. An animal's grunt. Her fingers grasping, desperately raking over hard muscle and rough leather. Fingernails catching on a purse string. Something unraveling. Terrible, searing pain in her stomach and chest. Warm wetness soaking her dress. And then gold. Gold coins like raindrops falling on her face and shoulders, flashing with cold brilliance until everything went black.

The ride to Fale took three hours. They followed the Chase River inland as it snaked between hills and wooded gorges. Forests of beech and oak spread far on either side of the river, occasionally giving way to stretches of yellow grass, or dense bushes, or slopes of crumbling white rock. Black-and-white houses crowded between the breaks in the forest, trailing lines of gray smoke between the chimney tops and the clouds. White stone shrines with tall spires and deep roofs sat close to the river's edge, their base stones darkened by damp.

A breeze gusted low from the east, cutting the river's surface into bobbing, flashing jewels and exposing the yellow underside of leaves.

Ravis explained that there were really only two rivers that counted in Rhaize: the Chase and the Thread. The Thread ran the length of the kingdom, running through the rich farmland of the south and then the quarries, salt flats, and copper mines east of Bay'Lis. The Chase was a different sort of river: deeper, slower, greener. It flowed through the moorlands of the north, linking Bay'Zell with over a hundred towns and villages on its long, rocky run from the Vorce Mountains to the sea.

"If Izgard captures Bay'Zell," Ravis said, pulling on his reins to guide his horse around a tight cluster of bushes, "not only will he be positioned to control sea trade to the north and east, and set himself up as sentry to the Bay of Plenty, but he'll have the run of the north as well. The Chase will be his. He'll be able to ship goods and arms north from Garizon, lay siege to Runzy, plunder the country north of Gornt . . ." Ravis shook his head. "The whole of Rhaize will be his within a year."

Tessa just nodded. She was having difficulty riding her horse. Although she had learned to ride several years ago while she lived in New Mexico, she was not an accomplished horsewoman. The reins, stirrups, and saddle were all different from what she was used to, and to add to her troubles, the skirts of her dress kept getting caught in the straps and stirrups. She should never have sold her clothes to Widow Furbish.

Ravis still hadn't said a word about his contract with Camron, but it was clearly on his mind. Whenever Tessa asked him questions about Rhaize, his answers would trail away into military strategy: the high hill to the west was the perfect position from which to launch an attack on the city, the castle spied on the horizon was one of several fortresses built by occupying Garizon forces centuries earlier and was therefore as much a weakness as it was a strength, and now the very river they walked along was a supply route waiting to be seized.

"Will Izgard be thinking the same way you are?" Tessa asked, feeling a little more confident about riding as she crested a sharp rise to find a surprisingly manageable slope on the other side. Now if only she could get herself comfortable on this hard, narrow saddle . . .

"Izgard won't be thinking of anything else. He's a Garizon, war is in his blood."

"You know him well?"

"I know Garizon kings well. They live to conquer: it's how they maintain their position, keep their warlords in line, judge themselves."

As her horse seemed to be doing just fine for the moment, Tessa risked glancing at Ravis. He smiled slyly back at her, knowing full well he had dodged her question. Tessa wasn't about to be put off that easily. "And is Izgard typical of these Garizon kings?"

"Even before the crown was on his head he planned to take Bay'Zell. So, yes, you could say he was typical." Ravis tugged on his reins as his horse began snuffling at a tuft of grass. "Then again, it's been fifty years since Garizon had a king, and you'd find many who'd say that all the old tales are just that. Old tales."

"What do you say?"

"I'd say Rhaize should keep a close watch on its borders."

Tessa frowned. Ravis was playing a game with her, a game involving deflecting sensitive questions. "Why has there been no king for fifty years? Who ruled Garizon instead?"

Ravis raised an eyebrow, yet he answered her question all the same. "After Berick of Thorn defeated the Garizon forces at Mount Creed, the surrounding powers—Rhaize, Drokho, Balgedis, and others—formed an alliance. They sent a massive force into the heart of Garizon, razed Veizach to the ground, and killed the king and his two sons. They issued a formal statement declaring that if anyone attempted to seize the throne, they would reenter the country, torch it city by city, and hack the arms off any man old enough to hold a sword."

The sun disappeared behind a bank of clouds, casting the road ahead in dark shadows. Tessa shivered, all games now forgotten. "It seems so brutal."

"It was brutal, but no less than Garizon deserved. For centuries Garizon has done nothing but cause wars: invading surrounding territories, plundering towns and villages, annexing land, pushing their borders. Five hundred years ago Garizon was a small duchy in the east, with poorly drained soil and no major waterway to call its own. Yet once its men took to war there was no stopping them. In the height of its glory, Garizon ran from Maribane in the north to the river Medi in the south. Garizon kings fought bloody, ruthless wars, and as long as the battle was won, they didn't care how many men—either their enemies or their own—wound up slain in the mud at the end.

"Look at Mount Creed—Berick's forces had to slay the *entire* Garizon army before the king would admit defeat. Any other leader would have pulled back, surrendered, cut his losses. Not a Garizon king. Garizon kings are like rabid dogs. There's no holding them back."

As Ravis was speaking, Tessa felt herself growing colder and colder. She felt small and insubstantial, out of her depth. This world she found herself in was so much more savage than the one she had left. Events moved with dangerous speed, people were more emotional, more threatening, more *real*. It was as if life had been boiled down, distilled, to a concentrated extract. Even the land itself seemed somehow richer. So many vivid shades of green and yellow, so many tones and halftones in between. Her own world seemed far away: a dreamscape complete with mist and muted colors. A watercolor next to an oil painting.

Tessa patted her horse's neck. Its warmth was familiar, comforting, yet it didn't halt the sensation that her past was fading away. Unsettled, she concentrated on the last thing Ravis said. "If Garizon kings are as bad as you say, why have Rhaize and the others allowed Izgard to take power?"

"Fifty years is a long time. People forget."

A pulse began to beat in Tessa's forehead. Ravis made the words sound flat and final, like a judge reading a sentence. People did forget. It was a simple truth. Here she was, sitting on a narrow saddle in a strange land, her whole life left behind her, yet already things that only two days ago had meant everything to her no longer seemed so important. She hadn't once wondered what the people at work would think when she didn't turn up on Monday morning or what her landlady would do when the rent wasn't paid. Bills, commitments, people, and relationships: they were all slipping away.

Tessa felt for the reassuring weight of the ring around her neck. The barbs didn't bite this time, but she almost wished they did.

Deveric's house was guarded by trees. It came into view when they rounded a bend in the road: a large, two-story building with a blue slate roof, stone walls, and narrow slits for windows. A line of blackbirds perching on the lintel above the door watched as Tessa and Ravis guided their horses through the trees.

In the cleared area at the front of the building, a small fair-haired man was loading a cart. Odd chairs, chests, tables, rolled-up carpets, and linens sat on the ground, ready to be loaded.

Ravis dismounted his horse, beckoning Tessa to do likewise. Just before he held out a hand to help her down, his fingers flicked to his waist. To his knife. Tessa pretended not to notice, but she couldn't stop her heart from beating fast.

As they led the horses through the last of the trees, a second man came out of the house. Folding his arms, he leaned against the door frame and waited for Ravis and Tessa to approach. Sandy haired and broad chinned, he sucked in air through his mouth, causing his cheeks to hollow, before exhaling in a series of short puffs. When Ravis and Tessa reached the cleared ground, he spoke out:

"If you're here for the auction, you're a day early. Come back tomorrow at first light."

"We're not here for the auction," Ravis said. "We've come to speak to Deveric's assistant."

The small man began loading the pile of linens onto the cart.

"What business do you have with Emith?" The man on the step looked Ravis up and down. He barely glanced at Tessa.

"Private business."

"*Private,* eh?"

"You heard. Now are you going to tell me if he's here"—the gracious tone Ravis had used to begin with abruptly slid away—"or will I have to find out for myself?"

As Ravis was speaking, the man on the step poked through the remaining linens with the toe of his boot. Finding something not to his liking, he bent over and snatched it from the pile. "This is Emith," he said, motioning toward the small man loading the cart. "Anything you have to say to him can be said right here. Out in the open."

The small man did not look up. He kept on loading his cart. Tessa noticed his hands were shaking.

Ravis' tooth caught at the rough skin on his scar. "What I have to say to Emith is no concern of yours." His gaze dropped to the sheet wrapped in the man's hands. "Why don't you run back in the house, make your bed, and lie in it?"

The man's face hardened. He kicked the side of the cart, sending pots and pans scuttering to the ground. "Go on! Get off my property! Now! All of you." Wiping the spittle from his lip, he turned to the man called Emith. "And you'd better keep your mouth shut. If I find out you've been blabbing around Bay'Zell about the will, then I'll come round to your mother's house and slice some silence from your tongue." He kicked the cart once more for good measure. "Now bugger off!"

Emith picked up the handle of his cart and tugged it into motion. In his haste he pulled too quickly and the contents shifted to one side, causing the cart to tip over. Wood cracked. A roll of carpet hit the ground like a felled tree.

Ravis shot forward. For a brief moment Tessa thought he was going to strike the man on the step—his eyes were dark and the tendons in his wrists were taut like wire—but he came to a halt by the cart and began pushing it back on its wheels.

An unmistakable look of relief rolled across the face of the man on the step. When he noticed Tessa was looking at him, he tensed, pumping up his chest and balling his hands into fists. "Get going! The lot of you! And don't come back."

"Come on," Ravis said to Emith as the cart juddered back onto two wheels. "Let's see if we can hitch this beauty to my horse."

As Emith drew closer, Tessa saw that he was older than she'd first thought. He was dressed neatly in a surcoat and tunic, but closer inspection revealed small patches and carefully darned threads. Avoiding Tessa's gaze as Ravis rigged the cart to the horse, he stared down at his hands, his feet, the ground.

The man on the step watched the proceedings. The sheet he had taken from Emith's pile now lay discarded in the dirt.

When the makeshift harness was in place, Ravis handed Tessa the reins and told her to walk on ahead. "I'll catch up with you in a few minutes."

Tessa glanced at the man on the step. "What are you going to do?" she whispered.

Ravis shrugged. "I haven't made my mind up yet."

He was lying. His mind was already made up. Tessa could tell by the way he gnawed at his scar: he was going to hurt the man on the step. She couldn't understand why he was so angry. The man was just a small-time bully, that was all. Like everything else that had happened in the past two days, it made no sense.

"Go," Ravis hissed, smacking his gelding into action.

Tessa turned the horses while Emith kept a hand to the cart to stop it from overturning. They made their way through the trees in silence. The grass underfoot was soft and damp, and gauzy long-limbed insects flew up as they passed.

Tessa didn't look back. She knew Ravis well enough by

now to guess that he wouldn't make a move until they were out of sight. To take her mind off what Ravis was about to do and why, she searched for something to say to Emith. Glancing over the contents of the cart, she said, "Are you going into the city?"

Hearing her words, Emith sprang into life. "I'm so sorry about Master Rance, miss. So sorry. Since his father died he just hasn't been himself." The man's voice was gentle, almost puzzled. "He's taking it very hard. Very hard indeed."

"And how about you? How are you taking it?"

"Me, miss?" Emith looked genuinely surprised that anyone had thought to ask how he felt. "I've been busy. Very busy. So many things to be tidied and put in their place, so many things to be sorted out. Master Deveric always said, 'Emith, you're here to keep things in order, that's your job.'"

Tessa smiled. "So now that everything is in order, you can leave?"

"Yes, miss. Master Deveric's equipment is stowed safely away. All his brushes and mixing bowls are clean—just the way he liked them." Emith smiled at Tessa. A sad, sweet smile.

Reaching the road, they were forced to slow down as a series of potholes on the surface caused the cart to lurch from side to side. For the first time all day, Tessa felt cold. It would be dark soon. Tall trees cast shadows on the path, and the moon, which had been a pale thumbprint in the sky for several hours, sharpened to a thin slice of bone.

"Here, miss." Emith tapped her arm. Tessa spun round to see the small man holding out a woolen blanket. "You look a little cold. You should wrap yourself up before you catch a chill."

Tessa took the blanket from him, suddenly feeling very sad. It had been a long time since anyone had spoken so softly and with such kindness to her. Longer than the past two days. "Thank you," she said, drawing the blanket around her shoulders like a shawl. "I didn't realize it would get so cold."

"You have to be careful, miss. Mother always says that unless it's high summer, you should never leave the house without your cloak."

Tessa smiled. Emith's mother must be very old. Indicating the mattress in the cart, she said, "Are you going to stay with your mother now?"

Emith nodded vigorously. "Yes, miss. Mother lives in the city. The gout's been troubling her for months now, so she'll be glad to have me home."

Glad to have me home. Something light, like a spider's web or an insect wing, brushed against Tessa's cheek. The ring was heavy around her neck. What would her own mother be thinking now? Would she even know her daughter was missing? Would the police visit the Arizona condo? *"We found your daughter's Honda Civic abandoned in the Cleveland National Forest. We know she stumbled across the missing security deposit boxes from the La Havra Bank robbery, but at this time we can't be sure of her movements after that."*

Tessa brought her hands to her mouth. Her parents would be worried sick about her.

"Miss, miss . . ." Emith touched her arm for the briefest moment. "Are you all right? You look a little pale. Here. Let's stop for a few minutes and rest."

"No." Tessa shook her head. "I'm fine. I was just thinking about . . . my family." Ashamed that she *hadn't* been thinking about her family.

Footsteps sounded in the dirt behind them. A twig snapped, and then Ravis emerged from the shadows of the trees. Tessa was surprised at how relieved she felt to see him.

He smiled. "If you two keep up this rate, you'll be lucky to get to the city by midnight."

As Ravis drew closer, Tessa searched his face for signs of what had happened back at the house. He looked calm, relaxed. A few strands of hair had worked their way loose from their binding, but apart from that he looked completely composed.

"Sir—" Emith began to speak, but Ravis cut him short.

"Don't worry, my friend, I did nothing to young Master Rance that a few days' lying on his stomach won't cure."

"He's just upset over his father's death, sir. That's all. He meant no harm."

Ravis began rearranging the items on the cart, laying all the heavy things on the bottom. "Emith, you are a considerate man, but I think we both know the real reason why Rance and his brother are so upset."

"But, sir, Master Rance has had a bad few days. He hasn't slept—"

"I bet he hasn't. He's so worried that someone's going to come along and take what he considers to be rightfully his that it wouldn't surprise me if he hadn't once closed his eyes to blink." Finished with the cart, Ravis kicked the wheels. "I suppose he didn't take kindly to Deveric leaving so many of his illuminations to you?"

"He may have got a little angry at first, sir, but that was only to be expected." Emith bowed his head. "It's the will, you see. It's very confusing. Master Deveric was so generous. He wanted to make sure that everyone got something, and Master Rance and Master Boice are just a little bit disappointed, that's all."

"Yes, that's why they are selling off the contents of the house tomorrow at dawn. They don't want to risk any further *disappointment*."

Tessa kicked Ravis' shin. Judging from what he was saying to Emith, it sounded as if Deveric's two sons were repressing the will and selling everything off before anyone could object. Even if that was the case, there was little point in upsetting Emith over it. The man was obviously trying very hard to think the best of his master's two sons.

Before Ravis had a chance to retaliate, Tessa said, "Emith, we came here to ask you about Deveric's work. His illuminations. Ravis saw them last night and said they were very beautiful."

"Marcel of Vailing showed them to me," Ravis added. "He thinks they may be worth a lot of money."

Emith shook his head. "That's not why Master Deveric left them to me, sir. Not at all. I would never sell them. Ever."

"Why not?" Ravis took the reins of his horse from Tessa, and their little party began to move again. "You could have a very comfortable life if you sold them."

"Master Deveric said I was to keep them until they were needed."

An owl called from the woods beyond the road. Tessa pulled the blanket close around her shoulders. The light was failing fast, and thin gusts of air hurried along her arms and down her neck.

"Needed for what?" Ravis asked.

"For whoever comes next." Emith held the side of the cart steady as the wheels rolled over a bad patch of road. "Master Deveric always said that someone would come after him, someone who could paint illuminations like him. Carry on his work."

Tessa's hand stole up to the ring. It was warm, as if it had been touched only seconds earlier. "And Deveric wanted you to keep all his illuminations to show whoever comes next?"

"No, miss. Not all of them. Master only gave me one set to keep." Emith's voice was soft, but he spoke each word carefully, as if he were anxious not to make any mistakes. "He left me the set he started work on twenty-one years ago. Not his most beautiful work, he left that for his wife, but his most . . ."

"Complex," Ravis said.

"Yes, sir. His most complex."

Ravis and Tessa exchanged glances.

Emith continued speaking. "Master Deveric would go years without working on one, and then one day out of the blue he'd say to me, 'Emith, I think you should run along and bring me the old set. Now feels like the good time to add another page.'"

Tessa shivered. "Deveric was working on a new page for the set when he died?"

"Yes, miss." As Emith spoke, his hands worked on Tessa's blanket, adjusting it so that all the gaps around her neck and shoulders were covered. "He started working on the page about five days ago: laying down the guidelines, hardpointing. He filled in one or two knots the day he started, and after that he worked on it for an hour or two each day. Then, the night before he died, he woke me up in the dark hours past midnight. 'Emith,' he said, 'mix up my pigments and soften my brushes, I have a sudden urge to go to work.'"

Emith's words left a deep silence behind. Tessa didn't know what to say, didn't want to be the first to speak. The wheels of the cart creaked, the horses' tack jangled, and the waxed leather of Ravis' tunic made a soft, swishing sound as he walked. The day seemed suddenly very long—the longest Tessa had ever known.

Ravis spoke. "Emith, I've seen designs like ones Deveric

painted only once before in my life. In a fortress I never want to revisit, commissioned by a man I wish I'd never met. At the time the man told me I wasn't to worry any longer about something that had been troubling me for many months—he had a special way to make it right." Ravis' voice was beautiful to hear in the darkness: gentle on Emith, yet somehow hard on himself. "I hadn't given the incident a second thought until last night when I opened the manuscript press and saw blood on a pattern barely dry.

"I have been to many places and seen many things, and have long forsaken the privilege of being anybody's judge. If there were things your master was involved in that may be considered ungodly, I would never condemn him or vilify his name."

In the moon-pale shadows of the road, Tessa could clearly see the line of Emith's shoulders moving up and down. Glancing from him to Ravis, she was struck by a sense that all of them—Ravis, Emith, and herself—were caught up in something that was too large to see or understand. As she had earlier in Marcel's cellar, Tessa felt that if she could just step *back* and view events from a distance, she would be able to trace a pattern from a seemingly random set of lines.

"Emith . . ." Tessa spoke into the darkness that lay between her and the scribe's assistant. "Yesterday morning I was pulled here, to Bay'Zell. I was somewhere else—somewhere completely different—and now I feel as if I've been placed in the middle of something important, and I don't understand what it is or why."

Emith did not reply. Tessa heard him breathing.

"Show him the sketch, Tessa." Ravis, so close now that Tessa could feel his breath on her cheek. They moved apart at exactly the same moment: he went to take something from his saddlebag, she went to take something from hers.

A dull, tapping noise sounded. Sparks flew, and then a golden flame lit up Ravis' face. Tessa stopped in midstep just to look at him. The scar on his lip was like a seam of precious metal running through a layer of rock. Light from the flame gilded the jagged flesh, creating an exquisitely detailed feature from a flaw. Tessa wanted to touch it.

Dismissing the impulse as foolishness, she took the

rolled scrap of cow's hide in both hands and unraveled it toward the light.

Emith caught his breath.

Tessa, who hadn't spared a glance for the sketch since she'd finished it last night, felt her face grow hot. The sketch was different from what she remembered: so much more *detailed* than anything she had ever drawn before. Curves spiraled into a labyrinth of shapes and forms, lines undulated in a dozen subtle ways while still managing to follow their path. Threads that first appeared to cross each other on closer inspection revealed themselves to be a series of intricately deceptive self-knots. Through it all, the ring was still identifiable as a ring, but it was so much more as well. It seemed to *mean* something.

Tessa shook her head, disbelieving. Had she really drawn this? She had been so tired last night, the light in Widow Furbish's stock room was bad, the smoke from the tallow stung her eyes, and the stick of charcoal kept breaking in her hand. But then . . .

Tessa's hand trembled. The page shook. She remembered feeling free. Her tinnitus, which for so long had been a hand on her shoulder holding her back, had taken the night off. There was nothing to stop her from going too far. There was no such thing as *too far*. No point where she had to stop because the space between her eyebrows was starting to ache or the blood in her ears was beginning to beat a pulse. No pain. No noise. And, after the first hour or so of drawing, no fear that the tinnitus would start.

The cow's hide was buttery yellow in the lamplight. The lines of the sketch were an eyelash short of black. Tessa studied the image of the ring as if looking at a stranger's face. Was this what she was capable of when her tinnitus was taken away?

"You drew this, miss?" Emith asked, pulling up the blanket around her shoulders again. She must have let it slip.

"Yes. Last night."

Emith made a curious sound in his throat. "I see. I see."

Tessa looked up from the sketch to see Ravis looking at her. His dark eyes looked too knowing by far. "Emith," he said, gaze still fixed firmly on Tessa, "tell us what you know about Deveric's illuminations."

He snapped out the light.

Emith spoke. "I was Deveric's assistant. I scraped, then stretched the hides, mixed pigments and glazes. I bound brushes, ground eggshells, cut nibs, and boiled quills. Whatever my master asked of me, I did. My place was to help, only to help. I created nothing, said nothing, merely saved my master time. It wasn't my place to ask questions. I was privileged to be where I was: with a great man, producing good work, getting paid to do what I loved.

"My master worked for the love of it, because he felt the shapes and forms in his heart and saw the inks and pigments in his dreams. He was a fine scribe, with a deep vision, and he would never do anything to hurt another living thing. He loved life and the one true God dearly."

Emith's voice conveyed pride and loyalty for Deveric, and although it was easy to see that he believed what he was saying, Tessa doubted it was the whole truth. The man wanted so badly to think the best of people.

"What did Deveric say about the one who would come after him?"

"Master said that his work was very hard, and it took a rare person to do it well. He learned the art of illumination from the monks on the Anointed Isle over half a century ago, and he hoped one day to pass along that knowledge to someone else." Emith sighed and began to shake his head. "No one came along: neither Master Rance nor Master Boice had the feel for the old patterns. Boys who started as apprentices didn't work out. In the end Deveric became resigned to the fact that he might never find the right person in his lifetime. Then one day he came to me—I remember it well, for it was the same day he finished the third pattern in his set—and said, 'Emith, after I'm gone I want you to watch and wait for someone to come along who has a feel for patterns just like this, and when you find him I want you to teach him all you know.'"

Him? Tessa frowned. "And what if this person turns out to be a woman?" Ravis smiled as she spoke—Tessa couldn't see his face in the darkness, but she could tell that he did. "Did your master leave any plans for that?"

"Why, no, miss. But I have seen work done by women scribes, beautiful work, light-handed work, and I'm sure my master meant no offense."

Ravis laughed. A noise that sounded very much like him slapping Emith on the back accompanied the laughter. "Emith, you would have made a fine diplomat. I do believe that if the devil himself turned up on this road, you'd stand there and tell us he's just a little misunderstood, that's all."

"But, sir—"

"Ravis. Call me Ravis. And my good, if rather indignant, lady friend here is Tessa." From the sound of his voice, Ravis seemed to be enjoying himself. Tessa found herself smiling along despite everything—what he said about Emith was absolutely true. Besides, it had been a long, hard day for both of them, and she was too tired to get angry. It felt good to laugh.

Reaching the point in the road where they had to change their path and cut across plowed fields, Ravis handed the reins to Tessa while he and Emith saw to the cart. The moon was high but not bright. The way ahead was little more than a dark sheet, and although Tessa could smell the salty, dead-leaf odor of the river, she couldn't spot any ripples or shimmers of light.

Once the cart was settled in the soft earth of the field, Ravis came back to walk beside Tessa. Emith stayed a few paces behind, keeping a hand on his cart.

"Why don't you ride for a while?" Ravis said. "I'll lead your horse, make sure she steps lightly."

Tessa shook her head. She was tired, but she preferred to walk in the dark. "How long before we get back to the city?"

Ravis shrugged. "An hour, perhaps longer."

"You're all welcome to come back to my mother's house for some hot supper and arlo." Emith sounded a little shy. "She makes the finest fish stew in all of Bay'Zell."

Following that remark, Ravis, surprisingly, entered into a long conversation with Emith about the best fish for stewing and whether it was better to poach in broth or arlo. Emith chattered along happily, beginning most sentences with, "Well, Mother always says . . ."

Tessa was content to listen. As they followed the river's course through dark, tree-striped ravines, night-fragrant fields, and steaming marshes that sucked at their feet as they stepped, the conversation shifted from local gossip, to rising prices, to tales of old princes and kings. No one mentioned Deveric and his illuminations again, but from time to time Tessa caught Ravis glancing over at her when he thought she wasn't looking, and although he may have been talking to Emith about the best places to buy Istanian leather or the reasons why the Sire of Rhaize would never move against Drokho, she knew his thoughts followed the same path as hers.

Could she be the one who was supposed to continue Deveric's work? And if she was, how did it tie in with everything else that had happened today?

EIGHT

essa's feet ached as she stepped onto the wooden camber of the bridge. She was so tired she couldn't think. It took all her strength to put one foot in front of the other and stop her chin from falling on her chest. Operating purely on instinct now, she knew it was time to sleep.

She and Ravis had just come from stabling the horses. Before that they had seen Emith to his mother's house—a small black-timbered building, filling a cleft between a bathhouse and a stable—and although Emith wanted them to stop, rest, and meet his mother, both Tessa and Ravis declined. All Tessa wanted to do was get back to Widow Furbish's stock room, roll herself and all the accompanying bugs up in a blanket, and fall asleep. They hadn't even stayed to meet Mother Emith, though Ravis was very careful and precise about passing along his respects. That sort of thing seemed to matter here, and Tessa found herself glad it did.

The clouds had long since kidnapped the moon, but the city created a smoky, mustard half-light of its own. The river stank. As Tessa walked across the bridge, she was aware of scratching, chittering, night-animal noises coming from the banks below.

Widow Furbish's house was much the same as all the others on the bridge; it leaned forward toward the center of the walkway, as if the original builder had decided that if his creation ever were to fall down, he'd be damned if it landed in the water. With nostrils shrinking from the stench and ears buzzing with sloppy, slapping, water noises and high-pitched, tiny-toothed gnawing, Tessa was inclined to agree with him.

Pale slashes of light marked the run up to the Furbish door. Ravis checked his knife. Tessa put her foot on the first step, but Ravis blocked her with his arm. "I'll go first," he said.

Tessa was annoyed at Ravis' theatrics. Why did he have to turn every arrival into an armed raid? Pushing back his arm, she said, "If there's anyone on the other side, they can have me. I'm too tired to care."

Ravis' fingers stabbed at her arm. Tessa winced.

"You will stay where you are." There was a cold, deadly authority in Ravis' voice that Tessa had never heard before. Suddenly she was reminded of what Camron had said about him in Marcel's cellar: Ravis was a mercenary, a man who trained others to kill. Kings paid for his services.

She stepped aside.

Ravis didn't climb the three steps. He stayed on the pathway, leaning forward to knock on the door. There was no answer.

Ravis sucked in his bottom lip. Tessa noticed his jaw working and realized that inside his mouth he was chewing on his scar.

Seconds passed, then Ravis shouted, "Swigg! Open up. My arms are full and I can't work the latch."

Nothing.

Ravis and Tessa exchanged glances. The bridge, which only minutes earlier had been alive with noises, suddenly seemed as quiet as a tomb. There was no one about. All doors were closed. All shutters were barred. A wheelwright's sign swayed in the wind, but if it creaked, the sound didn't carry.

Tessa's heartbeat quickened. The exhaustion she felt was slowly re-forming itself into something else. The aching muscles in her legs began to tingle.

On the first step now, Ravis lifted his free foot and sent it slamming into the door. The door swung open. Ravis drew his knife. As he called out Swigg's name, Tessa got a whiff of the smell.

A musky, dog-blanket smell. An animal smell.

And then she saw the blood. Red blood, blue flesh, white bone.

Tessa gagged.

The lights went out.

Two dark figures appeared at opposite sides of the door.

They lunged at Ravis, knife hands drawn back to their shoulders, blades poised to strike. Ravis' left elbow shot up and outward as his right hand traced an X in the air with his knife. The blade wasn't wielded to injure the attackers—there was too much distance between them for that—more as a warding device to give Ravis an instant to step back.

Tessa didn't know if she was too tired or scared to scream. She breathed quickly, though, for the first time in her life unafraid of holding on to tension. No matter what she did now—scream, panic, run, or fight—she knew the tinnitus wouldn't bother her. She was free to act as she pleased.

Ravis' foot found the path. He had a second, perhaps less, to free himself from the confines of the doorway before the first of the two figures shot down the steps.

The rangy smell of animal musk got stronger. Tessa could barely see the two attackers—it was dark and they moved too fast. When the first one swung his knife at Ravis, she caught his profile. Only it couldn't be his profile, because it didn't quite look right. Something about the bridge of his nose: it was too flat.

Tessa shuddered. She must be mistaken.

The two attackers were out of the house now. Cloaks whipping around their bodies like shadows, they moved without making a noise. One was on the walkway to Ravis' right, the other glided down the steps. Tessa could see him waiting for a chance to slip behind Ravis' back. Ravis, aware that the two were working together to outflank him, had to keep feinting attacks to give himself chance to move wide. Both men held their long, thin-bladed knives high at their shoulders. Ravis kept his own knife close to his waist.

The first man grunted and took a swing at Ravis. Occupied with fending him off, Ravis didn't notice the second man attack from behind.

"*Ravis!*" Tessa screamed.

Ravis swung round. He wasn't quick enough. The second man's knife glanced along his arm, slicing into the skin just below the shoulder. Even before Ravis could pull away, the first man was on him.

Tessa's legs kicked into action. She found herself running toward the first man, fists out. A noise ripped through her eardrums: the sound of her own screams. The first attacker's head whipped round. Hardly aware of what she was doing, Tessa punched him in the jaw. Even as the blow landed, she was conscious of the smell and the look of the man, and something deep within her warned her to get away.

Tessa fought the impulse, standing her ground, guarding her face with her fists, and screaming her throat raw. Blood barreled through her veins. Her lungs ran hot, sore, and ragged.

She felt completely terrified and exhilarated.

The blow barely made the man flinch. Turning away from Ravis, he hissed as he caught Tessa's eye. His eyes had a golden cast and his lips were peeled back, revealing the pink knuckle of his gums. Suddenly he shot toward her, cloak lashing out behind him like a tail.

Tessa stepped back, stumbled.

Ravis seemed somehow *attached* to the second man. Chest pumping, he glanced over his shoulder at Tessa.

Her attacker circled. His knife was poised at his shoulder like the beak of a carrion-feeding bird. His breath smelled ripe and fatty. The contours of his face were streamlined, almost fluid. With a quick movement he stepped out of Tessa's field of vision

Tessa tried to keep track of him. It was so dark.

Crack!

She heard her neck snap back as something smashed into her skull. She felt no pain, only a sick-spiraling blackness and a sense of outraged surprise: *she hadn't seen it coming!* Tessa's legs buckled under her, and there was nothing, absolutely nothing, she could do to stop them. The world started rippling away, and the last thought she had before losing consciousness was that she'd been right about the tinnitus. It was never coming back.

It was a gift from this world to her.

Sucked back, Tessa opened her eyes. She had read enough stories to know that when heroines blacked out in perilous situations they were supposed to awaken many hours, often days later, in a large feather bed, safe and sound. Thin broth, a motherly looking matron, and a crackling wood fire were usually somewhere in the picture, too.

No such luck for her.

Tessa awoke to find herself looking at the exact same sky she'd passed out under. And judging from the ragged breaths and sounds of fighting coming from somewhere to the side of her, minutes had ticked by, not hours.

The wooden boards of the bridge rocked under her back, set vibrating by the footfalls and lunges of the two men to her left. Tilting her head a fraction to see what was going on, Tessa was hit by a tunneling wave of sickness. A blasting, scissoring pain in her head bored all the way down to her gut. Eyes watering, she vomited onto the deck.

A low-pitched howl sounded. Hearing it, Tessa felt the hairs on the back of her neck prickle. Wiping her mouth, blinking furiously, she concentrated on the single shadow within her view.

The shadow was large. It moved smoothly for a moment like a bat gliding into land, then it began to twitch. A spasm rippled through its pooled blackness, and then the shadow cleaved apart. Tessa heard a breath taken sharply, followed by a thick gurgling noise. The shadow separated into two. The larger shadow rocked back and forth for a moment before collapsing into an oblique line and then receding from Tessa's sight. The boards under her back jerked as the body casting the shadow crashed to the ground.

Suddenly Ravis was beside her, face spattered with blood, chest pumping, smelling like the man he'd just killed. He pulled her to her feet. "Come. Hurry!"

Tessa would have liked gentler treatment just then. Her skull throbbed like a sore tooth, and her legs felt too thin and powerless to hold her up. Ravis didn't seem to care. His eyes were focused on the near end of the bridge. With his free hand he cleaned his knife, first flicking the blade downward, then wiping it against his leg.

Struggling to her feet, Tessa fought the tight braid of sickness stretching between her stomach and head. Ravis held her firm. He moved in close and whispered, "Someone waits at the end of the bridge."

Tessa squinted into the darkness. The bands of shadow

and light along the bridge's length played tricks with her watering eyes. She couldn't see a thing.

"Over there." Ravis made the minutest gesture with his knife. His shoulder was bleeding. "In the shadows."

Tessa decided she'd take his word for it. "Let's leave over the other side."

Ravis' teeth flashed into view. "I don't think," he said, speaking very precisely, "that would be a very good idea."

"You think there'll be more of them?" From where they stood, just short of the crown of the bridge, they could see only a short distance in the opposite direction.

Ravis nodded. "Men on each side. It's what I'd do."

And that, Tessa supposed, meant a whole lot more than she cared to think about at this particular moment. She said, "Well, we've got to go one way or another. Make a choice." As she spoke, she felt the tail ends of her words slurring like a drunk's.

High up in the opposite building a shutter rattled open, and somewhere in the distance a dog began to bark.

Guiding Tessa's arm around, Ravis said, "I choose this way."

At first Tessa thought he had decided to risk the far side of the bridge, but instead he led her toward Widow Furbish's door. The body of the second man lay across the step. Ravis had stabbed him in the back, and there was very little blood. As Tessa got close enough to see his features, she was surprised to see they were normal: not distorted or streamlined. He was just a man. Tessa shrugged. Her imagination had been playing tricks on her.

"Look up," hissed Ravis in her ear as she put her first foot on the step. "I'll tell you when to look down."

Tessa responded to the authority in his voice immediately, though it took her a second to work out the reason behind the strange request. He didn't want her to see Swigg's body. Too late, she thought; already seen it. But she didn't look down again.

It was dark and cold in the house. The smell of blood caught in Tessa's throat: she didn't want to breathe it in. She stood, staring at the dark expanse of ceiling, and waited while Ravis locked and barred the door. Finished, he took her arm and guided her toward the stock room where she'd spent the night. "Stay here a moment," he said as he moved back into the other room. Seconds later golden light spilled from the doorway.

Outside the house, the sounds of barking became louder. Footfalls drummed against the boards of the bridge.

When Ravis returned to the stock room, Tessa tensed. With the light behind him, he looked just like one of the attackers. Their meaty, wet-fur odor was on his clothes and in his hair. Did she smell the same? she wondered.

"Now," Ravis said. "We haven't got much time. It won't be long before whoever is waiting outside realizes we aren't coming out. I'm counting on them thinking we never spotted them, and that the only reason we came in the house is to pick up our belongings." He waited until Tessa nodded, then knelt on one knee before her. Wiping his blade one more time against his leg, he said, "This will only take a minute."

Alarmed, Tessa stepped back. Ravis grabbed the skirt of her dress, stopping her from taking another step. "I'm only going to cut it off at your knees. I'll be sure to keep your modesty intact."

Cutting it off at her knees? What on earth was he talking about? Tessa wished that her head weren't pounding so much and she could think straight.

Seeing the confusion on her face, Ravis smiled. "If we're going in the river, I don't want to risk your skirt getting caught around your legs. Now hold still." Pulling one section of her skirt taut, he began hacking away at the fabric.

"The river?"

Ravis nodded. "It's the best way. I'll lower you down from the window first, then follow you out. Don't worry, it shouldn't be too cold this time of year. And I'm pretty sure it's mostly mud down there, not water." He cut the final fistful of cloth, and the bottom of Tessa's skirt fell swishing to the floor. "Though it's best not to take any chances." He thought a moment, then added, "You can swim, can't you?"

Tessa nodded.

Standing up, Ravis gazed at her bare legs. "Good. Let's go."

Ridiculously, Tessa felt embarrassed by Ravis' attention.

She was only showing her knees, she told herself. It wasn't as if she were half-naked or anything.

Ravis opened the shutters. Sounds that had only been dull echoes earlier grew sharply louder. Barking, shouting, thudding. Tessa glanced at Ravis. "It's all right," he said. "The more noise the better—it will serve to cover our own."

He held out his hand. "The drop isn't bad—about fifteen paces."

Tessa joined him by the window; glad that the thumping in her head prevented her from concentrating. This wasn't a situation that would benefit from deep thought.

The smell rose up like smoke from a poorly burning fire. After the stench of blood and animals, the foul air from the river was a welcome change. Peering out, Tessa saw the river itself glinting darkly below. Gray silt banks flanked the sides, and beyond the black line of the river wall, the city crowded close like a milling, angry mob.

Thrmp! Thrmp!

The door. Someone was trying to break in. Tessa glanced at Ravis, and although he looked calm, his tooth raked against his scar.

He helped her up onto the windowsill. His touch was surprisingly gentle, and he paused a moment to push a strand of hair from her face. "Don't worry," he said softly, eyes looking straight into hers. "I'll be down a second later. Spread your arms wide, don't fight the current, but try to steer your way to the west bank."

Tessa barely nodded. She suddenly felt sick again. The face of the man who attacked her flashed through her mind. She saw teeth and gums and shining eyes. This was a world filled with mad, dangerous choices.

Thrmp! Thrmp! More banging at the door.

Ravis took her hands in his, and she scrambled out of the window. A cool draft blew over her bare legs as he lowered her down toward the water. His eyes were locked on hers and his grip was rock firm. He didn't want to let her go—even through fear, pain, and confusion, she could sense that.

"Only an instant behind you," he murmured as he released his grip.

Tessa dropped. Her stomach rose up to her chest and her

heart found its way to her throat. Cold air buffeted her body, and then she crashed into the oily, viscous water of the river.

Strangely, it wasn't as cold as she had expected, and its thickness helped buoy her up. Her head barely went under. She had no way of knowing how deep the river was, and she had no desire to find out. Her eyes, mouth, and nose were not going under again. There was no way she was going to risk any of this stinking, chunk-filled water finding its way down her throat. No way at all.

Unaware she was moving with the current, Tessa was surprised to see how far away from the bridge she had moved. As she looked up, a dark form dropped from a half-lit window into the water. Ravis. Tessa raised an arm, waved, considered shouting, then decided it was wiser to wave some more. Remembering Ravis' advice, she stretched out her arms on the surface and tried to steer herself toward the west bank. Her feet were kicking frantically, yet the water was so thick that she felt as if she were paddling through mud.

The smell didn't bear thinking about. Neither did the soft and bulging floaters that kept bobbing past her face. Grease formed a slick film on the water's surface, a rainbow of night colors swirling within. Tessa thought she saw patterns within the swirls. Intricate, shimmering lines of color, coiling around and upon each other like age rings on a tree. Like the golden threads in her ring.

The ring! Panicking, Tessa felt for the ribbon around her neck. Swollen fingers fumbled over drenched wool, desperate to feel the smoothness of silk. Finally her fingertips seized upon the ribbon, and she threaded it through her grasp until her thumb was pricked by barbs. Breathing a sigh of relief, she let the ribbon fall. She still had the ring.

Increasingly aware of the heaviness of her dress, Tessa forced herself to paddle harder to keep afloat. Her arms and legs obeyed her as best they could, but she'd had a long, exhausting day, and she could feel herself tiring. Funny, but her head had cleared up entirely. Her skull still ached where she had been hit, but now the pain seemed to be more of a needling, wake-up pain rather than a dull, throbbing sleep pain.

Shouting, splashing, howling noises sounded in the distance behind her. They seemed a long way off.

"Tessa," came a voice, rippling across the water's surface like a breeze.

Swinging her head back, Tessa spotted Ravis only feet behind her. She stretched out her hand, and within seconds he took it.

"This isn't normally where I take my lady friends in the evening," he said, moving alongside her, "but it does have its rewards." With that he brought his arm around her back and drew her close. "Now. Let's get to the bank."

Kicking together, they made good time. Tessa could feel Ravis' muscles working to hold her up. He didn't so much swim through the water as *attack* it: slicing, cutting, lunging. A few minutes later Tessa's foot hit the bottom. Feeling its soft, sludgy texture, she decided to continue paddling for as long as she could. Gradually she was forced to walk, feet sinking ankle deep into the sludge with every step. That in itself was bad enough, until Ravis hissed at her to get down. Almost clear of the water now, he didn't want to risk their pursuers catching a glimpse of them.

Cursing, Tessa fell onto all fours. The water began to look decidedly inviting as the silt sucked at her knees and wrists and her sodden dress hung on her body like a dead weight. She tried to take thin, fast breaths so as not to take in the terrible stench of dead things gone bad, but her lungs actively fought her. They needed all the air they could get.

As they crawled toward the river wall, Tessa risked glancing back. It was too dark to see if anyone had entered the water after them, but she thought she heard splashing noises in the distance.

Carcasses, bones, bloated bodies of rats and birds, rotting leaves, driftwood, and offal littered the silt. The nearer they got to the river wall, the worse it became. Long past disgust, Tessa actually found herself wanting to laugh. Here she was, running for her life, soaked to the skin, crawling through a mudbank that smelled like an open sewer. This wasn't how adventures were supposed to be.

The river wall was a pattern waiting to be read. The ground-level bricks were large and well cut, though very old. The higher the wall became, the less care had been put into its construction, and boulders, pebbles, and chips of stone had been added with little thought to either long-term preservation or aesthetics. The top layer had crumbled away completely. Streaks of mottled, yellow mortar laced between the bricks and stone like fat marbling through meat. Tessa studied the wall a moment longer, then shrugged. Patterns where everywhere she looked in this strange new world.

Once she had scrambled over the wall, she didn't dare stand. Crouching down, teeth chattering from cold, she turned to Ravis and said, "Where do we go from here?"

Ravis' eyes flicked from the wall, to the river, to the city. He chewed on his scar a while, then caught at her hand. "You know what?" he said, his lips curving to half a smile. "I think we may have been wrong to decline Emith's invitation earlier. Perhaps we should pay our respects to his dear old mother after all."

"We will begin the border attack tomorrow at dawn. Go forth and give the order to your men." Izgard of Garizon regarded the faces of his warlords and generals, looking for signs of weakness. A blink, a muscle twitch, a failure to meet his eye: anything that suggested fear or doubt. No man moved, not one of them. Izgard was well pleased. Snapping his wrist in dismissal, he turned his back upon them as they filed out the door.

There were emotions of his own he had no wish to betray.

Only when the door was closed and guarded seconds counted did Izgard let the stiffness ripple from his frame. Excitement was hot in his blood. As always these days when his thoughts dwelled on battle plans, he found himself trembling and short of breath. Crossing the great war room that formed the lead-and-granite heart of Sern Fortress, Izgard passed oak chests deep with maps, solid tables thick with scrolls, and bare stone walls crossed with weapons. In the corner of the room lay a dozen panels covered with cloth—paintings newly arrived from Veizach. Izgard had insisted they be ripped from the walls of Castle Veize: he had a craving to see images of war.

After tearing the cloth from the back of the first panel, Izgard angled the painting to catch the light. It was a battle scene depicting Hierac's great victory at Balinoc. The panel was alive with all the crimson shades of carnage, crowded with all the dark horrors of war. Broken limbs, weeping wounds, clenched fists, open mouths, and eyes wide, but blank, with terror.

Izgard's gaze was drawn to the deep crimson slash marking the death wound of Alroy, duke of Rosney. Slick and gleaming, his bloodied guts seemed to spill right off the board.

Izgard licked his lips. No one could paint blood like a Garizon. The Veizach Masters had named five hundred shades of red.

Letting the panel fall to the floor, Izgard stood and walked over to the nearest desk. Grasping one of several brim-full jugs, he did something he very rarely thought to do when alone. He poured himself a glass of wine. Red to match the blood on the paintings, strong to match the beating of his heart. He didn't bother to call for his taster. He knew the wine was safe, as two of his warlords had drunk from the same jug earlier. He always kept note of things like that.

Warming the glass in his fist, Izgard took a breath to calm himself. Tomorrow marked the true beginning of his reign. Only when the blood of the enemy had been spilled by his men and the emblem of the Barbed Coil had been raised over territory gained could he truly count himself a king.

Izgard swilled the wine on his tongue. He didn't taste it. He had never tasted anything in his life. Those who were born to wear the Barbed Coil always came into the world with one crucial flaw. Evlach the First had two fingers short of eight, his son Evlach the Second had been born with a clubbed foot, and his son after that had a disease that caused bone and flesh to grow at random on his face. He looked like a monster but won wars like a king: such were the rulers of Garizon. Even Hierac himself had been born blind in one eye. Yet he saw more with his one good eye than most men did with two, and it was that sense of something lost in order for something greater to be gained that united all the wearers of the crown. It was a thread, though not the only one, that linked kings past and present and added mystery and potency to the weft of the Coil.

No *whole* man could wear it.

Izgard swallowed the wine. It was so much lukewarm fluid to him. He could smell it—that enjoyment had not been denied him—but the taste eluded him completely.

Food was nothing but texture in his mouth. Soft, runny, oily, brittle, or rough: his smooth lizard's tongue could tell him that much, nothing more. He took no joy in eating. It was a physical chore, like urinating in a chamber pot, or clipping one's toenails, or rubbing fat into skin that was too dry. Izgard ate because he had to, because if he didn't, he would die.

As a child, he had once come close to death when he'd simply refused to eat anything set before him. Like fools, the kitchen staff thought to give him the richest joints of game meat, hoping to build up his strength. Meat was the worst thing to eat without taste. Leathery, fibrous, grizzled: it needed to be endlessly chewed and ground by the teeth before swallowing. And when one could not taste it while performing the task, the rewards were disappointing to say the least. The four-year-old Izgard had simply spat it out. After eight days of spitting, the physicians had become involved; they'd poked, prodded, postured, and puzzled. "What's wrong with you, boy!" they'd exclaimed. "Can't you taste how good the meat is?" Only when Izgard had shaken his head and replied, "I don't know what you mean," had they finally suspected the truth. Tests had been given. All sorts of foul-tasting potions had been dropped upon his tongue—iodine, castor oil, verjuice, and strong vinegar—and his reactions duly monitored like an insect under glass.

When finally the doctors had realized that he simply could not taste food, they'd nodded their heads as if they had known such a thing all along and murmured privately to themselves that this young smooth-tongued boy would one day wear the Coil.

He had the flaw for it.

By the time he'd reached his manhood, he could travel nowhere in Veizach without people whispering, "There is Izgard, son of Abor. They say he has a taste for nothing except blood." In any other city in the western continent those words would have been meant as an insult. In Veizach they were considered high praise.

Izgard swallowed the wine. He did not take another sip. He placed the goblet upon the desk, then took the necessary strides toward the door. Other matters needed his attention. He had been rough with Ederius earlier, and it had been preying on his mind ever since. The scribe was everything to him. Everything. He was the only man in Garizon Izgard trusted to hold the Coil. Yet whenever they were together Izgard found himself losing control and lashing out.

Mind set on making amends, Izgard burst into the scriptorium. Two figures froze at his entrance: Ederius, sitting at his scribing desk, leaning back in his chair, knife and quill resting motionless atop the illumination set before him; and Angeline, standing at his back, pretty-painted fingernails resting upon the coarse brown wool at his left shoulder. The Barbed Coil rested on a plinth behind them. Gold it was, but the shadow it cast matched the color of blood.

Both Ederius and Angeline stared wide-eyed at Izgard for an instant and then quickly sprang apart.

"Izgard," breathed Angeline in her high little-girl's voice. "Poor Ederius' shoulder was aching so. He has been working so hard and his muscles began to cramp, and the bone is badly broken—"

"Ssh," hissed Izgard.

Angeline's mouth closed. Her right hand fluttered by her side. Her left hand sidled up to the desk and silently slid a piece of parchment away.

Izgard was beside her in an instant, fingers gripping her wrist. "Give me that."

Angeline's face crumpled. Her blue eyes began to tear. "It's mine. I won't show it."

Furious, Izgard hit her with a half-closed fist. Her neck snapped back. She went sprawling sideways, falling onto the bare stone floor.

Ederius took a sharp breath.

Izgard raised his hand for a second strike. Catching himself at the last moment, he snatched the sheet from Angeline's hand instead. Crushing the parchment in his fist, he worked to control his rage. Minutes passed before it left him. No one moved or spoke.

Abruptly, Izgard's vision sharpened and cleared. The blood pumping through his temples slowed. Uncurling his fist, he smoothed out the sheet of parchment. It was a line drawing of a dog. All its limbs had been filled in with different colors, and his head and tail shone out in gold. A child's coloring page.

"Sire," Ederius said softly, "I just drew a small fancy to amuse the queen. Her Highness enjoys painting along with me."

Izgard nodded absently. He knelt by his wife and offered her his hand. "Come, my love," he said in his most gentle voice. "Take my hand. Let me help you up."

Angeline didn't move. A fat bead of blood welled up on her lip. Her gaze darted to Ederius.

Moving his hand upward, Izgard wiped the blood from his wife's mouth. As his knuckle grazed across her lips, Izgard felt something deep within his chest turn. Angeline was trembling; her small fingers clutched at the fabric of her dress. What had possessed him to hit her? She had only been comforting Ederius, that was all. Confused by the sudden switch of his emotions, Izgard pulled his hand away. "Go now, Angeline," he said, straightening to his full height. "I would talk to my scribe alone."

Angeline knew enough about his voice and moods to recognize those times it was best to do as she was told. She stood, brushed down her dress, and walked out of the room, closing the door behind her as gently as a scolded child.

Izgard turned his attention to Ederius. The scribe's left shoulder was a bulky, bandaged lump beneath his robe. Izgard wanted to touch and soothe it. Instead he said, "I never want to see you and my wife alone again. Is that clear?"

"But, sire, the queen is like a child to me, a daughter. I would never—"

Izgard cracked a fist onto Ederius' desk. Papers jumped, glazed pots chinked. A jug tippled over, spilling water onto Ederius' latest illumination. "I said is that clear?"

Ederius hung his head. Water dripped from the desk onto his lap. "Perfectly, sire."

"Good." Izgard nodded. The effort of holding himself back had left him drained. Now his anger had cleared, he realized that Angeline and the scribe were involved in nothing unseemly. Angeline had doubtless seen the scribe's work and wanted to try it for herself. The old scribe, anxious to please his queen, had probably gone out of his way to amuse her, and Angeline was always so grateful whenever anyone showed her kindness. Here in Sern Fortress she was isolated from her friends, and with both her father and brother now dead, she had no family to call her own.

An eternal little girl, Angeline had doted on her dear, drunken brother and her pockmarked papa. Izgard could still recall the first time he had ever set eyes on her. She was kneeling at her father's feet, warming them in her hands to improve his circulation. A vision of daughterly devotion. During the meeting with her father, Izgard could hardly take his eyes off her. She was the ideal Garizon beauty: pale, full hipped, and fresh faced. When she spoke she revealed yet another charm: her sweet, uncultured nature.

Izgard shook his thoughts away. Angeline was a fool. She meant less and less to him as the days went by. War and the Coil were all that mattered now.

Gaze circling the scriptorium, Izgard sought out his crown. The Barbed Coil shone gold in the candlelight. Hammer welded at white heat like a greatsword, fine rods of platinum, iron, and latten had been twisted into the molten gold. Once forged into a single billet, the cooling metal had been folded in upon itself a thousand times, then extruded to form a single strand of incalculable length before being beaten into a coil to fit a man. The gold looked like no other metal Izgard had ever seen. Its color and texture changed by the moment. And although it had once been tested and found to be ninetenths gold, it was harder than the finest fighting steel.

Worked in such a way that it reflected more of itself than its surroundings, the Barbed Coil seemed to glow with a private, inner light. Each strand of gold had been etched with its own set of designs. Cut deep to reveal the dark, multilayered interior of the metal, subtle patterns and markings chased their way across the gold. Recently Ederius had taken to re-creating the patterns and markings in his illuminations. It was how he made the harras more than men.

Turning to Ederius, Izgard said, "Let us consider the matter of my wife behind us. Tell me, have your sketchings been successful tonight?" As he spoke, Izgard reached out and stroked Ederius' thinning gray hair. He liked to touch those who were close to him.

Ederius tried hard not to flinch. "I have failed you, sire. Lord Ravis has escaped us again."

Izgard shook his head sadly. There was nothing for Ederius to be afraid of. Spying a lock of hair out of place on the scribe's temple, he smoothed it back. "What happened this time?"

A rivulet of sweat spilled from the hairline above Ederius' ear. "I'm not sure. There were six men in all—a pair waiting in the house and a pair apiece keeping watch on either end of the bridge. As you instructed, no one took action until Lord Ravis tried to enter the house." Ederius' voice rose higher as he spoke. "From what I can tell, Lord Ravis overcame the two harras in the house and then evaded the others by jumping into the river."

"And the remaining harras?" Izgard ran a finger along the scribe's cheekbone. "Did they not pursue him into the river?"

Ederius' nod was quick in coming. "Yes, sire. Two of the harras jumped in after him, but it was very dark at water level, and no one could be sure if they had swum to the east bank or the west, or followed the river downstream."

"They?" Izgard's finger moved across Ederius' brow to the bridge of his nose.

"Lord Ravis had a lady with him at the time."

"A lady." Izgard spat out the word. He twisted away from Ederius and stalked toward the crown. Ederius let out a tiny, almost imperceptible sigh of relief behind his back. Izgard heard it nonetheless. Born with one sense short of five, he took pains to ensure that the remaining four stretched themselves to fill the void. Izgard had the hearing of a creature of the dark.

Reaching out to touch the threads of the Barbed Coil, he said, "I don't think any woman who chose to be with Ravis of Burano would dare call herself a lady. A whore, certainly; a deluded fool, perhaps; maybe even an unwilling victim dragged away against her will." Aware of where his thoughts were leading him, and reluctant to pursue further, Izgard worked to change the course of his words. "I want Ravis of Burano dead. I will order more harras to Bay'Zell, and I want you to ensure they do their job well and swiftly." He ran his thumb over a cluster of golden barbs. He hadn't changed the subject at all, just honed it to a single deadly point.

In his anger, Izgard pressed his open palm against the crown. He closed his eyes as the barbs bit into his flesh. The pain was as pure and piercing as a Garizon prayer, and Izgard felt stronger for having suffered it. Straight away, his mind refocused on what was important: winning the coming war.

He turned his attention back to Ederius. Moving close to the scribe's side, Izgard set the fallen water jug back on its base. The pattern beneath was ruined; various colored inks had run into one, and the wet stain that remained was the color of blood.

Touching Ederius' broken shoulder as tenderly as Angeline had before him, Izgard said, "Come, my old friend, you must sleep. You have had a long, hard night, and now it is time to rest. I need you to be here at daybreak. A new pattern must be started before the battle at dawn."

The scribe patted Izgard's hand gently. "Yes, sire, you are right. I must rest."

Izgard's smile was gentle as he helped Ederius' out of his chair. He loved the old scribe very much.

NINE

ercury-rich vermilion ink slashed across the page, a thousand times more deadly than the sum of its poisonous parts. Honeyed gold spiraled behind it, a gilded viper at its heels. Red lead pinpoints blistered onto the parchment like venom from a snake. White lead would come later: red's lethal sister was best kept to last.

A complex mixture of folium purple and copper blue came next. If mercury vermilion formed the arteries, then copper folium formed the veins. Skeins of amethyst ink pumped from the scribe's brush, forming a varicose of lines. Yellow arsenic followed. Thickly mixed, it wept onto the page like pus suppurating from a wound. Through it all—through the yellow and blue and purple and red—the gold ink coiled like the serpent it was. Fat-bodied curves entwined scarlet vessels, constricting the flow of pigment to the upper left quarter of the page. Made from powdered gold, honey, and glair, the gold ink cut through all the lines in its path like an assassin slitting throats.

The scribe felt each deadly blow. He felt them in his temples and in the slowly mending bone at his collar and the muscles surrounding his heart. His eyes ached, his robe was damp with sweat, yet although his upper arm cramped with the strain of steadying his grip, his fingers never shook.

No one, not even an assassin, needed a steadier hand than a scribe.

The scribe didn't waste his energy on a smile, though he did let his bitterness work its way onto the parchment, where he could be sure it would do nothing but good.

He *was* an assassin. A deft hand, a clever eye, and a knowledge of poisonous substances: the two were surely one and the same. Here, in his grip and lying flat under his palms, were his weapons and poisons of choice: brush, parchment, pigment. His victims lay twenty leagues to the west, and as in all expert assassinations, they didn't suspect a thing. Seeing only a troop of armed men—not enough to be named a company, nor sufficient to be perceived as a threat—they let the men approach. "Look, they aren't heavily armed," they said. "They surely mean us no harm."

Ederius saw through the eyes of the creatures he had created from men: his pulse beat with their pulse, he felt what they felt. And even though he had created the raw need to kill within them, its sheer ferocity chilled him to the bone. They smelled their victims' breath like a hungry man smelled a meal. His tongue wetted with theirs, and he was powerless to stop it.

Briefly Ederius glanced up from his illumination. The Barbed Coil rested on a plinth before him, the gold weaving a secret maze for his eyes alone. The frame of light and shadow burned an image on his retina like the sun. When he looked down at the parchment, he saw the design he was working upon through the filter of the crown. The two images fit together like the pieces of a puzzle, and suddenly and irrefutably Ederius knew what he must do.

The brush became an extra finger and the pigments gushed from it like blood from a wound. Colors he mixed were deeper than any he'd mixed before. The brushstrokes he made were both swift and audacious, executed with the careless grace of a devil and the accuracy of a marksman taking aim.

The men approached their victims—Rhaize villagers in the border town of Chalce—blades warm against their thighs, vision showing all that moved, teeth unfamiliar shapes in their mouths. Minds were sharp, senses keen, and, as the illumination began to shift toward its final form, a feeling of unity swept through the group. Before the Barbed Coil they had been separate beings; now they acted and thought as one.

Ederius was a master magician, orchestrating his show with a cool hand, a swift eye, and an unshakable vision of all he could achieve. Scarlet ink sprayed the page as the men fell on the villagers. The scribe heard their cries, saw their horror at the breadth of savagery unleashed, and, without as much as a blink of an eye, incorporated the terror within the page. It was binder for the ink.

"So few," he heard one young man whisper. "Who would have thought so few could bring such—"

A spearhead of gold cut through a dark vein of purple, and the man neither said, did, nor thought anything more. Ederius dropped dots of red lead around the severed edge for no other reason than it felt the right thing to do. Brushstrokes followed knife strokes, knotwork became strategies, and spirals became movements in the drama to the west. The Barbed Coil was a ghost on the page. A terrible, bloodthirsty muse.

Nine men there were. Nine harras hand-picked by Izgard for their weapon skills and intelligence, and somehow the illumination forming on the scribe's desk brought all their training together, creating a whole being from the sum of their nine parts.

Ederius wanted more. He could control twenty, thirty, a hundred men. A company, a battalion, an army could be his! He knew everything they knew, their strengths were his strengths, and their weaknesses sank to the bottom like pigment settling in ink.

Line after line, the scribe carved upon the page. Original hardpoint guidelines, so painstakingly measured and worked out earlier, were ignored. Rules of symmetry, mirroring, and repetition fell away. Nothing was important, only reproducing his vision of the Coil. As villager after villager was slain, new designs emerged from the flood of colors bleeding over the parchment. Complex, beautiful, fascinating: they challenged the mind and quickened the heart and sent a white-hot excitement to the core.

Still the carnage continued. No longer any men left to slay, the harras turned on the women and children: spines snapped, jaws broke, bladders emptied. Ederius used each cry of terror and plea for mercy as fuel for his great feat of scribing. He fed off their fear. When finally there were no more people to kill, the harras turned their fury on the animals. Dogs, hens, pigs, calves: anything that moved was hacked until it moved no more.

Nine men there were. Nine lightly armed men. Yet they massacred a village of over ten times their number. And they did it in less than an hour.

When finally there was nothing more to kill and messages were sent to the army waiting on the far side of the pass, Ederius felt himself beginning to fail. With hands stained red and gold, he made the final penstrokes, following the imagined lines to their ultimate, eloquent end. He was close to losing the harras. He was even closer to losing himself. A feeling of well-being washed over him. He had created a magnificent design. The Barbed Coil held a world full of secrets, and it had chosen to let him glimpse one for a while.

Ederius felt his eyes closing. His brush fell from his grip and rolled from the desk onto the floor. If it made a sound when it landed, the scribe never heard it.

He awoke. Blinking, he ran a hand over the edge of the page. It was a reflex reaction of all scribes: *How dry is the paint? How long have I slept?* The paint was sticky, almost dry. An hour and a half, perhaps two, had passed.

Ederius wiped his old eyes, worked the cramp from his right arm, rubbed his aching collarbone, and then looked down at the illumination he had scribed.

A sharp pain coursed though his heart. Random bands and splashes of color met his eye. He searched and searched but could perceive no design. There *was* none. It was pure chaos.

Seeing it for what it was, Ederius hung his head low and wept.

"Emith! Emith! Come quickly and turn my chair. The young lady is beginning to stir."

Tessa opened her eyes. She was looking at a rafter hung

with herbs. A second rafter bristled with bacon joints, and a third was agleam with copper pots. Smells, good ones, sailed up her nose along with heat, steam, and smoke. Rising, Tessa saw that she was in a large firelit kitchen, cluttered with pans, teapots, bowls, and odd wooden devices she couldn't begin to name, dominated by a large figure of a woman sitting on an oak-framed chair facing toward the fire.

The woman, who had her back to Tessa, turned her head and nodded. "Morning, my dear. Emith will be here in a minute, then I can take a proper look at you."

Tessa swung her feet onto the floor. She had been sleeping on a wooden bench softened by a mattress filled with straw. Blankets smelling of things pickled and preserved slid down over her knees, and a nightgown the color of hazelnuts brushed against the floor. Her muscles felt stiff, her feet were aching, and her head felt decidedly heavy.

"Miss," called Emith from the doorway, "I'll just wait here until you're decent."

Tessa spun around. Emith was staring intently at the door frame. Glancing down at her nightgown, Tessa could only smile. *Decent?* She couldn't remember the last time she had worn anything as decent as this: the sleeves fell to her wrists, the hemline covered her toes, and the neckline was high enough for strangling. And judging from the slight chafing she felt directly under her chin, it may well have started out even higher.

"There's a robe hanging on the larder door, my dear. Could you be a helpful honeybee and fetch it yourself? My legs are just a little achy today." The bulky figure swiveled round a fraction farther. "And as for you, Emith, go into the larder until I call your name. I'll have no one saying that anything untoward goes on in my household. Stepping into a room where a lady is standing in her nightgown, indeed! What on earth would your father have said?"

"Sorry, Mother," came Emith's reply as his feet pattered away in the distance.

Feeling as though she'd made a terrible mistake, Tessa dove for the larder door. She reminded herself that this wasn't her world now: things that meant nothing to her meant everything to these people. It wasn't that attitudes were necessarily different here—her own mother wouldn't have approved of her appearing in a flimsy nightdress in front of strangers—but they were certainly more condensed.

"I'm sorry," she said to the back of Mother Emith's head as she shouldered on the robe. "I didn't mean to offend anyone." Noticing a set of ribbons sewn high up on the collar, Tessa tied them tight for good measure before walking into the old woman's line of vision.

She was met by a face that was somehow both long *and* round, boasting a pair of deep-set blue eyes that twinkled as brightly as the fire. "Nothing to worry about, my dear. 'Twas my own fault. If it weren't for my old legs here, I would have brought you the robe myself."

Tessa looked down at Mother Emith's legs. Everything but her feet and ankles were covered by her dress. The skin on her ankles was red and swollen, and her feet had a purple tinge. Mother Emith patted her knee. "Come closer, my pet, so I may see you more clearly." Then, shouting over Tessa's head: "You can come back now, Emith. Pour us all a cup of warm milk."

Tessa moved closer. Mother Emith leaned forward in her chair and slapped a warm palm upon Tessa's forehead. "Hmm. No fever. Open your mouth, my dear. Wide." Tessa did as she was told. "No swelling. Good. Good. Now turn around so I can see the back of your head."

Mother Emith *hmm*'d a bit more, then Tessa felt a bright flare of pain above her ear as the woman touched a tender spot. "Easy, my dear," soothed the old lady. "You've a lump the size of a crabapple up there."

"Here you are, miss," Emith said, drawing close with two bowls full of steaming milk. He handed the first to Tessa with a shy smile. "I added a sprinkle of cinnamon."

"I hope you put the cinnamon in while the milk was warming, Emith?" said his mother. Emith nodded. Satisfied, his mother tapped Tessa lightly on the shoulder in dismissal. "You'll need some witch hazel on that, my dear, and perhaps we should brew up a pot of wort-leaf tea just to be safe."

"Should I do it, Mother?" asked Emith, placing the second bowl of milk on the small hand table at his mother's side

Emith's mother patted her son on the arm and smiled.

She was very old. "You're a good boy, Emith. I'm glad you're home. If you could just turn my chair a shade for me first. It's getting a little too warm facing the fire."

Tessa watched as Emith worked to shift his mother's chair while his mother sat in it. How had such a large woman managed to have such a small son? Despite their differences in size, there were similarities between them: they shared the same dark blue eyes, and both dressed with extreme neatness. Comb lines could be spotted in both Emith's graying hair and the few snow white tufts that were left of his mother's.

Glancing around at the room, noticing the way it was laid out, Tessa got the distinct feeling that the solid oak chair that Emith was currently struggling to move marked not only the geographical center of the room, but also its very heart. Tessa had an odd image of Mother Emith and her chair slowly turning to face various points in the kitchen as the day went by, ticking around like the hands on a clock.

"Where is Ravis?" Tessa asked, pushing away the bowl of milk. She had never cared for warm milk; it reminded her of being ill as a child.

Emith wiped a sheen of sweat from his brow. His mother was now in place, and after settling her feet on a small footstool, he said, "Lord Ravis went out very early this morning, miss. He asked me to tell you not to worry, he would be back later."

"Oh." Tessa tried not to sound disappointed, tried not to *feel* disappointed. At some point during all the madness yesterday, she had begun to think of Ravis and herself as a team. Foolishness, she told herself. What use was she to a man who was in as much trouble as Ravis?

Tessa shivered as details of all that happened last night flashed through her mind: Ravis fighting the two attackers at Widow Furbish's door, the yellow glint of teeth, Swigg's broken body, the mad leap into the river. The journey back through the city had been little more than a blur.

Tessa had never thought of herself as physically weak, yet after she'd dragged herself up from the mudbanks she'd barely been able to stand. She remembered leaning heavily against Ravis and then not leaning at all. Ravis had picked her up and carried her through the dark, silent streets of

Bay'Zell. By the time they'd arrived at Mother Emith's house, it had taken all of her strength to lift her head off Ravis' shoulder, and Tessa now found she couldn't remember any of what had happened once they'd crossed the threshold into the warm, fragrant shadows beyond. She and Ravis had turned up wet and filthy, yet Emith and his mother had taken them in all the same.

"I want to thank you," she said. "Both of you. You've been very kind to me, and I—"

"Ssh, my dear," Mother Emith said. "There's no need to thank me and Emith. Emith warned me you might be coming to stay last night when you dropped him off."

"He did?" Tessa was immediately suspicious.

"Yes, miss." Emith was in the process of replacing Tessa's bowl of milk with a bowl of something else. "After we talked about Master Deveric's illuminations on the way home from Fale yesterday, when you showed me your drawing, I began thinking that perhaps you were the one my master was talking about. Perhaps you were meant to carry on his work."

"Be sure to drink all your tea, my dear," Mother Emith cut in. "There's nothing like wort-leaf tea for soothing achy muscles."

Tessa took the bowl in her hands. Odd flakes of dark matter floated on the surface, bleeding green pigment into the liquid. "You have no way of being sure it's me, Emith. All I did was sketch a ring."

Emith nodded. "You're right, miss. But the thought niggled away at me all the way home." As he spoke, Emith cleared a space on the huge trestle table that dominated the far wall of the room. Fat sacks of flour and spices were shoved to one side, along with pots, pans, cleavers, and root vegetables. "There was something about your sketch, miss. The way you draw curves reminds me of my master."

"You should listen to Emith, my dear." Mother Emith twisted around in her chair to face Tessa. "He's not one to rush to judgment on anything." Slapping her hand against her thigh, she said, "I know, just to be sure, why don't we all take another look at the sketch, here, in God's good light of day?"

The sketch? The last thing Tessa remembered about it

was folding it up and stuffing it down her bodice on the road back to Bay'Zell. "I must have jumped into the river with it," she said, walking into Mother Emith's sphere of vision. She didn't like seeing the white-haired lady strain.

"It was a charcoal drawing, miss. There's a fair chance it would have survived a wetting—ink or paint and it would have run clean away." Having cleared a good portion of the table, Emith was now taking things out of a chest: small glazed pots, brushes, scrolls, wads of cloth, flight feathers, and rolls of cork. "Your clothes are in the basket by the fire, miss."

"If you don't mind, my dear," Mother Emith said, "could you just fetch the basket yourself? I'm afraid you've caught me on a bit of a bad morning. Any other time and I'd be scurrying around the kitchen like a lost ant. Wouldn't I, Emith?"

Emith nodded softly. When he spoke his voice was subdued. "Yes, Mother."

Tessa walked past Mother Emith, trying hard not to look at her swollen ankles. The basket by the fire contained the remains of Tessa's dress and her shoes, nothing more. The scroll must have floated from her bodice when she was in the river. "I can't find it."

"It doesn't matter, miss," Emith said, mixing water and matte black powder into a bowl. "I'll soon have everything ready for you to try your hand at something else."

"Yes," echoed his mother from her chair. "Never mind about the sketch, my dear. Some things were made to be lost."

Thinking it a rather odd thing to say, Tessa looked up at Mother Emith. The old woman looked back at her, eyes twinkling.

"Come on, miss," Emith said, knife and flight feather now in hand. "I've just cut you a fresh nib. Let's see if you can scribe something to match the sketch you lost."

Tessa looked at Mother Emith a moment longer, then crossed over to her son. The kitchen was a large, low-ceilinged room with so many items hanging from the rafters that she had to duck constantly to avoid them. The floor was good, plain stone of the sort that she had seen a lot of during the ride to Fale. Light came mostly from the fire burning in the hearth, but thin strips of sunlight banded the room, spilling from two unglazed windows cut high into the wall.

"Here, miss," Emith said, taking the bowl of wort-leaf tea from Tessa and handing her the quill. "I've cut a fine tip, perfect for detailed work. It's a hard one, too. I boiled it myself a week ago, and it's spent all the time since in sand."

Tessa ran a finger over the nib. "Boiled? Sand?" She didn't understand what Emith was saying.

Gently Emith corrected her grip, moving her fingers so she held the quill like a fountain pen. "Yes, miss. You can't just pluck a goose and expect to write straight away with the feather. It has to be boiled to clean it and to make it soft and ready for shaping. While it's still hot I take my dutching hook and flatten the nib and the shaft. See?" He pointed to the areas of the quill that had been shaped. "And once that's done, I bury it in sand to make it good and hard. The longer you keep the feathers buried, the harder they become."

The nib felt as tough and smooth as a fingernail. It was almost the same color too. Looking at the eager expression on Emith's face, Tessa felt she should say something complimentary. "This feels like a good one," she said, weighing it in her hand. "I'm sure it will last a long time."

Emith shook his head. "Master always said it's the best ones that last the least."

Tessa was beginning to feel like a fool. "Why?"

"Because the better the pen, miss, the more a scribe will favor using it, and the more times the nib will have to be recut. I've seen Master Deveric whittle down as many as three pens in one day."

"So the nib wears down?" Feeling its hard toughness, Tessa found it hard to imagine.

"Yes, miss." Emith spoke softly and without a trace of impatience. "But you needn't worry about that. I'll be here ready to recut it for you as soon as the line thickens."

"Be sure to listen carefully to Emith, my dear," said Mother Emith. "There's no one in Bay'Zell who knows more about scribing than my son."

Emith actually blushed. He hurried on, pulling out a chair for Tessa to sit. "Here, miss," he said, guiding her hand toward a pot of ink. "This is how you dip to pick up the right amount of ink. You need to do it at an angle. See?" Tessa nodded. "And then you bend your wrist a little to keep the ink in the pen when you move it."

Tessa did as she was told, though a large drop of ink splashed onto the table. Emith was ready with a cloth. Drawing the pen over the square of parchment, Tessa was surprised at how difficult it was. Not like using a fountain pen at all. The nib scratched a furrow in the parchment and the ink pooled, then soaked into the lines created.

"Emith, could you bring the vegetables over? I'll need to peel them for the herring bake."

As Emith collected vegetables, bowl, and knife for his mother, Tessa concentrated on getting the nib to do as she wanted. The parchment itself was a problem because it was so much rougher than the paper she was used to. By the time Emith got back she had made a complete mess of the page.

"You don't have to press so hard, miss," he said, looking over her shoulder. "Let the ink do the work for you, not the nib."

"The ink?" As Tessa spoke, Mother Emith began humming a tune. Vegetable scraping sounds soon followed.

"Yes, miss," Emith said. "You only need to touch the page lightly. The ink will soak in of its own accord. It's made from gallic acid, you see, so it burns right into the page. Scrape too hard with your nib and the ink will sear the page like a cattle brand."

"This is acid?" Tessa found herself becoming interested in what Emith was saying.

Emith nodded. "Gallic acid, gum, and lampblack. I make it myself. Of course it's going to be more difficult for me to find gallnuts now I'm in the city. I'll probably have to buy them at market, so they won't be nearly as good." Seeing Tessa's puzzled expression, Emith explained further. "Gallnuts grow on the bark of oak trees after they've been stung by laying insects. There's a grove of fine oaks just at the back of my master's house, and all I ever had to do when I needed ink was take a walk and gather them. I'd chop them off, soak them in water overnight, and by the following morning they'd be ready to take the lampblack."

Tessa raised an eyebrow.

"Carbon powder," Emith explained without being asked. "It's what forms on the glass of burning oil lamps."

"Emith, could you set these vegetables to boil?" Mother Emith held out a copper pan. "And while you're up could you bring over the fish to be gutted?"

Tessa wondered how Emith's mother had gotten along before her son came. It was beginning to look as if she *couldn't* move from her chair. Yet the kitchen was so tidy and fragrant, and good things were cooking on the hearth. Tessa smiled: Emith's mother had a rare talent for asking people to do things without seeming bossy or troublesome. That probably had a lot to do with it.

Doodling with pen and ink, Tessa marveled at all Emith had told her. She liked hearing the details of scribing, ink making, and quill shaping. She even liked the feel of the quill in her hand. Carefully she began to trace spirals similar to the coils in the ring, turning the nib every so often to broaden the line to a barb. It was good to be here, in a warm kitchen, with Emith and his mother taking care of her. After all the madness of yesterday, she welcomed the peace and quiet. Funny, but she didn't feel like relaxing, though. She was determined to make the quill do what she wanted and make the ink go where it was supposed to. And as Emith turned his mother's chair another degree and put the vegetables to boil on the hearth, Tessa turned her full attention to the parchment. She was going to draw a better pattern than the one that had gone missing in the river, one that wasn't made to be lost.

Ravis walked through the streets of Bay'Zell. He knew Camron of Thorn would be waiting in Marcel's house to meet with him, yet he felt disinclined to be prompt for his new master. Let him and his newly inherited fortune wait.

Bay'Zell was a slow city at noon. Ravis walked down Fortune Street with its stylish pastry shops, elegant cobblers, and discreet pawnbrokers, then headed north into the Hemming Quarter, where the well-to-do middle classes and the respectable prostitutes shopped.

Prostitutes in lace hoods and carefully muted dresses of gray and brown greeted Ravis with a raise of an eyebrow or a slight incline of the head. The middle-class women simply ignored him. Sitting in shaded arcades, they sipped warm arlo thickened with honey and nibbled at apple tarts laced with sloe gin. Later on in the afternoon they would head over to Fortune Street and rifle through the pawnbroker's stores, anxious to buy anything that had been sold off by noblemen who had fallen upon hard times.

The middle-class women all knew their husbands visited prostitutes, but it gave them some satisfaction to say, "At least it is a girl from the Hemming Quarter, not one of those cheap, gaudy trollops from the docks." Still, no matter how stoically they regarded their husbands' indiscretions, the main reason they frequented the Hemming Quarter was to keep an eye on the prostitutes, lest they develop a taste for finery and fine airs to go with their heavy purses. The prostitutes, for their part, saw fit to play along. And although they wore enough red silks and golden threads by night to upholster a dynasty's worth of thrones, they always dressed discreetly during the day. Such were the moral standards of Bay'Zell.

Ravis was well aware of how he appeared to the middle-class women: his dark coloring marked him a foreigner, and his dark clothing marked him as dangerous. Yet, they thought as he approached their dainty arcades, he holds himself like a nobleman, and his clothes, although unfashionably black, are surely of the finest cut and cloth. Then he got close enough for them to see his scar, and each and every one of them looked away.

Normally Ravis would force them to look at him by bowing and offering the greeting "Ladies." Today he passed them right by.

Down Enameling Street with its slight, shabby shopfronts boasting goldsmiths, silversmiths, scribes, clerks, money lenders, and jewelers, down onto the north quay, where the rough cobbled road gave way to smooth dirt and a fresh easterly breeze blew away the smell of smoldering metal, acid, and once good timbers turned to rot.

Occasionally, out of the corner of his eye, Ravis would

catch a glimpse of a man dressed in a dark green tunic with a silver insignia on his breast. Thorn colors. The man dodged sunlight only tolerably well and was slow to move from his mark's line of vision when spotted. And considering he was wearing a bulky winter cloak for the sole purpose of concealing a crossbow beneath it, he succeeded only in drawing more attention to himself. No one in Bay'Zell had business wearing such a thick cloak in late spring. All in all, the poor man wasn't doing a very good job. Camron had obviously sent him to track down and then follow his new hired hand, and the only question that currently interested Ravis about the matter—for he guessed the man had caught up with him just after dawn when he returned to the brothel to check on Camron's story—was the dire possibility that this guard was one of Camron's best.

Ravis chewed his scar. If he was to do what was agreed in Marcel's wine cellar, then he would need good men around him. And judging from the lackluster performance of Camron's guard, he was going to have to train them himself.

Increasing his pace, Ravis walked along the quay. The northern harbor was smaller and less important than the western one. No large merchant ships anchored here, no spice boats or silk boats or pleasure crafts. No huge merchant vessels were built in the dry docks, and no tariff keepers could be spotted on the wharf, busy with their pens and scrolls. Fishermen, their boats, their lines, their nets, and their women, were what made the north harbor what it was. If you didn't look back at Bay'Zell, you could almost believe that the harbor belonged to a small fishing town, not the foremost port city in the west.

Picking a path between thick coils of rope, crates of fish—some still skipping—and fishermen mending their nets, Ravis made his way along the wooden wharf. The north harbor was busy without being bustling. Fishermen who spent their lives sailing their two-masters in search of sole and turbot, and their three-masters in search of cod, had little time for show. They worked long hours with little fuss, drank hard before sunset, and rose before dawn, and as long as their nets were sturdy and their hulls were sound, they counted themselves lucky and set sail for the horizon each day.

The north harbor wasn't a place to come in search of clever conversation, fine scenery, or fancy food, but Ravis liked it all the same. It was a useful place to know and be known in. The most up-to-date information to be had in Bay'Zell could be garnered from fishermen landing their catch.

The world was full of organizations—brotherhoods, knighthoods, leagues, and guilds—yet none of them spanned borders and countries with such regularity and unsung freedom as fishermen. Merchant sailors swapped positions and berths too often to build up relationships with crews of matching vessels. A merchant crew could change literally by the day. But fishermen spent their lives at their work, sailing the same run, on the same boat year in, year out—their small crew never changing, their friends made and kept for life. Even though fishermen from Rhaize, Balgedis, Istania, and Maribane were rivals, they depended on each other for their lives. Storm warnings, changing information on dangerous undertows and shallows, pirate sightings, and dire prophecies were exchanged in the no-man's-land of the sea. When a fishing boat ran aground, no fisherman ever asked what flag the boat sailed under. They simply sailed as close as good sense would allow and did whatever they could.

Of course, not all exchanges were a matter of life and death. As much idle rumor passed from boat to boat as stories about the sea. Fishermen were notorious gossips. Fish*wives* lived to hear the tales their husbands brought home with the catch.

Ravis made it his business to befriend fishermen in every seafaring city he passed through. You never could tell when a salty old seadog might bring back a gem of a bone.

Spying a familiar dark-haired figure tying his line to the far bulwark, Ravis cut a path to the end of the wharf. Soon he would return to Marcel's town house and meet with Camron of Thorn, but he wanted to gather whatever information he could before he set things in motion that could not be reversed.

"Pegruff!" Ravis called, lifting a hand in greeting. "How has the sea been treating you lately?"

"A good sight better than my wife," came the reply. Pegruff finished looping a knot around the bulwark and then waited for Ravis to approach. Bay'Zell fishermen never walked any more than they had to.

The two men clasped hands and exchanged a brief, searching glance. Pegruff's face was a tribute to the scouring effects of sea salt. His skin was red, his lips were flaking, and what was left of his eyebrows was not sufficient to form a frown.

"Where's Jemi?" Ravis asked as they pulled apart.

"I've sent him to the market for wax."

Ravis nodded. Jemi was Pegruff's only son, and the first time Ravis met him was on a small street leading off the east harbor when Jemi had begged to be recruited into the life of a mercenary. He was tired of mending nets and waxing timbers. Ravis had talked the gentle and sweet-natured boy out of it. Some men weren't cut out to be soldiers. Some were made for the sea. Ravis sent Jemi back to his father—not with harsh words, but with the simple truth that a mercenary's life was neither glamorous nor rewarding, and he would only be swapping one form of hard labor for another. It wasn't kindness that made Ravis speak—he only recruited men he knew he could teach to kill—but Pegruff had chosen to think it was, and Ravis never wasted breath on denials.

"He's got a girl now, you know," Pegruff said, pulling out a flask of arlo and offering it to Ravis. "Sturdy thing, she is. Just the sort to settle him down."

Ravis took the offered drink. Pegruff might not have a fortune to match Marcel's, but he always managed to have the best arlo to be found in the entire city of Bay'Zell in his flask. Wiping his lips, Ravis said, "What's the word from the sea, my friend?"

Pegruff took back his flask, pausing to polish the pewter against his sleeve before he took a drink. Magpies and sailors: neither could resist anything shiny. "There's a Maribane brig anchored off Balinoc. Gillif, friend o' mine who keeps lobster nets near there, swears he saw a scull full of Garizons row out to it last week in the middle of the night."

"How did he know they were Garizons?"

"You mean besides 'em rowing badly?" The fisherman's smile was not as wide as it might have been. As a country that had no sea to call its own, Garizon was eyed with open suspicion by old seahands like Pegruff. They believed that every country that didn't have a coastline would do anything in their power to get one. And in Garizon's case they weren't far wrong. "Gillif says they were carrying 'em new-style pikes and not one man among 'em had a beard."

Ravis nodded. He had introduced the new, broader pike blade to Izgard's harras. "Anything else?"

Pegruff looked a little disgruntled that such a juicy tidbit had been so quickly set aside. He handled this by taking a decent swig of arlo and moving on. "Troubles brewing between Medran and Istania over the eastern passage. Why, this month alone a dozen Medrani barks have been pirated. Medran swears it's the work of Istanians, and there's been talk of sending galleons into the Gulf."

"There hasn't been a warship in the Gulf for . . ." Ravis paused to think.

"Fifty years," Pegruff finished for him. "I tell you, Lord Ravis, things don't look that rosy from out at sea. All I ever hear about these days is trouble. Ever since Bay'Zell doubled its port tolls last week, the bay has been rife with pirates, warships, skirmishes, and secret dealings. Drokho is about as snappish as a crab in a bucket. Taken to sending armed sloops into the bay, they have. 'Course, Maribane's madder than anyone. The Bay'Zell tolls are crippling their exports, and they're worried that Istania and Drokho will follow suit. Maribane's even moved its two largest galleons down from Port Shrift to Hayle. Officially they say it's to protect their hulls from northern storms, but every fool knows those storms won't hit for another month."

Pegruff took a swig from his flask. "I've been fishing these waters for thirty years now, give or take a few catches, and I can't remember the last time I felt less like setting sail in the morning than I have done these past couple o' months. There's trouble coming for sure—the sea knows it."

With a shake of his head, Pegruff breathed on his flask, polished the moist bit, then finished off the last of the arlo.

After slipping the flask in his tunic, he turned back to his lines and began running them through his fist. In his typical fisherman's fashion, he was indicating the conversation was done.

Ravis thanked him and made his way back to the quay.

TEN

"The harras who killed your father, did you notice anything unnatural about them?" Ravis turned away from Camron of Thorn as he waited upon his answer.

They were sitting in Marcel's study. Beech logs crackled in the hearth, vintage berriac smoked in deep glasses, and an easterly breeze rattled the very shutters that Marcel had taken great pains to close. Despite the fire burning away, the room was not brightly lit. A bronze fireguard prevented any rogue sparks from falling on the nearby silk rug, and all the silver lanterns were capped with colored glass.

Marcel had a deep fear of fire. He didn't want any of his precious paperwork going up in smoke. Although he had lost no gold in the Great Banking Fire twenty years earlier, he had lost a fortune in bills—codicils, payment orders, promissory notes, deeds, bills of exchange, and leases—and he was obsessed with the possibility that it might happen again.

Briefly Ravis toyed with the idea of nudging over a lantern and watching as lamp oil and flames spilled onto Marcel's desk. After what the banker had done to him yesterday, it would give him a certain satisfaction to see the man scrambling to put out a fire. He didn't act, though. Ravis had learned many years ago that there was no real pleasure to be gained from revenge: just a brief, breathtaking stab of spite that hurt oneself just as much in the end.

Instead he turned his gaze back to Camron and forced his mind to the question at hand. He needed to be sure of certain things before he said his piece.

Camron was speaking. "When I first set eyes on the harras in my father's study, there was a moment when I thought they were monsters." He shrugged, but not at all lightly. "It all happened so fast. My heart was pumping, my hands were shaking. I wasn't thinking properly. And then I saw . . ." He shook his head, ran his hand through his hair. "Then I saw my father, and nothing else mattered after that."

Camron of Thorn looked worse than when Ravis had seen him last. His hair was lank, dark circles ringed his eyes, and his clothes hung loose on his frame. Ravis could see the man was in pain, but he could muster little pity for him. The world they lived in was a hard one: people died, friends lied, and family was quick to betray you. Camron's father may have been savagely murdered in the sanctity of his own home, but in many ways the death was a clean one. Camron was the only son of an only son. He had no brothers, half-brothers, uncles, or stepmothers to bicker with him over his wealth. What he inherited was his and his alone. And in that regard Camron of Thorn was more fortunate than he would ever know.

Ravis gnawed at his scar. It suddenly felt like gristle in his mouth. Deliberately he made his voice hard. "I need you to remember all you can about the harras. What they looked like, acted like, smelled like."

Hearing the word *smell*, Camron looked up.

"Really!" exclaimed Marcel from behind his satiny desk. "I don't see the need to bring up such an indelicate subject. Lord Camron is distressed quite enough as it is."

Ravis made his leather gloves crackle as he curled a fist. "Go back to your counting, Marcel."

Marcel was about to protest when Camron stopped him by saying, "It's all right, Marcel. While I'm sure our friend here is capable of idle curiosity, I don't think this is one of those instances." He looked at Ravis. "Is it?"

Ravis didn't care for Camron's tone, but he let it pass. "Yesterday you said the harras were like animals. What did you mean?"

Rubbing a hand over his face, Camron said, "I saw teeth, gums . . ." He struggled for details. Not finding any, he shook his head. "They were shadowy figures. It was hard to see them clearly . . . but there was a smell."

"Of what?"

"Animals. Like the stench in the stables when a mare is foaling: blood, sweat, damp horsehair. That sharp tang that comes off beasts when they're agitated or excited." Camron looked at Ravis. His gray eyes were dull and flinty. "Why is it important?"

Ravis glanced at Marcel. The banker was busy *pretending* to be busy: shuffling papers, dipping his quill, furrowing his brow as if unhappy about some discrepancy showing up in his figures. He really could have made a half-decent actor.

Leaning forward in his chair, Ravis spoke as softly as he knew how. "Last night after we took our leave of Emith, Tessa and I were attacked on Parso Bridge. Two men came at us, and there was at least another pair flanking both ends. If we hadn't jumped in the river to escape, I don't think you and I would be sitting here, talking, today."

Camron nodded. He didn't look surprised.

Marcel had stopped all pretense of counting but quickly resumed when he caught Ravis looking at him.

"I've never encountered men with such raw strength," Ravis continued. "It took all I had to finish them. They kept coming and coming and wouldn't stop. I had to stab the first man a dozen times in the chest before he fell. As I looked at his face, his features changed. Receded. He began to look more like a man. Both of them smelled exactly like you described—like animals."

"You trained them," Camron said, mouth curling to a sneer. "They're your men."

Ravis bit his scar as other people bit their lips: to stop himself from speaking rashly. After a second to control his anger, he said, "Yes, I trained them. And they set the ambush up exactly as I would have done myself—two lying in wait, more closing in to block off escape routes—but they weren't *my* men. I train men to kill quickly and with little ado, to back off as soon as they're injured, and to remain detached at all times. These men wanted blood, and they weren't going to stop until they got it." Despite his detached tone, Ravis couldn't stop a shiver from working its way down his spine.

"What's your point?" Camron was concealing his interest under a layer of contempt.

"My point is that these men have been altered in some way. Probably by sorcery."

Marcel choked on his berriac.

Camron merely nodded.

A moment passed while Marcel of Vailing coughed and spluttered and spat up his wine, and Ravis of Burano and Camron of Thorn stared at each other across the room. One of the lanterns went out. Dark smoke filled the amber glass, then escaped in a black thread toward the ceiling. Marcel's mercury-filled clock reached the hour, and its hammer hit the cast-iron bell, producing a note that was neither mellow nor bright.

Finally Camron spoke. "Let me tell you about what I found after I took care of my father's body, when I went down to the barracks to take a head count of those who were left." His gaze did not leave Ravis for a moment, and though his eyes were hard, his voice was rough and uneven. "I ended up counting bodies instead. Two dozen men had been butchered. Good men, whom I counted as friends. Some were like brothers to me. One man first taught me how to sit and handle my horse. And all of them, each and every one of them, had put up the fight of their lives. Blood didn't lie in neat pools, bodies weren't downed by a single blow. Guts and fingers and hair and teeth were smeared across the walls. I've been on battlefields, I know what death looks like, but this . . ." Camron finally looked away. "This was carnage."

Ravis closed his eyes. At some point while Camron was speaking, he'd actually begun to feel pity for him. He knew what it was like to lose good men. When he spoke, however, he made sure his sympathy didn't show. Experience told him Camron would want none of it. "Last night I saw a similar sight myself. The people who owned the house I was staying at were slaughtered by the harras."

"It doesn't mean that it's sorcery, though," Marcel said. "Everyone knows Garizons are as good as animals."

"It didn't stop you from taking their money, though," Camron said, stealing the words right from Ravis' lips.

Marcel stood. "Gentlemen," he said with bankerly dignity, "I see emotions are running high and imaginations are running wild. I think it best if I leave you two alone for a while. Perhaps when I return we can all sit down and talk about this rationally, like the educated men we are." With that he bowed, first to Camron and then to Ravis, gathered up his papers, and stalked out of the room, head held high.

As soon as the door was shut, Ravis turned to Camron and said, "How much commission is he getting on this deal?"

"Forty percent."

"*Forty?*" Ravis threw back his head and laughed. "Izgard paid him ten."

Camron looked stricken for a moment, but then gave way and smiled.

Leaning over Marcel's desk, Ravis grabbed the decanter of berriac and filled both their glasses to the brim. "Look," he said, handing Camron his glass, "I don't know what we're dealing with here, and that scares me. I trained Izgard's men and recruited mercenaries for him, but I had nothing to do with what has happened these past few days. While I was in Veizach, I saw some things that I didn't understand, and right now I'm doing my best to piece everything together."

Camron nodded. "How soon do you think Izgard will move against Rhaize?"

"As soon as he possibly can." Ravis took a deep draft from his glass. He felt more relaxed now that Marcel was gone—even though there was a distinct possibility that the Bay'Zell banker was still listening at the door. "He can't afford to wait. The land barons and warlords will be expecting him to move quickly. He needs to conquer and be *seen* to be conquering: that's the way a Garizon king keeps his crown."

Camron no longer bothered to feign disinterest or contempt. He leaned forward in his chair. "How can you be so sure he won't move against Balgedis first? If it's a saltwater port Izgard's after, they've got a dozen to spare."

"Two things," Ravis said. "First, no port in Balgedis can give him access to the Bay of Plenty and the Gulf. If he seizes Bay'Zell, then he secures passage not only to the north, but also to the warm-water ports of the lower south and far east. Second, I think Izgard and the duke of Balgedis have already come to some arrangement, where Izgard won't invade Balgedis as long as it remains neutral."

"What makes you say that?"

"There's a Maribane brig anchored off the Balgedis coast. Garizons have been spotted rowing back and forth to it."

Camron tugged his dark golden hair out of the way of his eyes. "And there's no possibility that Balgedis doesn't know about this?"

"No." Ravis put down his drink. He stood and began pacing around the room. "Balgedis knows it's there. What's more alarming, though, is the fact the ship's showing a Maribane flag. That means Izgard is doing deals with them too. And somehow I doubt very much that Maribane will be content to remain neutral. They want Rhaize blood. Maribane has always resented paying Rhaize tariffs to ship their goods into the continent. Just last week, Bay'Zell doubled its tolls, and no Maribane ship can sail into the Bay of Plenty without paying them. So right about now Maribane is looking for ways to strike back. All Izgard has to do is tell Maribane that once he's conquered Bay'Zell, he'll reduce the tolls to a copper on the pound, and they'll be lining up from Hayle to Kilgrim to help him. It couldn't be easier."

As he spoke, Ravis unlatched one of the shutters and looked out into the street below. Two of Camron's men wearing the green and silver of Thorn stood on the opposite street corner, keeping watch on Marcel's house. Ravis continued scanning: buildings, doorways, alleyways, the snakepit of shadows that was forming with the dusk. Although he could see nothing suspicious, he decided he would take no chances when making his way back to Mother Emith's house. He didn't want to risk bringing any harras to the old lady's door. Besides, Tessa was there, and as the hours ticked by, keeping her safe was beginning to matter more and more. He was beginning to regret mentioning to Marcel that they had both met with Emith yesterday.

Ravis closed the shutter. "Did Marcel show you the illuminations he's holding for Deveric's assistant?"

"Yes," Camron replied. "I took a look at them just before you arrived." The second glass of berriac had put some color in Camron's face but no brightness in his eyes. He looked tired, and the hand that held his glass shook. He probably hadn't slept in days.

"What did you think of them?" Though he hadn't intended it, Ravis was aware that his voice was almost gentle.

Camron looked at him sharply, and Ravis immediately regretted his lapse into sympathy.

"I thought they were beautiful," Camron said, his words cool. "I've seen Anointed Isle illuminations before, but none as detailed as those."

"Where have you seen them?"

"My father has one"—Camron caught himself—"*had* one on his study wall. Some old scribe stayed at Castle Bess centuries ago and showed his gratitude by painting an illumination. It's a much simpler work than the patterns I saw last night, and the pigment is so thick in places that it catches as much dust as a statue, but my father loved it."

Ravis took a quick breath and said, "I think Deveric's illuminations have something to do with what we've been seeing these past couple of days. It looks like Izgard's found himself a new trick, and if we're lucky, we've seen the worst of it."

"And if we're not?"

"Then God help us all."

Ravis moved across to the door. He suddenly wanted very badly to get back to Tessa. "Look," he said to Camron, resting his palm upon the smooth beechwood beams bonded by teeth of gilded iron, "I need to be somewhere now—"

"Back to the woman with red-gold hair?" Camron interrupted. "And the strange, lilting voice?"

Ravis hid his surprise. "I may pay her a visit. What's it to you?"

"She has something to do with this, doesn't she?" Camron's drawn features took on a new, shrewd light. Despite his attempts to look nonchalant, Ravis realized his face must be giving something away, for Camron added, "Come now, Ravis, it's obvious she's not from Bay'Zell."

Annoyed, but not sure why, Ravis said, "There are too many things I don't know or understand yet. If we are to work together to overthrow Izgard, then we must gather as much information as possible, leave nothing to chance. Marcel might throw choking fits over the possibility of magery and witchcraft, but you and I have both seen things that he hasn't. And when he's safely at his desk, toting up his receipts and writing entries in his ledger, it will be you and I setting ourselves against Izgard of Garizon. Not Marcel and his forty percent."

As Ravis was speaking, Camron's fingers tapped a beat against the armrest of Marcel's prized orangewood chair. He stopped tapping at the exact instant Ravis finished speaking. "I want Izgard dead, not overthrown. That was what we agreed yesterday in Marcel's cellar."

"You won't be able to assassinate Izgard as long as he wears the crown. I trained his personal guard myself, I—"

"Then you will know their weaknesses."

"They have no weaknesses." Ravis was losing patience. He was eager to be on his way. While he stood here, arguing tactics with Camron, a world of shadows was quietly forming outside. If *he* were in Izgard's place, Marcel's house would be the first site he would order the harras to watch. "Right now, Izgard is either at Sern Fortress or on his way there. Of all the Garizon-built castles I've stayed at, I've yet seen one to match the defenses at Sern. It's impenetrable. There is only one possible approach, and the minute Izgard takes up residence, it will be so heavily guarded that even the ghost of his own mother couldn't get through."

"If his army's there, surely we could smuggle some attendants, some women, into the camp?"

Ravis ran a tooth along his scar, then smiled. "No servants, no camp attendants. No whores. I put together this force. It's not some band of elegant knights and their entourages. No one is paid to shine armor and cook meals—the men do all that themselves. Infiltration is out of the question: I trained them how to spot intruders a league away. The camp perimeter will be guarded by enough troops to man a fort."

Camron did not look pleased. Ravis could see him thinking. "What about the castle servants?" he said finally, standing. "Surely you could find someone willing to slip poison into Izgard's wine?"

"*Poison* Izgard?" Ravis threw back his head and laughed. His amusement wasn't genuine, but he was getting increasingly more annoyed with Camron, and he knew from experience that the best way to cut a man dead was to laugh at him.

Getting back to Tessa was becoming more important by the minute. "No one on the continent could get near Izgard with poison. The man was born with no sense of taste. The one thing he fears above all others is the possibility that he might be poisoned and never know it. He could eat pure extract of belladonna and never taste a thing. He's so obsessed with being poisoned that he won't eat or drink anything, *anything*, that hasn't been tasted by a score of men first."

Ravis shook his head. "No, my friend, if you want to murder Izgard of Garizon, you will have to come up with something much, much cleverer than that."

Camron's cheeks were flushed. His golden hair fell across his face in dark tangles. When he spoke his whole body shook. "Seeing as you know so much about Izgard, you tell me what's the best way to kill him. Or has he got you so frightened that you'd rather take your chances with a Rhaize hangman than risk moving against him?"

Although Ravis knew he had driven Camron into making the accusation, it did little to lessen his anger. "You," he said coldly, "know nothing about the situation we're dealing with. When I tell you there's no way to get close to Izgard while he holds the throne, I don't do so to hear the sound of my own voice. I know the man, I know his army, and I know how Garizons view their kings. He is more than just a leader now. He is his country personified, and until he loses a battle or makes a mistake, they will lay down their lives to keep him safe. The only way to reach Izgard is to meet him on terms he and his country understand. We need to be ready when he invades. We need to smash his forces and counter his advances and match whatever witchery he uses. Then and only then will we be able to get close enough for the kill."

Camron looked at Ravis as if he were a madman. "Smash his forces? The Rhaize army is more than a match for Garizon. We have the bravest and best-trained knights on the continent. Izgard won't stand a chance."

"Knights!" Ravis put a world of scorn into the word. "You think Izgard gives a damn about Rhaize knights, when he has five companies of Maribane longbowsmen who can take out a knight or his horse at five hundred paces, using arrowheads that can rip through steel? Rhaize knights will ride to their deaths not ever having seen the men who killed them. And God help the ones who don't, for they won't find themselves staring into the eyes of fellow noblemen, matching them in sword length, armor refinements, and knowledge of battlefield etiquette. Once the longbowsmen have done their work, Izgard will send in his pikesmen, and believe me, those men don't go in for dainty exchanges, elegant sword-fights, and honorable deaths. Their blades are designed to tear out a man's guts. And Rhaize knights, charging into bat-tle expecting Izgard to comply with their outdated rules of exchange, will find themselves little more than highly visible moving targets."

Cheeks bright with blood, Camron cried, "No common foot soldier with a pike or a longbow can ever hope to match a Rhaize knight."

Ravis' palm hovered above the door handle. "That is ex-actly the sort of thinking that will lose the coming war." Voice still ringing, he hit the latch.

The door sprang open and Marcel fell into the room.

"Marcel," Ravis said, inclining his head as he worked to regain his composure. "Oiling the lock, I take it?"

"Nothing of the sort," Marcel said, trying his best to look dignified as he picked himself up off the floor. "I was just coming to offer you gentlemen a spot of supper."

"Well, I'm sorry, but I must decline." Turning back to Camron, Ravis sketched an elegant bow. He pretended not to notice the look of pure hatred on the young nobleman's face. Practice made such things easy. "I shall see you tomorrow by the fish market at dawn." Then to Marcel: "No offense, my friend, but I won't be coming here again for a while. For some strange reason that I simply can't understand, I feel as if every move I make is being watched." One charming smile, one final bow, and Ravis was off: heading down the stairs and out of the door into the waiting darkness of the night; hand on his knife, gaze darting sideways, trusting his feet to choose the least obvious path.

Angeline, once lady of Halmac, now queen of Garizon, sat on the end of her bed and rubbed her little dog's belly. Snowy loved to have his belly rubbed. He just lay on his back, legs splayed outward, head rolling from side to side, tail wagging furiously.

More. More.

"Silly Snowy," cried Angeline, delighted. "Who's a silly, silly Snowy?"

Snowy wagged his tail in agreement.

Silly Snowy. Silly Snowy.

Snowy was a no-good dog. That's what her father had said when he first clapped eyes on him. Last to come out of his mother's belly, last to be licked clean and to suckle, Snowy had been marked for drowning before his ears had chance to dry. "That dog is no good," her father had said to the houndsmaster. "Wrap him in a blanket and throw him in the Veize."

Angeline was at her father's side, as always in those days, and although she disliked the thought of drowning puppies, her father had explained to her many times that it was a kindness to them in the end.

Then the puppy picked up his too large head and looked at her with his new blue eyes, and all good sense drained from Angeline's head and turned into something warm and itchy inside her heart. He was a no-good dog and he knew it, and Angeline fell in love with him on the spot.

Father could always tell the difference between things that Angeline *thought* she wanted, because they caught her eye and were pretty or bright, and things she really, really wanted. Like Snowy. Even though he had given an order to his houndsmaster, and he never liked to take back his word, Father made a rare exception and let the no-good dog live.

Angeline felt her eyes begin to ache. "Oh dear, Snowy," she said, stroking the soft fur under the little dog's chin. "Father was good to us, wasn't he? He loved us very much."

Snowy's tail drooped.

Loved him back.

And the funny thing was, Snowy and Father did end up loving each other. Not in the same way that she and Snowy did, of course, but in a mutual no-good dog and aloof-master sort of way. Angeline had learned enough since her marriage to know there were many different types of love.

"Izgard loves us now, though," she whispered, tickling the silky bit behind Snowy's ears. "He loves us just as much as Father."

Snowy growled.

Not as much.

Angeline laughed. She tried not to think about how much Izgard had changed since their marriage. "Snowy, you're a no-good dog. You can't possibly know everything."

Growl over, Snowy scrambled to his feet, tail wagging once more.

No-good dog. No-good dog.

Straightening herself up, Angeline glanced out of the slit between the stones that was the nearest thing to a window one could find in the lower levels of Sern Fortress. The sky was fully dark now, and a few stars twinkled from very far away. Izgard would be returning soon, and Angeline knew she should make herself nice for him. Put on the gown with the boned bodice and call Gerta in to tie the laces tight. In fact, Gerta was probably on her way right now; hairpins bristling between her teeth, brushes, buffers, and tweezers hung like weaponry around her waist. Angeline actually preferred it when the pins were in Gerta's mouth, for the moment they were out it would be "Your first duty is to Garizon, my lady. You must provide an heir." With that as her opening statement, Gerta would launch into comments and advice about lovemaking that Angeline, depending on how heavily her wine had been watered at supper, found either unpleasant or vaguely amusing.

Well, she certainly didn't feel like listening to any lovemaking chatter tonight. Besides, she wasn't entirely sure that Gerta knew what she was talking about. Some of the things that she advised doing to inspire "child-begetting passion" in her husband were nothing short of strange. Oh, Izgard seemed to like them well enough at the time, but more and more often these days he was bad tempered afterward, stalking out of the room and slamming the door behind him. Angeline preferred the times when Izgard was so tired from working hard all day that he simply fell asleep in his chair. She had a sneaking suspicion that Izgard preferred those evenings too. But, just like Gerta, he knew the importance of providing an heir.

Angeline sighed. She slapped her thigh and Snowy came scampering over. "Things were a lot simpler when there was just you, me, Father, and Bors, weren't they, Snowy?"

Snowy wagged his tail in agreement.

Things better then.

"I know what, Snowy," Angeline said, an idea unfolding in her head. "I'll go and visit Ederius." Gerta had told her that Izgard was riding all the way to the pass today, so he might not be back until late. And although Izgard had warned her not to go and visit Ederius again, if she was clever, he'd never, ever know she'd been. "What do you think, Snowy?"

Snowy tilted his head to the side and wagged his tail only halfway.

Not sure.

Angeline laughed. "You're not happy because you know you can't come. No-good dogs have to stay in their rooms, don't they?"

Catching a glimpse of his tail, Snowy froze, eyed it with suspicion, then pounced. Not put off by his quarry mysteriously disappearing out of reach, he chased in mad, happy circles after it.

No-good dog. No-good dog.

Smiling, Angeline opened the door. Snowy would be asleep by the fire when she returned. Chasing his tail always wore him out.

Guards snapped to attention as Angeline walked through the narrow, rough-hewn corridors of Sern Fortress. Somehow, even though it was spring and it hadn't rained in a week, the air inside managed to be cold and damp. When she had first arrived at the fortress, Angeline had thought the bare stone walls were pretty—if you looked close, there were all sorts of patterns and colors twinkling within the gray. Now she hated them. They felt clammy when you touched them, and no matter what went on behind them, they never gave away a sound.

After turning into a staircase cut out of mountain rock,

Angeline made her way up to the top of the fortress. Just as she passed the halfway point, she stopped in her tracks. She should have brought Ederius some food! He worked so hard at his desk all day, never stopping to eat or drink. He could be hungry, cold, and tired and never know it. Just like Father before he got sick. But . . . Angeline's foot wavered on the lower step as she weighed up the risks. She dared not go down to the kitchens; the whole thing would take too much time. *I know,* she thought, *once I've finished seeing Ederius, I'll ask Gerta to make sure he gets some food.* That decided, she hurried up the remaining steps.

There was no answer when she knocked on the scriptorium door. As mistress of the house, she knew she could walk into any room in the fortress unannounced, but somehow it never felt right. Not like when Izgard did it. Balling her fingers into a fist, Angeline banged loudly on the door.

"Ederius. It's me—Angeline. Are you there?" Angeline didn't like the sound of her own voice much. Before she had married Izgard, other women used to make fun of it, saying it was too high and childish sounding. Now she was Izgard's wife, no one dared say a thing. Funny, but the women's silence didn't feel nearly as satisfying as she had expected. If anything, it made her feel sad.

A soft, scraping noise came from behind the door. Sounds of coughing followed, and then a thin voice said, "My lady, please go away."

Distressed by what she heard, Angeline pushed open the door and came face-to-face with Ederius. Her mouth dropped open. Ederius looked sick, very sick. His eyes were bloodshot and his face was bathed in sweat.

"Oh dear," Angeline whispered. She didn't say it, but Ederius looked just like Father during a bout of wet fever.

"My lady," Ederius said, not looking her in the eye, "you must go. The king has forbidden me to see you." The last words were spoken amid a hail of coughing.

Angeline knew all about coughing. Father always developed a terrible cough before the wet fever took him. Everyone in Castle Halmac—grooms, servants, attendants, and poor relations—lived in fear of hearing Father cough. Coughing meant sickness, and sickness meant death. The minute

Angeline heard Father coughing, she would run to the kitchens to warm up some honey and almond-milk tea. Though servants and physicians always did the same, Father blatantly refused to take any of their medicines. "I'll take a sip of Angeline's honey cup," he would say, "nothing more." Angeline's heart always swelled to hear him say it. Only she could make Father well.

Ignoring the scribe's protests completely, Angeline walked into the room. Ederius needed looking after, and she was the person to do it. "I don't care what Izgard says," she cried, knowing it wasn't true but enjoying saying it all the same. "He can't stop me from doing whatever I choose." With that, she took Ederius' arm and walked him back to his desk.

The scriptorium was a little cold and lofty for Angeline's tastes. The ceiling was high enough for bats, and the windows, being large, let in dust and drafts and moths. Angeline *did* like all the tiny pots of pigments laid out around the edge of Ederius' desk, and the rainbow of powders they held were as pretty as could be, but some of the more brightly colored ones smelled strange, and she knew from experience that if she inhaled their scents too deeply, they would cause her head to ache.

Gently Angeline helped Ederius into his chair. The old scribe moved slowly. He felt cold and stiff, and Angeline could tell he was nervous. Once he'd resigned himself to receiving her attention, though, he seemed strangely affected by it and kept touching her wrist and fingers, as if to ensure himself she was real.

"There," she said, patting his good right shoulder. "You sit and rest while I go and fetch us some tea."

Ederius shook his head. "No, my lady. Please. I will be fine. I have just had a tiring day." As he spoke, Angeline noticed that his fingers quietly pulled an unfinished leaf of parchment over a brilliantly colored painting on his desk.

"You've been working too long at your patterns," she said, trying her best to make her voice stern, like Gerta's. "Izgard has been making you do too much." She reached over to pull out the painting from beneath the vellum.

"No!" Ederius slammed his palm upon the desk.

Frightened, Angeline jumped back.

Realizing that he had acted harshly, Ederius said quickly, "Forgive me, my lady, I did not mean to startle you. The painting is not fit for anyone to see. I . . . I am ashamed of it."

Angeline wasn't sure how to react. She dearly wanted to see the painting now, but Ederius looked genuinely distressed. Then the scribe began to cough, and the matter was settled. Her expert healing skills were called for. She couldn't go to the kitchen to make honey and almond-milk tea—it would take too long and Izgard might be back at any minute—but she could at least fetch Ederius a glass of water and pat his back until the coughing stopped.

Painting forgotten amid the greater excitement of playing nurse, Angeline scanned the room for a water jug. She found what she was looking for on a side table set back against the wall behind Ederius' chair. Rushing over, she spied a handful of glazed cups farther along down the table. Picking one of the cups at random, she filled it to the brim with clear, sparkling water.

Ederius was bent over his desk. He was no longer coughing, but his face looked very red.

"Here," she said, holding up the cup of water. "I brought you this. I'll just take a sip first to make sure it's not too cold." Pleased with herself for thinking of such a nurselike thing to say, Angeline brought the cup to her lips.

"*Stop!*"

Angeline froze. Her gaze moved from the rim of the cup to Ederius' face.

"Don't drink from that cup," he said, standing up and walking toward her. "You must never, ever, drink from anything in here. Ever." He snatched the cup from her. "I use these to mix pigments in, and some of those pigments are very dangerous. They could kill you if you drank as much as a drop of them. Do you understand?"

Angeline nodded, not really sure if she understood or not. She was too upset. Ederius had never spoken to her like this before. All she had wanted to do was be a good nurse.

Seeing her expression, Ederius softened. He placed the cup on the desk and raised his hand toward her; not quite daring to touch her but wanting to nonetheless. "I'm sorry, my lady. When I saw you were about to drink, I was frightened. I wouldn't want any harm to come to you. Some of my pigments are very strong poison. I should have explained that to you before."

"Poison," Angeline repeated, understanding exactly what Ederius meant now. She knew all about poison: both Father and her brother, Bors, had feared it, and Izgard was so afraid of being poisoned that he ate or drank nothing that had not been tested. Sometimes he even made her try things first.

"Yes, my lady," Ederius said very gently. "You must always be careful when touching anything you find in here. Not everything is dangerous. The plant dyes you painted with yesterday—the saffron yellow and turnsole purple—they're both safe."

Ederius worked hard to stifle a cough, and Angeline felt herself softening toward him once more. He had just been trying to protect her, that was all. Just as Father would have done.

"And the red one?"

"Yes, kermes red is safe, though that comes from insects, not plants."

Angeline thought the idea of pigments being made from insects rather unpleasant, but didn't say so. "Which ones are dangerous, then?" she asked as she moved to stand behind Ederius' chair. Laying her hands on Ederius' good shoulder, she forced the scribe to sit.

Patting her fingers, he said, "The sparkling white color over there on the shelf." He pointed to one of the pots. "That's white arsenic, and the scarlet color beside it is mercuric sulfide. Both can be very dangerous."

"But you have other whites and reds you can use," Angeline said, gently working her fingers across the scribe's broken shoulder bone. "So why do you paint with them at all?"

"As the nature of my work changes, so must my pigments." Ederius suddenly appeared to get agitated again. He shrugged her hand from his shoulder and glanced toward the tall windows. "You must leave now, my lady. People will be worried about you."

Angeline opened her mouth to object, but she knew Ederius was right. Gerta would be looking everywhere for her, and Izgard may have arrived back from the pass. Reluctantly

she nodded. "I'll make Gerta fetch you some honey and almond-milk tea."

"You're such a good girl, Angeline," Ederius said, using
her name for the first time. "I'm sorry I frightened you earlier. I don't know what I would have done if anything had
happened to you."

Angeline felt her eyes prickling. Father had said something very similar to her once when he'd pulled her off a
mean-mouthed horse. "That horse has a mean mouth," he
had said. "And a temper to match. I can't risk him turning on
you the moment you're out of sight. What would I do if anything ever happened to my best girl?"

Feeling sad, Angeline bent over and kissed the scribe on
his old cheek. His skin was very frail. It reminded Angeline
of Mother's old silk dresses: even locked away in a chest to
prevent insect damage and weathering, they had still managed to fade to nothing over the darkness of twenty years.

As she straightened, a wisp of night air ruffled the papers
on Ederius' desk, lifting up the sheet of unfinished vellum
and allowing Angeline a peek at the painting beneath. What
she saw made her mouth go dry.

There was something monstrous on the page.

A terrible, unnatural design.

Then the wind withdrew and the vellum fell back into
place, and Angeline doubted she had seen anything at all.
Just a lot of jumbled colors thrown together with little thought.

"Are you all right, my lady?" Ederius asked, unaware of
what she had seen.

"Yes, quite all right. I must go now." Angeline made her
way toward the door. She was shaking but didn't know why.
The idea of being back in her own chamber, with Gerta spitting
pins and the no-good dog chasing his tail, suddenly seemed ap-
pealing, and Angeline took the stairs two at a time. She needed
very badly to get back to the ordered boredom of her life.

"Any finely ground powder is called pounce," Emith said,
running his hands through a dish of white powder. "I mostly
use chalk to whiten the hides, but others use ash or bread-

crumbs, and a few use ground-up bones. Sometimes when the hide hasn't been soaked for long enough before being scraped, I'll rub it with a little pumice to take away the grease." As he spoke, Emith took a handful of the white powder and began working it into the hide with a small wooden block. "Just before Master Deveric started work on an illumination, he always insisted I pounce the parchment one last time, to raise the nap and make it ready to take the ink."

Tessa nodded, trying hard to remember everything Emith told her.

They were sitting around the large table in Mother Emith's kitchen. Mother Emith and her chair had done a full turn from this morning and were back facing the fire. The old woman's head was resting on her shoulder, and a faint snoring noise could be heard escaping from her lips. According to Emith, she wasn't sleeping, though. Merely resting.

Pots of delicious-smelling stews, stocks, and sauces were bubbling in copper pots over the fire. Tessa had already eaten two meals since this morning, but she found herself eager for a third. Mother Emith could cook like a demon. Well, Emith did all the actual cooking, but his mother was the master chef: supervising spicing, boiling, blanching, and garnishing all from the safe haven of her chair.

Emith had explained to Tessa that before Deveric died, he always spent two days in every seven in town with his mother. Deveric had insisted upon it. During the five days when Emith was in Fale, his mother relied on a local girl to come and help her in the mornings.

Tessa had yet to see Mother Emith move from her chair, and as it was now full dark outside, and the shutters were closed for the night, leaving trapped moths to busy themselves around the flames, she had finally given up waiting. Perhaps, like the toys in children's stories, Mother Emith only moved when everyone else was fast asleep.

Tessa liked Emith and his mother. They were both kind, if a little odd, and they seemed very anxious to please. If she shivered, Emith would dash off and get her a blanket. If her stomach rumbled, bread would be buttered and sent her way. If the light wasn't bright enough for her to sketch by, enough tallow would be brought to illuminate a church, and all she had to do was hold up a hand to test the swollen lump on her head to be regaled with ointments, herbal teas, and advice.

Although she had never received such attention before, Tessa found herself growing used to it rather fast. It was nice to be here in this warm, busy kitchen, so unlike her own sterile, cheerless one at home, and just sit and listen and learn.

It was a new experience for her to be able to concentrate completely on what she was doing, not have to worry about her tinnitus recurring, and so be free to immerse herself in just the kinds of details she'd always avoided before. Work for her was normally a series of reflex actions: hear something, acknowledge it, encounter an awkward question, evade it. Her job in telesales had been about saying what *she* wanted to say, while delivering it into a form that others wanted to hear. Tessa could do it in her sleep. Her mind was neither challenged nor engaged—that was the way she'd liked it. It was the way she had liked all her life: no commitments, no details, no thought.

She'd fallen into telesales after she'd dropped out of college. As always, the big changes in her life were precipitated by tinnitus. The first year at New Mexico State had gone smoothly enough. She attended all the usual run of classes, made a few close friends, kept up with her coursework. Everything was fine until she began her second year. Art history was her major, and as soon as she started classes after summer break things started to go wrong. She couldn't concentrate in class. The slightest noise would distract her; the drone of the air-conditioning, a car pulling out in the car park below, someone in the row behind clearing his throat. Tessa became snappish with her roommate, Nyla, no longer able to tolerate Nyla's endless chatting on the phone and late night music sessions. Work started to suffer. Books piled up waiting to be read. Whenever Tessa tried to concentrate, noises grated in her temples, itching away beneath her skin like something wanting to get out.

Full-blown tinnitus attacks grew more frequent. Tessa bit her nails down to the quick. *Waiting.* She was always waiting for another attack to begin.

She started dropping classes. Soon Professor Yarback's course on the Byzantine empire and the Coptic art of Egypt was the only class she could bring herself to attend. It was the patterns that drew her out of bed in the morning, made her pull on her clothes and brush her teeth. The stonework of the period was rich with patterns and geometric designs. Intricate, fantastic devices slithered up stone columns, over door frames, and under arches.

Tessa would spend hours in the library, copying, tracing, and researching the designs. And in the long afternoons when Professor Yarback talked of the "naturalism of human figures" and "the importance of religious iconography," Tessa found her mind drifting away in the lecture hall, hands doodling on her notepad, trying to reproduce the last pattern she'd seen.

They always made such perfect sense to her. She could see how they had been constructed from a basic set of lines. How even a seemingly complicated design could be traced back to the simplest of grids.

It was during the last of Professor Yarback's lectures, "Coptic Influences on the Insular Art of Ireland and Britain," that Tessa had her worst attack of tinnitus ever. Professor Yarback was clicking slides at his usual snail's pace—Egyptian manuscripts, murals, stonework—when he stopped at a slide of the Lindisfarne Gospels.

"See how the panels resemble the key patterns and fretwork found in Coptic design?"

That was the last thing Tessa heard Professor Yarback say. The world began to fade away as she studied the pattern on the slide. She had never seen anything so minutely detailed before in her life. It buzzed with life and movement. Strange, elongated birds chased their tails across the page, twining and retwining around themselves, all claws, scalelike feathers, and beaks. On top of this seething bed of blank-eyed birds were laid self-contained panels filled with geometric designs: fretwork, knotwork, trumpet spirals, and interlaces.

Tessa felt her head begin to ache.

The controlling hand of the scribe was a palpable force in the room. It was the only thing that stopped the birds from breaking into a chaotic frenzy and spoiling the ordered symmetry of the page.

Softly, very softly, Tessa's ears began to burn. A high-pitched noise skittered through her eardrums, and the muscles on either side of her temples began to throb.

The slide dominated the entire front wall of the room. Its colors reflected off the faces of sixty students. The lecture hall smell of close bodies, old sweat, new varnish, and pine detergent faded away with the sound. Tessa caught a whiff of something strange—like paint, only spicier, more fragrant.

The sound in her ears sharpened to a knife point of gray noise.

Tessa couldn't take her eyes off the slide. It was an enchanted tangle of lines, curves, and forms, and she wanted very badly to make sense of it. Her gaze fell upon a single bird in the top left quarter of the page. Its wings were painted with stripes, not scales. It was the only one of its kind.

Professor Yarback was speaking, pacing, and pointing. In no rush to change the slide, he held the clicker limply in his hand.

Tessa's head was pounding. Her vision began to blur. Tears glazed her eyes, distorting the patterns on the slide. The dull eyes of the birds all looked her way, their beaks moved, scissoring up and down along the talons and body parts that were held in their grasp.

Tessa felt rather than heard her pencil drop to the floor. Professor Yarback stopped pacing. His head formed the center of the slide. Bird features projected over his own features like a mask, transforming him into a tattooed man.

Hardly aware of what she was doing, Tessa began pressing her fingers into her temples, trying to squeeze out the noise. It was unbearable now, a steel wire cutting through her thoughts. There was the pattern and the pain, nothing more.

Tessa's books slid from her desk onto her lap. Dimly she was aware of people around her, mouths open, hands up, eyes as black and glassy as birds'. Tessa wanted none of them. They blocked her view of the pattern, stopped her from getting to the source.

A high shriek, like the call of a sea bird, sounded. And then Tessa's world faded to so many shades of black.

She awoke a few minutes later in the campus infirmary. The tinnitus was still with her, but it was now little more than a vague background noise, like traffic heard in the distance. She could live with it like that. The nurse, a large Puerto Rican woman in a crisp white coat and high heels, explained that Tessa had fainted at her desk. She gave Tessa two Percodans and a can of soda and made her promise to go straight to a doctor.

Tessa took the Percodans, drank the soda, went straight to her room, and stayed there for a week. The tinnitus got steadily worse. Every time she tried to catch up on her work, read a course book, or even flick through a magazine the noises would beat away in her head. Every night she dreamed of the slide in the lecture hall, and every morning she awoke ill rested and drenched in sweat.

After the fifth day, Tessa knew the tinnitus wasn't going to go away on its own. As long as she stayed where she was, it would give her no peace. This she accepted as a simple fact. She needed to get away.

The next day she loaded up her car with a mattress, bedding, clothes, a few books, a potted plant she had given a name to, and a Rand McNally road atlas and drove west along I-8. At the time she had every intention of returning. Just a few weeks, she told herself. But she never did come back.

Her original destination was Los Angeles, but somehow she found herself in San Diego, selling office products over the phone. The job suited her perfectly. No responsibility, no dress code, flexible hours, and little paperwork: once she got her phone pitch down pat she barely had to think. Telesales was a numbers game. Phone enough people and a percentage would always say yes. Tessa was good at it. She made the calls, met the quotas, and always followed up. After two months at First Stop Telesales she was promoted from reworking existing lists that every operator in the shop had called before to pursuing fresh leads. In telesales terms that meant she'd arrived.

The tinnitus disappeared almost completely. In those increasingly infrequent times when she did suffer an attack, it was always a mild one, nothing to match what had happened in the lecture hall. The memory of that day was never far from Tessa's mind, though. All she had to do was walk in a bookstore, pass an art exhibit, spy a pattern in tilework on a restaurant floor, or spend too long sketching on her yellow legal pad to feel the ringing start. She never pushed it. At the slightest hint of an attack, she stopped what she was doing and relaxed. Took a walk, sat and listened to music, went for a drive . . .

Tessa felt a sharp pain in her thumb. She looked down to see she was holding the ring between her fingers. She had no memory of pulling it out from under her dress. Quickly she glanced at Emith. He was busy tending the supper by the fire. Mother Emith was still snoring away in her chair.

Tessa looked down at the ring, recalling the events that led her to finding it: the phone call, the drive, the pickup driver, the tinnitus. Why was it that whenever she had a bad attack of tinnitus she always seemed to end up somewhere else?

"The soup is ready now, miss," Emith said, cutting into her thoughts. "Would you like a bowl?"

"Have you remembered to add the pepper and the cream?" piped up Mother Emith, proving that she had, in fact, despite all evidence to the contrary, been resting, not sleeping, in her chair.

"Yes, Mother."

Tessa slipped the ring beneath her dress. "I'd love a bowl," she said, not entirely sure what sort of soup it would be but led by her nose into thinking that beef might have something to do with it.

Standing, Tessa began clearing the table in front of her. Emith's pigment pots tinkled as she pushed them into neat little lines, but his brushes, quills, styli, and lead sticks defied all attempts to be rolled into piles. Tessa was surprised by what she had learned about the various instruments in just one day. The styli were made from either copper or bone, so the point would be strong enough to trace lines in wax. Emith had explained that parchment was too costly to use for casual sketching, so most scribes used wax tablets whenever they wanted to experiment with something new. A wax tablet could be used over and over again, as the wax could be heated and then smoothed back to its original form with the flat end of the stylus.

Lead sticks were used for outlining an illumination or providing guiding points on a page. The lead could be handled as a plain stick or placed in a protective metal casing called a plummet. Emith said the best scribes always used them raw.

What surprised Tessa most about the things Emith told her was the sheer effort involved in each separate process. Hardly anything was purchased ready-made: ink, pigments, quills, parchment, wax tablets, glues, and thickeners were all formed by Emith's own hand. It seemed like a lot of work to Tessa, and she was beginning to understand why someone like Deveric needed an assistant. He wouldn't have time to paint a thing if he had to spend his days burying goose feathers in sand.

Just the parchment making alone could be a full-time job. Emith purchased raw animal hides at market—he said goat and sheep hides were the least expensive, but stillborn calves were the best—brought them home, and soaked them in a bath of lime to deflesh them. Then, while they were still damp, he stretched them on a frame and scraped them clean with something he called a "lunular knife."

Earlier, when Tessa had gone into the yard to use the privy, she had seen various wooden frames and metal-banded tubs and wondered what they were for. Now she knew. Emith had explained that the liming stage could be quite malodorous, and Deveric preferred that he took care of such matters in town. Which, Tessa supposed, went quite a long way toward explaining why Deveric so kindly let Emith spend two days out of every seven in Bay'Zell. She didn't say anything, though. She'd already learned enough about Emith by now to realize he wouldn't hear a word said against anyone he knew. Most especially his recently deceased master.

"Here, miss," Emith said, handing her a steaming bowl of something that looked far too thick to be called soup. "Sit down and I'll fetch you some bread to soak it up with."

"And a glass of arlo," added Mother Emith, reviving once more. "I think we can offer our guest a glass, seeing as it's after dark and the clerics have all gone home." She looked at Tessa and winked. "And I may just take half a cup myself."

Tessa smiled. She got the distinct feeling that Mother Emith took a cup or two every night.

"Oh, be careful, miss," said Emith as Tessa went to place the bowl of soup on the table. Dashing in front of her, he whisked away the sketch she had drawn earlier. "We wouldn't want anything to spill on this."

"No." Tessa sat at the table and began plumbing the depths of the stew for anything she could identify as meat. Behind her, she could hear Emith's footsteps pattering away, then pattering back. "Is the sketch really as good as you say it is?" she asked when he returned from dropping off a cup of arlo with his mother.

For the first time all day Emith took a seat. "I think it is," he said, moving his chair only as close to Tessa as his strong sense of politeness would allow. "I'm no expert on such things like my master, but I've seen the work of many scribes, and the one thing that separates the good scribes from the middling ones is a sense of detail. Master always said, 'Anyone can draw an illumination, but it takes a keen eye for detail to make it shine.'"

Detail. Tessa put down her spoon, not hungry anymore. Until three days ago she had been incapable of coping with details. For years her life had been without long-term relationships, financial commitments, career plans, savings plans, vacations, paperwork, or goals.

There *was* no detail in her life. It had been the one thing she'd avoided above everything else. When offered promotions, she turned them down because more responsibility meant more paperwork. When boyfriends became serious, she became distant; when friends got too close, she pushed them away. When bank tellers pestered her about putting savings in CDs, she'd threaten to take her business elsewhere just to stop them droning on about their "extra half a percent over prime." She didn't own a computer, daily planner, or even an address book and never bought anything mail order, as that meant filling out forms.

And now this small, unassuming man, sitting a polite three feet away from her, calmly told her that he thought she had an eye for detail.

Tessa laughed. She didn't think it was especially funny, but *some* sort of reaction was called for.

Emith looked hurt. "I'm only telling the truth, miss. To paint the sorts of patterns that Master Deveric did, you need to be able to see things others don't. I only got a glimpse of the ring you copied, but it was enough to see that you caught its likeness well. You managed to translate a complex weave onto the page. Not only did you capture the intricacy of the ring, but you found the pattern at its heart."

"The ring *has* a pattern," Tessa said, pulling out the ribbon around her neck. "I didn't find anything."

"May I?" Emith moved forward and took the ring from Tessa's fingers. He smelled of mint and pigments. "I look at this and I don't see a pattern," he said softly, turning the ring in his hand. "I see random threads of gold. Layers upon layers of metal laid down with no design. You look at it and you see a pattern, and not only do you see a pattern, you have the ability to transfer what you see onto a page. When I look at your finished drawing I get a glimpse of the ring through your eyes—I see the same pattern you do—yet when I look at the ring directly, I see nothing but random lines." He let go of the ring and it fell back against Tessa's chest.

Tessa suddenly felt very tired. She didn't know how to react to what she had just heard. Emith believed what he was saying, that much she was sure of, but it didn't mean he couldn't be mistaken. "What if I invented a pattern of my own? Just made one up that wasn't there. How would you know the difference?"

Emith's smile was a gentle reprimand. "The pattern felt right, miss. It wasn't forced or contrived, and for just a second when I held the ring, I almost understood what you were getting at."

"Be sure to listen carefully to Emith, my dear. There's nothing my son doesn't know about scribing." Mother Emith tapped her now empty cup against the chair and beamed at both of them. "I'll take an extra sip of arlo, Emith. It would be rude of me to let a guest drink alone."

Blushing at his mother's words, Emith seemed glad of an excuse to get away and dashed out to the yard, where a keg of arlo had been set to cool.

Tessa raised her cup in toast to Mother Emith, and the old woman returned the gesture with a decidedly regal wave before resting with her eyes closed once more.

Drumming her fingers along the wooden tabletop, Tessa thought about what Emith had said. She *had* seen a pattern in the ring, he was right about that. It was the reason she had wanted to draw it in the first place—to make sense of what she saw. All through her life she had seen patterns in things: flowers arranged in a bowl, chairs stacked in the back of a concert hall, cars on the street, clothes in a closet, roof tiles, book covers, cushion covers, and maps. As a child she was always trying to draw the things she saw, but somehow she'd fallen out of it. Normal growing up, she supposed. Or was fear of tinnitus holding her back even then?

Emith opened the door, sending a gust of night air whipping through the kitchen.

Tessa shivered.

Just as Emith stepped into the room, a gloved hand appeared out of the darkness and grabbed at the edge of the door. Something wet dripped from one of the fingers onto the floor. A fraction of a second later, Ravis appeared in the doorway.

"Good evening," he said, nodding first at Mother Emith and then to Tessa and Emith. "I trust I'm not too late for supper?" Noticing Tessa's gaze on his glove, he stripped it off and tucked it beneath his tunic. Meanwhile his foot was busy working the wet spot into the floor.

"Step over here by the fire, Lord Ravis," Mother Emith said. "Emith will fetch you a bowl of ox marrow soup and a cup of arlo."

Ravis crossed to the old lady and kissed her on each cheek. "Ox marrow soup! Why, I swear you read my mind, madam. I've been thinking of nothing else all night. Point me to the right pot and I shall get it myself." Turning to Emith, he said, "Hand me that jug, my friend, so I can top up your mother's cup."

Mother Emith beamed up at Ravis from her chair as he proceeded to take over the kitchen, pouring drinks, putting logs on the fire, tasting sauces, and talking spices.

Neither Emith nor his mother appeared to notice how fast Ravis' chest rose and fell when he spoke, the fine film of sweat on his brow, or the wine-dark stain on the collar of his shirt. Tessa noticed them all. Details, she thought with a quick, humorless smile.

Ravis proposed a toast to Mother Emith and another to her cooking and one more for the night. Tessa didn't realize what he was doing until he held the empty jug to the light and said, "Why, I do believe we've finished it off. I'll just go out to the courtyard and fill it from the keg. Tessa, could you follow me out with a candle? Having eaten Mother Emith's delicious marrow soup, I now have the strength of ten men and the mental capacity of a college full of scholars, but I still can't see in the dark." He smiled charmingly to Mother Emith, who smiled charmingly back.

"I'll fill the jug, Lord Ravis," Emith said, stepping forward.

"Wouldn't hear of it, my friend. You've done quite enough already." Ravis pulled out a chair. "Why don't you sit right here and let someone wait on you for a change." Emith succumbed to the considerable power of Ravis' charm and sat down. "Come along, Tessa, you can show me where the keg is."

The second they were out of the door, Ravis turned to Tessa and said, "I won't be coming back here again after tonight. It's too dangerous. Three of Izgard's harras followed me from Marcel's house. I managed to lose two of them, but the third"—he patted the bulge in his tunic formed by the dripping glove—"gave me a little trouble before he finally lost my trail. I can't risk leading them back here again. They don't know about this place, so as long as you're here you should be safe. Never leave the house, and make sure that both Emith and his mother keep your presence here a secret. Don't show yourself to anyone who comes to the door, especially Marcel, and take this." He drew his knife from his belt and held it out toward Tessa.

Hardly aware of what she was doing, Tessa reached out to accept the knife. Her head was spinning. *Ravis leaving?*

Ravis' fingers caught in hers over the silver wire of the knife's haft. His dark eyes were exactly the same color as the night. The light from the doorjamb caught on his scar, sending a shadow over the right half of his lip. "I don't know how long I'll be gone. I have to form and train a force for Camron of Thorn, and right now Bay'Zell is no place to do it. But I *will* return. And when I do, I will come for you and together we'll discover the reason why you're here."

Tessa nodded like a dumb child. She felt foolish, but what could she say? She couldn't object. This man didn't owe her anything. He had no obligation to take care of her.

Ravis leaned forward and kissed her on the lips. She felt the rough break of his scar, then the soft tissue of lip flesh. He smelled of blood and sweat and the sharp apple tang of arlo. His hand came up to press against the small of her back, and three seconds later he pulled away.

Before she could stop herself, Tessa stepped toward him, mouth open, wanting more. Embarrassed, she worked to control the impulse, glad that Ravis was already turning away and hadn't seen what she had done.

"Come," he said, leathers cracking as he bent over to tap the keg. "Let's get back inside. Mother Emith will be expecting us back, and she'll doubtless want me to propose another toast—this one to fond farewells."

Not trusting herself to reply, Tessa followed him into the house.

ELEVEN

The fish market at dawn formed the center of Bay'Zell. Without help, directions, or signposts, a man could find his way there in the dark. The smell was a pointing finger, and the sounds of fishmongers crating, squabbling, laughing, and bartering provided a more reliable beacon than a lighthouse on a rocky coast.

As a rule, Ravis didn't care for early mornings, but as far as they went this one wasn't too bad. The sky was clear of clouds, and the day promised to be fine and warm. Seagulls wheeled and dipped in the lightening sky, and a lively, salty, seaweedy breeze blew in from the east with the sun.

From where he stood, at the top of the white marble steps leading up to the entrance of the Old Shrine, Ravis could get a clear view of the fish market below. Ever since the new shrine, with its vaulting spires, brass-capped warding towers, and stone facing shot with seams of quartz, had been completed fifty years earlier, the forecourt of the old one had been taken over by fish. It was only fitting, really, thought Ravis. After all, both shrines had been paid for with income hauled in from the sea.

Looking down at the market, Ravis shifted his gaze from stall to stall, from face to face, from hand to hand: searching. He had already spotted Camron's dark gold hair in the crowd. The man was standing close to a mussel seller and his many baskets, two of his guards milling with the crowd nearby. Ravis wasn't ready to contact him just yet. He wanted to make sure the market was safe. After last night's run-in with the harras, he was in no mood to take chances.

One man had followed him from the moment he'd left Marcel's door. A second and a third joined their friend as the roads narrowed and the district took a turn for the worse. Remembering the previous evening's encounter, Ravis decided it was better to evade than fight and had managed to lose two of the men, only to find himself in the shadow of the third. Surprisingly, the fight was a quick one. The harrar was just that: a well-trained fighter, nothing more. There was no terrible blood lust, no whip-sharp reflexes, and no sense that the fight was destined to end in death. Ravis doubted that sorcery had been used to alter him. Once stabbed in the arm, the man wisely fled. Which, while being fortunate in many ways, only gave Ravis more cause for alarm.

He knew Izgard. If the Garizon king wasn't using his newfound trick to hunt him down, then he was using it for something worse. How long since his crowning: three, perhaps four days? Time enough for Garizon warlords to grow impatient for Izgard to make his move.

Ravis chewed on his scar. Even as he stood here, scanning the fish market, searching for anyone who looked as though he could be searching for him, an invasion could be taking place to the east. Funny, but just four days ago he had thought he had seen and heard the last of Izgard of Garizon. A commission had ended and gold had been paid and a ship's passage had been booked in his name. His short-term plans had involved little more than sitting out the war in Mizerico with a certain dark-haired beauty at his side. Now everything had changed. Izgard had moved against him, Marcel had betrayed him, and Camron of Thorn had him by the throat.

Or at least he thought he did.

There were a hundred different ways to leave Bay'Zell, and Ravis doubted very much that Camron knew half of them. If he wanted to, he could skip the city right now without leaving a trace. Pegruff was not the only fisherman in the north harbor who owed him a favor, and it would be easy enough to secure passage to Maribane or Balgedis. But for many different reasons, Ravis now chose to stay in Rhaize.

Gold, for one.

Izgard's attempt on his life, for another.

And a woman with almost red hair and a stubborn streak, for another after that.

Making one final scan of the crowd, Ravis made his way

down the steps. If there were harras in the market, then they must be concealing themselves in the barrels along with the mackerel and the cod, for he'd been standing here for over an hour now and had yet to see anything amiss.

At ground level the stench was vigorous, to say the least. Tables were layered with sea salt and fish, and men as crusty and weatherbeaten as the crates they toted called out to passersby, extolling the virtues of their catch. No cod was just a cod; it was "white and flaky and fit for a sick grandmother. Fresh enough to skip a path to the oven on its own."

Camron spotted Ravis approach from across the courtyard. Neither of his guards did. Walking back and forth with the throng, the two men had let themselves become distracted by the sights and sounds of the market. Matters weren't helped much by the fact that a pretty fishmonger's daughter, all dark curls and dimpled flesh, was currently bending over to pick through a barrel of hake. Since hearing that most of Camron's guards were killed the same night as his father, Ravis was inclined to judge the remaining men less harshly. Still, it didn't make the task ahead any easier, and Camron was better off relying on himself than placing his faith in ill-trained men who lacked the experience to stay focused in a crowd.

As he walked, Ravis' hand was on his knife—a new one, thanks to the fact that he had given his previous one to Tessa last night in Mother Emith's yard. It had neither the pattern-welded blade nor the silver-bound hilt of the one he was used to, but Ravis found he didn't mind the difference at all. There was still a part of him that found romantic gestures—such as handing over a knife worth fifty crowns to a woman in the dark—gratifying. Tessa could have protected herself with any number of knives from Mother Emith's kitchen, but it pleased Ravis to let her have his. He did not want any harm befalling her while he was away.

"Ravis," said Camron of Thorn, walking to greet him through the crowd. "I see your idea of dawn is later than everyone else's."

Ravis showed a smile. He was pleased to see that Camron was looking better than the night before; his hair was clean, his tunic well brushed, and the fingers that danced around his blade had been scraped clean of dried blood. Seeing how his hand worked in unison with his eye, Ravis revised his opinion of the man: Camron obviously wasn't placing all his trust in his guards.

"Walk with me," Ravis said, gaze flicking around the crowd.

Camron fell in at his side. "What happened last night?"

Again, Ravis' opinion of Camron went up. The man was bright enough to guess there was a reason behind his caution. "Three of Izgard's harras followed me after I left Marcel's last night. Gave me a spot of trouble. Nothing much, but it means I can't afford to stay in Bay'Zell any longer. As long as I'm here, Izgard is going to keep sending more men after me, and sooner or later I'm going to end up dead."

"We all end up dead in the end." Camron's tone was sharp. With his left hand, he made gestures to the two guards in the crowd, beckoning them to follow him.

Ravis chose to ignore the remark. Pushing past barrels of thrashing lobsters and trays of snapping crabs, he said, "We have to move fast. Bay'Zell isn't the place to assemble and train a force. I'll need somewhere where I don't have to worry about being knifed in the back. Somewhere discreet, with land and barracks to call its own, preferably situated along the Chase."

Camron nodded. "How far along the Chase?"

"Anywhere between Runzy and Gornt. I want to be able to ship in men and armaments, keep an eye to what's happening in Bay'Zell, and still be within striking distance of the Vorce Mountains."

"My father has—" Camron corrected himself. "I have a small manor house just north of Runzy. There's land, plenty of outbuildings that could be used as barracks, and the Chase runs through the neighboring estate to the east."

"How long will it take to ride there?"

"Three days. Two if we change horses along the way."

"Good."

Reaching the far end of the market where the salted and smoked fish was sold, Ravis paused to buy a hand of smoked herrings. He waited while the fishmonger heated the halved and boned fish on his brazier, then asked that the portions be split into two. The fishmonger was happy to oblige. "Plenty of salt and pepper," Ravis added as the fishmonger rolled the fish in sedgeweeds, "and how about adding a couple of pats of best butter on top?"

The fishmonger nodded enthusiastically, pleased to have such a discerning client. "Would sir care for chives and parsley?"

Ravis ran a finger over his scar, thought for a minute, and then said, "Just parsley. Chives would kill the aroma of woodsmoke."

"Sir knows his smoked fish," said the fishmonger, passing the two packets of herrings to Ravis with an impassioned bow.

Ravis thanked, then paid the man. Spinning around, he crooked a finger in the direction of Camron's two guards. "Gentlemen," he said as they approached, "I've taken the liberty of buying you both breakfast." Smiling, he offered a packet of the hot buttery fish to each man. The guards looked nervously at Camron, but the smoky aroma was too much for them to resist and their hands came up to accept the food.

Camron did not look pleased.

Ravis ignored him and continued smiling at the two men. "Now you two stand here, enjoy your breakfast, get yourselves a jug of beer"—he pressed a silver coin into the palm of the nearest man—"and Camron and I will be back before you know it. We have a little business to discuss."

"Sir—" began the first guard.

"It's all right, Scrip," interrupted Camron. "Do as he says. I'll be back within an hour."

Both guards nodded. The second one already had his mouth full of fish.

Ravis inclined his head to both men, waved farewell to the smoked-fish vendor, and then led Camron away from the market.

"Perhaps you'd like to tell me what that was all about?" Camron said as they walked through a series of covered arcades leading down toward the west harbor.

"Your men make me nervous." Ravis crunched salt crystals and seashells beneath his boots as he walked. "We might as well be followed by a town crier ringing his bell. Two run-ins with Izgard's harras in as many days is trouble enough for me. My neck suits me better in one piece."

Reaching the harbor, Ravis cut away from the crowds milling around the waterfront and headed for a collection of small huts teetering on the edge of the quay. "You should watch yourself, too. Just because Izgard decided not to kill you the same night he killed your father doesn't mean he won't change his mind. As soon as he learns you're behind this force we're putting together, he'll send his harras out to finish the job."

Camron turned to face him. He ran his hands through his hair. "I'm not afraid of Izgard and his men. If he comes, he won't find me hiding under my covers like a child frightened of the dark."

This was the first chance Ravis had to take a proper look at Camron in daylight, and he was surprised to see that Camron looked perhaps five years younger than he had in the soft, flickering light of Marcel's town house. Ravis had been about to shape a reply telling him that only a fool would not be afraid of Izgard of Garizon. Instead he said, "You know he'll think you're after his crown?"

"Let him think whatever he wants. My father never made a claim upon the throne. Nor will I." Camron resumed walking in the direction of the wooden huts. "It isn't about taking power. It's about vengeance."

"So," Ravis said, matching him step for step, "before Izgard murdered your father, you were content to let him be?"

Camron's hands curled into fists at his side. "Seeking to depose another is not necessarily the same thing as seeking power yourself. My father had a claim on Garizon just as strong as—some would say *stronger* than—Izgard's. Berick of Thorn was second cousin to the old king. His blood ran just as deep and was just as rich as Izgard's, yet he never sought power, never wanted anything for Garizon except peace."

Ravis ran a tooth along his scar. "Just as well, really. As I hardly think the good people of Garizon would have tolerated having the hero of Mount Creed as their king. How many Garizons died in that battle?" Ravis kept his tone light, as he feigned ignorance of a subject he knew well. "Fifteen, twenty thousand?"

Whipping around, Camron landed a blow squarely on Ravis' jaw. Although Ravis had been expecting it—goad a man enough and he *will* hit you—he was surprised by the sheer force of the punch. It didn't send him reeling, but it did send his head snapping back.

Seeing the punch, two old ladies in black bonnets and shawls scuttled away from the quayside like ants caught in candlelight. A whiskered longshoreman stopped in his tracks, folded his arms, and waited to see what would happen next. When Ravis made no move to fight back, he spat on the deck and moved on.

"Don't you dare speak of Mount Creed to me," Camron cried, eyes blazing at Ravis, fist held close to his chest. "You have no idea what my father went through on that mountain, how the memory wounded him until the end. He fought because he had to—because there was no one else to do it, and he had sworn his allegiance to the Rhaize king. Not because he wanted power. He had already disavowed all claims to the Garizon throne. Ruling Garizon held no interest for him."

Ravis tasted blood in his mouth. It reminded him of the day, seven years ago, when his bottom lip had been sliced in two. The bitter tang was just the same. Wiping the corner of his mouth, he said, "You're right. I shouldn't have mentioned Mount Creed. I apologize." Suddenly nothing seemed worth the fight.

Camron's gray eyes looked into his; scorn, accusations, and anger weren't enough to mask his grief. Ravis saw it, recognized it, knew what it felt like. After all this time, and all that had happened afterward, he still remembered the grief.

Ravis took a second look at Camron. Both of their fathers had died unexpectedly, leaving hard fights to be fought in their wake: perhaps they weren't so different after all.

Overhead, seagulls shrieked in a cloudless blue sky. The sea sparkled all the way to the horizon, then shimmered away to an indigo line. Ships of all sizes dotted the bay: sails fat as well-fed cats, prows gleaming with wax, rigging an ever-changing framework of rope. Easterly breezes, clear skies, and a busy sea: a perfect morning in Bay'Zell.

Something shifting in the corner of his eye caused Ravis to swing his gaze away from the sea, back toward Camron.

Was the man going to take a second swing at him? Even as Ravis balled his hand into a fist, he realized that Camron was offering his hand.

Ravis halted his own protective reflexes, ashamed. If Camron had seen him make a fist, he pretended not to notice, simply looked at Ravis with his mercury gray eyes and said, "I accept your apology, Ravis of Burano. And I'll even admit I acted rashly myself."

A tiny, bitter voice inside Ravis told him that in all his life, Camron of Thorn had probably never had his hand refused by any man. That every time he held it out—confident in the assurance that he was doing an honorable thing for honorable reasons—it was always quickly taken. Part of Ravis wanted to be the first to turn him down. Cut him dead, walk away, destroy just a grain or two of that unwavering blind pride.

Another part of him—not the one that had been turned to the light by the taste of his own blood in his mouth, but the small, older, immeasurably damaged part that had been brought to life by the sight of grief in Camron's eyes—urged him to hold out his hand. There was nothing to be gained by causing further pain.

So Ravis raised his hand to meet Camron's, telling himself he needed gold from this man and that was as good a reason as any not to antagonize him further. Yet when Camron's fingers circled his forearm and his gray eyes looked straight into his, the small lie Ravis told himself began to matter less. There was a genuine pleasure to be found in gripping someone's forearm, of knowing you were joined in cause and destined to fight side by side.

A wisp of a memory, fine as Istanian-spun silk, light as the touch of the long-nailed women who unraveled the cocoons, filtered down through Ravis' thoughts. Two young brothers, clinging to each other with a fierce, brotherly love as they watched their father's powder white body being carried into the crypt. *"Malray and Ravis of Burano,"* people whispered to each other beneath the chanting of the gray-robed clerics. *"Surely there have never been two such brothers as devoted as they."*

Abruptly Ravis pulled back from Camron. Threads of

memory proved hard to break. Even when his fingers no longer circled Camron's arm, he still smelled the myrrh-scented candles burning in the crypt, still felt the warmth of his brother's body next to his, still tasted Malray's tears on his lips.

Camron spoke, and even though his words seemed strange and distant to Ravis, he recognized their importance and realized how much it meant to Camron to say them out loud.

"In all the years my father and I were together, he never mentioned his Garizon claims to me. Not once, by either word nor deed, did he ever encourage me to stake a claim of my own. I am not seeking a crown. I simply want to be rid of Izgard. At first it was purely because of what he is and what he stood for; now it is because of what he did. Izgard of Garizon picked the wrong person to kill and the wrong point to make. He should never have killed the father, he should have slain the real threat, his son."

Camron's words were bright and piercing in the clear air of that perfect Bay'Zell morning, solemn against the cloudless backdrop of the sky. Listening to them was enough to chase away the last trace of Ravis' childhood memory. Things were not, nor would ever be, the same as they had been. And he wasn't the only person standing on the quay at that moment who had to live with pain and regrets.

"Come," he said to Camron, motioning toward the end of the quay. "There's a man in that hut over there staying awake just to see us, and every minute we keep him from his bed will end up costing *you* more gold." Ravis headed up the path, Camron less than two steps behind.

Segwin the Ney shook his large, fleshy head. "Ravis, you said dawn." With surprisingly slender hands for a man who was undeniably fat, he tapped the nearby window frame, indicating the clear blue sky beyond. "What do you call this?"

Ravis shrugged. "Your gain."

A noise that might have conveyed either satisfaction or displeasure escaped from Segwin's colorless lips. With a practiced movement he shut and latched the shutter, closing out the light. Segwin the Ney didn't like daylight. He swore it ruined his night vision, gnawing away at his special talent, developed and nurtured meticulously over half a lifetime, for spotting illegal activity in the dark.

Segwin the Ney was a Bay'Zell port officer, yet his name could not be found on any roll and his job did not officially exist. Segwin watched the harbor at night. Every evening at dusk he opened his shutters, made himself comfortable on his well-cushioned chair, brought his custom-made glass to his eye, and stared out to sea. Unlike bailiffs, harbor officials, tax examiners, and other functionaries whose main business was to police the bay, Segwin had no desire to catch smugglers, tariff dodgers, black-marketeers, known criminals intent on entering the city, or wanted criminals intent on leaving. His job was simply to record.

The merchant fathers of Bay'Zell knew that sometimes it was better to ignore the sins of a smuggler or a foreign merchant, and so gain a bargaining tool to be used at a later date, rather than take a man to task, make him pay all tariffs due on goods smuggled, or penalize him for illegal activities, and ultimately turn a friend and beneficiary of the city into a watchful, resentful foe.

Obviously such enlightened and liberal thinking wouldn't sit well with Bay'Zell's own hardworking merchants and harbor officials, nor indeed with the Sire of Rhaize himself, who as overlord of the city took a healthy portion of all monies levied from the port. So the whole thing, much like Segwin the Ney himself, was kept very much in the dark. To anyone who asked, Segwin was just an aging drunkard whose wife had left him in a fit of pique because he never rose before dusk. In keeping with this fiction, empty beer barrels, arlo kegs, and spirit bottles were always stacked outside his door.

Although it was dim inside the hut with the shutters closed, Segwin didn't offer to light a candle. He enjoyed having his visitors at a disadvantage, for while they could barely see his silhouette, he saw every nuance on their faces. It made for good bargaining, and although there were several men in the city equally clever, quick-witted, and resourceful as Segwin the Ney, none struck a harder deal.

"Gentlemen," he said with a short, impatient sigh, "first you keep me up, now you keep me waiting. Am I to take it you intend to see me recompensed for my ordeal?"

"Ordeal?" Camron began. "Why, I see no evidence—"

Ravis quieted him with a quick jab in the ribs. "Of course we intend to see you recompensed, Segwin. My friend here has assured me he values your time highly, and he will personally see to it that on top of whatever payment we agree upon here and now for your services, there will be an extra silver piece included for every minute you have been kept awake beyond the break of dawn."

Satisfied, Segwin nodded. For some reason, the pale rolls of flesh under his chin were the only part of his visage that caught the light. The rest of his face remained dark. "Go on."

Ravis focused on what was visible of Segwin's many chins. "My friend and I have need of your expert help. Men, supplies, armaments: the usual requirements. Only this time I will need them sent upriver to Runzy. I will not be here to arrange pickups or to inspect the men personally, so I will need to rely on you and Thrice."

Again came that sound that might have been pleasure or disapproval. The chins wobbled. "I keep Thrice very busy these days."

Thrice was Segwin's assistant. All the various side deals that Segwin made to supplement his income—selling confiscated goods, extortion, turning a blind eye, dealing in weapons, mercenaries, and occasionally slaves—were carried out by his man in the field. Ravis had never actually spoken to Thrice—merely nodded to him from a distance over crates of Istanian helmets or the heads of Maribane archers—but judging by the quality of men and weapons he selected, the man obviously took pride in his work. Some of Ravis' best mercenaries had been hand-picked by Thrice of Culling.

"As busy as both you and Thrice are, I'm sure you'll find time to help us out." Ravis jabbed Camron in the ribs. The moment called for a little verbal support.

"We'd be most grateful," said Camron.

"Not to mention generous," added Ravis for good measure.

Segwin the Ney held perfectly still for a moment, then let out a deep sigh. "Very well. Men, you want? Arms and supplies? I'll see what I can do."

"I need archers—longbowsmen if you can get them, though crossbowsmen would do. I'll want at least five dozen fine yewwood longbows, and double that number of Drokho pikes—not the lowland ones, mind, the ones made in the mountains with the broad blades and hooks. I'll need boiled leather armor, no plate—"

"No plate?" interrupted Camron. "Do you like sending men to their deaths?"

Ravis' first instinct was to lash out at Camron: now was not the time to discuss tactics. A deal was being struck. Controlling his anger, however, he spoke very softly, all the while keeping his facial features relaxed, aware that no detail would escape Segwin the Ney's all-seeing eye. "Any force I assemble has to be light on its feet. I've seen too many men die because they were wearing full armor and couldn't right themselves after a fall from a horse—an eyeblink is all it takes for an enemy to move in with a blade."

"At least they'll be well protected when they're in such a vulnerable state."

Ravis was losing patience. "A man wearing leather can be up and back on his horse before anyone realizes he's down. Speed and agility are all the protection he needs." To end the subject once and for all, he turned toward Segwin's chins and asked, "How much gold will you need to get started?" It was an indelicate way to broach the subject, and normally Ravis would use an entirely different approach, but he needed something to stop Camron's tongue.

The question had the desired effect. The tension drained out of Camron's body as he leaned forward to hear Segwin's reply.

Segwin the Ney acted as if nothing were amiss. Several noncommittal noises emanated from the area directly above his chins. After a bout of nodding, some finger drumming, and a slight retraction of his chins, he said, "Well, I can't guarantee numbers on the mercenaries, but I'll see what I can do. As for the other items, they shouldn't be too much of a problem. Though Thrice *is* very busy, and I myself am fully burdened as it is." Segwin paused, waiting for appropriate words of understanding and sympathy.

Which Ravis happily gave. "You push yourself too hard, Segwin. No man in Bay'Zell works such long hours as you."

The chins wobbled in what Ravis hoped was gratification. A moment passed, and then Segwin rustled into action. "The cost will be five hundred crowns. I'll take two hundred and fifty on deposit, plus the extra silver promised for my inconvenience. Payment must be in coin and should be received no later than sunset tonight." He stood up. "Now, if you gentlemen will excuse me, I must sleep. Two hours you have kept me awake. One hundred and twenty silvers, and not a minute less." The chins headed for the door.

Sensing that Camron was about to speak—either to object to the price or the terms—Ravis spoke up loudly instead. "We wouldn't dream of keeping you from your sleep a moment longer, Segwin. So, seems we're all agreed on the price, I say we discuss the details later. After dark." Negotiation may have brought down the cost somewhat, but it would have taken so long to convince Segwin to drop his price that any money saved in gold would be more than matched in compensation at the rate of one silver coin per minute. Besides, Ravis felt disinclined to save Camron's money. As one of the wealthiest men in Rhaize, he could well afford to pay the price.

Camron didn't say anything, but judging from the way the silhouette of his hand tugged away at his hair, it was obvious he wasn't pleased.

"After dark, gentlemen, and not a moment before." Segwin the Ney opened the door. Light flooded into the hut, blinding Ravis completely. By the time his vision had cleared enough to see details, Segwin had ushered him over the threshold. Before he had chance to shape a farewell, the door was closed in his face.

"Five hundred crowns!" Camron said, sweeping into Ravis' line of vision. "Five hundred crowns for leather armor, pikes, and mercenaries! Are you quite out of your mind?"

Ravis was more than a little annoyed at the fact that Camron had recovered from the shock of being thrust into the light faster than he himself. He began walking back up the quay. "You forgot the longbows."

"Longbows! Archers! What use will a man with an arrow be against a troop of fully trained knights?" Although Ravis was moving quickly, Camron had no problem keeping step.

"You obviously haven't seen the Maribane longbow in use. It can cut down a cavalry line faster than any other weapon I've seen."

"I've seen archers before now. The only thing they're good for is taking out their opposite numbers: archers to kill archers."

"The new longbows can shoot three times farther than a shortbow. They fire arrowheads that can cut through steel, and for every arrow loosed by a crossbowsman, a longbowsman can loose two. Archers don't just kill archers anymore: they stop charges, break defenses, win wars."

Having reached the main harbor thoroughfare, Ravis cut a path back toward the market. He cared little if Camron followed. The man was typical of all Rhaize lords—living on memories of a glorious past, where knights in gleaming armor fought other knights in gleaming armor, and any common foot soldier in the field, or archer stringing his bow in a trench, wasn't worth wielding a sword at. War was a nobleman's affair.

Izgard didn't play by those old rules, though. No one who wanted to prevail on the battlefield these days could afford to.

Camron caught up with Ravis on the steps leading up to the market. Some fishmongers were already closing shop for the day, and they marched down the steps, crates above their heads, buckets sloshing in their hands, tunics straining with the round-edged bulk of coinage. Children, dogs, and seagulls competed for scraps. Snapping at the salt-strewn steps, they fought over sprats, whiting, cockles, and clams. Whatever scales, shells, and fins the scavengers left behind were cleared away overnight by the rats.

Ravis heard Camron order him to stop so they could talk face-to-face, but he was damned if he was going to explain any more of his tactics to a man who would neither listen nor understand. He carried on up the steps, pushing against the market crowd, fixing them with his dark Drokho eyes, causing all but the poor sighted and reckless to move swiftly out of his way.

"I said stop," cried Camron, grabbing a fistful of Ravis' tunic.

Ravis slammed the heel of his hand into Camron's knuckles, forcing him to release his grip. "I didn't choose to heed you."

"Well, you'd better heed me from now on." Even though Ravis knew he had delivered quite a blow to Camron's hand, the man didn't stop to nurse it. He continued speaking, his low, aristocratic voice taut with fury. "You work for me. I'm financing this force. I'm the one who decides who's party to it, and what they wear and how they fight. I intend to pull men from Thorn and Runzy—trained knights, fine horsemen. Good, solid Rhaize troops, not some mismatched concoction of foreign mercenaries and common foot soldiers. I'll pay the five hundred crowns to the fat man with the chins, but I warn you now, I don't want to see, hear, or cross paths with any man you bring down to Runzy. And I certainly don't want them fighting by my side. In battle I need men I can rely on, ones who won't leave injured soldiers to die on the field, or turn tail at the first sign of a rout."

Camron drew level with Ravis on the steps. Bringing his face close, he said, "You're here to help me get to Izgard, not to tell me how to fight. Is that clear?"

Ravis chewed on his scar. Many things came into his mind to say—objections, sarcastic put-downs, verbal lessons in tactics—but he let none of them out. He'd been a hired hand for too long to let anger get in the way of business. Camron wasn't the first man to remind him who was master, and he probably wouldn't be the last. A man who inherited neither land nor wealth from his family could expect to have many different overlords through the course of his life. He learned early on to do and say what was expected, and he always knew when to bite his tongue or, in Ravis' case, his scar.

Camron was angry. His pride had been hurt, and a few of his dearly held beliefs had been challenged. One day would not make him a convert.

With one quick movement Ravis reached inside his tunic. Camron tensed for a moment before realizing that Ravis was merely taking out his gloves. With slow movements just short of insolence, Ravis pulled on the gloves, pausing to ensure that each finger slid down to the bottom seam and that the leather sat well over his hand. Only when he was satisfied with the fit did he look Camron in the eye and say, "I will do exactly as you wish."

To his credit, Camron neither frowned nor gloated. He nodded once, then started up the steps. Ravis followed after him, and together they headed back to the market, where Camron's two guards—lips still greasy with butter, breath smelling of beer and smoked fish—came running up to tell them that a rumor was sweeping the city that Izgard had invaded Rhaize to the east.

"What happened yesterday at dawn? What did you do?" Izgard of Garizon was tired of getting no answers. He was sick of seeing his scribe's head shake and his good shoulder descend from a shrug. The warlords were pressing to drive farther into Rhaize. They wanted to see plans. Move forces. Fight.

"I have told you already, sire. I drew my normal pattern, nothing more." Ederius twisted his purple-stained fingers into knots. The tendons on the back of his hands looked like bird claws. Izgard swore he could hear the man's heart pounding beneath the rough-woven fabric of his cloak.

The room smelled vaguely of urine, of a chamber pot tucked in the back of a cupboard or a bed wet in the middle of the night. Izgard didn't normally notice such things—in a fortress this large and cold, men pissed wherever they could rather than get up to use the latrines after dark—but Ederius was different. Once a monk on the Anointed Isle, he was a man of strict personal habits and always took care to keep himself and his rooms well tended. At this moment, though, both the scribe and his scriptorium looked a little unkempt, and even though it was an hour past noon only one of the great windows had been opened to let in the light.

The sky above the mountains was filled with plump white

clouds, and as the wind was high they continually blew in front of the sun, plunging the room into cool gray shade for minutes at a time. As the sun emerged once more from behind a bank of feathery down and shone through the tall window onto Ederius, his desk, pigment pots, brushes, quills, and works in progress, Izgard took a closer look at his hands. The purple stain wasn't as it first seemed. It was made up of two distinctly separate colors: red and blue. The blue sat over the red, masking, altering, filtering out the hue. The skin on Ederius' hands was sore and flaking, and it looked as if the scribe had first tried to scrub off the red stain, and when that failed, he had worked in blue pigment to veil it.

Excited, but not sure why, Izgard licked his lips. Stepping into the sun's rays so his shadow fell upon the scribe and his desk, he whispered, "Let me see the pattern you drew yesterday."

Ederius' gaze flicked from his red-blue hands to the eyes of his king. "I threw it on the fire."

"Why?" As Izgard spoke the word, his breath plumed white across the space separating him from the scribe. It was not cold, merely cool, but sometimes his breath did that: changed, became something else entirely in his lungs.

Eyes blinking away the moisture, Ederius said, "After I finished the pattern, I knocked over a cup of tannic acid . . . it spilt upon the page. The pattern was unsavable. The parchment was ruined."

Izgard nodded. "I see."

Ederius waited for his king to say something more, but Izgard merely curled his hands around the edge of the desk and leaned forward. After a moment of silence the scribe felt compelled to speak. "Forgive me, sire. I did not stop to think. The acid was everywhere. I was worried it would burn through to the parchment beneath—destroy new designs I was working on, things that could prove valuable in the months to—"

Raising up his index finger to silence the man, Izgard said, "What fire?"

"I . . . I don't understand, sire." Ederius was looking worried now.

As well he might. One of the bones in Izgard's wrists cracked softly as he pivoted farther forward, drawing face-to-face with his scribe. When he spoke, his voice was softer than the cracking bone. "What fire did you throw the design on? The one in here hasn't been lit in a week."

Ederius glanced toward the great fireplace. It was cold, black, swept clean.

"The one in your bedchamber, perhaps?" Izgard's lips stretched to something close to, but not quite, a smile. "Should I go there and check for myself?"

"No! No, sire," Ederius said quickly, his hands fluttering up toward his king. A bead of old man's sweat trickled down from the white hair at his temple. "I gave it to one of the maids. Told her to take it away and burn it for me."

Izgard smashed his fist into Ederius' jaw. Knuckle blasted against bone. The scribe's head shot back. The base of his skull slammed against the headrest of the chair, sending the chair teetering onto its back two legs. Izgard stopped it from falling over by slapping a hand down onto the armrest. The chair thudded back onto all four feet, jolting Ederius forward, so he was once more within striking distance of his king.

"Where is the pattern?" Izgard demanded. The urge to lash out again was strong, and Izgard had to grind his fist into the armrest to fight it. The imprint of his hand was clearly visible on the scribe's face, and for a brief moment Izgard found himself wondering when it had become normal to strike him.

Muscles contracted in Ederius' throat as he worked to contain a cough or bout of choking. A tear, just one, spilled out of his right eye.

Izgard moved his hand from the armrest. A splinter driven deep into his fingertip had drawn blood. Izgard felt no pain. Reaching over, he went to touch Ederius. The scribe had such an old and beautiful face, hair so perfectly white. When they had first met five years ago it had just been turning gray.

As Izgard's fingers brushed against his cheek, Ederius jerked back, eyes wide, inhaling sharply. Izgard caught himself. Surely Ederius wasn't afraid of him? "Don't be scared," he said. "I won't hurt you again."

Ederius hesitated, glanced into Izgard's eyes, and then moved forward. The mark on his jaw was now a bright, flaming red.

Izgard's touch was gentle as he stroked Ederius' cheek.

"Remember before I was king, Ederius? When there was just you and me and old Gamberon? Remember how close we were, how we swore we would do anything to help each other? How we were all united in the desire I should be king? They were good days, weren't they? You, me, Gamberon: friends and scholars first, master and servants second. I miss those days, my old friend. I miss Gamberon's wisdom and our special closeness. I miss the dreams we spun in Veizach after dark."

All the while Izgard spoke, Ederius sat perfectly still, accepting, but in no way responding to, the touch of his king. It looked not so much as if he were afraid to move, but rather that he physically couldn't. That somehow he had been lulled into a trance by a sly Gypsy or a master magician and his body was no longer his own.

Izgard smiled warmly at the scribe; his heart felt very full. "Oh, to go back to those days when there was just we three. The discussions we had! The books we pored over! The bonds of love, friendship, and obligations we shared!" The scribe's face was smooth—hot where he had taken the punch. Izgard enjoyed feeling the fine old flesh slide beneath his fingers. Touch was important to him. "Do you miss those days too, Ederius? Do you miss Gamberon?"

The questions were an enchanted kiss. They broke the spell that bound the scribe. Ederius moved, not away from his king's touch, but toward it; tilting his cheek so it was parallel with Izgard's finger. Touching all he could of his king. "I do miss the old days, sire. I miss Gamberon more than I can ever say."

A second tear glistened in the scribe's eye. Izgard felt its pull in his own. The muscles in his chest tightened. "Gamberon didn't have to die, did he, my old friend? He didn't have to move against me?"

The tear ran down Ederius' cheek and then slid along Izgard's finger, glazing his skin with its thin, salty wetness. The sensation of cool tear and hot flesh moved Izgard deeply. Perhaps because he had been born with one sense less than other men, he appreciated the ones he did have all the more. There was a world of beauty to be found in one's fingertips: the sweet beating warmth of another's pulse, the exquisite texture of aging skin stretched over smooth bone, and the sharp pain of snuffing a candle by hand. Sometimes Izgard thought he had been born with a sense of taste after all, only his tastebuds lay beneath his fingertips, not his tongue.

Ederius nuzzled his wet cheek against Izgard's finger as he shook his head. "Gamberon should not have done what he did, sire. He acted rashly, without thinking. . . . He should have stopped to discuss his fears with you."

Izgard leaned close and laid a kiss on his scribe's forehead. The man may have lied and prevaricated earlier, but surely now he spoke the truth? Gamberon *should* have come to him. Should have shared with his one master and his sworn friend all his fears about the Coil. Instead he had taken the crown from the convent at Sirabayus, where it had been kept safe for fifty years by the holy sisters of Martyr Ehlise and, with his own hands, tried to destroy it. By the time Izgard caught up with him on a dark, storm-lashed hillside a league east of the convent, his arms and chest were torn to shreds; flesh hacked, gouged, and split by the action of the barbs around the Coil.

Weak, raving, and losing cup after cup of blood, Gamberon still might have lived if it hadn't been for the fact that Izgard's blade slipped between his ribs mere seconds after he released his grip upon the crown.

Friends they had been, but a traitor was a traitor, and any man with desires upon the Coil was either a rival or a foe.

Drawing back from the kiss, Izgard said to his scribe, "You want me to win this war, don't you?"

Sensing a subtle change in his king's mood, Ederius was quick to nod. "Yes, sire."

"And you would do anything to help. Anything?"

"Yes, sire."

"And you would not turn upon me like Gamberon. Try to destroy that which is mine?"

Ederius took a short breath. For a second his face looked older and heavier, as if burdened by invisible weights upon his eyelids, nose, and cheeks. "No, sire. I cherish all that is yours. I would destroy nothing that belonged to my king."

"Swear it." Izgard's breath plumed white once more.

And even before the water crystals faded to nothing, the scribe whispered, "I do."

Satisfied, Izgard nodded. The desire came upon him to

touch Ederius' face once more, but he checked himself. The business in hand wasn't finished yet. Turning away from the desk, Izgard pulled himself up to his full height and began to move around the room.

When he spoke to the scribe this time he did not look at him. "You know that in the coming weeks I plan to push the border raids farther and farther into Rhaize territory? I aim to steal through the mountains into the heart of Rhaize, and as soon as my feet hit level ground I'll turn north toward the Mettle Sea and restake Garizon's claim on Bay'Zell. I have confidence in my army. I know we will prevail. Yet many months of bloodshed lie ahead. Men will die—*our* men. Sons of Garizon, brothers to you and me, husbands to our women and fathers to our children, will find themselves cut down in the prime of their lives.

"And although glory will belong to their eternal souls, their bodies will rot in shallow graves and their earthly remains will be claimed by Rhaize."

Izgard spun around to face his scribe. "Yet you and I both know that our men don't have to die in such numbers. Yesterday at dawn in a little mountain village called Chalce, just beyond the Garizon-Rhaize border, I watched as nine of my brave men fought their way to victory over a force that outnumbered them ten to one."

"A force! Sire, they were defenseless villagers, not a force!" Ederius actually rose from his desk. "It was slaughter, not battle. Women and children were killed along with all the rest."

"Sit, Ederius." Izgard kept his tone gentle, though in truth he felt annoyed. Aware that his anger was building and not wanting to hurt Ederius again, he moved farther away. Picking a spot against the far wall where he could see but not touch the scribe, he said, "You were there, weren't you? You were behind those men. You saw what they saw, you made them do what they did."

Ederius went to speak, but Izgard waved him to silence.

"It wasn't the same as the times before, was it? The men acted in unison, like a close-knit fighting force. They warned each other of dangers, watched out for each other's backs. Their desire to destroy was still the same, and their bodies changed in the usual way, but their methods were different, more calculating. They fought and acted as one."

Izgard ran a finger along the rough coolness of the scriptorium wall. No castle or fortress he had ever stayed at had stone that felt as good as Sern. It had the texture of fossilized suede.

Now that Ederius had the opportunity to say something, he chose not to. He sat, purple hands knotted on his desk, eyes either closed or gazing very far down, pressing his lips together as if afraid his tongue might turn on him and somehow force him to speak.

Nodding as if the scribe's silence were the answer he looked for, Izgard said, "When I saw what those men had done and with what speed and efficiency they had done it, I said to myself, Ederius has been working with the Coil. No longer just repeating patterns he had rubbed from the outer rim, but using the structure itself as the base for his design—just as we discussed all those weeks ago in Veizach. Just as he promised me he would do."

Pushing himself away from the wall, Izgard began to move toward the scribe. Each word he spoke brought him one step closer to the desk. "That's what you did yesterday morning, wasn't it? You worked from the Barbed Coil itself." Izgard came to a halt by the pedestal that held the crown. A thick sheet of linen had been thrown over it, like a shade to block out the sun. Red handprints were stamped around the cloth's edges. Ink, thought Izgard. Yet it looked just like blood.

Slowly, carefully, Izgard lifted the cloth from the Coil. As the crown emerged from beneath its linen wrap, the sun slipped out from behind a cloud, making the metal flash and sparkle like a crackling fire and causing specks of golden light to spray across the room.

Ederius put his hands over his eyes.

Izgard rubbed his fist over his mouth. His lips were wet with saliva. "Show me the pattern," he said quietly, not really to the scribe at all. "You must keep no secrets from me. I own you and respect you, and as long as you do my bidding, I swear you will come to no harm. Now show me what I need to see and help me win the war."

Izgard heard wood scrape against stone. Out of the corner of his eye, he saw the scribe rise from his chair, watched him walk across the room, then bend at the waist as he reached down to open a chest.

"You should not let what happened yesterday upset you, my friend," Izgard called after him, feeling the need to say something kind now that there was no question he would get what he wanted. "War has many horrors. Innocents are often killed: we will not be the first army to make such tragic mistakes. Yet if we win the war swiftly, we will actually save lives—and not just those of our own Garizon sons. In a long, bloody war people on all sides die unnecessarily. The shorter and more decisive the war, the fewer the deaths."

Ederius pulled something from the chest, looked at it briefly, murmured a few words to himself or his God, and then walked back to his king. In his arms he held a square of parchment no bigger than two outstretched hands, and before offering it up to Izgard, he pressed it close to his heart.

Izgard thought how beautiful he looked, like a holy man carrying a relic to his savior or a martyr poised to enter the underworld. It thrilled Izgard's heart just to look at him. "Kneel before me," he said, instinctively knowing the moment called for his scribe's complete supplication.

Ederius did what was asked. As his knees hit the stone, the sunlight withdrew from the room, sending shadows gliding in to fill the void. The light dimmed, the temperature dropped, the air rustled for a moment and then was still.

The scribe held out the parchment.

And as he did so, Izgard's own words slipped from his lips. "The shorter and more decisive the war, the fewer the deaths." They were spoken as part question, part excuse, part magic spell to ward off harm.

TWELVE

T hat's it, my dear. Don't be afraid of adding a little more indigo to the pot. The darker the wax, the better Emith likes it."

Tessa glanced over at Mother Emith, who was sitting facing the fire. "I don't understand why it has to be so dark." As she spoke Tessa wiped a bead of sweat from her upper lip. Standing so close to the fire, stirring a tub of beeswax that sat in a bath of boiling water, was beginning to make her a little uncomfortable. The wax was taking forever to melt.

Mother Emith settled back in her chair. A question had been asked—though granted it was about scribing, not cooking—and Mother Emith liked nothing better than to give answers. "Well, my dear, if you're scraping a design in wax with a stylus, then unless the wax is as dark as you can make it, you're not going to be able to see your own work. Try running your fingernail against a white candle—see how far that will get you. Won't be able to spot a thing."

The old lady had a point there. Nodding, Tessa added a few more drops of indigo to the wax. The dark blue plant dye rippled through the translucent wax, darkening on contact. Emith was running low on parchment, and rather than use up his remaining supplies, he had decided to make a scribe's tablet for Tessa so she could practice pen movements and knotwork as much as she liked and not have to worry about wasting any more vellum. Just this morning, Emith had hollowed out a square-shaped wooden block and given it to her to fill with wax. Now all she had to do was dye the wax and pour it into the block. Mother Emith was guiding her, as always, and together they were getting the job done nicely. Later there would be supper and tale telling.

For over a month now Tessa had been living with Emith and his mother in their narrow little town house on the south side of Bay'Zell.

Ravis had left in the middle of the night, pausing only to lay a handful of gold coins on the dresser and warn Tessa one more time to keep herself safe. After he had gone, Tessa wondered what she would do with herself. Alone in a world where she knew nothing and no one, she would surely take a wrong turn down a dangerous street and run straight into Izgard's harras.

Surprisingly, the weeks had passed safely, quietly, and quickly. Following Ravis' warning, Tessa never ventured far outside, and for the first week or so she waited for familiar feelings of restlessness, of being cooped up in one place and needing to be on the move, to take hold of her. Nothing came. In fact, as the days went by she found herself more and more content to be where she was. She liked sitting at the large oakwood table and learning about scribing from Emith, hearing about history and design one moment and washes and glazes the next. She enjoyed helping with the meals: slicing, dicing, boning, and scraping. And although no amount of teaching would ever make her a master chef, she had developed quite a talent for chopping things with Ravis' knife.

Tessa felt more at home, more at ease, in this strange household, presided over by an old woman sitting in the center of the kitchen who never left her chair, than anywhere else she had ever called home. Part of it was her newfound ability to just sit and listen and learn. She wasn't afraid to trace a finger over the tabletop and follow the grain in the wood. When Emith sketched something to illustrate a point, Tessa could concentrate fully on what he was doing and saying without fear that her tinnitus would start.

Her old life had been a series of mad dashes—calls to be made, meetings to be scheduled, short-lived relationships that always seemed to be beginning or ending with no middle to speak of in between—and she had lived that way for so long, she had assumed that was who she was and what she wanted to be. Only now was she beginning to suspect that without the fear of tinnitus hanging over her, she was turning into someone else. Still herself, only different, more thoughtful.

Her days now revolved around food: its preparation, cooking, and eating. Breakfast would be something hot, usually whatever was eaten the night before braised slowly overnight so the meat was so tender, it fell off the bone and the vegetables disintegrated into soft, nameless lumps that all tasted the same. At midday there would be cold pastries filled with creamed herrings, or smoked mackerels mashed with butter on heels of freshly baked bread. The rest of the afternoon was usually dedicated to the preparation of supper.

In the four weeks Tessa had stayed at Mother Emith's house, she had yet to eat an evening meal that hadn't taken five hours to prepare. Sauces simmered in tiny sauce pots, meat roasted on a broad spit over the fire, fish floated, belly up, in kettles filled with liquor, and red cabbage, white cabbage, and sliced onions huddled together in shallow dishes catching steam. Smells built throughout the day like a growing darkness before a storm. And during the final hour before eating, Tessa had learned to put down whatever she was working on, bring her chair close to the fire, and just sit and enjoy all the wonderful cooking fragrances, taking pleasure in anticipating the meal ahead.

Nothing in the household happened fast. At first Tessa had felt a few twinges of impatience at Emith and his mother when she asked for things like hot water for a bath, soap to wash her face, or a cold drink of anything that wasn't alcoholic. Now she realized that everything had to be done by hand: water had to be heated in a pot over the fire, so the meat would have to be moved aside, which meant the supper would be late to table. Soap had to be made in a tub in the yard, boiled down from bones and ash and other things Tessa didn't care to think about, then scented with rosemary oil, kneaded, and formed into pats.

Gradually Tessa's expectations changed. Days were long but never full; food was to be savored, discussed, and enjoyed; and evenings were made for huddling close around the fire, telling old tales, brewing strong drinks, and nodding off to sleep in your chair.

Wax candles were expensive, and tallow, which Tessa had learned was made from animal fat in much the same way as soap, burned with a flame that was too smoky and acrid to be borne for too long, so although Emith never stopped teaching and showing Tessa things in the daylight, after dark they didn't do much work.

Sometimes, when the fire dimmed, ready to be banked, and Mother Emith was resting, though not sleeping, in her chair, Emith would tell Tessa some of the history of manuscript illumination. After pouring them both cups of mulled arlo, more to hold between their hands for warmth and comfort than to drink, he would pull his stool up to the hearth and whisper stories of bygone days.

He told of how all the great scribes traditionally came from across the Mettle Sea, from an island off the island of Maribane. The Anointed Isle, it was called. It was where all the great scribes were trained: in an ancient monastery linked to the mainland by a long, sandy causeway that was completely covered by the sea at high tide. The scribes were monks in those days, boasting names that sounded as vivid and intricate as the patterns they created: Brother Ilfaylen, Brother Fascarius, Brother Mavelloc, and Brother Peredictine.

"The Holy League used to believe it was wrong for a scribe to try to reproduce the perfection of God's work," Emith began one night as he and Tessa sat around the fire. "Scribes were men of God first, men of letters second. They were forbidden to draw anything from nature. Instead they were forced to create new forms themselves that didn't rival any living plant or animal the four gods had created.

"So scribes began to illustrate their work with patterns and designs that borrowed shapes from nature, without copying them precisely. It wasn't long before scribes began to draw creatures from their own imaginations: four-legged animals with long bodies, flat ears, and curling tails. Serpents with gold eyes and segmented bodies and scales that never quite met at the edges, revealing dark underbellies beneath."

Emith shivered. "These paintings only pleased the Holy League for so long, though, miss. They began to see heathenness in the bright eyes and full curves of the scribe's creations. Rumors started that those on the Anointed Isle who had taken the art of creating patterns to its highest form were sorcerers. Demons who drew the devil out through the nibs of their pens, set him free from the black ink in their jars."

Emith paused for a moment. Tessa noticed his hands were shaking.

"Over the next few centuries, those on the Anointed Isle became more and more isolated, flouting the Holy League and common opinion alike. Rumors increased, terrible happenings were reported. The abbot at the time died suddenly one night in his sleep. Then one of the brothers at the abbey set about reforming the Anointed Isle: burning all the old manuscripts and bringing in artists from Rhaize and Drokho to teach the scribes the new lifelike styles that had become so popular there. He forbade anyone from drawing the old patterns ever again and reestablished relations with the Holy League, putting all heathenness behind him.

"Brother Ilfaylen was his name. And in his day it was said that he was the greatest scribe that ever lived. He didn't mix pigments, he wove spells of light and shade."

Hearing Emith speak so wistfully of the man's work made Tessa long to see it. "What happened to Brother Ilfaylen to make him change?" she asked, fingers curling around her arlo cup, gaze darting to Mother Emith, checking that her words hadn't disturbed her.

Emith shrugged. "I don't know, miss. They say he left the Anointed Isle for half a year and traveled to the continent to work on an illumination for Hierac of Garizon. Yet no trace of that commission has ever been found, and even though he wrote books and memoirs afterward, he never mentioned the trip."

"Was he involved in sorcery?" Tessa thought for a moment, then added, "Was Deveric?"

Emith chose that moment to stand up. "Miss, I know nothing of such things. I am a scribe's assistant, not a scribe."

It was always the way with Emith. He could tell her the most intricate details about how to apply gold leaf to a page—how the surface should be raised first with a thick, chalky paint called gesso, how pink earth should be added if the work called for richer tones, and how either agate, metal, or bone could be used to burnish the gold if a patron requested a finish with high luster—yet he would tell her nothing of the reasons behind it all.

Sometimes Tessa thought that Emith had deliberately

avoided learning anything about the true nature of Deveric's work: if his master was up to something ungodly, he didn't want to know about it, making it easier for him to believe his master was a good man. Sometimes Tessa thought her suspicions had been wrong and the patterns were just patterns after all. But every now and then something would happen to make her stop and think and guess again.

Last week Emith had begun teaching her how to rule and mark pages before starting work on a pattern. It was while he was demonstrating how Deveric went about constructing complex designs from basic geometric shapes—showing her how trumpet spirals were drawn from simple circles, how most knotwork was based on a continuous row of *XXX*s, and how all key patterns were built upon a diagonal lattice—that Tessa began to perceive something hidden between the lines.

Emith had pulled out an old parchment that Deveric had ruled and pricked years earlier yet never gotten around to filling in with ink and paint. Looking at it, Tessa immediately saw the patterns he had intended to construct. She had no way of knowing what forms those patterns would take— whether they would be elongated birds, vines, ribbons, animals, or just plain threads—but she could make out the overall design. She saw the way the lines would dip, curve, and cross each other. She knew the lay of the page.

It was as if a secret code had been revealed to her eyes alone. She cried out to Emith, "Can't you see it?" and although he nodded and said, "Yes, miss," she knew he didn't see it the same. The design didn't jump out of the vellum at him, demanding to be finished there and then.

Before Emith could stop her, Tessa took up a horsehair brush and began painting over the leadpoint markings. She quickly inked in the major lines, moving from curve to curve, knowing instinctively when to turn and raise the brush. In her mind she no longer saw Deveric's rough outline, but the finished design, complete with shadings, colors, borders, and background.

Emith *uhm*'d and *ahh*'d and didn't seem at all pleased that Tessa had taken it into her head to paint over his master's work, yet after a while of pacing, hand wringing, and anxious murmurs, he grew quiet and came to stand at the back of

Tessa's chair, peering over her shoulder to watch the design unfold.

Tessa was aware of him, but as the brush whisked across the page, trailing a line of acid and lampblack ink in its wake, the world around her began to matter less and less. She became caught up in the angles of the pattern. Lines were no longer just lines, they were secret passageways leading to other places. The page itself was no longer stretched and beaten lamb's hide, it was a landscape to be navigated, shaped, and explored.

Deveric might have laid down the blueprint, but all of a sudden Tessa realized she was in control. The brush did her bidding, no one else's, and as her gaze darted ahead to the next pinprick on the vellum, she decided to strike out on her own. Deveric's intentions were perfectly clear—too clear—and she felt a mad, intense itching to create something new.

Palm gliding two knuckles above the tabletop, fingers gripping the hog-bone handle of the brush, Tessa veered the line away from Deveric's pinprick, sending it reeling toward the virgin whiteness in the middle of the page.

Over her shoulder, she heard Emith catch his breath.

Under her hand, the pattern stopped being Deveric's and became Tessa McCamfrey's instead.

The brush turned and spiraled, broadening into the deep cleft of a curve, then thinning into a whipstroke on the turnout. Tessa no longer saw the pattern in terms of points to be met and rulings to be guided by. She saw a complex grid, many-faceted like a fly's eye, with jutting, eclipsing angles and a mesh of potential lines. She could move anywhere on the page, manipulate the design in any possible way, and as long as she kept to the grid laid down a decade earlier by a dead man, a pattern would emerge from the ink.

Tessa felt herself *entering* the design. She felt her mind crowded with fragments of lines, brushing against her thoughts like insects' antennae, bristling against her skin like hair just cut.

A faint noise sounded. Ringing.

Tessa panicked. She had let herself concentrate too deeply, opened up the door and let her tinnitus come in. She should have known better. Angry with herself, she pulled back, dragging the brush tip away from the parchment and her mind away from the design.

She closed her eyes. And as she did so, she caught a glimpse of something hidden beyond the screen of meshing lines. A land of dark curves, like rolling hills seen by night. A spark of something glinted in the valley between the slopes: a pool of black oil.

"Miss, are you all right?" Emith touched her shoulder, gently, as was his way.

Tessa nodded, suddenly feeling uncomfortable inside her body. Looking down, she saw where she had let her brush go idle for too long, causing the ink to run into a puddle on the page. Seeing its dark, shiny surface, she shrugged. The vision of the pool wasn't a vision after all.

A week had passed since then. A week where, depending on her state of mind, Tessa either excused the sensation of entering the pattern as mere foolishness or tried to recapture the feeling in her head.

Sometimes the ringing sound came back to her. For the first few days she froze when she heard it, yet only last night it had woven its way into her dreams and in the half-light, half-consciousness of sleep, the ringing no longer seemed like a threat. It wasn't the same as noise caused by her tinnitus. It began in a different place.

"That's enough, my dear," Mother Emith said, pulling Tessa back to the present, back to the task she was doing with no thought whatsoever. "The wax should be hot enough by now."

Tessa wrapped her hand in a cloth and lifted the pot containing the beeswax from the bath. "I'm sorry if I left it too long," she said, not knowing how long her mind had drifted away or what her hands had been up to in the meantime. "I was just . . . daydreaming."

Mother Emith nodded. "No harm done, my dear. Daydreaming never hurt anyone."

Funny, but Tessa almost knew what Mother Emith was going to say before she said it. The old lady was always so good to her. Always.

Tipping the pot on a angle, Tessa poured the hot, liquid wax into the hollow tablet, filling it to the edge. Almost as soon as the wax hit the wood it began to cool, growing duller and more opaque by the second. That done, she set the pot to one side and placed the tablet on the table, ready to show Emith when he returned. The wax was a fine dark blue color now, and she couldn't resist scoring her fingernail along the cooling surface. Mother Emith was right: the mark showed up perfectly.

Tessa crossed to the fire and poured Mother Emith a cup of celery tea to help the circulation in her bad legs. "Why are you and Emith being so kind to me?" she said, handing over the cup. "You've looked after me for all these weeks, yet you didn't have to. No one made you."

Mother Emith put the cup on the small stand she always kept close to her chair. Knitting, darning, dried herbs ready to be packed in oil or vinegar, and fish ready to be scaled: all her works in progress rested atop the three-legged stool.

Mother Emith took so much time settling the cup down, then settling herself back in her chair, that Tessa didn't think she was going to answer the question. Perhaps she had been too forward? Or rude? It was hard to judge these things. Her only points of reference were Ravis, Emith, and his mother. In the short time she had spent with Ravis, Tessa had got the distinct impression he would say and do whatever he liked and not care a jot what anyone thought of him. Emith and his mother were different, though; more considerate.

"How does Emith look to you these days, my dear?" Mother Emith said, startling Tessa by finally speaking up.

"Fine," she answered automatically. "Very well."

"Yes. He is, isn't he? And you know why?"

Tessa shook her head.

"Because of you, my dear." Mother Emith beamed at Tessa. She was looking very wise, enthroned upon her chair with all her instruments of power surrounding her. "Emith worked for Deveric for twenty-two years, you know. Twenty-two years of hard work, long hours, and unquestioning devotion. For Emith to lose his master so suddenly was a terrible blow—*terrible*. Yet having you here has helped ease his pain. By teaching you all he knows, he feels as if he's carrying on his master's work. It gives him a purpose, gives him chance to pass on the skills he loves, and stops him from brooding over Deveric."

"So that's why you keep him as busy as possible all day?" Tessa said, beginning to see things in a whole new light. "To stop him from brooding?"

Mother Emith neither confirmed nor denied Tessa's assertion, merely smiled and said, "It's so very hard for me to get around."

Tessa smiled with the old lady. What she said made such sense that Tessa wondered why she hadn't figured it out on her own. Sometimes the most obvious things passed her right by.

"In many ways Emith is like his father, you see," continued Mother Emith, her thin voice falling into the cadence of a much repeated phrase. "Both Maribane men at heart. And if there's one thing Maribane men like more than the feel of rain beating against their faces in a storm, it's feeling sorry for themselves in the dark. Such a damp, drizzly island. Made for brooding, it is. Why, if my dear old husband hadn't married me when he did, he would have brooded himself right into the grave."

As she spoke, Mother Emith rocked back and forth in her chair, and for some reason Tessa found herself doing the same on her little stool by the fire. Rocking was obviously contagious. "Has Emith ever been to Maribane?" Now that she and Mother Emith shared a secret, Tessa was hoping to coax her into talking a little more about her son.

"Been there?" Mother Emith sounded surprised. "Why, he lived there for six years."

Tessa felt the hairs on her arm prickle. "Did he visit the Anointed Isle?"

Mother Emith nodded. "That's where he learnt his trade. Of course he was only a young boy when he sailed there—not even old enough to scrape a razor across his cheek—but he was quite determined to go. Nothing would stop him, and his father all but tugged the ship out of the harbor for him. Never was a man more eager to see his son visit the land he once called home."

"What did Emith do once he learned how to scribe?"

"Oh, he never learnt how to scribe, my dear." Mother

Emith's voice was a gentle reproof. "He learnt how to be an assistant, not a scribe."

Annoyed with herself for making a mistake just as she was getting Mother Emith to open up, Tessa stopped rocking. "Did Emith work for any Anointed scribes?"

"Why, yes, my dear, I believe he did." Mother Emith picked up her cup of celery tea and blew off some imaginary steam. "What was his name now . . ."

Tessa stood. She was afraid of revealing how interested she was in what was being said. Looking around for something to do, she caught sight of the iron poker by the fire.

"Avaccus. That's it." Mother Emith nodded to herself. "Brother Avaccus."

The poker felt good and heavy in Tessa's hand as she began poking at a beech log near the bottom of the fire. "Did Brother Avaccus do the same kind of work as Deveric?"

"Why, I think so, my dear. But then it's all pretty much the same to me." Mother Emith drained her cup. Tessa noticed how well tended her fingernails were. They looked as strong and bright as a young girl's. "Terrible shame what happened to him in the end, though. Terrible shame. Emith had to leave Maribane straight after. The holy fathers insisted on it, seeing as he had been working for Brother Avaccus at the time it happened."

Tessa tended the beech log as if it were an only child. When she spoke her voice was as casual as she could make it. "What happened?"

Mother Emith didn't reply. After a minute or so her chin fell to her chest and her eyelids batted a few times, then closed.

Realizing that Mother Emith was launching into one of her rests, Tessa made a sudden jab with the poker, sending logs tumbling forward in a flurry of smoke, sparks, and steam.

Mother Emith sat bolt upright in her chair. "What? What?" she cried, head jerking left and right.

Stepping away from the fire, Tessa hid the poker behind her back. She felt bad about shocking the old woman. "Oh, it's nothing. Just a log rolling onto the hearth. Here," she said, moving forward and taking Mother Emith's cup from the stand. "Let me fetch you some more tea while you tell me what happened to Brother Avaccus."

The old woman regarded Tessa suspiciously for a moment, looked at the fire, then out of the window to check on the time of day. Finally she said, "Brother Avaccus, you say?"

Tessa poured tea in her cup. "Yes. Remember how you were telling me how Emith had to leave Maribane because the holy fathers sent him away?" To keep the old woman busy, she thrust the brimming cup into her hands.

"Aah. Yes, yes." Mother Emith struggled to get a proper hold on the cup. "Well, it had something to do with demons. The abbot said Brother Avaccus was drawing them, you see. Drawing craven, ungodly things to stir up the devil and his kind. Of course Emith was the one assisting him at the time the illuminations were found, so naturally he was sent away."

Craven, ungodly things. Tessa ran her hand across her chin, thinking. If Avaccus had been working on designs similar to Deveric's, that would explain why Emith had avoided knowing the purpose behind his master's work: because he knew it was considered ungodly.

Suddenly feeling hot, Tessa moved away from the fire. "What happened to Brother Avaccus?" As she spoke she glanced up at the window. It was almost dark now, and Emith would be back soon.

Mother Emith made a soft, clucking sound in her throat. "They severed the tendon on his right thumb. Stopped him from ever taking up a pen again."

Tessa looked down at her own hands. Her own thumbs. "Did he leave the Anointed Isle with Emith?"

"Oh no, my dear. He was one of their own, a fellow brother; they would never let him leave. Thóse hard Maribane holy men pride themselves on expelling demons and breaking the spirit of a man. They like nothing better than redeeming the sinned, that's what my dear old husband used to say. Probably did all manner of things to the poor man in the name of saving his immortal soul." As Mother Emith uttered the last words, her chin began to drift downward toward her chest. Another fit of resting was coming on.

Unwilling to shock the old woman twice in one day, Tessa let her be. She'd gotten enough to think about for the time being. Moving around the room, she began to make the usual preparations for the evening: taking butter from the larder and placing it near the fire so it would be good and soft by supper, pushing wicks into the bowls of tallow, stirring the fish stew so the bottom wouldn't burn, and sprinkling dried hellebore roots on the windowsill to keep out moths and gnats.

Strange how quickly she had become accustomed to this new world of hers, she thought as she pulled a linen square out of a bath of oil and wrung it between her hands. Here she was, preparing the cloth to be hung over the window in the morning—oiled, so it let in as much light as possible—as if it were the most natural thing in the world. Back home she let everything collect dust.

Things were different here. Jobs needed to be done, so she did them: it was part of staying in the house. She couldn't imagine it any other way.

Back over at the fire, Tessa grabbed hold of one of the small, thick-bottomed copper pots. She felt like trying her hand at making sauce. She wasn't sure what sort of sauce it was going to be yet, and had serious doubts about whether or not fish stew even *needed* a sauce, but the idea of cooking something had suddenly caught her fancy, and sauce seemed the easiest place to start.

As she scooped a spoonful of butter from the crock, the latch on the door rattled.

Tessa froze. An image of the night on the bridge shoved the kitchen from her sights. The harras. The misformed faces. The smell.

The butter crock slipped from her hands. It thudded onto the hearth stone, cracking but not smashing.

"What? What?" cried Mother Emith.

The latch lifted. The door swung open and Emith walked in, arms filled with bundles, cheeks reddened by fresh salty air. "Greetings, all!" he called, nudging the door closed with his elbow. "I'm sorry I'm late. It took me an hour to push through the crowds in Fullers Square. I think the whole city is out on the streets tonight." After shrugging off his parcels onto the table, he crossed the room, kissed his mother on each cheek, and then turned to Tessa. "I've brought lots of things to show you," he said. "And perhaps even a surprise for later."

Tessa smiled automatically, but her mouth was so dry that her lips caught against her teeth. Her heart was beating fast. The memory of the harras on the bridge was slow to leave. At her foot, butter began to run out of the crock, warmed to a glistening yellow ribbon by the heat from the hearth. The fatty, animal smell sickened her. "Why are so many people on the streets?" she asked.

Emith glanced at his mother, then leaned in close to Tessa and whispered, "News has just come today that Izgard has taken Thorn."

"Thorn?" Tessa remembered the man who bore the name: dark gold hair, gray eyes that shifted from light to dark, and a voice used to snapping orders.

"Yes. It's a town northwest of the Vorce Mountains." Emith made a small movement with his head, motioning Tessa to step with him, away from his mother and her chair. "People are saying Izgard's harras have done monstrous things: slain women, children, and old men, slaughtered pigs in their pens and cows in the fields, not stopping until everything and everybody was dead."

Tessa shivered. The butter began to sizzle, then burn, on the hearth.

Camron of Thorn ran until he could run no more. Until his lungs were bursting and sweat stung his eyes and his throat was raw and scorched. He ran until his legs buckled beneath him and he collapsed on the wet earth of Runzy, chest heaving, breath steaming, muscles cramping in his stomach, chest, and back.

The summer rain stung him. He imagined he heard it hiss as it touched his flesh. He hated the fact it was warm. In the darkness it might have been anything dripping onto his body, rolling along his cheeks, soaking through his shirt. It might have been his father's blood.

Bringing his knees up toward his chest, Camron curled into a tight ball and tried to ease the tightness in his chest. The smell of damp earth reminded him of home. Not Bay'Zell with its two harbors, two shrines, and two faces, but real home. The small community nestling in the joint shadows of the Boral and Vorce Mountains, that anywhere else in Rhaize would have been named a village yet in the northeast was called a town.

Thorn, with its hillsides dotted with meadows, its soil heavy with clay and rich with lime, and its people so full of local pride that they taught their children to tell strangers they lived but a valley away from God. No poets, philosophers, or artists had ever come from Thorn. Farmers, grape growers, dairymen, blacksmiths, wheelwrights, and charcoal burners crowded in the taverns at night for a platter of smoked goose livers and a glass of berriac. The town black sheep was a man who made clocks. The town prostitute was a sensible matron called Amy, and every man in Thorn, Camron included, had partaken of her delights at some point in their lives.

Thorn was where his father's ancient stablehand Phelas had first sat him on a horse and showed him how to ride; where Mari of Merly, the old Vennish cook who knew only a handful of Rhaize words, most of them curses, had plied him with gooseberry tarts until he felt sick and then forced clove oil down his throat until he felt better. It was where he had slit open his cheek trying to shave like his father, broken his arm trying to fight like Hurin, and shaved his head in an attempt to look like Mollas the Bald, the man who was his father's second at Mount Creed and widely held to be the greatest fighter in Rhaize in his day.

All gone now. All those fine, mountain-bred people gone. Phelas, Mari of Merly, Amy, Mollas, Sterry the clock maker, Barleaf the innkeeper, Dorsen, master of his father's estate: so many friends, casual acquaintances, and loved ones, dead. Men whom Camron had grown up waving to in the streets or fields, women he'd nodded to in the chapel or marketplace, children he'd raced and fought with in the forests, stables, and limestone quarries: all slaughtered by Izgard's men.

Camron grabbed at the soil, filling his palms with its warm, grainy wetness, plowing it inward toward his heart.

What was it the messenger had said? *"Izgard has taken*

Thorn. By all accounts he sent his harras in first to kill those who refused to surrender. You should be proud of your countrymen, my lord, for not one of them gave in."

What he really meant was that none had escaped alive. The harras had killed them all. They hadn't been given the chance to surrender; Camron felt the truth of it in the soft insides of his bones. The Garizon king had first killed his father. Now he had destroyed his home.

And for what? A claim, centuries old, never mentioned, never pressed, that linked the Thorn family to the barbed Garizon crown.

Camron punched the wet earth. He and his father had done nothing to deserve this. The townsfolk of Thorn had done even less. For centuries the Garizon-Rhaize border had shifted back and forth across the Vorce Mountains, and the town had belonged to both countries in its time—named Thorn or Thoren, depending on who held it. Yet fifty years ago, eight weeks to the day after Berick won his victory at Mount Creed, the townsfolk met in the market square and declared themselves for Rhaize. And from that day on the town had been known by its Rhaize name: Thorn.

Only now there were no townsfolk, and without them there was no name.

Camron shook his head so hard, his entire body shook with it. He couldn't bear the thought of Izgard's boots sinking into Thorn soil. He couldn't bear what his mind showed him every time he closed his eyes to blink. Heaving himself up, he struggled to his feet. Exhaustion rippled across his chest, but he fought it. Wiping the dirt from his cheek and hands, he began the long walk back to the manor house.

"It's too early to move against Izgard yet," Ravis had said only two hours earlier in the flickering candlelight of the great hall. "Half of the mercenaries won't arrive in Bay'Zell until next week, and I haven't finished training the ones we do have. Your men may be excellent knights and horsemen, but Izgard's archers will shoot the horses from beneath them the moment they take the field. And a knight without a horse might as well paint a bull's-eye on his breastplate and call himself a moving target. Though moving might be too generous a description. With the full body armor that's popular in Rhaize these days, a knight has a better chance of staying on the ground and *rolling* to safety than he does trying to stand and walk away."

Camron's back stiffened as he walked. How he hated Ravis of Burano's cool, mocking voice. The man picked apart all that was good with his biting wit, excusing a hundred years of military development with a single, sarcastic remark. He didn't care about people and causes. He thought only of himself.

War was about more than tactics: it was about heart and soul and *belief*. Rhaize knights hadn't won victory at Mount Creed because they had superior expertise; they'd won because they had a great leader they believed in and were fighting to defend their families and homes.

Camron brushed his wet hair from his face. He had no home now and nothing and no one to believe in. Responsibility was the one thing he had left. He owed something to those who had been slaughtered because they lived in the town bearing his name. He had to take action—leave right now. Tonight. It couldn't wait. He owed it to Mari, Amy, Phelas, and the clock maker. He owed it to himself.

The pale golden glow of the manor house came into view on the horizon, and Camron hurried toward it, a dark figure on a dark night, perfectly alone.

THIRTEEN

The scribe sat alone in his scriptorium. Pigment pots and brushes lay waiting to be cleaned, the shutters needed closing for the night, and hides hung from a hook set into a ceiling beam, waiting to be cut to size. From as far back as he could remember, from his first eight years spent growing up in Garizon and the next twenty spent in study on the Anointed Isle, Ederius had been taught that it was wrong to be idle. His mother had feared idleness would lead to sin. The holy fathers on the Anointed Isle had sworn it would turn him into a weak-minded fool. Yet right now Ederius found himself wishing that he had not been quite so hardworking all his life. Hard work had led him to this.

Sending the chair legs scraping backward as he stood, Ederius moved across the room toward the small trestle table that held the pure grain alcohol he used to clean his brushes. Even now he could not sit inactive for very long. Both his mother and the holy fathers had agreed upon one thing: idleness led to idle thought.

Izgard had not paid his daily visit yet, and as Ederius poured alcohol into a glazed bowl, he found himself listening for the first sounds of his king. When a wolf howled far in the distance, Ederius jumped at the noise, spilling alcohol over his fingers. The liquid tingled as it evaporated into nothing. Ederius attempted to shrug his fright away, but a needle of pain shot through his healing shoulder. Face crumpling, he shook his head.

He wished Izgard would come and get it over with. The pain he could stand, the blows he could stand, but the waiting was too much to bear. It turned him into a frightened old man.

Ederius grabbed the bowl, pressing his fingers hard against the glazed edge. He was an Anointed-trained scribe—he would not forget that—and nothing and no one could take that from him.

With a firm step, he walked back to his desk. After collecting all the pigment-caked paintbrushes in his fist, he dumped them into the bowl to soak them a while before cleaning.

One other thing that he must not forget was that he had brought this upon himself. Ambition had led him to the man who had then been known as Izgard of Alberach. Five years ago they had met. Izgard arranged a meeting in Veizach's Arlish Quarter in a perfectly square room above an inn. The smell of the Veize wafted up through the open window as Izgard laid out his plans.

"You must work with me, Ederius. I need you. Gamberon tells me you are the best scribe in all of Garizon, the only one who knows the old patterns and the old ways. The only one who can help me. Garizon must have a king again. We must be strong. We are a great country, with great people, yet here we are trodden beneath so many boot heels that we barely remember our victories and have long forgotten our pride."

Izgard knelt and took Ederius' hand. *"Do you not love your country, Ederius? Do you not want to see Garizon restored?"*

In all his life Ederius would never forget the look on Izgard's face as he'd asked those two questions. His eyes were shining and his skin was flushed. He looked like an angel, and his touch was warm and full of need. Ederius was deeply moved. This brilliant young man needed him. As he gave his reply, Izgard raised, then kissed, his hand.

Even now, Ederius felt his heart ache at the memory. Izgard had been different back then. Ambitious, yes. Violent to those who opposed him, but fiercely protective of those he loved. Ederius still remembered the time he fell ill that first year, catching a chill from working long hours in cold, unheated rooms. Izgard was at his side night and day. He would let no one else take care of him, insisting on being the one who sat with him day and night, not sleeping until the fever broke some three days later. When Ederius finally woke, Iz-

gard was there leaning over his bed. Tears glistened in the
young man's eyes.

"*A gift,*" he said, fingers brushing against Ederius' cheek.
"*I have been given a precious gift. I don't know what I would
have done if you had died.*"

Ederius closed his eyes. That seemed like a lifetime ago.
When there were just he, Gamberon, and Izgard. The scribe,
the scholar, and the man who would be king. Four good
years passed until things turned. Gamberon had been worried for many months. The more he researched the Barbed
Coil and its history, the more nervous he became. Late one
night he burst into Ederius' sleeping chamber. Spittle sprayed
from his lips as he spoke.

"*We cannot allow Izgard to take the crown. Come with
me now to Sirabayus and help me destroy the Coil before another sunset darkens the Veize.*"

Grabbing the paintbrushes in his hand, Ederius lifted
them free from the alcohol. Pigment had turned the liquid red.
With quick, almost frenzied movements, he began to scrub
the brush heads clean.

He had loved Gamberon like a brother, but Izgard like a
son. The choice was surprisingly easy. Gamberon left straight
away, alone. Ederius waited in the darkness for one hour,
counting seconds, then went to wake Izgard.

"*You must make haste for Sirabayus,*" he said. "*Gamberon is on his way there to destroy the Coil.*"

Ederius made a soft, rasping sound in his throat. It had
been the longest night of his life. He had been unable to move.
He sat in the darkness on the edge of Izgard's bed, his bladder
aching with fullness, his breaths shallow as a dying man,
waiting.

Daylight came and half a day passed before Izgard returned. The Barbed Coil was tucked under his arm. Slivers of
Gamberon's tissue still clung to the barbs. Ederius remembered thinking it strange that Izgard had managed to carry the
Coil all the way back from the convent without his own skin
being broken. Izgard did not speak as he entered the room. He
placed the crown on a chest, crossed to where Ederius sat,
and smashed his fist into the right side of Ederius' jaw.

Shaking his head, he left the room. "*You did not come to*

me straight away," he hissed, disappearing into the darkness beyond. *"You gave him an hour's start."*

Ederius raised his hand to his cheek as the memory of the old pain gripped him. It was first time Izgard ever struck him: the night he took possession of the Coil.

The door hinge creaked and Izgard stepped into the scriptorium. Lost in the past, it took Ederius a moment to come back. He had not heard his king approach.

"Ederius," Izgard said softly, pushing hides out of his way as he walked forward. "I'm glad to find you still at your desk. We must talk about my plans for Thorn."

Nodding, Ederius dropped his hand from his cheek and listened as Izgard spoke. Perhaps if he was lucky, his king would not strike him tonight.

"And this," Emith said, handing Tessa a swath of cloth, "is the plant dye turnsole. As you see, this is pink, but turnsole plants can produce rich purples, too."

Tessa took the small section of cloth from him. It felt stiff. Her fingertips came away deep pink where she touched it. "Someone didn't do a very good job of fixing the dye," she said.

Emith gave her a rather curious look. "It *is* the dye," he said. "Clothlets are how most plant dyes are transported overseas. All I have to do now is put that small piece of cloth in a bowl of clarified egg white, let the pigment bleed out overnight, and then the next day I'll have fresh pink paint to use for glazes or to add to other pigments."

"Oh," was all Tessa could think of to say as she regarded the small square of cloth with renewed appreciation. There was so much she didn't know.

Emith had come back from the market loaded down with pigment samples to show her. Tonight he was teaching her about how to make the various inks and paints used in illuminating. He was very excited about the whole affair, so much so that he had even lit two fine wax candles, which gave out sweet-smelling, smokeless light. Mother Emith was resting in her chair. Supper had been eaten, pots had been cleared away, the fire was burning quietly on fuel of old, pressed wood, and a light rain pattered against the shutters like insects against glass.

"What's in that?" Tessa asked, indicating a small cork-stoppered jar Emith had just taken from his pack. As the days went on, she found herself wanting to learn more and more about scribing. She wanted to know all the details.

Emith held up the jar to the light. "This is murex purple. It's a stronger pigment than turnsole, though more expensive. It's made from warm-water shellfish."

"Shellfish?" Tessa took the stopper from the jar and let a drop fall on the back of her hand. The pigment was an inky purple.

"Oh yes," Emith said, eyes twinkling. "There's a pigment made from cuttlefish secretions, too."

Tessa held out her free hand. Emith didn't disappoint her. After a little rooting in his pack, he produced a second jar, identical in every way to the first.

"Cuttlefish ink makes a warm sepia-colored dye. Good for glazes or backgrounds."

Tessa decided not to test the cuttlefish pigment. The shellfish one had sunk into her skin like a tattoo. As she tried to rub off the stain, Emith went on to produce a yellow powder made from crocus stamens; a deep maroon paste called reng that was a mixture of henna and indigo; a red dye called kermes that was prepared from the dried bodies of insects found on evergreen oaks; powdered gold and silver for fancy inks; yellow and orange ocher extracted from iron-rich soil; verdigris, a greeny blue powder that was scraped off weathered copper or bronze; and red, yellow, and white lead powders that Emith warned her not to get on her hands. Last he pulled out a tiny mother-of-pearl box not much bigger than a thimble.

"This," he said, flicking open the lid with his thumbnail, "is lapis lazuli. The rarest of all of the pigments. This box cost me double its weight in gold."

Not daring to breathe, Tessa leaned forward to examine the contents of the box. A deep, brilliant blue powder sparkled against the white pearl. So this was what Widow Furbish had got so excited about? A pigment the color of the sea. Look-

ing at the powder, Tessa felt her mind working on something
else. As soon as she realized what it was, she sat back in her
chair and asked the first question that came into her head.

"So, how do you go about making it into paint?" Her
mind had shown her the last picture she had of Widow Furbish—her broken body doubled up in the doorway of her
house, her skin shiny with blood—and she didn't want to
dwell on it. Not tonight. Not after Emith had told her that Izgard's harras had done the same thing to a town full of people.
And not just any town: Camron of Thorn's home. It didn't
take much intuition to guess where he and Ravis would be
heading this night.

Tessa rubbed hard at the murex stain on her arm, even
though she knew it wasn't coming out. Would she ever see
Ravis again? She honestly didn't know. Without realizing
what she was doing, Tessa felt for the ring hanging from her
neck. Whenever she thought of the future or the past, her fingers always found their way to the ring.

Emith began placing a collection of glazed pots on the
table. Some of them, like the large one normally stored in the
larder that contained clarified egg white for binding, she had
seen before, but most of them were new to her. Up until now
she had been doing most scribing work in plain black or
brown ink with a quill pen, and this was her first real sight of
Emith mixing and binding his pigments.

He used shells as his palettes, oyster or mollusk depending on the quantity of pigment he needed. He began with egg
white, added pigment either in powder or liquid form, stirred
it with a tiny stiff brush until the mixture was all one color,
and then, depending on what his needs were, added various
other items to the mix. Sometimes he added a few drops of
water if the paint needed thinning, or a glistening bead of
fish glue to increase the pigment's adherence to the page.
Chalk was added to increase opacity and lighten or modify
the color, and for some pigments Emith used ground-up
eggshells instead.

Emith moved like a head surgeon: confident, well practiced, graceful. Tessa felt as though she were seeing him for
the first time. No longer was he the short, neat, aging man
who jumped when his mother spoke and treated Tessa with

such polite deference that in the month they had known each other he hadn't once called her by her name: he was a skilled craftsman now. His movements were quick, his eye sure, his lips pressed firmly to a tight line.

This was his element. This was where being a scribe's assistant reached its highest form: the preparation, mixing, and modifying of pigments. Tessa could imagine Emith mixing away in the background as Deveric worked on his latest design, calling out what colors he needed next.

Powdery orange ocher was given a smooth gleam by the addition of a spoonful of honey, kermes red was thickened to a gel by the addition of earwax, and indigo blue was thinned and paled by adding just three drops of stale urine—Tessa didn't ask who or where it came from. Acacia gum, a dairy glue called casein, pink earth, gallic acid, powdered sulfates of green and turquoise, soot, lampblack, red wine, white wine, woad, ground bones, and gesso all modified the pigments in some way: thickening, creating textures, darkening, lightening, and altering color, shine, and absorbency.

By the time Emith had finished, the tabletop was filled with dozens of shells, bright pigments nestling in their midst like fantastic sea creatures pulled up from the deep. From a base of perhaps ten pigments, Emith had created a complete palette of colors ranging from the subtlest flesh pink to the bloodiest crimson, from the palest worm gray to the deepest midnight blue.

Tessa was dazzled by the colors. Each one was a jewel set in an iridescent casing of shell. Just looking at them filled her head with possibilities. She saw bands of color crossing a page, dots of shining silver, steps of gold and red, and knots of darkest purple throwing shadows of purest black. She wanted to pick up a brush and paint.

When she held out a hand to grasp a paintbrush, Emith clamped a palm upon her wrist. "You're not ready to use the full palette yet," he said, gently returning her hand to the tabletop. "Before you start illuminating properly, you must understand the colors completely, know what they represent and how and why they are chosen."

Tessa looked at Emith. How much did he know about his

master's work? Judging from his reluctance to meet her eye just then, enough to know it could be dangerous.

Pulling a small rectangle of vellum from his robe, Emith said, "Sometimes, especially when working from copies, it's important to match the colors exactly." He laid the sheet on the table, at the point where the two circles of light from the candles met. The design painted on it was simple, just trumpet spirals surrounding a central medallion, but the colors used stopped the design from appearing crude. Shades of green, gold, yellow, and mustard darted across the page.

"Some dyes are impossible to get hold of," Emith continued, wiping his hands with almond oil to remove the last traces of pigment. "Take this yellow color here. It's made from a rare type of mullein plant that only grows in high meadows in a remote mountain region of Drokho. It's not an especially good pigment—saffron would have done a better job—but scribes who live in remote areas tend to use whatever is readily available. The makeup of pigments changes from region to region, depending on local tradition and resources. Even here in Bay'Zell, you'll find more scribes using turnsole purple rather than murex purple, because it's cheaper and easier to get hold of in the north."

Nodding, Tessa picked up the sheet of vellum.

"As a scribe's assistant, one of my jobs is to match pigments as closely as I can. Copying existing patterns is at the heart of all illuminating done by the old-style scribes like Deveric. They never create purely on impulse, but always work off existing models—either copying them exactly or adding a few touches of their own. Unlike the new scribes today who all want to create something new, something original, the old scribes just wanted to rework the past."

While Emith was speaking, Tessa had noticed something odd about the vellum. When she held it up to the light, thousands of tiny pinpricks appeared on the page. More than just marking points, they were actual holes punched through the page. Candlelight streamed through them in crisp, golden lines.

"Those are pinpricks made with the tip of a knife," Emith said, seeing what had caught Tessa's eye. "Whenever a scribe wants to make an exact copy of a pattern and doesn't have the time or patience to construct a grid by measuring lines and angles, he'll place the original on top of a blank sheet of parchment and puncture the major points of the pattern with the tip of his knife. That way the parchment below will be marked with an outline of the original and a scribe can then go on and reconstruct the design from the pinpricks. Copies have been made that way for centuries."

Tessa traced her finger over the vellum. It felt stiff, which meant it was very old. As she looked at it, one particular color caught her eye: a silver black pigment that didn't fit in with the rest of the design. Its cool tone was at odds with the warm yellows, greens, and golds. "Was this used for a special purpose?" she asked, pointing to a spiral outlined in the color.

"That pigment was originally red lead," Emith said, obviously pleased that she had noticed the discrepancy. "Over years, metal-based pigments can weather in the air and either fade, as that did, or bleed into other colors. Some copper greens can even eat through the parchment completely as they age. That's one of the more difficult things about my job—sorting out what pigments the original scribe used. It helps if they finish their paintings with a vegetable wash or an extra coating of egg white; that way the pigments retain their original color longer."

Tessa ate up all the details Emith gave her. She fed on them like a hungry child, grabbing all she could to fill up the hollow space within. For years she had been starving herself of details, knowledge, and involvements. Coming here, to this world, to this house, was like sitting down at a banquet table and being allowed to eat until she dropped. She didn't have to pass things by anymore.

There was nothing about her old life she missed. Nothing. She had grown accustomed to chamber pots and the accompanying bail of straw, water that came from a pitcher and not a tap, lighting that had to be carried, dresses that had to be laced, fires that had to be tended as if they were a rich but sickly relative whose generosity everyone in the household depended on, floors that had to be swept clean one minute and then sprinkled with hay and herbs the next, wool

stockings that scratched and bagged at the knees, no under-
wear, toothbrushes, or toothpaste to speak of—Tessa had
learned to clean her teeth with a slice of marshmallow root—
and pig lard, lanolin, and animal soap as the only available
beauty treatments. There was no mirror in the house, so she
hadn't seen what she looked like in over a month, and although there was still a part of her that wanted to look her
best, right now it didn't seem so important.

There was little from her past that *did* seem important.
When she looked back on it—how she lived, what she chose
to do, the distance she always kept between herself and the
people she knew—it was as if she had been waiting, bags
packed, all along.

A sharp rap on the door startled Tessa from her thoughts.
Immediately worried, she glanced at Emith. He was already
rising from his chair.

"It's all right," he said. "It's only Marcel. I sent a message to him earlier, asking him to bring Deveric's illuminations to the house."

Marcel. Tessa remembered Ravis' words: *Don't show yourself to anyone who comes to the door, especially Marcel.* . . .
"Does he know I'm here?" she asked.

Emith thought for a moment, then shook his head. "No,
miss. I didn't mention you in my note. But surely there's no
harm in Marcel knowing? After all, he's a very good friend
of Ravis'."

Tessa had seen Marcel of Vailing in action. She had seen
him double-cross his very good friend, betray him without
blinking an eye. There was no point in explaining all this to
Emith, though. He'd believe the best of someone stabbing him
in the back. Instead she said, "Emith, I'm going to hide in the
larder. Promise me you won't tell Marcel I'm here. Promise."

A second rap came at the door.

"What? What?" cried Mother Emith. "Who's there?"

Emith turned toward the door, clearly anxious to open it.
Now that he was no longer at the table creating pigments, he
had reverted back to his normal soft-spoken, eager-to-please
self. "I won't say anything, but hurry now."

Tessa was already at the larder door. She pulled it open
and stepped down into the darkness. As the latch clicked shut

behind her she heard the main door swing open. A pocket of cool air swept under the larder door, and then a voice called out: "Emith, my dear, dear friend. How are you and your excellent mother this evening?" It was Marcel of Vailing.

Tessa took a deep breath. Meaty ham smells raced up her nose, followed quickly by the ripe, fatty smell of triple cream cheese. Despite everything, she felt her mouth watering.

Emith said something that Tessa couldn't hear.

"Yes, I have them," Marcel replied. "Just last week a gentleman passing through Bay'Zell on his way to Calmo made me quite an offer for them. Enough to keep you and your excellent mother in silks and fine lobsters for life."

"Can't eat lobster more than once a month," said Mother Emith. "Gives me terrible wind."

Tessa smiled. She wished she could have seen Marcel's face just then.

Footsteps echoed on the floor. The noise of something being placed, not gently, on the table followed. "Well, here they are," Marcel said, his voice as smooth and level as ever. "If you ever need hard cash, I could forward you a fair amount on the strength of the last one alone. You know, the one marked with blood."

"They are not for sale."

Tessa was surprised by the heat in Emith's voice. She had never heard him speak so harshly before. Taking a step toward the door, she risked placing her ear against the wood. She didn't want to miss anything that was said.

"Working late, aren't you?" Marcel again. Tessa detected a suspicious catch in his voice.

Emith started to say something, probably a poor excuse, but was cut short in midmumble by his mother saying loudly, "And what if he is, Marcel of Vailing? Do you know of any law he is breaking?"

It was Marcel's turn to mumble this time. Tessa was beginning to realize that being a very old lady had its advantages: no one dared contradict anything you said.

Letting herself relax a little, Tessa leaned back against the wall. To reduce vermin, the floor in the larder wasn't covered with rushes like the kitchen, and she could feel her feet growing numb with cold. The entire larder was built two feet lower than the rest of the house, to keep the food as cool as possible in summer. Up until this point Tessa had doubted the worth of those extra two feet. The goose pimples on her arms told her the true story, though.

Turning her attention back to what was going on in the kitchen, she listened to the rise and fall of voices. Marcel was talking about the war.

"Oh, there's nothing for us here in Bay'Zell to worry about," he said. "Izgard will never make it this far. Now that it's obvious he's set on invading Rhaize and not just flexing his newly crowned muscles, the Sire will bring his armies up from Mir'Lor and stop him before he crosses the Chase."

Tessa's lip curled. Marcel of Vailing was simply repeating a well-practiced phrase. He probably had a second one ready just in case Izgard did happen to make it to Bay'Zell. Tessa could imagine how it would begin: *These may be hard times, but we must endeavor to make the best of them.* . . .

She stopped in midcomposition as the name *Ravis* filtered through the cedarwood door.

"He and Camron will put up quite a battle, of course," Marcel said. Unlike the last time when Tessa had met him, he seemed to be doing all the talking. "Their force should reach Izgard before the Sire's army does. Where were they based again? The name of the place escapes me."

Tessa clicked her tongue against the roof of her mouth. The name didn't escape Marcel at all. Ravis hadn't told him where they were going, she was sure of it. The man was rooting for information.

"I don't know where Lord Ravis is," Emith said.

Marcel let out a long, wistful sigh. "And what about his pretty lady friend? The one with the reddish hair and strange voice. I believe you met her once. Do you happen to know where she might be?"

Sucking in her breath, Tessa listened for Emith's reply. All of a sudden the larder seemed unbearably small and confining. She knew Emith would do what he promised, but he wasn't the sort of man who could lie easily, and his nervousness might give him away.

A long moment passed. Even though she was in the dark, Tessa closed her eyes.

Mother Emith's voice broke the silence. "How would we know where Lord Ravis keeps his women? Does this kitchen look like a brothel to you?"

"No, madam," Marcel replied quickly. "I just thought—"

"Well, don't. Don't waste any of your time thinking about Emith and me and what we get up to, and we won't waste any time thinking about you."

Tessa fought back a cheer. Old Mother Emith was turning out to be more than a match for Marcel of Vailing. All that resting in her chair must have given her plenty of time to hone her tongue.

Footsteps pattered, rather quickly, across the kitchen floor. Marcel said something, probably a farewell, but for the first time since entering the house he whispered and Tessa didn't catch what it was. Mother Emith wished the banker a fond farewell and the door was duly opened, then seconds later closed. Tessa began counting to five just to be safe, got impatient before reaching halfway, and pushed open the larder door. She was greeted by the sight of Emith and his mother both grinning from ear to ear.

"Come over here by the fire, my dear," said Mother Emith. "A person could catch their death in that larder."

Tessa walked over to Mother Emith's chair and caught Mother Emith herself in a long, deep hug. The old woman protested, just as Tessa knew she would, but she hugged her even harder when she did. She owed these people so much. They had taken her into their home, fed, clothed, and lied for her, but most of all they had protected her. And that feeling of being protected, of knowing someone cared enough to put themselves out and, in the case of Emith and his mother, put themselves at risk to keep her safe, was something she hadn't felt in a very long time.

Emith circled the two women, drawing nearer and nearer with each pass, until he eventually plucked up courage to step forward and pat Tessa's arm. "Mother and I would never tell anyone where you are," he said softly. "Never."

Ravis stood, hand pressed against the great stone mantel, booted foot resting upon the hearth, eye to the sand drizzling down within the hourglass, and waited for Camron of Thorn to return. Briefly he had toyed with the idea of having a measure of berriac waiting for him when he did. Ultimately deciding against it, he had drunk Camron's portion himself.

Noticing that the mud caked on the tip of his boot had finally dried, Ravis knocked it against the hearthstone. Pale gray powder sifted to the floor. Camron of Thorn was not the only man who had ventured outside tonight.

A few minutes after he and Camron had argued and Camron had stormed off across the grounds, Ravis had pulled on his cloak, lit one of the sturdy glass lanterns that the seneschal kept gleaming in the entry hall, and walked across the courtyard to the stables.

He talked to the grooms first. Walked with them along the stalls, discussed the condition of the horses, listened to their opinions and advice, and then asked them to have four dozen horses groomed, saddled, and ready within two hours. The grooms hadn't liked the order, for it was past dark and one skittish horse could affect the mood of them all. Yet Ravis had taken time to get to know the grooms at Runzy, both the ones who had arrived with Camron's knights and the ones who had lived here all their lives, and once he had explained his reasons, they were willing to do what he asked. One or two of the older men had even been expecting it.

Next Ravis went to the kitchens. The cook and the servant girls were sitting around the table playing cards, tippling on strong local-brewed beer, and eating slices of the sweetened carrot tarts that were so popular in Runzy. The cook threw her shawl over a large baked ham when he walked through the door, and one of her girls slipped a flask up her sleeve. Ravis pretended to see neither. Camron's food and wine were nothing to him. The goodwill of the kitchen staff, however, was a valuable asset to a man planning a journey.

Having complimented the cook on the fine dinner she had cooked that evening, and flirted with the shyest and plainest of the kitchen girls, Ravis asked them, very kindly, if they would be so good as to prepare and pack enough travel food to feed four dozen . . . no, he corrected himself, six dozen men for six days and have it ready within the hour.

The cook's plump arm rested on the shawl that rested on the ham. Ravis could tell what she was thinking: with the master and his men away she could sell off the extra food that had been purchased at market that week. Fresh venison would fetch a premium price at this time of year.

By the time Ravis left the kitchen to head to the great hall, pots, pans, knives, chopping boards, parsley, hard-boiled eggs, and fruit were flying through the air like dust from a saw.

Most of Camron's knights—two dozen seasoned campaigners, a dozen or so young bucks, a handful of arrogant nobles, a few men past their prime, and one or two truly outstanding fighters—waited in the great hall. They fell silent when Ravis crossed the threshold. All were tense: ale had gone flat in tankards and pitchers, the fire had burned low from lack of tending, and the normal bevy of tavern wenches and servant girls was missing. The massacre at Thorn was on everyone's mind. Three of the men had been born there. All were shocked by the news. They were Camron's men and, in some cases, his personal friends, and an attack on his land and holdings was as good as an attack on their own.

Watching their hostile stares as he cut to the center of the room, Ravis judged it wise to speak plainly. "Get your packs, weapons, and armor ready. We ride tonight for Thorn."

The knights, who had spent a good portion of the past month questioning every instruction, drill, and order he had given, immediately did as they were told. All wanted to go. Their eagerness crackled through the room like ice on a thawing lake. One of the men even patted Ravis on the back. Up until then Ravis had been the villain who forced them to watch senseless weapon drills, talked nonsense about swapping their plate armor for chainmail or boiled leather, who was opposed to taking quick, decisive action against Izgard of Garizon, and whose harsh words were responsible for sending Camron of Thorn running out into the night.

The last thing wasn't true, of course—Camron's torments were of his own making—yet as no one else had been party to the conversation, the knights had naturally assumed that their leader's sudden departure was all Ravis' fault. It was easy to hate a man who wanted you to change your ways. Most especially when that man was a foreigner who brought in mercenaries to show you how you should fight.

Ravis had met that sort of resistance on every job he had tackled. Time was the only solution. Time and perhaps a practical lesson in technique.

"Take only what is necessary," he had said as the last of the men filed out of the hall. "There will be no wagon trains or packhorses to carry your dress armor. We need to be light on our feet." None of them acknowledged the order. He had not expected them to.

After topping the lantern up with oil, Ravis had made his final excursion of the evening: across the forecourt, through the palisades, past the dairy, and toward the barracks. The mercenaries and longbowsmen Segwin the Ney had sent from Bay'Zell were housed there with their horses. Ravis met with the men, gave them his orders, then left.

The rain beat against his face as he returned to the manor house. It was a bad night for travel, and they wouldn't make good time in the muddy and moonless darkness, but that really wasn't the point. The simple fact they were on the move would be enough to satisfy Camron of Thorn.

Ravis knew that when Camron returned from whatever place his grief had driven him, he would want to do just one thing: leave straight away for Thorn. Ravis had known this from the moment the news came in from Runzy. Still, he had to say his piece, raise objections, and give cautions, for first and foremost he was a professional fighter and it was his duty to give his considered opinion to the man who was paying his way.

The truth was they *weren't* ready. The mercenaries had been training for less than two weeks, the longbowsmen had arrived from Bay'Zell only eight days ago, and Camron's knights were a mixed bunch brought together in haste. They had no real knowledge of what the situation was in Thorn, whether they would encounter a full occupation, a minimal safekeeping force, or just a ravaged, deserted town. They didn't know the location, intent, or makeup of Izgard's forces, and they still didn't know what lay behind the terrible blood lust of the harras.

All in all it was a bad situation. Ravis didn't like launching blindly into a campaign with no foreknowledge of the enemies' tactics. He didn't like it at all. But he had been in similar situations before now, and by the grace of the gods—all four of them—he had always managed to survive.

There were a number of reasons Ravis had held off making his preparations, some of them petty. By moving now, while Camron was away from the manor, Ravis effectively took control away from him. He prevented Camron from returning in a lordly rage and cracking orders like whips. Ostensibly this would be Camron's campaign, but ultimately, beneath the surface and behind the scenes, Ravis would be in charge. He had to be—Thorn was too emotional a subject for Camron. He saw it through a mist of grief and rage, and although fiery emotion bred bravery in men, it seldom bred anything as useful as common sense.

Strategy aside, though, the real reason Ravis chose to wait was not nearly so significant or high-minded.

He liked to throw people off guard. He knew that when Camron of Thorn walked up to the manor house the last thing he would expect to find in the courtyard was a force provisioned, ready, and mounted. Ravis smiled to himself just thinking about it. It had been many years since a man had last taken his measure correctly. If someone knew you inside and out, could gauge your beliefs before you stated them and guess your decisions before you made them, then that made you theirs to manipulate. They could play on your weaknesses, goad you in your sore points, and appeal to whatever vanities you nursed.

Twenty-one years ago Ravis had thought he knew his brother completely, yet Malray had held something back. While Ravis himself had been open and trusting, his elder brother, whom he had loved above all others, had kept a bracelet of knives up his sleeve.

These days Ravis liked to keep things just as close. No man would ever find him gullible or predictable again.

Footsteps sounded in the entrance hall. A long shadow cast by a lantern hung at chest height stretched a dark line across the doorway. Ravis glanced at the hourglass: the last grains of sand raced through the middle to the fat globe below. Everything would be ready as planned, yet Camron would not be aware of anything. He had entered by way of the main doors, which meant he wouldn't have seen all the activity going on in the courtyard to the rear.

Camron stepped into the room. His hair was a dark mat against his face. There was mud on his clothes and his left cheek. His eyes had given up all semblance of gray; sunk deep into their sockets, they were black. Even as he crossed the threshold his right hand was massing to a fist.

"We leave for Thorn tonight," he cried, marching toward Ravis. "And you will be with me, riding by my side, and God so help me I will hear no word against it."

Ravis had waited with delectable anticipation for this instant for exactly an hour. He had planned what he would say and the careless manner in which he would say it. He had even stripped off his gloves so he could make a nonchalant show of pulling them on as he said, "Come, my Lord Camron, your men grow restless waiting. Not all of us can afford the luxury of running out into the night like lovesick fools." Yet seeing what state the man was in, watching his chest rise and fall with exhaustion, hearing the desperation in his voice, but most of all, listening to the words he said, made Ravis catch his breath.

And you will be with me, riding by my side. . . .

Ravis felt the muscles in his chest tighten. Surely Malray had said those words to him once? Long ago when their father first died, when the whole world seemed set against them and they were as close as two brothers could be.

Standing there, booted foot resting on the hearth as he watched the last grains of sand trickle to the bottom of the glass, Ravis suddenly felt old and cynical.

He didn't like himself very much.

Camron despised him, yet the first words from his mouth were as close as an appeal as a proud man like him could manage.

Ravis looked into his face. There was little of Camron's arrogance left. Grief and rage had taken something from him. His father had been murdered, his childhood home had been destroyed, and the burdens of loss and revenge fell on no one's shoulders but his.

Ravis took his boot from the hearth. Reaching down along the mantel, he caught hold of the hourglass, then turned it upside-down.

"After you left," he said to Camron in a voice carefully measured to be neither gentle nor harsh, "I gave some thought to what our next course of action should be, and I came to the conclusion you were right. We cannot allow Izgard of Garizon to get away with what he's done. The Sire will move against him now, but it will take him at least two weeks to rally his army from the Drokho border and Mir'Lor. In the meantime you and I can take a close look at Izgard's forces, jab a thorn in his side, and gather what intelligence we can."

Camron nodded. "And Thorn?"

"I can make no promises. It depends what kind of force, if any, we find there."

The words were the simple truth, and although they weren't what Camron wanted to hear, he accepted them without protest. "How long will it take to get the men ready? Can we move by first light?"

Ravis bit his lip. All his earlier delight over the situation had gone, erased by a handful of words from the past, still yet he managed a ghost of a smile as he told Camron they would be leaving that night.

FOURTEEN

nowy was up to his no-good dog tricks. He was barreling around the courtyard chasing sparrows, shadows, dandelion puffs, and fresh air. Anything that moved—and a good few things that didn't—found themselves the object of the little dog's pursuit. Snowy liked being outside in the courtyard; inside he had nothing to chase but his tail. There were always rats, of course, but Snowy was afraid of them. He was a *no-good* dog, after all.

Gerta watched Snowy's performance from the thinly cushioned stone bench opposite. Angeline had brought out two beautifully plump cushions for them both to sit on, but Gerta had said it wasn't fitting for a maid to sit as well as her mistress and had promptly produced her own thin cushion from the vast storage space under her skirt. Angeline, not wanting to give away how disappointed she was that Gerta had turned down one of her matching cushions, now sat high atop of both of them.

Gerta disapproved of the whole concept of being outside. She had a way of saying the word that made it sound about as unsavory as a witch-hunt. "Outside?" she would exclaim. "*Out*-side?" Even now, as she sat there, unraveling a silk surplice thread by thread, fingertips peeking out through gloves that had been sliced off at the knuckles, thumbs encased in leather protectors, pins, as always, forming a pinecone around her teeth, she had an air of a martyr about her. Her fingers picked at the silk surplice as if it were a horsehair shirt.

Going outside in Sern Fortress wasn't the same as going outside anywhere else. The courtyard was about the size of four large tablecloths laid edge to edge. Stone battlements so high they limited the view of the sky to a distant blue square fenced in the area. Sunlight shone directly onto the courtyard for only an hour every day. A few plants did manage to grow, poking through the hard soil in the boxed borders dug long ago by some hopeful cook or gardener, but Angeline didn't recognize any of them. There were no violets, rosemary, fennel, or tansy, just stout-stemmed yellow things that looked as dour and invulnerable as the fortress itself. Even Snowy could muster up no interest in them.

The truth was Angeline wasn't fond of being outside either. Not here, anyway. Not in Sern Fortress, with its thin mountain air, pale mountain sky, and chilly mountain breezes. It wasn't anything like being outside in Castle Halmac. Within the grounds at Halmac there were hedged gardens, rose gardens, walled gardens, herb gardens, fountains, a fish pond, pretty pink paving, and a holy martyry for Martyr Assitus. The sun shone all day, not just for an hour at noon, and butterflies, dragonflies, and all sorts of nice birds darted through skies that were a proper shade of Garizon blue.

"Angeline," Gerta said sharply. "Come and help me roll this thread onto a bob."

Angeline blushed. Gerta always knew when she was thinking about the old days in Castle Halmac. "I can't help with the silk, Gerta," she said, brow furrowing as she tried to come up with a feasible reason to get out of the hateful thread reeling. Her eyes alighted on Snowy's muddy feet. "Petting Snowy has made my hands dirty."

Snowy, hearing his name spoken, stopped chasing whatever it was he imagined he was chasing and looked his mistress's way.

Snowy did something wrong?

Angeline laughed. Snowy's face looked funny. Patting her side, she beckoned the little dog over.

"Let me see them, then," Gerta said, nodding at Angeline's hands. "I'll be the judge of just how dirty they are." Gerta was the only woman in the entire world whose voice was actually clearer when speaking through a mouthful of pins than without them.

Angeline glanced at Snowy for support. The little dog had caught wind of the situation and had suddenly found something very interesting to sniff at in the corner of the yard. That was the sort of thing no-good dogs did all the time. Slipping down from her cushions, Angeline dragged her feet across the courtyard and came to stand next to Gerta. "My hands aren't as dirty as I thought," she admitted. "They look clean enough to hold the thread."

Gerta nodded. "Hold them out, then."

Still standing, Angeline spread out her hands and let Gerta weave silk thread around them. She was beginning to feel a little sick in her stomach, just like yesterday morning. Coming outside hadn't been such a good idea after all. Neither had eating in the kitchen last night, or lighting a fire in the great hearth, or searching through the dungeons for treasure. Now that Ederius had left, nothing was fun anymore.

According to Gerta, Izgard was doing very well in Rhaize—so well, in fact, that he had occupied all the towns and villages directly west of the Vorce Mountains. Towns and villages, Gerta was fond of saying, that were rightfully and legitimately Garizon's. Gerta usually went on to say why and how they rightfully belonged to Garizon, but Angeline never listened past the first sentence or two.

She hadn't minded much when Izgard left. There were times when her husband frightened her, like after lovemaking, when he would get angry and force her to dress and leave the room. Sometimes he called her names, and if he became really agitated, he would hit her. He was always sorry afterward, of course. She had to give him that.

The first week after he left was heaven for Angeline. She could run up and see Ederius whenever she wanted. The scribe would draw things for her, tell her stories, and let her paint with his fat-headed brushes. In turn, Angeline saw to it that his room was kept tidy and well brushed and his food was always delivered hot. Although she passed along those mundane chores to the maids, she saw to his nursing herself. Whenever Ederius' cough got bad or his head ached, she would run to the kitchens and brew up her special honey and almond-milk tea, just as she had for Father. Ederius was always so grateful. He would pat her hand and smile gently and drain every last drop from his cup.

Angeline frowned. She missed him so much now he had gone. Izgard had called him to the front. Two weeks back a message had arrived saying that the scribe's skills were needed imminently and he was to leave straight away for Rhaize. Ederius had packed all his pigments and brushes into a great birch trunk and departed the fortress in the company of a dozen armed men. He'd barely had chance to say good-bye. *"Take care, my sweet one,"* he had said. *"May the good Lord keep you from harm."*

"Hold your hands steady, m'lady!" cried Gerta, breaking into her thoughts. "While you've been busy daydreaming, the silk's been getting slack."

Even though her arms ached with the strain of holding them up for so long, Angeline did as she was told. It wasn't wise to disrupt Gerta in midravel.

Gerta tutted. The pins in her mouth stood to attention like guards. "It's being outside that's turned your head this morning, if you ask me. No good has ever come to a lady while she was *out*-side. No good at all."

Snowy picked that moment to come bounding up to his mistress's heels.

Snowy here! Snowy here!

Angeline dearly wanted to bend down and pet him, but Gerta had her handcuffed in silk.

"Have your menses come on yet, Angeline?" she asked. "You look a little pale."

Gerta felt she had a right to know all of Angeline's most delicate affairs. Angeline would have liked to tell the old maid to mind her own business, but she couldn't quite bring herself to say the words. Reluctantly she shook her head.

"Another couple of days and you will surely be late, m'lady." The pins in Gerta's mouth twinkled as she spoke. "If that's the case, there'll be no more talk of you joining Izgard across the mountains."

"What talk?" Angeline had heard no such thing. Izgard never sent messages directly to her. He sent them either to the seneschal, Gerta, or Lord Browlach, the man currently in charge of defending Sern Fortress.

Gerta lifted the last of the silk thread from Angeline's hands. "Why, m'lady, if you're not pregnant at the end of this month, then you may have to join Izgard in Rhaize. The king needs an heir almost as much as he needs to win land for his warlords. The campaign could go on for months—years, even—and whilst you're here in Garizon and the king's hundreds of leagues away in Rhaize, there's no chance of you providing the son the country needs."

Angeline's mouth fell open. Joining Izgard in Rhaize? Why, she had never even dreamed such a thing was possible.

Mistaking Angeline's surprise for trepidation, Gerta patted her arm. "Never mind, m'lady. If you are with child, then you won't have to go anywhere—I promise you that. You'll be safe and sound here, with me, for the duration of the war."

Briefly Angeline recalled the sick feeling she'd felt in her stomach earlier. "Surely if I were pregnant, I'd be allowed to go to Veizach? Or home to Halmac?" The idea of spending nine months holed up in Sern Fortress with only Gerta to talk to and no outside to speak of, only the dismal little courtyard they stood in now, was more than a little distressing to Angeline. Snowy was her only friend here.

"Izgard won't let you travel back to Veizach if you're with child, m'lady," Gerta said. "What with all those narrow mountain roads, sheer drops, and rock slides, it's just too great a risk. All it takes is one rock tumbling onto the road to scare a high-strung horse. Look what happened on the way here: that good-for-nothing dairy maid Enna was thrown from her filly when a doe ran across the path. Of course, if the girl hadn't been flirting with the chamberlain at the time, the whole thing might have been prevented."

Angeline didn't see how Enna and the chamberlain's flirtation had anything to do with the doe crossing the path, but she was willing to let the point drop, as she had another more important one to make. "No harm came to the girl, though," she said. "Her leg was bruised a little, but she got on her horse straight after and never once cried out in pain."

Gerta shook her head for what seemed to Angeline to be a very long time. "Makes no difference, m'lady. When a woman is with child her womb is as delicate as white-fired Istanian lusterware. One little bump in the road, one skittish horse, one sudden storm, and"—Gerta spat her pins out into her hand—"your innards could shatter like glass."

Feeling a little queasy at the thought of her innards shattering, Angeline bent to pet Snowy. The little dog was snoozing by her feet. Not feeling confident enough to meet Gerta's ever-vigilant eye, she kept her gaze firmly on Snowy as she said, "How will you know if I'm pregnant or not?"

If there was anything Gerta liked more than talking about women's matters, Angeline had yet to discover it. At the sound of the question, Gerta's face came as close to lighting up as was humanly possible in a gloomy courtyard on an overcast day in the mountains.

Sliding her pins into one of the many pouches that hung from her waist like meat on a hook, Gerta said, "Well, the first indication is the menses. If they don't come in the next few days, then that will be a very good sign indeed. But"—a warning finger came up—"that doesn't necessarily mean you're pregnant. You could just been sickening after your missing husband, or be poorly from not eating enough meat. No, the real signs are feeling sick in the morning, soreness in the breasts, and a tendency to feel flushed for no reason."

Down on the ground by Snowy's feet, Angeline felt her face growing hot—*for no reason!* She had been feeling sick this morning, too. Angeline frowned. She didn't want to be pregnant if it meant being locked up with Gerta all summer. Silently she counted out nine months on Snowy's toes. Why, she'd be cooped up here until next spring! No butterflies, no pretty birds, no *real* outside, and no friends.

Snowy, awakened by the indignity of having his toes poked one by one, scampered to his feet and began to dart around his mistress's heels.

Snowy ready to play now.

Angeline wasn't. Her glance shifted from the little dog to the nearest of the fortress walls. Blocks of square-cut stone rose up and up into the pale blue sky. Dark, damp stone. After a moment Angeline looked at the adjoining wall, and then the next one, and then the one after that, spinning around until she was right back at the first one again. Apart from a few differences in arrow slits and crenellations, they all looked just the same. Like jailers.

Funny how they hadn't seemed that way when Ederius was here. The scribe would be in Izgard's camp by now: his painting things getting dirty from lack of care, his cough getting worse from lack of her honey and almond-milk tea.

Angeline contemplated the walls for a few seconds more and then made a decision. Pulling herself up to her full height, she turned to Gerta and said, "If I do get my menses, that means I'm definitely not pregnant, doesn't it?"

Gerta was in the process of tucking her thin cushion under her fat skirts. "Yes."

"And if I'm not pregnant, that means I'll have to go and stay with Izgard until I am?"

"It's not what anyone wants, but it may well come to it, for the king dearly needs an heir." Gerta crossed the court-yard as she spoke. "You shouldn't worry about that happen-ing, m'lady. My hopes are high that you're with child." Picking up Angeline's two cushions from the bench, she said, "Come on, m'lady, we've had quite enough time out-side. It's getting chilly now the wind's started cutting from the east."

Although Angeline wasn't feeling chilly at all, she patted her thigh to bring Snowy to heel. "What's Rhaize like at this time of year?" she asked, following Gerta inside.

"Use the peat salt, not the sea salt, for the filling," said Mother Emith from her chair.

"Peat salt?" Tessa said.

"Yes. It's in the jar above the mantel to keep it dry." Mother Emith was giving Tessa instructions on how to cook plaice and shrimp dumplings for their midday meal. Tessa was anxious to get the whole thing over and done with so she could take a proper look, in full daylight, at the illuminations Marcel had dropped off last night. The manuscript press lay on the table, sunlight slanting across the etched-wood frame, pins loosened ready to be pulled. Emith had given her a peak at one of the patterns last night, but the light wasn't good and it was very late and they had both decided that any serious examination was best left until the morning.

Hurrying over to the mantel, Tessa grabbed the jar that Mother Emith had pointed out. Inside she found plain white salt, a little finer than table salt back at home, but essentially the same color and texture.

Seeing her examining the salt, Mother Emith beamed with pride. "Beautiful, isn't it? Nothing's as fine for cooking as peat salt. It's a little more expensive than the usual, but for special dishes like dumplings and savory custards I wouldn't use anything else."

"What makes it so expensive?" Tessa asked, sprinkling a small portion into the creamy mix for the filling. Mother Emith liked to be asked questions about all things related to cooking: it was how they passed the time whenever Emith was outside chopping wood or scraping hides or seeing to his arlo stocks.

"The trouble taken to make it is what makes the price so high. The peat burners first have to burn the seawater peat to get the ashes, then they stir the ashes in water until the mixture runs clear, and then boil the whole thing up for a day and a night until there's nothing left in the pan, only salt." Mother Emith shook her head in grudging respect. "The only task harder than burning peat is digging it out of the ground in the first place."

Tessa nodded absently, only half listening to what Mother Emith said. She'd heard enough stories by now about the way things were done to know that similar tales of drudgery, long hours, and complicated processes involving boiling, burning, scraping, and soaking lay behind even the simplest of household items. Mother Emith had yet to answer one of Tessa's questions with a simple, "Oh yes, that takes but five minutes to make from scratch." To her mind that would be sacrilege. Anything not laboriously produced at great expense by a team of hardworking professionals was not worthy of space in her kitchen.

Transferring the saucepan over to the table, Tessa mixed in the mushrooms, shrimp, shallots, and flaked plaice that would make up the filling for the dumplings. As she stirred the mixture together, the manuscript press kept catching her eye. The corners of vellum peeked out from beneath the wood, their colors aging from snow white to warm amber. Two decades had passed between the painting of the first pattern and the last. Twenty-one years, yet Emith said he could remember the day his master picked up his brush and began the series as if it were yesterday.

"Deveric chose red to begin," he said. "I had six other colors mixed and ready, but his hand went straight for the red."

Tessa's own eye fell on the one glimpse of color that was visible from the manuscript press: a thin curl of yellow reaching out toward the corner on the whitest of the leaves. A very bright, glossy yellow the color of her Honda Civic at home.

"Saffron, my dear," reminded Mother Emith from her chair. "Don't forget to add a pinch or two to color the sauce."

Tessa blinked. An idea, half-formed in her mind—not really an idea at all, just one thought linked to another by a thread as fluid and tenuous as a string of saliva flashing between teeth—disappeared from her mind upon hearing Mother Emith's words. By the time the blink was finished she'd forgotten what it was.

The yellow color on the illumination was the same one used every day in this kitchen: saffron yellow. There was nothing unusual about it at all.

Opening up the spice box, Tessa searched out a few of the golden crocus stamens and then flaked them into the sauce. Gradually, as she stirred the sauce, the cream took on a pale lemony hue. Mother Emith, had she been standing over Tessa's shoulder, would probably have advocated adding more saffron to the mix: her eyesight was failing somewhat, and the more subtle tones didn't register too well. Tessa glanced over at the old lady, remembering how she had taken care of Marcel last night. Perhaps a few more sprinkles wouldn't go amiss.

As Tessa's fingers found their way back to the spice box, Emith walked in the door. He had been out in the yard, doing one or other of those unpleasant tasks that could only be done outdoors: skinning, butchering, plucking, scrubbing the pots with hay and ashes, boiling up bark and lye to make kindling for the fire. Judging from his red face, he had been doing something that involved steam or hot water. Tessa decided against asking him what he'd been up to. She didn't want to know.

"You sit down, miss. I'll finish the dumplings," he said as he rinsed his hands in small bowl kept by the door. "You've had no time to rest all morning."

Tessa opened her mouth to protest, but the edge of the manuscript press caught her eye: she dearly wanted a chance to look at the illuminations properly. "I'll just put the sauce on the fire."

Emith moved over and took the saucepan from her. Tessa didn't object.

Reaching over, she grabbed the press and then dragged it across the tabletop. The metal pins rattled as it moved. Seen up close, the carvings on the wood were exquisitely detailed: serpents coiled around quills and paintbrushes, their fangs sinking deep into their own tails. Behind her, Tessa was aware of Emith rotating his mother's chair, turning it away from the window toward the fire. In front of her, the sunlight moved to catch up with the manuscript press, circling onto the frame, her hand, the pin between her fingers.

She pulled out the first pin, sent it skittering over the table and off into the shadows. The second and third pins followed. The fourth pin was warm to the touch. It wasn't as loose as the others and needed twisting before it came free. As Tessa pulled it from the frame, a fine mist of sawdust came with it. Free from its constraints, the press cracked softly like a ceiling timber at night. Tessa ran her hand along the top edge, feeling the serpents' bodies as thin furrows against her skin, and then opened the press like a book.

The sweet-sharp chemical smell of pigments and binders prickled the inside of her nose as five leaves of vellum fell like playing cards into her hand. The leaves were not large. Tessa had learned enough by now to know that their small size and smooth texture marked them as uterine vellum. Emith said only the most precious of documents were scribed upon the hides of stillborn calves.

Tessa fanned the leaves out in her hand. It seemed important to see them all at once in her first real look; get a feel for the colors, designs, and patterns that ran through the series as a whole; work out their common elements; and discover how and why they were connected.

The sunlight, having circled swiftly to catch up with the press, now seemed in no rush to go away. It shone on and through the five pieces of vellum, warming umber-toned inks, glowing on moss-colored greens, shimmering on amethyst and ruby glazes, but most of all glancing off gold.

Threads of gold ink shot through the series like arteries through an outstretched palm. Lines were joined, bridged, severed, or diverted by hooks and knife edges of gold. The golden pigment seemed to *feed* the designs, sending spirals spinning and curved lines lashing and knotwork buckling across the page. Looking at the sheer movement in the illuminations made Tessa catch her breath. It was difficult to take it all in.

Dipping her head downward, she moved even closer to the leaves. She wanted to breathe in the chalk smoke, see the details of the patterns up close. The sunlight reflected off the vellum onto her face, and only when she'd blinked away the dazzle in her eyes did she see the minuscule barbs on the gold. The golden thread that traced its way through each illumination, pattern, border, side panel, and interlace bristled with rosebush thorns.

It had its tiny little hooks into everything.

Tessa became aware of a dull weight around her neck. For a moment she thought it was just the strain of holding her head forward for so long, but then she felt something itch against her skin near the base of her throat.

It was the ring.

The sunlight slipped away between Tessa's fingers, leaving the five sheets of vellum to the shade. The illuminations felt thick and rough in her hands, and suddenly she didn't want to hold them anymore.

Tessa shivered. She placed the sheets side by side on the tabletop, then reached for the ring around her neck. Its warmth wasn't a surprise, but the color of the gold was. It matched the pigment used in the illuminations exactly. Its shades, highlights, lowlights, and middle tones were all captured, with perfect precision, on each page.

And then there were those tiny little barbs. . . .

Running a finger across the gold, Tessa recalled the image that had sparked an idea minutes earlier: the plume of yellow curling toward the manuscript's edge. The saffron pigment the same color as her car.

Even before she looked down at the illuminations, she guessed that the yellow thread would only be on the lightest, and therefore newest, of the leaves.

She was not mistaken.

The only illumination containing that particular color was the one Deveric had died completing. One of his drops of blood had splashed across a yellow curve.

Tessa felt her scalp tighten. Her mouth was as dry as the chalk-finished vellum beneath her hands. Eye muscles aching, she scanned the pattern.

Yellow spirals were interlaced with a zigzagging line of green. Odd, she thought, that color is usually reserved for plant forms. Yet the meandering peaks of green looked like no other plant designs she had seen. They looked like a string of miniature pines.

Something shifted in Tessa's brain. An idea—skirted around earlier but excused as nonsense before it was fully formed—unrolled within her mind like a bolt of cloth. Her car. The Cleveland National Forest. The ring.

Tessa swallowed hard. She could hardly believe where her thoughts were pushing her. The idea was too fantastic, but even as she tried to dismiss it, it wouldn't let her go. The pattern portrayed her drive through the forest. It was an illustration of the journey that had led her to the ring.

A smooth yellow line weaving through a forest of green braid to a spiral of barbed gold.

The hairs on Tessa's arm bristled. Her scalp seemed to contract, pulling at her forehead and temples. The skin just behind her ears flushed hot. She could feel the blood pulsing past the tendons in her neck.

Her eyes darted across the page, searching.

There were some sections that meant nothing to her—spirals of red, knots of sea blue, and ribbons of waxen violet—but her gaze fell upon the single gold coil that formed the center of the illumination. Surrounding the coil was a fretwork panel of niello ink. The lead-based pigment, consisting of silver, copper, lead, and sulfur, had a drab plate-metal finish one shade darker than slate. The fretwork panel was little more than a ring of dull, gray squares: the safety deposit boxes.

Tessa's stomach condensed to a tight, heavy ball. She felt physically sick. Deveric had *drawn* her here. He had picked up his brush and quill and painted away at her life.

This illumination was a *summons*. It was no coincidence she'd found the ring, no coincidence at all. Deveric had led her to it.

"Emith!" she cried, angry, excited, breathless. "Come here and look at this!"

Her voice must have sounded strange, for Emith was at her side in an instant. "What is it, miss?"

Tessa hit the vellum. "This is me—the day I found the ring." Her knuckle grazed along the yellow line. "This is how I got here."

A ripple of anxiety crossed Emith's features. "I don't understand, miss."

Tessa watched him closely. How much did he know? He looked worried, but then he often looked that way. "Deveric brought me here," she said, testing the words as she spoke them, seeing if they sounded sane. "This pattern he painted guided me to the ring."

Emith began shaking his head.

"How much do you know about this?" asked Tessa before he had chance to speak.

"I never questioned my master's work, miss. It wasn't my place."

"You were afraid of knowing what he did, weren't you?" Tessa was angry now. Someone had interfered with her life. Some man whom she had never met—and never *would* meet— had pushed her car along the freeway that day, sweeping everything else aside with the tip of his brush. "Mix your pigments, sharpen your quills, ask no questions, and take no blame. You knew Deveric was interfering in people's lives. You just didn't want to be burdened with the details."

Emith shrank back from Tessa, visibly upset. "No, miss. It wasn't like that—Deveric wouldn't do anything to harm anyone. He was a good man."

"He brought me here against my will."

"Did he?"

Emith's softly spoken question stopped Tessa in her tracks. It had been *her* decision to put on the ring; Deveric had not forced her hand. And in the five weeks she had been here, she had made no effort to get back. Annoyed at Emith for bringing up the subject and, if she were honest, feeling guilty for not thinking about home in so long, Tessa searched for something cutting to say. "Deveric did hurt me," she said finally. "He brought on the noises in my head to force me to change my path."

As she spoke the words, Tessa's gaze flicked over the remaining four patterns. A twenty-one-year series, Emith had said.

The lead ball in Tessa's stomach turned. The skin on her scalp felt as tight as a drum. Emith was speaking, but she didn't hear a word he said.

Twenty-one years.

Grabbing hold of the newest illumination, Tessa brought it within blinking distance of her face and scrutinized the yellow-and-green weave on the page. Running alongside the saffron pigment was a fine corkscrew spiral of gray. Fine as a strand of hair, it was so pale that it looked more like a shadow than a line. Yet it had force. Like a cheese wire, it sliced through objects ten times it size, severing plump yellow veins and entrails of gold.

Tessa looked down at the other four illuminations. This time she didn't allow herself to be distracted by the gold, she just searched for more of the fine gray spirals. They were hard to spot at first. The silvery filaments had been applied with a quill pen, not a brush, and as the pigment itself was fluid ink, not paint, the lines produced were so fine that they almost disappeared into the vellum. *Burnt in,* Emith would have said. Yet once Tessa's eyes spotted the first gray thread, twisting its way around a border like a chain around a gatepost, she began to see them everywhere. The whole series was marbled with the cobweb-thin coils.

Taking a deep breath, Tessa told herself they weren't what she thought. They couldn't be. Turning to Emith, she asked, "Do you know the dates on these illuminations?"

Emith, who had stopped speaking some time earlier and now stood over Tessa's shoulder, keeping watch, didn't hesitate before answering. "Before my master put ink to parchment, I always scribed the date on the underside. Turn the leaves over and look in the bottom left-hand corner."

Before Emith had even finished speaking, Tessa was looking at the date on the newest parchment. Fresh black script read: "At this juncture, being the first day in the Lord's fifth month, in the thirteen hundredth and fifty-second year since He revealed His True Self, Deveric of Fale began this work with the intent of glorifying, not imitating, the Lord."

Tessa counted back seven years from thirteen hundred and fifty-two and then flipped over the second-to-last illumination in the series. Emith's neat, now not-quite-so-black script, proclaimed the date as "the twelfth day in the eleventh month of the thirteen hundredth and forty-fifth year."

Seeing it Tessa leaned back against her chair, her body suddenly seeming too heavy for her bones. The date on the manuscript—the month and the year—corresponded exactly to the last major tinnitus attack she'd had before the incident on the freeway. The lecture hall at New Mexico State. Professor Yarback. The slide from the Lindisfarne Gospels. It was the attack that had forced her to leave college and move to California, to San Diego. Where she stayed for seven years until she found the ring.

Tessa put her hands over her face, covering her eyes and nose and mouth. She couldn't believe the scale of what Deveric had done. The depth of his interference in her life. He had used her tinnitus as casually as he used Emith's pigments. It was just another of his scribing tools, like his leadpoint plummet, his wax tablet, and his knife.

Those pale gray coils that hung suspended within each page like smoke trapped in glass were a record of her tinnitus.

Five major attacks in her life. Five illuminations in Deveric's grand design.

Hands enclosing around the yellowest and stiffest leaf, Tessa took a quick guess at the month she had experienced her first ever tinnitus attack. She remembered being outside at the time, wearing a short-sleeved dress and feeling warm: sometime in high summer, perhaps July or August. She already knew, without seeing the date, that the year would be exactly right. Twenty-one years ago it had happened: she had been five years old at the time.

Once again, Emith's script, now faded to a pale, uneven brown, proclaimed the date: "The third day of the eight month in the thirteen hundredth and thirty-first year."

August. Twenty-one years earlier.

Deveric had been manipulating her all along.

Tessa's head was reeling. Not in a fast, chaotic way, but in one slow, incredulous turn. She couldn't begin to imagine the implications, couldn't begin to think what it all meant.

Two months after that first attack, she and her family had moved from England to New York. Her father had been offered a job in his company's U.S. office, and Tessa could still recall her mother urging her father to take it: "The change might do Tessa good. We don't want her having another of those attacks like the one on the lawn."

With a quick breath, Tessa picked up the second illumination in the series. "The eighteenth day of the eleventh month in the thirteen hundredth and thirty-eighth year." The year and the month were not a surprise. She was twelve at the time, living at an apartment on Riverside Drive with her parents. She was on her way home from school when the tinnitus began.

The traffic was bumper to bumper along Broadway. Tessa remembered getting off the school bus before her stop, thinking she could walk the distance home faster. As soon as her feet hit the road, things began to go wrong. A car cut alongside the bus, brakes squealing. The driver screamed abuse at Tessa for causing him to stop. When she reached the sidewalk a second car sped through a puddle, sending cold muddy water splashing over her coat. In a nearby doorway two men were arguing, their rising and falling voices jarring against Tessa's nerves. Suddenly the whole street seemed full of noises: horns blasting, music blaring, children shrieking, metal shutters rattling as shop owners shut up shop for the night. A woman in a camel coat too short to cover her calf-length dress walked past Tessa, pulling a thin, yelping dog at her heels. Somewhere in the distance a police siren began to wail.

Tessa ran all the way home, palms pressed close to her ears to shut out the noise. By the time she got to her building she realized she was no longer keeping outside noises out, but rather keeping her tinnitus in.

Looking back on it now, seeing it through the filter of the gray spirals on the vellum, Tessa realized the attack coincided with another move. Her father again: some sort of reshuffle at work had left him unhappy, and he was contemplating leaving to take up a position as sales manager to a distribution firm in St. Louis. Tessa's doctor saying to him, "Your daughter will be better off away from all the noise and bustle of the city," may not have been the deciding factor, but they had moved the following month all the same.

Tessa placed the illumination on the desk. All her earlier excitement had drained away, leaving her feeling too tired to be angry or amazed.

She didn't have to look at the date on the third illumination to know what it was and what it corresponded to. A company picnic: Tessa, fourteen years old, sitting at the executives' table with her parents, her father gripping her wrist and refusing to let her leave. Flies buzzing past her ears, sweat trickling down her back, children shrieking around the "little people's table." The tinnitus came on so quickly and with such venom that Tessa blacked out. Right there. She fainted in the middle of the sales director's speech, falling across the executive picnic table, upsetting paper cups and plates and checkered paper towels, sending plastic ketchup and mustard containers rolling to the floor.

Everyone had been as kind as they could be. They'd picked her up, given her water and aspirin. The sales director's wife had even brushed down Tessa's dress. But the next week, during an unscheduled management meeting, the sales director had informed Tessa's father that a promotion he had been expecting was going to "Jack Riggs in the Lexington office. There's a lot of traveling involved in the job, and we felt it was best tackled by a younger man who doesn't have a family to worry about."

Three months later, faced with the possibility that if he stayed with his current firm, he would always be passed over for promotion, Tessa's father had moved his family to Albuquerque, New Mexico. Another job. Another state. Another move westward toward the ring.

"Here, miss. Drink this. Mother says you're looking a little pale." Emith's voice was gentle as it broke through Tessa's thoughts. A hand touched her arm very lightly, and another laid a steaming drink on the tabletop beside the illuminations.

"Are you feeling quite well, my dear?" came Mother Emith's voice from her chair.

Although she wasn't feeling quite well at all, Tessa nodded. Her head ached with a deep, splitting pain. Her eyes were sore, and the muscles around her heart felt oddly tight. Somehow, while she had sat here, something that started out as almost impossible to believe had hardened into plain fact.

Deveric had manipulated her life. And not only her life, but the life of her family too. His pigment-stained fingerprints were stamped upon every move she and her parents had made.

Just how deep did it go? Where did it end? Things that had seemed like mere chance before, such as finding herself living in San Diego after she'd left college when her intended destination was Los Angeles, began to take on the look of a sinister plot, every bit as intricate and carefully planned as the patterns Deveric drew. A night spent in a San Diego motel because her tinnitus had begun to bother her on the freeway, a newspaper left outside her room, a Help Wanted ad asking for telesales operators with "no experience necessary," suddenly didn't seem like coincidences anymore. Deveric had been pushing her all the way.

Tessa picked up the steaming cup. It was warm in her hands. Lemon and honey smells curled up with the steam.

"Drink it all up, my dear," Mother Emith said. "It will put some color back in your cheeks." Then, turning to Emith: "Take the dumplings from the pot and see to it that Tessa gets a good portion—plenty of sauce."

The old woman sounded worried. Normally Tessa would have spoken up to reassure her, but right now she didn't trust herself to speak. The enormity of what Deveric had done to her was settling in her mind like a fine but heavy dust. It lay like lead ash on her tongue.

Was her tinnitus real? Or had it been something Deveric conjured up at will, a magician's sleight of hand? Either way he had used it against her, summoning it forth with his fine-cut nib and his diluted lampblack ink, directing her actions with a crack of his thumb knuckle and a practiced flick of his wrist.

Tessa shivered. For the first time since she had come

here, Mother Emith's kitchen actually seemed cold. The chair she sat in felt like stone.

Tessa's eyes gazed straight ahead without seeing a thing. Her mind looked backward and saw a life that had never quite been her own. Opportunities missed, friendships overlooked, interests, relationships, and ambitions pushed aside. Deveric had drawn her a shell. The gray threads that spiraled through each of his illuminations might as well have had barbs all their own. They kept everyone and everything away.

Tessa took a sip of the lemon honey tea. It was bitter and sweet all in one.

As soon as she put the cup down, her hands strayed back to the vellum. Why had Deveric gone to all this trouble? Why was it so important to bring her here? Fingers grazing across the bands of green, yellow, and gold pigments, Tessa slowly shook her head. She didn't know. Yet, she thought, stretching the word out as her gaze came to focus on the barbs around the gold, the answer was here, in the parchment.

Watching the gold wink slyly in the shade, Tessa made a decision.

"Emith," she called, sitting back in her chair, "forget about the food. Come and show me all the things I need to know about selecting and using pigments." Tomorrow she was going to paint a pattern of her own and discover for herself what no one seemed willing, or able, to tell her.

Gerta pulled back the sheet as if it concealed a wanted criminal beneath. "Aha!" she cried, gaze locking onto the red stain that formed the center of the bed. "When did this happen?" she demanded, moving in closer to touch the offending mark.

Angeline kicked Snowy into action. The little dog scrambled onto the bed and snapped at Gerta's hand, all the while barking his piercing no-good bark and wagging his short no-good tail. Shocked, Gerta yanked back her outstretched hand, returning a moment later with a fist.

"Bad dog!" she cried, swinging a punch Snowy's way.

Snowy defended the red stain. Little paws dancing, hackles rising, teeth snapping, and fur bristling: having a thoroughly enjoyable no-good dog time. Seeing him in action, Angeline suspected that Snowy had harbored a secret desire to bite Gerta's hand all along.

Having missed with the first punch, Gerta tried a second, but her heart clearly wasn't in it and she missed by a margin as wide as her own formidable Garizon head. "Angeline! You really should discipline this dog," she said, turning away from Snowy, the bed, and, most important of all, the deep red stain.

Angeline hadn't realized she had been holding her breath until she went to speak, and it rushed out ahead of her words like a draft rushing in through an opening door. "I'm sorry, Gerta. I don't know what's got into Snowy these days."

As she spoke, Angeline moved toward the bed, casually picked up the sheet Gerta had pulled away, and threw it back over the mattress: Snowy, stain, and all. Snowy didn't take kindly to being covered and began jumping up and snapping at the descending sheet as if it were a large, gliding bird. The sight of Snowy attacking the covers very nearly made Angeline laugh out loud, but she hadn't spent an afternoon planning for just this moment to give herself away at the last minute.

What she needed to do now was draw Gerta away from the bed and get her mind working on something else. "The blood came on earlier when I went to take a nap before supper," she said quickly. "I hadn't been feeling well since midday, when I had that pheasant pie Dham Fitzil warmed up—"

"Dham Fitzil is a born fool!" interrupted Gerta. "No one in their right mind reheats pheasant pie two days after it's been cooked. Why, she might as well give us all a dose of henbane and poison us on the spot!" Gerta shook her head vehemently, her entire body and its many attachments—girdle book, sewing bag, scissors, handkerchiefs, combs, tweezers, perfume flask, and cosmetic purse—swinging with it. "I swear one day she'll kill us all!"

Angeline nodded in complete agreement. Gerta hated the cook. She and Dham Fitzil were the two highest-ranking female servants in Sern Fortress, and the rivalry between them was neither friendly nor subdued. They disliked, distrusted, and disagreed with each other at every given chance. Both women felt it was their right to oversee the housekeeping and all the remaining women servants in the fortress. Angeline didn't care a jot either way who was in charge, she just knew that Gerta liked to criticize Dham Fitzil almost as much as she liked to discuss women's troubles.

Walking away from the bed toward the fire, Angeline said, "This means I'm not pregnant, doesn't it?"

Gerta glanced back toward the bed. Snowy, who had successfully managed to extricate himself from the sheets while Gerta was speaking, growled right on cue. Gerta made a noise that sounded just like a growl right back at him, then turned toward Angeline. "From what I saw of the blood it looked good and dark, m'lady." She lowered her voice slightly, made a minute eye gesture toward Angeline's stomach, and said, "Is it still flowing?"

Angeline nodded. She thought for a moment and then sat on the bench nearest the fire. Sitting suddenly seemed more appropriate than standing.

Gerta sighed. "It's menses, then. I've been hoping against hope that you would have conceived, but it doesn't look like it's to be." Her smile was gentle. "Perhaps next time, m'lady."

Feeling a teeny bit guilty, Angeline nodded some more. "I'm sorry, Gerta," she said. "I did everything you told me."

"I know you did, m'lady. I know you did." Gerta patted her shoulder. "I just don't like the thought of you being dragged across the mountains to Rhaize, that's all. A military camp is no place for a young lady like you."

"You'll come too, won't you, Gerta?" The idea of traveling to Izgard's camp without Gerta was unthinkable. Gerta might be many things—bossy, nosy, and overly familiar, to name but a few—but Angeline cared for her all the same. She had grown accustomed to having her around.

Gerta nodded. "Of course I'll come, m'lady," she said in her most motherly voice. "What sort of lady's companion could I call myself if I let my lady travel to Rhaize alone, with only guards and horses to speak to?" As she spoke,

Gerta moved back toward the bed. "Well, I'll just take these sheets to the laundress and then go and advise Lord Browlach about your condition. He'll be wanting to send a message to the king this very night."

Angeline darted from the bench. Snowy, whose sole job in this whole scheme was to guard the red-stained sheet until Gerta left, was nowhere to be seen. The little dog was up to his no-good tricks.

Diving into the rapidly diminishing space between Gerta and the bed, Angeline cried, "I'll take the sheets downstairs, Gerta. You go straight to Lord Browlach and tell him the news."

A moment of silence followed. Gerta's face registered bewildered surprise, followed by something that may well have been suspicion. Angeline's heart beat against her rib cage so hard, she was sure the old maid could hear it. The stain on the sheet wasn't blood at all. It was pigment. Vermilion ink she had found in a chest in Ederius' scriptorium after she and Gerta had left the courtyard this morning. Slipped into her bodice, brought to her chamber, and spilled into the appropriate dip on the bed: it had both the look and feel of blood.

Angeline didn't want to stay in Sern Fortress. Not for nine months. And although she wasn't sure whether or not she was pregnant, she was taking no chances. If Gerta needed to see blood to let her go to Rhaize, then blood she would see. Only now it looked as if she wouldn't see blood at all. The pigment may have been the exact same color and consistency of blood, but it didn't smell the same, and if Gerta got her hands on it, she would surely be able to tell the difference.

"Nonsense, m'lady," Gerta said, pouncing into action. "I can't let you walk up and down the stairs feeling as you do at the moment. You need to lie down, not go running about the fortress with laundry." With that she pushed Angeline aside and made a grab for the sheet.

Angeline furrowed her brow, stamped her foot, and *willed* a clever excuse to come into her head. Nothing came. Her mind was a blank, Snowy was nowhere to be seen, and Gerta's hand was making a beeline for the stain.

Cursing her own stupidity, Angeline gritted her teeth and closed her eyes, preparing to be caught. Why couldn't she be as clever as other women?

A second passed. A soft, sheet-swishing noise came from the bed. One of Gerta's old bones cracked as she bent forward.

Angeline couldn't bear to look. She was in just about the worst trouble a person could be in. What would Izgard say when he found out? Angeline shuddered. What would he *do?*

A noise that sounded suspiciously like a finger being poked against a mattress was followed swiftly by a sharp intake of breath.

"Why, that dirty, disgusting dog!" exclaimed Gerta, voice rising to an indignant squeal. "Snowy! You come here this minute!"

Confused, Angeline opened her eyes. She had been gritting her teeth so hard, her jaw ached.

Gerta yanked the sheet from the bed and thrust it toward Angeline. "Have you seen what that no-good dog has done?" she cried.

As Angeline shook her head she caught a strong ammonia whiff in her nostrils. The stain on the sheet was larger and pinker than she remembered it.

"That dog of yours has wet the sheet—right on the bloodied spot." Gerta waved the offending linen in front of Angeline's nose as if it were a severed head. "It's disgusting. If you don't start training him soon, m'lady, then by all five gods I will!"

Gerta was shaking so hard that all of her various maidly attachments chimed together like tinkling bells. Fuming, she bundled up the sheet into a loose ball, dog urine and bloodstain packed out of sight in the center, and stormed toward the door. "If this happens again," she said, spinning around on the threshold, "then I'll get the seneschal to slice off his tail." With that she stalked out of the room, one solitary corner of the sheet trailing behind her like a train.

Angeline stared at the door, stunned. She was so amazed that she hadn't been caught out that she could barely take it all in. *Snowy wetting the bed?*

As if aware that his name was being thought of, Snowy waddled out from under the bed. He looked about as smug as it was possible for a dog to look. Tail up and wagging, he scampered over to his mistress's side.

No-good dog. No-good dog.

FIFTEEN

awn could offer a thousand shades of gray, and in his time Ravis of Burano had seen all of them. As they walked the horses alongside the limestone cliff, the sky was the color of charcoal. A thin line of silver cut across the horizon, illuminating clouds of ash, trees of lead, and hills of naked slate. Even the mist was gray. It swirled around the horses' fetlocks, dampening all that it touched and most of what it didn't. Ravis could feel it as a dank greasy film next to his skin, between his thighs and his horse, and deep within his lungs. It was everywhere yet nowhere, and there was no way to stop it. At least a man could put on a cloak against the rain.

"The town is just over that rise," hissed Camron of Thorn. "We could be there in less than an hour."

Ravis nodded. For the past two hours words had been kept to a minimum. They were in the valley just northwest of Thorn. It had taken them two full nights and a day to reach here, and although most men had slept for less than five hours during that time, none were drowsy. Even now, in the thin mists and subdued grays of predawn, all were alert, sitting forward on their mounts, eyes darting from side to side, hands never far from the hilts of their swords.

Two men rode half a league ahead of the rest. Trained scouts brought in from Istania, they rode horses whose vocal cords had been cut at birth, lest they whicker at an inopportune moment and give away their riders' position. Minutes earlier Ravis had noticed a circle of hoofprints on the trail marking where the scouts had stopped and dismounted. A single snippet of leather discarded on the side of the path was enough to tell Ravis that they had stopped for the express purpose of binding their horses' hooves with cloth. They were getting nervous. And when an Istanian scout got nervous it was wise to be nervous oneself.

Ravis reined in his horse. The gelding had been straying away from the shadows cast by the cliff, following its natural inclination to walk in the lightest possible path. Ravis patted its neck, glanced over at the horizon, then checked the looseness of his sword in its scabbard for the eighth time in less than an hour.

"We'll stop soon," he whispered to Camron. "Wait for the scouts to report back."

Camron shook his head. He was riding barely a neck in front of Ravis. The two horses were so close, their barrels touched from time to time. "We've only got an hour before daylight. We can't afford to wait."

We can't afford to take any chances, Ravis thought, but didn't say it.

Something moved in the foliage to the left of the path. A pair of geese took to the air, their undersides lit by the broadening light on the horizon, their wings beating against the mist.

Ravis glanced over at Camron. "That could have been one of Izgard's harras lying in wait." As he spoke, he felt the mist curl along his tongue. It tasted of things from the earth. "We need to know what sort of forces we're dealing with before we approach the town. Izgard could have two hundred men stationed there."

"I don't see why he would," Camron snapped. "Everyone is dead. The animals have been slaughtered, the crops have been burned. Why in God's name would he set men to guard a derelict town?"

Ravis could name several reasons why Izgard would set men to guard Thorn, yet he chose to disclose only the most obvious one. "It's his territory now. From what we've seen so far, I'd say this marks his deepest thrust into Rhaize, and I tell you now, he won't be prepared to give it up without a fight."

Camron's face was a gray mask against the cliff side. His grip on his reins was too tight. In the quarter-light of dawn his knuckles showed up whiter than his eyes. Seeing them,

Ravis knew anything he said would be ignored: Camron heard only the cries of the slaughtered inside his head.

Kicking his gelding, Ravis rode on. The light level was increasing steadily, and the horses responded to the dawn by becoming restless. Behind him, he heard a gust of nickering and blowing. Tack jingled as a fretful horse pulled against his reins and another shook out his mane. The gray mist thinned. No longer steaming clouds, it formed itself into thin wisps, then glided toward the earth.

Ravis chewed on his scar. He didn't like any of this: riding blindly into enemy territory, not stopping to hear the report from the scouts, not knowing what, if any, forces they might run into. They didn't even have a proper purpose—not one they agreed upon, at least. The only thing a force this size was good for was spying or sabotage, and judging from the look on Camron's face and his white-knuckled grip on his reins, he plainly wasn't interested in either of those. He was spoiling for a fight.

And knowing Izgard, he would probably get one.

Ravis stood on his stirrups and looked back along the column. Beyond the four dozen mounted men, deep in the shadows perhaps three-quarters of a league behind the main party, rode the mercenaries and archers supplied by Segwin the Ney. Camron hadn't wanted them riding with him—none of his men did—and although Ravis knew he could have forced Camron's hand in this matter, he'd chosen not to. The mercenaries were exactly where he wanted them: bringing up the rear.

Wheeling round in his saddle, Ravis spotted a smoke trail breaking the line of the horizon ahead. A second later he tasted woodsmoke in his mouth. Woodsmoke and something else.

"Someone's cooking breakfast," hissed Camron.

Ravis nodded. Though in truth he wasn't sure if it was breakfast at all. Glancing down at the path, he searched for the hoofprints of the scouts' horses. The light was growing brighter by the minute, and the two pairs of hoofprints, softened and distorted by the thick cloth covering that now bound them, were clearly visible to the eye. Seeing them, Ravis felt only a small measure of relief.

He couldn't shake off the feeling they were walking into a trap.

They had come within a league of what was, presumably, an occupied town without seeing any signs of soldiers: no campfires, no camp waste, no lookouts, no tracks. And now a single line of smoke had mysteriously appeared on the horizon, and even as Ravis guessed it was a foil to lure them away from the path, Camron pulled on his reins and turned his horse toward it. The rest of the party followed without a word.

Ravis held his position, letting the men pass him. He heard their breath coming sharp and fast, saw faces slick with sweat and backs held so straight, they had to be in pain. Plate armor did that to a man: wound him up in a tight metal case where every move was weighted, every breath was forced, and each bead of sweat had nowhere to go and nothing to do but form a damp haze against the skin. It was cool now, but the clouds were clearing and the earth was sucking back the mist, and it was only a matter of hours before the sun would be up and shining. By noon Camron's men would be steaming at the neck.

They had made a short, cheerless camp through the darkest hours of the night. No fires lit, no voices raised, no tents to cordon off the mist. Some men had chosen to sleep, most had sat in silence polishing their swords, waiting for the signal to strap on their armor and move. The mercenaries and archers had made a separate camp on the far side of the limestone cliffs. Ravis had ridden over to them. Handing around flasks of berriac still warm from being pressed against his horse's flank, he had run through his last minute instructions. By the time he had returned to the main party it was time to up camp and head east.

Hand slipping from his reins to his sword, Ravis scanned the area ahead as he waited for the rest of Camron's men to pass him by. The source of the smoke was unclear: it could be coming from before, or beyond, the ridge. In the shifting gray light of dawn, distances were hard to judge.

Briefly, just before he turned his horse to follow Camron, Ravis glanced back at the limestone cliff, his gaze traveling upward to the rocky brow above. If *he* were setting a trap, he'd have lookouts positioned there.

Nothing met his eyes but chunks of jagged rock and bands of thinning clouds. Shrugging, he kicked his horse into motion and followed the rest of the men from the path.

Tessa worked the pounce into the vellum with a small wooden block. Even so, she managed to get the chalk-and-bread-crumb mixture under her fingernails. Emith had offered to do the job for her, arguing that preparing the parchment to take the ink was the work of an assistant, not a scribe, but Tessa had refused his help. This was her first real illumination, and it seemed important to do as much as she could herself.

She and Emith had stayed up most of the night going over all the rules and proper procedures for illumination. The rules seemed strangely primitive to Tessa: plant forms and animals forms must be kept separate at all times, every line within an animal pattern must turn out to be part of an animal, and no matter how fantastically elongated a creature became as its body formed a latticework of knots across a page, its various parts had to adhere to the rules of nature: two eyes, four legs, one tail. Plant forms had to be seen to come from a source, like the ground or a pot, and they could not trail arbitrarily around the page, unattached to the earth. Colors had to be chosen from nature; certain forms had to be mirrored on both sides of the page and others repeated a set number of times.

Tessa had sat in silence while Emith told her all he knew: nodding occasionally, repeating things back to herself in her head, concentrating hard on all the details.

At some point during the night the tallow had gone out, and as neither she nor Emith had made a move to relight a fresh pat, they had spent several hours in the dark. As Tessa listened to Emith speaking through the darkness, her eyes conjured up the lines and forms of Deveric's illuminations. Against a black backdrop, she saw green spirals, yellow ribbons, gold coils, and silver cord. Her life was caught up in those angles and curves, and seeing them there, in the shadows long past midnight, made Tessa more determined than ever to draw out the truth.

She had to know why she had been brought here.

"Do you want to put a stain over the parchment before you begin?" Emith asked, his voice gentle, as if he had known her thoughts were elsewhere. "Or are you going to put the pigment straight onto the pounce?"

Tessa looked down at the even, now almost white surface of the vellum. The chalk and breadcrumbs had raised the nap, making it ready to catch and absorb the ink. Emith had ground the pounce coarsely, and the rough grains of chalk had irritated her skin. All her fingertips were red. One was bleeding.

As she stared at the parchment, its perfect unmarred whiteness began to look too clean and new, like a child's coloring book waiting to be filled in with colored crayon. She needed a more personal beginning for her first illumination. The ink should burn into a color of her choosing. It suddenly seemed important to exert her control over every element on the page.

Glancing up through the window to the broadening dawn beyond, Tessa felt the skin on her scalp tighten minutely. A headachelike pressure pulsed in her temples as she gazed out at the dull expanse of sky.

"Gray," she said softly after a moment. "The vellum should be stained ash gray."

It took them forty minutes to track down the source of the smoke. They rode through row after row of scorched vines, their charred branches rising from the earth like monstrous many-legged insects, and then down along a dried-up stream bed and through its accompanying maze of reeds.

Camron knew every rock, bush, ridge, goat path, and cattle path they crossed. He knew the lay of the land, the colors of the trees in full sunlight, and the quality of wine produced from each particular row of vines. This was his home, and as he rode past torched dairy farms and vineyards, deserted fields and decaying animal carcasses, a hard core of rage hardened in his gut. Izgard of Garizon had destroyed his homeland, his friends, his family, and his life, leaving him nothing and no one to fight for but his memories and himself.

The column of smoke came from a rocky outcropping at the far side of a narrow valley. Chunks of limestone broke through the thin soil around the slopes, and pine trees ringed the area, creating a barrier between the valley and the dawn. Belts of dim gray light banded the valley as the sun, still below the horizon, sent ghost light filtering through the trees. The ground underfoot was hard.

Strangely enough, the smell of woodsmoke and cooked meat had receded as they drew nearer to the source. Perhaps the breeze was blowing in the opposite direction. Yet when Camron looked up he saw the smoke rose in a level line, indicating little or no wind.

Briefly, Ravis' words of some fifteen minutes earlier crossed Camron's mind. "Take a look around. We're heading from high ground to low ground, from an open road to an enclosed valley. This is a trap, and we're walking straight into it like fools."

Glancing up at the fringe of rocks and trees enclosing the valley, Camron had to admit there was something to what Ravis said. He only wished it mattered more than it did. The truth was he had followed the smoke *knowing* it could be a trap. He was in Thorn country now. He had come here to fight, and Ravis could advise, plan, and strategize from dawn to dusk, yet it would do little but postpone the inevitable.

People had died here: good, honest men and women who had loved their country, respected the land, reared God-fearing children, and taken pride in their work. And somehow to approach the place of their death like frightened clerics at dawn, clinging to shadows provided by cliff sides, accompanied by foreguards, rear guards, and mercenaries, seemed like sacrilege. The people of Thorn deserved more than that. They deserved a tribute from brave fighting men.

"Over here!" came a cry, breaking the silence of dawn. "I've found the fire."

Camron looked ahead at the dense cluster of rocks and bushes that formed the far side of the valley. Although he hadn't been aware that any of his knights had ridden ahead of him, he took a grim pleasure in discovering that at least one had. He was not the only man who needed to fight.

A sharp intake of breath, like a hiss, echoed around the valley. A muffled thud followed seconds later. Hearing it,

Camron kicked his horse into a canter and rode toward the rocks.

The column of knights was close at his heels. No one was concerned with silence anymore, and tack jangled, horses whickered, plate armor cracked, swords rang from scabbards, and curses were spat into the air. Camron felt his chest muscles tighten. His mouth was perfectly dry. As he fell under the shadow of the rocks, Ravis' words were like dust in his mind's eye. *This is a trap, and we're walking straight into it like fools.* . . . Almost unaware of what he was doing, Camron shook his head. No, not fools. Brave fighting men.

Even as that thought brought him comfort, his eyes circled the valley's slopes, searching for signs of movement.

They found the knight's horse roaming loose by a thick heel of limestone. The smoke, little more than a wiry gray line now, rose from the center of a crown of rocks. They would have to dismount to reach it. As Camron swung his feet down from his horse, he glanced behind him, looking for Ravis' face in the crowd. He half expected the man to speak up, telling him that it was pure madness to dismount now, while they still didn't know what they were dealing with. No words of warning came, however, and although Camron searched, he could find no sign of Ravis.

A dozen men dismounted along with Camron, unbuckling shields from leather pouches, sliding daggers from sheaths, and adjusting grips on their swords. One man whispered a prayer. Another man tapped Camron on the shoulder and begged to be the first to go in ahead of the troop to check for dangers.

"No," Camron said, trying to find words to sum up the way he felt at that moment. "We must act and be as one in this."

The man nodded and fell in by his side.

Camron turned to the remaining troop on horseback. "Spread out around the rocks and keep watch until we return. No man is to ride so far that he cannot see his companions at his front and his back." He waited until all men nodded. Looking into their faces, Camron realized that during the last few minutes the collective mood had changed. The troop was no longer merely watchful, it was ready. By unspoken consent they had decided the time was fast approaching when they would fight.

"May God watch over us," Camron said, his throat aching as his gaze passed from man to man, "and see fit to lend us His strength and His light."

The words were a simple enough prayer, spoken by Thorn farmers every morning in the field, whispered by Thorn women to their children every night; but as he said it, Camron heard it spoken through his father's voice. A blessing from the grave.

Abruptly, he turned from the troop. He couldn't trust himself to say more. As if aware of his leader's mood, the young knight who had begged to go alone into the rocks gave the order to move on.

Camron headed in the direction of the smoke. Almost daybreak now, the light changed by the minute, altering shadows and perspectives. Someone called out to the knight who had found the fire. There was no reply.

Up close the rocks were larger than Camron had first thought. They towered above him, blocking the view ahead and casting dark shadows on already dark ground. Jagged splinters of stone poked through the earth like spikes, and Camron was forced to watch his footing, lest the soles be ripped from his boots. Somewhere in the distance water dripped onto rock. Hearing the sound, a memory slid into place in Camron's mind: he had been here before. Twenty years ago, when he was just a boy. The Valley of Broken Stones.

It had been midwinter and the snow was thigh deep. A sudden storm had isolated the entire flock of Long Angrim's sheep, and everyone in Thorn—from Camron and his father to Sterry the clock maker and Bowleg the village drunk—turned out to look for them. It wasn't done as a great favor, it was just what people did in the mountains: looked out for everyone else. Of the three dozen sheep that were missing, thirty were swiftly found, huddled together in a high pasture; their bleats drew the search party to them in less than an hour. As the morning wore on, the search was extended westward onto rockier terrain. Four sheep were spied high atop a snow-covered cliff, and another was found, scared and disoriented, skirting the banks of a frozen lake.

With dusk approaching and only one remaining sheep unaccounted for, any other farmer would have counted himself lucky, said a prayer to Martyr Assitus, the fabled shepherd who had died defending his flock, and headed home. Long Angrim refused to return until he had found his last sheep.

Eventually, as the sun set over the limestone cliffs, the search party came to the valley. As they waded through snow three paces deep, Long Angrim heard the sound of a sheep bleating. His flock were like children to him, and to hear one crying out was more than he could bear. Shouting, "Papa will be with you soon," he ran ahead toward the rocks.

Afterward people said it was the snow that killed him. Blown into shoulder-deep drifts against the rocks, the snow covered all the sharp edges of stone with a smooth blanket of white. Long Angrim, the sound of his lost sheep ringing in his ears, stepped onto one of the drifts, expecting the snow to be packed solid. It wasn't. The snow had formed into a loose, grainy layer. And the instant Long Angrim's weight fell upon it the drift collapsed, sending Long Angrim's body crashing to the spears of rock below. His skull was smashed and his spine was broken, and by the time the search party reached him, he was already dead. The lost sheep stood over the body, nuzzling gently at Long Angrim's hair.

Camron's father hadn't let his son see the body, but Camron remembered getting close enough to hear the sound of Long Angrim's blood, dripping drop by drop onto the chunk of limestone below his neck.

Even back then Camron had known that the villagers weren't telling the truth about the real cause of Long Angrim's death. It wasn't the snow that killed him. It was the rocks.

Shivering, Camron clambered over stone slickened by the retreating mist. "Rhif!" he called to the missing knight. "Rhif!"

This time when there was no reply, Camron wasn't surprised.

With a dozen men right behind him, Camron made his way through the rocks. As he stepped onto a knuckle of limestone, the faint smell of charred wood met his nostrils. Looking ahead, he spied smoke escaping from a nest of tall, lichen-covered stones. There was no sign of Rhif. Running his sword hand through his hair, Camron took a deep breath. Almost against his will he found himself looking over his shoulder, checking for Ravis of Burano. No matter how much he disliked the man, he valued his opinions. And right about now, faced with a situation that looked benign enough on the surface but his every instinct told him was dangerous, he could do with the Drokho mercenary's advice.

Ravis was nowhere to be seen. Although he didn't much feel like it, Camron shrugged, jumped down from the rock, and made his way forward.

Entering the nest of broken stones was like entering a tomb. The temperature dropped along with the light level. The ground underfoot was no longer soil; it was solid stone. A small burned-out campfire formed the center of the ring. A few lingering breaths of smoke escaped from its loosely built timbers. Cutting toward it, Camron was aware of his men, steps behind.

As he drew close, he spied a vaguely familiar shape set amid the blackened timbers of the fire. Seeing it, a warning pulsed high in Camron's temples; and even as he took the last few steps toward it, he knew he wouldn't like what he found.

It was a human forearm, burned black near the elbow where it had been thrust into the fire. Camron would not have been able to recognize it for what it was, had it not been for the fact that the hand had barely been touched by the flames. It protruded from the charred, smoking firewood like a salute from the underworld. All the fingernails had been removed, and the index finger had been crooked into a slyly beckoning curve.

Swallowing hard, Camron tried to look away. Something caught his eyes, though, some tiny little detail on the hand. A gold ring resting at the base of the fourth finger; an amethyst stone sparkling in its center like a lizard's eye. Camron recognized the ring immediately. The man who wore it had been the first to show him how to handle and care for his sword. His father's second at Mount Creed. Mollas the Bald.

Camron's stomach turned. He bit down on his lip, right down until his teeth pressed against bone and his mouth filled up with blood. What had the harras done to him? Why had they left part of him here to burn? Camron fell onto his hands and knees and pulled the arm from the fire. He couldn't bear to see it there amid the burned timber and ash.

That was when he smelled it. The foul animal stench

from the night his father died. The stench of blood and sweat and urine decomposing within warm fur.

Smelling it, Camron felt himself falling into a deep black pit where the sides were formed from a coven of shadows and the bottom was amethyst wax. He was in his father's study again. Men who weren't men at all glided around the room like witches. And no matter how hard he tried, how fast he ran, and how loud he shouted, the dagger still slid into his father's chest.

"May God help us all," came a cry to Camron's left.

Camron blinked back to the present. His breath was coming in short, quick bursts. His hands were shaking, and something deep within his chest ached like an old wound. He felt lost.

"We've found Rhif," came a second cry.

Camron struggled back to the present.

From the tone of the second man's voice, he guessed that what the men had found wasn't Rhif at all. It was his body. Adjusting his grip on his sword, Camron pulled himself upright. The animal stench had gone. All he could smell now was charred timbers and burned flesh. His mind must be playing tricks on him.

Walking over in the direction the shouts had come from, Camron tried hard to control the beating of his heart. He had to appear calm and in control before his men.

He found the men just outside the nest of stone, gathered around Rhif's body. Their faces were grim. Hands were bunched into knots. Lips moved, in prayer or warding, Camron didn't know. Seeing their leader approach, they parted, allowing Camron a clear view of Rhif of Hanister's body.

He thought he was prepared to see the worst. He thought after what he had seen in his father's study and what he had found on the fire, nothing would shock or surprise him.

He was wrong.

Rhif wasn't dead. Not quite, not yet. The skin on his chest had been torn off, and the chest cavity had been ripped open. The rib cage had been pried apart, and flesh and muscle had been scraped away to allow a clear view of the heart. It was still pumping. Rhif's eyes were open, and his breath came in powerless gasps. The muscles in his right hand contracted involuntarily, and a small wound in his leg dripped blood onto the ground. The fabric of his britches was soaked in urine.

Camron closed his eyes. His throat felt raw. The air in his lungs felt as heavy as water. Taking a quick breath, he fought back the memory of racing down the stairs in Castle Bess and finding Hurin's nephew laid out on the bottom step.

This wasn't about him now. It was about this young man who had wanted to fight so much, he'd ridden ahead of the troop.

Camron knelt beside him. Dimly he was aware of someone saying the Lord's True Prayer. Rhif's eyes were dark with pain. He was trying hard not to look frightened. Camron took hold of his right hand, gripping hard to still the spasms. There were many things he could say to him just then—questions about what happened, where his attackers had come from, how many there were, what weapons they had. Yet he chose to ask nothing. Instead he moved his whole body close to Rhif's, hugging the young man to his chest, and murmured, "May the Lord take and cherish you. May you find your way home. May your deeds be neither forgotten nor in vain, and may you rest in eternity knowing your loved ones could not have loved you more."

With that Camron took his knife from his sheath and slit the arteries leading to Rhif's heart. Laying down beside him, he held him tight until the last breath left his lips.

The men above were silent, swords pointing toward the earth, eyes closed.

When the contractions stopped, Camron let go of the young man's hand. Leaning over, he laid a single kiss on his cheek. Strangely, he felt calm. The words he had spoken had been wrapped around his heart since the night his father died. Now, finally, they had been said. Not for his father—they had always been too late for his father—but somehow that didn't matter anymore. The words had been said and a brave young man had heard them, and that was, surprisingly, enough.

Camron stood.

A sharp breeze cut from the east.

The stench of animal excretia caught in Camron's nostrils. Thinking his senses were failing him, he glanced at the nearest man.

"Something reeks around here," the knight said.

Even as the words left his mouth, the nature of the dawn changed.

The air was filled with harsh, animal braying. Hundreds of torches blistered to life, creating a ring of fire around the valley and the stones. Swords rang. Horses squealed. Hooves drummed over rock.

The shadows of the stones seemed to come to life, and dark forms slid from even darker recesses, knives catching, then reflecting, the sun's first rays. They came from everywhere— from beneath rocks the troops had scrambled over, behind bushes they had walked past, and from the trees they had leaned against to catch their breath or lace their boots.

More and more poured from the rocks, the valley's slopes, the periphery of the broken stones. Within seconds they were everywhere, like a spill of black oil. Cloaked and dressed in darkest gray, they seemed to crawl from the very earth itself. Swords held high at their shoulders, they *stalked* rather than moved. Their shoulder movements were strangely fluid, and their heads remained level as they drew close. Cloaks whipped from side to side, eyes darted, mouths were open, revealing notched pink gums, white in places where the bone and roots pressed against the surface. Saliva, thick as mucus, flashed between crowded teeth.

The foul animal stench of meat left rotting in a lair was overpowering. It caught in Camron's throat, making his gorge rise.

The harras brought a hail of light and shade. Their torches robbed the dawn of its glory, creating a fistful of shadows for each man and standing stone.

The smell. The shadows. The light. Thin blades, bared teeth, gums like animal vertebrae in their mouths. Camron swallowed bile. He gripped the hilt of his sword so hard, veins broke in the meat of his hand.

It was the night his father had died all over again.

That terrible, damning night.

Camron looked at his men and saw they were ready. He looked at the body of Rhif of Hanister and saw a man at peace. The carnage of his flesh was nothing compared to the expression on his face. It was faith Camron saw nestling there between Rhif's eyelids and his mouth.

Pure, unquestioning faith.

Camron felt a weight so heavy on his heart, he was sure it would break. Every man here was his father, son, and brother. And if he couldn't save them, he would go down with them, and a terrible wrong created the night his father died would finally be redressed.

He should have died saving him.

With the harras calling to each other in their howling half-animal voices, and the stench of animal waste and naphtha-soaked torches heavy in the air, Camron called out the order to take up positions.

The enemy was a dark fluid line spilling closer as, without a word being passed between them, a dozen men formed a circle around the body of Rhif of Hanister.

The ruling and leadpointing was done now. A gray-washed leaf of vellum, stiff from being dried on the hearth, lay waiting beneath Tessa's hand. As she looked at it, she was aware of her stomach muscles contracting in a long-drawn-out wave. She felt sick with anticipation.

"Here's the first one, miss," Emith said, handing her a bone-and-sable brush. "I'll oil a finer one next, just in case."

Tessa nodded. She couldn't speak. Already, in the seconds between finishing the ruling and Emith handing her the brush, the world had started falling away. Behind her back and to her sides, she felt shadows railing her in. As she dipped the brush into the gleaming, viscous blackness of pitch and lampblack pigment, she felt the room around her contract to a single square of light. The vellum, her hands, the pigment, and the brush were all that mattered now. Even the air felt heavy on her fingers, as if that had contracted, too.

Emith was speaking, perhaps giving last minute advice or first-time encouragement, but Tessa could no longer understand what he said. His words were so much dust in the ink.

The knuckles in Tessa's right hand cracked as she drew

the paintbrush down toward the page. The loaded tip trailed a line of purest, deepest black onto the vellum. Tessa imagined she heard the pigment hiss as it settled against the chalk.

With a practiced flick of her wrist, she sent the line curving upward toward a guide mark on the top left-hand corner of the page. The movement was swift, and Tessa could feel the brush gathering speed, see the pigment racing behind. Halting the trajectory of the brush, she used the built-up momentum to send a wide band of ink flaring on the page. Brush freshly dipped, she then sent a curve spiraling downward to the baseline ruled in lead.

As the brush moved in her grip in a series of slow, repetitive loops, and the pigment slid from the tip in a succession of ever-thickening lines, Tessa felt her head begin to spin. Her stomach contracted sharply. The skin on her scalp bristled, as if a thousand tiny insects were crawling through her hair. The brush slid in her hand, sweat oiling the grip.

She caught a whiff of woodsmoke and something else. Before she could identify it, it was gone.

The black curves drew her in like a beckoning hand. Thick, shiny, and guarded, they promised secrets if she would follow their path. Tessa's eyes and hand moved as one. She felt her physical self dimming to a silhouette of lines. A flutter of panic rose in her chest, but the urge to keep painting was too strong and she half swallowed, half willed it away. The brush turned, pigment flowed, spirals uncoiled like silk from a reel. Leadpoint lines and pinpricks glowed against the gray: no longer simply guidelines, they were a roadmap to another world.

A soft noise hummed in her head, but she ignored it. It was a ghost attack of tinnitus, that was all. Deveric, his finehaired brush, and his even finer ink were no longer here anymore. They couldn't do anything to stop her. Not this time. Not here and now. Not ever, *ever,* again.

From now on she could do what she wanted.

Feeling a mad rush of adrenaline, Tessa pushed the brush across the page. A skitter of sound grazed her eardrums: harsh metal clanging muffled by stone. She tried to focus her mind upon it, but the noise trailed away like smoke.

Down she went, down deep into the vellum with the lampblack and the pitch; down to where the pigment seared the hide, and the bristles touched flesh, and the page gave birth to the design. Tessa's head spiraled with the brush. Her thoughts soared with the ink. Catching a glimpse of the landscape that lay beyond, through, and behind the design, she began mirroring the pattern on the right-hand side of the page. This time there was no going back.

As her brush turned curve after curve, the shadowy territory beyond the design grew clearer. A pool glinted darkly in the center. Almost unaware of what she was doing, Tessa took a second brush from Emith's outstretched hand, dipped its tip into niello ink, and began painting knots. A string of *XXX*s wove their way off the brush as Tessa moved closer to the pool. The landscape was a construction of shadows and shadings. Not really a landscape at all anymore, rather a series of lifting veils. Black, gauzy, and infinitely thin, they rose from the illumination like fumes from the paint.

Suddenly uneasy, Tessa bit on her lip. Just like Ravis, she thought.

She tasted blood in her mouth. Or was it the ink? Both tasted of copper and salt.

The line between what she was, and what she was painting, began to fade away. A shiver passed down her spine. A cool breeze brushed against the left side of her face. The smell came again. And this time Tessa recognized it at once: the stench from the night on the bridge.

The rangy, spoiled-meat odor of the harras.

Blood, ink, whatever it was, turned to powder in Tessa's mouth. Something soft and malleable pulled at her stomach, causing a sickening hollow to form beneath her lungs. The dark, shifting forms of the harras—knives held at shoulder height, knuckled gums wet and dripping—fixed themselves in Tessa's mind. Their images passed along her body to her fingers, where they became slants in the brushstrokes. Shadows in the ink.

A spine of knots spilled from the brush, propelling Tessa further, deeper, into the world on the other side. Tinnitus rang its ghost chimes in her head, as the harras' cloaks formed a whipping, undulating pathway to the pool. Panic began to beat in Tessa's temples, and this time she couldn't will it away. Her scalp felt as tight as a bowstring. She didn't want to go, didn't want to see, but the patterns kept spinning from her fingertips, illuminating the way.

Remember Deveric, she told herself. Remember what he did.

Grinding her teeth, Tessa forced an image of the damning gray spirals to come before her eyes. Lines as fine and abundant as facial hair that had held her back most of her life. Twenty-one years she had been misused and manipulated, and now she had a chance to find out why.

She could and *would* take that one last step.

"Be careful, miss. Please don't go too far." Emith's voice was a vague undertone. By the time he'd finished speaking, Tessa had forgotten what he said.

Through the pigment, vellum, and chalk she moved, down to somewhere deeper, darker, and immeasurably distant, far on the other side.

While her mouth counted knots and her eye controlled the brush, Tessa McCamfrey *entered* the design. A shearing sensation passed along her body, and the tissue lining her nose and throat became sharply and suddenly dry. Taking a running man's breath, she forced her way through to the pool that lay at the heart. Human cries and animal cries and sounds of fighting followed her. The smell of the harras no longer tantalized, it overwhelmed.

As she moved forward, Tessa was overcome with the feeling that she was walking into familiar territory after all. She knew this place, or at least the feel of it. The darkness was as warm as her belly and as soft as her skin. On the vellum, her hand worked its magic, drawing a warren of predatory lines. Another dip into the ink, one final knotted *X*, and Tessa found herself at the pool's edge. Taking a deep breath, she leaned forward and looked into its black, glassy depths.

She saw nothing but her own face staring back.

She should have been surprised. But she wasn't. Some small part of her had already guessed the truth. She hadn't stepped into some fantastic otherworld, summoned up by sorcery or sleight of hand. She had withdrawn inside herself.

Slowly Tessa's head began to shake. Deveric had used tinnitus not only to manipulate her, he had used it to mask who she was. By preventing her from concentrating, from thinking too deeply and going too far, he had kept a portion of her mind locked away. Something inside of her had been cordoned off: out of sight, out of use. Out of mind.

"No," she murmured, not knowing if the words were thought or spoken. "No." Slamming her palm upon the vellum, she stamped her fingerprints in the ink. What had given Deveric the right to interfere with her life? *What?*

"Miss! Miss! Are you all right? Please speak to me. Please." Even though Emith's voice seemed to come from far away, Tessa could tell he was genuinely distressed. Hearing the concern in his voice helped calm her down. Emith and his mother cared about her, and she cared about them. Deveric and his patterns may have robbed something from her, but his assistant had given something back.

"I'm fine, Emith," she said slowly, her tongue almost a stranger in her mouth.

Emith's hand brushed her shoulder. "I think you should stop now, miss. Come and sit by the fire and rest."

Tessa shook her head. The brush was already back in her hand. She had to return to the place she'd just found. Follow the stench of the harras and the clashing of their knives, and discover why she had been brought here.

Running the brush along the page, she said, "Pass me the blood red pigment, Emith. This pattern isn't finished yet."

SIXTEEN

The harrar's gold-cast eyes appraised him. Saliva dripped from its dog-toothed maw as it swept closer with the pack. Back bent, shoulders crouched, it swayed from side to side as it moved. A thin knife held at chest height projected from its leather body armor like a spike. It was no longer recognizable as a man. Its nose was flattened and streamlined like a snout. Its cheeks were bone-hard hollows, and its eyes were slits. It didn't blink. As it padded over ridges of rock and twisted fists of brushwood, its gaze never left Camron for an instant.

It smelled like a butchered carcass, the gamy odor of blood no longer fresh, mixed with the harsh ammonia tang of stale urine and the cloying ripeness of fecal matter.

The knife it held was unclean. A dark stain ran along the edge, and something white and loose, like a gob of animal fat, clung to the blade near the hilt.

As Camron watched, the harrar let out a low, yelping sound. Others responded, and within seconds the Valley of Broken Stones rang with the sounds of their calls. The air bristled. The sun rose. Golden eyes glinted with hunger and need. Camron swallowed hard. The sword in his hand—the twice-fired, lead-weighted steel falchion his father had given him as a naming gift—felt as light and flimsy as a bamboo cane.

By his side the troop held their circle, waiting for the harras to approach. Lured, trapped, and surrounded: there was nothing else they could do.

Smoke from the harras' torches formed a swirling, noxious haze around the rocks. Camron felt his eyes watering. Behind him, one of his men began to cough. Paces away now, the harras didn't move as much as *spill* over the remaining space. Cloaks cracking behind them like bullwhips, they drew a writhing black ring around the troop. Camron watched the face of the harrar whom he knew without question had come to kill him. There were many things he had expected to see shining in the creature's eyes, yet cunning wasn't one of them. It was there, though: cold, calculated cunning.

Camron shuddered. The harras weren't animals after all. Even as Camron forced his body to still, the harras fell on the troop. Blades hacking downward, teeth bared and dripping, they shot forward as a single, unified mass.

Camron sucked in air. Swinging his sword in a mighty half circle around his chest, he stepped forward to meet the monsters who had slaughtered his father.

His blade glanced against the first harrar's knife. Metal screeched. The gob of animal fat on the creature's blade was sliced in two. Before Camron had a chance to draw back his sword for a second blow, the harrar's knife was already on its way down again. As a reflex action, Camron raised his left forearm to protect his face. The harrar's blade blistered down on the steel gauntlet, puncturing the plate with a soft-metal hiss. Serrated edges of steel gouged Camron's flesh. The blade tip jabbed against his wrist bone. Grinding his teeth together, Camron forced himself to swallow the pain.

In the half second it took the harrar to free his knife from the metal trap of the gauntlet, Camron sent his sword hacking into the soft flesh of the creature's side. The harrar's eyes widened. Its jaw unclenched and its spiked yellow teeth sprang apart. A breath of foul air escaped from its mouth as it let out an explosive sigh. Springing forward, it threw its entire body against Camron.

Blood sprayed Camron's hands and cheeks. The harrar's knife was like a machine: up and down it went in a single hacking line. The hairs on the back of Camron's neck prickled. His skin felt like a heavy cloak weighing his body down. He was so close to the harrar, he could smell its breath, see the gray cast of its skin, and feel the terrible, unnatural heat from its body.

It wasn't going to stop until it was dead.

Weighing his sword across his chest, Camron used it as a shield. To either side of him, he heard the grunts and ragged breaths of his men. The dark forms of the harras bore down upon the troop, always moving forward, never back. Ahead, he could see more still coming. Cloaks snapping, knives raised, wasp eyes glinting black and gold, they poured down the valley's slope toward the rocks. There was no end of them.

Briefly Camron wondered what had happened to the three dozen men who had been left on the other side of the rocks. Not liking what his mind showed him, he pushed the thought aside.

A second harrar came to back up the one Camron was fighting. Covering his partner's wounded flank, he slashed at Camron's sword arm, rib cage, and thighs. A low growl sounded deep in his throat as he fought, and his buckled maw clenched and unclenched as if he were crunching invisible bones between his teeth.

Camron was forced to step back. Making quick sweeping motions with his blade, he moved side on to the two harras, giving them less of a target to aim for. There was blood in his eye—he didn't know whether it was the harrar's or his own. His left wrist felt as if scalding water had been poured on it. Blood pumped through the puncture hole in the gauntlet, spilling down his arm and onto the rocks below.

The sun slanted upward through the trees. Camron could feel its warmth on his shoulders and the back of his neck. The smell of burning grass was carried on the breeze. Grass and something else. Camron switched his mind back to the fight. It was yet another thing that didn't bear thinking about.

The long, thin knives of the harras were no match in size or weight for the troops' broadswords, yet that hardly seemed to matter. The harras were fast—faster than any fighters Camron had ever known—and their leather armor kept them light on their feet. They lashed out with deadly, unstoppable focus. They wanted blood, and nothing, absolutely nothing, was going to stop them from getting it.

To Camron's left, a man went down. A harrar's blade punctured his breastplate above his heart, and he stumbled forward, breaking the circle formed by the troop. As Camron sent his sword glancing in a series of defensive broadstrokes, he watched as half a dozen harras fell on the wounded knight. Saliva frothed between their teeth, spilling down their jaws in thick, viscous strings. Long knives flashed in the sunlight as they hacked away at the downed man. Arm raised above his face to shield himself, the man was helpless to stop them slicing away at the exposed flesh of his forearm, neck, and throat.

"Get up," Camron willed him between gritted teeth. "Get up."

The knight didn't respond.

Ravis' words filtered through Camron's mind: *"I've seen too many men die because they were wearing full armor and couldn't right themselves after a fall. . . ."*

A wave of anger swept over Camron and he lashed out with his sword. The blow caught the wounded harrar in the center of his flank, slicing through muscle and kidney tissue. Even before the creature could react, Camron switched his grip on the leather-bound hilt, adjusting it so the blade was facing inward toward himself, and sent the pommel of his sword smashing into the second harrar's snout. Bone cracked, teeth caved, blood spilled down from its nostrils. As the creature stumbled back, Camron switched his attention to the wounded harrar. Sword whirling in his hand, he regained his grip on the hilt, and using the built-up momentum of the blade to add power to the blow, he hacked at the harrar's throat. He felt the blade go in, yanked it out, and then moved swiftly sideways toward the downed knight.

By all the gods, he was going to *make* him get up!

Blood stung his eyes. Trapped sweat steamed beneath his armor. The muscles in his sword arm ached with the strain of wielding his sword. All around him, he was aware of the changing nature of the battle. His troop was tiring. No longer grunting, thrusting, and parrying; breaths came quick and shallow as they held their swords close to their chest. Faces were red and dripping sweat. Slowly, step by step, they backed inward in an ever-decreasing circle toward Rhif of Hanister's body.

Hacking a path toward the downed man, Camron risked

casting a glance over the dark, mewling forms of the harras.
Teeth glinting, chests pumping: they were just getting started.

Sword slashing Xs in the air around his torso, Camron
approached the pack that had fallen on the wounded knight.
The man's armor straps had been cut, and the harras were
busy tearing off his breastplate. The leather ailettes over his
shoulders and upper arms, and the cuisses protecting his
thighs had been sliced to ribbons. The harras clawed at the
remaining armor, tearing at the padded undershirt beneath in
their eagerness to get at flesh.

There was a lot of blood. The knight's helmet had come
off, and two harras were stabbing at his head, ears, and
throat. The knight's arm was still up, protecting what he could
of his face. The arm itself was a bloodied mass of raw meat,
the gauntlet long since cut away.

Camron bore down on the pack. He saw them through a
red haze of blood and anger. That could have been any one of
the Thorn villagers lying there, defenseless, unable to stand
against the savage frenzy of the harras. It could have been his
father, that night in Castle Bess.

Not caring anymore about protecting his back and sides,
Camron took swings at anything that was in front of him.
Again and again his sword came down, on limbs, shoulders
blades, skulls, and breastbones. The harras were monsters.
Monsters.

If blades cut into his flesh, he didn't feel them. If the harras cried out to each other in warning or support, he no
longer heard their calls. All that mattered was getting to the
downed man and pulling him away from their black, night-
mare clutches. His sword was an angel in his hand: flashing
silver in the sunlight, it formed a protective halo of steel
around his chest. Cutting a path through razored teeth and
spiked blades, he stepped through blood and viscera toward
the clearing where the injured knight lay. Keeping the wall of
lashing, furious harras at bay with his sword, he held out his
left hand toward the man.

"Come," he said, the words stinging the raw flesh of his
throat. "Fall in behind me. I'll keep you safe as long as I can."

The knight grasped Camron's hand. His flesh was hot,
sticky with blood, yet never had a single touch meant so much

or felt so good. With one mighty tug, Camron pulled the man to his feet. Even before he was fully upright, Camron stepped in front of him, shielding him from the harras' blades.

"Step back into the circle," Camron murmured, eyes aching, lungs burning.

The knight didn't move.

Puzzled, Camron glanced over his shoulder to the circle at his rear.

A fist of lead twisted in his stomach. The steam in his armor turned to ice.

There *was* no circle. The troop was gone. The harras were everywhere he looked: dark, eager, triumphant. A high-pitched cry rippled through the pack as they moved forward for the kill.

The paintbrush became a dead weight in Tessa's hand. All the silver ink was used up. There was no more left: not on the brush, or in the shell, or in the glazed pot Emith used for mixing.

A band of pain ringed Tessa's forehead. She felt as if metal plates were being pushed against her temples, only they weren't really her temples at all.

She was *there*. With Camron amid the rocks. She could smell his sweat, taste the blood in his mouth, feel the pressure building in his temples. Her stomach churned with his. The wet-fur stench of the harras was all around her, yet at the same time it was nowhere at all. Her hands, which had stayed so steady through everything, through what seemed like hours of painting and concentration, shook for the first time against the page. She felt drop-dead tired.

Then again, perhaps she wasn't tired at all. Perhaps she was feeling Camron's exhaustion as if it were her own.

She had drawn herself to this battle. To a valley she had never seen before in her life, to a forest of broken stones. The harras' smell and the ringing of their blades had been her paper trail. She had followed their tracks on the vellum, sent ink curling into the imprints left by their footsteps, painted an interlace of keywork tiles to pave herself a road.

She had even drawn the harras themselves. Carbon and gallic acid ink, dimmed minutely with sulfur, then thinned once more with stale urine, had been their medium. The black pigment had a yellow cast where it caught the tallow's light. Its fumes stung Tessa's eyes. Even though she knew in her mind the harras were men, she painted them as four-legged creatures with dog's snouts, claws, and thick, muscular tails.

"Quadrupeds," Emith had called them, his voice sounding oddly strained.

The pattern was not pretty. A graveyard of bleak colors ran across the page: grays, charcoals, blacks, deep reds, and cold, fleshless blues. It was almost as if the colors weren't really colors at all, more shadows cast by pigments after dark. Looking at them, Tessa felt her mouth go dry. What had Deveric drawn her into? What was she, Tessa McCamfrey, doing sitting here creating these monstrous designs?

All of a sudden she wanted very much to go home.

Running a finger along the edge of the vellum, Tessa sighed. The breath ached in her throat as it came out. How could she return home, though? Even if the ring could take her back, how could she leave Camron among the rocks, with the harras closing in on him and the man whose life he had just saved?

Tessa turned the paintbrush in her hands. She had drawn the pattern in search of answers, yet it had only raised more questions instead. She knew how she'd got here; how she had drawn herself a path along the vellum; and how the path didn't really lead outward at all, but rather inward toward herself. Yet she didn't know how to *affect* anything. She was just an observer, that was all. She couldn't change anything. She didn't know how to.

A bead of sweat trickled down Tessa's temple. Curving inward with the line of her cheek, it ran into her mouth. It tasted of bad things. Tessa shivered. Her vision of Camron was already beginning to fade away. She could hold on to it only as long as the brush pushed pigment across the page.

"What can I do, Emith?" she asked, not really sure how much Emith knew of what she was doing or where she had been. "How can I change what the pattern shows me?"

The air above her left shoulder shifted as Emith shook his head. "I don't know, miss. I don't know."

The bone brush snapped in Tessa's hand. Splinters punctured the meat of her thumb muscle. "There has to be something. Think. *Think!*"

Emith's hand brushed her shoulder. "Come away, miss. Leave the pattern now while you're—"

"While I'm what?" Tessa cried. "While I'm still safe?"

With every second that passed, Camron and the battle were sliding away from her. She felt as though she were deserting him. Even though Emith was busy explaining what he had really meant to say, Tessa cut him short. "I need a new brush—and more pigment. I'll use whatever colors you have left." Knowing her words sounded harsh, she added, "Emith, someone is in great danger. I can't leave the pattern now. I can't."

Emith made a soft sound in his throat. She could tell he didn't approve of what she was doing, yet he handed her a new brush all the same. Tessa felt bad—she knew he was worried because he cared about her—but she had to carry on. All her life she had shirked involvements and responsibility, but she couldn't go on doing that anymore. Things were different now. *She* was different.

There was no walking away this time.

"This is the only pigment I have left," Emith said, sliding a shell of gold ink along the tabletop. "I'll mix up some more while you work."

Tessa nodded. She wasn't surprised at the color of the pigment: everything in this world began and ended with gold. After dipping her brush into the ink, she trailed the loaded tip onto the page. This time when the pigment touched the vellum it didn't hiss, it sizzled.

Ederius stopped in midbrushstroke. A sharp pain raked along his brow bone, just above his eyes. His vision blurred. The ink on his brush pooled onto the page.

"What is it?" hissed Izgard.

The words made Ederius flinch. He had forgotten his

king was at his side. "Nothing, sire," he said quickly, bringing his left hand up to his forehead. The greater, duller pain of the slowly mending bone in his shoulder canceled out the pain in his brow. "A muscle cramp, that is all."

"What is happening in the Valley of Broken Stones?" Izgard's breath fell like cold mist on Ederius' ear. His fingertips hovered a moth's wing above Ederius' face, not touching the skin itself, only the raised hairs. Oh, he wanted to touch more—Ederius knew just how much his king loved to touch those he considered his—yet even he dared not interrupt an Anointed-trained scribe at his work. Even now, five hundred years past the golden age of the isle and its scribes, the stories and rumors still retained a power all their own.

People had died, they said.

Men had burned.

Ederius smiled, but even though it was his first in twenty-one days, there was no joy in it. People were right to be afraid. There *was* power. Not in the ink, or the parchment, or the designs, but in the act of creation itself. When the ink burned into the vellum in a well-practiced curve, when a scribe's vision of a pattern took form upon a page, and when a thousand years of tradition gave rise to something new, a summons was sent out into the overworld. Power was demanded. And those scribes who had the ability to sense and accept it could shape themselves a weapon, or a shield, or an ivory tower from its fabric. They could bring their weight to bear on lives that were not their own.

Ederius never questioned where the power came from. He had stopped asking himself hard questions the day Izgard slaughtered Gamberon on the hillside east of Sirabayus. It was how he survived from day to day. It was how he lived with the choices he had made.

Another spasm clawed across his temples. Vision blurred by many different types of pain, Ederius looked down at the design he had created. He didn't see the page itself as much as a fine tapestry of meshing, vibrating lines. Something wasn't right. The pattern was being interfered with in some way: a faint tremor resonated in the background like an irritant. A fly in the ink. Aware that Izgard's gaze was upon him, Ederius tried to give nothing away.

He didn't succeed, for Izgard's breath plumed cold across his neck once more. "What is it, Ederius? Tell me what is wrong."

Ederius shook his head. "I don't know, sire." As he spoke he cleaned his brush of gray ink, then reached for the deepest, blackest pigment in his palette: pulverized jet and obsidian in a binding of mineral pitch. Dense, gleaming, and razor edged; minute slivers of volcanic glass were suspended in the mix.

"I don't want anything going wrong this time," Izgard whispered into Ederius' ear. His breath smelled of sweet things turning sour in an absence of light. "This trap has been planned for too long. The town was taken for one purpose alone: to lure Camron of Thorn and his latest hireling here for a fight. I want both of them dead now—*both of them*. Thorn was given a warning and he chose not to heed it, and that wasn't only his mistake, it was mine. I should have had him killed the same night as his father.

"And as for Ravis of Burano—" Izgard's hand shot from Ederius' face down toward his desk. By the time it slammed into the wood, it was a fist. "That man will find himself well received in hell."

Izgard's voice was a distant murmur. Ederius heard the hate but little else. His mind was smoldering with the ink. Borne inward and downward, his thoughts raced along a well-worn trail to the valley and the battle to the east. Izgard kept speaking, and as his emotions suited Ederius' purpose well enough, the scribe let him be. Something wasn't right and his job was to fix it, and if that meant destroying whatever was interfering with his design, then so be it. A master scribe had to master so much more than mixing pigments and drawing lines.

Blood pounded through Camron's veins. His chest was pumping so hard, it pushed against the metal plate above his heart. Sweat poured down his neck and his chest, running in rivulets beneath his armor before hissing, then turning to steam. Wounds in his legs, side, arms, and neck blistered with white-hot pain. Every breath he took scorched his lungs. His sword was glued to his palm by dried blood, and as he wielded it before the harras, his grip had never been surer, and strike after strike landed true.

Broc of Lomis, the knight he had pulled free from the pack of harras, was at his back. Not only had the man managed to stand, but he'd also found the strength to lift his blade. His right arm was unusable, but he could do enough with his left arm to keep the harras at bay.

Just knowing he was there, behind him, his torn shoulder plates brushing against his own, gave Camron a feeling of well-being. He wasn't alone in this.

The sun was working for them. Oblique morning light shone directly onto the harras' faces. Camron could see the gold filaments in their pupils and the fine saliva strands between their teeth. Their jaws worked furiously as they fought: palates grinding, lips spreading, tongues lashing in mouths that seemed too small for the fist of gums and teeth they contained.

Camron's sword never stopped—it couldn't. The constantly moving edge was the only thing that stopped the harras from tearing him limb from limb. He and Broc stood a head above them on a smooth shoulder of rock. All torches had burned out now, and the smoke had long dispersed. The spoiled-meat stench of the harras was the only thing that marred the air.

The other knights were nowhere to be seen. As he fought, Camron tried to pick out their forms amid the dark, milling mob. He hadn't spotted them yet, but it didn't stop him looking or hoping. Perhaps somehow they had managed to escape.

Whether it was the effect of being dazzled by the light or something else, Camron couldn't tell, but for some reason the harras were beginning to slow. They were becoming more wary of his blade, giving it a wider berth on the thrusts, and hesitating before springing forward after withdrawals. Even their features seemed to be shifting. As Camron looked on, the gold light in their eyes wavered and their lips fell slack over their gums. They began to look more like men.

A breeze suddenly picked up from the west, and Camron got his first whiff of fresh air since dawn. Risking a glance over his shoulder, he locked gazes with Broc of Lomis. Broc didn't smile—events were too far gone for that—but his hazel eyes were no longer filled with fear.

He sensed it, too. The harras were beginning to fail.

Grasping the hilt of his sword in both hands, Camron hefted it high above his head, ignoring the ripping, straining muscles in his arms and chest. Even though he knew hope was a reckless luxury he couldn't afford, he couldn't stop himself from being filled with it. Perhaps somehow, by the grace of God, they just might get out of this.

Tessa painted with a mad, intense fury. She didn't know what she was doing, or how she was doing it; she just knew she had to keep pigment pumping onto the page at all costs. Everything depended on it.

Her head ached. The muscles in her arm felt as if they were being clawed by some invisible sharp-nailed beast. Her left hand was numb from supporting the weight of her chin for so long. Behind her, Emith mixed up pigments she knew she would never use, and his mother sat ticking away in her chair.

Time no longer had meaning. Tessa couldn't tell if ten seconds or ten hours had passed since she'd first dipped her brush into the gold. The only way she had of keeping track of the world was the developing pattern on the page. It was not turning out as she had imagined. Somehow it had taken on a life of its own. Thick branches of color swerved across the vellum. Thin-limbed, many-jointed creatures crawled through spirals and under knotwork, their tongues and tails curling around fretwork borders like vines suffocating a tree.

Tessa felt as if she were swimming in the dark. She had no idea where she was heading or what she might encounter next. Her only guide was herself. She could only do what felt right. The gold ink was right—that much she knew. And when she sent gold lines slashing across the sulfur-tinted forms of the harras, tying them up in knots, she felt sure it was having some effect on the battle amid the broken stones. The pads of flesh on her fingertips tingled as she worked, and she took that to be a good sign.

Mostly she relied on willpower. It pushed every brush-stroke she made, gave momentum to curves, and kept key-work and knotwork in line. She was going to help Camron of Thorn. She had to. Deveric had brought her here for some-thing, and as the brushstrokes built up on the page in increas-ingly tangled layers, and as forms emerged from the ink like landmarks from lifting mist, she began to realize that he had brought her here for this. To work against the harras.

They were unnatural beings—aberrations. She could feel their wrongness burning away in her stomach like acid. When her mind showed her visions of the writhing, baying pack, the hairs on her scalp bristled. From above they looked like cockroaches teeming over a carcass. Eyes and teeth flashed amid the winged darkness of their cloaks.

Then, as she looked on, paintbrush dancing beneath her hand, one of the creatures looked her way.

One moment it was just another harrar in the pack, head thrashing in time with the rest. Abruptly it stopped moving, held still for a moment, then turned its streamlined maw to-ward her in a slow liquid arc. Sulfur eyes focused through a haze of light and shadow, their gaze finding, then resting, on her face. Without blinking, the creature regarded Tessa with the narrow-eyed leer of a predator. After a moment its lips stretched to a unhurried smile and its jaws sprang open like a trap.

Tessa jerked back. The legs of her chair skittered across the stone floor. The paintbrush jumped in her hand, sending the line running askew.

"Tessa! Tessa! Are you all right?" Emith, using her proper name for the first time since she had met him. "Come away now. Let the pattern be."

Tessa's heart was racing. Her body felt hot and cold all at once. "I'm fine, Emith," she said, trying hard to make her voice sound level. "It was nothing. Just . . ." Words failed her. "Nothing."

"I think you should stop right now, miss. Right now."

"I can't, Emith." She wanted to say more, to explain that she couldn't leave Camron alone and helpless surrounded by harras and that she had to carry on no matter what, but instinct told her it was best not to speak. Anything she said would only turn to hysterical nonsense in her mouth.

Adjusting her grip on the brush, she dipped it once more into the ink. Already her mind was working to calm her: how could anything she saw through a pattern cause her harm? She was far away from the battle, here, in Mother Emith's kitchen, safe and sound. The harras weren't about to come bursting through the vellum. It wasn't possible. Telling herself she was foolish to feel frightened, she brought the gold ink down onto the page. Her hand shook, and the curve she drew wasn't as smooth as she would have liked, but it was enough to push her back toward the battle.

Sounds of grunting and metal whistling against metal greeted her. The stench of animal waste caught in her throat. There's nothing to be afraid of, she told herself as she began painting over the dark, snaking forms of the harras.

Gold ink skimmed across black. Colors bled. Pigment smoked. Tessa's hand wouldn't stop shaking, and sable hairs began to work their way free of the brush, catching on the vellum like splinters. She thought of the harras, imagining them fleeing, gone, dead. Not knowing what to do, she hemmed them in with strips of gold, fettered them with a manacle of knots.

It was working. She could feel them slowing down.

Wanting to do more, she struck through a row of harras with a single, slashing line. As the gold soaked into the parchment, Tessa caught a whiff of something else.

Another pigment, freshly applied.

And even as she realized it was not her own, a splitting pain seared across her forehead. Her vision blurred, then dimmed. Gold-cast eyes glowed from the darkness, seeing her, knowing her, gloating. A second wave of pain tore through head. It felt like ground glass was being rubbed into her flesh. Tessa tried to take a breath and couldn't. Her eyes burned. Falling forward against the tabletop, she felt another spasm rack her skull. The pain blinded. She couldn't see anything except the gold eyes. Brush still in hand, she stabbed at the vellum. A blast of heat scorched her palm, but she couldn't let go of the brush.

Pain stopped her from thinking, breathing, acting. Tears streamed from her eyes. Razors raked along her temples.

She couldn't bear it.

Breath wouldn't come. Darkness opened up before her: cold and infinitely deep.

Something tugged at her hand. Fingers prying her palm open. A terrible cleaving pain as the brush was stripped away from her flesh. Arms tugging her away from the chair. Sobs, hysterical sobs.

The gold eyes winked closed, and then everything went black.

The harras turned. It happened in the space of an instant. One moment they were sluggish, wary, their features shifting gradually inward, revealing them to be nothing more than men. The next they were like rabid dogs. Baying, clawing, thrashing: they pressed forward in a continuous black wave.

Breath caught in Camron's throat. His stomach clenched shut, leaving a sickening vacuum between his ribs. There were too many harras. They were coming too fast. His sword arm ached with a deep bone weariness. He could feel himself slowing, see his blade tip dipping as he drew protective rings around his chest. He didn't know how much longer he could keep this up.

Behind him, Broc of Lomis was struggling for breath. Blood and spittle rasped in his throat. His sword wasn't down yet—it hovered in increasingly slack circles around his lower abdomen—but it wouldn't be long before it fell by his side. The man was losing a lot of blood. The soles of Camron's boots stamped footprints entirely in red.

"Pull closer," Camron cried, reaching back with his left hand to touch the young, dark-haired knight. "Draw to my back so I can shield both our flanks."

A second passed, and then Camron felt Broc's shoulders knock against his. He let out a sigh of relief. It wasn't much, but it was all he could do. Broc only had to worry about the harras directly ahead of him now. Camron would take care of those to either side. It meant hefting his sword in broader, deeper circles, exerting further pressure on muscles already ripped to shreds, but there was no other choice. They had to keep fighting.

Although his throat felt as though it were on fire, Camron forced himself to take long, deep breaths. He may have ridden here to perish, to fight against his father's killers until they hooked him with their long knives and sent his soul spiraling to heaven or plunging down hell. But as every minute passed he realized he didn't want to die.

Not here. Not now.

He wanted to live.

Dying wouldn't bring his father back. It wouldn't change the course of events that night in Castle Bess. Nothing could or ever would change that: not this fight or a thousand others like it, and certainly not his death. His death would mark the end of Thorn the town, its people, and the family who had shared that name. It would mark the end of everything his father had known and loved.

Glancing out over the wet and snapping jaws of the harras, Camron tried not to feel afraid, tried not to think anymore about dying. All that was left now was to fight.

A thin cry sounded behind him. Metal screeched. Caught in the middle of a deflective blow, with three harras' blades raking against his sword and more on the way to meet it, Camron couldn't look round. Another cry sounded. A sharp, desperate breath followed, then Camron felt Broc fall against his back. Bringing a foot forward to steady himself, pulling in his sword close to his ribs, Camron turned toward the knight. His left hand shot out. Harras blades stabbed against the punctured gauntlet. Something sharp pierced his undefended right flank.

Broc was on his knees. His sword was gone. Harras clawed away at legs, feet, and arms. Broc saw Camron's outstretched hand but didn't have the strength to reach for it. A muscle pumped in his forearm, but the arm itself didn't move.

Camron felt a blade slash the back of his head. A second later another slashed his ear. Pain came in sharp waves. Tears flooded his eyes. Bending down, he reached for Broc's arm. Even as his armor creaked at the joints, he felt a salvo of knife stabs at his back. The metal plates fell from his chest and back. His mouth filled with blood. He looked into Broc's hazel eyes and saw a reflection of his own. Fear made his mouth go dry.

The harras closed in. Dog maws grinding, knives hacking downward, they filled the remaining space like tar poured into a ditch.

Camron braced himself. Pain scorched his body in a dozen places as he raised his sword high above his head. One harrar broke from the path and made a lunge for him with his knife. Camron mouthed the words "Forgive me." Whether it was to his God, his father, or Broc of Lomis, he didn't know. Perhaps it was to all three.

His sword rang against the harrar's blade. He didn't have the strength to match the attacker's blow, and the hilt went spinning from his grasp. Even as the sword left his hand, it was snatched away by a black-gloved grip. The first harrar's lips curled to a sneer as it tilted its blade to an angle fit for slipping between ribs.

Defenseless, Camron could do nothing but cross his arms over his chest. Bracing himself for the impact, he tensed the muscles in his right leg: he would go down kicking.

A soft *thuc* sounded. It was so soft that Camron doubted he heard it.

The harras' gold eyes widened. A hiss of breath puffed from his lips and he fell forward against Camron's chest. An arrow jutted from his spine, shaft still humming.

As Camron stepped back, something soft whirred past his ear. Another *thuc* sounded, then another, then another after that. Before Camron's foot fell flat against the rock, the air was filled with a hailstorm of arrows. Wooden shafts skimmed past Camron's cheeks and shoulders. Flight feathers grazed his temples. Steel heads exploded into harrar flesh, finding muscle and ligament and bone. Harras dropped to the ground, eyes bulging, hands clawing at the oak and ashwood shafts. The pack began to break up. Some scattered, others crouched low or crawled behind rocks.

Camron didn't move. He held perfectly still, letting his

hot skin be cooled by the breeze the arrows created. Broc lay flat against the rock. His face was dark with blood. He was breathing, though. Camron didn't take a breath himself until he was sure of that.

Still the arrows kept coming, finding their marks as surely as prodigal sons returning home. More harras fell. They thrashed on the ground at Camron's feet; their features slowly re-forming, their cries becoming lower, more human. Within seconds none were left standing. Scattered, lying low, playing possum, wounded, or dead: Camron didn't know or care. He was so weak, it took all his strength to stop his legs from buckling beneath him.

The hail of arrows tapered off. An order was shouted. Tack jingled. Camron raised his head in time to see a man riding clear of the rocks. A second riderless horse trailed behind. As Camron watched, the man slipped a shortbow into his saddlebag. Then he looked up and smiled.

Ravis of Burano inclined his head. "Gentlemen," he called. "Forgive me, I am a little late."

A snap of his wrist brought a ring of archers into view. Like the harras before them, they appeared from behind rocks and trees. They carried staved longbows taller than themselves. Less than a dozen in all, they held their positions, arrows nocked and ready.

As Ravis drew nearer, Camron saw that he wasn't as cool and unruffled as he appeared from a distance. There was blood on his gloves and sleeve. Sweat dripped from the hair at his temples, and his breath came in quick, shallow bursts. He didn't waste any time. Drawing his sword, he trotted the spare horse through the ring of downed harras. As soon as he reached the crop of rock where Camron stood, he dismounted, crossed to where Broc lay, dragged his body off the ground, and hefted him over the back of the spare horse. That done, he turned to Camron.

Arrows shot through the air, picking off two harras who chose that moment to move.

Ravis looked Camron in the eye. "I would have come before now, only I had business to take care of on the far side of the rocks." His voice was lightly mocking, but his eyes told a different story. They were dark, shining, filled with pain. As he helped Camron onto the back of his horse, Camron saw where a blade had sliced open a gash in his side.

Camron didn't say anything, just closed his eyes, dropped his head against Ravis' shoulder, and waited to be gone from that place.

t took Tessa a while to realize she was awake. She was warm and comfortable in a softly scented cocoon. Pain barked away in the distance like a neighbor's dog: annoying, but not worth making any effort to stop it. In fact, the idea of doing anything other than lying still and thinking of nothing didn't appeal to her at all. It was only when someone *told* her she was awake that she actually started believing it.

"There, there, my dear," came a gentle voice. "You're just coming round. There's nothing to worry about." A little patting followed. Tessa felt some part of her body being touched, but she didn't have a name for it just yet. "Emith, hurry. She's waking."

"She's awake? Thank all four gods. I'll be right there."

Tessa couldn't help but feel a little annoyed. All this talk of waking up was making her feel as if she had to *do* something. Bracing those parts of herself she still didn't have names for, she made a break for the surface. Rolling her neck in the direction the voice had come from, she opened her eyes.

A large meaty hand slapped against an even meatier chest. "Emith! Quickly! Linden flower tea and hot broth."

Tessa's eyes traveled upward past the hand, the chest, and the neck to the face. Mother Emith. *Standing!* The shock of seeing such an unnatural phenomenon had a profound effect on Tessa's brain. Everything snapped into place at once: names of body parts, memories of where she was, how she had got here, and what she had last done and why. She even found her voice.

"Mother Emith, sit down."

Mother Emith looked at Tessa as if she were a kitchen pot that had suddenly decided to talk. The hand descended from her chest and landed, slap, in the middle of Tessa's forehead. "The tea, Emith. The tea!"

"Here it is, Mother." Emith appeared in Tessa's line of vision, looking older than she remembered him. Older and more frail. "Oh, miss, miss. Are you all right? Are you in pain?"

Tessa nodded, even though she knew everything wasn't all right. Not all over. Her head felt heavy and stuffed up as if there were no room for her thoughts. The muscles in her neck ached, and a niggling soreness was working away at her right hand.

"Miss, just lift your head so I can slip this under." Emith held out a pillow. His voice was so gentle, it made Tessa's throat ache. Already, in the back of her stuffed-up mind, some tiny bit of her knew they would soon be parting. She didn't say anything, though, simply did as she was told and tried not to let the pain show on her face.

"Here you are, my dear. Drink up." Mother Emith bent forward with a bowl of steaming liquid. Tessa moved quickly to drink it—more to minimize the time Mother Emith had to spend on her feet than in eagerness for a strange-smelling, scalding drink.

"It's good," Tessa said after swallowing a mouthful. She knew Mother Emith was waiting expectantly to be asked what was in the tea, how it was made, and in what way it would make a person better, but she didn't have the heart for it. Catching Emith's gaze, she tilted her head toward his mother.

Emith nodded. Laying a hand on his mother's arm, he said, "Come, Mother. Come and sit down. I'll turn your chair so it's facing this way."

Mother Emith grumbled a bit, ran her hand over Tessa's brow, made her promise to finish all the tea in the cup, and then let herself be led back to her chair. She moved so slowly, it was painful to watch. Tessa reached out her hand toward her, wanting to touch the soft woolen fabric of her dress before she walked away.

Pain sizzled in Tessa's palm as she straightened out her hand. Although she tried, she couldn't keep herself from inhaling sharply. Her right hand was heavily bandaged. Only her fingertips were visible from beneath a swath of linen strips. Tessa remembered stabbing the vellum with her brush, feeling her palm burn. Letting her hand fall back against the sheet, she tried not to think about all that had happened. It didn't work. Her mind showed her flashing images, like sunlight on a lake, of the pattern she had drawn and the things she had seen.

Tessa drew her body into a tight ball beneath the sheets. It wasn't fair. She had only just woken up, yet already her world was shaping into something she didn't like. She had responsibilities now: of all the things that had happened while she painted the pattern, that one fact was perfectly clear.

She had been brought here to destroy the harras. Stop those who made them what they were. Someone was behind them, turning them into monsters, creating their need for blood, and shaping them into a pack. Tessa had smelled the pigment that pushed them, got a whiff of the man behind the beasts. And he, in turn, had spotted her. That was why one harrar had stopped and looked at her. It was why she was lying here, head aching, palm burned. Someone had seen her and wanted her dead.

Suddenly aware of a lump in her throat, Tessa swallowed hard. It didn't go.

"Have you drunk all your tea, miss?" asked Emith. "It will take away any pain you might be feeling. Help clear your head."

Although she didn't feel like it, Tessa smiled. She doubted if any medicine in the entire city of Bay'Zell could clear her head just then. "Emith, how long have I been asleep?"

"A full day, miss." Having settled his mother in her chair, Emith moved back toward Tessa. "You collapsed yesterday morning and slept through the day and night."

Tessa nodded. Her hand felt as if it were on fire. "You pulled me away from the table, didn't you? And tore the brush from my hand?"

Emith didn't answer her question. Pulling up a stool to sit beside her, he said, "It's a bad burn, miss. More your palm than your fingers. Mother washed it and put pot-marigold paste on the worst part, but I doubt if you'll be scribing again for a good few weeks . . . and there might be a scar."

"Ssh, Emith," said his mother. "Just keep it bound up for now, my dear. I'll clean it again tonight. I don't want to be causing you any more pain just yet. You need to rest. Eat. Emith, has she got that broth?"

"I'll give it to her as soon as she's finished the tea, Mother."

"Be sure you do." With that Mother Emith turned her attention to some vegetables in need of scraping. Tessa wondered if the old lady knew they wanted to talk.

Nursing her hand against her chest, Tessa said to Emith, "What happened yesterday morning? Have you ever seen anything like it before?"

Emith shook his head. He rubbed his temples and then glanced quickly at his mother before speaking. "I'm so sorry, miss. I should have pulled you away before I did. I wasn't thinking. I've heard stories of scribes being burned as they worked, but I didn't know whether they were true or not. When I saw you fall forward onto the table I knew something was wrong, so I did the first thing that came to my mind—I pried the brush from your hand and dragged you away. It was all my fault." Emith looked down. "I don't know what Mother and I would do if anything ever happened to you."

As Emith was speaking, Tessa glanced around the kitchen. Soft buttery light filtered through the oiled panels over the windows, and the fire crackled within the hearth, giving off a golden glow. She had come to love this place and the people in it. "It wasn't your fault, Emith," she said at last. "You can't protect me against things you don't know."

Tessa glanced at Emith, anxious to see how he reacted to her words. He was still looking down. His hands were in his lap. When he made no motion to reply, Tessa decided it was best to continue speaking. She needed to say these things to herself just as much as to Emith. "We both know Deveric drew me here for a reason, and now I think I know what that reason is. Only I don't know what to do about it, or even how to start. You've taught me the important things, given me the bones, now I need to go and learn the rest.

"Those five patterns Deveric created were a summons,

and whether I like it or not, he's given me something to do. There are terrible things out there, Emith. Terrible things. I've seen them. And I think I'm meant to fight them, and unless I know what I'm doing, I have a feeling I'll end up getting hurt." Tessa smiled, almost laughed. She felt as if she were saying things a madwoman would say.

Still Emith said nothing. He did not look at her.

Tessa shifted beneath the sheets. Her hand burned. Suddenly she didn't feel like laughing at all. She felt tired, and her body seemed to be growing heavier by the minute. If only she could clear up the stuffiness in her head.

"Deveric kept a part of me locked away," she said, willing Emith to look up at her. "A part that has something to do with scribing, that helps me see through the vellum as if it were glass."

Emith's head came up. His eyes were red. "If my master kept things locked away from you, miss, I'm sure it was to keep you safe."

Tessa nodded. She knew how important it was for Emith to think the best of Deveric. "Yes, judging from what happened yesterday, I think you might be right. I went in blind, drew a pattern without knowing what I was doing and why, and I ended up with this." She raised her bandaged palm toward Emith. Pain made her bite her lip. A long moment passed before she could speak. "I think Deveric knew that what I did would be dangerous, and he didn't want to risk me hurting myself before I was here, in this place, and could be properly taught." Words came from her mouth only a fraction of a second before the ideas formed in her head. It was almost as if her brain were too tied up to work properly, so her tongue was doing the thinking instead.

"I can't teach you any more, can I, miss?" Emith said, not really asking a question at all.

Tessa considered replying several ways, but in the end she said, "No." Camron of Thorn had surely died yesterday, and if she had only known what she was doing, she might have saved him. Things were different now: what she said and did mattered. For the first time in her life she had real responsibilities. People's lives depended on her. She might not like it, and she certainly wasn't prepared for it, but that was the way it was. She was going to have to learn a lot more about a lot of things, and scribing was only the first of them.

Emith glanced over at his mother. When he saw she was resting with her chin against her chest, he said to Tessa, "I don't want you to leave us. Not ever. But you're right; what you are doing *is* dangerous, and I don't think Mother would ever forgive me if I let anything happen to you." Emith's hands were in knots. His voice was very low. Tessa thought he was finished speaking, but after a moment he carried on.

"There is someone who can teach you things I can't. A man in Maribane, on the Anointed Isle. He was a master scribe once. Now——" Emith shook his head. "Now I don't know what he does. He won't have forgotten, though. Nothing the holy fathers could have done would make him forget. He was too great a man for that."

"Brother Avaccus?"

Emith's eyes widened. "Yes, miss. Brother Avaccus."

"I got your mother talking one day," Tessa said quickly, not wanting to leave Emith hanging. "She told me a few things about what you did before you began work with Deveric."

"Brother Avaccus didn't do any of those things the holy fathers accused him of, miss. He was a scholar, he wanted to learn. He drew patterns to gain knowledge, not to draw forth the devil like they said."

Tessa nodded. The need to defend people he cared about was in Emith's blood. He would do no less for her when she was gone. Feeling the lump return to her throat, she said, "Do you think Brother Avaccus will help me?"

"Yes, miss. If he knows that I sent you, he will."

"If he's still alive."

Emith shook his head. "Oh, he's still alive. I'd feel it in the ink if he wasn't."

Tessa looked into Emith's dark blue eyes, and she knew what he said was true. Scribes' assistants obviously had a little magic all their own. "How long will it take to get to the Anointed Isle?"

"Four or five days, usually. The nearest port is Kilgrim. From there you travel overland to Bellhaven and then cross the causeway to the isle."

"Will you make the arrangements for me?" Tessa continued to look into Emith's eyes. "I need to leave as soon as I can."

"You need to rest for a few days, miss. Get your strength back. Your hand wasn't the only thing that was hurt." Emith seemed agitated. His hands buckled in his lap, and his gaze traveled from Tessa, to the floor, to his mother, to the window. "The weather at this time of year can be very unpredictable—terrible winds. Hailstorms. You haven't even got a cloak. And a young woman shouldn't travel anywhere on her own without a comp—"

Tessa cut him short. "Will you make the arrangements?"

Even though Emith only let out a gentle sigh, his whole body seemed to deflate; his chest shrank inward and his shoulder slumped. His gaze fell to the floor. "Yes, miss. I'll make the arrangements."

Although she had got what she wanted, Tessa felt no satisfaction. She didn't want to go, leave this place and these people. She didn't want to cause them pain. Reaching out with her left hand, she brushed Emith's arm. "Thank you," she said softly. "Thank you."

Emith patted her hand. He smiled, but it wasn't convincing. "I'll go down to the harbor first thing tomorrow morning. See about securing passage." With that he stood, walked across the room, drew his mother's shawl around her shoulders, picked up his lunular knife from the bucket near the sink, and let himself out into the yard. He didn't slam the door, but Tessa felt as if he had.

She shouldn't have been so hard on him, should have said things differently, explained things better. Been kinder. More like . . . What? Her old self? Surely the old Tessa McCamfrey would have handled it even worse. Or would she? Tessa didn't know the answer. Head hurting, she drew her hand up to massage her aching temples. Forgetting about the burn, she used her right hand instead of her left. The movement caused pain to tear along her arm. She closed her eyes, held her breath until it was gone.

Apples, chestnuts, and onions roasted on the fire. Although every man present had meat in his saddlebag, none had the stomach for it.

It was getting dark. A breeze cut from the east, from the mountains and the passes that marked the Garizon-Rhaize border. There was no moon. A few bright stars twinkled close to the horizon, but a bank of clouds was sweeping across the sky and soon there would be nothing but darkness left.

No one spoke. They huddled around the fire, though in truth the night was not that cold, and drank heavily from pewter flasks that passed from hand to hand as silently and fluidly as whispers from ear to ear. By unspoken agreement the fire had been built both broad and tall. Every man had helped collect wood for it. Every man who could walk, that was.

Ravis looked from man to man. Mercenaries sat next to knights, archers sat next to noblemen, their faces all looking the same in the warm glow of firelight. Fear could be seen in the hollows beneath their eyes and the lines leading down to their mouths. The rational part of their brains told them the harras would not come after them, but it didn't stop them from being afraid. Ravis had been on scores of campaigns in a dozen different countries, been set against the odds and natural wisdom more times than he cared to recount, yet he'd never seen anything to match what had happened yesterday at dawn. The men were right to be afraid. *He* was afraid himself. The harras were not creatures of God.

Glancing through the flames and rippling air, Ravis picked out Camron's form on the far side of the fire. He was tending to Broc of Lomis. The man had lost a lot of blood yesterday, and Ravis didn't know if he would survive another night. Yet Camron seemed determined that he would. And if time spent and care given counted for anything, then there was a chance Broc might live to see dawn.

Camron, as if aware someone was looking at him, turned to meet Ravis' gaze. The two looked at each other for a long moment, and then Ravis nodded once, handed his flask to the man next to him, stood up, and made his way around the fire. He and Camron had things they needed to talk about, and although Ravis would have liked nothing more than to get drunk with the troop just then, he knew that he would better serve his men by staying sober and keeping watch. There were not many things in life that mattered to him, but the responsibility of having a troop under his command was one thing he never took lightly.

"Is Broc sleeping?" Ravis asked as he approached.

Camron nodded. "I hope so."

Ravis thought Camron was in need of sleep himself; his skin was gray and blotchy, his neck was shining with sweat, and wounds on his hand and leg had reopened and fresh blood was soaking the bandages. Frowning, Ravis said, "Let's go and sit by those trees over there. I need to rest my legs."

Camron glanced down at Broc's motionless form. "I don't want to go far."

They settled on a patch of grass a short distance from where the wounded lay. Camp had been made on the high slope of an east-facing meadow—no man trusted valleys after yesterday—and even though it meant the troop was more exposed, it suited Ravis just fine. The first sign of movement from the east and they could up camp and withdraw to the west within minutes. They would not wait around for a fight. Luck had been with them yesterday morning. It would not be so again.

"Do you think the fire is a good idea?" Camron asked, wincing as he lowered his body onto the ground.

Ravis shrugged. "It's a fine fire. The men need it."

"No. I mean do you think it will draw the harras to us?"

"If Izgard's looking for us, then yes, the fire will give our position away, but I don't think he'll come after us tonight."

"Why are you spending so much time looking over your shoulder, then?" Camron pressed his fist into the wound on his thigh. He closed his eyes for a moment. His arm and chest shook, and his breath came in a series of halting rasps. Ravis waited until he took his fist away before he spoke.

"Because I can't predict Izgard's moves as well as I thought I could. He's involved with things I have no knowledge or experience of. I don't know the game anymore. And that makes me nervous."

"You appeared to know the game well enough yesterday at dawn."

Ravis bit on his scar. While his teeth raked over the rough

tissue of knitted flesh, he reminded himself that Camron of Thorn was a wounded man and that he must have gone through hell yesterday fighting the harras in the Valley of Broken Stones. Of the twelve men who entered the rocks, only two got out alive. All bodies had been left behind. Ravis didn't want to think of what had become of them.

Taking a deep breath, he said, "I didn't know what the game was yesterday. I guessed it was a trap. From the moment we first heard Thorn had been taken, I had a suspicion that the whole thing—the burnings, the mindless destruction, the mass deaths—was meant to draw us there. Izgard could have taken a hundred villages between the Vorce and the Borals, but he chose to take Thorn. And not only did he take it, but he took it in such a way that the news spread like wildfire. He wanted us there." Ravis looked into Camron's dark gray eyes. "You and me."

Camron ran his hand through his hair. His knuckles still bore the blood from his wound. "You knew all this, yet you didn't try to warn me?"

"Would you have listened?"

That was enough to silence Camron of Thorn for a while. His chin dipped to his chest, and his hands found each other, matching fingers clasping tight. Both men were silent, looking out past the camp and the fire down the slope to the east. The wind picked up, blowing sparks into the air with the smoke, and somewhere on the far side of the camp a man began to sing. It was a low, mellow song that mothers sang while their newborn babies slept, to keep evil spirits at bay.

After a few minutes, Camron spoke. "It was wrong of me to lead the men down into the valley, I know that now. I wanted to die fighting. I thought that somehow, if I fought hard enough and took as many harras down with me as I could, that it would make up for—" He took a breath, closed his eyes. "Not being there the one time I was needed."

As Ravis listened to Camron speaking, he traced a furrow in the soil with his thumb. The cut on his right side pained him, but he'd had worse in his time, and his body had reached the point where it could deal well enough with flesh wounds. In a few weeks' time it would be just another scar. Like the one on his lip.

Looking up at Camron's face, Ravis said, "I didn't hang back to teach you a lesson. I've lived for over thirty years now and still have none to teach. The dangers were obvious—you were being led into an enclosed space ringed with rocks and trees. Someone had to stand by while you went there. I made mistakes myself. Men died because I didn't get there soon enough. And for all my cleverness and forward planning, I never imagined Izgard would send a force such as he did."

While he spoke, Ravis was aware that Camron was watching him closely. Even with all the bruises and lesions on his face, the Rhaize nobleman looked very young, and Ravis found himself envying that.

Slowly Camron began to shake his head. "I shouldn't have done it. Shouldn't have led those men into the rocks. Everything I've done since my father's death has been a mistake."

Ravis slapped his tunic for his flask before realizing he had given it to the man sitting next to him around the campfire. With no drink to offer as comfort, he was forced to speak instead. "Strong emotions breed mistakes. They create them. There's not one man here tonight who hasn't done something in anger or rage that he didn't later regret."

Camron tilted back his head and looked at the night sky. "And what about you? Have you made mistakes?"

Ravis made a hard sound in his throat. "Me more than any man."

"And how do you live with yourself?"

"You move on. Always on."

Still looking at the sky, Camron nodded. The clouds had long since covered the stars, but strangely enough the night seemed better for it. Smaller. More comprehensible.

After a minute or so, Camron said, "So, what do we do now?"

"We make plans. Move forward. Try to understand what happened and why."

"Well, if you're right about the whole thing being a lure from the start, then that means Izgard now wants me dead."

Ravis smiled. "You're in good company."

Camron managed half a smile himself. "Would you say Izgard knows you and I are collaborating?"

"Say it! I can guarantee it. And not only that, I can tell you the name of the man who told him."

"Marcel of Vailing?"

Ravis nodded. Camron was catching on just fine. "Marcel would sell his own mother's soul for a handful of promissory notes and a bankable bill of sale."

"How much do you think he knows?"

"Enough to be dangerous." Ravis shrugged. "Marcel isn't the real threat here, though. Izgard is. If he's not stopped soon, he *will* make it to Bay'Zell. You've fought against the harras, you know what they're like. Do you really think Rhaize knights are capable of putting up a feasible resistance?"

"But the longbows. You shot the harras down. You—"

Ravis cut Camron short. "First of all, the Rhaize army has no longbowsmen. The longbow isn't like a sword or a pike—you can't just pick it up, have a few lessons, perform a few drills, and then expect to know how to use it. A good longbowsmen is *grown* into his bow. In Maribane they start training early; they take young boys who are at an age where they still hate girls and thrust a bow with a thirty-pound pull in their hands. When the boys have learned to shoot with them, and their muscles and reaches have developed, they give them a forty-pound bow, then a fifty-pound one, then a sixty-pound one after that. And they keep doing it until some ten years later they have a full-grown man on their hands, whose body has been shaped *for* and *by* the bow, and who's capable of drawing a longbow with a hundred-and-fifty-pound pull and shooting arrows as heavy as your fist to targets at over four hundred paces."

Camron went to speak, but Ravis didn't give him the chance.

"Second of all, we were lucky in the valley. Nothing more. Izgard failed to back up his harras with archers—why, I don't know. But more important than that, he hadn't counted on us having any. The harras were taken by surprise. They weren't expecting any real resistance. They saw a few of their own go down, and they got scared. They won't be next time. Next time they'll be prepared. Whatever or whoever is behind them will see to that."

Ravis saw Camron's expression change as he spoke. Too bad. He still wasn't finished yet.

"The harras weren't mounted. They were using long-knives. They were equipped purely for close combat against foot soldiers—that was why Izgard lured you into the rocks, that's what he planned for. But don't think for one minute he won't plan something entirely different when he meets a fully mounted army on the field. Izgard knows war, and he won't join a battle lightly."

As the last of Ravis' words rang off his tongue, they seemed to hang in the air like the chime of a bell, resonating long past their saying.

Camron sat in silence, head hung low, right hand skimming the bloody bandage on his left. The wind blew across his face, lifting his collar and tugging his hair away from his forehead. Ravis knew what he said sounded harsh, but he couldn't see anything to be gained from speaking otherwise. Things had gone too far for smooth words softly spoken. Izgard of Garizon had seen to that.

When minutes passed without Camron saying anything, however, Ravis began to wonder if he had said too much. Sometimes he took pleasure in presenting the worst side of things—he couldn't stop himself.

"There are things we can do, though," he said, tearing the sleeve from his tunic and offering it to Camron. Blood from his leg wound had soaked right through the bandage. "Actions we can take."

Camron looked up at Ravis. His gray eyes, which had seemed so dark earlier, suddenly seemed light. Silver almost. After a moment, he reached out and took the length of sleeve. "What can we do?"

Ravis felt unaccountably pleased that Camron had taken the cloth, and when he spoke it showed in his voice. "First thing tomorrow morning we send the Istanian scouts back home. They have the fastest horses of any man amongst us and they can be in Bay'Lis and on their way to Mizerico before we reach Bay'Zell."

"And what's in Mizerico?"

"The best longbowsmen to be had outside of Maribane. I

did a commission for the Lectur there a few years back—he'll send me a company if he's asked nicely enough and his palms are well greased enough. Draft him a letter promising him payment in full for his inconvenience plus a suitably sparkling bauble for the real power in Mizerico—his wife—and within a month or so we should be in command of a hundred-plus archers."

Camron nodded. Ravis thought he might smile, but he didn't. Instead he thought for a moment and said, "And what do you and I do?"

Ravis took a breath, looked north. He was getting tired and the knife wound in his ribs was beginning to bother him. Some of the harras had unclean blades—they lined their scabbards with unwashed pigs' intestines and worse—and he was beginning to think the cut might be infected. He would have to deal with that later. For now he had a difficult question to answer.

Planting his fists on the ground and levering his weight forward, he said, "We go our separate ways from here. You need to go to Mir'Lor, force the Sire to meet with you, tell him what you've seen the harras do. Warn him. Let him know what sort of enemy he'll be fighting. Get him to recruit foot soldiers and archers—crossbowmen, longbowmen, shortbowsmen—anyone he can get his hands on quickly. Make him see that unless he meets Izgard on equal footing his army will be destroyed."

Camron nodded so slowly, it hardly looked like a nod at all. "Why me?" he said, his voice low and difficult to read. "Why not you? I haven't been to court in five years—not since my father and the Sire disagreed over Izgard of Alberach. My father advised the Sire to watch him closely; to send emissaries, make overtures of friendship, minimize the chance of war. The Sire wasn't interested. He couldn't see why he, the Sire of Rhaize, should consider a rogue Garizon nobleman a threat."

Ravis caught and held Camron's gaze. "You are the only one who can do this. The Sire would never accept the word of a Drokho mercenary. He'll listen to you, though. Past disagreements count for little. You're the son of Berick of Thorn, sole survivor of one of the oldest and noblest families in the country, joined by blood to the Garizon throne: he'll *have* to see you. And if you're direct enough, he'll take heed.

"You go to Mir'Lor, take the troop with you and put the fear of God into the Sire of Rhaize."

Camron had gone back to pressing the wound in his leg with his fist. He didn't look young anymore. The pain in his eyes aged him. "And you? What will you do?"

"I've got to find out what's behind the harras." For some reason Ravis found himself whispering. "They aren't turning *themselves* into monsters—someone is doing that for them, and unless I find out what or who is behind them, then Rhaize isn't just going to lose the coming war, it's going to be annihilated. Thorn was just the start. Izgard wants land. Only land. He's not interested in people, families, farmhouses. He's promised his warlords territory, and he'll do anything to get it. The harras are perfect for him; they go in, kill everything in sight, clear the land before it's occupied.

"Unless we do something about them, every time we meet Izgard on the field, the odds will be in his favor. The harras terrify men. They stop them from thinking or acting rationally. They force them to make mistakes."

"And how do you intend to find out more about them?" Camron's voice was subdued.

Ravis could tell he didn't want to go to Mir'Lor. He would go, though. Two days ago he would not have even considered it. But he was a different man now. The battle in the Valley of Broken Stones had changed him. And Ravis didn't know if that was a good or a bad thing, he just knew he could use it to his advantage.

"Remember the woman who was with me in Marcel's cellar?"

"The girl whose hair is one shade short of red?"

"Yes, Tessa. I think she has something to do with this. She draws patterns, and I once saw Izgard's scribe drawing similar things. I didn't think much about it then, but it's been a lot on my mind these past weeks. I've got to go back to Bay'Zell, talk to Tessa, find out just what she knows and how she got here."

Camron raised an eyebrow. "And make sure she's safe?"

"Yes." Ravis saw no point in denying it. "I don't want her

to come to any harm." He shrugged. "I may take her to Maribane, to the Anointed Isle. That's where Deveric and Izgard's scribe were trained."

Sucking in his cheeks, Camron said, "So, you're asking me to take the men and head to Mir'Lor, while you sail to Maribane and search for answers?" He did not wait for a reply. "How do I know I can trust you? And that you won't just ride away and I'll never see you again?"

"Because I give you my word."

Camron didn't blink. For a long moment he just stared into Ravis' eyes. The singing had long stopped and the wind had died down, leaving the east-facing slope perfectly quiet. After what seemed to Ravis to be an eternity, the muscles in Camron's throat started working. Still looking at Ravis, he swallowed hard and said, "That is guarantee enough for me."

Until that moment Ravis had been unaware he was holding his breath. He exhaled deeply, and as he did so a small trace of bitterness escaped with the breath. No one had trusted him in so long, he had forgotten what it felt like. Good. It felt good.

Not wanting to give away his emotions just then, Ravis pulled himself to his feet. Offering a hand to Camron, he said, "We'll arrange to meet in three weeks' time in Castle Bess."

Even with Ravis' help it took Camron a few moments to rise. Knife wounds crossed his back, arms, and legs. "In three weeks' time, then," he echoed.

Ravis nodded and made his way back to the camp. He needed to find a quill and ink. There was a certain dark-haired beauty in Mizerico who was owed an apology, and right now for some reason he felt like offering one. The Istanian scouts could deliver it along the way.

In the darkness the girl's flesh felt so frail that Izgard could imagine he was touching the bone beneath. That was what excited him: the feeling that he was touching something deep, personal, *inside*. Something never touched by any man before.

The girl was emaciated. Starved. Izgard had spotted her along the roadside, begging for food. Bones shone white through her skin, and her eyes had receded so far back in their sockets, they hardly seemed like eyes at all. More like two coals burning at the bottom of a deep pit. Dressed in a tattered red cloak, mud caking her face like dried blood, Izgard had ordered his men to pick her up.

The girl slapped her hands on either side of him as he entered her. Even that touch thrilled him. Dry palms. Eager. There was so little meat left in her thumb and finger pads, Izgard could imagine he was being clutched by a corpse. His breaths were ragged, short. The girl hardly seemed to breathe at all, as if over time her skeletal body had grown accustomed to surviving without air as well as food.

Izgard's eyes were open. The darkness in his private tent was complete, and he could see nothing before or under him. It was the way he wanted it. If the lamp was lit, he would have to look at the girl's face, and that wasn't what he was interested in at all.

Saliva rolling from his tongue, Izgard reached back to touch the girl's hand. His finger found the smooth, parchment-like skin of her wrists and then moved down over the back of her hand, fingertips trailing over the protruding veins—counting, caressing, feeling the blood pump through. More excited than ever, he moved his fingers down along her thumb. The skin stretched over the knuckle was the thinnest yet, and Izgard lingered long over the joint. When finally he'd had his fill of that, he edged his hand down to the hard skin above the girl's fingernail and then to the nail itself.

Something jagged pricked against his fingertip.

Izgard inhaled sharply.

Although some distant part of him knew it was only a rough edge of the girl's thumbnail, another greater, deeper part told him it was a thorn on the Barbed Coil. In the darkness they felt like one and the same.

Izgard froze. He could feel nothing other than the point digging into his flesh. The darkness in the tent thickened. He was aware of it pushing against his back, settling in his lungs, and coating his thoughts like molasses rolled around a glass.

The Coil shone in his mind's eye as its surrogate barb pricked his flesh. He saw his own face reflected in the twisting bands of gold. Other images, shifting so quickly that individual portions could not be recognized, flashed within the metal like salt crystals thrown on a flame. Even though Izgard was unable to name the parts, the whole was perfectly clear.

He licked his lips. The Coil was showing him images of war.

Suddenly they were no longer before his eyes. They were in his head, spinning, thrashing, cutting a path to his core: blood, sliced flesh, the hollow O's of opened mouths and the immaculate glint of steel. Izgard saw things he didn't understand and many that he did. The images scorched the raw tissue of his mind, branding him with the mark of the Coil and destroying whatever matter lay beneath. When finally the visions slowed, and all ideas obstructing their path had been converted or consumed, one final image lingered within the smoking embers of his thoughts.

He, himself, standing in the great western harbor of Bay'Zell, master of the trade routes to the west, far east, and lower south, master of Rhaize, the Bay of Plenty, and the Gulf that lay beyond.

And all that was just the start.

Izgard pulled away from the girl and struggled to his feet. The girl clutched at him, but he didn't even acknowledge her. Her emaciated body repulsed him now. Desire had left his body to nestle solely within his mind. He wanted what the Barbed Coil showed him. All of it. He wanted the glory of victories won, power taken, and acclaim given freely by land barons and lords. Yet he wanted the dark side too: rotting carcasses, festering wounds, muck and dirt and flies.

Heart pumping, palms damp, Izgard moved around the darkened tent, pulling on his clothes. He hadn't done enough. He should have pushed harder, fought longer, not stopped for either breath or sleep. If he wasn't careful, everything could be lost. Everything. He needed to talk to his scribe.

Cool night air buffeted his body as he stepped out into the camp. The girl knew her place and didn't call after him. And he might spare her just for that.

Guards snapped to attention as he made his way through the ordered lines of tents. Situated a day's ride east of Thorn in the foothills where the Borals rose to join the Vorce, the camp formed the heart of territory gained. No man who was not a Garizon by blood or leaning now lived within a circumference of thirteen leagues. It was the harras' doing. They killed for the sake of it, because they needed to see blood and smell fear, and because any breath that was not a man's last burned like poison in their lungs.

With a few exceptions, Izgard was well content with their services. They cleared the land of all impurities, made it fit for occupation by Garizon sons and lords.

Ederius' tent was in darkness. As Izgard had brought no torch with him, he slipped through the slit unannounced. The scribe was sleeping. His dark form lay curled up on the ground, knees raised close to his chest. Even in the grainy quarter-light, Izgard could tell he was shivering. The blanket covering his chest rose and fell in tiny, shallow bursts. The battle yesterday morning had left him weak. He had been in the care of the physicians ever since.

Izgard knelt by the sleeping scribe. Reaching over, he covered Ederius' face with his hands, blocking his nose and mouth. A second passed while Ederius' lungs tried to suck in air, then the scribe's body convulsed and his eyes flew open. Izgard pressed harder, keeping the man down.

"Awake now, I see," he murmured.

The scribe blinked furiously. The whites of his eyes were very bright. His hands jerked by his side and the muscles in his jaw worked a silent cry.

Still Izgard did not allow him to breathe. "Look at me," he hissed, bringing his face within a thumb length of the scribe's. "Look at the man who wears the Coil."

Panicking, Ederius tried to struggle free. His chest thrashed from side to side and his heels kicked the ground, but he was weak and lack of air was taking its toll. After a few seconds the scribe settled, his hands falling limp and his back lying fast against the ground.

Izgard nodded. His palm was pressed so hard against the scribe's mouth, he could feel the curve of his teeth. "Am I your master, Ederius?" he whispered. "Am I?"

Ederius' eyes were bulging. His lungs sucked his chest into a cavity as he managed something close to a nod.

"And you have sworn a sacred oath to me?"

Again Ederius nodded, the action more in his eyes than his face.

"And if there were any dangers, you would—you *will*—tell me?"

The scribe's body convulsed. His rib cage beat against the blanket, and his shoulders and arms began to twitch. Tendons rising like cords in his throat, he forced himself to nod.

Feeling a bite of misgiving, Izgard withdrew his hand.

Ederius bolted forward, coughing, choking, hands out, chest pumping wildly. Tears spilled from his eyes.

Watching him, Izgard let out a long breath. The air exhaled from his lungs was white. "There, Ederius," he said, turning away to hide his confusion. "It's all over now."

Wheezing noises that may or may not have been words escaped from Ederius' lips.

Glancing around the tent, Izgard searched for a jug of water. Even though it was still dark, he could see objects clearly and, spotting a flask sitting on top of a chest, he grabbed it in his fist. "Drink this," he said, flicking off the cap and handing it to Ederius. Judging from the smell, it was spirits, not water.

Ederius took the flask, drank, swallowed hard, and drank some more. His body was still jerking and twitching, not quite in his control.

As he watched the scribe drink, Izgard felt his anger returning. The man was weak. *Weak.* He leaned forward. "What happened during the battle yesterday? Why did my harras fail to kill Camron of Thorn and Ravis of Burano?"

"Archers, my lord." Ederius forced the words out between coughs. "Surely you already know that. The harras must have returned to the camp by now." The scribe's words were halting. Spittle frothed from his mouth as he spoke.

Izgard went to step back, away from the scribe and the temptation to strike him, but he caught himself. He was king. He wanted answers, and he was going to get them. "Why did the harras back off? Why didn't you force them to keep fighting regardless of the archers and their arrows?"

Ederius rubbed his hand over his face. He didn't speak.

"You have promised me answers, scribe," Izgard reminded him.

Hand shooting to his heart, Ederius cried, "Because I was too weak to do anything more. Someone—a girl—interfered with my illumination. I was forced to use all my strength to stop her. She was dangerous, untrained—" The scribe shuddered. "There was no telling what she would have done if she had been allowed to carry on."

"A girl." Izgard ran his fingertips over the skin on his own throat. "Who is she? Why was she trying to interfere with my plans?"

"I have seen her face once before." Ederius took long, deep breaths to still his body. "She was with Ravis of Burano the night the harras attacked him on the bridge."

Izgard beat his fist against his thigh. "Ravis of Burano! Ravis of Burano! Always his name. His filthy, sordid name. What is this girl to him? What is he involved in now?"

Drawing the blanket up around his body, Ederius backed into the corner of the tent. "The girl is a scribe, sire. A raw beginner. But she does have knowledge of the patterns, and she was working to stop the harras."

"Did you destroy her?"

"I tried."

Izgard caught the end of the blanket and yanked it away from the scribe. "*Tried* is not what I want to hear. Is she dead or isn't she?"

Ederius shook his head. Without the blanket he was naked except for a linen wrap around his hips. "I don't think so. Burned, certainly, but not dead."

"That's not enough. She must be sought out and destroyed. You say this girl is untrained, yet she diverted your attention, your resources, stopped you from doing your job. She is a threat to the harras, to myself, and to the Coil, and she cannot be allowed to carry on." As Izgard spoke, the vision of the crown beat in his temples like a pulse. He felt excited, anxious, eager for action. "Where is she now? Do you know?"

Ederius was shivering. His knees were pulled up to his chest. "Bay'Zell, perhaps. I'm not sure. I saw a kitchen and her face, nothing more."

Izgard nodded. "Bay'Zell is a good place to start. I will send a pack of harras there tonight." Throwing the blanket back to Ederius, he said, "Cover yourself up, old man. I don't want you catching your death."

"There may be patterns I can use to search for her, sire. I shall look through my books at first light."

"Look through them now, old man," Izgard said, stepping out of the tent. "Within minutes I will have this camp lit up like day. I am here for war and war alone, and I will not rest, sleep, or pause until all my enemies are defeated and I name myself master of Bay'Zell."

EIGHTEEN

Angeline sat very gingerly on her horse, choosing her path with almost fanatical care, intent on preventing her innards from shattering like glass. Every so often Gerta would look over at her from high atop her huge old nag, and at such times it took all Angeline's powers of determination to stop herself from blushing. Sometimes she dug her fingernails into her thigh, but even that didn't work all the time. These days *everything* made her blush.

They were traveling up through the Vorce Mountains toward the Rhaize border and the pass. Izgard had called for her presence at the camp, so a small party had been assembled—her, Gerta, Snowy, a dozen armed men, and a trail cook—and they had left the morning after the messenger from Rhaize had arrived. Angeline had been a little surprised by how fast it had all happened, and only now was the whole thing beginning to sink in.

She was on her way to an armed camp. To war.

Angeline frowned, not liking that thought very much, and reached down to pet Snowy.

Snowy was packaged up in her right-side saddlebag and was about as miserable as a no-good dog could be. He looked up at Angeline with his big dark eyes, cocked his head in puzzlement, and squeaked like a mouse.

Snowy down. Snowy down.

Angeline thought he might be suffering from riding sickness and would have dearly liked to stop and nurse him, but although she knew she was officially head of the party and so could call a stop whenever she liked, she didn't dare do it. What if she gave an order and everyone ignored it? What if the armed guards, all twelve of them, started laughing at her voice? When Father was alive all she had to do was go and tell him what she wanted and seconds later he would boom out orders in his deep, rumbling baritone. No one ever ignored him, not even Izgard himself.

Feeling sad all of a sudden, Angeline tickled the silky bits behind Snowy's ears. "There, there, Snowy," she said. "We'll just have to make the best of it, you and me."

The truth was she wasn't feeling much better than Snowy. And even the excitement of being properly outside on a beautiful, blue-skied, flower-scented day in the mountains wasn't nearly enough to take her mind off feeling sick. It didn't help that Gerta was watching her like a mother hen, making her feel about as guilty as a girl who had lied and deceived *could* feel, and that the path they were riding along was bumpier than the crust on one of Dham Fitzil's apple-and-hazelnut pies.

Apples and hazelnuts. Just the thought of them made Angeline feel queasy. In fact, the idea of any food whatsoever, even her favorite—strawberries and clotted cream—made her stomach turn, and not at all silently at that. Gurgling, watery noises kept emanating from deep within her belly. Distressed, Angeline let out a faint sigh. To top it all off she was starting to feel flushed again!

"Are you feeling well, my lady?" called Gerta from across the path. Minus her usual grooming paraphernalia and mouthful of pins, Gerta looked ill at ease, like a fiddler without a bow.

"I'm fine, Gerta. Just a little"—Angeline glanced around for inspiration: she saw high cliffs of gray stone, small patchwork meadows filled with flowers, odd little bushes that even odder little birds flew out of, and the sun, large and yellow, hanging in a cloudless sky—"hot. That's it. I'm just a little hot."

"Well, we'd better stop for a while, then." Gerta swiveled around in her saddle. "All halt! All halt! Tents up! Her Highness needs to rest in the shade for a while. You over there. Yes, you with the polearm, run and find some cool stream water for the lady. And you with the saddlebags, unroll one of the best blankets and lay it on the ground. Now! Not when you've finished inspecting the dirt under your fingernails."

Watching Gerta in action, Angeline felt a mixture of guilt

and relief. She greatly admired the way Gerta made everyone do what she wanted when she wanted and was extremely grateful for the chance to rest a while, but she couldn't help feeling bad all the same. Gerta cared for her, truly cared, like Snowy did, like Father had, yet here she was keeping up a terrible deception.

Frowning, Angeline slid off her horse. She felt very queasy, and not even holding Snowy tight could make her feel better. If it was just guilt that was making her feel ill, she could probably cope with it, but she knew in her heart it was much more than that.

She was really, truly pregnant. All the symptoms were there: the blushing for no reason, the sickness, the soreness in her breasts, and the absence of womanly bleeding. She was pregnant, yet she couldn't tell anyone. Gerta would be angry that she had been deceived, and Izgard would be furious that she was jeopardizing her unborn child by crossing the mountains on a horse. Why, her innards could shatter at any turn of the path! Everyone would be mad at her. Everyone.

Dropping Snowy to the ground, Angeline sat on a nearby rock and watched as the midday camp took shape. The truth was she wanted this baby very much—much more than she thought she would—and the idea that she might be harming it by riding was so upsetting, it made her chest ache. Father had dreamed of having a grandchild. "A bonny little baby, just like my best girl," he would say. Only now there was no Father, and she was no one's best girl.

She was a bad girl. She had lied, fooled Gerta, and tricked Izgard into sending for her. And for what? To be *out*side? Angeline looked around. The mountains were gray and hazy in the warm air, and dandelion puffs and insects floated past her face. It was a lot prettier than Sern Fortress, but she wasn't going to stay in the mountains, she was going to live in the middle of a warring camp, surrounded by armed men, guarded at all times, pregnant, yet not daring to tell anyone, with Izgard close by, temper ready to boil over like water above a fire if she as much as put a foot out of place.

Angeline shivered despite the heat. She had made a terrible, terrible mess of things.

As always when she was afraid or upset, the first thing

she did was slap her thigh and call for Snowy. The little dog came straight away—he just wasn't his no-good self at the moment. Bending down, Angeline scooped him up in her arms. Fighting off another bout of queasiness, she laid one hand on her stomach and the other on Snowy's neck and whispered, "You and me are all alone in this, Snowy. Just you and me."

"And, miss, here's an extra ten silvers for hiring a horse." Emith handed Tessa a second purse. "There should be a little extra in it for emergencies. Oh, and remember to keep this one in a separate place from the other. And be sure to watch yourself at all times. All times."

Even though Emith had given her the same piece of advice at least a dozen times since breakfast, Tessa nodded. She took the purse—which felt as if it contained at least double the number of coins Emith had stated—and tied it to her belt.

They were standing on the quay, in the shadow of the three-masted vessel that would take Tessa to Maribane. Longshoremen pushed past them, toting barrels, chests, and crates up a series of gangplanks to the ship. Sailors called to each other from high atop the riggings, crying insults, warnings, and instructions. Seagulls shrieked, wood warming in the morning sun creaked, passengers waiting to board chatted in subdued groups on the wharf, and high up on the quarterdeck, a man wearing a turban and chewing on licorice root shouted orders to everyone in sight.

Tessa couldn't really believe she was going. Only five days ago she had wakened in her bed, head sore, palm burned, and asked Emith to find her passage to Maribane. Things in the Emith household had moved quickly after that. Emith, although reluctant at first, had been as good as his word. Better, even. Tessa now had new boots, gloves, a cloak and a dress, a scabbard for Ravis' knife, a leather belt and pouch, and a leather sack for her belongings. Emith had even purchased combs and ribbons for her hair, though granted they were probably his mother's idea, not his own. No one could think of everything quite as emphatically as Mother Emith.

From the safe haven of her chair Mother Emith had directed the whole operation: supplies to be bought, items to be pawned for cash, meat to be dried for travel food, leather sacks to be patched, and tales to be spun to explain why Tessa, as a woman, was traveling alone. Mother Emith was a planning demon: ship schedules, weather reports, local custom, and word of mouth had all been taken into account in the raveling of her grand design.

Tessa herself had been scrubbed, laced in, and primped to the point where she looked "respectable" without appearing too comely. Mother Emith had spoken long and hard about the dangers of catching the eye of a lecherous man while at sea.

"At least you're at an age where everyone will assume you're wed," she had said earlier as she'd pinned up Tessa's hair in a tight, matronly knot. "And be sure to insist that everyone on the ship, most especially the captain, calls you madam, not miss."

Tessa drew a hand over her newly styled hair and smiled. It had been hard to say good-bye. Very hard. Mother Emith had almost, yet not quite, risen from her chair, and she had hugged Tessa so tightly that Tessa thought she might never let go. She did, though, and by the time Tessa was at the door she had already taken up her little knife and begun scraping vegetables for the pot. No matter what happened in a day, there was always supper to be prepared.

Swallowing hard, Tessa swung around to face Emith. He was kneeling, tying the drawstring on her sack, checking that nothing was about to fall out.

"All aboard! Captain says: All aboard!" The man with the turban spat out his licorice root. "We sail within the quarter. All aboard!"

Passengers started gravitating toward the gangplanks, bags in hand, trunks in tow. Tessa counted over a dozen men and women boarding, though according to Mother Emith *Tarrier* was first and foremost a merchant ship, carrying cargo between Kilgrim and Bay'Zell.

"All aboard!" shouted the turban man, looking directly Tessa's way. "All aboard!"

"Here, miss. Here's your pack." Emith handed Tessa her

sack. Out of his normal setting of the kitchen, he looked small and lost.

Just like she felt. Looking into Emith's dark blue eyes, Tessa felt her throat begin to ache. All her life she had loved journeys, loved the excitement of being on her way, of traveling somewhere, anywhere, always to another place. Yet here she was today, finally free of Mother Emith's kitchen, about to embark on a journey to an unknown land, to an island off the island of Maribane, and all she wanted to do was follow Emith home.

She didn't want to go. For the first time in her life she didn't want to walk away.

Tessa let out a quick breath, considered launching herself at Emith, and then decided against it. The affection would just embarrass him. "Take good care of your mother while I'm away. Tell her I said good-bye."

Emith appeared suddenly interested in his sleeve. "I will. I will. If it wasn't for her, I'd—"

"I know. You'd come with me." Tessa tried to smile, found she couldn't so turned it into a lopsided grin.

"All aboard! All aboard!"

"You really should go, miss. Remember to watch yourself at all times. Don't talk to strangers, and always try to stay in the company of other women."

Tessa stared at Emith's sleeve along with him. "I won't forget anything you said. Anything."

The sleeve rose. Tessa felt Emith's hand upon her arm. "Go, miss. May all four gods watch over you, and bring you back to us safe and sound."

Reaching up, Tessa put her left hand over Emith's. She felt so many things just then. New things, like being afraid and not wanting to let go.

"Last call! All aboard!"

Tessa heaved her sack over her shoulder, looked into Emith's face for a moment until he finally met her eye, then turned and walked away. She had a journey to begin.

The sun was warm on her back as she made her way up the gangplank. After seven weeks of being secluded in Mother Emith's kitchen, the throng of noises, people, and smells was overwhelming. Tessa felt as if she'd emerged from a protective cocoon. Funny, but during the time she had spent with Emith and his mother, she had almost forgotten where she was. Now, today, it all came back to her. She was in a strange land, with strange people, an impossibly long way from home.

Without conscious thought, Tessa's hand stole up to the ribbon around her neck, to the ring tucked beneath her bodice. Forgetting to use her left hand instead of her bandaged right, she felt heat scorch across her palm. Wincing, she took the golden band in her fingers, deliberately pressing the barbs into her flesh. The tiny jabs of pain seemed to help.

"Here, missy," called a young, gap-toothed man, reaching out a hand as Tessa's foot landed on the deck of the ship. "Let me help you with that sack."

Remembering all of Emith's advice, Tessa shook her head. "No. It's not heavy. I can carry it myself. And it's not miss, by the way, it's madam."

As she spoke, Tessa felt some of her old strength coming back. She hadn't slept well the past five days. Blisters had erupted along her burned palm, oozing blood and pus, pulling on her skin and cracking open healing flesh. Pain had kept her twisting in her sheets at night. When she did fall asleep, she got little rest. The harrar with gold eyes watched her from the dark edges of her dreams.

The gap-toothed man backed off, and Tessa walked onto the ship. *Tarrier* pitched lightly in the water, reminding her she was no longer on dry land. Pushing past a gaggle of squabbling children and a woman wearing a pointed hat with a veil that barely covered her eyebrows, she made her way to the rails. Her right hand hovered above her sack, while her left lay beneath the shifting folds of her cloak, fingers resting not at all lightly upon the hilt of Ravis' knife.

Emith was easy to spot on the quay. Among a milling, chattering, disheveled mob, he was an island of quiet neatness. He had taken great pains to dress well today, and catching a glimpse of his wine-colored waistcoat beneath his outer coat, Tessa wished she had thought to tell him how very fine he looked. Leaning forward, she waved wildly, determined to catch his eye.

She needn't have gone to such trouble. Emith waved back straight away, as if he had never lost sight of her once.

Seeing his gentle, well-known face lifted up toward her, Tessa felt the soreness come back to her throat.

Tarrier lurched sharply as the lines from the rowing tugs pulled taut across the water and the ship began to feel the pull.

"All hands! All hands!" The turban man stood, bare feet wide apart on the quarterdeck, and began to direct operations. "Anchors up! Hatches down! Lines in!"

Sailors darted from quarterdeck to midships, from the prow to the stern. Knives between their teeth, ropes looped over their shoulders, metal cups filled with wax and grease bobbing at their waists, they moved through the passengers like dancers among statues. Overhead, the masts swayed in the rising breeze, stays humming, sails dropping, rigging wrestling with the weight of swinging booms.

Tessa felt the breeze tugging at her hair, pulling tendrils loose at her temples, ears, and neck. Under her feet, the ship juddered and pitched as it began to move away from the dock. Emith looked up at her from the wharf, his face small and pale. No longer waving, Tessa just watched him, left hand curled fast around the rail.

Suddenly horses' hooves thundered along the quay.

"Make way!" called a voice. "Make way!"

Tessa watched as a horseman blasted through the crowd, dressed in black, crop in hand. People ran screaming from his path. Women fled. Children cried. Seagulls took to the air. Undeterred, the rider kept up his pace, wooden boards splintering beneath him as he drove his horse toward the wharf. Tessa thought he must be mad; he would surely ride himself and his horse straight into the sea!

Then the sunlight caught his face.

Breath hung in Tessa's throat. Her fingertips ground into the rail. It was Ravis.

"Run a plank!" he cried, pulling in his reins, sending the crowd of well-wishers scattering like ants. "As God is my witness, I will not miss this ship."

Tessa glanced down at the gap widening between the ship and the jetty. The sea was the color of mud below. On the main deck, two sailors slid out a plank to bridge the gap. It didn't reach. More sailors came. The plank was retracted to half its length and then all five sailors leaned their weight to the ship's end.

"You're gonna have to jump," shouted the first of them, spitting into his palm. "If ya have the balls for it."

Ravis' horse skittered to a halt. One hand grabbing his saddlebag, the other flinging his crop to the ground, Ravis leapt off the saddle and raced along the wharf. Boards pumped under his feet, his hair pulled loose from its bindings. The tendons on either side of his neck were as white as the gulls he sent flying. Tessa saw his hands ball into fists and his teeth come down on his scar as he tore toward the end of the jetty. Knuckles bristling around the rails, she watched as he reached the final board and launched himself toward the ship.

For a fraction of a second Ravis was nothing more than a dark blur. He ripped through the space between the ship and the jetty like a bolt from a crossbow. A soft rasping sound escaped from Tessa's lips. The sailors waiting on the plank huddled close. Ravis' body seemed to hang in the air for an instant before blasting onto the plank.

Right leg extended, his foot slapped down hard against the wood.

Crack!

The wood split. The outstretched section of the plank dropped beneath Ravis' foot, yet although he fell downward, the momentum of his body kept him moving forward toward the ship. Fists beating air, Ravis whipped his left hand forward, trying to reach the deck. Tessa didn't blink or breathe. Ravis' body was as quick and malleable as mercury. His fingers caught the deck. The sailor who spat into his palm slapped his hand on Ravis' knuckles. A second man gripped his wrist, and a third man went for his arm. Together they hauled in Ravis' body as if it were a catch: arm, shoulder, head, second arm, chest, body, then legs.

Tessa let out a deep breath.

Chest thumping, limbs shaking, Ravis was dragged to his feet by the sailors. He was quick to recover. Very quick. Running a hand through his tangled hair, he turned to face the passengers and crew, who, like Tessa, had been watching from the aft deck. After taking a few long breaths to control himself, he bowed deeply, sweeping around to include everyone on the ship, and said:

"Forgive me, ladies and gentlemen. I had hoped to arrive some ten minutes later, when I really could have put on a show."

A huge cheer went up.

Crewmen banged their cups against the deck, children ran forward, and the sailors who had saved Ravis all slapped him on his back.

Tessa smiled, then, catching Ravis' eye, she laughed. He really did look quite magnificent just then.

"When Mother Emith told me you were sailing to Maribane, I took for the docks straight away." Ravis shrugged. "I may have flattened a few rats underfoot."

He had just come from paying the captain for his passage and was in the process of making himself comfortable in Tessa's cabin. His riding boots, cloak, and saddlebag formed a small pile near the hatch.

The cabin itself was tiny and oddly shaped—like the spaces found under stairs—and was barely long enough for a grown man to lie down in and just high enough for Tessa's hair to snag on the wooden ceiling beams. This close to the hold the air smelled of dried spices going stale between cracks in floorboards and narrow corners missed by the broom. A boxed pallet that seemed to be made mostly from nails, not wood, took up most of the available space. The place was lit by a hanging lantern capped with brass, and as it swung back and forth with the motion of the ship, it drew an arc of light and smoke in the center of the room.

Ravis sat on the pallet, back against the cabin wall, while Tessa knelt on the floor. Up close, he looked pale and tired, and although he tried to hide it, he winced as he moved. Tessa wondered how he had managed the jump from the jetty to the ship, as he was obviously unwell. Even though twenty minutes or more had passed since the jump, his chest was still pumping.

"How far did you ride today?" she asked, not wanting to betray her concern.

"I'm not sure—twenty, thirty leagues." Ravis' dark eyes met hers. "You wouldn't happen to have any berriac in that sack of yours? I drained my own flask a league past Runzy."

Nervous but not sure why, Tessa dragged her sack to her side and began to look through it. Ravis suddenly seemed like a stranger to her. She didn't know him at all. They had spent only one full day together what seemed like a very long time ago. Yet here he was sitting before her, taking up most of the space in the cabin, smelling of sweat and horses and faraway places, having raced through a city to be with her.

Tessa rummaged through the packages in the sack until her fingers brushed against the smooth coolness of a pewter flask. Pulling out the cork stopper, she brought the flask to her nose. Volatile fumes rose up her nostrils, making her blink. "Here," she said, handing the flask to Ravis. "This should help."

Ravis took it from her and drank without pausing to smell or sample. Judging from the tilt of the flask, he drank a good third of its contents before stopping. Wiping his mouth dry with the back of his hand, he said, "I see you still have my knife."

Tessa glanced down at her waist. The knife was not visible beneath her cloak.

Seeing her puzzled expression, Ravis stretched his lips to a smile. "I caught a glimpse of it as you leant over to hand me the flask."

"Do you always watch the people you are with that closely?"

"Always."

Feeling challenged by the self-assured expression on his face, Tessa said, "So what else can you tell me about myself?"

Ravis inclined his head. "Very well, if you insist. You have a bad wound beneath the bandage on your right hand. So bad, in fact, that you had to take the cork from the flask with your left hand instead of your right. You've put on weight since last time I saw you—and, may I say, you look better for it. And despite Mother Emith's attempts to make you appear less attractive by pulling back your hair like a sister in a convent, she has only succeeded in making you more beautiful instead. Any man looking at you now will be forced to look at your eyes, not your hair."

Annoyed with herself, Tessa blushed. She looked down at her hands, unable to meet Ravis' eyes. What had possessed her to ask such a stupid question?

Ravis handed her the flask. "Perhaps you could do with a drink right now?"

Tessa snatched the flask from him. Although she couldn't see whether he was smiling or not, his amusement was evident in his voice.

"And you," he said softly. "What can you say about me?"

Tessa didn't hesitate. "You're in pain, yet you're acting as if there's nothing wrong." Still feeling nervous, she took a hefty slug from the flask.

Ravis watched her for a moment without blinking. When he finally spoke all his former amusement had drained from his voice. "I was wounded a week ago in battle. The tip of the blade was unclean, and the wound has become infected." He brought a hand to rest upon his ribs. "I don't think five days of hard riding has done it much good."

Tessa handed back the flask, suddenly not angry or embarrassed anymore. "Battle? Were you with Camron of Thorn amid the broken stones?"

Ravis looked at Tessa hard and long. He did not take the flask from her. "What do you know of that battle?"

The burn on Tessa's hand flared, sending pain sizzling over her palm and wrist. The ship pitched sharply and the lantern smacked against a ceiling beam, causing the light to dim and black smoke to stream from the wick. Although she wasn't cold, Tessa pulled her cloak close around her shoulders.

"I was there," she said slowly, not wanting Ravis to mistake her meaning in any way. "I saw Camron of Thorn surrounded by the harras. I saw him trying to save the other man's life, and I watched as he tried to keep all those monsters at bay."

"You drew a pattern."

It was not a question, but Tessa nodded all the same.

"Yes. I drew a pattern. And at some point everything began to slip away from me. I could smell the harras. Hear them." She shuddered. The burn throbbed away in her hand. "I kept painting, and it was almost as if I were seeing *through* the parchment. I could see everything clearly: Camron, the harras, their knives, the blood."

Aware that her voice was starting to break up, Tessa cried, "I tried to help him. I just didn't know what to do, didn't know how to start. At one point I thought I was having some effect—the harras began to back away—but then . . ." She shook her head, unable to speak.

"What happened?" Ravis' voice was hard.

"Something came after me. It saw me, knew I was there, and came through the vellum to get me." The pain in Tessa's palm was unbearable, and she rocked back and forth over her hand. "I saw eyes watching me, felt a terrible pressure in my head, and then my hand began to burn." Tessa made a small, helpless gesture with her shoulder. "The next thing I knew I was waking up in Mother Emith's kitchen and a whole day had gone by."

Ravis bit on his scar. "How could you have done something so foolish? Didn't Emith warn you? Didn't you stop to think? You could have been killed. *Killed*. This is not a game we're involved in. The dangers are real. You should have stopped the moment you smelled the harras. Put the brush down and walked away. You should never have tried to interfere. Never."

Tessa was stunned by Ravis' anger. She couldn't understand it. "I'm not a little girl. I knew what I was doing was dangerous, yet what choice did I have? Camron was surrounded by harras. I couldn't leave him there. I had to do something—*anything*. I had to try."

"There was no need for you to risk yourself. I had everything under control." There was something besides anger in Ravis' voice that Tessa couldn't quite name.

Ignoring whatever it was, she cried, "You didn't do too well, though, did you."

"What do you mean?"

"I mean Camron is dead. And if I had known more or

tried harder, he might be on this ship today." As Tessa spoke, she felt herself close to tears. Why was she acting so emotionally? She didn't recognize herself anymore.

"Camron isn't dead." Ravis' voice was only a fraction softer than earlier. "He's alive and on his way to Mir'Lor. I pulled him away from the harras."

The wooden braces in the cabin creaked and strained as Tessa tried to make sense of Ravis' words. The pain in her hand, together with the rocking motion of the ship, was combining to make her feel sick. "You saved him?" she said finally, feeling like a small child who needed everything explained in the simplest terms.

"Yes. Me and a dozen bowmen." Ravis ran a finger along his lip, pausing to linger over his scar. "I held my company back. I knew the whole thing was a trap, yet I didn't know what form that trap would likely take. The last thing I expected to encounter was a troop of harras like the ones you and I met on the bridge."

"Someone is behind them," Tessa said. "I felt them come after me."

Ravis nodded. "I think it's Izgard and his scribe."

"Yes. There was a scribe." Tessa felt her heart beating fast. "Before I blacked out I smelled pigment, and I'm sure it wasn't my own."

"Can you remember anything else?"

Tessa shook her head. She was still trying to accept the fact that Camron of Thorn wasn't dead.

"Think. *Think!*"

"There's nothing else to remember. I was painting a pattern, I saw the harras attack Camron, I tried to help, didn't know what I was doing, and got caught." Tessa's temper was coming back. "That's all there is."

Ravis didn't even blink at her raised voice. Instead he said, "So, whoever it was—Izgard or his scribe—only noticed your presence when you tried to work against them?"

"I can't say for certain. I'm not sure." Seeing another question ready on Ravis' lips, Tessa halted it with one of her own. She didn't like being the one under attack. "You haven't said why you are here yet. Or did you just happen to find yourself in Bay'Zell and thought you'd look me up?"

Ravis' smile was dazzling in the dim, smoky light of the cabin. It changed the mood instantly, warming the very air itself. "I seem to have overstepped my question quota."

Tessa didn't want to be charmed by his smile, yet she couldn't help herself. His dark eyes twinkled with delight, well aware he had accurately pinned down her motives. "Just answer my questions," she said, pleasantly surprised at how serious her voice sounded—that, at least, was still under her control.

Ravis eased himself forward on the pallet. The only sign he was in pain was a slight deepening of the lines around his eyes and a flicker of white tooth biting down on his scar. Details, Tessa thought as he spoke.

"I came to Bay'Zell to find you. To make sure you were safe, and *keep* you safe, and try to find out why you're here." Ravis' voice was low without being a whisper, rough without being harsh. "You're connected to this whole thing in some way—even before you told me you'd seen Camron in the valley, I guessed that. What you've just said proves it.

"I don't know what you're capable of, but I've seen what Izgard's harras can do, and it frightens me. I've never fought men like them before. They're not like normal troops, they have no fear or sense of responsibility. They keep coming and coming and don't stop. I sliced one man open from the throat to the navel, yet he didn't go down—his face didn't even register pain—he just kept on attacking until he was so weak from loss of blood that the knife fell from his hand."

Ravis shivered. His fingers hovered around his rib cage. "When a man's that badly injured his first instinct should be to back off and save himself—not fight until it kills him.

"What frightens me more than anything else, though, is the thought of *thousands* of men like that. I don't know how many harras there were in that valley—probably a lot less than there seemed at the time—but their numbers were nothing compared to what Izgard held in reserve. He has an army of twenty thousand men. *Twenty thousand.* And over a quarter of them have been trained to the point where they can handle weapons, horses, and drills well enough to be called harras. What if Izgard can turn them all into animals? We've seen what can happen when the harras are let loose on a town:

they annihilated Thorn. Women and children, armed men or animals: it made no difference to them. They kill everything that moves."

Ravis gnawed at his scar. "Believe me, if Izgard has got the means to turn his entire army into monsters, he won't hesitate to use them. And if he does, I don't see any way that Rhaize can stand against him."

Kneeling quietly in the corner, Tessa closed her eyes. She knew Ravis had deliberately spoken to frighten her, yet it didn't make any difference. She *was* frightened. Her stomach ached, and a dull pain sounded in her temples. No tinnitus, though. No tinnitus ever again.

Not knowing if that thought made her feel strong or angry, she said, "I know why I'm here. Deveric drew me to Bay'Zell so I can stop the harras."

Ravis looked at her, the lids on his eyes dropping to conceal his thoughts.

Tessa rushed on. "Those patterns Deveric died completing, the ones Emith gave to Marcel of Vailing to keep safe, were a summons. They brought me here. They're a series of five illuminations that Deveric began working on twenty-one years ago, and every time he completed one of them it brought me closer to finding the ring. I've checked out the dates—they match exactly. Deveric has been pulling me along for most of my life, and the day he finished the final pattern was the day I found this." She pulled the ring out from her bodice, held it up toward Ravis. "And when I put it on it brought me here."

Ravis made no move to touch the ring. He held his position on the pallet, looking neither worried nor surprised. He didn't ask where she had come from; instead he said, "And that was the morning I found you by the docks?"

"Yes."

"And a week ago, when you were drawing the pattern and saw Camron fighting the harras, there was a point when you thought you were actually making a difference?"

Tessa nodded. "I'm sure of it. The harras began to slow down, to change. They began to seem more like men, and if I'd known what I was doing, I think I could have stopped them."

"So that's why you're on your way to Maribane? To learn what to do?"

"Yes. Emith can't teach me anything else—he's a scribe's assistant, not a scribe. He only knows so much." Tessa found she no longer minded answering Ravis' questions. Saying these things out loud seemed to make them more comprehensible. It helped that Ravis accepted everything she said without question.

"When I was painting that pattern last week, just before I saw Camron, I found something inside of myself, something buried deep beneath my skin. It was as if a part of me has been hidden away for twenty-one years, and only by coming here did I get to find and use it."

Ravis felt the flesh around his rib cage. He suddenly looked tired and pale. "So you're going to Maribane to find answers as well as advice?"

"Emith has given me the name of a man there, Brother Avaccus, who he thinks might be able to help."

As she spoke, Tessa began rummaging through her sack. Mother Emith had supervised the packing of all sorts of herbs and pastes—"You never can tell what dangers might befall a woman alone on a ship," she had said—and Tessa thought she might be able to find something to help Ravis. The pot-marigold paste she used on her burn might help his wound heal cleanly, and the dried willow bark Mother Emith had included for aches and fever could ease his pain. After opening various small packets wrapped in sedgeweeds and tied with string, Tessa found what she was looking for. The willow bark would have to be boiled in hot water first, but the paste could be used right away.

"Take your shirt off," she said.

Ravis' eyes widened. "So soon? We've only just left dry land."

Tessa saw the smile playing around his lips and frowned. "You know what I mean. I want to take a look at your wound, put some of this on it."

"What is it?"

"Pot-marigold paste."

Ravis nodded. "It might help." After tugging the lacings from his tunic, he dragged it over his head and then pulled off his undershirt. Part of the linen was stuck to the wound, and he winced as it came away.

Tessa drew in her breath. The wound was caked in dried blood, and the skin to either side was bloated. All that she had picked up about healing from listening to Mother Emith in those long afternoons around the fire didn't seem nearly enough to cope with anything like this.

"See that knife in my saddlebag?" Ravis motioned toward his belongings piled by the hatch. "Pull it out and heat the blade over the flame."

Glad that Ravis appeared to know what he was doing, Tessa did as she was told. Once she'd unhooked the lantern from the ceiling hook, she flipped off the brass cap and exposed the flame. The blade blackened as she heated it, and when it started to smoke Ravis said, "Enough. Wipe the edge with the paste and bring it to me."

The ship pitched sharply as Tessa stepped forward, and she was forced to grab the cabin wall to stop herself from falling. Her stomach appeared to move independently of her body, though, and even as she managed to steady her feet, a wave of nausea rippled up from her gut. Biting down on her tongue, she handed Ravis the knife.

Ravis didn't waste a second. He pivoted the handle in his grip, bit down on his scar, and sliced the skin just above his bottom rib. Grimacing, he grabbed his shirt and pressed it into his flesh, forcing out blood and pus. Tessa wasn't normally squeamish about such things, but her stomach wasn't playing fair right then, and the sight of thin yellow fluid oozing from Ravis' wound made her gag.

"Have you got any ginger in that pack of yours?" Ravis asked, wincing as he pushed against a tender spot.

"I'm not sure. I'll check." Tessa was glad for a chance to turn away. "What do you need it for?"

"It's not for me. It's for you. You look pretty green from where I am."

"Green?"

"You've got a bad case of seasickness. Ginger is the best thing for it." Ravis lifted the shirt from the wound, then concealed the blood and fluid stains by rolling it in a ball. "Pass me the rest of the paste and a clean cloth if you have one."

As he tended and bound his wound, Tessa searched for ginger among all of Mother Emith's various packages. "How come you know so much about medicine?" she asked, bringing something yellow and disk shaped to her nose to smell.

"I need to. It's part of my job. If I ship men expecting them to fight on arrival, then I'd better be sure that they don't spend the entire voyage losing their meals and groaning in their bunks. Same with sending troops into battle—you have to know how to deal with the wounded, how to stop bleeding and prevent infection using whatever materials are close at hand. If the word gets round that in your company you leave your wounded to die, then no amount of gold will help you recruit more men."

Having discovered that the yellow disk was in fact dried, sliced ginger, Tessa popped it in her mouth and began chewing on it. What Ravis said made cold business sense, and she found herself strangely disappointed by it. Changing the subject, she said, "How long will your wound take to heal?"

Ravis finished tying a knot around the bandage and then reached for the berriac flask. Although he had given no verbal indication of being in pain while he tended his wound, beads of sweat trickled down from his brow and there was blood on his lip where his tooth had bit through his scar. Having swallowed a mouthful of berriac, he said, "By the time this ship docks in Kilgrim the wound should be dry."

"Three days?"

Ravis laughed. "This old heap of nails will take more than double that to reach Kilgrim."

"But Emith said the voyage took three days."

"It can if you happen to be sailing in an Istanian bark or a Medrani cutter. In an old merchanter like this one we'll be lucky to get there within a week."

Tessa didn't understand. "But it has three masts—"

"And it needs all three of them just to pull its load."

"But Mother Emith chose *Tarrier* because it had the highest masts and broadest sails of any ship leaving for Maribane."

"Emith and his mother are very dear people and they may well know a lot about food and scribing, but neither of them knows the first thing about ships." Ravis made himself comfortable on the pallet. He seemed amused. "You can't judge how fast a ship is by the number of its masts. You look at the shape of its bow, the length of its hull in relation to its beam, and the cut of its riggings. You can hardly tell the bow of *Tarrier* from its stern, and it's nearly as wide as it is long." Smiling, Ravis shook his head. "Not a good sign in a ship you're hoping will get you somewhere fast."

Annoyed at Ravis' smugness, Tessa spat out the ginger into the palm of her hand and said, "I suppose you make it your business to know all about ships so you can move your men into battle faster?"

Ravis shrugged. "Not really. I just pick things up as I go along." He thumped the cork into the flask and let it drop to the floor. Pulling a blanket over his chest, he said, "If you don't mind, I think I'll take a short nap. You need to keep chewing on that ginger, go on deck, breathe in some fresh air, and get accustomed to the motion of the ship. We have a long journey ahead."

Still mad, yet unable to think of anything to do or say about it, Tessa crossed to the hatch. Despite all his sarcasm and bravado, Ravis was genuinely sick and he did need some rest. Feeling an odd mixture of anger and excitement, she made her way up through the ship. Part of her old self came back to her as she climbed the steps to the main deck: her old love of traveling to new places and seeing new things and waiting for adventures to happen.

arcel's cellar was dark, and that was the way he liked it when he was receiving guests. He didn't like to look at the harras. They scared him. He didn't like to smell them, either, but there was nothing to be done about that. After they left he usually burned cinnamon-scented candles to cancel out the smell. It was not the sort of thing a connoisseur like himself would normally do in a wine cellar containing such rare vintages—the aroma of cinnamon might slip through the corks and casts, corrupting the wine beneath—yet he did it anyway. The smell of the harras really did bother him quite badly. He even had to wash it off their gold.

Just one harrar had come through the gate in the back courtyard. Pulling open the wooden trap door, he had let himself in. That was another thing Marcel didn't like, but he knew from experience that if he bolted the door against them, they would simply tear it off. Unannounced guests were one thing, suspicious noises in the early hours of the morning were another thing entirely. There was no worse sin in the banking business than drawing unnecessary attention one's way.

"What do you people want this time?" Marcel asked, the actor in him injecting the words with a measure of impatience and mastery he did not feel. "I've already told you that I do not know where Ravis of Burano is."

The harrar's face was in shadow, and all Marcel could see of him was the whites of his eyes and the glint of saliva on his teeth. This one looked more like a man than the last one, but the smell was still the same.

"We need to find a girl—a woman. The one who was with Ravis of Burano the night we attacked him on the bridge."

The harrar spoke in a whisper, his jaws smacking together as he pronounced the words *woman* and *bridge*.

"The girl's name is Tessa. She's a foreigner. Ravis brought her here that same morning." Marcel edged away from the harrar as he spoke. Sometimes he wondered how he had got himself into all of this. Things had started out simply enough—a nice middleman deal between Izgard of Garizon and Ravis of Burano—but ever since the night Berick of Thorn was murdered at Castle Bess, events had taken a more serious turn. Izgard didn't want him in the middle anymore, he wanted him firmly on his side. And Marcel of Vailing always prided himself on being accommodating to his clients. Most especially those who mattered.

Izgard of Garizon had manpower and might, and it didn't take a clever man to see he'd soon have more. He wanted Bay'Zell and he was likely to get it, and Marcel planned on being one of his sympathizers when he did. Just because power changed hands didn't mean that money had to. Fiscal continuity was what really counted.

"Where is the girl now?" Saliva slapped around the harrar's mouth as he spoke, giving the impression he was chewing on something tough like gristle. His thin-bladed knife was hooked on a strap beneath his armpit, and the leather-bound hilt was stamped with blood.

Averting his eyes from the knife as he spoke, Marcel said, "I have no idea where she is. She could be anywhere." Feeling his voice wasn't doing the best job it could, and knowing how very important it was that the harrar believed he was telling the truth, Marcel threw his hands into the air for extra emphasis. "Anywhere."

The harrar's boots made no noise as he stepped toward Marcel. "We think she is in the city. Where is she likely to be?"

All of Marcel's actor's instincts weren't enough to stop himself from shaking. The harrar might not be one of those mad-dog men now, but he had been, and it wasn't only the smell that still clung to him. Seen close up, the whites of his eyes had a faint golden cast and his gums were a splintered ridge of bone.

Marcel attempted a nonchalant shrug as he cleared his

throat before speaking. "I can't begin to think where the girl might be. I . . . I . . . I just don't know."

"She was in a kitchen. There was a broad table spread with pigments and brushes."

Still recovering from the blow of his voice giving way, Marcel attempted to rally his thoughts. Kitchen? Table? How could he possibly be expected to pin down such things? Why, there must be ten thousand kitchens within the city gates alone!

The harrar leaned close and breathed on Marcel. His breath was moist and gamy, like the mist steaming off mud-banks at night. "I need to know where she is. *Think!*"

Marcel thought; it seemed the wisest thing to do just then. Kitchen . . . table . . . *pigments!* His plump lips pulled tight as he recalled the night he'd dropped off Deveric's illuminations at Mother Emith's house. The table had been loaded with pigments! And neither Emith nor his old bat of a mother could wait to be rid of him. Emith had been about as nervous as an Istanian courier carrying gold, and his mother had all but pushed him out the door. That was it! They were hiding the girl.

Glancing at the harrar, Marcel let his new discovery settle around his body like a fine silk cloak, enjoying the feeling of confidence it gave him. This time when he spoke he didn't bother to clear his throat. He had a feeling his voice would come out well. "There may be one particular place worth a look."

"Where?"

"A small town house on the west side of the city, in the same street as the old milkstone martyry."

The harrar's hand flicked from his waist to his knife. "Who lives there?"

Marcel hesitated, wondering whether to give details about Emith and his elderly mother or leave matters as they were: vague. Surely there was no danger in telling? After all, the harras would probably only put a watch on their door, and what was the harm in that? Indeed, thought Marcel, he could probably get himself into worse trouble by *not* telling. Izgard's men were notorious for ferreting out lies and evasions.

Glancing from the harrar's knife to the shelves of his

own prized vintages, Marcel took an actor's breath and then spoke. He had to think of himself first. Besides, he *was* rather fond of the sound of his own voice.

Tessa was on the foredeck, leaning against the rails, the bridge house behind her and nothing but the sea in front. It was early morning and the sun shone at an oblique angle on the water, creating veins of silvery light on the surface. If she watched the shifting silver threads for long enough, she began to see patterns within their forms. Shapes winked at her, then vanished, like letters written in invisible ink.

Frowning at her own foolishness, Tessa deliberately shifted her gaze to the sky. No clouds, no birds, no banks of lifting mist: the uniform grayness suited her just fine. She didn't want to spot patterns wherever she looked. She wanted to look at the sky and see the sky, not some grand and intricate design.

Pulling her cloak over her arms, she turned from the railings and moved across the deck toward the steps. Her new boots made good, slapping noises against the wood as she walked, and a handful of sailors turned to look at her as she passed. Tessa's frown turned to a smile. She was beginning to feel at home on the ship.

The ginger Ravis had prescribed worked. In fact, everything he had said yesterday worked: the ginger, the walking, the fresh air, and the suggestion that she familiarize herself with her surroundings. The seasickness had gone completely, and barring high storms and spoiled food, it didn't feel as if it were coming back.

Tessa had spent most of yesterday just walking around the deck. It felt good to be outside after so many weeks of staying in. The female passengers on the ship mostly ignored her, either sending disapproving looks her way for daring to walk around deck unaccompanied or glancing nervously at the knife she wore at her waist. Tessa quite enjoyed those glances: it amused her that people thought she might be dangerous.

The male passengers made her thankful for Ravis' presence. They stared at her openly, and Tessa couldn't tell whether they were interested in the contents of her money pouch, her body, or both. Nothing she did—either staring them down, making a show of feeling for her knife, or walking away— could stop them until she mentioned loudly to a passing deckhand that her husband needed an extra pallet belowdecks. No one had bothered her since. Tessa didn't like to think what she might have had to do if Ravis wasn't with her. This world was no place for a woman to be on her own.

When she had finally returned to her cabin she found Ravis still asleep. No food was supplied on board, so she had taken an apple and a wedge of cheese from her sack, eaten a quiet supper, curled up on the second pallet that the deckhand had somehow managed to squeeze into the room, then quickly fallen asleep.

She'd woken early. Hand throbbing, muscles aching, and shivering with cold, she had brushed down her dress, clipped on her cloak, grabbed the chamber pot that had so thoughtfully been supplied with the cabin, relieved herself in the deserted silence of the latrines, then made her way above deck. The few sailors who were up and about gave her no trouble, and after she had bathed and dressed her burn, she'd gone to stand on the deck to watch the sun rise.

The yellow, haze-stretched sun looked just the same as ever. And until Tessa spotted its first rays glowing on the horizon, she hadn't realized how important it was for her to see it. Like the ring around her neck, it was a connection with home. It was the same sun that had shone down on her the day she'd found the security deposit boxes, she was sure of it. When she had first put on the ring in the clearing in the forest, and the world had begun to switch beneath, above, and around her, the sun may have changed angles, but its heat and light remained the same.

Tessa didn't know what it meant, but leaning over the railings, watching the sunlight glance off the waves, she decided it was a good thing. Her old world and her old home couldn't be far away.

"Just in time for breakfast."

Tessa spun around. Ravis was standing in the hatch that

led down to the galley, steaming jug in one hand, a basket filled with bread and pastries in the other. Tessa felt a wave of pleasure seeing him, then told herself she hadn't.

"You will join me, won't you?" Ravis smiled. He looked a lot better for his long sleep. "I haven't just bribed the ship's boy, two scullions, and a very irritable cook to eat all this by myself."

Finding herself smiling along with him, Tessa said, "I thought passengers had to bring their own food on board with them?"

"Well, they do if they want to arrive in Maribane with anything more than holes in their pockets. I could have bought a chainmail vest and matching leg arms for what this stash just cost me." Ravis stepped out of the hatch and onto the deck. "Follow me. I have it on good advice that the aft deck is the place to be at this time of day: quiet, sunny, and sheltered from the worst of the wind."

Ravis walked on ahead of Tessa, assuming she would follow. Tessa hesitated for a moment, wondering whether to protest his assumption by staying put or just go along with him as expected. The old Tessa McCamfrey would certainly have objected. But then, thought Tessa, planting her foot in the space just vacated by Ravis, the old Tessa McCamfrey would have missed out on breakfast.

The aft deck was just as Ravis said it would be: quiet, warm, and sheltered. One crewman was busy adjusting the sails on the aft mast, but if he noticed Ravis and Tessa sitting on the sun-bleached bench by the railings, he didn't show it, just kept winding in the rope and squinting into the wind.

Ravis surprised Tessa by serving her breakfast. He pulled two square cloths from the basket and laid one on her lap, passed her a bread roll and two fat pastries, poured a brimming cup of cider and, after pausing to blow off the steam, handed it to her.

"Is there anyone on the ship you haven't bribed this morning?"

Ravis grinned. "The captain, the first mate, the helmsman and the ship's cat." He poured himself a cup of cider. "Though in fairness, if I could have *found* the cat, I may well have bribed it."

Smiling, Tessa tore a chunk off the bread roll. While she had been spending the morning leaning against the railings, gazing out at sea, Ravis had obviously been busy arranging things belowdecks. "So that's how things are done around here: bribery?"

"Not just bribery, no. I always make it my business to get to know the men around me. You never know when you might need their help."

Tessa nodded. Everything Ravis did seemed to have a calculating edge behind it. "How are you feeling?" she asked, motioning toward his right side. "How is the wound?"

"I won't lie. It's as sore as hell, but the skin's resting flat and I think it's starting to dry out."

"What about Camron? How was he when you left him?" As Tessa spoke, she broke open the pastry, checking to see what was inside. It was some kind of chopped-up sausage filling, so she put it back in the basket and broke open another. She liked to know what sort of meat she was eating.

"Camron was in a poor way. He lost a lot of blood and his legs were cut up badly, but he's young, strong, and where he's going he can be seen to by the best doctors in Rhaize."

Tessa tried to remember the name of the place Ravis had mentioned yesterday in the cabin. "Mir'Lor?"

"Yes." Ravis split open his own pastry, inspected the contents, then handed it to Tessa. "It's where the Sire and his mother, the Countess Lianne, are. Camron's gone to warn them about Izgard's army, tell them what to expect when they meet the harras."

"And will the Sire listen to him?" Tessa examined the pastry Ravis had given her. It contained slices of ham, the meat clearly identifiable, packed between layers of pale yellow cheese. She was quietly impressed. Not only had Ravis been watching what she was doing, he had guessed the reason behind it.

"Sandor is not a stupid man, but he's not a clever one, either. He'll listen if enough people tell him to."

"You know him?"

Ravis shrugged. "I've met him once or twice."

"Why didn't you go to Mir'Lor instead of Camron? If you know the Sire, surely he would listen to you?"

Ravis made a hard sound in his throat. "The Sire of Rhaize would not listen to any warning given by a mercenary."

Tessa looked up from her pastry. Even though the sunlight shone down on his face, Ravis' eyes were the darkest she had ever seen them. His bottom lip moved minutely, and she realized that inside his mouth, he was chewing on his scar.

The sailor who had been adjusting the sails picked that moment to take his leave. After knotting the rope around the lanyard, he stripped off his gloves, spat over his shoulder, and leapt from the masthead to the main deck below.

When Tessa's gaze returned to Ravis, she caught him with his hand around his ribs. He grabbed the fabric of his tunic as soon as he realized she was looking at him; made as if he were straightening his clothes rather than easing his wound. Tessa pretended she hadn't noticed anything and took a deep draft of her cider. Later she would make sure he got some rest.

"What do you think Izgard will do next?" she asked.

"Izgard will push for Bay'Zell as quickly as he can. He won't be pleased that Camron and I are still alive, and he'll be worried about what harm we can do him now that we know what sort of men he's fighting with."

"I think he'll be worried about me, too." As Tessa spoke, she pulled the edges of her cloak together. Her voice sounded unfamiliar to her: serious and firm. "Someone spotted me when I drew the pattern. They looked into my eyes and saw my face. They knew I was trying to work against them."

Ravis nodded slowly. "Then that makes three of us Izgard's after."

Tessa shivered. A sharp spasm of pain coursed up her arm from her burn. She almost expected the sun to slip behind a cloud, but it didn't, just kept shining down on the bench, her cheek, and Ravis' face.

The ship's timbers creaked all around them and the sea had a sound all its own, yet to Tessa everything suddenly seemed too quiet, and she spoke to fill the imagined silence. "What do you know about sorcery?"

Ravis ran a hand through his hair, thinking a moment before answering. "Not much—rumors, hearsay, like everyone else. Sorcery is like the devil: some people think it exists, some don't, and no one wants to talk about it either way. Years, decades, even centuries pass with no mention of it. A thousand years ago in Drokho they burned old women who lived on their own, saying they were witches who had communion with demons. Five hundred years later every Maribane scribe on the continent was hunted down and hanged. The Holy League claimed they summoned devils as they painted."

Ravis shrugged. "The stories still carry to this day. You can walk around any town or village in Rhaize and Drokho and find people who are afraid of scribes, old spinsters, and holy men from the Anointed Isle."

"But there is some truth to the stories, isn't there?" Tessa pushed aside her food as she spoke. She wasn't hungry anymore. "Deveric is proof of that—*I* am."

"I don't think you'll find many people on the Anointed Isle willing to admit it. They're very careful these days about what they do and say. Officially they don't even admit to scribing the old-style patterns anymore. They paint pretty pictures now, with proper subjects: landscapes, portraits of the great holy men, recognizable plants and flowers. Nothing shocking or abstract. Their work is still sought after on the continent, though, and I've seen people pay good money for a manuscript transcribed and illuminated by their holy men."

"Yet Deveric learned how to draw the old-style patterns there," Tessa said, "and so did the man I'm going to see: Brother Avaccus."

Taking a deep draft of cider, she looked out toward the horizon as she listened to Ravis' reply. Even though his voice was pitched low it carried well over the sound of the sea.

"Izgard's scribe was trained there as well. And Izgard himself has exchanged letters with the abbot." Ravis eased himself forward on the bench. "We have to be careful when we get there. Garizon and the Anointed Isle have had a long association with each other. They share secrets, histories, God knows what else. When Hierac himself needed some patterns scribed, he commissioned an Anointed Isle scribe to do the job."

"Hierac?" Tessa felt like a fool. There was so much she didn't know.

"The greatest war king Garizon has ever known. Or the worst, depending on who's writing the history books." Ravis poured cider into Tessa's cup. Tessa was surprised to see it was empty. Had she drunk that much already?

"Hierac was the first man to wear the Barbed Coil," Ravis continued. "Before his reign Garizon was nothing more than a poor duchy surrounded by uncleared forests, with no major waterways to call its own. Hierac built it up field by field, league by league, stream by stream. There was no stopping him. His army was ruthless, his strategies as cool as a blade packed in ice. By the time he died Garizon wasn't just a country. It was an empire."

"Did he take over Bay'Zell?"

"Not just Bay'Zell, but all of Rhaize. The Istanians ruled most of the continent at the time, and Hierac broke their hold on it. He drove them out of Rhaize, Drokho, Medran, Balgedis, and Maribane. He killed millions of people. Millions. Even so, there were many who were glad to see him come—rather a Garizon overlord than an Istanian. At least Garizon was one of their own."

"But I thought Istania was just across the sea from Bay'Zell? Surely that counts as part of the continent?"

"The country does, but its ruling classes don't. They originally came from the distant east, across the stretch of barren land that rings the Gulf. Their language and customs were foreign to the west, and they were cruel in different ways from Hierac and his Garizon warlords."

The bench Ravis and Tessa were sitting on was covered by a fine layer of sea salt, and while Ravis spoke, Tessa found herself tracing a design in the dust. "What happened after Hierac died?"

"Other Garizon kings followed. Some were greater than others, but all pushed for territory: for trade routes, for cold-water ports, then warm-water ports, for passes and rivers and land. Hierac may have been the first of the great Garizon war kings, but he definitely wasn't the last."

As Ravis said the word *last,* Tessa put the final flourish on her pattern in the salt. It was crude, with thick, fingertip-wide lines, yet the design was unmistakable: it was the ring she wore around her neck. She hadn't realized what she was drawing until Ravis stopped speaking. Unnerved, she swept her hand across the pattern, wiping it out. "Let's take a walk around the deck," she said, standing.

If Ravis was surprised at her request, he didn't show it. He merely inclined his head, gathered the breakfast things into the basket, and came to stand at her side. "Lead the way."

Tessa led Ravis down to the main deck. Remembering his injury, she moved slowly, feeling guilty at making him walk. The sea was calm, and the ship hardly rocked at all beneath Tessa's feet. Every passenger and crewman on the ship seemed to be above deck, and children ran yelling along the main deck while sailors worked on the sails and women worked on themselves. The woman with the veil that covered her eyebrows was busy patting powder and something that looked like pig's lard onto her face, and farther up the deck, two old ladies were soaking their feet in barrels of warm, soapy water.

It was turning out to be a fine day. The sky was very blue and the wind was high enough to fill the sails, nothing more. There was no land in sight, and after a while Tessa gave up trying to spot any. It was more interesting watching people's reactions to Ravis.

His presence drew some sort of response from everyone they passed. He had a way of meeting people's eyes, of forcing them to look at him and then holding their gaze until they were obliged to look away. The woman with the veil had sneered at him, but Tessa also noticed that she drew in her breath and smoothed down her dress as he approached. The two old women laughed nervously as he walked by, bobbing their heads and smiling quick, worried smiles.

It was partly his scar, Tessa supposed. It made him look dangerous, hardened. And his coloring was so much darker than the fair-skinned, fair-haired people of Bay'Zell. She could tell they thought he was a foreigner. In fact, she had a feeling that was exactly how Ravis wanted to look. The dark clothing he wore only enhanced his foreignness. He was the one man on the ship dressed in black.

For some reason, as she walked alongside him, Tessa

found herself thinking about the night he'd kissed her. Six weeks ago now, yet it seemed like much longer. She wasn't the same person anymore. Living with Emith and his mother had altered the way she looked at things, made her realize that being tough and self-sufficient wasn't everything.

Ravis hadn't realized that yet. Every glance he gave was designed to say, *I don't want or need your good opinion or respect.*

Feeling an odd mixture of emotions, and remembering the feeling of Ravis' lips against hers, Tessa slipped her hand through his arm.

At last she had managed to surprise him, for he tensed for a moment and turned to look at her face. Tessa didn't know what was showing in her eyes just then, but after a second Ravis made an almost imperceptible movement with his lips and, relaxing slightly, switched his gaze back ahead. During his next few steps, he gradually altered the angle of his arm, making it more comfortable for Tessa to hold.

"What's Drokho like?" she asked, steering him toward the relative calm of the quarterdeck. It was time he sat and rested for a while.

Ravis took a breath but didn't answer. He gazed straight ahead, yet Tessa had a feeling that the last thing he was seeing was the ship. After a moment he took a second breath, held it in his lungs for a long while as if he were trying to draw strength from it, and said, "Drokho is many different things to many different people."

"What's it to you?"

"Home I can never return to."

Tessa felt Ravis' words in her heart. He spoke softly, yet there was no mistaking the pain in his voice. It ran through the words like the scar on his lips: deeply rooted, long shadowed, irrevocable.

Tessa's free hand stole up to the ring around her neck.

Home I can never return to.

She could have said those words herself, yet she knew she would never say them with the same raw longing as Ravis. Her home meant a different thing to her, and although it wasn't easy to admit, she knew that if it wasn't for her parents, she wouldn't have spared her old life a second thought.

This world was becoming her home now. And Emith and his mother, waiting patiently back in Bay'Zell for her to return, were her family.

Unsure what to say next, Tessa gently increased her pressure on Ravis' arm and decided not to speak. She didn't know Ravis at all, couldn't begin to guess what had made him so bitter.

Ravis kept walking until they reached the end of the quarterdeck. Turning so his back rested against the railing and he could look Tessa in the face, he said, "What? No more questions?"

Tessa thought he might be angry, but she wasn't sure. His voice was soft enough, but the tendons at either side of his neck were raised and taut. A muscle pumped high in his cheek. Seeing him like that, she remembered the day they'd ridden to Fale to find Emith. She remembered how Ravis had left her and Emith walking down the road while he went back and beat up Deveric's son. Before he had gone, he looked just as he did now.

"Why was it so important for you to hurt Deveric's son in Fale?" she asked. "He was just a small-time bully, nothing more."

Ravis flashed a quick, dark smile. "You do have a way of getting to the heart of things, don't you?"

Tessa didn't like Ravis' smile, and she didn't like the sharp edge to his voice. If it hadn't been for something else shining in his eyes, she might have turned and walked away. Drawing closer to him, she said, "I don't think you were upset with Deveric's son because he was mean to Emith. I think there was another reason behind it."

Ravis looked at Tessa. He drew his hand across his mouth so his scar didn't show, lowered his heavy-lidded eyes, and searched her face. Seconds passed. He didn't speak for a long time, just kept taking deep breaths and watching Tessa with a steady gaze. His eyes were so dark, most people would have mistaken them for black. But they weren't. They were a rich, sable brown. The color of sepia ink.

Finally something in his gaze shifted, and the muscles surrounding his eyes and mouth shaped his expression into something new. Inclining his head toward Tessa, he dropped his hand from his lip. "You're right, of course," he said, speaking more gently than she had ever heard him speak. "I wasn't angry over how the man treated Emith. I wasn't really angry at him at all. More at the way things are done, conventions, people's greed." He shrugged. "Myself.

"Death brings out the best and worst in people. Deveric's son was just protecting what he thought was rightfully his. And likely his brother, sisters, and mother were busy doing the same thing too." Ravis spun around so he could stare out to sea. "I don't know. I just hate to see people scrambling for possessions."

"Why?" Tessa came and stood by his side. She tried to follow his gaze, but his eyes were focused on a point far beyond the horizon, and she could see only so far.

"Because I did it myself once, and it brings back memories I don't care to recall."

"Bad ones?"

"No." Ravis shook his head. "Not all bad memories. Some good ones as well."

He let his words hang for a few seconds and then spoke into the distance. "When my father died he left his estate in Burano in chaos. He was a gentle man, not a great leader or a manager of men, not even a good custodian. His one ambition in life had been to become a village cleric, but his older brother died without producing a legitimate heir and the lands and title of Burano fell to him. He never wanted them. Didn't know what to do with them." Ravis smiled. "He spent the first ten years managing the duchy in a sort of bewildered daze. He just wasn't cut out to be overlord of a great estate. Sometimes I would run into the small library and find him immersed in his prayer book, planning sermons in his head, blind to the mountain of paperwork that surrounded him.

"Malray and I were young at the beginning and couldn't help him, but over the years we grew to love the land. We worked on it together: clearing forests for planting, building up the estate stock, introducing new breeds, and planting new crops. Malray was four years older than I, but we took decisions together, worked always together. We were so young—boys, really—yet we built that land up. Toiled on it for five years. And then our father died."

Ravis paused. His knuckles were white where he gripped the railings. A droplet of sweat trickled down from his brow, and Tessa suddenly remembered he was ill. She didn't say anything, though. She doubted he would hear any words spoken just then.

"He never left a will." Ravis' voice was flat, unemotional. "He wasn't that sort of man. The only thing the executors could find that even came close to one was a letter he wrote and sent to the Lectur at Jiya. In it he stated that after his death he would like to see his wealth divided fairly amongst his family.

"Fool's words.

"What family? His sons, Malray and me? His sister and sister-in-law, his nephews and nieces, his younger brother, his elder brother's bastard son?"

Ravis beat his fist against the rail. *"What family?"*

Tessa flinched. Her own hand was on the rail, and she felt the impact of Ravis' punch like a blow. Even before the rail stopped vibrating, Ravis had managed to control himself. His tooth was down on his scar, reining in his anger. When he spoke again, seconds later, his voice was calm.

"In a normal case the fact there was no will wouldn't have mattered—the estate would have passed over to Malray, the eldest son. Yet by that time people began coming forward with claims of their own. A bastard son of the original duke was the first to press his claim. He brought papers, conveniently smudged by spilt wine, that stated his father had been about to legitimize his parentage when he died. The old duke's widow was next. She claimed she had been left part of the estate in a separate codicil that had just come to light. Our own aunt, Rosimin, who had lived off our father's generosity for twelve years, claimed that he had promised to set aside a third of his wealth to be distributed evenly among his nephews and nieces upon his death. There was even a great-uncle, my grandfather's brother, who claimed he owned the rights to all fish pulled from the river and game shot down from the sky above Burano."

Ravis made a hard sound in his throat. "It was madness. Everyone who was brazen enough to make up a lie and stick to it claimed part of the estate for their own.

"It was because there was no will, you see. It brought out the worst in people. They saw a weakness and used it."

Still staring straight ahead, he ran a hand through his hair. The wind had picked up while he spoke, and the sails of the mizzenmast were making tearing, snapping noises behind him. Tessa didn't need to look round to know that a sailor was up in the mast, adjusting the riggings, as his shadow formed a dark slash that ended at her feet. The sun was in the west and the day was wearing on.

Part of Tessa wanted to guide Ravis away from the railings, make him sit down, rest, sleep. Another part wanted to hear the rest of his story. It was almost as if he were casting a spell with his words, taking them both to a place that was neither past nor present, suspending them in the warm light but hard substance of memory.

Knowing that by speaking she would break the spell, Tessa said nothing. She waited, and after a while Ravis carried on.

"I was seventeen. Malray was twenty-one. The day of our father's funeral was the last day of peace we had in seven years. We clung together as they carried Father's body to the crypt. Both of us tried to be strong, but one of us started crying—I don't know who—and then we were both crying. Leaning against each other and crying. And the strange thing was it didn't matter. As long as we were crying together and had each other it didn't matter. We loved each other that much.

"The next day the fighting started. The first duke's bastard son, Jengus of Morgho, led a force onto the estate. Malray and I had no choice but to defend our home. By more luck than skill we managed to force them from the grounds. The only real advantage we had was our knowledge of the estate. It was just after spring thaw, and a handful of the smaller streams had overrun their banks, turning some of the low-lying valleys into marshes, and somehow we managed to drive Jengus and his men onto them. As he withdrew, Jengus threatened to be back with more men within a week."

Ravis halted for a moment. Tessa glanced up at his face and was surprised to see he was smiling faintly.

"Malray and I were terrified, though we both pretended

not to be. Jengus was ten years older than us, a fighting man with real experience on the battlefield and with contacts in all the mercenary companies in the north. We were just two young boys who knew how to tend the land and little else.

"To make things worse, other people began to press their claims that same week. Magistrates came to the gates, armed with clubs and torches, demanding money and goods to the value of a third of the estate in the name of Rosimin and her six children. The next day, Savarix, duke of the province bordering Burano, sent out his steward to warn us that if any fighting occurred on land adjacent to his property, he would be forced to come in and occupy as much Burano land as he judged fit to protect his borders.

"Vultures were closing in. Jengus would be back in a few days, the magistrates could only be put off for so long, and as young as Malray and I were, we knew enough to realize that Savarix wasn't really interested in his borders at all. He wanted Burano land.

"Two nights after we drove Jengus from the estate, Malray came and woke me in the middle of the night. 'Ravis, we must learn to fight,' he said. 'This land is ours by right and by use. We have loved it and worked on it and called it our home for fifteen years. No one is going to take it from us, even if it means waking up every morning and buckling on a breastplate and sleeping every night with a knife close at hand. I will neither rest, negotiate, nor relent. And you will be with me, fighting by my side, as my brother and my friend.' "

As Ravis spoke the last sentence, Tessa felt the hairs on the back of her neck bristle. The words sounded like a prayer spoken without belief. She felt them resonating in the space within her inner ear where the tinnitus used to start. They made her long for something, but she wasn't sure what. Family? Love? The past?

Ravis' gaze had shifted from the point beyond the horizon, and he now looked down at his hands. Tessa wanted to touch him—she even moved her hand up from her waist—but at the last minute she stopped herself. She didn't have the nerve.

Head tilted down toward the railings, breath coming in deep but irregular bursts, Ravis continued. His voice was rich with opposing emotions, yet as his words wore on and he spoke of fighting alongside his brother, all his pain seemed to slough away. And the one emotion left behind was, surprisingly, joy.

"So Malray and I fought. Together, always together. We made mistakes, a few terrible ones, yet somehow we managed to learn from them.

"Jengus came close to defeating us more times than I can remember. He was a fine fighter. He never stopped pushing, never stopped testing, searching for our weak points. Years passed that were no more than one crisis after another. Jengus burned our crops, poisoned the groundwater, slaughtered our cattle, and burned all the outbuildings. He never did love the land. At one point he joined forces with Rosimin and her sons, and Malray and I spent six months barricaded in the manor house, and to this day I can't remember if it was because we *couldn't* come out or wouldn't.

"One wet spring Savarix sent out his men and claimed the long stretch of Burano land that ran adjacent to his southern borders. All hell broke loose after that. Jengus didn't know whether to fight Savarix, join with him, or ignore him and carry on his own campaign." A gentle laugh escaped from Ravis' lips. "You know, to give him credit, I think he tried all three.

"And through all this madness—terrible bloody fights, sieges, ambushes, shifting alliances, and double crosses—Malray and I were always by each other's sides. We recruited men of our own, fought on hard ground and in the courts. Learned what it was to fight, really fight, over weeks and months and years.

"We relied on each other completely. Trusted each other completely. We anticipated each other's moves, compensated for each other's weaknesses. If I went first into a battle, then I knew without question Malray would be at my back. If I was on the ground and wounded, I knew all I had to do was wait until he found me and brought me home. When Malray was sick, I tended him. When he was worried and thought everything was about to collapse around us, I could not rest until I had eased his mind.

"And he"—Ravis shook his head slowly—"he did no less for me.

"We were young and we grew into manhood fighting. And sometimes it wasn't easy; sometimes we had to fight those we loved, like our cousins and Rosimin. Yet as long as Malray was at my side there was no question of right or wrong. We were brothers fighting for what was ours.

"Seven years we fought. Seven long years, where hardly a day passed without some new challenge sent to try us. Rosimin tried to have us evicted, Jengus turned the gatehouse into an armed camp, and Savarix sent letters to the Lecturs at Jiya and Parafas, demanding our excommunication, swearing that one night he spied us fighting on the consecrated ground of the estate martyry.

"Somehow, by sticking together and not giving up, we managed to live through everything. And the day I killed Jengus the madness finally stopped.

"I suppose, if I were to judge honestly, I was a better fighter than Malray. It was I who planned the strategies, trained the men. Even back then I had a talent for it. Malray had passion, though. He was stronger than I, and when he fought a rage came upon him and nothing, absolutely nothing, could make him put down his sword. One morning, he and a few men rode out to the edge of the estate to check the traps we'd set for Jengus. Jengus was lying in wait. He had three times Malray's numbers. If I had been there, I would have withdrawn, got the hell out of there as fast as I could, made sure I lived to fight another day.

"Malray didn't withdraw. He stayed and fought. He was sick and tired of fighting. He wanted the whole thing over— we both did. But he felt it more than I. He was nearly thirty, and I think he wanted what other men his age had: a wife, family, peace.

"As the afternoon wore on and Malray didn't return, I went out to look for him. I finally came across the battle. Found Malray lying in a plowed field, blood pouring from a gash on his thigh, Jengus standing above him, sword poised to enter his throat."

Ravis' hand flitted up from the railing in a small gesture

of self-denial. "After that I hardly know what happened. I have heard accounts, but whether I believe them or not I can't say. I remember only rage. Absolute, blind rage. Malray was all I had. And Jengus was about to take him from me.

"According to some, I rode my horse over four men to get to him. Crushed the skulls of two, cracked the ribs of another. Some say I screamed as I rode. Others say I was silent as the dead. I felt only the weight of the sword in my hand and the sheer terror of losing Malray in my heart.

"Jengus barely had time to straighten his back. I came at him, swung my sword, and beheaded him in a single blow."

Tessa closed her eyes, pressed her lips to a tight line to stop herself from making a noise.

"After that I didn't stop—*couldn't* stop—until all Jengus' men were dead." Ravis' voice was soft, almost bemused. "Malray had to pull me off the last man's corpse. He'd been dead for God knows how long, but still I couldn't stop beating him. I don't know what happened to me, don't know what I became. I think by the time Malray reached me it was already too late."

Something like a shiver passed down Ravis' spine. Tessa could see Ravis harboring its momentum, using it to give his body strength.

"Things moved swiftly after that. Jengus had always been our greatest threat, and with him gone all other disputes fell away. Savarix could no longer claim his borders were threatened, Rosimin could find no one new to back her suit, the local magistrates were sick of the whole thing, and everyone else who had ever raised a greedy eye or a clutching hand toward Burano finally backed away."

As Ravis spoke, Tessa was aware of the light fading around them. How long had they been standing here? Hours?

"So you won?" she said, filling the pause after he finished.

A hard, bitter laugh burst from Ravis' lips. "Not me. No. I didn't win anything. Only Malray won.

"A month after the whole thing ended and the lawyers finally agreed to sign the estate over to us, he turned on me. My own brother, whom I had loved and fought with for seven long years, turned. He said I had tainted everything by what I did that day in the plowed field. He said I still smelled of the blood. He didn't want me on his land. His land. *His!*"

The fist at Ravis' side shook so violently, it made the rest of his body shake with it.

"He said our father's property was his now, and to split it would diminish it. A great estate like Burano had to be preserved intact. He told me I wasn't made for the land. Told me I was a born fighter and should go away and fight." Ravis' voice dropped abruptly, as if he himself could hardly believe what he was saying. When he spoke again he sounded as confused as a child who had grabbed something shiny only to find that it burned. "Offered me five hundred pieces of gold and pointed the way to the gate."

Tessa swallowed hard. Her eyes ached. Stretching out her hand, she touched Ravis' arm. "I'm sorry."

Ravis reacted to the words as if they were acid. Snapping back his arm, he pushed himself off from the railing and turned to walk away. "Don't be sorry for me," he said. "I made sure I got my revenge."

Spying a handful of drunks on the nearing street corner, Emith scurried across the road to avoid them. He had two hot, butter-drenched lobsters wrapped in grease cloth in his hand. And if the drunks got as much as a single whiff of them, his mother's favorites wouldn't stand a rowboat's chance in a storm of ever making it home.

Mother really loved lobster, you see. She only said she didn't to Marcel of Vailing to stop him from asking questions about Tessa. Mother was good at things like that—far better than he himself. Which was just as well, really. Every household needed one person capable of showing troublesome guests the door. Not that Marcel was bad, of course. He just had a way of asking questions in his commanding banker's voice that made it impossible not to give answers.

Well, nearly impossible. Emith had yet to meet the person who could get Mother to say anything she didn't have a mind to.

Smiling, Emith clutched the package containing the lobster to his chest. He didn't want them going cold before he got home. It wasn't often Mother had lobster, and it was even less often that it arrived on her doorstep shelled, hot, and ready to eat. It would be a nice treat for her and one Emith hoped would cheer her up.

Mother had been lonely since Tessa left. Oh, she tried to hide it—this morning alone she'd gutted enough fish and peeled enough onions to make a mountain of herring bake— but she was all the same. Emith knew it. She couldn't fool him. He saw the way she stared into the fire and never once wiped the tears from her cheek when the onions made her cry.

Mother missed Tessa. They both did. Tessa was so full of life, so strong. The house just wasn't the same without her.

Emith had tried various things to cheer his mother up. Last night he had opened their second-best flask of arlo, lit wax candles instead of tallow, and picked out her favorite tunes on his fiddle. He wasn't a very good player, but that didn't matter to Mother. In her mind she heard the music as if it were played by angels—he knew it because she had told him so a very long time ago. And Emith never forgot things like that.

No matter what she heard, though, it had only seemed to make her sadder. So Emith had decided that tonight they would have a makeshift feast: lobsters, a nip or two of the berriac that was kept in the back of the larder for feast days, medical emergencies, and special guests, and this time no music, just some tale telling instead. Mother liked to be read to, and Emith still had a few of Master Deveric's books lying around the house. One of these days he really must return to Fale and hand them over to Master Rance.

It was just getting dark as Emith turned into his street. Two shadowy figures passed him by on the far side of the road. Emith paid them little heed: they looked in too much of a hurry to bother a man about lobster. Besides, this street was a safe one, unlike other parts of the city. He would never have agreed to work five days a week in Fale if he hadn't been sure of that.

Working out the earliest day in his head when Tessa might arrive back from Maribane, Emith made his way to the house. It just might be possible that Tessa could be back in less than nine days' time. If he remembered rightly, the passage only took three days, and Tessa as a laywoman would only be allowed to stay one night on the Anointed Isle itself. The abbot was very strict about things like that.

Feeling excited about the idea of telling his mother that there was a chance Tessa could be back earlier than they first thought, Emith made his way to the back of the house.

Mother *had* a front door, but in the thirty-four years she had lived here, Emith had only seen it open once. That was the day Mother's sister, Aunt Pelish, had arrived from Mir'Lor to stay for a month. At the time her own house was being refurbished with the latest and most fashionable of amenities—a red brick oven—and Mother said she was far too grand to enter via the yard.

The smell of lye and quicklime bristled at Emith's nostrils the moment he opened the yard gate. Judging from the faint sweetness accompanying the smell, the hides would soon be ready to be scraped. Nowadays he didn't need nearly as much parchment as when he'd worked with Master Deveric, but old habits died hard. Making parchment was a link to his old life with Master Deveric, and the idea of giving it up was as unthinkable to Emith as jumping into the sea in midwinter. He was a scribe's assistant, and although he had no scribe to work for and, with Tessa gone, no one to train, he still had to do his job. It was what made him who he was.

Shouting out to his mother he was home, Emith reached for the door.

It was ajar. A narrow band of light spilled out onto the cobbles.

Emith frowned. Surely he hadn't left it open?

Grabbing the handle, he opened it fully, then stepped into the kitchen.

A cool breath of air replaced the smell of lye with something else, like wet animal fur, only stronger. Something sticky caught at the sole of Emith's shoe, and he looked down to see what it was. A hard knot twisted in his stomach. The package of lobster meat in his hand suddenly felt as cold and greasy as pig fat left overnight in the yard.

Almost unaware of what he was doing, Emith shook his head. Just because the stain was red didn't mean it was blood. . . . It could be one of his pigments—he was always spilling those—or one of Mother's raspberry sauces.

"Mother?" Although he hadn't intended it, the word turned to a question in his mouth.

The room was dim. The fire was burning low, and no lamps had been lit. The knot in Emith's stomach rippled into a liquid band as he looked over to his mother's chair. The back of her head was visible above the headrest. Even from behind, Emith could tell her hair was mussed.

"Mother?"

There was no response.

She was resting, that was it. Just like her to be resting the one day he returned home with cooked lobster.

Smiling faintly and shaking his head, Emith crossed to the fire. Other red stains pulled at his soles, but he tried not to think about them. He'd clean them up later, after he'd woken Mother. As he took the last few steps toward her chair, Emith twisted the package of lobster meat in his hands. He twisted it so hard, butter squeezed through the cloth.

A trickle of grease ran down his thumb as he spun around to face his mother.

A short noise, like something broken, escaped from his lips. His grip gave way on the lobster meat and the package hit the floor.

Mother was covered in something. Covered.

Emith sprang forward. How could she sit there, sleeping, and not be aware of it? Even as part of his brain formed that thought, another part warned him that something was terribly wrong. He pushed the idea away.

She was resting, that was all.

"Mother," he called, trying to roll saliva in his mouth so he could spit on his sleeve and wipe the dark stuff from her chin. No saliva would come, though. His mouth was completely dry.

Collapsing at the foot of the chair, Emith hugged his mother's lap and begged her to wake up. She didn't hear him. He grabbed at her wrist to shake it, and as he did so a scrap of paper fell from her grip.

Emith recognized it straight away. It was a copy of Tessa's bill of passage to Maribane. Mother had scrunched it up into a very tight ball, as if she had been trying to hide it. The bill contained all the details about *Tarrier*, its tonnage and ports of call, and Mother had insisted on keeping it close in case anything should happen to Tessa's ship. Anyone holding a bill of passage would be sure of receiving disaster information first.

Emith picked up the scrap of paper, smoothed it flat in his hand, and then slipped it onto Mother's side table, where she liked all her important things to be kept. That done, he turned back to Mother and sat and waited for her to wake up, until the dairyman found him the next morning and forced him to come away.

T W E N T Y

arrier had a smooth and peaceful voyage to Maribane. There was no bad weather or high winds, no close brushes with jagged rocks, sea creatures, or pirates. Just long days and short nights and sunsets that were broad and blood red.

Tessa lost count of how many days she had been aboard the ship—certainly more than seven, but surely not as many as ten. The extreme monotony of the days made them hard to track: they all felt like one and the same. Up at dawn, breakfast, walk around the deck, midday meal, sit on the deck, evening meal, and then bed.

Talking to Ravis was the only thing that broke the monotony, but ever since the day he had spoken about the fight for his father's estate, Ravis had been subdued. He had made it clear that he didn't want to discuss his past any further and had kept all talk impersonal since. He wasn't rude exactly, just guarded. The stories he told were never about Drokho, and the people he mentioned were casual acquaintances or former employers, never family or friends.

His wound got better, but slowly. Pain kept him awake late at night, made him toss and turn and throw off his sheets. Even now, a week later, sudden movements could still make him wince. The burn on Tessa's palm was healing well, and scabbed skin broke off in flakes revealing a hard, raised scar beneath. Tessa hated to look at it. When she ran her finger over the scarred tissue, it didn't feel as if she was touching herself at all. All sensation had gone.

Thanks to Ravis' powers of persuasion, they had been well taken care of along the way. At least once a day the ship's boy would knock at the cabin door, bearing a tray loaded with fresh bread, hot cider, and joints of meat. Tessa couldn't be sure whether or not Ravis was still bribing the crew for food; his purse never looked any lighter.

"Land ahoy off the port side!"

Tessa turned to see who was shouting. It wasn't a seaman. It was a young boy imitating one, but when she followed his gaze port side she saw he was right: land, a hazy gray wall of it, looming to the northwest of the ship. Something tingled in her stomach. Maribane. Another journey ended.

Making her way to the foredeck, Tessa pushed past excited women and children, dodged deckhands, and gave all male passengers a wide berth. She was at home on the ship now, sure of herself in every way. Even her long skirts no longer hampered her, and she scrambled up ladders and jumped from deck to deck with the skill of an old hand. Ravis laughed at her sometimes. Told her she'd never make a proper Rhaize lady. The words might have been an insult, but Tessa had a feeling they weren't.

The midday sun beat down on the crown of her head as she leaned over the ship's railings and tilted her body out to sea. A seagull shrieked overhead—the first one in days—and Tessa convinced herself the air was fresher, less salty, now that land was in sight.

"There's a sight to warm a man's blood."

Hearing Ravis' voice behind her, Tessa nodded without turning to greet him. "Wonderful, isn't it? How long before we get there?"

A warm, throaty laugh sounded from behind. "It wasn't the land I was admiring."

Embarrassed, Tessa swung about and stepped back from the railings. She tried to issue an indignant snort, but it ended up sounding more like a peeved squeak instead. Ravis always managed to throw her off guard.

He smiled. "I didn't mean to embarrass you."

"Yes, you did. That's exactly what you meant to do." Spying a crease in her skirt, Tessa went about smoothing it with venom. The purse at her waist jingled as she moved.

"Have you got all your belongings from belowdecks?" Ravis asked. "Right about now, when everyone is so excited by the sight of land that they forget their own good sense, is when most thievery takes place."

Still irritated, Tessa motioned toward the pack at her foot. "I carry all my things around with me. When will we dock?"

Ravis gazed out to sea. "Not as soon as you think. That land over there isn't close to where we're headed. We won't dock until a good few hours after dark."

Ravis was right; *Tarrier* didn't pull into port until the moon was high and the sky was completely black. The approaching dock was ablaze with torches, and standing where she was right at the prow of the ship, Tessa could smell their smoke and feel their bitter fumes sting her eyes. Rowboats clustered around the ship's hull, some drawing so close that she wondered how they managed to avoid harm. All sails except the aft had been reefed, and *Tarrier* glided into port with little help from the waiting tugs.

Only a mild wind blew, but somehow the night managed to be the coldest of the voyage so far, and Tessa had her cloak tied at the neck and chest. The lights of Kilgrim were muted compared to Bay'Zell's, and the town seemed scattered and loose, with buildings dotted across the surrounding hills, robbing the town of central focus. Ravis said Kilgrim was a wayport, not a real destination in itself—just a place people passed through on their way to somewhere else.

Tessa hadn't seen Ravis for over an hour. He was probably plying the crew for information about the best place to spend the night, eat, and hire horses. He was always busy with things like that.

As she looked on, the ship drew alongside the dock. Longshoremen jumped across from the wharf, and the crew threw ropes and secured lines. The Maribane men had strange voices, harsh and guttural, and they swore outrageous curses, pausing only to bow low to the ladies and wink at any awestruck child.

Within minutes the ship was transformed. Everyone was on the move: passengers, seamen, longshoremen. Hawkers boarded the ship and did brisk business selling hot pies and cold beer to people who had seen neither in over a week.

Tessa held back from the crush. The blazing torches, harsh

cries, and flickering shadows made her uneasy. They reminded her of the battle amid the stones. Without being aware of what she was doing, she drew her burned palm up to her face. The skin was hot against her cheek.

"I thought I'd find you here."

Tessa jumped at the words, even though she realized straight away it was Ravis. He had changed clothes since she had seen him last, slicked back his hair, and put a shine to his boots.

"Are you all right?" he asked. Not waiting for an answer, he held out his hand. "Here, let me take your pack."

Tessa handed it over. She didn't feel in the mood to make a point by insisting on carrying it herself.

As their hands met over the rough canvas of the pack, Ravis said, "There's no need to be afraid, you know. I'll be with you all the way."

Tessa hadn't heard him speak so softly since the day on the quarterdeck by the railings. She met his gaze for a moment, long enough to see that he meant what he said, and then turned on her heel and stalked away. She didn't like the way he pinned all her emotions down. It made her feel vulnerable.

"Come on," she said, calling over her shoulder. "Let's get off this ship and into the town." Feeling her voice sounded harsh and knowing her actions were, she added, "Last on dry land buys the other supper and a jug of ale."

Ravis didn't reply, but somehow he managed to beat her to the ladder, and when he jumped down to the main deck, she noticed his eyes were sparkling.

Without saying a word, Ravis bade farewell to what seemed like the entire crew. Meeting the eyes of every seaman they passed, he either nodded, inclined his head, or pressed his lips together in some kind of sailor's salutation that was halfway between a frown and a smile. Watching him, Tessa was drawn to the scar on his lip. It was the first time she had noticed it in days. Strange, she thought, how quickly she had grown accustomed to it.

Ravis picked that moment to turn and offer his arm. "Are your legs ready for the shock of dry land?"

Not knowing what he meant, she nodded. Her legs felt fine to her.

Together they walked down the gangplank and onto the wharf. Ravis held back slightly, allowing her foot to hit the wooden boarding first.

He sighed amiably. "Looks like I'll be buying supper."

Again Tessa was surprised by him. She had been sure he would try to win the bet.

"Carry your bags, sir?"

"Trinkets for the lady? Ribbons?"

"Horse and cart to take you to the best inn in Kilgrim?"

People crowded close. Hawking, begging, and propositioning, they thrust out their hands, speaking in fast, thick dialects that Tessa had to strain to understand. Ravis shook them all away. Unlike with the other passengers who had disembarked earlier, one flat rebuff from Ravis and they left him well alone.

The torch smoke was so thick it made Tessa's eyes water, and flecks of burned matter caught in her mouth and throat. As she walked along the wharf, her legs began to ache. The bones felt heavy, and every time the pads of her feet hit the ground, she felt a jolt coursing up through her ankles as high as her knees.

"Sea legs," Ravis said, placing his hand beneath her arm for support. "Happens to the best of people when they've been on a ship as long as we have. Bones get used to the give and take of a ship. Land just takes, doesn't give." He smiled like a rogue. "It'll get worse when we reach the hard ground of the dock."

"I suppose that's another of your military considerations?" Annoyed by Ravis' smugness, Tessa tried to walk as steadily as she could. Every move she made seemed to give something away.

"A minor one." As he spoke, Ravis released his hold on Tessa's arm. Coming to an abrupt halt, he stared into the crowd of people waiting at the end of the wharf.

Looking up, Tessa followed his gaze through thick bands of smoke, shifting shadows, and bright bursts of torch light, to a hooded figure dressed in black. As Tessa watched, the figure drew hands to the hood and pushed it back. Tessa caught her breath. It was a woman with violet eyes and gleaming dark hair. A murmur passed through the crowd as everyone turned to look at her. She was strikingly beautiful. The torch light, which succeeded in making everyone else look red faced and haggard, made the woman's skin glow with soft, golden tones.

Quickly, Tessa glanced at Ravis. His tooth was down upon his scar. Without returning his hand to Tessa's arm, he moved forward. Tessa had no choice but to follow after him. As Ravis walked, the crowd parted before him, opening up a path to the woman standing on the flight of steps leading up from the wharf to the dock. Taking deep breaths to calm herself, Tessa inhaled the sharp, sweet odor of violets.

As Ravis drew close, the woman's eyes darkened and her lips curved minutely. Suddenly feeling grubby and plain, Tessa brushed back her hair and smoothed her dress. The woman with violet eyes let her own hair blow in the wind. Glossy curls framed a heart-shaped face and flawless skin. When a sharp breeze cut from the east, her cloak parted to reveal a dress of scarlet lace beneath.

Without looking once at Tessa, the woman remained motionless until Ravis came to a halt before her. "We need to talk," she said, her voice low and husky. Not waiting for a reply, she turned, climbed the steps, and began to walk along the dock. Ravis moved to catch up with her.

Tessa stood on the bottom step, watching them. They shared the same dark hair and quick, fluid movements. For a moment she felt as if she were looking at two people made from the same substance. Then Ravis turned. His expression was strained as he searched out Tessa's face in the crowd. When their gazes met, he relaxed imperceptibly, beckoning her forward with a brief tilt of his chin. The violet-eyed woman saw, but in no way acknowledged, the exchange.

She led them along the dock and up into the city. The streets were wet and slick with grease. Horses, litters, covered carts, and laden donkeys choked the roads. When a barrow boy wheeling a cart full of apples strayed too close, Ravis took hold of the woman's elbow and drew her away. Tessa tried not to notice how long his hand stayed upon her arm afterward. Crossing a busy thoroughfare, the woman guided them through a series of short turns and then up the steps of a sandstone building, into the light and warmth of an inn.

They entered a room dominated by a fireplace large enough to stable a horse. Spits ran from one side of the fire to the other, thick with roasting chickens, onions, and joints of meat. The sound of fat hissing above the flames competed with the sounds of laughter and singing. The air was heavy with smoke, smells, and liquor fumes. Men and women sat in close groups, their cheeks flushed from drinking, their hands busy with gaming chips, ale tankards, coins, and drawstring purses.

The moment the small party appeared in the doorway, a short man standing by a row of beer casks made his way forward. Rubbing his hands against his apron, to brush off either dirt or sweat, he bowed deeply as he approached the violet-eyed woman. "Lady Arazzo, you have returned. Please, come this way. Such a night to be out! You must be cold and parched. I've had Mulch baste a brace of good pheasants, and I've personally taken the liberty of setting a jug of berriac to warm by the fire."

Ignoring the man completely, the violet-eyed woman turned to Ravis. "We must speak in private." Although she didn't so much as glance at Tessa while she spoke, Tessa felt the words like a cool draft upon her cheek.

The short man with the apron moved toward a doorway that led through to a small, dimly lit room. From where she stood, Tessa could just catch the gleam of rich furnishings beyond: dark woods, crimson silk, and silver-capped lanterns.

Ravis turned to Tessa. "You will sit here," he said, guiding her toward a table in the center of the main room. "And will not move until I say so. I'll have the innkeeper bring you food and drink."

Tessa blinked. She thought of many things to say, but in the end she simply nodded. Ravis' face was dark and unreadable, his voice hard.

"And you," he said, spinning around to face the innkeeper, "will extend the same courtesy to this lady as you have to the Lady Arazzo. See she gets the same plump pheasants and fire-warmed berriac. And be sure the word gets around that she is to be left well alone. Any man coming close enough to cast a shadow on her chair will have me to contend with." Ravis made a point of pushing back his cloak to reveal his knife. Those watching him from various alcoves and corners dotted around the inn all found reason to look away.

With one final glance at Tessa, Ravis let himself be ushered into the private room.

Tessa watched him go. The violet-eyed woman waited by the doorway until Ravis had passed into the room, then put a pale, unjeweled hand upon the door, meaning to close it behind him. Ravis said something to her, and a second later her hand dropped from the wood, door unclosed. As the two receded into the darkness of the room, Tessa strained to see more, but the light level dropped further as the woman moved to snuff out oil lamps, and soon all Tessa could see were shadows.

"Here, my lady. Pheasant and berriac." The innkeeper startled Tessa by depositing a tray upon her table. "Mulch has boned the bird, and I've taken the liberty of pulling the stuffing out myself. I know how you ladies hate catching grease on your sleeves." The innkeeper spoke pleasantly enough, but his gaze was fixed firmly upon the darkness in the private room.

Tessa nodded. She suddenly felt sick. Trying to convince herself it was the smell of pheasant, the long day, and the smoke from the tallow that was making her queasy, she let the innkeeper go. A moment later she let out a small sigh and called him back. The smells weren't bothering her at all. Something else was.

The innkeeper was quick to return, wiping his hands against his apron as if somehow, in the minute he had been away, he had managed to get them dirty. He leaned close. "Yes, my lady?"

"Who is the lady in the private room?" Tessa said, hating herself for asking yet wanting to know all the same.

"Violante of Arazzo," the innkeeper replied, obviously pleased to be asked. "The most famous beauty in Mizerico. The Lectur's bastard daughter."

Feeling the muscles in her throat contract, Tessa waved the innkeeper away. Mizerico. That was where Ravis was headed the day she'd met him.

"What did you come here for, Violante?" Ravis glanced through the doorway into the main room as he spoke. He could just see the edge of Tessa's table. Although the inn-keeper had left a tray laden with food minutes earlier, Tessa had not touched it.

Violante of Arazzo walked across the room, coming to stand directly in front of the partially closed door. Silk rustled as she moved. "I've come to warn you," she said, her pale fingers working on the ties of her cloak. With one quick shrug of her shoulders, the cloak fell to the floor, revealing her lace-clad body beneath. "Your brother means to kill you."

"Tell me some new news, Violante." Ravis looked away from her, turning his attention to the jug of berriac by the fire. Even after all this time he still found Violante of Arazzo's beauty unsettling.

"Malray knows you have left Rhaize. He also knows you have come here, to Kilgrim."

"And how does he know that?"

"Does it matter?" Violante's curved lips were so perfect that every female portrait commissioned in Istania for the past five years boasted a copy of them. "Make my lips fuller, more curved," the fine ladies of the court would plead with their portrait artists, "just like Violante of Arazzo's." Some ladies even went so far as to have their maids slap their lips before dances and banquets, just to give them that flushed, swollen look of Violante's.

It was the peasant in her, the fine ladies of the court were fond of pointing out, that gave Violante her charm. Her fine-cut bones and her violet eyes would be nothing without those peasant lips.

Ravis tugged a hand through his hair. "Just tell me the truth, Violante."

Violante's expression changed imperceptibly. Ravis thought he saw her bottom lip tremble, but then she stepped into the shadows against the far wall and he was no longer sure. "Malray was in my house the day the two Istanian scouts delivered your message. I tried to hide it, but he guessed it was from you." Violante took a quick breath. "He tore it from me, read it, found the part where you mentioned your travel plans, then raced out of the house. He didn't even stop to collect his cloak."

All the time Violante was speaking, Ravis watched Tessa's table through the doorway. One man had strayed close, only to be intercepted by the innkeeper carrying half a dozen foaming tankards. After a brief exchange of words and ale, the stranger moved away. Relaxing a bit, Ravis turned his attention back to Violante.

In the narrow, dimly lit room with its red-painted walls and its crimson silk upholstery that Ravis suspected was normally used for cushioning prostitutes and their wealthy clients, Violante looked liked a creature from another world. While the red furnishings surrounding her had the cheap look of cherry and vermilion dyes, the fabric of Violante's dress looked as if it had been dyed by grinding rubies, distilling fine red wine, and reducing blood.

It wasn't worth asking her what Malray had been doing in her house. Ravis knew Violante well enough to guess. Left alone in Mizerico for nearly a year while he finished his commission for Izgard of Garizon, she had no doubt taken other men to her bed. It was hardly surprising that one of those men should be his own brother. Malray would have made it his business to seek her out. Any woman who interested Ravis always interested his brother as well.

"How long ago did this happen?" Ravis asked.

Violante sent dark curls tumbling as she shook her head. "Six or seven days back. Malray sent his assassins out that same evening. The next morning I set sail on a local bark."

That explained why Violante was here, ahead of everyone. No one could build a hull as fast and smooth as an Istanian shipbuilder. Their bows sloped so wickedly from the stem that their ships were able to slice clean through oncoming waves.

Pouring two cups of berriac, Ravis said, "When do you think Malray's men will arrive?"

"The captain of the bark said we passed a Drokho cutter two nights back, so perhaps late tonight or early tomorrow morning."

Ravis glanced into the main room.

"Why does Malray still hate you so?" Violante asked, directing his attention back toward herself. "He got the money, the land, the title. What did you take from him?"

For the first time since meeting her on the wharf, Ravis smiled at Violante. It was a cold smile and she knew it, for she looked quickly away. Seeing the faint blush on her cheeks and the way her slender fingers plucked at the fabric of her dress, Ravis wondered why she had come. Violante of Arazzo was beautiful enough to choose any man she wished. Even the highest-born noblemen crumbled beneath her cool violet gaze, presenting her with extravagant gifts of land, gold, and family jewels. Glancing at her unadorned neck and wrist, Ravis shook his head softly. Although Violante had received a fortune's worth of jewelry, she never wore any. She didn't need it.

Ravis crossed the room and handed her a cup of berriac. "What makes you think I took something from Malray?" He had meant his tone to be light, but somehow it wasn't.

"Because I saw the look on Malray's face when the scouts arrived with your letter. I saw the hate."

Closing his eyes, Ravis bit down on his scar. Seven years had passed since his last contact with his brother, yet he could still feel Malray's malice pressing against him like a splint bound to a bone.

"What did you take from him, Ravis?" Violante said, her voice low. "Was it a woman?"

Ravis turned away. In the main room he saw Tessa shifting in her chair. She had rolled back her sleeves and was about to start on her food. A quick scan of the room assured him that no one was paying her any special attention. He wanted to go to her anyway.

When he spun around, he caught Violante watching him. In that unguarded moment she looked young and unsure of herself. Ravis ran his hand across his face. Violante had traveled all the way from Mizerico to warn him about Malray, even though she knew she was no longer wanted. The note Ravis sent her had been a farewell. At some point during the past six weeks he'd come to realize he'd been mistaking his eagerness to be gone from Bay'Zell for a desire to see her.

Suddenly feeling tired, Ravis said, "What difference does it make? The past is gone. Dead." Glancing up at Violante's face, seeing the question repeated again in her eyes, he sighed and gave in. "Malray was betrothed to a girl once— fourteen years ago, when he first took legal possession of the estate. When I heard of the betrothal I couldn't stop thinking about it. It ate away at me. Malray had the land, the wealth. Why should he have a wife too? As soon as I learned who the girl was I sought her out, made her fall in love with me instead of him." Ravis shook his head, laughed coldly. "It was easy. I told her about the rift between Malray and me, cast myself as the villain . . . women always love black sheep.

"A month later we ran off to the east and got married. Malray was publicly humiliated. He'd had a grand wedding planned, invited heads of state, dukes, duchesses. He'd even arranged to have the ceremony performed at the Liege's palace in Rhiga. Then to have to tell everyone that the wedding was canceled because his betrothed had run off with his own brother . . ."

"He took it badly?"

Ravis made a hard sound in his throat. "So badly that when I finally returned to Drokho some seven years later he had one of his men welcome me home with a knife."

Violante's gaze dropped from his eyes to the scar on his lip.

Ravis nodded. "Half a second later and it would have been my throat."

Fingers grazing across her own perfect lips, Violante said, "How is it that no one ever talks about this?"

"Both Malray and the girl's brother had an interest in seeing the story buried with time. No one gained from what happened. No one."

"What about the girl?" Violante drained the berriac from her cup. "What became of her?"

Ravis' teeth found his scar. It felt like cold wire in his mouth. "She died two years after we were married. She wasn't made for the sort of life I lived in the east. I took work as a mercenary, living in mercenary camps, following the winter campaigns east and the summer ones south, moving from one stinking dugout to the next. Within a matter of months she caught *hura aya,* swamp sickness. It took her over a year to die. She was blind for the last month. 'Ravis,' she would say, 'I'm frightened. Hold me. Tell me what you see—' "

"Stop it!" cried Violante, her voice sharp. "Stop it." Their gazes met. Violante's eyes were bright. A high flush blazed across her cheeks. After a moment she looked away.

"My lady. Sir." The innkeeper stepped into the room, carrying a silver tray loaded with food and a second jug of berriac. "I'll just put this near the fire so it won't go cold."

Neither Ravis nor Violante acknowledged what he said. They stood looking at each other while he laid out salt dishes, silk napkins, and little silver bowls for spitting gristle.

"Who was the girl?" Violante asked the moment the innkeeper was gone. "Malray isn't the sort of man to marry for love. She must have been someone highborn. An heiress, perhaps?" Although she tried, Violante couldn't quite keep a trace of bitterness from edging into her voice. A bastard herself, she was feted by society while never quite being allowed into it. The noblemen who wooed her seldom had marriage on their minds.

Ravis made a negligent gesture with his hand. "Just a girl from Veizach."

"Just a girl from Veizach? Yet the Liege offered to marry her in his palace?" Violante shook her head. "I think not, Ravis of Burano."

Turning to face the fire, Ravis took a deep breath. The past was long gone. Why should it still hurt? After a long moment he let his wife's name out. "Lara of Alberach."

Violante let out a short gasp. "Izgard's sister?"

Ravis nodded to the fire.

"Yet you've spent the last three years working for him. How can he—"

"Because he needed my services. And that's just the sort of man he is."

As Ravis said the word *is,* voices rose in the main room. Something wooden, like a chair or a table, crashed to the floor. Ravis spun around. The door was shut—the innkeeper must have closed it on the way out. Cursing himself for not checking sooner, he raced across the room. As one hand came down upon the latch, the other reached for his knife.

The door swung open. Tessa was sitting exactly where he had told her, only now two men were standing over her. One man had his hand on her shoulder. Straight away, Ravis took in their dark hair, blood red cloaks, and the square-shaped clasps at their throats. Malray's men. Two more were busy pressing the innkeeper against the wall, and another pair was guarding the door.

All six men stopped in their tracks when Ravis appeared in the doorway.

Behind him, Ravis heard Violante take a step forward. "Stay where you are, Violante," he hissed. Then, sending his gaze in an arc to include all six of Malray's men before coming to rest upon Tessa, he said, "Gentlemen. This *is* a little disappointing. I had hoped you'd come all this way to see me, not some two-copper trollop from the docks." With that he launched himself into the main room, heading for the back of the inn, away from Tessa and the door.

"*Run!*" he cried at the top of his voice, launching his body toward the area where the two men held the innkeeper. "*Run!*" The words were for Tessa, only for Tessa, but it suited Ravis that every patron in the inn—every old man supping barley beer, every drunken sailor with a hand down a girl's blouse, and every old maid getting quietly potted—chose the exact same moment to heed his advice and make toward the door. People began screaming and pushing, and when Ravis looked over his shoulder he could no longer see Tessa or her table for the crowd of people rushing to escape. Telling himself that was good, he turned his full attention to the two red-cloaked men by the wall.

With no finesse whatsoever, he sent his elbow cracking into the first man's face. The man was young and sallow skinned, and he was wearing a high silk collar that quickly soaked with blood. Deliberately making as much commotion as possible, Ravis paused to push over the wooden frame that supported half a dozen beer barrels on a slant designed for settling dregs. As barrels rolled onto the cobbled floor, he stepped onto the downed frame and hiked himself above the crowd, ensuring that all six of Malray's men had a clear view of him. He wanted them coming after him, not Tessa.

Immediately, Ravis felt a blade jab against his spine. Bucking his shoulders backward, he wheeled around and slammed his forearm into the blade holder's wrist. The blade, a shortsword inlaid with curls of silver wire, spun out of control and dropped to the floor. The man who wielded it slid his hand into the shadows of his cloak, meaning to draw a second weapon. Briefly, Ravis got a whiff of the man. He smelled like all fighters: of sweat and linseed oil and dirt. Yet there was something else. A faint undertow of plain herbs and dry grass. And even as he recognized it as the smell of Burano and home, he sent his dagger plunging into the man's flank. The man's blood red cloak, his wool tunic, and the loose-knit chainmail beneath were all driven deep into the wound. Sickened, Ravis pushed the man away, turned to face whoever was next.

Ravis fought savagely after that. Lashing out with brutal force, breaking bones and slitting skin, he tore his own knuckles to shreds in his frenzy. Always he moved away from the door and the place he had last seen Tessa. Dragging down smoke-yellowed tapestries, spice racks, and meat hooks and even kicking the spits clear from the fire, he worked to buy Tessa time. He wasn't sure if Malray's men knew whether she was with him or not, but he was taking no chances. Fourteen years ago he had run away with Malray's betrothed, and Malray still held him responsible for her death. Ravis bit down on his scar: he still held *himself* responsible.

Three of Malray's men were down: one dead, one too busy stanching a knife wound to be interested in further fighting, and one groaning on the floor amid the beer barrels, nursing his groin. The man whose face he had smashed earlier was madder than ever, and despite a continued stream of blood and mucus running from his nose into his mouth, he had managed to maneuver Ravis into a corner. Carrying a cleaver-shaped falchion with rain damage along the hilt, Bloody Nose was clever enough not to draw too close until his two remaining companions joined him.

The main room of the inn was empty now, except for the innkeeper himself, who was crouching in the shadows behind the bellows, and one old man in an alcove near the door who appeared to have passed out, either from drunkenness or shock.

Seeing the last three of Malray's men moving to form a half circle around him, Ravis glanced from side to side, searching for anything he could use to throw them off guard. Nothing. He was backed into a corner with not so much as a soup ladle within striking distance. In vain, he tried to catch the innkeeper's eye—all he needed was a short disturbance to distract the attacker's attention—but the innkeeper seemed intent on wiping grease stains from his boots and wouldn't look up.

Shifting minutely to the left, Ravis was aware of a strained tightness hugging his ribs: the battle wound inflicted by the harras. Lowering his knife arm a fraction to decrease the strain on the muscle beneath, he looked into the faces of Malray's men. Their features were hard, focused. All three were wary of him—he could tell that from the number of times they exchanged glances—yet they knew the advantage was theirs. Slowly, Ravis felt back with his free hand, testing the distance between himself and the wall. Recent encounters with the harras had made him careless. He had forgotten that men didn't have to be monsters to be dangerous.

Blood from knuckle wounds trickled between Ravis' fingers as he settled his knife at his chest. Falling back against the wall, he took a quick breath as he waited a split second for Malray's men to start forward, then kicked off with all his might, meeting the attackers head-on.

It wasn't much of a strategy, but it gave him a moment of stunned surprise as all three men were forced to reposition their weapons for defense. Already Ravis was working out what he could afford to lose. This wasn't a fight he was about to emerge from unharmed.

Pain sizzled across Ravis' ear as Bloody Nose's blade found his lobe. Hot blood rained down his neck and shoulders. Black dots streaked across his vision as a second man cracked something hard against the back of his skull. Ravis bit down on his scar, biting back pain, nausea, and blurred vision. Sticking his knife into the tangle of arms and weapons attempting to rein him in, he gathered his strength for a break toward the door. The harrar wound on his ribs tore open as he pulled his knife free of a tough, boiled-leather gauntlet. Pain gripped his chest. Flaring outward along old fever lines, it shot toward his heart. Ravis felt his strength drain away.

A knife stabbed at his shoulder, and another slid across the blood at his throat. As Ravis spun around to strike the two men who were attacking him from behind, Bloody Nose screamed. His body stiffened, and for a moment he seemed to grow taller as his chest and shoulder muscles stretched forward. A fraction of a second later, Bloody Nose fell to the floor. Ravis didn't spare a glance for his body. Strange things happened in fights, and those who stopped to wonder wound up dead.

Ravis grabbed hold of a cloak tail and wrenched it down toward the floor. As its owner reached up to loosen the ties at his throat, Ravis stuck him with his knife. Two blows: one into the ribs, cracking them, one sliding into the muscle between, puncturing lung tissue. Taking a ragged breath, Ravis spun around to face the last man. Only he wasn't there. He was on the floor, one of the inn's metal spits embedded in his throat. Bits of chicken skin and slivers of onion were squashed into a lump against the entry wound.

"You," came a cool female voice. "Yes, you. Innkeeper. Bring me some hot water in a bowl, clean towels, good brandy, and a hand of valerian root if you have one."

Such was the crisp authority in Violante of Arazzo's voice that the innkeeper emerged immediately from behind the bellows stock and began to do her bidding, stepping over Malray's men with only a minor shudder of distaste, as if they were drunk rather than dead or mortally wounded.

Brushing back hair wet with sweat and blood, Ravis turned to face Violante of Arazzo full on. He thought of saying something clever about her newly discovered talents in the kitchen, but he saw that as she cleaned blood and grease from her hands, her fingers were shaking. A quick glance at Bloody Nose's back revealed that she had used her own personal knife on him before picking up a spit and impaling the third man. Ravis spat blood and cloak wool from his mouth, then pressed his fist against the harrar wound.

"What? Do I get no thanks, Ravis of Burano?" Violante

dropped the rag she had been using to clean her hands. "Would your fair-haired friend have done so much?"

Ravis took a deep breath. He hoped Tessa was far away across the city in another inn, safe. "Thank you, Violante," he said after a moment. "You saved my life."

A quick, sad smile flashed across her face. "Not enough, though, is it?"

Seeing two bright spots shining behind her eyes, Ravis suddenly knew why she had come all this way to see him. It made him feel ashamed.

"Come," she said, stepping forward. "That wound on your ear needs stanching. You're losing blood."

Ravis let Violante care for him. With gentle hands and crisp words, she cleaned and bound his wounds, administered brandy and valerian root, massaged almond oil into the stretched flesh surrounding the harrar wound, warmed sheets before he lay upon them, and removed all his worries about the bodies, the state of the inn, and the financial loss to the innkeeper by spreading good portions of her own Istanian gold. It wasn't the sort of thing Ravis would normally do— give someone else leave to take care of his body and his problems—but Violante wanted to do it. And after all she had done for him this night, it was little to give in return.

TWENTY-ONE

I know! Let's count Snowy's toeys." Angeline of Halmac dragged her no-good dog onto her lap and began counting its no-good toes. Well, she wasn't actually sure if dogs had toes, but whatever they were she was counting them. "One toey, two toey, three toey . . ."

Snowy was more than a little indignant at having his toes counted, but he made no effort to struggle away. Here, in Izgard's armed camp, there was little else for mistress and no-good dog to do.

They couldn't leave the tent. Gerta said that just the sight of Angeline's golden hair could create a riot among the men. She was the only woman here, you see. Not counting Gerta, a few ancient cooks, and one or two hangers-on, of course. Gerta herself said she just didn't figure as a woman anymore. According to her, all men suffered from what she called "old maid's blindness," which meant they simply couldn't see women over a certain age. Angeline had thought it rather a strange condition and wondered if there were any cure.

Anyway, they *could* see Angeline. And queen or not, everyone said it was best for her to stay inside.

Which, Angeline thought ruefully, probably served her right. It was the desire to be outside that had got her into this whole mess in the first place. *Out*-side. *Out*-side. Angeline could almost hear Gerta's voice telling her that's what ill-scrupled liars got for scheming to be *out*-side.

Frowning, Angeline pushed Snowy from her lap. Father had hated liars. Angeline remembered the time he'd discovered his treasurer had been fiddling the estate accounts. "That man is an ill-scrupled liar," he had said. "Bind a rope around him and flog him till he bleeds."

Angeline shivered. She was a liar now.

Snowy, having recovered from the upset of being pushed onto the floor, came and sat at his mistress's feet. His tail was down and his eyes were big, and when Angeline ignored him he rolled on his back and howled.

Snowy here! Snowy here!

Angeline laughed despite herself. Snowy always knew when she needed cheering up.

As she leaned forward to pet him, a spasm tore along her side. Angeline screwed her face up tight, dug thumbnails into her palms. It wouldn't do to cry out. Just wouldn't do at all. Gerta was in the adjoining chamber, separated only by a stretch of cloth no thicker than Snowy's ear, and even the softest of noises had a way of carrying like war cries. The walls of Izgard's tent couldn't hold a candle against Sern Fortress when it came to muffling sound. Why, sometimes at night she heard Gerta breaking wind!

Bringing a hand to her side, Angeline massaged the bruised flesh. Izgard had been rough on her last night.

Not wanting to think about that, Angeline patted the bench for Snowy. "Hungry, Snowy?" she asked, suddenly feeling hungry herself. "How about I get us some supper?"

There was no mystery about what Snowy's answer would be. No-good dogs were always hungry. It was the main reason they did so many no-good things.

Jumping up, Snowy wagged his tail wildly.

Snowy starved! Snowy starved!

"Gerta!" Angeline called. "Gerta!"

Gerta now controlled all the food in Izgard's tent. All cold things like cheese, fruit, smoked sausages, bread, butter, and pies she kept locked in a wide-bottomed chest, metering them out through the day as needed. Isolated from her normal surroundings and with no female servants to boss over, Gerta needed *something* to be in charge of. Normally Angeline wouldn't spare a thought for such things, but these days she was hungry a lot. And asking Gerta for food every time she had a craving was beginning to annoy her just a bit.

"Yes, m'lady?" Gerta's large head emerged from the tent slit. "Is it your hot milk you'll be wanting?"

"Not milk, no. I'm—" Angeline glanced at Snowy.

"Snowy's hungry and needs some supper." She had already asked for two extra lots of food today. A third might make Gerta suspicious. After all, she was an old maid and Angeline knew they were trained to look for signs.

"That dog's getting no supper off me!" Gerta stamped her way into Angeline's chamber. Even at this late hour she was still equipped for battle: tweezers, scissors, brushes—three separate kinds—crochet needles, and curling irons were all hooked around her waist. No pins in her mouth, though. Angeline supposed she had to spit them out sometimes.

Angeline made her eyes as big as Snowy's and tried not to think of the fate that awaited ill-scrupled liars. "Please, Gerta. Just some cold chicken and a sausage. Snowy's sad at not being allowed to go outside, and some supper would help cheer him up." As she spoke, Angeline poked Snowy's belly with her foot.

The no-good dog took the hint, howling dolefully on impact.

Two sets of large blue eyes pleading with her was too much even for Gerta. Turning on her heel, she went back the way she came, muttering something about old bones.

Angeline felt bad. She didn't like deceiving Gerta. Gerta loved her, really, and she loved Gerta back. The trouble was that her one little lie had gotten out of control. Others popped up around it like mushrooms around a tree. She couldn't seem to open her mouth these days without adding to her sins. Lies about how she felt, why she didn't want her lacings tied as tightly as normal, and why she was sick so often tripped off her tongue so frequently, they were beginning to feel like truth. Now she'd demanded food for Snowy that she really wanted herself.

Tickling Snowy's chin, Angeline sighed. If she was only clever like other women, she could think of a way out of this.

It didn't help matters that since she'd arrived at the camp, Izgard had barely taken notice of her. He was different from before. Colder. There was a dullness in his eyes. At least it looked like dullness until you got very close, then you saw it was something else instead. His pupils looked as though they'd been etched by barbs.

He wasn't interested in her a bit—not in a husbandly sort

of way. All he thought about was war. He spent all his days riding out with his men and all his nights with his maps, his warlords, and his scribe. Gerta said the Garizon army was doing very well and had yet to meet any organized resistance. Every town they entered, they took, and the camp now moved northwest on an almost daily basis. Angeline was draped in cloaks and veils for the duration of each ride.

Sometimes Angeline thought Izgard asked for her just to keep up appearances, like last night. He wasn't interested in kissing or anything, and when she had touched him, he'd pushed her aside. What happened next was her own fault entirely. A clever woman would have known when to stop. Angeline shook her head. Not her. She thought that if she could just get close enough to him, he'd forget about his maps and scrolls and start acting the way he used to in the days before he acquired the crown. She had been wrong, though.

Angeline's hand stole to her side, and as she touched the bruised flesh she winced. Just as wrong as she could be.

The problem was she had to keep trying. Her only hope of getting out of this mess was to pretend she had conceived at the camp. That way she could admit she was pregnant, confess openly to the sickness, soreness, and blushing, and leave all the mushrooming lies behind. Only Izgard wasn't interested in her anymore, and if Gerta didn't already know it, her old maid's nose would sniff it out soon enough.

From her side, Angeline's hand curved across to her belly. She couldn't feel anything, but she could tell her baby was there all the same. Gerta had once said, "A woman knows about these things," and she was right. Angeline *did* know. She knew because she felt such love.

It was like the first time she'd seen Snowy, only more so. Her heart ached sometimes when she thought about it. She wanted her baby very much, and every day that went by she wanted it more. When Izgard had pushed her into the table last night, she had very nearly pushed him back. There was a minute or two when she was so angry that she forgot every caution Gerta had ever given her about dealing with her husband. All she wanted to do was hurt Izgard for hurting her. Balling her fists, she had scrambled up from the floor and actually gone to strike him.

One look from those dull gray eyes was all it had taken to stop her. Angeline had seen something she didn't like nestling within the dullness. Something that made her afraid. If provoked, Izgard could do much worse than push her. The truth of it was in those eyes.

Feeling her lip trembling, Angeline bit down on it before any sound escaped. She wished Father were here. Father would make everything right.

Father had loved babies. He always kissed them and stroked their heads. Sometimes he took them in his big, rough hands and held them up for Angeline to see. "Look, Angeline," he would cry. "You'll have a beauty like this one day. A sweet granddaughter for your old papa to fuss over."

Still biting on her lip, Angeline shook her head slowly. Father wouldn't have stood for Izgard pushing her. He would have taken her to Castle Halmac and spoiled her until his grandchild was born. Angeline stamped her foot on the packed, carpet-covered earth of the tent. And afterward he would have spoiled her more.

"Here you are, m'lady." Gerta said, emerging platter first into the chamber. "I've found some drumsticks and a little chicken skin. More than enough for that no-good dog."

"Oh." Angeline's face dropped. She had been hoping for sausages and breast meat. Remembering that the food was for Snowy, not herself, she forced herself to nod. "Thank you, Gerta. You can go now."

Gerta's eyes widened. Angeline never dismissed her. "Go?"

"Yes, go. I'll take care of my own toilette tonight."

"But, m'lady, your hair—"

"Go, Gerta!" Angeline tried her best to copy the tone of voice Gerta herself used when barking orders to servants in Sern Fortress. It seemed to work, as Gerta's lips came together rather quickly and her forehead dipped in something close to a nod.

"Yes, m'lady," she said. After slipping the platter onto a nearby chest, Gerta pulled the tent flap to one side and stepped through to her private chamber, an offended sniff following her from the room. Hearing the sniff, Angeline very nearly gave in and called her back. She hated giving orders. Somehow she never got them right.

"Here, Snowy," she called, standing up and crossing over to the platter. "Supper for you and me."

The drumsticks were thin and greasy, but Angeline tore at them all the same. Her own hunger surprised her these days. She was sure the court ladies at Veizach would never stoop to gnaw at bones. Snowy dutifully ate the chicken skin, though he knew quite well there was meat. When Angeline had finished with the bones, she teased Snowy with them, making him jump high, roll over, and fetch. Snowy only went along with these games for only so long before pouting in his doggy way and skulking to a corner. Angeline wasn't fooled. It was just another of his no-good ploys.

After a while of playing, bone munching, belly tickling, and resting, a noise sounded from the adjoining chamber. Angeline held her breath, listening for the noise to come again. Which it did. Good. It was Gerta snoring. The old maid was fast asleep.

"You stay here, Snowy," Angeline whispered, grabbing her cloak from its place near the entrance. "I'll be back before you know it. I'm just going to see Ederius."

Snowy was lying, belly up, on his cushion, too well stuffed with chicken bones for any meaningful sort of protest. Angeline patted his no-good head and slipped out into the night.

The camp smelled of woodsmoke and horses. A mild wind forced Angeline to keep a hand on her hood as she walked, and the ground was muddy enough to make her watch her step. The two guards posted outside the tent stood to attention as she passed. Emboldened by the fact that she didn't recognize either man, Angeline acknowledged them with a little wave. It was always easier to act queenly around those she didn't know.

The coldness of the night had little effect on her. Halmac born and bred, she could endure a lot worse than a mild chill and an easterly breeze. Father always said that in all of Garizon there was no winter to match Halmac's when it came to matters of frost and sleet. Once, when Angeline was very young, she had gone running to Father in tears because they'd been snowed in for weeks and she was tired of being cold and bored. "We should be thankful for the snow, Angeline," he had said. "Every day it stays here it teaches us how to be strong. It's what puts the steel in Halmac bones."

Angeline frowned as she made her way through the camp. Her bones didn't feel much like steel now.

The lights in the command tent were blazing. A dozen separate shadows flickered across the canvas, and although Angeline could not pick out Izgard's form among them, she was sure he was there.

Slipping into the darkness, she avoided the command tent guards, veering off to the quiet side of the camp, where surgeons, clerics, and aides pitched their tents. Ederius' tent was among them. Angeline spotted it straight away, as it was the only one brightly lit. Izgard had him working hard these days. Sometimes Ederius even jotted patterns in his girdle book as he rode.

"Ederius! It's me—Angeline." As soon as the words were hissed, Angeline stepped into Ederius' tent. She didn't want to risk anyone catching her loitering outside.

Ederius' head came up from a book as she entered. "M'lady?" The scribe sounded more startled than angry. His gray hair looked as if it had been slept on, then not brushed. His tent didn't smell nice, and books, scrolls, and paint pots were scattered on the floor.

Angeline pushed back her hood. "I've come to see how you are," she said, conjuring up an image of Gerta scolding scullery maids in an attempt to sound commanding.

"You must go, m'lady." Ederius' eyes flicked to the tent flap. "At once. It would not be fitting for you to—"

"Ssh," Angeline said, cutting him short. "I've come to see how you are, and I'm not going until you tell me." Rather pleased with the way her words came out, she walked into the center of the tent and sat on the tallest of Ederius' chests. Made from satinwood and thick with varnish, the chest was polished so smoothly that Angeline felt her bottom sliding as she settled herself on the lid.

"So, how are you, Ederius? You look terribly pale."

"I am well, m'lady. Very well."

Angeline doubted that. "Izgard works you hard, doesn't he?"

Ederius, as if becoming resigned to the fact that Angeline wasn't about to leave until she got some answers, pushed the book he had been reading to one side. "I am the king's servant to command, m'lady."

"And he commands you to read books after midnight?"

Ederius began to nod, paused, then shook his head instead. "It is by choice I work this late, m'lady. There are things I must study."

"Like your patterns?"

"Yes, like my patterns."

Angeline frowned. Ederius really did look ill. He sounded ill, too. Like Father had the year before he died. Reaching forward, she brushed her hand against Ederius' cheek. The scribe flinched.

Realizing what he had done, he shook his head softly. "Forgive me, m'lady. My nerves are not what they were."

Angeline had seen dogs flinch like that. Dogs beaten by Father's houndsmaster for being cowardly or bad. Before she had time to think, words spilled out of her mouth. "Does Izgard hurt you, too?"

Ederius looked at her a very long time before answering. His old face looked worried and sad. "My lady," he said gently, his hand hovering above his lap, as if he wanted to touch her but didn't dare, "you must promise me never to make the king angry. Try to say nothing that will upset or agitate him, and if he ever does become angry, you must always run to Gerta straight away."

"But—"

"Promise me."

Angeline had never seen Ederius so firm. He sounded just like Father, the time he forbade her to ride past the boundaries of Halmac land. "There are brigands on the free roads," he had said, "I will not have my best girl riding on highways that are unsafe."

For some reason Angeline found it hard to meet Ederius' gaze. Her eyes ached. Head bowed toward the floor, she said, "I promise."

Even as she spoke it, she knew it would be impossible to keep. There was no telling what would make Izgard angry these days. The slightest word or look might provoke him. Yet even knowing that, Angeline was glad Ederius had made her promise. Father would have done just the same.

Ederius stood. "Good. Now you must leave, m'lady. I sent a messenger to the king but a few minutes back, asking him to join me in my tent. He could be here any moment."

"But—"

"No, Angeline. Remember your promise: you must do nothing to anger the king."

Angeline closed her mouth. She felt as if she'd been tricked, yet when she looked into Ederius' eyes she knew she was wrong. "Very well, I'll go," she said, slipping from the chest to her feet. For a moment she considered asking Ederius to make the same promise as she had made to him, yet she didn't quite have the nerve for it.

Instead she said, "Izgard won't be angry with you tonight, will he?"

"No," Ederius said. "I have just found something that should please him greatly."

"What?"

"A pattern that lets me find people in the dark."

Angeline shivered; she didn't like the way Ederius said the word *dark*. Pulling the hood over her face, she slipped out into the night.

As she made her way across the camp Angeline passed within three paces of Izgard, yet by some miracle he failed to stop her. His gaze was turned inward, toward himself.

Izgard looked over his shoulder, watching the silhouette as it receded into the darkness of the camp. Any other time he might have turned, tracked the figure down, and demanded to know what they were doing walking through this section after dark. Small things were beginning to matter less and less, though. He had just spent the past four hours in conference with his warlords, and anything not directly concerned

with war and its making had a hard time finding purchase in
his mind.

Pulling back the canvas flap, Izgard stepped into Ederius'
tent. The scribe stood motionless in a halo of golden light.
He was holding a quill pen, and the veins of the feather shook
along with his hand. For a brief moment Izgard found himself surprised at how frail Ederius looked. Had he always
been that pale? How long had those dark circles ringed his
eyes? Shaking aside his unease, Izgard said, "What news do
you have for me, scribe?"

Ederius moved behind his desk before he spoke. "Sire, I
have been looking through Gamberon's old books and have
come across a sequence of patterns that allow me to track
certain people down over great distances."

"What kind of people?"

"Those who venture into the darkness beyond the ink."

"Scribes, you mean?"

Ederius shook his head. He dragged one of the large pigment boxes from the corner of his desk, bringing it to rest directly in front of him. Izgard got the impression the scribe
was arranging his defenses.

"Not all scribes, sire," Ederius said. "Only those who
deal in the old patterns and draw forth power through the
vellum."

"The girl?"

Ederius nodded. "I believe I can find her. Once someone
has passed through to the other side, to the folds that lie beneath the ink, traces of power cling to them like pollen to an
insect's wing. I think I can paint a pattern that will illuminate
the way."

Excited, Izgard stepped forward. Ederius moved back.
"You have done well, my friend," Izgard said. "Of all those
who surround me, you are the only one I love and trust."

A small, sad smile stretched Ederius' lips. "I know, sire."

Hearing the catch in Ederius' voice, seeing the way his
entire body strained backward away from him, Izgard paused
in midstep. How long had Ederius been afraid of him?

"Tomorrow I will discover where the girl is," Ederius
said, breaking through Izgard's thoughts.

"And send the harras after her?"

"If she is still in or around Bay'Zell."

"What if she is somewhere else, out of range of the harras?"

Ederius pulled upon a piece of cloth and uncovered the Barbed Coil. "Then I will use someone close to hand instead."

Izgard's eyes were drawn toward the Coil, all his earlier concerns about Ederius forgotten. "You can change others in the same way you change the harras?"

"I believe so." Ederius' voice was low. "The Coil harbors far worse demons than those loosed upon harras."

"What else?"

"Gathelocs."

Izgard shuddered at the word, and as he listened to Ederius' description of the creatures he shuddered more. By the time the meeting was over and Izgard spoke the words "Kill her quickly but discreetly," the chill he felt had passed down to his lungs, where it turned the air he exhaled into mist.

Tessa walked. She walked until her feet were sore, her leg muscles were stiff, and the darkness took on the grainy look of predawn. She didn't know where she was headed, didn't even know why she was walking at all. Sometimes people called to her—men, usually—yet for the most part the night folk of Kilgrim left her well alone. She supposed she looked like one of them. Her cloak was long gone, her dress was ripped, and she had a gash on her left shoulder from being pushed against a nail-encrusted door frame by someone rushing to escape from the inn.

Kilgrim was a dark, dripping maze. Water gurgled beneath drains set deep amid the cobbled road. Moisture glistened on walls and seeped from crumbling mortar; overflow ran along storm channels and bubbled from lead pipes. Archways rained water on Tessa's back as she passed under them, and every dip in the path formed a wet and glistening pool.

It drizzled for an hour or so in the middle of the night.

Tessa was glad of it at first, as it cleared her head a bit and emptied the streets of the few people who were still about. Then the rain began to soak through her dress and make her shiver. Just when she decided she really should find some shelter, the rain stopped, robbing her of all resolve. She hadn't gotten around to making another decision since.

Somehow, when the air cleared from the rain she found herself outside the inn Violante of Arazzo had led them to. The building was quiet now, shut up for the night. Tessa approached the door, but as she raised her hand to knock, she smelled violets. Hours later, and the air still smelled of Violante of Arazzo's perfume. Suddenly unsure of herself, Tessa turned and ran away.

She tried not to walk in circles after that, and somehow her mind had picked up on this idea and turned it into a game. She was never to walk down the same street twice or backtrack and retrace her steps. There were times when she became so caught up in the game that she walked streets out of her way just to end up on the far side of a promising wall or forced herself to march past dodgy-looking men to prevent breaking her own rule about doubling back.

As the night wore on the game grew more elaborate, involving counting steps, dodging archways, and never falling under the same shadow twice.

Tessa knew it was madness, but it didn't stop her from playing. At least while she played, she could push all decisions to the back of her mind, and she didn't have to think about Ravis.

Ravis. No—Tessa turned down an alleyway at random, daring it to be a dead end—she wouldn't think about him.

Tessa's throat felt sore for a moment, and she had to swallow once or twice to make it better, but by the time the alleyway's shadows engulfed her she was caught once more in the game.

The gash on her shoulder stung from step to step, and Tessa used the distance between stingings to judge her pace. For some reason, now that the darkness was lifting and dawn was on its way, she found herself walking faster. She hadn't walked down every street yet, seen what lay beyond every dripping archway and moss-lined wall. Gaze fixed firmly on the cobbles beneath her feet, Tessa rushed down the alley-way into the shadows and away from the dawn.

A dead end stopped her in her tracks. A tall wall, twice her height, blocked the way ahead. Seeing it, Tessa felt her heart sink inside her chest. The game was over now. She'd have to break all her own rules just to get back onto the street.

Tessa spun around, put her back against the wall, and slowly let her body sink to the ground. She ached all over. Muscles in her calves, ankles, feet, back, neck, and arms all throbbed in disunion. The soreness in her throat returned, and no amount of swallowing would make it go away.

The sky grew lighter by the second, revealing steaming banks of thick gray cloud whipped by invisible winds. It was going to rain again some time soon. Tessa smiled weakly. Mother Emith had been right to call Maribane a damp, driz-zly island made for brooding.

Resting her head against her knees, Tessa sighed. What was she going to do now? The game was over, dawn was breaking, and she had to get out of Kilgrim. This place wasn't safe. A shudder started in Tessa's ankles and worked its way up her body to her shoulders. Her mouth burst open and a high, choking sound came out.

What had become of Ravis?

Tessa ground her forehead against her knee bone. Every-thing had happened so fast—armed men bursting into the inn, demanding to know where Ravis of Burano was, then Ravis appearing in the doorway, the first words from his lips a warning to Violante of Arazzo. Tessa swallowed hard. He had been afraid for Violante, not for *her*.

Lifting her head, Tessa took a long, hard breath. What did she expect? She'd only known Ravis for a few weeks. Violante acted as if she had known him for years. They had planned to meet in Mizerico. And Violante was so beautiful . . . Tessa shook her head. She couldn't compete with a woman like that.

Suddenly uncomfortable with the turn her thoughts were taking, Tessa forced her mind back to the present and strug-gled to her feet. She still had to get to the Anointed Isle. Nothing had changed that.

Her body had grown heavier while she crouched. The

sting on her shoulder felt sharper than she remembered, and she suddenly became aware she was cold. Glancing down the alleyway, back the way she'd come, Tessa forced her mind to go to work. She needed a cloak, somewhere to freshen up and eat, and someone to point her to Bellhaven. Ravis would be all right without her, she was sure of that. It would take more than six armed men to get the better of him. Besides, he had Violante now.

As Tessa thought, her hand felt for and then curled around the money purse at her waist. Now she was no longer playing games, it seemed dangerous to have it swinging in full sight, and she plucked it from her belt, took out one silver and two gold coins, then tucked it deep inside her bodice. This one small act of decisiveness calmed her, helped her remember who she was. Taking a quick breath to brace herself, she began walking down the street, breaking three of her own rules with her very first step.

TWENTY-TWO

Sandor, Sire of Rhaize, laughed. A fraction of a second later his entourage laughed, too. When he stopped, so did they. "You mean to tell me, Camron of Thorn, that you think my armies, my knights, my strategies, and my wits are no match for the Garizon king?"

Camron felt his palms sweating. Sandor's entourage—knights, generals, lords, and lectures—all looked his way for an answer. Finally, after a week of appeals, the Sire had granted him an audience. Camron had prepared every word, every gesture. Broc of Lomis waited in the back of the hall to bear witness to his story if needed, and more men waited outside.

"Yes, sire," Camron cursed himself. "I mean no, sire." Rushing on to cover his blunder, he said. "What I mean is that I have seen Izgard's army—fought them. They're not like other men. The harras are . . ." Camron bunched his fists, willed the right word to come.

"The harras are what?" Sandor's voice was light, his gaze flicked around the court as if they were all party to some clever joke.

"Monsters." Camron spat out the word. It silenced the court.

Sandor regarded Camron. After a moment he stroked his fingers across his close-trimmed beard. "You tell me nothing I do not know, Thorn. I received reports from the town bearing your name. I have read the catalog of Izgard's sins. I know his men built a bonfire and threw women and children upon it." Sandor paused. He no longer looked at the court; his blue eyes gazed solely at Camron. "That is why my forces are on the way to intercept him, and why tomorrow I go forth myself."

Silence followed the Sire's words. The court shifted uneasily, transferring their weight from foot to foot. Camron glanced around the Hall of Kings at Mir'Lor. Burnished candelabras as large and many branched as pear trees blazed against walls and ceilings of midnight blue. Stars, comets, moons, and winged creatures voyaged across the make-believe sky. The floor was a glittering patchwork of stone. Quartz, granite, marble, slate, mica, bluestone, onyx, shale, and more: samples of every kind of stone mined in Rhaize shone beneath Camron's feet.

Camron suddenly felt tired. This was no place for him to be. There was nothing for him to do here. "Sire," he said, knowing it was not his place to speak into his king's silence, but helpless to stop himself, "I beg you, take precautions with your men. Do not fight at close range, use arrows and missiles, lances if you have to. But do not head into anything blindly. Know that the harras will fight until their legs are hacked from under them."

A buzz erupted in the court. A woman near the back inhaled sharply. Someone coughed.

Sandor tapped his hand on his chin. "But you survived, Thorn." His smile was faint but unmistakable. "As did the man behind you."

"Sire—"

Sandor's hand shot up from his chin, silencing Camron. "You hire and fight with mercenaries, do you not?"

Camron tugged his hair in frustration. "And if I do? That has no bearing on why I am here. I came to warn you, to help you prepare." He was losing them; he could tell from the way they refused to look him in the eye. In his desperation, he motioned toward Broc. "Ask Broc of Lomis, ask any of my men—they will tell you what the harras are like. Rhaize knights will die if—"

"Enough." Sandor cracked the word like a whip.

Camron pressed his lips together. He was dealing with this badly. Not so long ago he could have shaped words smooth enough to convince Sandor's urbane and worldly court of the dangers, yet now he knew only how to speak plainly. Too much was at stake for anything less. Stepping forward, he spoke again. "Sire, I want to travel north with you. My men can help you with the harras, tell you what to expect."

"Camron of Thorn," Sandor said, addressing the court rather than the man he had named, "I am not a fool, and will turn down no one who offers me help in this hour. I have seen your men and I know they are worthy, and you yourself, despite a certain rashness of manner, seem young and strong and able. Indeed, just for your name alone I would bid you ride at my flank—your father's victory at Mount Creed has not been forgotten."

Sandor paused, better to pounce on his next sentence. "But you must remember that Rhaize knights have remained unbeaten in battle for the past fifty years. *Fifty* years. No small feat, I'm sure you'll agree." The court was favored with a deprecating smile. "So, while I note your concerns and those of your men, you must forgive me for remaining uncowed by your warnings. I am a leader and must lead my armies without fear."

A second passed, then the court erupted; men stamped their feet and spear butts against the glittering floor. Silk rustled, palms were slapped against silver cups. "Aye!" was shouted loudly by many.

Camron's heart sank. He tugged at his hair, cursed himself again. Sandor's speech was faultless—putting Camron in his place in the most disarming of manners. There was nothing to speak up against now. Sandor had maneuvered himself onto the high ground of kings.

Locking gazes with Camron over the uproar, Sandor smiled. Camron didn't know whether it was out of sympathy or satisfaction. He didn't even know if he cared.

He had failed.

"Have your men report to Balanon tonight. You will find him camped on the east side of the hill." Sandor. It was a dismissal.

Camron inclined his head. "As you wish, sire."

The uproar had died down quickly, and all eyes were on Camron as he walked toward the double doors. Camron didn't bother to hide his limp as he had upon entering. He was wounded—let them know it. Broc came forward to join him, lips stretching to a sympathetic curve. Camron was glad of a smile he knew was genuine. Despite the fact that great sections of his arms, legs, and lower abdomen were still bulked up by bandages, Broc had dressed with care. The brass on his belt and buckler shone like gold, and beneath his tunic he wore an undershirt of bright red silk. Broc had admitted earlier, a little gingerly, that his younger sister had made him wear it.

Sandor chose not to say anything as the two men left the room. Perhaps he knew the sight of the two men limping was more succinct a statement than any words he could think of just then.

Camron held out his arm to Broc, taking as much of his weight as he could while still allowing Broc the appearance of walking freely.

"I can't believe the Sire didn't listen," Broc murmured as they passed under the shadow of the door.

Camron didn't reply. Truth was, he had acted in just the same way with Ravis only two months earlier. Rhaize pride was hard to break—Sandor could hardly be blamed for that. Camron held his breath a long moment before letting it out. The fault was all his own: he should have handled things differently, spoken more eloquently, played the court at its own courtly games.

"My lord Thorn?" came a soft voice.

Camron swung around to see who had spoken. A young girl, dark haired and dressed in white, curtsied. Camron nodded. "I am he."

The girl glanced around, curtsied again, then spoke in a whisper. "Sir, the lady Lianne requests that you visit her apartments tonight at dusk."

Sandor's mother. The countess of Mir'Lor. What could she want with him? Camron found himself glancing around the antechamber just as the girl had. The doors leading to the Hall of Kings banged shut as he spoke his reply. "Tell Her Highness I would be honored to attend upon her."

The girl bobbed once more and then scurried off down a corridor, silken slippers pitter-pattering against stone.

Broc made a soft sound in his throat. "Some say the countess is the real power in Rhaize. You should try to get her on your side."

"I'll try, but I'm no ladies' man."

"Well, perhaps you *could* be a little less direct with the mother than you were with the son. Try not to mention hacking limbs in her presence."

Camron managed a grim smile. "I made a mess of things, didn't I?"

"No, you didn't. You spoke honestly and bravely, and I think people will leave the hall thinking about what you said."

Hearing sounds of strain in Broc's voice, Camron resumed walking across the antechamber. It was a mistake to have brought Broc here. The knight should be resting in his bed, not walking around leagues of palace corridors on the chance that his support might be needed. Edging closer, Camron took more of Broc's weight upon his arm.

"How can I get Sandor to understand, Broc?" he asked. "How can I make him see that the harras are—" Camron checked himself. Broc knew what they were just as well as he.

"Use the journey up north to talk to people. If you can get them to be cautious, that should be enough."

Cautious. Camron flinched at the word. If he hadn't been so caught up in his own problems the day they rode into the Valley of Broken Stones, they might never have encountered the harras. Men would be alive today. Caution could have saved them. Feeling a sickening pull in his stomach, Camron forced himself to speak. "I'll do what I can."

Broc nodded. "I know you will."

They were both silent for a while after that.

"Canna give it yer gratty, lovey. Why, me wife would pollox me on the spot."

Tessa nodded wisely, though in truth she hardly knew what the stall holder was saying. She guessed his tactics, though. "Well, I'll be off to look somewhere else. Thank you for your trouble." She spun around, sending her skirts swishing after her, and began to walk away from the used-clothing stall.

The stall holder called after her. "I mebbe able to rub a little suet off the top."

Tessa carried on walking as she cried, "I can't give you any more than a silver for it. I'm sorry for wasting your time."

"Come back, lovey. I'll see what I can do."

Tessa held her ground. "One silver."

The stall holder sighed. "One silver it is."

Resisting the urge to jump on the spot, Tessa returned to the stall. The cloak she had just negotiated for was made of dark blue velvet, and as she approached, the stall holder ran his fingers along the fabric, raising the weft.

"A bargain, lovey! A bargain!" He sighed again, shook his head. "Me wife will surely pollox me."

Tessa handed him a silver coin. She really did want the cloak. "Where can I get some breakfast around here? And freshen myself up before my journey north?"

"Wicks Supper 'n' Board will be the place ye're after, lovey. All thems that head north start their journey at Wicks."

Tessa nodded. While the stall holder was speaking, she had been pulling the cloak off his table, winding the fabric around her wrist. The marketplace she had stumbled upon seemed safe enough, and the stall holder looked as honest as any, but she felt better taking precautions. "Which way is Wicks?"

"Down th' Aspeys and short right on Kings. Canna miss it. Big red shutters, lots o' smoke." As he spoke, the stall holder rolled his eyes to indicate the direction. "Going to Palmsey, are yer?"

"No, to Bellhaven. To the Anointed Isle."

The stall holder sucked at the insides of his cheeks. He let go of the last corner of the cloak, allowing Tessa to pull it away. "Best be getting a move on, then. Y'ill be wanting th' early start."

Tessa took the cloak, threw it over her shoulders, thanked the stall holder, and walked away. She told herself it wasn't fear she had heard in the man's voice at the mention of the Anointed Isle, just surprise.

Rain began to drizzle softly as Tessa walked the length of the still-forming market. Merchants were busy setting up stalls, packing tables with wares, unloading mules, and throwing curses at the rain. The place had a different feel to it than Bay'Zell; it was drabber, more subdued except for the cursing, not a good place to linger now she wasn't protected by mindless games. Tessa wished she weren't here.

She couldn't go back, though. She had to do what she was brought here for: to fight against the harras, send them back to wherever they belonged. Deveric had believed she could do it, and there was some small part of Tessa that believed she could too. She had felt many things that morning in Mother Emith's kitchen when she'd picked up her brush and painted the pattern, yet looking back on it now, in the damp and dismal light of a Maribane dawn, Tessa realized the most potent thing she felt was power. For a few seconds she, Tessa McCamfrey, had held the harras back.

Tessa snuggled her shoulders against her new cloak. She didn't feel any better, but she was clear about her job. She had to get to the Anointed Isle.

Wicks Supper 'n' Board was easy to spot. Shutters as large as doors were flung open onto the street, and clouds of water vapor burst from them like steam from a geyser. Puzzled, Tessa looked up, squinted, then nodded. No chimney.

"Breakfast, board, or delivery?"

Tessa spun around to see a young boy tugging her cloak tail. The boy's cheeks and forehead were flushed red, and a film of sweat gave a high gloss to his nose.

"Breakfast, board, or delivery?"

"Breakfast."

As if she had uttered a magic word, the boy grabbed her elbow through the fabric of her cloak and led her through one of the open shutters into the dark, steamy interior of Wicks. "Don't have no doors at Wicks," the boy offered without prompting. "Missis Wicks won't have 'em."

Tessa blinked, trying to accustom her eyes to the darkness.

"Don't have no candles, either." The boy spoke in a matter-of-fact manner. "Missis Wicks says only God-given light is right and proper to eat by."

Tessa wondered what Missis Wicks' customers did at night. The smell of fresh-baked bread, fried onions, and smoked bacon soon put a stop to all conjecture. Yes, Tessa thought to herself, mouth watering despite everything, I'd sit here and eat in the dark.

The boy ushered her to a long bench beside a long table and bade her sit. The room was noisy and packed with people eating, drinking, and chatting. Tessa scooted along the bench so she could sit in the shadows of the wall. She didn't want to draw any unnecessary attention her way.

" 'Ere yöu are, lady." The boy returned with a jug of something hot and a loaf of bread with the middle scooped out and melting butter and honey spooned in its place. "I'll be back with the rest soon's it's done."

Tessa went to thank him, but he had already moved away. There was no cup—Missis Wicks probably didn't believe in those, either—so she drank from the jug. It was some sort of tea, spiced and very sweet, and absolutely delicious. Tessa drained the jug—she hadn't even realized she was thirsty. The bread was warm and filled with nuts and grains. As she ate, Tessa leaned back against the wall, put her feet on the base of the table, and rested her aching muscles. She wasn't tired in a yawning, stretching sort of way—she had long since walked her way through that stage—she was just plain exhausted.

" 'Ere you are, lady. Sausages and bacon, with a slice of ham thrown in gratty. Compliments of Missis Wicks."

"Gratty?" It was time she learned what the people of this strange, drizzly island were talking about.

"Free, lady. Missis Wicks always gives new customers a free slice of ham." The boy dabbed at his brow with his sleeve. "You'll be needing a cloth for it, though. Cart leaves for Palmsey within the quarter."

"I'm not heading to Palmsey."

The boy took this piece of information and chewed on it. His jaw worked for a moment and then he spoke. "Where you be heading, then?"

"Bellhaven."

Glancing into the banks of steaming clouds that obscured the fire and cooking range from view, the boy repeated the word as if it were an answer to some long-mulled-over puzzle. He spun on his heels and headed back into the steam. "I'll be gone just a spit."

Tessa let him go. She didn't know what he was up to, but she didn't sense any danger. As she went to pull the platter containing the bacon and sausages toward her, the pain in her shoulder flared. She tensed her jaw, counted to three, then relaxed. The pain was slow to recede. The muscle, which she had kept loose all night by walking, was beginning to stiffen up.

The fatty smell of the ham and bacon caught in her throat, making her feel sick. Against her will, her mind replayed what had happened last night at the inn. She heard Ravis warn Violante to step back and then watched as he launched himself toward the two armed men holding the innkeeper, shouting at everyone else to run. Tessa shoved the platter to one side. She had to believe he was all right.

"Are you the young woman heading to Bellhaven?"

Startled, Tessa looked up. A woman with fat red cheeks and high gray hair stood before her. Annoyed to find herself shaking, Tessa worked hard to regain her composure. "I am."

"And do you intend to leave this morning?"

The pain in her shoulder made Tessa snap. "What's it to you?"

The woman's chin receded into the folds of her neck, and she blinked several times in quick succession. After a moment the chin came out again, looking blunter than before. "I've been meaning to make that journey for weeks now, but as a woman I refuse to take the road alone. Simply won't do it." The woman shook her head emphatically. "No, by God's good name I won't."

Something in the woman's manner prompted Tessa to ask, "Missis Wicks?"

The woman nodded. "One and the same."

"And you're going to Bellhaven, too? This morning?"

"I am if there's another woman by my side for decency's sake."

"No other women travel to Bellhaven?"

"None that are decent."

Tessa thought a moment. "How long is the journey?"

"Day and a half. There's a party of three leaving within the half hour." The woman sniffed. "Though a word from me will slow them down soon enough."

Tessa didn't doubt it. "Is there anywhere I can freshen up before leaving?"

"This is Wicks Supper 'n' Board. If a traveler has a God-given need, we attend to it. Follow me and I'll show you to a room."

Tessa followed. She walked in Missis Wicks' considerable wake through billowing clouds of steam and ever-increasing darkness, too tired to be surprised at her own willingness to let someone else take charge for a while.

Camron tugged down his tunic, smoothed a hand through his hair, and knocked on the gold-and-white-striped door before him. Despite its delicate look, the door was made of solid oak and Camron's knock sounded muffled and flat.

"Enter," called a soft voice.

Camron pushed on the wood and took his first step into the room. Glancing at the edge of the door, he saw the wood was almost a fist thick. How had someone's voice managed to penetrate its thickness while sounding so soft?

"Welcome, Camron of Thorn."

Camron looked up to see a woman dressed in a shimmering gray dress, with hair perfectly white and eyes so blue that even from this distance, in the failing light of day and the flickering shadows cast by candles just lit, they drew one's gaze as surely as jewels cast upon a jet black cloth. As if well aware of the worth of her eyes, the woman did not blink once as she crossed the space to the door.

"Your Highness." Camron bowed to cover his surprise. He had not imagined he would meet the countess so soon upon entering her chambers. Where were her ladies, her attendants?

As if he had spoken the question out loud, the woman held out her hand and said, "Come, I am too old to waste my time standing on ceremony, and have well passed the stage where I need an entourage to excite respect." A well-arched eyebrow arched one degree more. "Pour yourself a glass of wine, then sit or stand as you wish."

Camron's fingers barely had chance to close around the cool palm of Lianne, countess of Mir'Lor, before the woman withdrew her touch. She turned her back on him, and he followed her toward the center of the room. Unlike the formal sections of the palace, the countess's private chamber was low ceilinged and intimate. Umber-painted panels glowed in the candlelight, thick saffron-colored carpets muted Camron's steps, and deep within a red stone hearth, a small but forceful fire blazed with purely golden flames.

Reaching a cluster of high-backed chairs, cushioned benches, and tables, the countess turned and made a small gesture to a silver tray laid with goblets and a single jug of wine. Even though his mouth was dry, Camron did not want a drink. Something told him he would need all his wits about him when talking to this woman. He could not refuse her request, though, and poured them both a cup of wine. As soon as he tilted the jug, the fumes of fourteen-year-old berriac rose up to meet his nose. Memories, brittle as autumn leaves, gathered in the back of his throat: Thorn, his father, long evenings sitting around the great hearth, talking weapons and supplies and estate business.

Camron swallowed hard. Aware that his hand was shaking, he forced himself to concentrate on pouring the wine as evenly as he could. When he looked up, he saw the countess was watching him.

"There is no wine to match that made in Thorn," she said.

Seeing her this close, Camron realized she was very old. Small, too, though he had not noticed it when he followed her across the room.

"What do you want from me?" he asked.

She seemed less surprised at the question than he was. Camron could hardly believe he had asked it. Was it the fumes from the wine or the sheer weight of the countess's presence that had forced him to speak so openly? He didn't know. But he did not take the question back.

Taking the second goblet from his hand, Lianne said, "You will be heading north with my son's forces at dawn." It was not a question, but she paused all the same, giving Camron time to realize that she knew all that had happened that morning in the Hall of Kings. Fixing him with a gaze as direct as only eyes that color could allow, she said, "Tell me, Camron of Thorn, when you meet Izgard's army on the field, what will you be fighting for?"

Camron felt blood flush up his cheeks. He looked down, away from the scrutiny of those perfect blue eyes.

"Vengeance?" she said. "Love for Rhaize? Or do you see it as a chance to step out from your father's long shadow and create a new generation's Mount Creed?"

Angry now, Camron shook his head. "I will fight for my father's memory, and for Thorn and the people who died there."

"Aah," Lianne said, ringing the goblet with her finger. "All three, then."

"No." Camron slammed the jug onto the tray. Silver goblets tinkled like bells. What was it about this woman? What gave her the right to say such things? Feeling almost drunk, as if he had swallowed rather than inhaled the wine before him, Camron stepped away from the countess and her nest of tables and chairs. "I did not come here to talk of myself. As you say, the Rhaize army moves north first thing tomorrow. I came to Mir'Lor to warn your son that Izgard is fighting with—" Camron checked himself, remembering his earlier performance in front of the Sire's entourage. "Unnatural advantages."

A husky sound that might have been a laugh sounded deep within Lianne's throat. Turning toward the light from the fire, she took a long drink from her cup. Camron saw then how beautiful she was: the long sweep of her neck, the upward tilt of her cheekbones. What was it people used to say about her? *All of Rhaize is met within her eyes.* There was something else, too. Something about her having had the two most powerful men in the country as her suitors. Besides the old Sire himself, Camron could not guess who the other man might be.

Lianne, countess of Mir'Lor, trailed a long finger over her lip. For a moment she looked just like her son. "What if I could give you another reason to fight, Camron of Thorn? What would you say to that?"

Camron tugged at his hair, frustrated. Men and women were dead. His father was dead. Why couldn't he get the people in this palace to see that? Why wouldn't they listen? "I have reasons enough to fight, my lady. Anyone who sees the harras cannot doubt that."

Unaffected by the force of his words, Lianne smiled slowly. "You are so like your father when you are angry, you know."

A muscle tightened in Camron's chest. He felt disoriented, as if he had been thrown into the middle of a game with no rules. "You knew my father?"

Lianne nodded. For the first time since Camron had walked through her door, she looked down. "You could say that. Many years ago now. Back in the days of war and Mount Creed."

Camron's first reaction was disbelief. How could his father have known the countess of Mir'Lor and not mention it?

"We were of an age, he and I," Lianne said, turning her back on Camron and walking toward the fire. "He and I were the only two left who remembered Garizon for what it was." She shrugged at the flames. "Now Berick is dead, and I am the only one."

Abruptly she turned from the fire. Her eyes were bright, and two spots of color blazed high on her cheeks. "So don't think you come here telling me things I do not know. All tales of Garizon and its kings are old news to me."

Camron bowed his head. Every time this woman spoke she stole a little more of the solid ground beneath his feet. "He never spoke of you."

"There was much he never spoke of."

"What do you mean?"

"He never spoke of Garizon to you, did he?"

"You are mistaken, my lady. He did speak of Garizon. He told me how, twenty-one years ago, he relinquished his claims upon the crown because he wanted to give the Garizon people peace. He said they had suffered enough at Mount Creed and a civil war would only tear them apart."

Lianne made a small flicking motion with her hand. "If your father relinquished all claims on Garizon, why then did he sign all his letters with the amethyst wax of Garizon sovereignty up until his dying day?"

Camron kept very still. His chest felt so tight, he didn't risk a breath. Amethyst wax. The same color he had used to seal the very last letter he'd written to his father. The same color that was caked under his thumbnail as he'd pumped at his father's heart.

Lianne watched him with a steady gaze. "He made you use it, too, didn't he?"

Camron felt the pressure in his chest shift down toward his gut. He shook his head. "It meant nothing. Nothing. It was just a family custom, that was all." Even as he spoke he felt the lie. The fire suddenly seemed close enough to burn his face.

"I don't think you really believe that, do you?"

And with that, Lianne, countess of Mir'Lor, took away Camron's last patch of solid ground. Camron felt himself falling. He was back in his father's study once more, kneeling over Berick's body. The room was full of light, the air tasted of wet fur and warm blood, and as the harras changed from monsters to men, they cast shifting, liquid shadows on his back. Camron watched them leave. He felt the vibrations of their boots on the stone beneath his knees and heard the dull thud as the last harrar threw something on the floor before he left.

Camron shuddered, coming back to the present with a jolt. His hands formed fists by his side.

Sealing wax. The last harrar had thrown a block of red sealing wax onto the study floor.

During all the madness that had followed—the terror of his father's cooling body, the men below stairs, butchered, their blood steaming in the heat from the furnace—he had pushed it from his mind. There was no space for anything except death that night. Camron pressed his lips into a hard line. He should have gotten to his father sooner.

"Sit, sit." A hand brushed against his shoulder, then up to his cheek. Camron looked up to see Lianne of Mir'Lor watching over him. How could he have been so wrong about her eyes? They weren't cold like jewels. They were soft and deep, with so many sorrows collected in their irises that they made his throat go dry.

She guided him to a chair, plumped a cushion for his back, brushed a lock of hair from his forehead, and handed him his cup of wine. "Drink," she said. "I know you do not want to, but do so because I ask."

He brought the cup to his lips, closed his eyes, and drank.

The wine tasted of home. He felt it slipping down his throat like a prayer mouthed in the dark. It calmed his pumping heart, released something in his chest, making it easier to breathe.

Lianne smiled softly. "See," she said, sounding just like a mother teasing a stubborn child. "I told you it would help."

Camron couldn't stop himself from returning her smile. She made him feel very young.

Raising her own cup to the light, she made a toast. "Rhaize." Camron repeated the word and drank. After a moment Lianne brought her cup down to her lap. Her eyes shone brightly, their focus shifting to some unknowable point before coming to rest on Camron's face. "You know I speak the truth about your father."

Camron didn't reply. He didn't trust himself to recognize the truth anymore.

"Izgard didn't kill your father because of the victory he won at Mount Creed." Lianne shook her head. "No. He was killed because of the amethyst wax. Izgard knew, you see. He knew that by continuing to use the wax to seal all his correspondence, your father—despite all his fine, selfless words of denial—was keeping alive his claim."

"But he said he never wanted to rule Garizon. He swore it."

"He wasn't doing it for himself." Lianne tilted her chin as she spoke, offering Camron the answer with her eyes.

Camron shook his head, refusing to take it.

Lianne shrugged and spoke it out loud anyway. "Yes, Camron of Thorn. He kept alive the claim for you, just for you."

The room seemed suddenly hot and dim. Camron felt sweat trickle past his ear. Even though deep down he knew the countess was right and that the block of red wax thrown by the harrar was a sign that Izgard knew it too—no one was to use amethyst except him—Camron still shook his head. To accept what she said changed too much.

Lianne continued speaking, her soft voice turning rough.

"Even though your father was cousin to the old king, he knew he could never rule Garizon after Mount Creed. They would never have him back. He was the great Rhaize hero, the man who fought and won the greatest battle in half a century, who slew twenty thousand Garizons on a mountain in midwinter and didn't leave a single man standing to bury the frozen dead."

Camron frowned.

"Make no mistake about it, Camron of Thorn, your father wanted to rule Garizon. He wanted it in his heart, his bones, his blood—he wanted to wear the Coil. Yet he could not take back his victory at Mount Creed, and fifty years wasn't nearly enough for the Garizon people to forget."

"But the people of Rhaize forgot. They forgot all about Garizon's past."

Lianne's smile was gentle, but her words when they came were hard. "The defeated always remember the longest. All Rhaize remembers, all this court remembers, is that half a century ago Rhaize won a magnificent victory over Garizon. Tomorrow my son rides north believing he will do the same."

Camron locked gazes with the countess of Mir'Lor. He was beginning to understand things now.

Lianne's hands made a swishing sound against the silk of her dress as she brought them together in a knot. "I loved your father once."

Camron nodded. He had heard as much in her voice minutes earlier.

"I would have married him, too."

"If he had taken the Barbed Coil?"

Lianne didn't blink. She regarded him with such a look that Camron felt his cheeks grow hot. What had possessed him to say such a thing?

Then she smiled; the countess of Mir'Lor smiled with such brightness and warmth that it took Camron's breath away. "I am too old for lies, Camron of Thorn," she said, "and have long forgotten the art of verbal dancing. So even though it hurts my vanity to do so, I will confess that you are right: I was young and ambitious and determined to marry a king."

She was so beautiful when she spoke, her eyes sparkling

with such dark brilliance, that Camron could see how she had gotten away with it. She could tell a man to his face she wanted him for his title and his wealth, and he would go right ahead and marry her anyway. She was that sort of woman.

Yet even as he admired her and fell a little bit in love with her himself, the tightness returned to Camron's chest. His father had given up so much at Mount Creed: his country, his future, the woman he loved.

Shaking his head, Camron murmured, "Fifty years is so long."

"Yes," Lianne said, knowing immediately what he meant, "it is, but he had his conciliations, you must not forget that. He had a wife who loved him dearly and his work as a peacemaker: to this day the Garizon people do not know that Berick saved ten times as many lives as he took. He stopped Rhaize generals from tearing Garizon apart after Mount Creed, forcing the destruction to be limited to Veizach. God alone knows how much suffering he saved by that."

Lianne paused, bringing her gaze up to meet Camron. Behind her, the fire crackled softly, throwing out a halo of wavering, golden light. "And then there is you, Camron of Thorn. Your father had a son to love and dream for."

As she spoke, Camron felt his body becoming heavier. He felt drained, as if he had run and run until he could go no farther. Looking into Lianne's dark blue eyes, feeling too many things to put names to, Camron made a decision.

"My father wanted me to rule Garizon in his place?"

Lianne smiled like a wise teacher. "Yes. Though for many different reasons he couldn't say it."

"Why?"

"He feared for you. Assassination is a way of life in Garizon. Izgard moved to kill his rivals the day he was crowned king. If you had openly opposed him, it would be you who are dead today, not your father."

Camron flinched.

Still Lianne wasn't finished. "Second, he didn't want to push you into it. If you were going to stake a claim on Garizon, he wanted you to come to him."

So much. So much he hadn't understood. Camron covered his face. All those years his father had been waiting . . .

that last night in his study he had been waiting. Yet his son never came.

"It's not too late," Lianne said, her voice gentle. "You can still fight for what he wanted. Even now."

"I—"

"Go and talk to Balanon," Lianne said, cutting him short before he knew what it was he was about to say. "He is the real leader of the Rhaize forces. My son talks a fair game, but he has yet to meet war full on. And when he finally does it won't take him long to realize how little he knows and turn to Balanon for help. Here—" Lianne crossed over to Camron, pulled his hand from his face, and pressed something warm and smooth into his palm. "Give Balanon this. He will know it's from me. It's enough to make him listen."

Camron closed his fist around the object. He did not look at it.

"For all its grand halls and corridors Mir'Lor is really a small place." Lianne smiled a small private smile. "Most here owe me a favor or two."

Camron stood. He had to be alone.

Lianne took a few steps with him, then halted, letting him find his own way to the door. "Sleep on what I said, then go talk to Balanon at dawn."

Grabbing the door handle, Camron said, "Why did you tell me this?"

Lianne, countess of Mir'Lor, pulled herself up to her full height. Jewels that Camron had hardly been aware of before flashed at her throat and wrists, and as she spoke her eyes reflected the golden light from the fire. "I tell you this because I am Rhaize's memory and its heart. I am the only one left who knows what Garizon is and what its war kings are capable of." She shook her head. "And perhaps I'm too proud to admit I made a mistake all those years ago by not marrying your father, but even so I still find myself living with regrets."

Camron tried to say something, yet the words wouldn't come, so he nodded once, then left.

TWENTY-THREE

Riding on the mud-mired, drizzly road that led north to Bellhaven, Tessa was beginning to realize two things. One, a velvet cloak was no good against the rain; and two, Missis Wicks had an opinion on everything. A farmhouse wasn't just a farmhouse, it was "a scandalous misuse of timber and a waste of good paint," and a bundle of logs wasn't just a bundle of logs, it was "oak: perfectly fine for chests, joinery, and milking stools, but wholly unsuitable for clocks, tables, and decorative bowls." Missis Wicks didn't as much say these things as *pronounce* them, as if she were a rather irritable god bestowing wisdom on mere mortals too dim to realize what was good for them.

"That meadow over there," Missis Wicks said, sitting high atop her horse, back straight. "That's owned by the monks on the Anointed Isle. Good land for grazing, but unsowable in spring."

Tessa nodded, hoping that Missis Wicks wouldn't see fit to elaborate further on why the land was unsuitable for sowing—she was feeling wet, miserable, and sore all over, and she really didn't care.

It was midday. The small party of five that had left Kilgrim yesterday at noon had spent the night in a tiny wayside inn that Missis Wicks had pronounced as "one large breeding ground for fungus, wet-rot, and sin." Tessa rather liked the place—at least it had candles and doors. Everyone had bundled down in a common room around a fire, and the only thing Tessa could remember thinking as she'd wrapped herself in a blanket was, I'll never fall asleep on this hard floor. She was woken from a deep, dreamless sleep at dawn by

Missis Wicks, who urged her to brush and clip up her hair for decency's sake and drink a bowl of whey for stamina on the road. Tessa had wound her hair into a tight knot but refused to drink the whey, which as far as she could tell was some thin, watery cheese by-product that smelled like sour milk.

One night's sleep hadn't been nearly enough. Tessa found her body ached more than ever now, and in new, alarming places: the base of her spine, her inner thighs, and the column of muscles to either side of her neck. The gash on her left shoulder was beginning to heal. Once all the dried blood had been cleaned away, she was surprised to see how small and shallow it was. Clean, too, which was good considering it had been caused by a rusty nail jutting from the inn door.

Tessa pulled sharply on her reins, guiding her horse around a ditch in the road. She didn't want to think about that night. She didn't want to think about Ravis or his relationship with Violante of Arazzo. Reaching the Anointed Isle was what counted, and anything that took her mind away from that had to be pushed aside. She had to carry on. There was no choice here, only the thought of the harras and what an army of them could do, and a series of patterns, twenty-one years in the making.

"What do you know about the Anointed Isle, Missis Wicks?" Tessa asked, keeping an eye on the way ahead. Rain was causing the road to deteriorate rapidly. The land they were traveling through was flat and unremarkable: low bushes, scrubby trees, the occasional plowed field, and whole banks of reeds growing in circular clumps or winding lines, marking deep-set ponds and hidden streams. If it wasn't for the fact that the road was built a few feet higher than the surrounding land, the whole thing would have been water-logged by now. Tessa wondered why anyone had bothered building it in the first place.

"The Anointed Isle is no place for a woman," Missis Wicks said, shaking her head with venom. "No place at all. My daughter's a match for you in age, young lady, and I can tell you now all the land between Kilgrim and Hayle would have to sink clean to the bottom of the sea before I'd even allow her to set foot there."

Tessa let out a small sigh. This wasn't going to be easy. Glancing around to check that none of the men were in earshot, she asked, "Why is that?"

Missis Wicks shook her head some more for good measure. "Because it's a bad place, simple as that. The monks don't like women, for one thing. Say they distract the monks from their work. My brother-in-law Moldercay would still be there today if it wasn't for some young baggage catching his eye." All the while she was speaking and shaking her head, Missis Wicks' hair never moved. Despite being rained on for over an hour, its height and style remained unchanged. "Not that it was a bad thing in the long term, you understand. Wicks were made for trade."

"Your brother-in-law used to live on the Anointed Isle?"

"Aye. Record keeper, he was. He had a good hand, but an eye prone to wander. And not just over women, I'll have you know. That man couldn't look at anything without wanting to unravel, unfold, or undress it!" Missis Wicks executed a forceful, pouting *tut.* "Of course, he didn't get that from the Wicks side. No, my good shoes, he didn't! That came from his mother's side: the Polliers. There's not a Pollier living who isn't famous for putting his or her nose into other people's business. Disgraceful, it is. Though it can make for good business from time to time."

"What does Moldercay do now?"

"Bone keeper." Missis Wicks spoke the words with grudging pride. "He runs his own charnel house in Bellhaven—keeps all the decent people's bones there. No trollops, beggars, or tinkers ever find their way into Moldercay's pot."

Moldercay's pot? Tessa shivered; she didn't like the sound of that one bit. "And he was cast out of the monastery for falling in love with someone?"

"No, girl. You're just like my daughter, Nelly—too busy thinking to listen. You should pay more heed to what I say. Moldercay wasn't cast out—no one is cast out of the Anointed Isle. It would take an act of God himself for those hardhearted stone-faced holy men to give up one of their own. Heaven forbid, no. Moldercay *chose* to leave so he could marry the girl."

Missis Wicks settled herself more comfortably on her

saddle while managing to keep her back ramrod straight. "The holy fathers put up quite a fight, I'll have you know. They had Moldercay fast for thirteen days before they finally agreed to let him go. Poor Moldercay was so delirious that he walked right across the causeway as the tide was rolling in. Had to swim the last ruvit to shore. Never been in the water since, and I can't say I blame him. Salt water might be good for the eyes and inducing the vomits, but it's murder on a person's skin and teeth. Wouldn't catch me dead in it. I'd rather soak in lye for a week."

Tessa could think of no suitable response to that, so she stayed quiet for a few moments, thinking. The three men in the party were riding a few paces ahead. Tessa hadn't spoken to any of them apart from the briefest of nods and greetings. Missis Wicks said it wasn't proper. And she said it in a loud enough voice, with a sweeping enough glance, that all three men had got the message and had duly kept their distance ever since.

"The Old Hoot's cummin' up, Missis Wicks," shouted the oldest man without looking around. "Will yer be wantin' a stop or press on?"

"We'll press on, Elburt. Stop now and we may not reach Bellhaven by dark. And I won't have us riding through unlit streets like mounted trollops or Vennish spies. I just won't have it."

Elburt grumbled, but quietly.

Tessa didn't pay much attention to the exchange; she had quickly grown accustomed to Missis Wicks' bossy ways. Her mind was still on the Anointed Isle. If she was lucky, she might be there tonight.

Fingers searching out the ring around her throat, Tessa said, "Why are the holy men so reluctant to let any of their own go?"

Missis Wicks sucked in a good amount of air to aid thinking. After a moment her brow lifted and she let the air right out. "Secrets, suspicions, and second nature."

Tessa didn't say anything, just waited for Missis Wicks to elaborate. Which she did.

"Those holy men have been keeping secrets for so long that it's just part of their nature now. They're a close bunch, I can tell you. Comes from them being isolated out there on that island year after year. At certain times during the winter they can be cut off for weeks on end, and even when the causeway's clear, visitors have to move across it sharpish, else risk being caught in the tides. Up there, perched high in their spiraling towers, with nothing below them, only sea and rocks, it's easy for them to forget about the real world. They won't have any dealings with the mainland Holy League. No, my spring greens, they won't! Have their own secret little world, they do, with their own hidden purposes and their own furtive alliances." Missis Wicks shook her entire body along with her head. "If you ask me, Moldercay is better out of it."

Tessa pulled her cloak close, suddenly acutely aware of the damp and the cold. She was aching all over, and sharp splinters felt as if they were working their way down her spine. Her scalp itched.

The Old Hoot turned out to be a low-walled, flat-roofed inn just to the east of the road. Smoke rose in a broken line from a short chimney, and the sign above the door had faded in patches, leaving only the letter *o*'s remaining. Looking at the dismal little place, Tessa was glad they weren't stopping.

"That man is quite mad, if you ask me," pronounced Missis Wicks as she and Tessa rode past the inn. "Business has been dry here for years, decades even, yet he still insists on keeping up that slop bucket."

Tessa sat up on her horse and surveyed the surrounding land. A few odd buildings were dotted across the green, reed-striped landscape, but none of them looked to be in use except the inn. No smoke trailed from chimneys, shutters banged loose, and many of the houses were without roofs.

Noticing where Tessa was looking, Missis Wicks said, "The Venns. That's who did this. Used to be a fair-sized village up until twenty years ago, when the Vennish raiders began besetting the coast. Now there's no small towns and villages within leagues. Everyone headed to the big towns ten years back, and no one's returned since."

"The Venns?"

"Dirty, weaseling dark-eyed raiders from across the northern sea." Missis Wicks pursed her lips. "Can't grow crops or rear cattle to save their lives, but they do have a way with salting fish."

Tessa brushed a lock of wet hair away from her face. She was coming to realize how large this world was. All the time she had stayed with Emith and his mother she had never once heard about the Venns. "And the big towns manage to defend themselves from the Venns?"

"Aye, Kilgrim, Palmsey, and Port Shrift do a fair job. They have to. Trade is their life blood—can't have the coast unsafe for merchant ships."

"What about Bellhaven?"

Missis Wicks regarded Tessa with slowly narrowing eyes. "Bellhaven's not one of the big towns, girl." She shook her head. "No, my winter coat, it isn't! Why, it must be less than a third the size of Kilgrim. If that."

Tessa sat back on her saddle. She was beginning to feel like a fool, and more important, Missis Wicks was becoming suspicious as to why she knew so little. Even though Tessa knew the best thing would be to change the subject—get Missis Wicks' mind working on one of her pet hates, like doors or candles—she had to ask one more question.

"If Bellhaven is such a small town, how do they manage to defend themselves against the Venns?"

Missis Wicks' eyes, still narrow from her last pronouncement, narrowed even further. "Because it's barely a league away from the Anointed Isle. Everyone knows that."

More puzzled than ever, Tessa tried to come up with a way of discovering what Missis Wicks was talking about while not revealing any more of her ignorance. Rain dripped down her neck, though, and the burn on her hand was aching from being wrapped around the reins for so long, and deep inside her boots ten toes simmered in a steam bath of damp wool. She was in no mood for subtlety, couldn't think of anything clever to say, she just wanted to *know*.

"What has being close to the Anointed Isle got to do with anything?"

"Young women these days!" Missis Wicks *tut*ted so hard, tiny flecks of spittle sprayed from her lips. "Really! It's quite bad enough you journeying alone in the first place, without being entirely ignorant of where you are going and what you are getting yourself into. If you want my opinion—"

"I don't want your opinion," interrupted Tessa, wet, sore, and rapidly losing her temper. "Just tell me what keeps Bellhaven safe from the Venns."

Missis Wicks jerked her head back as if Tessa's words were something unpleasant thrown her way, like a rotting tomato or a dog-chewed bone. Her lips moved a moment, and Tessa could almost swear she heard the sound of grinding teeth. Finally Missis Wicks nodded once rather solemnly and said, "You could be a Wicks with a temper like that."

Tessa kept her face stony. She wasn't sure whether to take it as a compliment or not. "Bellhaven?" she insisted.

"Right, right." Missis Wicks tugged at her reins, pulling her horse away from an especially eye-catching clump of grass. "Well, it's nothing to do with the town, that's for sure. It's the abbey on the Anointed Isle. Been there for nine centuries, it has, and for the last five hundred of those nine hundred years no invading force has ever set foot on it. In my lifetime alone, we've had the Venns, the Balgedins, and the Hoks all seizing parts of the coast, yet not one of them has ever ventured within twenty leagues of the isle." Missis Wicks nodded as if such a thing were only right and fitting. "It's tradition. No one takes the isle."

"Why not?" As she spoke, Tessa caught a glimpse of the sea. It was a white-flecked band of gray to the east. The wind was beginning to pick up, and the rain driving against her face tasted of salt. Shivering, she patted her mare's neck. It was a gentle old horse, hired from Missis Wicks' own stables, and Tessa was glad of its warmth.

Missis Wicks was also looking out to the east, but just before she spoke, she made a point of shifting her gaze back to the road ahead as if she didn't want to risk being distracted by whatever she saw out at sea.

Tugging her reins to the left, she said, "Well, by all accounts, it's a mixture of history and hearsay. It all started five hundred years ago when Hierac of Garizon conquered Maribane. There was no part of the country he didn't take, not one stream trickling down a hillside or one pebble lying flat in the sand. The man was a bloodthirsty demon." Missis Wicks pursed her lips. "To give him his due, though, he *did* know how to fight. Anyway, being the sort of arrogant brute that Garizons usually are, he went on a tour of the country—making sure everyone knew who he was, executing any pour soul who didn't cheer at the sight of him, and having every farm, stronghold, and village counted."

Bouncing her chin against her thumb, as if it were just the sort of thing she would have done in his position, Missis Wicks continued. "Well, eventually Hierac arrives at Bellhaven. Now, by all accounts the tide is in when he gets there, and waiting around for the causeway to clear so he can cross to the isle makes him about as mad as an archer in the rain. He'd heard tales that the holy fathers keep gold and other treasures hidden away in the abbey, and he was quite determined to have them.

"Anyway. Eventually the tide goes out, and he and his forty best men gallop across the wet sand to the island, swords out and ready.

"To this day no one knows for sure what happened when they got there—some say the holy fathers put a spell on them, others swear they beguiled them with their clever talk and sly ways—but one hour to the minute later, the forty best men ride back. Hierac has ordered them away. He wants no armed men within a shadow's fall of the island.

"Hierac himself spends the next day and night in conference with the holy fathers on the isle. When he finally emerges the following morning, riding through the rising tide, water up to his horse's flank, he announces that the Anointed Isle will be free from the rule of Garizon law and all Garizon tariffs. No Garizon officials will set foot on it ever again, and all Garizon soldiers will leave with him, never to return."

Tessa felt her scalp moving slowly as Missis Wicks spoke. Despite the rain, her throat felt dry. She suddenly wished she were back in Mother Emith's kitchen. She missed Emith and his mother very much.

"Well, Hierac was as good as his word," Missis Wicks said, breaking into Tessa's thoughts, "and he and his men withdrew from Bellhaven that very same day. And throughout his forty-year reign and then the reign of his son—in fact, right up until the Garizon occupation ended some hundred years later, the Anointed Isle remained free of Garizon rule."

Missis Wicks twisted around in her saddle, rummaged in her saddlebag, pulled out a glazed and stoppered jar, and handed it over to Tessa. "Here, drink this. It will warm you up a portion. It's no hard alcohol, mind. It's what I give to my Nelly when she looks like she's catching a chill. You remind me of her, you know. Both headstrong and uppity, the pair of you."

Tessa, touched by Missis Wicks' sudden kindness, thanked her and took the jar.

Missis Wicks waved away the thanks with a broad sweep of her arm. "Wicks can't notice a need without tending to it."

Pulling the stopper from the jar, Tessa said, "What happened when the Garizons withdrew from Maribane?"

"Well, after that any force who invaded Maribane made a point of keeping well away from the Anointed Isle. If Hierac of Garizon, the greatest war king ever known, refused to take it, then he must have had a spitting good reason. Tales spread, fears grew: it was considered bad luck even to *attempt* to take the isle. The fact that no one really knew what happened between Hierac and the holy fathers just added more spice to the pot. Some say that Garizon still protects it to this day."

Missis Wicks drummed her gloved hands against her horse's neck. "Anyway, one way or the other, the Anointed Isle became no-man's-land. Still is. The holy fathers are many things, but they're definitely not stupid. Officially they say all heathenness and superstition is well behind them, that they are men of God: scholars, clerics, and monks. Yet they still keep those old tales alive. I swear by my summer petticoats they do."

"It sounds to me," Tessa said, wiping a drop of honey beer from her lips, "that Hierac and the holy fathers reached some sort of agreement on the isle during the night and day he stayed there."

"Exactly!" Missis Wicks pounced forward in her saddle. "That's what I've maintained all along—Wicks can smell out a deal a league away. If you ask me, it was good old give and take, not some superstitious fish-kettle of spells and curses, that transpired that day on the isle." Missis Wicks' smile was almost motherly as she turned to look at Tessa. "Have you ever considered going into trade?"

Tessa smiled. Missis Wicks was beginning to grow on her. "So, if it was some sort of deal that was struck, why is the isle still benefiting from it long after Hierac and the Garizons have gone?"

"Those holy fathers are no fools. They know as long as people are scared of them and they remember the old tales, they'll be left well alone."

Tessa nodded, even though she thought there must be more. Five hundred years free of invasion due to one visit from a Garizon king? Almost unconsciously, she felt for her ring around her neck. The metal was several degrees warmer than when she'd touched it last. Abruptly she let it go.

"I'm surprised Bellhaven isn't a lot bigger than Kilgrim, seeing as everyone who lives there is guaranteed protection from invasions."

Missis Wicks snorted. "You won't be when we get there. Thoroughly miserable place, it is. No harbor to speak of because of the long beaches, no decent freshwater source, soil that's fit for turnips, little else. To say nothing about the people themselves!" Motioning to Tessa to hand back the jar of honey beer, she said, "And then there's the weather. I make this journey once a year to visit Moldercay—God and female traveling companions permitting—and no matter what season I come, I can count on there being a storm."

Tessa looked out to sea. The sky had darkened, and flashes of white foam streaked across the water's surface as low winds sliced away at the waves. Missis Wicks' storm was right on cue.

"How long before we get to Bellhaven?" Tessa was surprised to hear a tremor in her voice as she spoke. It's just the cold, she told herself. That and the damp.

"Roads permitting, four hours. Maybe even a little less if those three"—Missis Wicks projected her voice forward, verbally aiming for the three men who rode ahead of her—"sluggards would kindly pick up their pace."

Elburt, taking the hint, kicked his horse into action, and soon the small party was trotting at a brisk pace. Fields, marshes, and reed beds fell behind them, giving way to yellow-grassed flatlands and long, sallow beaches. Mud splashed up around Tessa's cloak and the rain beat against her face. The path was slippery and uneven, and she forced herself to focus on the way ahead. The sea kept catching her eye, though. Its color bothered her: it was a different shade of gray from the sky. The line of the horizon where they met seemed unusually dark and dense. From where Tessa was it looked almost black. Then, far in the distance, she spotted a dim silhouette. A blank speck against the sea, it had shape but no mass, like a shadow or the hollow cavity of an open pit.

Breath froze in Tessa's throat. When she exhaled the air came out white.

The Anointed Isle.

Shivering, Tessa whipped her head forward, determined not to look out to sea anymore. That was when the wind began to bother her. It whistled past her ears, high and piercing, sounding just like tinnitus.

Ravis walked with Violante down to the dock. The wind was beginning to pick up, and far to the east a dark band of cloud was moving in. The four masts of the Istanian bark *Fine Shore* creaked and listed, and her furled sails snapped impatiently against their posts. Already lines had been secured, connecting her to the thirty-man tug *Bullser.* She'd be ready to set sail within the hour.

"A storm's moving in from the east," Violante said, her voice carrying well above the wind. "It should give the ship an extra push from the harbor."

Ravis listened for sounds of hurt or bitterness in her voice but could detect none. He glanced over at her. Any other woman would shy away from the wind, pull up her hood to protect her hair, clasp her cloak seams tight. Not Violante. She stepped into the wind as if it were another layer of clothing to be worn. Cold gusts heightened the color of her lips and cheeks, sharp breezes teased curls free from their bindings, and a steady push of air served to mold her cloak against her body, revealing the form beneath.

Ravis reached out and touched her arm. "You should be safe from Malray in Mizerico. I've had a word with the captain. He'll escort you back to your lodgings."

Violante smiled slightly as she stepped onto the wharf. "You forget who I am, Ravis of Burano. My father may be Lectur, but my mother's mother was a bandit who worked the roads and foothills north of Sullin for thirty years before she died. So you'll forgive me if I'm not afraid of Malray or his men."

"You're not going to see him again? Not after what happened at the inn?"

Violante turned to face him. "You lost whatever sway you held over me the day two Istanian scouts delivered your letter. Besides, I have business of my own with Malray."

Ravis caught at Violante's wrist. "You're not—" Abruptly he stopped himself.

"Not what, Ravis?" Violante asked softly. "Not going to harm him? Kill him?" When he didn't meet her eye, she said, "You still love him, don't you? After all these years and all he's done."

Ravis shook his head.

Violante made a soft clicking sound in her throat and moved on. Neither spoke again until they fell under the shadow of *Fine Shore*.

"So," Violante said, elegantly skipping aside as two deckhands toting a pallet loaded with sheepskins attempted to pass. "From here you'll ride east? Catch up with the girl you brought here? I heard you talking to the red-faced boy from Wicks. You'll have to hurry. The girl has nearly two days' start."

Ravis nodded.

"You didn't have to stay here with me last night and today. You could have left the other morning. Your wounds weren't so bad you couldn't ride."

"I wanted to see you safely on your ship."

Violante smiled her full dazzling smile, her eyes suddenly bright. "You think you owe me, don't you?"

"I don't want to see you hurt."

"I'm not." Violante's smile failed. She looked away. "You can leave my bag here. I'll have the ship's boy carry it to my cabin."

Ravis started to say something, thought again, and then laid Violante's bag on the striped oakwood boards of the wharf.

Violante boarded the ship. Ravis stayed on the dock and watched as *Fine Shore* was pulled from the shallow anchorage of her mooring into the deeper, quicker waters of the harbor. He continued watching as her crew worked to drop her sails, adjusted them to catch the wind, then set her under way. Only when the bark's red-and-gold pennant finally disappeared into the inky darkness of the open sea did he turn and make his way back to the quay.

A ye, yer be lucky, lovey. Tide's just rolled out."
Elburt motioned across the sandbars to the
causeway and the mountain of rock beyond.

The Anointed Isle was a black fortress against a
nearly black sky. Tiny pinpoints of yellow light flickered
within its charcoal form. As Tessa looked on, a series of
them snuffed out. It wasn't late—early evening as far as she
could tell—yet it was very dark. The wind screamed past her
ears, reminding her of tinnitus, making her temples ache.
Thinking straight wasn't easy. She was so tired, it took all
her strength to sit upright in the saddle. All she wanted to do
was sleep.

Bellhaven lay just ahead of them. They had approached
the town from across a broad beach of wet sand. It was too
dark for Tessa to make out any details of Bellhaven itself except for the varying levels of rooftops, the occasional puff of
smoke from a chimney, and the bright sheen of water on var-
nished awnings and doors. Missis Wicks had insisted the
party travel past the causeway before entering the town. She
wasn't happy about Tessa riding to the isle alone and in the
dark. Tessa guessed Missis Wicks had been hoping the tide
would be in.

"Tide'll be out till just past midnight, lovey," Elburt said.
For some reason that Tessa couldn't understand, he had taken
off his cap as they approached the causeway, and he used it
now to indicate the way. "Yer just ride straight for the rock.
'S best to keep t'middle, where sand's at its driest."

Tessa nodded. The distance to the isle was difficult to
judge. Sand stretched out endlessly before her. High on the
horizon, a line of foaming water marked the receding tide.

"It's madness to cross the causeway after dark. Madness."

Missis Wicks' whole body quivered as she spoke. "Come into town with us, Tessa. Get a proper night's rest, a hearty traveler's breakfast, and give that wet blanket of a cloak chance to dry. Velvet indeed! What sort of material is that to wear in the rain?"

"I can't stay in town. I've got to get to the abbey tonight." Tessa dug her heel into her horse's flank, guiding the animal round. She was tempted by Missis Wicks' offer, but she knew she had to go. This was her duty now. Deveric had chosen *her* with his patterns, summoned *her* with his sorcery. People were dead, and more were going to perish, and she didn't know if she could prevent it from happening, but she knew she had to try.

"I must be on my way." Tessa's gaze took in the whole party and then came to rest on Missis Wicks. "Thank you for everything." She kicked her horse, slackened her hold on the reins, and trotted onto the causeway.

Elburt's voice called after her: "Y'ill be guaranteed a bed 'n' meal for the night. T'holy fathers never turn travelers away."

And then Missis Wicks: "Watch yourself, Tessa. Long robes, bald heads, and prayer books mean nothing if you ask me: men are always men."

Tessa's mare found its way with little prompting. It was a good horse, gentle, affectionate, seemingly impervious to the rain and wind. "You must be tired, too," Tessa whispered, rubbing its neck. "Tired and hungry and sore."

Even though the sea was far away, its spray beat against her face. Carried on low, gusting winds, it stung her eyes and the inner lining of her nose and left a sharp, salty taste in her mouth.

Ahead, the lines of the abbey and the isle emerged from the artificial darkness of the storm. Two towers reached up from a skeleton of black rock, piercing the leaden clouds overhead. Structures rose around the towers, protecting, strengthening, then ultimately falling away, leaving the spikes of curving stone alone in an unstable sky. Light shone from slits in the lower walls. Tide pools rippled at the base of the rock and to either side of the causeway.

The wind shifted momentarily and Tessa caught a whiff of the abbey. It smelled of old things dredged up from the sea with the silt. She heard a sound, focused on it, yet the noise trailed away before she could pick out any details. It sounded like voices chanting. Tessa swallowed. Not for the first time that day she found herself wishing she was back in Mother Emith's kitchen, sitting around the fire, safe and sound.

Chunks of rock and stone began to litter the causeway as Tessa drew near the isle. Shells crunched under her horse's hooves, and tendrils of seaweed wrapped around its fore-locks. Dead things decayed in the sand. Jellyfish lay dying; stranded by the tide, they quivered with every turn of the wind. Tessa's horse needed no prompting to avoid them.

Then, all of a sudden, she was there. The Anointed Isle. One moment it seemed impossibly far away, like a castle in a fairy tale, and the next it formed a barricade between Tessa and the night. Breaking through the rock like the roots of a powerful tree, the abbey walls blocked everything else from sight. Thick and curving, they were laid out in a pattern Tessa couldn't quite grasp. Spying a path winding between boulders and crumbling wedges of stone, she guided her horse toward it, glad to be on firm ground. Ahead, she caught sight of a gateway sheltered within an alcove in the wall.

The wind seemed louder as she took the path, and it bounced from rock to rock, blowing in all directions. Tessa's ears ached with the pressure and the noise.

The gate was twice as tall as Tessa. The metal crosspieces that held the door to the hinge were as big as her horse's head. Any varnish the door boasted had long since been blasted away by the wind. There was nothing to knock with, so Tessa pulled Ravis' knife from her belt and rapped smartly on the wood with the butt. The sound pleased her. It was loud and carried well, and it made a nice change from the wind. While she waited for a reply, she dismounted from her horse.

As she worked out a cramp in her thigh, the door swung open. Straightening, Tessa took a breath and held it in. A young man stood in the gateway. He was dressed in an un-bleached linen robe and held a lit candle in his hand. "Welcome," he said. "Come inside and take shelter from the storm."

Tessa let out her breath. For some reason she hadn't expected to be greeted by a young man. All Missis Wicks' talk of holy fathers had made her think everyone on the isle was old or aging.

"Allow me to lead your horse."

Nodding, Tessa held out the reins. She was suddenly aware of how weatherbeaten she must look. Bringing up a hand to push wet hair away from her face, she said, "Does Brother Avaccus still live here?"

The young man led the horse through the gate and into the courtyard beyond. He did not answer Tessa's question. Thinking he hadn't heard it, she repeated it again.

"Brother Avaccus is no longer with us, my child."

Startled, Tessa whipped her head around in time to see a second man emerge from the shadows behind the gate. Clean shaven and white haired, he was old without looking frail.

"I'm sorry I startled you, my child," he said, coming forward and taking Tessa's arm. "I am Father Issasis, the abbot here. Come, let me find you something hot to eat."

Tessa allowed herself to be drawn through the gate. The abbot smelled strange—not unpleasant, just of things she had no name for. His grip on her arm was firm.

"Where is Brother Avaccus now?" Tessa asked.

The abbot took a heavy breath. "Alas, my child, we all must pass on."

The young man holding the candle snuffed out the flame by hand. Tessa heard his skin sizzle.

"Come, this way." The abbot guided her away from the young man and the gate.

Tessa pulled back. "What about my horse, my saddlebag?"

"Child, Brother Erilan will see to your horse, and you may bring your bags with you if you choose."

Feeling foolish, Tessa shook her head. The only thing in her saddlebag was a loaf of bread and some oats for her mare. Her knife hung from the belt around her waist, and her money was tucked away down her bodice.

The abbot led her across the darkened courtyard to a

stone arcade far on the other side. The sound of voices chanting accompanied them as they walked.

"Cerallos," said the abbot. "Our prayers to thank God for
the blessings of the day and to beseech his protection for the
night." As he spoke, the abbot pulled on Tessa's arm, guiding
her toward a doorway. "Come, we must hurry if you are to
eat and find a cell by Eighth Toll."

"Eighth Toll?" Tessa suddenly didn't like the abbot's
hold on her arm, and she pulled away. She thought it strange
that such an important man would come to the gate to greet
visitors.

The abbot tried to pull Tessa back for an instant, then
abruptly let her go. "Eighth Toll is when the last light goes
out. No one may eat, raise their voices, or move from their
cells once it sounds."

A door opened before them, pulled back by a shadowy
figure who slipped quickly away as they entered. They stepped
into a long corridor set with many doors. Finally free of the
wind, Tessa let out a sigh of relief. She thought the ghost
ringing in her ears would stop. But it didn't. It kept sounding, like an alarm bell heard over a great distance.

Tessa shivered. The temperature inside the abbey was
colder than outside in the courtyard. The floor beneath her
feet was formed from an intricate mosaic of thumbnail-size
tiles. Worn and faded from centuries' worth of wear, patterns
branched out in all directions, inhabiting every shadow-filled
corner, following each curve in the wall. Tessa recognized
some of the designs from Deveric's illuminations.

The chanting was very loud now. Tessa couldn't make out
any words, but listening to the tone of the men's voices, she
found it hard to believe they were giving thanks. Briefly she
considered leaving, tracing her steps to the gate, sending for
her horse, and riding back over the causeway into the town.
After grumbling a bit about the dangers of women riding
alone, Missis Wicks would welcome her in. She was so tired,
though, and the thought of wind, wet sand, and an extra half
hour in the saddle was disheartening. Besides, she wasn't sure
if she believed what the abbot said about Brother Avaccus.
Emith had seemed sure he was alive.

"How long ago did Brother Avaccus pass away?" Tessa

asked as the abbot led her into a large, high-ceilinged room. The room was split in two by a long refectory table running straight down the center. Two neatly placed rows of chairs ran down either side of the table, and the top was laid with pewter candlesticks and bowls. A few men dressed in the same un-bleached linen robes as the abbot were busy cleaning away the remnants of the last meal. Dishes and goblets were piled into wooden tubs, then carried off through a small door in the opposite wall.

Ignoring her question, the abbot crossed to the nearest man, spoke a word in his ear, touched him lightly on the arm, and bade him go. The man slipped away into the darkness beyond the far door.

"I said when did Brother Avaccus pass away?" Tessa was surprised by the strength in her voice.

"Child, you are tired and soaked to the skin. Sit down a moment while Brother Llathro brings you some bread and hot soup from the kitchen." The abbot pulled the nearest chair from the table. "Sit."

The seat looked tempting and her entire body ached, but Tessa made no move toward the chair.

The abbot shrugged. "Very well, child." He pushed the chair back under the table. "Brother Avaccus died five days ago. He was very dear to us here at the Anointed Isle, and I'd be grateful if you would refrain from any further mention of his name." The abbot's voice sharpened. "It grieves me to hear it spoken so harshly."

Tessa looked down at the floor. She felt her cheeks growing hot. If what the abbot said was true, then that meant Emith had been right in believing Brother Avaccus was alive. The man had died later, while she was at sea with Ravis.

"Brother Llathro, take this child to a cell."

Glancing up, Tessa saw the man the abbot had given orders to minutes earlier return to the room, carrying a wooden tray laden with a bowl, a jug, a loaf of bread, and a thin wedge of cheese. He crossed to the abbot and spoke so softly, Tessa cold not hear what he said.

"No, Brother Llathro," replied the abbot. "You will take the food along to the cell with our visitor." He met Tessa's eye. "We will leave it to her own conscience to respect the conventions of Eighth Toll."

Tessa's cheeks burned. The abbot had a way of making her feel like a disobedient child.

"This way, my sister." Brother Llathro walked past Tessa to the door. His shadow felt cold as it glided over her face.

"You will be woken at First Toll," said the abbot as Tessa walked out of the door, "and shown to the gate. Unfortunately we cannot allow visitors to stay more than one night." The abbot's smile was brisk. "God's rest, my child."

Tessa didn't reply, simply followed Brother Llathro into the corridor beyond. She felt drained of all strength. Coming here had been a mistake.

Brother Llathro led Tessa down a maze of curving corridors. Stone arches braced the walls and supported the weight of floors above. Patterns were everywhere: in the masonry, in the woodwork, on the rise of every step. Loose tiles rocked beneath Tessa's boots as she walked. The chanting had stopped, and the only sound as they walked was the patter of footsteps and the faraway thrum of the sea. The ringing in Tessa's ears receded to a mild buzz.

"Here, my sister," Brother Llathro said, stopping by a door located at the end of a long, remote corridor. "This will be your cell for the night." He pushed open the door and walked in. Tessa followed him through. Using the flame from the candle on the tray, he lit a second candle, waited for the top layer of wax to melt, then fixed it upright on the floor in a pool of its own wax.

The cell was tiny and very cold. A draft blew around the room. Shutters blocking the only window rattled along with the wind. It sounded as though the storm were moving in.

"God's rest, my sister."

Tessa looked around in time to see Brother Llathro closing the door behind him as he left. The tray he had been carrying now lay on the floor next to the candle. The soup in the bowl rippled with every gust of the wind. Tessa took a deep breath, ran a hand across her temples. She was so tired, she could barely think. Tomorrow. She would decide what to do tomorrow.

A woven rug laid over with a blanket was the only item
in the cell, and Tessa collapsed onto it, unhooking her cloak
and unpinning her hair. Pulling the food tray forward, she
tore a piece of bread from the loaf. Her mouth was so dry she
could barely swallow, and she didn't take another bite. As
she lifted the bowl of soup from the tray, a bell began to toll.

Eight times it tolled: long, hollow notes that hung in the
air minutes after sounding. Eighth Toll.

*No one may eat, raise their voices, or move from their
cells once it sounds.*

Tessa put down the bowl. She didn't want to tempt fate.

Lying on the mat, she pulled the blanket up to her chin.

Patterns. There were patterns etched into the wood-and-
plaster ceiling overhead. Too exhausted to pick out any details, Tessa closed her eyes and began to drift off to sleep.
Dimly, in the back of mind, she remembered the abbot
saying Eighth Toll was when the last light went out. Only her
candle was still burning, and before she could make the decision to snuff it out, she fell into a dark, dreamless sleep.

Izgard held out his hand and ran his fingertips over the
scribe's shadow. The canvas was rough and streaked with
dried mud, yet the sensation pleased him all the same. The
only part of the shadow that moved was the section cast by
the scribe's right arm. Ederius was inside his tent, putting the
final touches to a pattern from the Coil. Izgard wanted to
enter the tent, wanted to sit quietly and watch the old scribe
work—just as he used to before he was king.

With a heavy sigh, Izgard pulled himself back from the
canvas and made his way across the camp. He could not risk
disturbing Ederius tonight. The design he was working on
was important enough, but nothing compared to the great feat
of scribing he would begin in the darkness before dawn.

The camp was unnaturally still. Men gathered around
low-burning fires, feigning or waiting for sleep. No one
sang, or drew a blade over a whetstone, or held a cup to the
barrel and tapped. There was no need for last minute prepa-

rations and no desire for the companionship of song. The Garizon army was ready for war.

Tomorrow at dawn the first battle would be joined. The Sire of Rhaize's forces would meet the Garizon army on territory south of the rise. Izgard had picked both the time and the place, and he knew in his heart, his liver, and his bones that victory would soon be his.

One battle was all he needed. One bloody, decisive battle to give him the war.

The brave, arrogant knights of Rhaize would advance into a valley marked for death. The Garizon army would surround them like the Barbed Coil itself: wounding, impaling, casting shadows red with blood. Sandor would be too proud to plan for retreat. His pride only allowed one vision of the battle, and his memories only began at Mount Creed. He didn't know what a Garizon war king was capable of. He had been told, but he didn't really know.

Tomorrow he would receive a lesson in the dangers of forgetting: he, his army, and the country for which they fought. Fifty years ago Rhaize knights had burned Veizach to the ground, and although little blood was spilled in a torching, a blood debt still remained. The Barbed Coil had been driven out of sight and out of mind, and it had fifty dormant years to reclaim. For half a century it had lingered, like an assassin in the shadows, in the darkest, deepest cellar in Sirabayus. The holy sisters couldn't wait to be rid of it. They said it robbed them of their peace of mind and poisoned all their dreams.

Coming to a break in the dirt path, Izgard considered walking the camp perimeter, talking to the latest scouts to return from the Rhaize camp, and checking that everything was going to plan. Deciding against it, he took the turn leading back to his tent. His troops had no need of last minute precautions. As their leader he would honor them the same.

All was ready. Traps had been laid. The harras who would be drawn together by the patterns on the Coil had been hand-picked by Izgard himself. One thousand of them. One-twentieth of the number gathered around Garizon campfires this night would emerge as a ruthless fighting force at dawn. Ederius and his patterns would see to that.

An animal cry broke the silence of the camp. The high, haunting howl drove through the night like splinters of broken bone through flesh. Although he had grown accustomed to such sounds by now, Izgard could not help but flinch. It meant one more harrar would have to be slain.

The Barbed Coil exacted a price for its gifts. One-third of the harras who had been sent into the Valley of Broken Stones to fight Ravis of Burano and Camron of Thorn were now dead. They had to be slaughtered for the good of the camp. When the illumination was finished and the ink long dry, there were those who held on to the patterns in the Coil. The bloodlust never left them. Their features shifted between man and beast. Bones thickened, appetites sharpened, claws curled inward and grew into flesh. The physicians didn't care to discuss what caused the harras so much pain that they howled, but Izgard only had to look at their jawlines and fingernails to guess.

They split open the first victim: the third rib on the left had detached from the sternum and grown into his heart.

They slaughtered all of them now the moment they felt any pain. Deaths as discreet as the howls of pain would allow, bodies carried from the camp in utter darkness. Izgard could not risk the wrong sort of fear sweeping the camp, so he had instructed his warlords to inform the troops that the harras were under attack by foul Rhaize sorcery. It made everyone more eager to fight.

Izgard approached his tent, noted the pale light still burning and the shadow cast by his wife's silhouette. Angeline was still awake, petting her silly, little girl's dog, talking to herself in her high, little girl's voice. Izgard pulled his lips to a line as he yanked the flap to the side and entered the tent.

"Izgard." Angeline jumped up from her chair at his entrance, sending her little dog rolling onto the floor. A guilty flush stole across her cheek. There was a plate of food next to her on a chest. Seeing Izgard's look at it, she said, "It's leftovers. For Snowy."

Izgard noticed Angeline swallowing something herself. He sucked at his cheeks. The stupid girl had now taken to eating scraps meant for her dog. She was getting worse. He wished he had never sent for her. "Go to your chamber and take that animal with you."

Angeline raised her hand toward him, took a step forward. "But, Izgard—"

"*Go!*"

He didn't know who flinched first: Angeline or her dog. Both of them stepped back. The creature moved to his mistress's heels. Bending down, Angeline petted the cowering animal. Izgard noticed the expression in her eyes change as she stroked the soft fur behind its ears. Fear was replaced with something else.

Angeline swallowed again, only this time there was no food in her mouth. "Gerta says we need an heir. And the only way we can get one is if you and I . . ." Her words trailed away as she suddenly became intent on plucking a bit of straw from her dog's coat.

Izgard was in no mood for Angeline. His mind was on war. Everything had to go as planned. He had an entire night to get through, and he knew he would not sleep. One decisive victory tomorrow and the road to Bay'Zell would be cleared. Oh, the Sire and what remained of his army would eventually regroup and reattack, but stories would have spread, and old memories would have stirred, and fear would have set in by then. Every Rhaize knight who survived the battle at dawn would have a tale of horror to tell: popping bones, tearing flesh, harras attacking in black waves. Word of demons would drip from every fever-bloated tongue, and fear of death would shine in every bloodshot eye. "Izgard is the devil incarnate," they would say, "and his harras are more monsters than men."

Terror would do half the work for him. Many would desert the Rhaize army rather than fight such unnatural forces. Those who stayed would be blighted by fear.

"Izgard, here, let me take your cloak."

Izgard's thoughts snapped back to the moment. Angeline. He had forgotten she was here. Mistaking his lack of response for consent, Angeline moved forward to unhook his cloak. Izgard raised his hand to stop her.

"I said go. Do you no longer understand what I say?"

Angeline froze, her arm suspended in midair. Blue eyes regarded him with a child's hesitant indignation. The little dog shrunk farther away.

Chin tilting upward, Angeline said, "I understand what

you say. I'm not a child. It's *you* who aren't making any sense. You brought me here to beget an heir, and now you do nothing but ignore me. How am I supposed to become pregnant unless you take me to your bed?"

Izgard felt a muscle pumping in his neck. How dare Angeline speak to him in such a way? She was picking up ideas from that fat, lazy servant of hers. "Do you know what tomorrow means?" he said, snatching her wrist from the air and twisting it. "Do you?"

"I . . . I . . ."

Izgard's finger dug into her tendons. Her wrist was so small, he could feel his fingertips pressing from the other side. "Tomorrow is the first Garizon battle since Mount Creed. *Mount Creed*. Twenty thousand of our sons died there—bodies frozen on that mountain until spring thaw brought them down, the Veize choked with their remains for two seasons."

As he spoke, Izgard pictured the scenes of carnage and corruption: the Veizach masters had painted them all. Inventing new colors as they worked, they detailed all the subtle variances of rotting flesh and crumbling bone. Izgard's heartbeat quickened. Saliva filled the dip beneath his tongue. Lying beneath the images, like initials etched into the trunk of an ancient tree, was the shadow of the Barbed Coil itself.

Angeline pulled against his grip. She looked frightened now.

"No," Izgard murmured, excited by the visions flashing through his mind. Angeline's wrist was damp beneath his finger. Damp and hot as it shook. "You wanted to stay. Well, stay you shall."

Digging fingertips through tendon to bone, Izgard twisted Angeline's arm back toward her body. Angeline was forced to lower her shoulders and step back. The tension on her forearm was enough to break the bones if she tried to fight. The dog howled and then slunk into the shadows well behind his mistress's back.

"So you want me to bed you, do you?" Izgard hissed. "This night before I head to war? Before I send Garizon sons to die?"

Angeline shook her head. Drops of spittle speckled her right cheek. Dimly Izgard realized he must have sprayed them from his own mouth.

"I'm sorry, Izgard," she said. "I'm sorry. Gerta said—"

"Gerta said! Gerta said!" Izgard jabbed Angeline's wrist toward her body with every word. Her back was almost doubled up. "Should I tell you what I say? I say that woman will be gone by morning. Gone. Get her in here now."

Angeline bit her lip. Although her face was only a hand's span away from his, she avoided looking into his eyes.

"Call her."

Angeline shook her head. "I'm sorry, Izgard. It's not Gerta's fault. It's mine. I just felt . . . lonely."

She was lying. Her cheeks were so hot, Izgard could see his own spittle evaporating before his eyes. Beneath his fingertips, Angeline's pulse throbbed as blood forced its way round his grip to her hand. She had a strong heart, this child wife of his. "Call Gerta," he murmured, his voice bearing the lode of his visions. He saw bone growing into a beating heart, felt the ground throb in time to Angeline's pulse as an army charged toward him, blades drawn. Tomorrow suddenly seemed too far away. He needed to see the blood of his enemies. Now.

"Gerta." Angeline's heart wasn't in the call. Tears reddened her eyes.

"Call again. Louder." To his own ears, his voice sounded calm. But Angeline must have heard something he didn't, for she called again straight away. Loud enough to draw sailors in a storm.

Looking at Angeline's plump, flushed cheeks and the awkward curve of her back, Izgard felt only contempt She became one more thing to break. Like Rhaize. He would soften her with fear first, take the fight right out of her before the battle was even begun.

"Mistress. Sire." The servant woman Gerta parted the tent slit with capable hands. Too large and graceless for curtsies, she bowed her way into the chamber as if the ceiling were too low for her to stand. Her eyes registered no surprise at the scene that awaited her, and after a quick glance at Angeline's face, she met Izgard's eye with a level gaze. "You have need of me, sire?"

Prepared to be angered by her shock, Izgard found himself even further enraged by her lack of response. She sought to rob him of the fear that was his due. "Your mistress no longer requires your services. You will head back to Garizon this night."

"This night!" Angeline cried. "But—"

Izgard silenced her with a twist to her wrist. Angeline drew in breath. From somewhere deep in the shadows, her dog growled.

Gerta stood her ground. Her large Garizon frame lost none of its sense of purpose by being bent in supplication at the waist. "If you give me but a few hours, sire, I can have both myself and your lady ready to journey back to Sern. We will need an escort of six armed men, a covered cart, and a—"

Releasing his grip on Angeline's wrist, Izgard sent his fist smashing into Gerta's square jaw. Angeline screamed. The old servant reeled back but didn't fall. Various metal items hanging from her belt jingled as she steadied herself against a timber.

"I said *you* will return to Garizon. Not my wife. You alone. Get your belongings together. Get a pony from the stablehand, pick an escort from the wounded, then make haste out of my sight." As he spoke, Izgard glanced toward Angeline to see her reaction. Blood drained from her face, making her skin look as if it were covered by a layer of rapidly cooling wax. Izgard wanted to touch her cheek, monitor the withdrawal of blood firsthand. He didn't, though. Other urges called with more powerful voices.

Returning his gaze to Gerta, he said, "Do my bidding."

Gerta hesitated. She looked at Angeline, passing along a message with her eyes, before bending her back into a deeper bow and murmuring the word, "Aye," deliberately omitting his title.

Izgard saw red. He saw the caked-in shadow of old blood and the bright flaring spill of new. His mind's eye fractured into a dozen separate images like the surface of a diamond-cut stone, each individual facet reflecting a vision of what it was to win a war. Glory, immortality, power, reverence, and fear: victory would inspire them all. *He* would inspire them all.

Mouth thick with saliva, Izgard watched as Gerta began the process of backing out of the chamber. He detected insolence in the way she dared to rub her injured jaw in his presence, defiance in the slowness of her gait. How dare this woman hesitate? How dare she raise her eyes to flash a warning to his wife? How dare she question the orders of the wearer of the Coil?

Izgard went for her. Tomorrow at dawn he would command an army. Garizon sons would jump at his bidding, eager to please their country and their king. Yet this woman, with her placid, old-maid toughness and her message-sending eyes, deliberately defied him in his own tent, in front of his wife. He would not have it.

Although Izgard had a knife sheathed at his side, it never occurred to him to draw it. He needed to touch, to *feel*. Hands grasping at the rolls of fat beneath Gerta's chin, Izgard felt a momentary satisfaction as his fingers slipped over skin slick with sweat. She had been scared all along and hadn't shown it. The woman was strong in her heavy-limbed way and fought back by pushing and slapping. But Izgard was fired by a dozen burning visions, and her blows fell like cushioned punches on his chest. Cupping her chin in his hands, he drove the back of her skull into the wooden timber she had used minutes earlier to steady herself.

Angeline screamed and screamed. Her dog came out of the shadows and danced a snarling, snapping circle around Izgard's heels. Izgard lashed out with his foot, sending the toe of his boot smashing into a nearby chest, barely missing the creature by a tail. Out of the corner of his eye, Izgard saw Angeline scoop the animal into her arms and hug it very tight. Both mistress and dog were quiet after that.

Again and again, Izgard rammed Gerta's skull into the wood. The pewter cup and brush suspended from the old maid's belt chimed like a cow bell with each blow. The pole itself began to loosen in its seating, and the oilcloth ceiling it supported began to shake. Izgard continued beating Gerta against the listing timber until he got what he wanted.

Finally blood flowed, running down from the back of Gerta's large Garizon head, across her jaw, and onto Izgard's hands. Gerta's body was limp, her arms dead by her sides, her eyelids fluttering as if in deep sleep. A thin stream of mucus ran down from her nose. Izgard felt the warm thickness of her blood coat his fingers. There was not much, really, barely sufficient to fill four thimbles, but it was enough to appease the visions in his head.

Like smoke rising from a once hot pot, the visions deserted him in thin, curling plumes. The need for victory passed, leaving him as disoriented as a man stripped of a blindfold and then pushed into the brightness of day. Removing his hand from Gerta's throat, Izgard lowered her body to the floor, careful not to cause any further damage. Looking down at the old maid's crumpled, bloodstained face, Izgard trembled so deeply that he felt muscles in his chest working to still his heart. He could no longer remember the reason behind his rage.

It was not midnight, yet Ederius chose midnight blue. The sea was over a hundred leagues to the north, yet he thinned his pigments with salt water. He hadn't stepped on the Anointed Isle for thirty-five years, yet he remembered its features as if it were yesterday, and its colors, textures, and smells he re-created in his inks.

No scribe trained on the isle ever forgot the shifting gray of the rising tide or the shrieking of the gulls.

Pigments all but mixed, brushes clean, parchment raised and pounced with chalk, Ederius moved from his makeshift desk, taking the four steps required to cross his tent. An hourglass rested on a camp table, its contents long settled, its time long passed. After pulling a fine linen square from his personal chest, Ederius picked up the hourglass and wrapped it in the cloth. Twisting together the four corners of linen, he made himself a makeshift handle, and after tracing the four steps back to the desk, he raised the bundle high above his head and sent it smashing into the wood. Glass shattered. Pigments pots chimed. Parchment fluttered and then was still.

Ederius released his hold on the twisted ends of linen, allowing the cloth to fall open. Shards of glass jutted like transparent teeth from a mound of glittering sand.

Slowly Ederius began to pick the glass away piece by piece. The large slivers were easy to remove, but some of the glass had shattered into splinters not much bigger than the sand itself, and after a while of sorting he finally gave up. Precious minutes were passing, and the illumination had to be started. The guiding points for the design lay etched inside the densest weft of the Barbed Coil. Ederius knew he would need time to grow accustomed to the unfamiliar forms.

He could not afford to make any more mistakes.

Once he'd gathered the cloth into a tight bundle, Ederius transferred it to the scribing side of his desk. Holding the package above the various pigment pots crowding around the parchment, Ederius took his knife and stabbed a hole in the fabric. A fine stream of sand flowed through the hole to the pigments below. Cupping a hand beneath the flow, he filtered it through his fingers, catching the last splinters of glass.

Sand was what he needed.

Yellow sand to mark the beaches that stretched around the isle.

TWENTY-FIVE

he buzzing noise grew steadily louder. She was running through a maze of patterns and could find no way out. Gold-eyed snakes hissed at her heels, and razor-edged barbs caught in her dress and hair. Something was coming after her; she could hear its footsteps padding against the earth, feel its breath curling past her cheeks. Gaining speed, it stepped on her shadow and then slapped its claws on her back.

Tessa snapped awake.

The cell door burst open.

Light from the candle flickered then died. Utter blackness was left.

Something entered the room. Tessa could feel it pouring into the cell, robbing the available space, sucking at the air she meant to breathe. A smell, like the harras, only different, older, deeper, bloodier, pushed against her face like heat from a furnace. The hair at the base of her scalp bristled. She tried to swallow, but something hard blocked her throat.

The thing moved closer, its weight setting the walls vibrating and its mass killing all drafts stone dead. Even though it was still feet away from her, Tessa could feel its presence pulling at her skin. Grabbing the blanket as if that could somehow protect her, she scrambled upright on the mat. There was nowhere for her to go except back. One step and her ankle hit the corner of the cell.

Pottery crunched like dry sand as the creature took another step. Its smell sharpened. Tessa didn't want to take it in, but she had to. Forcing her lips apart, she took a breath through her mouth instead of her nose. Blood. The taste of blood smothered her tongue. A tiny quivering noise sounded in her throat. She couldn't move.

The thing that matched the darkness sprang at Tessa. Air pushed past her face. Something flashed—tooth, eye; she didn't know what—and then the creature fell on her. It slammed her rib cage into her lungs, sending air exploding from her mouth. A wet claw raked across her cheek. Wet fangs sank into the meat of her shoulder.

Tears rushed to Tessa's eyes. The darkness blurred. Pain tore along her arm and down to her chest. She had no breath to scream. Yanking the blanket up toward her face, she beat against the creature with bunched fists. It was like beating against solid ground. Driving up her right hand, she sent her knuckles blasting into its snout. The creature's jaw sprang apart, and it lost its grip on her shoulder.

Head shooting back, the creature exhaled. Its breath was hot and sweet. Tessa felt the vapor condense as it hit her face. She smelled blood and something else—the stench of old, hateful things rotting away in wet soil.

Tessa was glad then of the darkness. She didn't want to see what was in the cell with her. She didn't want to know what it was.

Hearing the soft click of bone as the creature pulled back its arm for a blow, Tessa threw the blanket in the direction of the noise. It was nothing—a handkerchief before a charging bull—but it gave her a quarter second as the creature tore it aside. Tessa sprang off the mat toward the window.

As her hand fell down by her waist, her wrist brushed against something hard. Ravis' knife. Before her fingers had chance to close around the shaft, something blasted into the back of her head. Tessa's teeth smashed together. Her upper torso fell forward into the deep alcove of the cell window. Her forehead cracked against the shutter. Everything dimmed. Thoughts and intent slipped away. Tessa's legs buckled and her body slid off the ledge toward the floor. Claws ripped down her back.

The cell began to spin. Tessa couldn't think, couldn't move. Specks of light shot across her vision, leaving white motion trails where they passed.

In the spinning, thrashing, sharp-clawed darkness, Tessa became aware of the ringing in her ears. The high-pitched noise that had begun burrowing through her mind at the start of the storm, accompanying her ride across the causeway and then infiltrating her dreams, grew louder with every beat of her heart.

It stopped her from forgetting who she was.

Forcing her thoughts into focus, willing her muscles to work, Tessa tried to curl herself into a ball against the ledge. Movement was difficult, as her limbs felt heavy, and there was a wet, sticky substance coating her skin. Surprisingly she felt no pain.

The creature tore at her back and shoulders, its claws shredding her dress, its fangs searching for muscle to grip. Tessa felt its mass pressing against her spine, crushing her ribs and lungs. The smell of blood was overwhelming.

Noise ground through Tessa's temples, forcing her to breathe, move, *think*. One small shift of her right arm brought her hand back in contact with Ravis' knife. The handle felt large in her palm. Drawing it from her belt seemed to take forever. It was heavier than she remembered; awkward to hold. As she turned the blade to face outward, the heel of the creature's hand smashed into her temple. Tessa's entire body was thrown sideways. The darkness flashed white for an instant, and then her hips and rib cage hit the floor.

That, thought Tessa as slowly and carefully as a drunkard reciting lines, was a very great mistake. The blow only made the ringing louder. She would never black out now with all this noise thundering through her head.

Belly flat against the stone floor, knife in hand, blade parallel to her chest, Tessa waited for the creature to come to her. Wet stuff poured down her cheek. Her left thighbone throbbed, her lungs burned, but her mind was perfectly clear. *One two three four five six seven eight nine*, she breathed. *One two three four—*

The creature shot toward her. Air pushed against her face, claws sank into her scalp. A frothing, saliva-thick breath sounded directly above her head. The noise was all she needed to aim her knife. Twisting around, she lashed out with the blade, hacking at the creature's jaw and snout.

A choked howl sounded. The creature stepped back. Something hot sprayed against Tessa's face. Struggling to her feet, she wiped away the wetness with what was left of her sleeve. Her legs weren't working properly, and as she took her first step forward, her knees buckled beneath her. She had to lean against the alcove for support.

Glancing into the darkness at the far side of the room, she tried to recall the exact location of the door. The creature was blocking her way out. Hearing a soft hiss of rage and feeling the air switch as if cracked by a whip, Tessa sucked in her breath. A wave of nausea rolled up from her gut. The creature was tensing for another attack. She was never going to make it to the door.

As she altered her grip on Ravis' knife, preparing to use it like a sword to defend herself, the blade tip scored against something metal. The clasp on the shutter. The noise in Tessa's ear shifted to a higher pitch. *The window.* The creature was too large to fit through the window.

But she wasn't.

Even as the thought formed in her head, the creature lunged at her. Tessa stabbed the darkness surrounding the clasp. Hands shaking, she drove the blade into the metal. The edge caught, a spark flashed, and then the creature yanked at her hair. The bones in Tessa's neck cracked all at once, but she managed to keep her grip on the blade. Desperate now, she drew back the knife and sent it plunging into wood.

The catch gave. The shutters flew open. A high, furious wind filled the room. Tessa smelled salt and seaweed and sand. A sheet of rain blasted against her face. The light level remained unchanged. It was as dark outside as it was within.

The thing, the creature that smelled like fresh blood and old earth, sank its fangs into Tessa's upper arm. Tessa wheeled round and stabbed the blackness above the area where she felt the pain. The creature's bite loosened for an instant, and Tessa wrenched her arm free. Pulling herself up into the alcove with her left hand, she swept the air behind her with her knife. The window opening was a fraction narrower than her shoulders, and she had to squeeze her way through. The blood helped; warm and slick, it lubricated her skin, allowing her shoulders to slip through the frame.

As she forced her way through to the exterior ledge, Tessa felt something sharp puncture the flesh on her right shin—the creature had bit right through the boot leather.

Close to hysterical, she wrenched her leg back. Skin split, pain sizzled down her leg, and then her foot came free of the boot.

Thrown off balance, Tessa careened off the ledge. She tried to grab the exterior wall, but it was too late, and she fell into the darkness below.

She landed in a shallow pool of salt water. Her body stung in a hundred different places. Pebbles and smooth rocks lay beneath her. Ringing sounds clanged through her ears like the toll of a mighty bell. They cleared her mind in an instant.

A cracking, splintering noise sounded directly above her. As she looked up to see what it was, the claw marks on her back pulled open. Tears filled her eyes. Wind and salt water blew in her face. She could barely see the outline of the abbey wall.

Something landed in her hair. Raking her fingers along her scalp, she pulled out the object. It was a thick splinter of wood. Tessa's stomach contracted to a solid mass. The creature was tearing away at the window frame. It meant to come after her. Scrambling to her knees, she plunged her hands into the water, searching for Ravis' knife. Her fingers felt nothing except the smooth surface of sea-worn rocks. She must have lost the knife when she fell.

The creature made a soft, throaty hiss. A wood-splitting noise followed, and then something heavy splashed into the water by Tessa's hand. The window frame was coming apart.

Abandoning her search for the knife, Tessa thrashed in the rock pool, trying to get her legs to take the weight of her body. Her thigh muscles were shaking. What was left of her dress hung like a wet curtain on her back. It was hard to orient herself in the darkness; the water from the pool dragged at her body, and the wind blasted her face from all sides. Slapping her hand against the abbey wall, she dragged herself to her feet. Water sloshed around the one boot she was still wearing. Briefly Tessa considered pulling it off, but she doubted she had the strength.

Smiling grimly, too tired to retain any thoughts more complicated than the need to get away, Tessa pushed herself off from the abbey wall like a rowboat leaving a jetty. Her body felt strange, heavy and slow to react. If it wasn't for the noises grinding in her ears, she had a feeling her mind would feel the same way too.

Walking was difficult. The ground beneath the window was little more than a mound of loosely piled pebbles. Stones dug into the arch of her bare foot, making her wince with every step. Blood dripped down her shin from the bite wound, and each time she transferred her weight forward, she had to fight the buckling action in her knees.

Ahead, she spied a gray line stretching across the coupled darkness of the storm and the night. It was either the sea or the mainland shore—she couldn't tell which. Squinting into the rain and sea spray, she tried to pick out more details: the rise of the mainland, the lights of Bellhaven, the angular forms of buildings in the town. Nothing.

Pebbles crunched directly behind her. The backwind carried a whiff of blood.

Tessa closed her eyes. The ball in her stomach twisted, pulling the muscles in her abdomen into a tight, quivering band. She was so tired, she felt physically sick. She just wanted to lie down on the pebble beach and drift away—to sleep or unconsciousness, whichever came first: she didn't care. Yet the high, piercing, cold-metal ringing wouldn't let her. It told her the creature that had just torn off a window frame to get to her would slice her body to shreds the moment she stopped for breath.

Tessa sucked in two lungs' worth of air and broke into a run. She'd lived with her tinnitus for too long not to listen when it spoke.

She ran and ran and ran. Heart pumping, lungs scorching, she headed into the oncoming wind. The ground underfoot gradually changed. The pebbles became smaller, smoother, more scattered, and then they gave way to sand. Tessa's feet splashed through tide pools clicking with crabs, stamped over lumpy patches of seaweed that made popping sounds as she passed.

The rain came in short, savage bursts. There would be nothing for seconds at a time, and then Tessa would be blasted with rain and sea spray. Specks of wind-driven sand flew into her mouth, lodging between her teeth and forming a salty, gritty layer beneath her tongue. Her eyes stung so much, she kept them closed as she ran. In the utter darkness of the storm there was nothing to see.

Hard, crunching footsteps gained on her. Tessa felt the creature's momentum as a palpable force against her back. It pushed her forward, made her take step after wavering step, forced her to flee into the black tunnel of the night. She didn't think. It took everything she had to breathe and run.

The noise in her temples grew louder. Before long it blocked out the sound of the wind and the storm. She heard blood pumping through her temples, sand shifting beneath her feet: little else. After a while the creature's footsteps seemed to recede into the distance. Tessa didn't trust her senses, though, and kept running on and on. Ringing meant danger, and the louder it became, the worse the danger was.

Beneath her feet the sand grew wetter. Channels in the beach began to fill with water and large patches of ground deteriorated into soft mud. Thinking she was veering off course, Tessa changed her direction, running away from the waterlogged channels.

Within seconds she ran into more.

Thin plumes of icy water spilled over the sand. Tessa felt the water foaming beneath her bare foot. A thick gust of wind sent a wave breaking against her ankle. The noise in her ears became so loud, she could no longer hear herself breathe. A second wave followed the first, and this time it didn't need the wind to roll over her foot; it flowed smoothly across the sand in air that was nearly still. Half a minute later another wave hit from the opposite side. The water level crested Tessa's shin.

Tessa stopped dead. Her heart and lungs seemed to collapse inward, leaving a hollow ache inside her throat.

The tide was coming in.

Rubbing her closed eyes, working the grit and sea salt into the outer corners, Tessa tried to take a deep breath. She didn't manage it. Two waves hit her shins from either side. Before the water had chance to recede, a third slapped against her knees. The ground underfoot was no longer solid; it was a rapidly liquefying mire of sand. Tessa felt her feet sinking in. Panicking, she dragged her booted foot from the bottom. The sand sucked at the leather, not wanting to give it up. Pivoting her weight onto her other leg, Tessa pulled her foot free of the boot.

A series of waves hit as she planted her newly freed foot in the sand. The water hardly retreated at all this time, just kept rising steadily against her leg. The hem of her dress floated like an open flower around her shins.

Working the last grains of salt free from her eyes, Tessa peered into the darkness. Ragged gray lines rolled out of the shadows toward her. Breaking waves, somehow managing to catch and reflect minuscule traces of cloud-filtered moonlight, rose and fell in the distance as far as she could see. Spinning around, she looked back toward the abbey. Only when she looked she wasn't sure if it was the right direction after all, as the view looked the same as dead ahead: a black curtain, featureless except for the tide-driven waves skimming across the sand.

Tessa pressed her lips together very tight, stifling a cry. There were no lights allowed in the abbey after Eighth Toll. She'd have nothing to guide her back.

A hard gust of wind sent water splashing up to midthigh. Below the surface, uncoiling like a rope pulled from both ends, a current was beginning to form. Tessa could feel it tugging against her ankles, shifting her weight from side to side.

Stay calm, she told herself. *Stay calm.*

A trickle of salt water ran into her mouth, depositing more grit beneath her tongue. Now that she had stopped running, the ringing in her ears seemed less intense. She had to think. *Think.*

Planting her feet well apart, Tessa spun back in the direction she had been headed. Looking into the darkness, she realized there was no way of knowing for sure if Bellhaven lay ahead. In the madness of the chase she had run without any thought. She didn't even know on what side of the abbey her cell was located: the window may have faced straight out to sea.

Tessa ran her hand along her aching temples. She had no choice but to try to make it back to the abbey.

Carefully tracking the degree of her turn, trying to recall

the exact angle she had used earlier when changing course, Tessa spun around once more. The water level reached past her knees now, and the skirt of her dress dragged behind, making it difficult to step clear of the waves. It had to come off. Bending, she grabbed a fistful of fabric and yanked it away from her body. The creature's claws had torn the dress to shreds, and a great portion of the skirt came away in her hand. Just as well, thought Tessa, bunching the skirt in her fist, as Ravis wasn't here this time to cut it away with his knife.

Flinging the skirt into the water, Tessa fought the desire to collapse into a small, defeated ball. A tendon in her throat began to quiver. Ravis. Why hadn't he spoken up to warn *her* in the inn? Why had his first thought been for Violante?

A wave broke against her hip. Sea foam splashed as high as her cheek. Below the surface, bands of cold, fast-moving water began to move in with the undertow. Tessa shivered. She wouldn't be able to keep her feet on the bottom for much longer. She had to find her way back to the abbey.

Thinking about Ravis, wishing for something she could never have, was a waste of energy. She couldn't let herself get distracted. She had to be tough, focused: more like the old Tessa McCamfrey. She had to think of herself.

Wind sliced across the rising tide, cutting the waves into lines and driving sea spray into her open wounds. As she leaned into the wind to keep herself steady, Tessa's thoughts turned to Emith and his mother: they would both blame themselves if anything happened to her. She shook her head violently, trying to dispel a sudden tightness in her chest. She didn't want to think about them being hurt.

The ringing in her ears altered pitch, becoming softer, deeper, more urgent. Time was running out.

Looking out over the darkness, Tessa searched for anything that would indicate the direction of the abbey. The sky and the horizon were perfectly black. The only variance in light was provided by the wave crests, which flashed a dull, barely luminous gray as they rolled together over the sand. Tessa watched the waves for a moment, studying the shapes they formed before disappearing into the dark swell of the sea.

As she watched the wave crests flashing then fading, something began to shift in Tessa's brain. Forms and lines caught her eye. Threads of light would disappear, only to be replaced by similar ones seconds later. The skin on her scalp slowly pulled tight, making her hair bristle at its roots. There was a pattern in the waves.

The point at which the breakers met, where the sea closed in from both sides over the causeway, a crude spiral pattern had formed. Waves hitting each other from opposite directions bounced back into the oncoming swell and were driven outward once more before rippling back into the join. The center of the causeway was marked by a flashing gray interlace of waves. Tessa followed the weave of light with her eye, tracking its course back into the darkness, seeing it as a roadway leading straight to the abbey.

Chest aching from too many hard breaths, thoughts full of all the people and places she missed, Tessa took her first step back toward the Anointed Isle. Pulling her foot from the bottom, she forced her leg through bands of jarring currents and columns of swirling foam, moving her entire body into the center of the swell. The pattern would lead her back.

Each step was a fight against the current and the rising water level. The water temperature was colder than the air, and as the level rose to waist height, Tessa could feel a chill settling against her bones. She was so very tired. All the energy she had left—what little she could pull from her muscles, lungs, and heart—she focused on moving forward against the crosscurrents. Eyes staring straight ahead at the shifting, repeating patterns of the waves, Tessa let her mind drift away.

She worried about Mother Emith, about her legs and her health, and Emith and their safety, and about how bad they would feel if she never came back. She tried not to think of Ravis, but her mind seemed to grow numb along with her body, and it was as difficult to switch her thoughts from subject to subject as it was to force her feet onto the bottom with every new step.

Water rose. Wind dropped. Rain came in ever-decreasing bursts. Tessa's body cooled so slowly, she was hardly aware of the change. Limbs became heavy and liquid like the water itself, and she began losing sensation in her feet. The ringing in her ears sounded far away now . . . not really like ringing at all, more like a mild hypnotic buzz. The patterns shimmered before her eyes, showing her the way.

By the time the water reached shoulder height, Tessa

could no longer keep her feet on the bottom. Spreading out her arms on the surface, she concentrated on keeping her head above water. Swimming was out of the question: she didn't have the strength to fight the waves.

Bitter, salty sea water washed in and out of her mouth. A deep cold gripped her chest, and the only breaths she could manage were shallow. The current tugged her back and forth as if she were as weightless and insubstantial as the seaweed that twined around her ankles and wrist. Only the flashing wave crests kept her on track. Floating through the darkness felt like being nowhere at all. She was completely and utterly alone.

Tessa hugged the surface of the water as if it were a living, breathing thing. The sea no longer seemed cold: it was the exact same temperature as her body, and it brought comfort as it pressed against her chest. In the black, edgeless night, it was all she had left.

She missed Emith and his mother and their warm, golden kitchen. She missed Ravis and his softly mocking voice.

Too tired to hold her chin up any longer, Tessa rested her head against the surface and let the motion of the waves ease her neck. Slowly, against her will and her very best efforts, her eyelids began to close. The ringing in her ears faded to a mosquito's hum, and the sea rocked her body back and forth. Strange how she felt the emptiness inside much more than she did the cold.

"Gerta. Gerta. Please, please, *please*, wake up." Angeline was too frightened of hurting Gerta to shake her, so she squeezed her arm instead. Snowy made an odd whining noise from his position at the base of the camp bed. Angeline could tell he wanted to jump on the bed and lick Gerta's face, but no-good dog's remorse kept him from it.

Snowy's sorry for not being brave.

Angeline smiled a small, relieved smile. She wasn't the slightest bit sorry Snowy wasn't brave. Izgard was brave. Gerta was brave. Being brave meant you either did bad things to others or got bad things done to you. Angeline didn't think she could stand it if bad things happened to Snowy. Bending, she reached out and ruffled the fur under the little dog's chin. Snowy was so pleased to be touched, his tail thumped against the floor double time.

No-good dog. No-good dog.

"I know Snowy," said Angeline, very softly. "I love you and I know."

"M'lady . . ."

Spinning around, Angeline looked up in time to see Gerta's eyes open. A milky film ran over her irises, and even when she blinked, it didn't quite go away.

Angeline squeezed her arm a fraction harder. "You're in the surgeon's tent, Gerta. Izgard had you moved. He ordered his best surgeon to stitch you up."

Gerta made a small movement that might have been a nod.

"I'm sorry, Gerta. Truly. I should never have said any-thing to Izgard. I'm so sorry." Aware that her voice was rising, Angeline forced herself to calm down. She took a breath. "The surgeon says you were lucky. He said you have a skull like a horse. No broken bones, just a split head. It took a dozen stitches to fix you up."

Gerta licked her lips. They were pale and looked very dry. "Did he hurt you?"

Angeline shook her head for a very long time. It pained her to see this woman, whose strength and sense of purpose she had always envied, in such a weakened state. It wasn't right. Speaking in a rush to stop her voice from breaking, Angeline said, "Izgard was just worried about the battle, that was all. It was my fault he—" Her words came to an abrupt halt as she realized that what she was about to say might be considered disloyal to her husband. It was hard sometimes to remember things like that. "Anyway. The good thing is you won't have to go home now."

"Is that what the king said?"

"No." Angeline was confused by the question. "He didn't say that. But you can't cross the mountains until you're well. You just can't."

"I see she's awake." The surgeon strode into the tent, forcing Angeline to step aside so he could reach Gerta's pallet. Angeline didn't like the surgeon. If it wasn't for the fact she was his queen, she felt sure he would never have remembered her name. He had neither love nor patience for women. The long dark apron he always wore was dry now, and Gerta's blood, which had wetted it earlier, was no longer visible. That was, Angeline supposed, the reason why surgeons wore black.

Suddenly feeling cold, Angeline went to pet Snowy. The little dog was already off, sniffing out dust and rat droppings and hairballs. His hind legs protruded from under a nearby pallet and his tail was suspended at half-mast, meaning he was on the hunt of some large hairy spider or poised to battle with ants. Angeline immediately felt better for seeing him. Some things never changed.

She turned around to see the surgeon grabbing hold of Gerta by the shoulders.

"What are you doing?" she cried. "You can't take Gerta out of bed."

The surgeon did not stop as he replied, "There's a cart and an escort of two armed men outside, waiting to take her from the camp."

"But . . . but . . ." Angeline was so surprised, she could find no words.

"Ssh, m'lady. Ssh," murmured Gerta. "The king gave an order. He cannot take it back."

"But . . ."

"The woman will be fine," the surgeon said, speaking as if Gerta weren't even in the room, let alone in his arms. "She's old, but I've given her tonic, pulled the splinters from her wounds. She's lucky the king thought well enough of her to send for me."

Angeline surprised herself by thinking of a nasty reply, then lost her nerve and didn't say it. "Please leave us a moment," she said. "I would like to speak to my servant alone."

The surgeon continued dragging Gerta from the tent, not even bothering to acknowledge Angeline's words.

"I said leave us!"

The surgeon stopped in midstep. Gerta drew in a thin breath. Snowy backed out from the pallet and cocked his head.

Angeline covered her mouth in shock. In all her life she had never spoken so harshly to anyone. What was the matter with her? Her first instinct was to apologize, to make an excuse about being tired and irritable, but as she formed the sentence in her head, she saw the surgeon begin lowering Gerta, very carefully, onto the floor.

Angeline felt a warm wave roll over her body. She felt dizzy with triumph. Standing a little straighter, forcing her shoulders back, and tilting up her chin, she said to the surgeon, "Get a pillow for Gerta's neck. Bring me a flask of honey and almond-milk tea and then leave."

"Yes, Your Highness." The surgeon's voice was different now. For the first time, Angeline noticed how small he was. Strange, how he had always seemed so tall before.

Watching him struggling to pull a pillow from the pallet with one hand while cupping Gerta's head in the other, Angeline was tempted to help out. She even stepped forward, but Snowy growled: *Stay.*

So she did.

The surgeon didn't only bring a flask of honey and almond-milk tea, he poured two cups to the brim with the pale, milky fluid. Angeline, frightened that if she spoke she might lose her resolution and start apologizing, acknowledged his services with a nod. The moment he stepped from the tent, Snowy came bounding up, yelping and jumping and demanding to be taken into her arms.

"Bad Snowy," Angeline said, laughing as she bent to pet him. How could a night manage to be so very bad and yet good all the same? "Bad, bad Snowy."

"M'lady . . ." Gerta's voice was weak. It immediately brought Angeline down to earth. "You must make the king find another woman to tend you."

"But I don't want anyone beside you, Gerta. I'm sorry I never listened. Sorry I was always bad." As she spoke, Angeline remembered how she had tricked Gerta into letting her come to the camp. A guilty flush spread across her cheeks. Without realizing it, her hand came up to rest upon her stomach. "Sorry for everything."

Gerta was very pale. Her skin looked heavy yet transparent, like wet linen hung to dry on a line. The milky film floated across her pupils as her gaze flicked from Angeline's face to her stomach. "You must take care of yourself when I'm gone. Eat right. Sleep properly."

Angeline frowned. First Ederius and now Gerta. Why did everyone warn her to take care of herself? "I'll be fine, Gerta. Honestly. It's getting you safely across the mountains that I'm worried about."

Gerta blinked slowly. She made a small motion with her wrist. Angeline, taking it to mean she wanted to be touched, grasped Gerta's hand in hers. The coolness of Gerta's fingers was a shock, but she tried her best not to show it.

"I'll be fine, m'lady," Gerta said. "It's high summer, I'm mountain born, and the king has cleared the passes of brigands. There's nothing for you to worry about. See?"

Even though she wasn't convinced, Angeline nodded—she knew that was what Gerta wanted.

A cough sounded behind. It was the surgeon. He waited for Angeline's attention before he spoke. "Your Highness, it's best if your servant leaves now. Dawn is only two hours away, and already some of the troops are moving to the east. Her party must clear the camp perimeter before daylight." He waited for Angeline to say something, and when she made no effort to reply he added, "It is what the king advises."

Angeline rubbed her aching wrist. She was tired of pretending to be strong, worried about Gerta, exhausted down to her bones. "Very well. You may take her." The surgeon took a step forward. "But," she said, halting him, "call someone else to help carry her. I will not have her dragged across the ground like a sack of grain." It wasn't much, but it was all she could do. Gerta was right: Izgard would never change his mind and let her stay.

Gerta's cool fingers pressed against hers as the surgeon slipped out of the tent. "You be strong like that every day," she said. "Be strong for yourself and the baby."

Angeline looked into Gerta's eyes without blinking. She didn't trust herself to speak.

Gerta spoke softly into the silence. "Do you think I didn't notice, my little one? An old maid like me?"

In all the time she had known her, Angeline had never heard Gerta speak with such gentleness. It made her heart ache. Leaning forward, she pressed her lips against Gerta's cheek.

Gerta smiled as she withdrew. "As soon as I figured it out, I started sending Snowy better scraps."

"You knew all along I ate them?" Angeline brushed a stray hair from Gerta's face. She was relieved Gerta knew. It meant she could stop being a liar.

"Not even a clever dog like Snowy could tear the meat right off a bone, while leaving all the fat." Gerta patted Angeline's hand. "Then there was the morning sickness and the redness around your neck and chest. Babies and the business of making them is my trade. I don't know many things, but I know when a woman's with child."

Angeline didn't like the way Gerta's voice grew weaker as she spoke, but even though she knew it was best to let Gerta rest, she had to ask one question. "Why didn't you tell Izgard? Wasn't your job to watch over me for him?"

Gerta closed her eyes. It took a few breaths before she was able to speak. "I know what my job was—and no one loves their country as much as me. No one. But you and that no-good dog of yours wheedled your way into my heart. I didn't mean to love you, but there it is."

Snowy issued a low howl. Padding over the floor, he came and rested his head on Gerta's ankle and stared up at her face. Angeline swallowed hard. She had gotten all three of them into such trouble.

"Right, There she is. Be careful with her." The surgeon entered the tent flanked by two other men. After a quick glance toward Angeline to check that it was all right to do so, he began moving Gerta out of the tent. Angeline and Snowy followed behind.

It was pitch black outside. The air was choked with smoke as campfires were extinguished one by one. Soft noises pierced the darkness: the catch of metal fastening to metal, the skim of leather hooked through a clasp, the blowing of nervous horses, and the clicking of bones as men straightened legs after six long hours of crouching. The ground beneath Angeline's feet trembled. Izgard's army was on the move.

Looking over toward the horizon, she caught sight of a line of troops cresting the rise. The harras. Even in the darkness, she could tell they moved too fluidly for men. Blacker than the night itself, they seemed to bleed from the shadows like juices from a roast. Angeline heard them call to each other, then told herself she hadn't. Men didn't sound like that. Wolves did.

Shivering, she turned back to the surgeon. He was directing the laying of Gerta's body in the covered cart. Angeline looked over the two men who would escort Gerta back across the mountains. They looked restless, gazes darting across the camp, hands twisting around their horses' reins. Like all Izgard's men, they wanted to fight.

"Take care of this woman for me," Angeline said, surprising even herself when she spoke. "I will count it as a great personal favor if she arrives at Sern Fortress in good health." Normally when she spoke to men, Angeline averted her eyes downward, preferring not to meet their gaze. But this time she looked both guards squarely in the face. And didn't look away until they answered.

Both fell to one knee, pledging to do her bidding. Angeline held out her hand and let each man kiss it in turn. Neither gave any indication of noticing the red weal Izgard had raised on her wrist. "Go," she said. "Take my servant home."

Mouthing the words, "I love you, Gerta," Angeline watched as her old servant was pulled away. Two men, one woman, three horses, a cart, and a pony. The pony had a longbow strapped to its flank. Good. That meant Izgard had sent along one of his prized longbowsmen to protect Gerta on the journey home. Recognizing it as an act of remorse, Angeline ran her aching wrist over her lips. Perhaps her husband wasn't so bad after all.

When the small party disappeared into the shadows, Angeline slapped her side for Snowy to come to heel and then cut a path across the camp. Even though it was an hour before dawn, she had no problem finding her way. There was still one bright spot left to navigate by: the oil lamps blazing like a furnace within Ederius' tent.

TWENTY-SIX

amron stared at the sky until he could no longer
see the stars. He crouched in the gorse until he
lost all sensation in his legs. He held on to his
breath until it turned to poison in his lungs.

Waiting on a hillside west of the Vorce Mountains, half a
league northeast of Izgard's camp, in the last hour of darkness before dawn, Camron waited. Sandor and his first-in-
command, Balanon, were camped on the opposite hill. East
facing, it would be the first to catch the sun's rays at dawn.
The Rhaize army would begin their first charge with the sun
in their faces. Sandor had no mind to such matters when he
picked the slope. He saw only that it was broad and clear of
rocks and afforded a good view of the land adjacent to Izgard's camp.

The enemy camp itself could not be seen. Izgard had
chosen the only spot for leagues that was sheltered on three
of four sides by cliffs and sharp slopes. The fourth side was
bounded by the quick-moving Hook River and then a forest
thick with birches beyond. Unlike Sandor, Izgard had planned
for retreat. Pontoons were in place at the narrowest point in
the river. If the retreat was sounded, Izgard's army would
withdraw across the river and then destroy the makeshift
bridge.

Camron himself had scouted the enemy camp. He went
in alone, for he wanted to skirt close enough to count numbers and could ask no one to share such danger. Izgard's
army was all Ravis of Burano had said it would be: a massive, well-organized fighting force. Even though the camp
was a temporary one, it had been planned with an engineer's
care. Row upon row of white tents were laid out in concen-
tric circles to protect the central corral for the warhorses and

an oiled-hide arcade for artillery and bows. Four sentry posts constructed of timber towered above the camp, huge, many-spoked wheels at their bases for ease of movement from site to site. Latrines to prevent camp waste from poisoning the water supply had been dug downwind and down river of the tents, and the entire camp was ringed by a circle of guard posts, man traps, and covered ditches.

As he looked over the arrangements, counting tents, campfires, and warhorses, Camron could not prevent himself from feeling a sting of bitterness. How much of this was Ravis of Burano's work?

Now, though, eighteen hours later, bruised from half a day scrambling over rocks and hard earth, cut in many places from shouldering through fields bristling with thorns, and with an eye full of blood following a bad landing into one of Izgard's branch-covered ditches, Camron had no mind for Ravis and his past.

His thoughts were all of his father.

Camron ran a hand through his hair, let out the air that burned in his lungs. Berick of Thorn. How could he have wanted so much for his son, dreamed of him taking the one thing he could never take himself, and yet never spoken out loud? Then, more important: How could his son have failed to see the one thing his father wanted most?

Rubbing temples that ached with a dull, persistent pain, Camron switched his gaze away from the night sky. There were no answers. None that he could live with. All he had to hold on to were the words of Lianne, countess of Mir'Lor. *It's not too late. You can still fight for what he wanted. Even now.*

And that was what he would do today.

Briefly Camron glanced over to the Rhaize camp. The first signs of movement could be seen above the rise. Sandor and his knights would be rousing from a night spent sleeping in half armor. They thought it would save time and demonstrate readiness for a surprise attack. In reality it meant sore muscles, aching backs, leg cramps, and painfully full bladders.

Camron caught himself, then frowned. He was beginning to think like Ravis of Burano. Feeling a strong sense of disloyalty for finding that thought less abhorrent than in the past, he turned his attention to his troop.

Fully awake for the past two hours, clad in chainmail or simple breastplates, shortbows strung to the backs of all except the longbowsmen, eleven score men crouched in the darkness behind Camron's back.

The morning following his meeting with Lianne, Camron had gone to meet with Balanon as she'd suggested, taken her token, and retold his story to the man who would stand beside Sandor in battle. Balanon had listened to the full account of the battle in the Valley of Broken Stones, interrupting Camron every few minutes to ask some detail about the harras, their weapons, and their tactics. Unlike Sandor, Balanon had not dismissed the story lightly. And although he'd promised little except increased caution, he had assigned Camron a troop of one hundred men and given him the task of alerting the main army to any unusual dangers posed by the harras. In addition to the hundred foot soldiers, Camron had a dozen of his own knights to command and two dozen longbowsmen, courtesy of Segwin the Ney.

Camron had no illusions about Balanon. He had listened only because of Lianne's token, allowed Camron his own troop to command purely because of favors owed to, or admiration for, the countess of Mir'Lor. Still, it was something. Enough to stop Camron feeling powerless. Enough to stop thoughts of his father eating a hole in his mind.

"Movement on the slope north of the camp."

Camron responded to the hiss of one of his men by raising his gaze to the north. He saw nothing at first, only the dark curve of a second slope tucked behind the camp slope like a shadow. Then, as his gaze skirted across the mushroom-shaped silhouette of a copse of trees in summer foliage, he spied a line of pure darkness spilling down the side of the hill. Camron's first thought was that it wasn't possible. A guard of eight dozen men had been set on that rise to watch the rear of the camp. And then there were the sentry posts: scores of men in tight-knit groups of six, set five hundred paces apart to form a ring around the camp. All were heavily armed, and one in each squad carried a horn to send early warning. Confident Sandor might be, but even he followed the accepted wisdom of securing the camp perimeter.

Camron's second thought wasn't nearly as rational. It was hardly even a thought at all. It was a reaction to the dark, undulating nature of the line. The harras were back.

Every hair on his body bristled. All moisture evaporated from his mouth. A tightness gripped his chest, pushing his ribs against the soft tissue of his lungs and his heart. He saw his father. Dead. He saw Hurin. Dead. He saw Rhif of Hanister, exposed heart still beating.

Alarmed by the sheer strength of his reaction, frightened that if he didn't act now, his memories would overpower him, Camron barked out an order. "Mills, Toker, Stango. Take a squad each. Make your way down the slope as fast as you can. When you've covered a quarter league, raise the alarm."

"Why not raise it now? The camp must be warned." Mills. He was one of Balanon's men.

"I don't want the harras knowing our position. They don't know we're here. Let's keep it that way." Camron looked at the three men, daring them to defy him. He was almost sorry when they didn't. Anger would be a welcome distraction. "Go. Keep your heads down. Don't return."

All three men scrambled to their feet and began gathering their men around them. Balanon's men were ready. Eager. But then they hadn't encountered the harras before. What did they know? Camron stopped himself. His bitterness was directed the wrong way. "Watch yourselves," he hissed.

Mills barely nodded. His expression was hard. "Any message for Balanon?"

Camron shook his head. "No." His gaze returned to the moving line on the horizon. The harras seemed to suck away the darkness from the night, keeping it all for themselves. "None, save we do what was agreed." Before the last word left his lips, the men were on their way, running down the slope, backs bent at the waist, swords sheathed to prevent telltale flashes of light from giving them away.

"Right," Camron said quickly, finding it hard to tear his eyes away from the black line descending on the camp. "Izgard's sending the harras around the rear, hoping to cause the camp to panic. By the time they realize what's hit them, his main force will have taken position for a full frontal attack. Izgard's using the harras as a diversion."

Working things out as he spoke, Camron paused to consider his next move. He found it hard to concentrate. A hundred and thirty pairs of eyes looked his way. Even in the darkness it was easy to tell which men were his and which were Balanon's. His men had fought the harras. Knowledge lay over their eyes like a film of ice.

Camron dragged his hand over his face, forcing himself to think. Should they move to intercept the harras? Block off the line? Or should they head into the valley and attempt to slow down Izgard's main force? Following Ravis of Burano's advice, Camron had equipped all his men with bows. Working quickly and at close quarters, they could target horses and take out the first few lines of the Garizon charge. Segwin the Ney's longbowsmen, with their greater skill and range, could target troop leaders, warlords, even Izgard himself.

But then, realistically, what impact could eleven score archers hope to make upon a force of twenty thousand? Tugging at his jaw, as if he could somehow pull the answers from out of his mouth, Camron considered what Ravis of Burano would do. The answer came straight away. Ravis would double back around the harras and take them by surprise. Play them at their own game.

The wind, which had been blowing at their backs for the past hour, suddenly switched direction and blew into their faces instead. As Camron's hair was pushed back from his cheeks, he caught a whiff of something carried on the breeze. All the muscles in his chest contracted as his body recognized the stench even before his mind had put a name to it. It was the fresh-urine, stale-kill stench of the harras.

Almost unaware of what he did, Camron took a step back. He felt something touch his shoulder. Glancing around, he saw it was Broc of Lomis. The battle in the Valley of Broken Stones had cost him his spleen, two fingers on his right hand, and loss of muscle in his thighs, arms, and chest. Still, he had come. Camron had begged him to stay in Mir'Lor, but Broc wouldn't hear of it. He said his place was by his leader's side. Camron hadn't known at the time if he meant Sandor or himself. Looking into Broc's face now, in the slowly draining darkness of dawn, the truth was plain to see.

It made Camron feel old.

Despite his injuries, Broc had slowed no one down. Working twice as hard as any other man to produce the same results, he had never once complained or shown signs of pain. He took breathers only when the troop did. Slept six hours each night like the rest. Camron felt responsible for him. He felt responsible for all those who had ridden with him that day into the valley. He had acted without thinking, yet they followed him anyway. They were owed a debt for that.

Moving his gaze upward, Camron looked on as the black line of harras flared out across the hill. They were near enough so that the sound of their movements should have roused the camp. Yet their increased speed and activity raised no cry, nor caused one oil lamp to be lit. Watching them, Camron saw how they moved as one body, like a plague of locusts massing before a feeding frenzy. They had one mind. One intent.

Camron found his fingers had dug deep into the muscles at his jaw. Should he circle around to the rear of the camp? Engage the harras? Or should he move forward into the valley instead?

At that moment, noise blasted through the night. A horn was sounded. Then another. Cries followed, and a covey of burning arrows was shot high into the air. The commotion came from an area directly below where the troop stood. It was Mills, Toker, and Stango. The alarm had been raised. Camron froze for perhaps half a second, waiting to feel some sense of relief. When none came, he refocused his attention on the camp—he didn't want to think why.

The horn calls had an immediate effect on the Rhaize camp. Horses squealed, torches blistered to life, dark silhouettes poured out of tents. From where he stood, Camron could just hear the ring of drawn steel. It sounded muffled, tinny. Powerless. The camp was not the only thing affected by the alarm. The harras broke into a full charge, skimming over the hillside like the shadow of a great bird of prey.

"Camron." Broc spoke his name with soft urgency, breaking through the wired cage of Camron's thoughts. Turning to look at him, Camron spied a line of bright yellow silk peeking out above Broc's collar. It came close to making him smile: Broc's sister obviously had something to do with the packing of her older brother's clothes. "What is the order?"

Camron looked back over his men. How could he send them to fight the harras knowing what they were? How could he fight them himself after the battle amid the stones? There was no glory in fighting them. No clean kill. No swift death. Yet what was the alternative? Attack the main force of Izgard's army from the sidelines? Let terror stop them from taking the one action that might have any real effect?

Camron's hand dropped from his chin to his chest, then down to the scabbard of his sword. He looked into Broc's eyes. Seeing something in the soft hazel irises that he could only describe as faith, Camron made his decision.

"We move to intercept the harras," he cried. "Double back behind the camp. Attack them from the rear." A hundred and thirty men moved at his word, drawing bows from their backs as they descended the slope. Camron waited a moment, his gaze defying him by coming to rest one last time upon Broc of Lomis. The young knight nodded. He knew the reason behind the choice: the harras' main weapon was fear. Any action other than attacking them would be an admission of defeat.

Abruptly Camron turned and followed his men down the bank.

It was the smell that woke her. As piercing as any sound, as persistent as the patter of rain, and as forceful as a shake of the arm, the smell pushed against her nostrils, forcing her awake. Tessa opened her eyes. Blinked. Above her lay a canopy of red rock. As she opened her mouth to breathe, a wave of sickness hit her. Rolling onto her side, she vomited onto the rock. The quick movement brought tears to her eyes. The muscles to either side of her shoulders burned. Her head began to spin, immediately bringing on a second wave of nausea. Tessa vomited again. Clear, salty bile.

Bringing up a hand to wipe her mouth, Tessa checked for her ring. It was something she did without thinking. A reflex action, like blinking dust from her eyes. Her hands skimmed over fabric and then skin. Nothing. Panicking, she sat up. She beat her hand against her chest, looked wildly around the area where she lay. *Where was it?*

"Is this what you are looking for?"

Tessa looked up. An old, old man held something toward the light. Dressed in a dull brown tunic, hair perfectly white and close shorn to his head, he regarded Tessa with a faint smile.

Without thinking, Tessa began to scramble to her feet. She wanted the ring back. Nausea twisted in her stomach like a fist. Her legs refused to stiffen beneath her, and she collapsed back down against the rock.

The old man made a soft, whisking sound in his throat. He tossed the ring toward Tessa. "Hold on to it as tightly as you can, my sweet one, but you will still find it lost in the end."

The ring landed on a flat plate of rock by Tessa's side. She snatched it up, closing her fist around the gold. It felt warm, as if it had been in the sun. Just having it back in her possession made her feel calmer, stronger. She pressed the meat of her thumb against the barbs, willing the nausea to pass.

Suddenly aware of how cold she was, Tessa pulled her knees to her chest. She was dressed in a coarse woolen tunic, and the only parts of her body that were visible were her shins. Her skin was crisscrossed with angry, red lines. Among the cuts and bruises was a bite mark. The imprint of three teeth could clearly be seen in the torn and puckered flesh. Shivering, she looked away.

She was in a deep cave. Daylight filtered from some unseen point high above the old man's back. The roof of the chamber dipped low above where she sat and then soared high into darkness in the center of the cave. The rocks ranged in tone from red, to umber, to soft sandy browns. A few were gray, but even they had red mineral deposits bleeding through them. Water dripped. When Tessa placed a hand upon the nearest rock, it came back damp. Specks of orange dust glistened on her drying fingers. There were many smells, but only one that demanded attention. The sharp, sour-milk odor of a dairy. Letting her gaze arch downward, she saw that the entire floor of the cave was laid with pale, circular objects. Lying on beds of something that Tessa guessed to be seaweed, the circular objects were an off white color and looked to be coated in coarse salt.

"Cheese," said the old man, following Tessa's gaze. "This is where we age our best wheels. A cheese cave, if you will." He made a negligent gesture with his hand. "Damp air, seaweed, salt, even the rock itself: they all lend their flavor to the wheels."

Tessa nodded. She felt as if she had fallen into another world. If it wasn't for the sound of the sea drumming far in the distance and the soft Maribane accent of the old man, she could easily have believed the ring had taken her to yet another place. "How did I get here?"

The old man sighed. "Yes, yes. Of course you'll want to know that." He looked quickly at Tessa, then away. "I should ask how you are feeling first, though, shouldn't I?"

"I'm fine," Tessa lied, impatient to hear what he had to say.

"Fine, indeed?" The old man raised his eyebrows. After a moment he nodded. "Well, I suppose that is for you to judge."

Tessa felt a faint blush come to her cheeks.

Picking a path between the wheels of cheese, the old man made his way toward her. He was small, smaller than Tessa herself, but his body had the dense look of something that had been compressed by weights. Briefly she glanced upward. Massive hands of rock dipped from the roof of the cave like stone chandeliers. Tessa imagined she could feel their weight pressing against her ribs. Shaking her head quickly, she drove away the sensation.

"Please, drink this." The old man stood before her, holding out a cup. "As you say, you are fine, so have no need of my medicine, but I am an old man with a hard head, and once it's taken me an hour to brew something, I'm loath to see it go to waste."

Chastened, Tessa took the cup. It was warm and made of bone. As the old man pulled his hand away, Tessa noticed that his right thumb lay tucked away in the palm of his hand. Mother Emith's voice murmured in her head: *"They severed the tendon on his right thumb. Stopped him from ever taking up a pen again."* Tessa looked from the old man's hand to his face. "Brother Avaccus?" she asked.

"And if I am? What of it?"

Tessa found she couldn't stop shivering. It wasn't the air

in the cave that was cold. It was something inside of her. She took a sip from her cup and then said, "They told me you were dead."

"Who did?"

"Father Issasis."

The old man looked genuinely surprised. "He did?" He shook his head. "That must have cost him dear. To lie like that to a stranger. That's not the sort of man he is."

"He seemed to lie smoothly enough to me," replied Tessa, instantly regretting it. Whatever was in the bone cup had gone straight to her head. She felt it drawing the blood to the surface, pumping away at her thoughts. Putting down the cup, then pushing it out of reach, she said, "Why didn't Father Issasis want me to see you?"

"Yes. That's the question." The old man who Tessa was now almost certain was Brother Avaccus lowered himself to the ground. Arranging himself into a compact form, he folded his hands in front of his chest. "Father Issasis does not like me to see anyone. That is why he has kept me here, in the cheese cave, turning the cheeses from month to month, from season to season, for the past twenty-one years."

Something clicked by Tessa's side. Looking down, she saw a crab scrambling over a rock. Its shell was covered in glistening specks of rock dust. Unnerved, she nudged it the way of the cup. Turning back to Avaccus, she said, "You never answered my question."

Avaccus' light-colored eyes twinkled for the briefest moment. "Which one? I don't believe I've answered any yet."

He was right. He hadn't told her anything so far—just some nonsense about cheese. Tessa wished she could think more clearly. She was so cold, though. As cold as the sea in the dark. Memories of the rising tide and the currents and the darkness pressed against her mind, crowding out the light of the cave. Tessa gasped for air. "What happened to me?" she cried. "Tell me how I got here."

Avaccus looked at her calmly. "I brought you here. I rowed a boat out across the causeway, found your body floating on the surface, dragged you aboard, and brought you home." He smiled. "You very nearly made it on your own, you know. Another hundred paces and you would have been back at the abbey. Remarkable. Quite remarkable."

Tessa didn't feel remarkable. She felt cold and edgy and out of her depth. Forcing herself to think, she said, "You knew I was out there?"

Brother Avaccus made a small, self-deprecating gesture with his damaged right hand. "I had an inkling."

"Do you also have an inkling as to why I'm here?" Tessa's voice was sharp. She felt at a disadvantage.

"I could make a guess," Avaccus said, his tanned and salt-reddened face forming a carefully placid expression. "But it would save us both time if *you* told me instead."

Tessa rubbed her eyes. Despite his soft voice and gentle facade, Brother Avaccus was as sharp as a tack. She took a breath. "I came here because a friend of mine, Emith, told me that you know about the old ways of scribing. I have a job to do, and I'm not sure how to do it, and I need some help. I need to know how to stop Izgard from turning his harras into monsters."

Avaccus greeted this information with a barely perceptible nod, as if it were something of minor interest, like a comment about the weather or a suggestion for a first course at dinner. Tessa felt disappointed. She was considering restating her purpose in stronger terms when he spoke.

"You do know that ring you have there is an ephemera?"

Tessa was losing patience. She shook her head. "An ephemera? I don't understand."

"A relic of an old age, when all the worlds were bound into one, before the Shedding began, before the layers fell away. Before time and space slipped into the breach, creating new worlds from each fragment shed." Avaccus spoke softly, his gaze focusing on some far distant point before coming to rest on the fist Tessa had formed around the ring. "It's very old and very precious, and the fact you have it with you tells me all I need to know."

Tessa felt her head spinning. The rocks in the caves blurred out of focus. They looked like the walls of a deep, red pit. New worlds? Shedding? Uncurling her fist, she held up the ring until it caught the light. She heard herself say, "What did you mean when you said I would surely find it lost in the end?"

"Aah. Lost. That's the thing." Avaccus shifted slightly, making himself more comfortable. Again Tessa was struck by how dense his body seemed. Even though the light in the cave was pale and diffused, he cast a shadow that was dark and well defined. "It is the nature of an ephemera to be lost. It is what they are, what they were forged for, what they strive to do. They pass from hand to hand, from time to time, from world to world. Slipping through cracks in ages, through fissures in time and space, they fall into the keeping of countries and men, only to disappear as quickly as they are found. Grasp it as tightly as you can, but you will never manage to hold it. Watch it day and night, and one morning you will wake, blink, and find it gone."

Tessa's gaze never left the ring as Avaccus spoke. The sparkling gold seemed to wink at her, as sly as an old married man slipping out to visit his mistress.

Avaccus continued, his voice tripled by soft echoes bounding from the walls around the cave. "Ephemeras never stay long in one place. They are ephemeral, temporary: a shooting star in the night sky, a sudden storm that rages and then is gone. They may lie, undiscovered and unused, for centuries. Tucked in the dark spaces between worlds, in the gaps and clefts of time, they bide their time and await their time, and then appear as they are called or needed. Ephemeras can incite causes, enflame conflicts, inspire transformations, and shape lives. There is power to them. They are where light and dark meet, where worlds converge and time becomes less substantial than the slow tick of a failing clock.

"They pass through all worlds; holy grails, magic rings, stone arcs, and sacred jewels. People believe they find them, but in reality it is they themselves who are found. Ephemeras are not a gift; they are not a bauble to be displayed or a treasure to be hoarded. They are a burden. A taskmaster. A force unto themselves."

As Avaccus spoke, Tessa felt herself growing warmer. The sea cold lifted from her limbs and chest, leaving her feeling drained yet relieved. She felt as if she had been waiting outside in the cold overnight and was finally being allowed in. Her aches and pains dimmed and her stomach rested flat. She didn't stop shivering, though. Weighing the ring in her hand, she said, "Are you saying this ring has some purpose?"

Avaccus tilted his head up toward the roof of the cave. He held it there a moment before finally bringing it down in a nod. "Oh, yes. Ephemeras always have a purpose. Some great, some not so great. Some have purposes that cannot be fathomed in a single lifetime. They cause something seemingly insignificant—the death of an infant, the birth of an idea, the loss of a time-honored custom—and only lifetimes, sometimes even centuries, later can the true importance of those events be judged.

"Ephemeras are catalysts for change. They slip into a world, slip out of a world, never leaving it the same." Avaccus sighed, his entire body collapsing inward. "And you, my dear girl, are in possession of one of them."

Tessa met Avaccus' gaze. The ring was heavy in her hand, and she wished for a moment that she could nudge it away like the crab and the cup. Even as she felt the urge, another part of her dismissed it. The ring was hers. Avaccus watched Tessa, his face devoid of emotion, like a scholar examining text. She didn't doubt what he said. All along, from the very first day in the forest, she had known the ring was special. "Is there magic in it?" she asked.

"Yes and no." Avaccus smiled. His teeth were the exact same color as the wheels of cheese he turned. "Ephemeras work through people. Whoever holds one is granted a portion of its power, or allowed a glimpse at its vision, but I do not believe it makes a magician out of anyone."

Tessa found herself nodding. "This has fallen into my hands because of Izgard's harras. I think I was brought here to oppose them."

"You do, eh?" Avaccus rubbed his smoothly shaven chin. His arms were bare, and despite his age, his flesh was solid. Not plump, but weighty with ligaments and bone.

Tessa waited, expecting him to speak and confirm her belief. He remained silent, breathing evenly, his face absent of expression. The light dimmed. Colors in the cave grew deeper, redder. Shadows cast were the color of blood. From somewhere to Tessa's side, the crab could be heard, clicking its way around the bone cup. The steady drip, drip of water droplets into some unseen pool suddenly stopped. The smell of curing cheeses mixed with the salty, bitter odor of old places once frequented by the sea. Although she was lying against the back wall of the cave, Tessa felt somehow she had been pushed to the center. That the ring she held made any place she chose to walk, crawl, or lie dead center of wherever she was.

The silence continued.

Tessa thought. She considered all she knew about Deveric, the harras, and Izgard of Garizon. She cast her mind back, trying to find any small thing she may have missed. It had felt so right when she'd scribed against the harras. Glancing down at the ring, she followed its golden folds with her eye, tracing the inner weaves as they expanded outward into the light. Perhaps the harras were only one small part of the whole. Perhaps it was Izgard himself she was meant to oppose. Abruptly her thoughts turned to Ravis and Camron. Both of them were committed to bringing about the downfall of the Garizon king. What if she were part of that same commitment? All three of them had been pulled together the day she'd put on the ring.

"Maybe it's more than just the harras," she said. "Maybe it's the man who commands them."

Avaccus flicked a finger. "Yes. No. Perhaps."

Again Tessa felt as if she were boring the old man with trivial detail. "If you know the answer, why don't you tell me?" she demanded. "I came all this way to see you. I've been attacked, chased, and nearly drowned. I've left people I cared about to be here, and now all you can do is sit there looking smug and keeping secrets. Worlds shedding, hidden causes, ephemeras: if you know so much, *tell me*." Somewhere during her outcry, Tessa's voice lost its sting. She felt more tired than she could ever remember feeling. Against her will, her mind conjured up the last image she had of Ravis, of him racing away from her in the inn. All the cuts and gashes on her body suddenly ached so sharply, they brought tears to her eyes.

When she spoke again, her voice was quiet, normal except for an undertone of rawness as she worked to control her emotions. "Please. I was brought here by this ring. I came from a different place—perhaps one of your worlds that split away during the Shedding. I don't know. All I do know is I was brought here for something. Deveric called me here. The ring brought me here. I have to find out why. Until today I thought I had to destroy the harras and the scribe who summoned them. Now you look at me and although you don't say it, I can tell you think I'm wrong. If I'm missing some piece in the pattern, I need to know."

Avaccus sat very still while she spoke. When the last echo of her voice died away, he blinked slowly, as if his eyelids were a burden to be lifted. He spoke, but not before he had taken a deep breath to fill himself. "I am eighty-two years old, young lady. Eighty-two. And for seventy of those years I have made the Anointed Isle my home. I first came here to learn my letters, as many young boys my age did. The holy fathers have long supplemented abbey stipends by teaching young boys to read and write. It was not my intent to become a scribe, not in those days. No. I do believe I wanted to be an astronomer, mapping the night skies from behind a thick round of glass."

Avaccus smiled at Tessa with genuine warmth. "It wasn't to be. Once the holy fathers found I had talent with pen and parchment they were loath to let me go. I could be a great scribe, they said. An illuminator the likes of Fascarius, Mavelloc, and Ilfaylen. I should stay, learn, be initiated into the brotherhood." The smile on Avaccus' face faded. "We are a possessive lot here on the island, and when we consider a man our own we like to keep him close."

Tessa glanced at Avaccus' thumb, tucked away, useless, against his palm. When she looked up, she saw Avaccus had followed her gaze. He made no effort to conceal his hand.

"The holy fathers are filled with love and fear," he said. "We all are, but they most of all. If you were to enter the abbey now, you would likely find Father Issasis lying prostrate on the floor of the great chapel, seeking forgiveness for the lie he spoke to you. In many ways he is a good man. In all matters save this he is an honest one."

"He came to meet me at the gate," Tessa murmured. "He showed me to a cell, and after I fell asleep I was attacked." The memory of that creature in the darkness came so strongly, it made her flinch. The smell, the sound, the sheer mass of the creature. It was like utter darkness condensed.

Avaccus let his damaged hand drop to the ground. "Father Issasis sent no creature to kill you. That is not the holy fathers' way. The threat came from another place."

"Yet Father Issasis allowed it to happen?" Tessa was only guessing, yet something in Avaccus' face told her she might be right. For a moment he looked immeasurably sad.

"I hope not. By all that this isle once stood for, I hope not."

"Is there a connection between the ring and the isle?" Tessa hadn't known what she was going to say until she said it. Avaccus' light brown eyes seemed to pull the words from her mouth.

His nod was slight but unmistakable. "Patterns can be used to draw knowledge. I learned that very early on. All one needs is the right designs painted in the proper sequences and proportions, and one can revisit the past. Not as it was, but what remnants it leaves behind. Everything sheds skin. Things are left for us to find. If we are lucky, we stumble across them: study, classify, come to our own conclusions. That's what illuminations enabled me to do: journey beyond these walls in search of truth."

Avaccus' voice began to falter. Tessa saw something shining behind his eyes. Something bright and sad and still young. "It was my talent and my downfall. Emith's too. Though he was young and only did my bidding, and knew very little of the nature of what I did, the holy fathers punished him the all same. They separated us, exiling him because he was not truly one of their own, not quite, not yet. Another year and perhaps he may have been. But they thought it best to let him go. And me—" He made a small gesture with his hand.

"They cut your tendon to stop you from scribing."

"They did. That and more." Avaccus arched his gaze across the cave. All the rocks were blood red now. "They have old secrets to protect, you see. Secrets five hundred years old."

Tessa pulled the hem of her dress down over her shins, disturbed by the color of her skin in the light. She didn't speak. In the distance she could hear the sea pushing against the shore. It sounded like someone breathing.

"That ring you have is a replica of the Barbed Coil," Avaccus said, his voice matching the cadence of the sea. "I believe they are bound together through time and space and forging."

"The Barbed Coil is an ephemera too?"

Avaccus smiled very softly. "Yes, perhaps the greatest one of all. It slips into a world with only one purpose beating deep within its heart: *to win wars*."

Tessa felt something pass along her body. The skin on her scalp puckered, causing her hair to bristle at the roots. She was suddenly aware of her body as an assemblage of parts. Her limbs seemed heavy like clubs, her hands no more than a useless coterie of bones. Her middle was like a soft, malleable waterskin. She was inconsequential, vulnerable. How could she have come so far and fought so hard with her body as her only protection? Surely it was madness.

Eyes painfully dry, Tessa blinked many times in quick succession. She tried to swallow and found she couldn't. So she spoke instead. "The Barbed Coil has been Garizon's crown for five hundred years. If it is an ephemera as you say, then surely it shouldn't be here? It should have disappeared centuries ago."

"Now that, my dear girl," Avaccus said, pronouncing every word precisely, "is the problem."

TWENTY-SEVEN

moke rose from the illumination as acid burned
the vellum. Black ink settled against black-
washed parchment, gliding through the fibers
like a panther hunting in the dark. Hair shed from
the paintbrush, a tear of drool gained mass beneath Ederius'
chin. Sunlight streamed through moth holes in the tent canvas, spraying pinpoints of light across the desk.

Ederius was aware of none of this. The only smoke he
saw came from the torching of the Rhaize camp, as the harras set light to a hillside Izgard had marked one week ago as
dry. "Those grasses will go up in flames the minute a torch is
taken to them," he had said. "Let's make sure Sandor finds it
a tempting place to camp."

It had taken Garizon troops nearly two days to roll rocks
and other impediments from the slope. Another day had been
spent building a dam five leagues downstream of a local waterway. The resulting overflow had been diverted northward,
turning a tiny, summer-dry creek into a water supply big
enough for a camp. Fresh water, a cleared hillside, and a pros-
pect that allowed a view of the land directly adjacent to Garizon's camp had been more than enough fuel to sway Sandor's
choice. Izgard hadn't even raised an eyebrow when the
Rhaize forces began pounding stakes into the hillside yesterday at noon. It was what he had planned on all along. That
and southwesterly winds to drive flames through the camp
and thick tunnels of black smoke onto the battlefield beyond.

Ederius saw, smelled, and tasted the smoke now. He
watched the havoc it created, and even as he noted its effect on
the Rhaize vanguard, he weaved the harras through it like
pieces on a board. Black moving through black: they knew
what all knew, saw what all saw, took orders as a single

corps. Their terrible half-human braying keened away in Ederius' ears. Any other time it would have chilled him. Here and now, though, he found his lips opening and closing involuntarily, mimicking their calls. He was one of them. All of them. Their leader, their creator, the thread that bound them to the Coil.

Ederius felt needs so deep and so base, they could only be expressed in images, not words. And although there was still some part of him that was afraid and appalled at the horrors his mind's eye showed him, his hands never shook against the parchment and he never lost sight of the design.

Black moving through black. The harras swept down the burning slope, longknives clawing downward, driving the confused and terrified Rhaize forces before them. Smoke stung eyes and choked lungs. Flames licked heels. The noise was deafening, maddening. It inhibited rational thought.

Herded as surely as cattle, the enemy fled down into the valley. Most wore full armor. All had blades. If they had stopped and thought and held council, they would have turned on the harras and fought—they outnumbered them ten to one. Yet there was no council. Or if there was, it went unheeded amid the roar of the fire and the howling of the harras. Panic overtook the camp, just as Izgard had said it would. Just as he had planned.

Seeing the Rhaize forces running at full charge into the valley, Ederius risked switching his attention back to his tent. His vision blurred for a moment and then came sharply into focus. The Barbed Coil lay before him on the desk, more vivid and more golden than he remembered. No longer gleaming like polished metal, it *shone*. Just one look was enough. Izgard had given him orders. The Barbed Coil offered him the means to carry them out. Quickly, eagerly, Ederius returned to his design.

Ink scorched the vellum as the harras moved to form a half circle behind the enemy: chasing, goading, and ultimately propelling them to a valley partitioned for death. Dark figures they were, darting through showers of soft, burned flecks and a barreling storm of smoke. Black moving through black.

"It was Hierac who found the Barbed Coil," Avaccus said. "Legend goes that the young king was battling the Venns in the Upper Vjorhad at the time. Seventeen he was. Not a clever fighter, so they say, but a tenacious one. He was leading a raid on a Vennish village in retaliation for some incident involving the slaughter of Garizon merchants the previous summer. It was a mountain town, situated within the folds of the great northern glaciers. The Venns knew their territory and had long since perfected the strategy of driving invaders onto the glacier. They knew the glacier, you see, knew where it was weak and likely to collapse. Knew just by looking at the texture of the packed snow which areas were unsafe to tread."

Avaccus paused in his telling to take a sip from his cup. It was almost dark in the cave now, and Tessa could no longer see the old monk's face clearly. She could not guess what time of day it was. Perhaps the sun had simply stopped shining through the cave entrance. Perhaps the sky was overcast. Perhaps it was night.

Avaccus had prepared them a light meal of butter-soft cheese, pale bread, and water. Tessa had no appetite, but she forced herself to eat a little of the bread. It was as dry and tasteless as rice paper, and it caught in the back of her throat. From the shadows behind a rock, Avaccus had brought forth a fat white candle and then spent many minutes trying to light it with a flint. Watching him struggling to strike the flint at the correct angle to produce a spark, Tessa guessed that Avaccus lit the candle only for her benefit. That either from frugality or choice, he usually spent the long hours of darkness in the dark.

The candle burned now, on the floor of the cave, sending a low tissue of light across the chamber. With candlelight grazing their curves, the wheels of cheese took on the look of craters on some remote alien landscape. Looking down at them from her position against the wall, Tessa felt as if she were floating in the darkness above another world. A loose pile of dried seaweed smoked away in the far corner behind Avaccus' back, giving off the sweetly decaying aroma of the seashore at low tide. Avaccus said the smell drove away bats.

Tessa couldn't decide which she thought was worse: the smoking seaweed or the cheese.

Strangely, she was no longer tired. Sore and hurting all over, shivering now and then as drafts took her, but wholly alert. She didn't want to miss anything Avaccus said.

Putting down his cup, Avaccus took a sharp breath, shifted his body from side to side as if it were some troublesome weight he had to bear, and then continued with his story.

"The Venns sent the entire Garizon raiding party over the edge of the glacier, driving them back until they had nowhere else to go. The shelf of packed snow they were forced onto collapsed beneath their feet, calving away from the dam the moment it bore their weight. All but Hierac died, their falling bodies crushed by walls of ice, their spines snapped by rocks impacted in the frozen snow.

"Hierac fell with all the rest. How far, I do not know. His body was flung outward as well as down, and by some miracle he landed on the rain-softened remains of the previous calving. His right leg was broken in two places, his rib cage crushed. He was unconscious for one night and a day. When he finally opened his eyes he saw it, shining gold in a stream of white glacial milk, embedded in the meal of gravel, clay, and sand. The Barbed Coil. It had been uncovered by the very calving that had sent Hierac's men to their deaths."

Hearing Avaccus speak, Tessa shivered so deeply she felt a trembling motion in her heart.

"It is always the way with ephemeras. They never enter a world quietly with a kiss; they claw their way through with a vengeance: diverting lives and history and nature itself. They like to make an entrance."

Tessa nodded. She knew. A long, tortured ride in the car, a head full of noises, and three hundred lives laid bare, courtesy of two robbers who likely thought it bad luck when the main safe wouldn't open, forcing them to raid the vault instead. How long could the thread be traced back? How long had the ring been waiting for her? Perhaps it had not waited one instant. Perhaps it had held off until the last possible moment before slipping between the envelope's folds.

Avaccus made a soft noise, drawing Tessa's attention

back. "Hierac took the Coil back with him to Garizon. How he managed the journey is a story in itself, but I do not see how you would benefit from the telling. Things were never the same for him again. Up until that day on the glacier, he had been a hard-fighting, hardheaded soldier duke, with modest ambitions and a limited vision incorporating nothing more sophisticated than border raids and blood feuds. Garizon was a small dukedom with small ideas and even smaller plans. Hierac changed all that.

"Within a month of crowning himself with the Barbed Coil, he won his first war. Fighting against Balgedis in the north, he managed to claim the pasturelands of the Berrans. From there he never looked back. Victory fired and inspired the Garizon army; appetites grew, ambitions expanded, possibilities opened up before them like fields of summer wheat.

"Most of the western continent was under Istanian control at the time. The Istanian infidels had conquered Rhaize, Medran, Drokho, west Balgedis, and south Maribane. They controlled the Bay of Plenty, the Gulf, the Mettle Sea, and were masters of the middle east. Terhas, the desert state where they had originally risen from, was theirs, along with Harassi, Ranypt, and Arpur. The world had never seen an empire like it. The infidels placed no value on life. They entered a country and slaughtered its men and women until they had robbed it of its heart. Goods were what counted: grain, silks, gold, wool, precious stones, and human flesh. They herded hundreds of thousands of Drokho and Medrani children onto slave boats and sent them to the east. Adults were too old, they said, too set in their western ways to be trained for service at infidel courts.

"All men of fighting age who were not slaughtered were maimed—the infidels wanted no army massing in the shadow of their turned backs. They favored pouring scalding oil into ear canals, ruining a man's hearing and sense of balance, and rendering him unfit to fight. The operation is painful in the extreme, and if not carefully done, it can result in brain damage, madness, and death. The Istanian infidels cared little either way. They had a saying: *The blood of a westerner washes quickly from the blade.*

"The same spring that Hierac found the Coil, the Istanians decided to invade Garizon. Some say the Istanians had become lax, that they had grown accustomed to meeting little or no resistance, and that they set out for Garizon ill prepared."

Avaccus pushed a hard noise from his throat. "They are wrong. The Istanian forces moved across the Veize in late spring. They had taken note of Hierac's victory over Balgedis in the north. They came expecting resistance.

"And they got it. The likes of which they hadn't seen in over a century. Hierac had been reborn in the brilliance of the Barbed Coil. It showed him visions of war, brought forth skills he never knew he possessed, endowed him with the confidence necessary for command. It made a war king of him.

"Not only did Hierac succeed in halting the Istanian invasion, he drove them back. Back into Rhaize and Balgedis, back across the Veize. Within three months Hierac claimed Balgedis for himself. One year later to the day he took Rhaize. There was no stopping him. His armies went from strength to strength. His strategies were bold, ingenious. The Istanians matched his brute force, but they could not compete with his sheer relentlessness. No one could stand in his way. Always he pushed forward, claiming one field, one village, at a time. Hierac changed the way the world fought. He didn't plan single battles or campaigns, thinking two, perhaps three moves ahead. He planned an entire war."

"He broke up the empire?" Tessa spoke more to hear the sound of her own voice than to ask a question for which she already knew the answer. The further Avaccus went with his tale, the less substantial she felt. Things grew larger with every word he said. Five hundred years. Empires. Thousands of deaths and countless generations. It didn't bear thinking about. The fact that she was here and caught up in it seemed some terrible mistake.

"It took Hierac only a decade to achieve what no other army had managed in over a century." Avaccus was as composed as a historian reciting dates. "The infidels were driven from the west; from Rhaize, Medran, Maribane, Drokho, and even the greater part of the Istanian peninsula. Garizon forces hounded them south and then east, and ultimately annihilated them. At the last great battle, on the red sandbanks of the river Medi, Hierac's army massacred one hundred thousand men. The Barbed Coil had a hand in every death."

Tessa closed her eyes. The silence following Avaccus' words seemed to press against her eyelids. She didn't want to open them again. Opening them would mean facing things she didn't want to face. Seconds passed and then, with eyes still closed, she let out a small, defeated sigh and said, "That was the reason the ephemera entered the world, wasn't it? To dismantle the Istanian empire."

Even though her eyes were closed, Tessa knew when Avaccus nodded. "I believe you are right."

"And somehow the ephemera outstayed its welcome? It failed to slip away?"

"Yes. Yes." A subtle change could be detected in Avaccus' voice. "Though *failed* is hardly the right word." He met Tessa's gaze, and in that instant she immediately knew the great weight of responsibility that came with the knowledge he had gained. Even as he spoke again, she felt a portion of that weight transferring to herself. It was shared now.

"The Barbed Coil was prevented from leaving this world," Avaccus said. "Hierac commissioned its binding."

Tessa pulled her knees to her chest and rested her head against them. Her body felt as heavy and brittle as slate. All around her the walls of the cave soaked up the light from the candle, converting its tiny golden flame into a dozen shades of red. It was like sitting in the middle of a glowing hearth. Only there was no warmth.

"It's why I'm here today, isn't it?" she said, looking Avaccus straight in the eye. "Not to rid the world of the harras or their leader, but to send the Barbed Coil away?"

Avaccus' hand flitted upward and then stopped abruptly, as if he meant to touch her yet quickly realized she was beyond his reach. "Yes," he said, dropping his hand to his side. "I believe that is why you were brought here. The ring and the crown are paired ephemeras. The ring is a sister piece to the Barbed Coil, and is working through you to free it."

"Tell me what I must do."

Avaccus' eyes widened, and Tessa realized she had spoken the words as a command. He looked at her a long moment and then nodded as if she had spoken something unpleasant but ultimately true. "To understand what you have to do, you must first know how and why the Coil was bound."

Something in Avaccus' voice made Tessa's heart race. She put a hand on her chest, to calm herself. As she pressed her palm against her ribs, she noticed Avaccus was looking past her toward the entrance to the cave. Somewhere up there lay the abbey.

Avaccus began speaking, his voice low enough to whisper secrets, his gaze flickering from time to time back toward the entrance. "After Hierac crushed the infidels at the river Medi, he traveled back to the west to consolidate his territories. He went on a massive three-year tour of all the lands, towns, and dukedoms he had conquered. He wanted people to know him as a king. He wanted them to see him on his mighty warhorse with his broadsword in his hand and the Barbed Coil upon his head and realize it would be futile to oppose him. Specially trained troops went into towns after Hierac had departed, slaughtering rebels, torching their homes and meeting places, seizing property, gold—anything of value—in the name of the king. Those who did not give willingly were forced to watch as their homes were drenched with naphtha and then burned.

"It is how the harras got their name: Hierac's arsonists, his bringers of horror. His harras."

Tessa felt a hand of ice slide down her spine. Bundling herself up into the smallest ball she could manage, she pressed her knees fast against her chest.

"During this time, Hierac made it his business to seek out scholars in every town he visited, as he was anxious to discover more about his crown. He was fiercely possessive of it, never allowing it to be handled by another or let out of his sight. He knew, you see. He knew it was the reason he won the wars he did. And he wanted to find out why."

"He came here, didn't he?" Tessa surprised herself by interrupting. Fragments of old conversations weaved through her mind, revealing connections as she spoke. There was a pattern here. She could sense it. "Hierac came to the Anointed Isle and visited with the monks. They knew what the Barbed Coil was, didn't they? They helped him bind it to the earth in return for . . ." As Tessa let the thought dangle unsaid, Avaccus supplied the word for it:

"Immunity." His entire body shifted downward as he spoke, as if someone were high above him, piling weights on his shoulders. He regarded Tessa a moment, his light eyes full of pain, and then said, "Yes, it is so. Hierac came here, lured by talk of holy relics, priceless manuscripts, and the reputation of the Anointed Isle for learning. He came to plunder, either gold or knowledge—whatever treasure he found first. The holy fathers came out onto the rocks to meet him. They were full of fear. They had heard all the stories of Hierac and his harras. They believed he would burn the abbey to the ground, rob their ancient treasures, and take lives.

"Instead he brought them the Coil. *Look at it,* he commanded. *Tell me of its nature and its history. Give me reason to spare your lives.*

"And they did. A full Quire of scribes was called to the abbey scriptorium and immediately began work on a pattern to reveal knowledge of the Coil. Twelve men there were. Twelve men working for twelve hours through the night, each contributing a pattern to the whole. It wasn't like today, where gathering knowledge through the painting of illuminations is considered a trespass against God and his domains. The holy fathers considered it a blessing, bestowed upon their scribes for their use alone."

Avaccus shook his head. "I do not know the right and wrong of it. I, of all people, am not fit to judge." His head sank against his chest and his breaths were labored for a while. After a few moments of working to control something inside of himself, he continued, his voice firm. "At dawn the Quire had their answers. They called the holy fathers to them and spoke what their patterns had revealed. They knew it all. They knew the Barbed Coil was an ephemera, one of many that slipped from world to world, each with its own intent. Winning wars was the Barbed Coil's purpose, and now that it had won one of such import it would surely slip away.

"The holy fathers made a decision. I believe they thought that even without the Coil, Hierac would still be a demon king, that they and the rest of the world would continue to suffer from whatever poison had been administered through its barbs." Avaccus shrugged heavily. "Whatever their reasons, the holy fathers went to Hierac within the hour and passed along the findings of the Quire. Hierac was immediately overcome with a deep fear that the Coil would be lost to him. He turned to the holy fathers and demanded they find a way to harness it to the earth, to prevent it from leaving his side. He threatened to burn the abbey to the ground and kill the monks one by one.

"The holy fathers turned him down. They could not in all conscience agree to it.

"Frustrated by their reluctance even in the face of his threats, Hierac then promised them the ultimate gift. *Bind the Coil for me*, he said, *and as long as Garizon is a country or even a memory of a country, it will protect the Anointed Isle from all invaders. Your monastery will never be torn asunder while the Barbed Coil remains in this world. You will be free of all Garizon taxes and levies, and my troops shall withdraw, never to return, unless it is for your protection and at your request. This I do hereby swear by all the blood the Barbed Coil has shed.*

"So that is what the holy fathers did. Not there and then. Not right away. But a promise was struck and a contract was drawn, and Hierac was as good as his word. Withdrawing his men that very morning, he issued a warning to all who gathered at the beachhead to meet him that from henceforth no one was to set foot upon the Anointed Isle unless they came in peace. Garizon would protect the abbey as its own.

"Meanwhile the monks set their most gifted scribe to work upon the problem of binding the Coil. Brother Ilfaylen spent six months designing the illumination that would hold the ephemera in place. Inventing new forms and new metaphors as he worked, Ilfaylen studied first on the Anointed Isle and then in Garizon itself. For the last month of the six he did nothing but trace designs directly from the Coil. It is inlaid with them, you see. Every strand of gold upon the crown is etched with patterns and devices. I have never laid eyes upon them myself, but I believe there is much power to be drawn from such markings."

Hearing Avaccus' words, Tessa couldn't resist glancing down at the ring. The gold strands formed smooth threads, broken only by the barbs. Nothing was etched into the metal.

Avaccus continued speaking. "Finally Ilfaylen judged himself ready to begin the illumination, and so presented himself to Hierac. By this time Hierac was a man possessed. He forced himself to stay awake for days at a time, fearing he might lose the Coil if he slept. When he did sleep, it was with the crown laid across his chest and a servant standing close to warn him of the slightest change. The moment Ilfaylen came to him, he bade the man begin, and for the next five days and five nights, the scribe worked on a pattern that was as good as a cage.

"Lashing the Coil with his brush, weighing it down with his pigments, Ilfaylen designed an illumination that defied all the magic of the Shedding. The Barbed Coil, the mighty ephemera that flitted from world to world like a harlot from lover to lover, became nothing more than an insect under glass. Ilfaylen bridled and contained it. He placed his hand upon it and pressed its nose to the dirt.

"During those five days it is said the moon failed to show in clear night skies, that dams dropped their foals before their time, that tides pulled high onto beaches and water levels dropped low in wells. Infants weak from jaundice and old folk weak from dropsy died in unheard-of numbers, and all cities on the continent reported a record number of flies.

"Ilfaylen did what he had been chosen for: he fixed his shackles to the Barbed Coil and chained it to the earth. When he had finished the ephemera became little more than a harnessed ox, destined to plow the same furrow on the same field, over and over again."

Seconds passed. The silence following Avaccus' words had an expectant quality to it, like the moment immediately following the end of a play, when the last line has been uttered and the actors hold their poses, waiting for the audience to respond.

Unable to resist the pressure, Tessa finally said, "So it's remained here ever since." Suddenly tired of sitting, she made an effort to scramble to her feet. Pain pulsed along her right thigh. The puncture wound on her shin pulled apart, and blood trickled down to her ankle. Frustration at her weakness made her fight her buckling knees and pull herself up in spite of the dizziness washing over her. She had to think. A wound she couldn't see on the back of her shoulder prickled as the rough fabric of her tunic rubbed against the scabbed flesh. Leaning against the cave wall for support, she said, "What happened to the pattern Ilfaylen drew?"

Avaccus made a sound that might have been a sob or a laugh. "My, my, young lady. You certainly know how to get to the point." He scratched his finely shorn hair. "It was sealed in a lead box and then buried in an undisclosed location in Veizach. All three men who worked on the grave were slaughtered before they had chance to clean the dirt from their fingernails."

Avaccus' use of the word *grave* made Tessa shiver. "Were there any copies made?"

"Copies?" Avaccus shook not just his head, but his entire body. "No. Right from the beginning Hierac forbade it. Whenever Ilfaylen left the scriptorium he was watched. Every night before he retired, he was searched from head to foot, his scribing materials were confiscated, his sleeping quarters inspected, and the parchment itself was held up to the light and checked for pinholes."

"Which would have been a sign Ilfaylen was keeping a copy?"

"Yes. But true to Hierac's orders, the manuscript was not pricked. No copy was ever made."

"What about Ilfaylen's sketches, his blueprints?"

"It was all done on wax tablets. Hierac insisted that nothing ever be put to parchment. After the illumination was completed Hierac himself stood over Ilfaylen's shoulder and watched as the scribe melted the top layer of wax from over two dozen tablets."

Tessa nodded. She thought for a moment and then said, "Two dozen wax tablets would have been a heavy burden to carry on a long journey. Did Ilfaylen have an assistant?"

"Yes. That is why we know so much about the scribing. His assistant kept a journal of his master's journey to and from Garizon: the places he stayed along the way, the food he ate, other matters such as that."

"And did he include any details about the illumination?"

"Little more than I have told you. He was bound by the same restraints as his master. He could write nothing about the contents of the illumination."

Tessa felt her legs giving way beneath her. She couldn't recall why it had been so important for her to stand and so let her body flop to the floor. She landed badly, twisting an ankle that was already weak. Thirst gnawed away in her throat, but she was reluctant to ask Avaccus for anything to drink. She wanted no more potions administered in bone cups. "Does the account of Ilfaylen's journey still exist?"

All the while Tessa struggled to stand and then keep standing, Avaccus maintained his cross-legged sitting position. Watching his composed stance, she got the feeling he was accustomed to sitting in one place for long periods of time. "Sadly the journey book no longer exists," he said. "Twenty years ago there was a fire in the abbey's west tower and many books and scrolls were lost."

So there was nothing to go on. No copy of the pattern. No record of its making. Tessa let out a long breath. If a pattern had bound the Coil, then it would take another to free it. One that incorporated all the elements found in the original design, then turned against them like a traitor in the ink.

"What became of Ilfaylen after he returned to the isle?"

Avaccus clicked his tongue against the roof of his mouth. "Yes. That's the thing. The man was never the same again. He took ill during the journey overland from Veizach, and it was several days before he had the strength to make the sea crossing from Bay'Zell to Kilgrim. By the time he finally arrived back at the Anointed Isle he was a different man. I think painting the pattern wasted him more than any illness. Whatever the cause, he had lost something from inside himself. He never painted another pattern again. For many years he lived the retired life of a scholar, writing, learning, rebuilding his strength.

"Eleven years later, when the old abbot died, it was Ilfaylen who came forward to fill his place. The holy fathers had thought Ilfaylen would be quiet, malleable, a defender of the old ways. Yet those eleven years of silence had distilled something in his soul. The day he was made abbot he changed everything. He broke up the Quires, forbade all painting of the old patterns, and had every manuscript containing details of the old designs thrown into the sea. He forced the abbey back into mainstream beliefs and spent the rest of his life working for peace."

"He never tried to undo his binding?"

"No. What was done was done. He had sworn terrible oaths that he would never revisit his work upon the Coil. And he didn't. He lived a long life and changed many things, but that was the one thing he left untouched."

"And the Barbed Coil?" Tessa felt herself growing sleepy. The sea coldness was slowly reclaiming her aching limbs. "That has stayed in Garizon ever since?"

"Yes." Avaccus stood. Weaving a path through the wheels of cheese, he made his way toward the candle. "The Barbed Coil has been the power behind the Garizon throne for five hundred years. Always, the king who wears it seeks to invade and destroy: claiming land, victories, lives. Their ambitions are never their own. People make the mistake of thinking that it is Garizon itself or its kings that have this driving need for conquest. They are wrong. It is the crown that directs every battle, pushes every blade, nestles at the heart of all ambitions. Even bound as it is, it cannot forsake its nature. War is, and always shall be, its purpose."

Very cold now, Tessa settled herself down amid the rocks. When she spoke, her voice dragged with exhaustion. All she wanted to do was sleep. Perhaps when she woke in the morning all this would turn out to be a bad dream.

"What if the Coil continues to stay in this world?"

Avaccus knelt in front of the candle, blocking most of its light. "I think the entire continent will be destroyed. The Barbed Coil is a mad dog chewing on its leash. It has been dormant, its powers uncalled upon, for the last fifty years. Now Izgard is the first king in half a century to wear it. It has lost time and lost battles to make up for. Its sphere of influence is growing. Its power is growing." Leaning forward, he snuffed out the light. "And ten days from now it will have been upon this earth for five hundred years."

The silence following Avaccus' words was broken by the sound of a bell tolling in the distance. The long, muffled notes set the air in the cave resonating. Tessa felt as if the darkness were pulsing against her skin. Even though there was no longer any light to see by, she could hear Avaccus returning to his place at the back of the cave. His joints cracked with the dull sound of striking weights. The bell continued tolling. On the fifth toll Avaccus stopped moving and said,

"There is power in the number five. Ancient power custom shaped to be used by ancient things."

The bell rang three more times, marking the beginning of Eighth Toll, and Tessa and the old monk spoke no more.

Camron spat blood. He squinted into the darkness, searching. Something moved. His right thumb released the trigger, and a crossbolt exploded from the plate. It hit nothing. Shooting off into the distance, it skimmed a bank of smoke, or a shadow cast by the moon, or a fleck of ash caught in Camron's eye. There were no targets left. All the harras were dead. It had taken them thirteen hours to die. Still, Camron kept his position on the skirt of the hill and watched. And even as the crossbolt fell wasted to the ground, he drew another from his pack, cocked it, and set his sights. He couldn't believe the harras were finally gone.

Fingers encrusted in dried blood, hands that wouldn't stop shaking, eyes so raw they hurt when he blinked, Camron lay belly flat on the ground and waited. Cuts striped his body, bruises blackened it. Exhaustion so deep it caused blackouts ate away at his muscles and his thoughts.

He was alone, that much he knew. The battle had been lost.

The stench was terrible. Blood in all stages from freshly spilled to burned dry could be smelled with every gust of wind. The rotting, animal-lair odor of the harras was everywhere. Camron could taste it mixing with the blood in his mouth. Smoke hung in tired bands, too heavy to be dispersed by the breeze. There was no longer any ash or burned matter in the air. It had settled to the ground before dark, turning all the surrounding hillsides black. The moon was full, but cloud cover robbed most of the light. Strangely, it was as warm as day.

Which, thought Camron, his mind stumbling from subject to subject like a blind man from step to step, was really just as well. As his cloak had been burned off his back hours ago. Or had it been sliced to shreds by a harrar's blade? He found he couldn't remember.

Frowning, he tugged his fingers through his hair. A fistful came free in his hand. Black and brittle as dead insects, he threw the charred locks onto the ground. A second later his finger was back on the trigger. Someone was coming.

They approached from the rear, forcing Camron to swing his body around in the mud. As he spun about, his bow stock jarred against a stone, causing the bolt to jump from the string. Camron hissed a curse. He hated crossbows. He had no memory of how he came to have one in his hands. Surely, at the beginning, he had started out with a shortbow? Shaking his head, he worked to fix the bolt back in place.

A dark silhouette drew nearer. Camron centered him in his sights. His finger felt large and awkward on the trigger. It wouldn't stop trembling.

"Who lays there?" The voice was challenging, aggressive, but the Rhaize accent was unmistakable. "Name yourself or be speared."

Camron didn't move. He knew he should take his finger off the trigger, but a part of him wouldn't let go. Blood pouring from a gash in his gum made it difficult to speak. "Camron of Thorn."

A quick inhalation of breath followed his name. "If you're injured, sir, I'll walk you back." The figure took a step forward. He was young and dark haired. Large eyes looked out from a face that was black with blood and soot. He stooped down toward Camron. "Here, let me help you stand."

Camron flinched.

The young man backed away immediately, raising his spear above his shoulders in a gesture of no harm. "Are there any others here with you?"

Camron shook his head. He wasn't sure of much, but that he knew. "They scattered. Most are dead."

The young man nodded. "I think you should take your finger off that trigger and come with me down to the river."

The river? Camron didn't understand. He felt himself blacking out.

He came to. Something that stung his sliced gum was being poured in his mouth. "Swallow," said the young man. "It'll do you good."

Camron swallowed. The fluid was both hot and cold. It

washed away the taste of blood. As he pulled his shoulders from the mud, he noticed the familiar weight of the crossbow was missing from his elbow. Looking around, he spied it, tossed aside, in a charred hand of grass.

Seeing where Camron's gaze was focused, the young man managed a tired smile and said, "There was a moment I thought you were going to use that on me."

Camron couldn't deny it. He nodded. Slowly the liquor was helping patch together his thoughts. All sorts of pain came with increasing reason. Grimacing, he took another drink from the flask. As he wiped his lips dry, he said, "How many survived?"

The young man looked down. He went to speak, but a muscle quivering in his jaw failed him. He shook his head. Claw marks raked along his throat. Camron handed him the flask, but he refused it. After a moment he said, "Five hundred. Perhaps less."

Camron closed his eyes. He was too tired to feel shocked. "What happened?"

"How can you not know?" The young man's voice was rough. Something shone from behind his eyes. "If it wasn't for you and your archers, everyone, even the Sire, would have died. You shot them. You shot all the harras. You had less than a dozen men in the end—I watched you from my post. The harras kept coming and coming, forcing our troops into the valley. We were cut off. The harras were blocking our retreat. There was smoke everywhere. Flames." The young man shuddered. "Balanon was burned alive."

There was still no shock. Camron felt dead inside. The Sire's survival meant less to him than the loss of his crossbow.

"You opened the retreat." The young man continued speaking. Camron heard something akin to awe in his voice but couldn't understand why. "No one else was fighting the harras. The Sire marshaled the charge into the valley. We weren't ready. There was no time. The harras were on our heels." Shaking off the memory with a violent snap of his neck, the young man cried, "It was like being in hell. The smoke. The harras. The screams."

Camron wanted to say something to comfort the young

man, but he had no words. Memories ripped through his mind: the soft tearing sound as naphtha ignited behind his back. The warm blast of air on his neck. A voice barking orders—*could it be his own?* Screams. Feet scrambling in mud. Arrows and crossbolts pulled desperately from dead men's packs. The snapping maw of a harrar tearing at his cheek.

Unbidden, Camron's hand rose to his face. Dried blood flaked between his fingers.

They had run out of arrows. Weaving in and out of the smoke, the harras had made poor targets. They could take half a dozen hits without going down. Arrows shot from the shortbow needed to be aimed well to cause damage, and except for Segwin the Ney's longbowsmen, none of the troop were skilled archers.

Hampered by smoke, low on armaments, their position had been overrun twice. The close contact fighting was the worst. Camron had seen a score of Balanon's men flee. He didn't blame them. He would have done so himself if he had paused to think. Strangely enough, the harras didn't fight with the same intensity as they had in the Valley of Broken Stones. At some point Camron remembered feeling more like an obstacle than a target. The harras had a specific job to do: to spread terror through the Rhaize troops and drive them down into the valley. Whole companies of longbowsmen waited there, cool, collected, ready.

Camron felt a sick pull in his stomach. Thrusting his hand out toward the young man, he said, "What is your name?"

The young man's fingers closed around his. "Pax."

"Help me stand, Pax. Take me down into the valley."

"But the Sire stands by the river, awaiting news of survivors. All those in the valley are . . ." Pax's voice faltered for an instant, but he worked quickly to control it. "Dead. Izgard's troops are looting their bodies. We can't go down there. It's not safe."

Camron was about to object, tell Pax that the darkness would conceal them, but something in the young man's face stopped him. He wasn't the only one who had fought today. "Take me only as near as we can safely go."

Pax glanced the way of the retreat, thought a moment, then pulled Camron up. He asked no questions, and Camron was grateful of that. Together they hiked down the hillside. Bodies littered the charred grass. Many had fallen to surprisingly light wounds. Slowed by their injuries, they had been caught in the smoke and forced to inhale the hot, reeking air. Some had burned to death, others had bled. Many bore the marks of the harras' claws and fangs on their necks.

In the darkness their features were hard to recognize. Camron found himself unable to walk past a body until he had seen each man's face for himself. Pax helped him turn them. Sometimes skin came away in their hands. Other times the bodies were still warm and blood was still damp upon their clothes. All of them seemed light. It took nothing to lift them. Bows and swords fell from their grips as they were turned. Pax was quiet as he worked. He breathed silently, as if ashamed of the sound of his own body laboring to keep him alive. Camron knew how he felt, but he also knew the dead couldn't hear, and his own breaths came hard and laden.

Camron put names to many faces. Those he was unable to identify troubled him. He spent longer with them, looked closer, committed them to memory.

Each time he and Pax turned a body, a muscle deep in Camron's chest tightened for the briefest instant. He feared finding Broc among the dead. Of all the people who had fought here today, Broc was the least fit to outrun the smoke and the flames. His old wounds were slow to heal. Camron tried to recall the last time he had seen him, the last word or glance they had shared. When no memory came to mind, he felt the muscle in his chest tighten once more. This time it stayed tight. Only when he and Pax finally made it down into the lip of the valley did he realize that the sensation he was experiencing wasn't a physical one at all.

It was anger.

The harras had robbed him yet again. First they'd taken his father, then they'd stolen his childhood home. Now they had lifted his memories. He could not recall when he had last seen Broc. He had no memory of what he had said to any of his men during the battle. Had he given encouragement along with the orders? Had he warned them to watch their backs? Stay clear of the smoke? Withdraw when wounded? Had he stopped to squeeze the hands of the dying? Or helped carry the injured away?

Camron pushed his teeth together until his jaw ached. He remembered the battle and the orders, but nothing else.

"Sir. We should go no farther than this."

Camron looked up at the sound of Pax's voice. The young man's eyes held no fear, just concern. Handling the dead had changed him. "I need to see the valley for myself," Camron said. "I have to see the bodies."

After a long moment Pax nodded. He made a small gesture with his hand, indicating a line of trees to the east. "If we use them as cover, we should be able to move closer without being spotted."

Camron nodded back. He was suddenly very glad he was not alone. "Let's go."

They skirted around the periphery: two figures winding in and out of the trees, the dried blood on their clothes and faces the perfect camouflage for the night. No owls called. No foxes or voles snapped twigs or rustled leaves as they passed. Black ash coated branches and bushes like a layer of negative snow. The moon came and went. Camron's muscles ached as he walked. A molar rattled loose in his jaw. Long past fatigue now, his body had emerged from the other side of exhaustion to be rewarded with a tooth-and-gristle sort of strength. He felt as if he had been stripped, skinned, and then pared to the bone.

The tree cover weaved down into the valley. Camron and Pax slowed their pace. Directly ahead lay the battlefield. At first Camron could make nothing out. The moon had disappeared behind a bank of clouds, and the valley seemed little more than a black pit. Slowly details began to emerge from the darkness: the curve of the land, the broken thread of a stream, the charred skeletons of bushes. The cloud cover thinned minutely, and Camron was able to pick out figures bobbing up and down across the entire stretch of the valley. Izgard's men. They were looting whatever dark forms lay on the valley floor.

A sharp wind cut across the valley. Camron's hair was pushed from his face. The last of the clouds blew clear of the moon, and the valley was suddenly filled with silver light.

Camron heard Pax draw breath. The young guard was a pace or two ahead of him. The butt of his spear trailed in the dirt at his heels. His knuckles cracked as they tightened around the shaft.

The valley was crowded with bodies. Heads, limbs, torsos, hands, necks, and shoulders were packed so closely together, they stopped being parts of individual men and became something else instead. Part of the whole. The Rhaize dead formed a single mass. Black with soot and dried blood, their bodies had set in a jagged clot of arms and legs and fingers and feet. Like debris dumped by a hurricane, they covered the valley floor with a cluster of broken parts. One man. One corpse.

One death.

Camron dropped his chin to his chest. He had never seen anything like it in his life. He had no words to use or images to compare it with. It was death, that was as much as his mind would allow.

Directly ahead of him, Pax fell to his knees. Camron himself was frozen. He felt lost. Ever since the night of his father's death he had been trying to find his way. Seeing the bodies was one more step back.

They could be anyone, he thought. Rhaize, Garizon. Anyone.

"Ten thousand," murmured Pax, breaking a silence so absolute that it seemed like blasphemy to speak into it. "Ten thousand men died here today."

Then, hearing Pax's words, Camron knew why he had come here. He had come to bear witness. Berick of Thorn had seen forty thousand die at Mount Creed, and now his son saw ten thousand dead in a valley north of the river Hook.

Camron looked hard. His eyes, still raw from smoke burns, stung and watered. But he didn't blink. He was seeing what his father had seen fifty years before. Bodies covered in ash, not snow; the breeze warm, not mountain cold on his cheek: yet it made no difference. The truth was the same.

No. Camron didn't know if he said the word or thought it. He didn't know if it was a denial or a promise. He only knew he had been wrong. No matter who had won today, he had lost. Just like his father at Mount Creed, he was in the middle. His countrymen died either way. Slowly, his gaze not faltering from the sight before him, Camron began to shake his head. He understood now why his father had fought with him that last day. He had not wanted his son to repeat his own mistakes.

Taking a step forward, Camron laid a hand on Pax's shoulder. He intention was to comfort the young guard, but as soon as his fingers closed around Pax's shoulder blade, he realized he needed support. It was all he could do to keep standing. Strength drained from his body with every breath. All this time he had been running around, looking for a fight, not once stopping to think about the future or the past.

The Countess Lianne had assumed Berick wanted his son to wage war against Garizon to win back the crown. Yet she was wrong. Berick wanted no wars. *"What value is victory when all a nation's sons are dead?"* They were as good as his last words.

Camron smiled grimly. He had been a fool.

"Come on, Pax," he said, his voice more level than he could ever have hoped. "Let's get away from here. We've seen enough."

Pax stood. Like Camron, he did not take his eyes from the bodies as he moved. When he spoke, it was in a child's frightened whisper. "This is just the beginning, isn't it?"

"No." Camron tried to look away from the dead and found he couldn't. "This is the end."

TWENTY-EIGHT

essa's breaths grew shallow as she slept. The air passages in her nostrils closed, and her mouth sprang open to take in air. Only the air wasn't right. It was thick and bitter, hardly air at all. It blocked her throat like a wad of cloth thrust down a pipe. Her lungs did the only thing they could: they contracted violently to expel the unwanted matter.

The muscles in Tessa's chest convulsed. Her eyes blinked open. Sheer terror hit her like a smash in the jaw. She couldn't breathe. Vaulting upward into the darkness, she called Avaccus' name. Smoke pushed out of her mouth with the cry. Smoke was sucked down into her lungs with her very next breath. The cave was filled with it. *What was happening?*

"Avaccus!" Tessa stumbled in the direction she had last seen the monk. Her lungs burned. Her heart pumped strangely, erratically. It kept missing beats. Smoke scoured its way down her throat. "Avaccus!"

No response. Blind panic seized Tessa. There was no air. As she rushed forward, her shin slammed against a rock. Pain exploded in her leg. Tears stung her eyes. Her bladder weakened but didn't give. Knowing it was foolish to do so, but unable to stop herself, she gasped for another breath. Foul, smoke-laden air choked her lungs. Retching and coughing, she thrust out her hands to feel the way ahead. Darkness had turned the cave into a shark's open maw. Every rock was a tearing tooth. The blackness closed about her like a swallowing throat.

"Help!" she screamed. "Help!" That was another foolish thing: screaming. But even as she scolded herself, she screamed again. Hysteria was close to overwhelming her. Someone had set a fire to kill them.

Dimly Tessa realized she must be taking in some small portion of breathable air with the smoke, or she would already be dead. A bout of coughing racked her body. Seconds passed before she brought the spasms under control. As she spat out a mouthful of thick saliva, a small noise sounded to her right.

"Avaccus." Tessa didn't wait for a reply. She made her way in the direction of the noise. The darkness pushed against her body like black steam. Taking rapid breaths through her nose to filter out what smoke dust she could, Tessa moved across the cave. Pain throbbing in her leg reminded her to step cautiously, but her lungs ached with a raw, near-to-bursting pain, and except for sweeping her arms out before her, she did little to feel the way.

The sound came again. Softer, shorter: it sounded like a last breath.

Tessa's foot stamped into a round of cheese. Rind broken, it released its sour-dairy odor like a flower releasing pollen. Tessa sneezed. Her lungs cleared for an instant and she sucked in more air. As she wiped her face with her wrist, she crushed another round of cheese with her heel. They were everywhere. Frustrated, she rushed forward, sneezing and stamping cheeses with every step. The sneezes helped, clearing smoke debris from her nose and throat in between each breath.

Just as she approached the area where the noise had come from, she stepped on a wheel of cheese that hadn't ripened. It collapsed beneath her foot like a soufflé, spilling out fungus-warmed liquid onto the rock. Tessa slid in the wetness, losing her footing and falling forward onto the cave floor. She landed well, cushioned by the cheese rounds. Her nose touched rock. When she took a breath to calm herself, she found the air was clearer. Her lungs didn't fight it tooth and nail. They drank it up.

Of course, she thought. Smoke rises. The best place to be was on the ground. Why hadn't she thought of that sooner?

Not stopping to consider the answer, Tessa bellied her way through the last of the cheeses, nose pressed firmly against the rock. Her throat still burned, but she could feel muscles deep inside her chest relaxing. Her rib cage released its lock on her lungs.

"Avaccus," Tessa cried. "Make a sound so I can find you."

Nothing. The silence made the darkness seem even darker. As she waited, she raised her hand to her neck to check for the ring. It was there. Before she had fallen asleep, she had tied it in place. Touching it, she remembered all Avaccus had told her about ephemeras. It hardly seemed possible she was holding one.

A thin scraping noise sounded directly in front of her. Letting the ring drop back to her chest, Tessa crawled forward. Smoke was moving in to fill the gap at the bottom of the cave. The air was beginning to get hot.

Shooting a hand forward, she grasped something smooth and heavy. If it hadn't been for the fact that it was warm, she would have assumed it was a wooden club or a metal bar. It was Avaccus' leg. Tessa shook it.

"Avaccus! Wake up! Wake up!" When there was no response, she shook harder. "Please. Wake up." Still no reply. Tessa lowered her nose to the cave floor and took a breath. Avaccus must have been lying down the whole time, in the center section of the cave. Surely he would have been breathing fresh air? So why wasn't he responding?

Cursing the darkness, the smoke, everything, Tessa leaned forward and grabbed Avaccus' shoulders in her hands. Panic and anger at the unfairness of everything that had happened to her since she'd reached this blasted place made her shake Avaccus' body with mad fury. He couldn't die. It would be her fault if he did. The smoke wasn't meant for him.

"Wake up!" she screamed at the top of her voice. "Wake up!"

A muffled choking noise gurgled up from Avaccus' throat. Tessa bobbed her head down to the floor, took a quick breath of air, and then pumped Avaccus' chest with her fist. His body felt as heavy and unresponsive as a lead jacket. What had living in this cave for twenty years done to him? "Come on, Avaccus," she coaxed. "Take a breath."

Avaccus' chest rose beneath Tessa's fist. His entire body trembled, and then the muscles in his chest contracted in a rhythmic wave. He took a breath. Immediately he began to cough and splutter, attempting to raise his head from the floor.

Tessa pushed him back down. She didn't want him repeating her mistake. Standing, even sitting up, was certain death.

Hot clouds of smoke pushed against Tessa's back. No longer curling idly around the cave, the smoke rippled through it with intent. In the distance she heard a faint crackling sound. Fire.

"Avaccus," Tessa said, not sure if the old monk was in any state to hear her words, "we have to get out here. Where is the entrance?"

More coughing, followed by the terrible thin wheezing sound of an old man struggling for breath. "Ahead, through the bed of cheeses."

It took Tessa a moment to realize that Avaccus had spoken. His voice was very weak. Sucking in a mouthful of air from the cave floor, she said, "Come on. Turn on your stomach. You have to keep your face against the rock. It's the only way to breathe." Even as she spoke, she was aware of smoke scratching away in her throat. The air at the bottom was no longer fresh.

"You go." Avaccus's voice was raw. He stopped between each word to cough. "I can't make it to the entrance. I would slow you down."

Without even giving it a thought, Tessa shook her head. The idea of leaving someone in this pitch black smoky hell was intolerable to her. She couldn't just run away. At one time she might have done just that. Running away was her specialty. Her party piece. The one thing she did well. But things were different now. Ederius and his patterns, Avaccus and his ephemeras, Emith and his mother: whatever or whoever had changed her didn't matter. The fact was she had changed.

Grabbing hold of Avaccus' left side, Tessa began rolling the old monk onto his stomach. He protested. She didn't listen. He slapped her hand away. She slapped it back. Strength came from somewhere—lots of it—and with one mighty heave, she flipped him over. He coughed and groaned, and his bones made terrible dull clicking noises, but Tessa ignored everything. She had to. Smoke was hitting them in hot, thick waves. The crackling sound grew steadily louder, and a warm breeze began to whip around the cave. In a few moments, smoke wouldn't be their only danger. Fire was somewhere close. Out of sight for the time being, but there.

Tessa tried to drag Avaccus across the cave floor, but the sheer density of the old monk's body was a problem. She might as well have tried to drag solid rock. The rough, uneven texture of the cave floor didn't help either, as the slightest protuberance could jab against Avaccus' skin, tearing and bruising his flesh.

"Breathe the air right off the floor," she reminded him, hoping the more air he got, the more alert he would become. Avaccus did as he was told. Tessa could hear him taking in air. "Come on," she said, realizing their only chance of escaping was if Avaccus could be made to move by himself. "We've got to start moving. One leg at a time." Her tone started out gently enough, but the same panic that had overrun her earlier began to reassert itself in her voice. The temperature was rising sharply. "Now! Now!"

Pulling at Avaccus' shoulders, his arms, his hands, his robe, Tessa dragged him into motion.

Fresh air was increasingly harder to come by. Tessa breathed in great wads of smoke with every breath. The urge to cough was overpowering. The stench of smoke drowned out the odor of cheese, and as she crawled through the maze of split wheels, she no longer had the urge to sneeze.

"Hurry," she cried, making no attempt to hide the fear in her voice. "Hurry!" Hot air blasted her face. Even though her eyes were closed, the heat penetrated her lids. The inside of her mouth felt as if it had been grated by hot sand.

Avaccus did his best, easing his body over the cave floor as quickly as he could. It wasn't enough. At this rate they would both be suffocated by the heat and smoke before they managed to make it to the entrance. Tessa knew she shouldn't get angry with him, but she couldn't help herself. He had to move faster. He was *going* to be saved.

Sending a hand through the soft, milky soil formed by the squashed cheeses, Tessa searched for Avaccus' arm. "We have to make it out of here," she cried, grabbing his wrist not at all gently. "You've still got things to tell me. I still don't know how to scribe properly. You have to show me what to do."

Avaccus made an odd sound in his throat. Tessa thought he might be laughing. She couldn't tell. "You've been taught by Emith of Bay'Zell, young lady," he said. "You should know all you need to know."

"But Emith is just an assistant. He doesn't know how to draw patterns."

Air brushed against Tessa's face as Avaccus shook his head in the darkness. "Emith knows more about scribing than any other man alive. If he's taught you all the rules of pigments and forms, then you have all the information you need to know. Paint the problem, then solve it. Emith—" Avaccus' words came to a halt as a blistering sheet of smoke hit them both. Hot flecks of burned matter flew into Tessa's face.

Tessa slipped her fingers from Avaccus' wrist and grasped hold of his hand. She told herself she wasn't scared, yet when the old monk's hand closed around hers, she was glad to her very core. Together they moved forward through the smoke.

With great effort, Avaccus began clearing his throat. It took several minutes of coughing and swallowing before he could speak. Tessa told him to concentrate on moving forward, not speaking, but he was set on saying what he had to.

"Emith is a modest man; you must not forget that. If it wasn't for his modesty, he would have become a brilliant scribe. He had the eye and the feel for it. He just never had the confidence."

Avaccus succumbed to a terrible bout of coughing. Squeezing his hand as his entire body was racked with convulsions, Tessa willed herself to be strong.

Orange light now marked the cave entrance. It flickered and hissed and grew brighter by the minute. The air was so hot, Tessa could no longer open her eyes. Beneath her body the wheels of cheese softened into a warm, grainy mush.

Avaccus forced out words as he coughed. Tessa could only guess what effort it cost him. "You must trust your own abilities, Tessa. Trust yourself and trust Emith. An ephemera did not fall into your hands by chance. It found you because you are capable of doing what is needed."

"Ssh, Avaccus. Ssh." Tessa patted the old monk's hand. She wanted to hear more of what he had to say but could no

longer bear to hear him struggling for breath. "Tell me everything when we are safe."

Avaccus fell silent. He didn't even cough.

Tessa nodded, pleased. "Right. Let's get out of here."
Scrambling forward, she released her hold on Avaccus' hand.
A dull slapping sound followed as Avaccus' hand fell to the
cave floor. Something in Tessa's stomach dropped with it.
Spinning around, she grabbed the monk's hand again. It was
limp.

Tessa drew a short, frightened breath. Scalding soot-
filled smoke poured into her lungs; she had taken the breath
without dipping her head into the layer of fresher air. She
started choking and couldn't stop. A searing pain ripped
through the back of her chest. Her eyes stung, but she couldn't
risk opening them to let out tears.

"Avaccus!" she screamed, shaking and then pulling on
the monk's hand. "Wake up. Wake up."

He wasn't going to wake. He needed help. He needed
fresh air. Tessa defied her good sense and glanced toward the
entrance. The smoke was so thick now, it stifled the light
from the fire. Heart pumping wildly, mouth so dry it ached,
she made a decision. She had to make it to the entrance on
her own. Avaccus didn't have much longer.

Placing her right cheek against the cave floor, she took
the deepest breath her damaged lungs could manage. As she
breathed, she ripped the collar from her tunic. Working
quickly, she flattened out the fabric and placed it over Avaccus' face. She didn't know if it would do any good, but at
least it would filter out the worst of the dust and ash. She
didn't waste any of her breath on speaking, but in her mind
she told the monk to stay where he was—she'd be right back.

Tessa scrambled to her feet and ran. Eyes and mouth
sealed against the ash, face scrunched up against the heat, she
tore at the smoke. Heat rose. Sweat streamed down her back
and throat. Scorched air blasted her from all sides. Finally
she could go no more. The temperature ahead was too high.
Tessa could feel the skin on her face burning. Although she
didn't open her eyes, she guessed she was only a short distance from the cave entrance.

The spent air in her lungs burned with a hot, searing

pain. She had to let it out. Yet when she did, she wouldn't be able to take another breath. This close to the fire there would be no more fresh air.

I'm sorry. Tessa formed the words in her head. They were meant for many people scattered over two worlds. Her mother and father. Emith and Mother Emith. Avaccus. All those who would fight and die because of the Barbed Coil.

Taking her ring in her hand, raising her head against the heat, Tessa braced herself for a moment, then let out the air in her lungs.

"So you have no recollection of a young woman coming here? Two, perhaps three days back?" Ravis thought he heard a faint cry as he spoke, but dismissed it as the wind or a night-flying bird. "Reddish golden hair, slight build? Stubborn?"

"No, my son. No young women have visited us since spring." The old monk smiled, showing even, white teeth. "I surely would have remembered if one had."

Ravis looked at the old monk. His manner didn't suit him. His teeth were too well cared for and his eyes far too sharp for the fumbling character he was playing. Five minutes earlier Ravis had presented himself at the abbey gate. The young man who had greeted him was quickly replaced by the one who stood before him now. Ravis' questions had brought the old monk here with such speed that he wondered if the man hadn't been listening the whole time in the shadows behind the gate.

Pulling his cloak close to his chest, Ravis said, "The young lady in question is called Tessa. She came to meet with one of your brothers. Avaccus, I believe his name is."

When the old monk met his eyes over the word "Avaccus," Ravis knew he was dealing with a man accustomed to deceit.

The old monk traced a prayer with his hand. "Brother Avaccus passed away early this summer." The words were a reprimand. "Now, if you will excuse me. My brother and I have already broken our vows by speaking with you this late, so I would be grateful if you could turn your horse and leave. The causeway should be safe for another hour at least. God's blessing on you this night." The old monk went to close the door.

"Father," Ravis said, choosing the word deliberately. He was rewarded by the old monk looking up at the sound of the honorific—he obviously wasn't the lowly brother he pretended to be. "I have spoken with several people in Bellhaven who claimed they kept watch from the tavern as Tessa rode across the causeway the other night. Are you telling me she never made it here?"

The monk shook his head and then closed the door. Ravis heard bolts being hastily drawn. A whole fist of them. He chewed on his scar. Behind him, his horse nickered softly, pulling on its reins. The old gelding wanted to be away. Ravis regarded the closed door. He had ridden nonstop for a full day to reach here. He hadn't paid a visit to Bellhaven, as he had claimed. The line to the monk was just that—a line.

Reluctantly Ravis turned from the door. Moonlight shone on the surrounding rocks, making salt and other mineral deposits glitter. A few ancient barnacles clustered down near the high-tide mark, clinging to the rock for grim life. As Ravis looked on, a breeze sent a series of shallow tide pools rippling. A second later he smelled smoke. Not woodsmoke, he thought idly. Or at least not wholly wood. Peat, dried seaweed, and pitch. The sort of mix Drokho fishmongers used for smoking fish, as it produced the greatest volume of smoke with the fewest flames.

Strange. If the monks in the abbey had vows about speaking after dark, then surely those vows would cover any kind of physical labor, too? Like tending fires or curing fish.

Ravis patted his gelding. Spying a rock with a narrow cap, he looped the reins over it. Once he was sure the gelding had enough slack for comfort, he checked his knife. He was going to take a look around.

Leathers creaking as he stepped from the path onto the rocks, Ravis made his way into the wind. The smell of burning grew stronger with every step, and patches of blue-gray smoke began to blow along the abbey's outer wall.

Rocks formed a jagged jaw around the abbey. Thick tails of seaweed and layers of crusted salt made the going difficult, and when Ravis looked ahead and saw the rock rising to form a cliff against the abbey's east wing, he was tempted to head back. Still, the worst thing that could happen here was he'd end up with some freshly smoked fish for his trouble. Yet even as the thought occurred to him, he realized something wasn't right. There was no fish smell accompanying the smoke. No delicate aroma of slowly cooking herring or trout.

Tessa. Ravis didn't believe in coincidences: first the monk had lied, now smoke burned at midnight with no purpose. The two things had to be related. Increasing his pace, he jumped from boulder to boulder. The rock face rose sharply, stretching high against the abbey wall. Ravis stopped jumping and began to climb.

Smoke choked the surrounding air. Rising in great clouds above the cliff, it was pushed into Ravis' face by the wind. Soft flecks of burned matter rained down on his hair and shoulders. Many feet above the high-tide mark now, the rock was easier to navigate. It was drier and smoother, free of all the churned-up refuse of the sea. Ravis reached the top with surprising speed.

As soon as he saw what was there he knew what was happening. The rock face he had just climbed harbored some sort of cave. The entrance to the cave had been blocked with a stack of wood, peat, seaweed, and anything else that could burn or give off smoke, and the whole thing had been set alight.

Ravis sucked on his scar. Now it could be that the good brothers were trying to rid the cave of bats—after all, it *was* the season for them. Yet Ravis didn't believe this for one instant. Scanning the abbey wall, he spied a small door set deep within a hood of cut stone, affording the monks easy access to the cave and its entrance. So if people in the abbey could reach here at any time of day they pleased, why not build the fire in broad daylight instead? Midnight was no time to smoke out bats.

Ravis pulled off his cloak and threw it onto the fire. The moment it was in place he kicked at the heart of the blaze, scattering the burning embers to the wind. The fire had been built in haste, and with its core disintegrating, it dwindled quickly. Abandoning his cloak to the flames, Ravis began stamping on burning logs and squares of peat. As the fire collapsed downward, a huge column of smoke started pouring out from the cave. Seeing it, Ravis grabbed a smoking log from the fire and started beating away at the flames. If his hands burned, he didn't feel them.

Anyone caught in the cave would surely be dead.

Not waiting for the last of the flames to die down, Ravis stepped inside the cave. Smoke enveloped him. He could no longer see the log he was holding. Every breath he took was loaded with reeking ash. "Tessa," he called into the darkness. "Tessa!"

Nothing. He went farther into the cave.

As he felt his way through the smoke, the toe of his boot hit something soft. Falling to his knees, Ravis sent out a hand to feel for whatever was blocking his way. A body. He risked opening his eyes. It was Tessa. He couldn't tell if she was dead or alive.

Ravis' chest tightened. He let out a single animal cry. He felt anger so intense that if the monk who had lied to him were here now, he would have snapped the man's neck with his bare hands. Then kicked the body until it was nothing more than splintered bones.

What had they done to her?

Gently and with great care, taking time to ensure he put no undue pressure on her wounds and bruises, Ravis scooped Tessa up in his arms and carried her out of the cave. Her cheek fell against his. It was hot and coated in soot. She felt so light, it made his throat ache. Although he tried to halt them, memories of his wife flooded his thoughts. During the last month of her illness, Lara had been so weak she could not raise herself out of bed. He had carried her everywhere. She had been ashamed of her weakness. He'd seen it as a chance to touch her more.

Ravis bit right through his scar. The brief stab of pain wasn't nearly enough to kill the memories, but it did force them back to their usual place.

Clear of the fire now, he searched for somewhere to lay Tessa down. Spying a shallow depression surrounded by chunks of weather-split rocks, he hurried toward it and carefully laid her on the ground. As her body came in contact with the rock, a faint noise, like an inhaled sigh, sounded deep within her throat. Hearing it, Ravis stopped what he was doing, closed his eyes, then tilted his head back as far as it could go. Most of the time he didn't believe in God. Then there were times like this. . . .

He opened his eyes. Stars shone down from a black sky. If anyone had asked about them in that moment, he'd have sworn they gave off warmth as well as light.

Shrugging at himself, the stars, and the night, Ravis turned his attention back to Tessa. He had work to do.

Smoke injuries were not uncommon in battles and an everyday hazard in sieges, and Ravis was familiar with the problems that came from inhalation. Crouching beside Tessa, he took a deep breath of air, held it in his lungs, then pressed his lips against her mouth. Softer than a kiss, he let it out. Air filled Tessa's mouth and then her throat, then traveled down to her lungs. Her chest rose and fell. Ravis took another breath and then breathed for her again. Her lips were as hot as her cheeks. They tasted of ash.

Slowly, gradually, breath after breath, Tessa began to respond. Faintly at first, her chest rose and fell on its own, and beneath her eyelids, her eyes began to move. Ravis talked to her, saying gentle, nonsense things he would never have said if she were fully awake. He stroked her hair and brushed the ash from her cheeks, all the time continuing to breathe for her. After a few minutes, Tessa's chest began to pump rapidly and she started to choke. Her shoulders flew forward and she coughed violently.

"Don't open your eyes." Ravis pressed her shoulders back against the rock. "You're with me, Ravis. You're not in the cave anymore, and you're safe." He spoke firmly, as he would with a wounded soldier; troops waking after being injured in battle needed to be told they were safe. "I won't let anyone harm you."

Tessa raised her hand. Muscles in her chest, neck, and jaw pumped wildly. She opened her eyes and winced. Quickly she closed them again. "Got to . . . got to . . ." Even though her voice was raw, she seemed intent on saying something.

"Ssh. It's all right." Ravis placed a finger on her lips.

Tessa jerked away from it. "Got to go back."

Ravis leaned forward. "Was there someone else with you in the cave?"

Tessa nodded. The tendons in her neck were white with strain as she forced herself to speak. "Ava . . . Avaccus is still in there."

Standing, Ravis said, "I'll be right back."

A good portion of the smoke had dispersed from the cave, and although the remains of the fire still smoldered, there were no more flames. Ravis found the body quickly. It was lying amid a bed of cheeses in a shallow cavern that appeared to form the center of the cave. A scrap of Tessa's tunic lay over the man's nose and mouth, and as Ravis drew closer he watched it for signs of movement. The scrap lay perfectly still.

Ravis took a hard breath. Judging from all the small footprints stamped in soot around the body, Tessa had tried her best to save him.

Kneeling, Ravis ran a finger over one of the many imprints of Tessa's bare feet. She was brave, this woman whom fate had thrust upon him.

Abruptly he turned his attention back to Avaccus. It was strange to touch a dead man whose body was so warm. When Ravis lifted up the body, its heat wasn't the only thing that surprised him. Avaccus' corpse was as dense as stone. Slowly, his thoughts in many places, Ravis carried the old monk's remains from the cave.

Tessa sat up as he approached. Despite his earlier warning, her eyes were open. She closed them when she saw the expression on his face. Ravis wanted to say something to her, to tell her he knew what it was to lose someone you had tried very hard to save. Yet after he had laid Avaccus' body across a crown of rocks, he found his arms painfully empty, and all he could think of doing was crossing to Tessa and holding her as close as he could.

And that was exactly what he did.

Izgard forced himself to take another mouthful of food. Judging from the look and smell of it, the dish was barley and vegetables cooked in a thin beef broth. What little meat there was had been sliced and then shredded into so many tiny filaments that it looked like little more than shaving stubble tapped out into a bowl.

Izgard didn't like meat. He didn't like to think of it trapped between his teeth. He liked to chew on it even less; with its thick, fleshy texture it was like biting into one's own tongue. Still, he forced himself to eat a little just the same, as he always had, as he always would. Physical strength had to be maintained at all cost.

Ederius had already finished his food. The same dish as his king, of course, begun some twenty minutes earlier just in case the food tasters had failed to do their job and there was still some small measure of poison gliding, undetected, through the broth. Izgard didn't believe in taking chances with his own life.

Not that he wanted Ederius to die. Far from it. Of everyone gathered in the victory camp this night, the scribe was the only one who meant anything to him. Ederius had stood by his side for the past five years. His loyalty was absolute. Izgard loved him, and that was partly why he chose to share his food with him. If, by some sleight of a clever poisoner's hand, a slow-working poison took Izgard, then it would also take Ederius. Izgard hated the thought of the scribe living on without him.

Brushing aside the pewter bowl, Izgard said, "So, my old friend, how did it feel to be on the field today? Did running with the harras make a young man of you?"

Ederius grew paler and more weak looking by the day. The circles under his eyes were the color of bruises. He had spent the past thirty hours at his scribing desk, painting patterns. Since Izgard had entered his tent some half an hour earlier, Ederius had done little but shake his head. He shook it now, no more or less strongly than before. "They are all dead. I sent them to die."

"No. *I* sent the harras to do a difficult job, to run into a camp where they were outnumbered ten to one, and drive the Sire's forces onto the battlefield. They were not sent to die. If it hadn't been for Camron of Thorn, most of them would have returned home."

Ederius made a hard sound in his throat. "Returned home to what? To a slow death, where their bones grow into their organs and the roots of their teeth split their jaws?" The scribe continued shaking his head. "Do not think I haven't seen the harras' bodies. Do not think I haven't seen them carried from the camp late at night. Your men may have been ordered to thrust wads of cloth down their throats, but still I hear their screams."

Izgard went to speak, but Ederius wasn't finished.

"I create them," he said. "I paint them and incite them, they are creatures born of my hand. Yet as soon as my purpose is done, I abandon them to their fates. Their bodies fight the sorcery, and the sorcery fights them back. Monsters they may be, but they are my sons in the ink. I am responsible for them. And today I sent them to their deaths."

Izgard had a dozen words, ready, upon his tongue—the harras were not Ederius' men, they were *his;* Ederius hadn't sent them into the camp, *he* had; the Barbed Coil created the harras, Ederius was just a cipher—yet he decided to say none of it. Ederius was very beautiful to him at that moment. There was fire in his old eyes and a damp sheen of sweat on his skin. He was tired, that was all. Overworked to the point of exhaustion. He needed to be tended by a physician, wrapped in warm blankets, and given herbs and ewe's milk to help him sleep. Izgard nodded softly. He would see to the arrangements himself.

"Listen, my old friend," Izgard said gently. "We won today. Garizon won. Harras may have died, but the vast majority of our sons survived. The harras made that possible. They gave to save the whole. Just as you do, just as I do. We must not lose sight of our mission. There are only hard choices in war, and every time I issue an order on the field I make one decision more." As he was speaking, Izgard felt for Ederius' hand. The scribe fought the contact only a moment. "We are alike, you and I. Our conscience troubles us over the means, even though we know in our hearts that the end is Garizon's due. You may have spent two decades on the Anointed Isle, but you were born a Garizon and are still a Garizon and will remain one until you die. Think not of those harras who were killed this day; think of all those you helped save instead."

Ederius shook his head some more. "I can't . . . I don't . . ."

"Hush." Izgard's voice sharpened. Remembering what had happened the last time his anger had been provoked, he released his hold on the scribe's hand and moved away. He did not want to risk hurting Ederius in the same way he had hurt Gerta. Abruptly he changed the subject. "Has the girl been seen to?"

Responding to the sharpness in his master's voice, Ederius was quick to reply. "Yes, sire. I contacted the holy fathers. They said they would deal with her themselves this time. The incident with the gatheloc troubled them."

"You called one forth?"

Ederius nodded. His voice was grim when he spoke. "I brought it to bear upon one of the holy brothers. It was caught in the rising tide and drowned. Its body washed up on the isle at dawn. Many brothers saw it before the holy fathers had chance to drag it away."

"And was it as you thought it would be?"

"Worse. It was a creature wholly of the dark. There are no words to describe . . ." Ederius shook his head. "It seemed older than the Barbed Coil itself."

Izgard glanced at his crown. Resting on a plinth directly in front of Ederius' desk, the Barbed Coil sparkled like broken glass. A moth darted around it, mistaking it for a light source. When Izgard leaned forward to touch the crown, he didn't bother to brush the moth away. Neither insects nor dust ever came to rest upon the Coil.

"There are many patterns for us to discover yet," Izgard said, his fingers tracing the inner etchings of the crown.

"Yes, sire. Many."

In the old days when they had talked about the Coil, Ederius' longing had always come through clearly—he had so badly wanted to possess its secrets and draw its patterns. Here and now, though, Izgard heard nothing but exhaustion in the scribe's voice. It worried him.

Turning to face Ederius, Izgard said, "Rest now, my friend. I will send the physician to you with herbs to help you sleep. Tomorrow at dawn you must contact the Anointed Isle and confirm the girl is dead. She associates with the wrong people and visits the wrong places. You say she can scribe patterns, and I say she has her eye on what is mine."

Ederius' gaze flicked to the Coil. "She should be dead by now, sire."

"Only if your precious holy fathers have devised a way to kill her without wetting their hands with blood." Seeing Ederius flinch at his words caused Izgard a moment of regret. Taking the few steps needed to cross the tent, he said, "You have done well this day, Ederius. Take comfort in that."

Ederius let his head slump forward onto his chest. He did not speak.

Izgard pulled back the tent flap. The sounds and smells of victory floated in with the breeze: men sang, meat sizzled, ale foamed into the mud. Izgard had promised his men women tomorrow, and he had already picked the town that would provide them. Merin, a market and dairy farmer's town, was half a day's hard march at most. Plump, milk-fed maidens could be harvested there, along with meats, grains, and supplies. Izgard had no appetite for meat and was losing his interest in women, yet he would make sure his men got both. It cost him so very little to do so.

Besides, Merin was en route to Bay'Zell.

Mistress of three seas, central to more trade routes than any other city in the west: Bay'Zell was the ultimate prize. From its harbors a man could take a continent. Five hundred centuries earlier, that was exactly what Hierac had done. He'd even built himself a fortress as a base. Castle Bess: now in the hands of Camron of Thorn, presently to be reclaimed by the wearer of the Coil.

As he thought, Izgard's fingers tightened around the tent canvas, imagining it was skin. Today the first battle had been won. Soon the first city must be taken.

"Rest, Ederius," he said, relinquishing his grip on the canvas. "Tomorrow we begin the journey north."

essa remembered little about the night Ravis pulled her from the cave. What memories she did have seemed patchy and unrelated. She recalled Ravis' arms around her as she sat on the cliff top catching her breath, heard him whispering in her ear that everything would be all right. Next she remembered the ride to the mainland. Bound to Ravis' back so she wouldn't fall from the horse if she passed out, she and Ravis had ridden across the causeway one step ahead of the tide.

After that a long period of darkness followed, where Tessa remembered nothing except varying degrees of pain and the creak of old floorboards as she was carried up a flight of stairs. The next thing she was fully aware of was waking up in a warm bed, in an oak-paneled, windowless room, listening to the sounds of drinking, arguing, and eating filtering up from what she guessed was a tavern below.

Three days later she was still here. Ravis stayed with her most of the time. Drawing up his chair to the bed, he would tend to her wounds, cleaning and binding them every few hours, rubbing ointment or grease into them, depending on what he found. He would feed her, too; blowing on each spoonful of broth until it was cool enough to run down her throat without causing further pain.

Swallowing hurt a lot. Breathing hurt even more. Her back ached every time she inhaled, and fresh air stung like vinegar in her lungs. Sometimes she had to force herself to breathe. Other times her throat closed off, blocking the path to her lungs. Two times she had woken in the night, unable to take a breath. Ravis would hold her tightly, smothering her panic as he rubbed something oily and sharp smelling under her nose. "Peppermint oil," he told her as he worked. "To ease the spasms in your throat."

Much of the time Tessa kept her eyes closed. It hurt when she opened them, and Ravis told her the longer she kept them protected from light, the quicker they would recover. She felt weak all over and could never get warm, despite the blankets and the fire. Cold chills shook her. Hot flushes heated her skin but left her insides cold.

She tried not to think about Avaccus. They had left his body on the top of the cliff. Tessa felt it was the right thing to do. Avaccus had spent his entire adult life at the abbey, and even though the holy fathers had exiled him to a cave for twenty-one years, it had been his own decision to stay there. He could have walked across the causeway any time he chose.

Tessa sighed. In her heart she knew Avaccus' choices weren't really as simple as that; he was old and set in his ways, and the severed tendon on his thumb prevented him from pursuing the only trade he knew. Even so, she still believed Avaccus' body belonged on the isle. It was, and always had been, his home.

Sliding down amid the blankets and pillows in her bed, Tessa tried to rest. She didn't want to sleep. Sleep brought dreams, and dreams brought all kinds of bad things. The night in the cave played itself over and over again in her dreams. Sometimes she woke sooner, or shook Avaccus harder, or ran to the cave entrance straight away and immediately kicked out the fire. Whatever she did, the outcome was always the same. Avaccus died, and she was left with the feeling that if she had just done something different, she might have saved him instead. When she woke the dreams faded, but the sense of responsibility remained.

Tessa's thoughts were interrupted by the sound of footsteps drumming along the hallway. A key was turned and Ravis entered the room. "How are you this morning?" he asked, placing a tray of food on a small trestle table near the bed. "You look better."

It was morning? With no window in the room, times of day were difficult to judge. Tessa could sometimes guess when it was midday or suppertime, as the sound coming from below was punctuated by the clattering of plates and the chiming of cutlery. "I'm fine," she said, not sure if it was the truth or not.

Ravis nodded. "Your voice sounds stronger. How is your breathing?"

"Better, I think."

"Good. Then you should be able to eat better, too." With that, he picked up a bowl from the tray and began stirring it with a spoon.

Feeling as if she had been tricked, Tessa pulled herself up reluctantly. She didn't want to eat.

Ravis blew across the bowl a few times and then handed it to her. "It's oxtail broth," he said, eyes twinkling. "A guest downstairs in the tavern was most insistent that you get some. Why, she even went to the kitchens herself to make sure the cook prepared it just right. She managed to upset so many people in the process that it's just as well she's leaving Bellhaven today. She actually told the cook her stock wasn't fit for washing dishes." Ravis laughed. "And the cook here has arms the size of beer barrels. I'd think twice before insulting her myself."

Tessa found herself smiling too. "Does the lady's name happen to be Missis Wicks?"

"One and the same. She wanted to come up here to see you, but I wouldn't let her. She's been visiting the tavern every day, hoping to find a lady companion to travel with her back to Kilgrim. One of the maids here is leaving with her at noon." Ravis patted his leather tunic, then pulled out a small handwritten card. "She gave me the name and address of her brother-in-law. Said if you didn't find what you were looking for on the Anointed Isle, you should pay him a visit." Ravis read the name on the card. "Moldercay."

The bone keeper. Tessa suppressed a shudder. "He used to be a monk. Missis Wicks said he kept records at the abbey for many years. She also said he had eyes prone to wander over anything—not just women."

"Sounds much like any other man of God to me." Ravis chose an apple from the tray and bit on it. "So," he said, "are you going to tell me what actually happened on the isle? Did Avaccus teach you about the old patterns? Or did you and he find something else to talk about?"

Tessa spooned her soup to give herself time to think. The man before her had worked for Izgard of Garizon. Could he be trusted? What Avaccus had told her was too important to be passed around lightly. She was the only one he had ever spoken to about ephemeras—she was sure of it. Now he was dead, and the burden of that knowledge fell upon her shoulders. It was yet another responsibility in her growing collection.

Briefly, Tessa glanced at Ravis. Part of her still couldn't believe he was here. She had assumed he would return to Mizerico with Violante of Arazzo. Only he hadn't. He had ridden all this way to be with her, Tessa McCamfrey, leaving Violante to sail home on her own.

Tessa raised a spoonful of broth to her lips.

"Be careful," Ravis said. "Blow on it one last time to be safe."

She met his eye. Over the past few days she had seen things in him that she could never have imagined before. He was gentle with her, careful. It was as if she were something precious that he was afraid might break. He was still the same man she had come to know on the ship, yet in between being his normal sardonic self she now caught glimpses of something else.

Returning the soup to the bowl, Tessa said, "Avaccus told me the real reason why I'm here."

Ravis raised an eyebrow. "And what is it?"

Tessa took a small breath. Ravis was the first person she had made contact with in this world, he had protected and saved her, and for the past three days he had tended her day and night. In all ways that counted she had trusted him right from the start.

Pulling her ring from its usual place around her neck, she turned it toward the light, waited a moment until there was a lull in the noise rising up from below, and said, "This ring is the key to it all."

Slowly, pausing as her breath left her or the pain in her back bit too deeply, taking long blinks from time to time to ease the stinging in her eyes, Tessa told Ravis all she had learned about the Barbed Coil. She told him about ephemeras, what they were, what little she knew of where they came from, how Hierac of Garizon had found one, and what it had caused him to become. She spoke of Hierac's visit to the Anointed Isle, of the agreement struck between the Garizon king and the holy fathers, and of the binding of the Coil to the earth. She explained why Avaccus thought she had been brought here and what he believed she must do.

Through it all, Ravis sat and listened. He never interrupted once. Sometimes he nodded or ran a hand through his hair, but mostly he chewed on his scar. If Tessa had been hoping to surprise him, she would have been disappointed, for his expression never changed during the telling. She could tell he was listening intently, but although he was hearing things he could not possibly have heard before, his face gave nothing away. Finally, when she had finished, he reached out to touch the ring.

"Five hundred years," he said, his fingers touching Tessa's over the gold. "And all this time we thought Garizon and its kings were responsible for their wars."

"Have you seen the Barbed Coil?" Tessa asked.

Ravis shrugged. "Once. From a distance. Izgard's scribe was drawing patterns from its base—I remember his fingers bled as he worked, yet he didn't seem to notice. Ederius is the only man alive Izgard trusts with his crown."

"Do you think Izgard knows about the Coil? What it is, what it does?"

"I can't say. Perhaps not all of it. Perhaps Izgard knows only that he cannot afford to lose it. After five hundred years old tales can become distorted and diluted, and the truth of the matter may well be lost. The agreement is still intact, though. Izgard is committed to the safety of the Anointed Isle, and judging by the attempt on your life three nights ago, the holy fathers still feel some sense of obligation in return."

Even though Tessa agreed with Ravis, she found herself shaking her head. Avaccus had been wrong about Father Issasis. He'd thought the abbot would take no action to harm her, that even the small lies he'd told her would trouble his conscience. Tessa pushed her lips together as hard as she could. She hoped Father Issasis' conscience troubled him into the grave.

"This pattern you have to draw," Ravis said, "how can we find out more about it?"

Tessa was suddenly very glad she had told Ravis everything. She liked the way he used the word *we*. "I'm not sure. Avaccus said I had to paint the problem, then solve it. To do that I need to have some idea of what the original looks like. I have to know how Ilfaylen worked."

"And there are no known copies of the illumination?"

"No. Every night after Ilfaylen had finished work on the manuscript, it was taken from him and checked for pin-pricks. Whenever he wasn't working on the pattern, all his brushes and pigments were removed, so he couldn't even make a rough sketch of it."

Ravis nodded. "And the original is in Veizach?"

"Avaccus said it was sealed in a lead box and buried in a secret location deep beneath the city."

"Hmm." Ravis stood up and walked over to the fire. "As Veizach is one of the five largest cities on the continent, I would say we have quite a problem."

"Perhaps Missis Wicks' brother-in-law knows something that might help us, or even Emith. Avaccus told me Emith could have been a great scribe if he had chosen to be."

"Only he had no faith in his own abilities?"

Tessa found herself surprised at Ravis' astuteness. "Yes. That's the same thing Avaccus said." As she spoke, Tessa was aware of her voice thinning. She took a breath, but it caused a sharp, stabbing pain in her back and didn't fill her up. As she took a second, deeper breath, she felt her lungs begin to burn.

"You need to rest." Ravis was beside her before she knew it, drawing the covers up around her chest, laying a hand on her brow to feel the temperature of her skin. "Close your eyes for a while. Don't try so hard to breathe." From his pack he pulled out a small greased-paper pouch and dabbed a little of its contents onto the skin directly above Tessa's upper lip. Peppermint oil.

Closing her eyes, Tessa allowed herself to be calmed by Ravis. Air passed easily enough down her throat, but the farther it went the harder its journey became. She felt as if her lungs were closing up.

"Easy now," Ravis said, stroking her hair. "One small breath at a time."

The urge to panic was great, but Ravis kept talking to her

and touching her, and gradually she began to relax, allowing air to pass down to her lungs. Tessa was left feeling physically drained. She couldn't stop trembling. The back of her nightgown was soaked in sweat, and she was aware of a salty, slightly chemical odor rising from her skin. She didn't even smell like herself anymore.

"Sleep," Ravis said. "You can't expect to get over injuries like yours overnight. They are too serious. Sleep now. I'll watch over you."

"You've looked after someone like me before, haven't you?" Tessa spoke mostly to test her breath and her voice. After a few seconds, when Ravis didn't answer, she opened her eyes.

He was looking straight at her. His dark brown eyes had lost the one subtlety of shading that stopped them from being black. Something shone through them, but it wasn't light, nor was it any kind of emotion Tessa could put a name to.

"I was married once," he said after a moment. "My wife died of *hura aya*. Swamp sickness." Seconds passed, and just when Tessa thought Ravis would say nothing more, he did. "*Hura aya* eats into the lungs first, and from there it travels outward to the kidneys, the liver, the brain. At first you think being unable to catch your breath is the worst part of it, and then you learn it isn't." Ravis ran his thumb knuckle over his scar. "*Hura aya* takes everything in the end: breath, sight, ability to move, urinate, think. Everything."

Tessa glanced down. She couldn't look into Ravis' eyes. She now realized what shone through them, changing their color from brown to black: self-control.

Not knowing what to say to him, and suspecting anything she did say would be wrong, Tessa closed her eyes. She didn't expect to sleep, but somehow she did, and when she opened her eyes again, Ravis was gone.

"Pass the word. Everyone in this village must leave their homes. Not later today, not this evening, but now. Take only what you can carry and flee to the west. Do not head to Bay'Zell looking for safety. Izgard will be there in less than a week. You must save yourselves and your children. Your village is directly in his path, and unless you act now you will all be dead by sunset. Now go."

Camron forced his jaw together as he regarded the dozen men and women gathered before him. He knew his words were harsh, but he also knew harsh words were the only way to reach them. He had spent his childhood in a small, isolated community like this one. People grew up thinking no harm would ever befall them, that the world and its changes would pass them right by. They were wrong. Izgard was coming. He and his army were on the move, and less than five hours' hard march separated them from the village of Shale.

"What about our grains?" said one man with yellow gray hair and patches of skin flaking from his sunburned nose. "Our summer stocks?"

"Leave everything you cannot carry. If Izgard burns the grain in your fields and the grapes on your vines, be glad you and your family weren't there to be burned as well."

A moment of shocked silence followed. A plump, well-dressed woman was first to break it. "But what about our animals? You can't expect us to leave those too." Her words met with grunts of approval from the others.

"No. Take only those animals you can safely load onto carts. Your herds must be turned loose."

"Turned loose! Why, that's madn—"

"Keep them in their pens and Izgard's men will seize and slaughter them. Take them with you and they will slow you down to the point where you'll be unable to outrun the Garizon forces. The only thing you can do is let them loose. Scatter them. Izgard's men won't have time to run down and catch individual animals. It's summer, there's plenty of grass in the valleys; the animals will be able to fend for themselves. When it's safe you can return and round them up."

The villagers didn't like that at all. Their faces were drawn, their shoulders hunched. They shot each other nervous glances. The well-dressed woman clutched at the fabric of her blue linen dress. Camron wished he could deal with them more gently, yet he knew fear was the one thing that would make them leave their homes.

"When will it be safe to come back?" It was the old man with the yellow gray hair.

Camron shook his head. "I don't know. Soon, I hope, but in truth it could be many weeks. Months, even."

"But, our homes, our livelihood, our—"

"If you stay, you will die." Camron's voice was as cold and sharp as an ax breaking ice. "Your daughters will be raped, your sons will be mutilated, your homes will be set alight, and your animals will be taken. These are not empty words. I have seen what Izgard and his army is capable of. He tore the town of Thorn apart. No man, woman, or child was left standing. And right now he and his men are frustrated and angry. They won a battle, yet there were no spoils. They need food, drink, women, and supplies, and they won't think twice about taking them."

"But if we leave, Izgard can still burn our homes, torch our crops."

A second man nodded in agreement. "We'll have nothing to return to."

Camron looked at the two old men who had spoken. He looked at all the villagers who had gathered in the plowed field to meet him. Morning sunlight shone in their faces, showing up wrinkles, broken veins, sunburned skin, and chapped lips. These people worked on the land, it was their life. He would not lie to them.

"Yes," he said. "Izgard could order everything to be burned, I will not mislead you in this. It comes down to a choice between your homes and your lives. What do you value the most? Three nights ago I saw ten thousand corpses laid out in a valley west of Hook River. Chances are the bodies are still there. With limited manpower and even less time, the Sire has little choice but to let them rot." Camron's gaze traveled from face to face. "Would you want to meet the same fate as those men? Would you want your children to?"

One by one the villagers looked down, away from his gaze. Camron didn't know what was showing in his eyes, but he was conscious of a catch in his voice. Three days' hard riding, moving from village to village and, in some cases, farmhouse to farmhouse, had taken their strain. But what else could he do? What choice did he have? Izgard was only half a day behind him. The towns and villages that fell within his path to Bay'Zell had to be warned. Camron had seen his lifetime's fill of dead bodies. He did not want to see any more.

The villagers shuffled their feet. Some shook their heads. More than one man glanced over his shoulder, in the direction Izgard's army would approach from.

The well-dressed woman spoke first, releasing her grip on her dress and checking the faces of her companions before she began. "I am a grandmother. I have four grandchildren and another on the way. I love my land and I tend it well, but it's been twenty years since I tended it with myself in mind. Every time I hitch my plow to my ox, I do it for my sons and daughters, that they might have something of value after I'm gone. Now, I'm no fool and I'm no spring lamb either, but I'd rather leave now and let Izgard run around after my chickens and pigs than risk having no one left to plow my fields for but myself."

A moment passed. No one moved. The woman stood perfectly straight, chin high in the air. A breeze rippled through the group, raising collars and tugging at hair, and the moment it died away everyone spoke at once:

"Send for Wells. He's got the fastest horse in the village. He can ride to the outlying farms and spread the word."

"We must keep the children calm."

"Let's tell them we're off on an outing."

"No. We must tell them the truth."

"Ethee, get Amis to pull out his four-wheeled cart."

"Let's all meet back here one hour from now."

"Make it forty minutes instead."

As he watched the villagers organize themselves, Camron took a long, deep breath. Checking that no one's eyes were upon him, he moved closer to his horse and rested his weight against the creature's flank. He was dead tired.

Each place he visited was different. Each group of people he spoke to reacted in a different way; some hurled insults at him, told him he was a liar, or a con artist, or a deluded fool. Others barely waited to hear the end of his story: they packed their belongings into a cart and left. In the three days he had been doing this, Camron had evacuated close to a dozen towns and villages, yet he still didn't know what to expect. He only knew it had to be done.

The night following the battle had been a hard one. Camron had no memory of how he and Pax had managed to pull themselves away from the bodies. They retraced their steps up the slope and spent the next hour looking for Broc of Lomis. Finally they found him, lying in a rocky depression on the west side of the hill. He was as cold as the stone that lay beneath him. Part of his face had been torn away, and a deep gash had severed his windpipe. Blood from the wound had turned the undershirt Broc had worn to please his sister from bright yellow to black.

Camron picked up the body and carried it back to the retreat. Many times during the journey Pax asked if he could help bear the weight, but Camron refused. He had no memories, no family, no hometown. Broc's body was all he had left.

As he laid Broc down close to the riverbank, the Sire sent for him. He wanted Camron to accompany him as he traveled first west, then north, and gathered a new army about him in preparation for a second battle in Bay'Zell. Camron refused. Sandor hadn't liked that. He would have issued an order, only Camron didn't give him the chance. Calling together the twenty or so men who were left in his troop, Camron rode from the retreat. Pax accompanied him. The young guard had seen the bodies in the valley; he had seen what was missing from Broc of Lomis' face. He shared Camron's need to get away.

Riding north from the camp in darkness, they had no purpose at first. Camron felt only loss. He had been too exhausted for anything else. Hours passed. The night passed. When dawn came the small troop happened upon a cleared road cut with freshly marked wheel furrows and followed it into a town.

His men were tired, dispirited to the point where they let their wounds bleed when heavy riding reopened them and fought viciously among themselves over the last drops of berriac. They needed food, rest, reason.

As they came to a halt by the town's first inn, a young boy came out to water their horses. An even younger girl tagged along on his heels, mimicking his movements, and breaking out in high, excited giggles whenever he turned to shush her away. Judging from their coloring and dress, the boy and girl were brother and sister, busy doing whatever mischief brothers and sisters normally did. Camron found himself smiling. They were such happy, bright-looking children.

That was when it struck him. Izgard would be on his way. Here, to this sleepy little town of Merin. An army that size needed supplies, grain, alcohol, livestock. High on victory, they would be looking for victims to torture and taunt. And women. Izgard would have promised them women to lie with.

Camron turned cold. His horse, feeling a sudden change in his master, brayed nervously and flicked its mane. He patted the creature's neck as he glanced around the town. But for the slanting copper awnings on the buildings and the partially paved roads, Merin might have been Thorn.

Camron looked back at the brother and sister. The boy had refilled his bucket at the well and was letting his younger sister help carry it back to the horses. They were laughing and pushing each other and losing great splashes of water to the dirt. Watching them, Camron felt a dull pain building behind his eyes. His vision blurred.

He had seen such terrible things in the past twenty-four hours, sights so appalling they had stripped all sense of normality from him, leaving him nothing inside but the kind of knee-jerk anger that wasn't really an emotion at all. Now, to see something good, something simple and normal from everyday life, was like walking from a darkened room into daylight. It dazzled him. It made the ground shift beneath his feet one last time. This wasn't only about soldiers anymore. This was about people and families as well.

Turning his horse, Camron gave orders to his men. The town had to be evacuated in less than an hour. Izgard's army could reach here by noon. As he shouted the orders, Camron heard his voice grow stronger. He took deep breaths and, for the first time since the battle, focused his mind on what he could do, here, in the present, rather than all he could not make up for in the past.

They made mistakes that first time in Merin. They caused panic and anger and confusion. Twenty bloody and battle-weary troops riding into their midst, ordering them to leave their homes and abandon their possessions, had been met with open hostility by the townsfolk. It had taken a lot of time to persuade them to go. Some chose to stay behind, yet most decided to leave in the end. The gashes and claw marks on the troops' thighs and chests persuaded better than words alone.

When Izgard and his forces rode up some four hours later, they found a ghost town.

Camron and his men had been moving steadily north ever since. Hugging the foothills, following the course of the Hook and then the Veize, sometimes half, sometimes a full day's march ahead of Izgard, they had moved from town to town and village to village, warning everyone of the enemy's approach. Fanning out, they had split up into groups to cover as many villages and outlying areas as possible. In four days' time they would meet up in Bay'Zell.

Camron ran his hand over his horse's flank, enjoying the warmth of flesh and blood. Most of the villagers of Shale had left the plowed field and only a few remained, discussing last minute changes to their evacuation plans. The woman in the blue dress was among them. Catching Camron's eye, she mouthed the words "Thank you" and walked away.

Nodding an acknowledgment to the shadow cast by her back, Camron led his horse from the field. What he and his men were doing was so little, and unless Izgard's army was somehow stopped at Bay'Zell, it was a temporary measure at best. Camron swung himself up in the saddle and headed due north. There had to be another way.

"Izgard has won the first battle. He slaughtered ten thousand Rhaize troops on ground to the west of Hook River." Ravis paced the room. His leather tunic snapped as he moved. "He'll be in Bay'Zell in under a week." Water droplets glistened in Ravis' hair and on his shoulders. His boots left wet imprints on the turquoise rug lying in front of the fire. He had just come in from the rain.

"We need to get back to Bay'Zell, don't we?" Although Tessa had been awake for some time, she hadn't been aware it was raining. She didn't like being in a room with no windows. "We should leave tonight."

Ravis shook his head. "No. We'll stay until you're stronger."

"We can't afford to."

Something in Tessa's voice caused Ravis to stop in midpace. "What do you mean?"

Tessa took a breath to steady herself before she spoke. "Just before I fell asleep the night of the fire, Avaccus said something to me. It was a warning."

"What was it?"

"He said that in ten days' time the Barbed Coil will have been upon the earth for five hundred years."

Ravis' tooth came down upon his scar. He closed his eyes for a long moment, then spoke, "This is what Izgard has planned for all along. He believes in all those old superstitions. He waited until the fifth day of the fifth month to make himself king. He even picked the year—crowning himself on the fiftieth anniversary of the last king's death." Ravis began to pace again. "Izgard will take Bay'Zell on the Barbed Coil's five hundredth anniversary. That means we have only six days left."

Tessa didn't like to hear Ravis sounding so openly worried. "So you think there's truth in what Avaccus said?"

"I think Izgard believes there is."

Gritting her teeth together, Tessa swung her feet onto the floor. All sorts of pain fought her, but she fought them back, fists clenched. "Let's get out of here."

Ravis abandoned his pacing. "You're not going anywhere."

Tessa smiled. "You don't know me very well, Ravis of Burano. If you did, you'd know that leaving is the one thing I do well. And you can either help or ignore me, but I warn you now, you won't even come close to stopping me."

Ravis' mouth fell open. He looked at Tessa as if she were

a bug he'd long dismissed as merely a crawler, only to find that if pressed in a certain spot, it stopped crawling and started flying instead.

Tessa's smile widened. She had finally succeeded in surprising him. "I'll use that new cloak of yours for now. We can buy more things when we get to Kilgrim. Have you got Moldercay's address? We should pay him a visit before we leave."

"You have to promise me to be careful."

Tessa nodded. "I will."

Ravis took her arm and helped her out of bed. The muscles in Tessa's legs hurt as she shifted her weight onto them. Her eyes began to water. Ravis stood behind her, letting her use his weight to support herself. Feeling foolish for her show of bravado seconds earlier, Tessa waited for the weakness to pass.

It didn't, not quite. But somehow she managed to get ready, brush her hair, splash water on her face, and pull the ties together on Ravis' cloak. Ravis was beside her every minute, helping only if she needed it, allowing her time to do things for herself. Getting down the stairs was difficult. She had to take them one at a time. Her back ached a lot, but it was the shortness of breath that bothered her most. She hated being weak.

Moldercay's address turned out to be on the same thoroughfare as the tavern, but on the far outskirts of town. Ravis led the horse while Tessa rode. A moderate rain set the street cobbles shining and made Ravis' wool cloak stink.

The dull afternoon light did Bellhaven no favors. Three-story buildings blocked the streets; their gray stone facades bird stained and salt stained, their gutterless roofs spilling great jets of water onto the streets. Ditches were choked with empty beer casks and wine skins. The few people they passed held bulky objects under their cloaks and seemed to be in a hurry to get somewhere. Little business was being done. Most shopfronts were shut up, and the ones that were still open had a feeling of being closed. No candles had been lit to illuminate the wares.

They smelled Moldercay's place before they saw it. An

odd, almost familiar odor of stale things, mineral salts, and mold was borne along the street on a ragged plume of smoke. Three-story buildings gave way gradually to cleared lots, fenced-off enclosures, and squat, window-starved constructions that might have been warehouses, granaries, or stables.

The last building on the street was two-storied and smart compared to its neighbors. It was the only building Ravis and Tessa had passed that was whitewashed. All the window frames and shutters were painted white too, and the roof was covered in a layer of gray white lead. A thick chimney stack swelled from the west-facing wall, and a large plot of land to the east of the building boasted freshly turned soil, spiked with white markers at regular intervals, looking, for all intents and purposes, like an oversize seed bed.

"You didn't tell me Moldercay kept a charnel house." As he spoke, Ravis laid a hand against Tessa's cheek. Feeling something he didn't like, he pulled a small envelope from his pack. "Here, swallow this."

Tessa did as she was told. The envelope turned out to be some semi-liquid substance wrapped in a coating of sugar paper. The taste of sugar did little to mask the herby tang of comfrey and thyme. "Missis Wicks called Moldercay a bone keeper."

Ravis rapped on the door. "The two are one and the same."

A minute passed. Ravis helped Tessa down from the horse, and together they stood and stared at the finely painted white door. A few seconds later a panel was pulled back and a pair of extremely light gray eyes regarded them through an ornate metal grille.

"Visitation or bereavement?"

Tessa looked to Ravis to supply an answer. She had no idea what the question meant. "Neither," he replied. "We've come to see Moldercay. This lady here is an acquaintance of his sister-in-law Missis Wicks."

The man whom the light gray eyes belonged to pondered this information a moment. He nodded once, pondered some more, and then drew back the bolt and let them in.

Tessa stepped into a small, carefully lit hallway. Candles burned on waist-high sconces, sending an equal amount of shadows darting upward as well as down. The odor she had detected earlier on the street sharpened. The air was clammy and cool, and condensation dotted the walls. Seeing where Tessa's gaze lingered, the gray-eyed man said, "It's boiling day today, miss."

"Boiling day?"

The man, who was dressed in a blue tunic with a white apron tied over it, nodded. "Yes, miss. We only dig and clean the bones once a week."

"Crust!" A cry sounded from somewhere within the building. "Who disturbs us at this hour?"

"People to see you, Moldercay." Crust regarded Tessa rather solemnly. "Acquaintances of Missis Wicks."

"Bring them in! Bring them in! Can't be leaving the bones for chitchat."

Tessa and Ravis exchanged glances. Crust wiped his hands on his apron and guided them toward the voice. The building was a warren of whitewashed passageways. Plaster had been molded onto the corners where opposing walls met, cutting down on angles and giving a round, cavelike appearance to what were otherwise normal rooms.

Crust led them into a large, tiled kitchen. A man stood with his back to them, tending an iron pot the size of a hip bath that was suspended on a grill above the fire. As soon as Tessa entered the room, her eyes began to sting and water. Without so much as a word to anyone, Ravis crossed over to the side door and opened it, letting the boiling fumes out and fresh air in.

Moldercay turned on them. "What's this! What's this! Crust, did you give these people permission to open the door?"

"No," Ravis said. "He didn't. I've had an aversion to harsh vapors for as long as I can remember. They make me break out in boils, and I'm sure you wouldn't want to risk aggravating such an unfortunate condition?"

"No, sir. I would not. I thank you for speaking plainly. Crust, open the shutters and pull up some chairs near the door."

Ravis walked Tessa to the door, supporting her weight until the chair was in place. The fresh air began to make her feel better.

Moldercay resumed stirring his pot. He was a small, angular man, bony and perfectly bald. Both he and his assistant, Crust, shared the same hunched shoulders and curved backs. "You don't mind if I carry on working, do you? This last batch is nearly done. They'll be clean as a pick before you know it. As soon as they're finished I'll rub them with a spot of spirits and set them to dry. Crust, bring this fine lady and gentleman some refreshments. Sage tea, perhaps, with honey and a splash of sloe gin. Let's have some spice cakes, too. Currant ones, I think." Moldercay turned to Tessa. "Unless the dear lady would care for candied peel?"

Tessa shook her head. Eating was the last thing on her mind. "Currants will be fine."

"Excellent! Crust, set them to warm on the griddle, would you?" Moldercay began stirring his pot with renewed vigor. Boiling water frothed and bubbled, belching out huge gasps of steam to the chimney above.

"You boil people's bodies?" Tessa found she could no longer contain herself. She had to know what was going on in that pot.

Moldercay slapped his free hand to his chest. "Good grief, no, miss. I boil the bones, not the bodies. Unless they're heretics or murderers, of course." Glancing over his shoulder, he spotted the puzzled expression on Tessa's face. "I can't speak from where you are from, miss, but here in Maribane no one who is an unbeliever or a murderer can have their bodies raised from the earth once they've been placed there. Just isn't fitting."

"Not fitting at all," chimed in Crust from the far side of the kitchen.

"You raise the bodies from the earth?" Tessa was aware of Ravis sending her a cautionary glance, warning her that she was asking about things she should already know, but she couldn't help herself.

"My companion here was raised in a convent." Ravis spoke in a condescending voice. "She knows little of the outside world and its customs."

Moldercay nodded knowingly. "Indeed! Indeed! Well, miss, Crust and I take the bodies from the bereaved—"

"In a cart," interrupted Crust.

"Yes, in a cart, bring them here, wash and prepare them, then bury their remains in our garden of peace."

"With quicklime packed around their bodies," added Crust. "To make 'em rot faster."

Tessa suppressed a shiver. The plot of land on the east side of the building must be where Moldercay and Crust buried the bodies.

"We never use quicklime on holy men, of course," Moldercay said. "Men of God are allowed the privilege of staying in the earth for as long as the process naturally takes. Up to half a year in winter. When a body's been limed, though, it's usually ready within a month. Crust here pulls them up for me and we clean and bleach the bones in my pot. Lye for normal folks. Ashes and calf urine for men of God."

Tessa nodded. She had learned a little of such matters from Emith, who used lye to remove flesh from hides. "What do you do with the bones when they're done?" she asked. "Give them back to the families?"

"Sometimes, my dear lady. Mostly, though, we keep them here, with us."

"That's what we like best," said Crust.

"We keep them in the catacombs that run beneath the house, the road, and the grounds. Crust keeps track of whose bones are where, how long they've been interred, and so forth. These days I can't remember a thing for myself. As soon as a fact's in my head, then poof! it's out again the other side." Finished with his pot, Moldercay called Crust over and together they moved it from the flames, setting it on the tiled floor. The water was murky and gelatinous, and Tessa was glad she couldn't see what was in it.

"How's your long-term memory, Moldercay?" Ravis asked. "Do you still recall your time on the Anointed Isle?"

"Take these outside and drain them for me, Crust," Moldercay said, tapping the side of the pot. "I'll be out a little later to wash them down." He waited until Crust had dragged the pot away before answering Ravis' question. Scrubbing his hands with a wet brush, he said, "I don't like to talk of the Anointed Isle in front of Crust, you understand. It might upset him. He's Bellhaven born and bred, and everyone in this town grows up believing that once those holy fathers have got their claws into a man, they hate to let him go. Crust thinks that one day I'll be dragged kicking and screaming across the causeway and confined to a high tower or low dungeon, never to be heard of again."

"They kept Brother Avaccus in a cave," Tessa said. "In the dark, alone, for twenty-one years."

Moldercay nodded. "Yes, it was so. The holy fathers feared him. He was too clever by far with his paintbrush and his ink. The things he could draw! Beautiful, they were. But worrying. Very worrying. Avaccus could learn things from them, they said. He must be a very wise man by now."

Tessa felt a stab of pain in her back. Moldercay didn't know Avaccus was dead. She closed her eyes. Why hadn't she managed to save him? Why hadn't she moved faster? Been stronger? Something touched her arm. She opened her eyes, looked down. It was Ravis' hand. Although he never seemed to, he always watched her closely.

"You were a scribe, weren't you, Moldercay," he said. "A record keeper?"

Finished with scrubbing his hands, Moldercay crossed to the kitchen and picked up a tray filled with steaming bowls and plates of hot spice cakes. "I was never an illuminator of manuscripts like Avaccus. No, indeed. No. I was a copyist. Chosen for my neat script and quickness of hand." He pulled up another chair next to Tessa and laid the tray upon it. "I was charged with copying all the old scrolls onto new vellum. They had been stored below sea level for centuries, you see, and were badly damaged. They'd fall apart in my hands as soon as I picked them up. Terrible to behold it was: all that old knowledge grown over with mold, ruined by salt air, water-stained by the damp."

While Moldercay spoke, Ravis handed Tessa a bowl of sage tea and a plate of spice cakes. Tessa hadn't wanted to eat or drink anything, but the toasty, buttery aroma of the spice cakes broke down her resistance, and she soon found herself munching and drinking. The tea was sweet with honey and bitter with sloe gin, and it made Tessa's toes tingle. Soon, she no longer thought it strange at all that she was sitting in a charnel house, having tea.

— Moldercay continued speaking. "The holy fathers made me work down in the cellar. They didn't want to risk moving the manuscripts upstairs to the scriptorium—the parchment was just too frail to be exposed to daylight. It suited me well enough at the time, I must say. Alone most of the day and a good portion of the night, no one looking over my shoulder except the good Lord himself. Brother Pettifar was supposed to come down each morning and sit with me, but between his bad knee and his fondness for gin-soaked oatcakes, he barely made it down the stairs once a week." Moldercay smiled fondly. "Those were the days.

"Of course, in the end the whole thing was a waste of time. The holy fathers took my newly copied manuscripts, packed them in open crates, and ordered them to be stored high aboveground in the west tower. One year later they sent in Brother Boddering to bind the loose leaves into codices. Boddering had been sewing books for thirty years, and no one could match his eye for detail on matters of kettle stitches and cording, but when it came to spotting obstacles from a distance he was as blind as a bat. Poor man tripped on an uneven timber the minute he stepped in the room. His candle went one way, he went the other, and by the time he righted himself the first of the four boxes was alight." Moldercay shook his head gravely. "Everything went up in smoke."

"What about the originals?" Ravis said. "Weren't they still in the cellar?"

"They'd been left to the devil. I never packed them away in crates. All it took was one damp winter for wet rot to take them. Three years of copying wasted."

Tessa put down her bowl. "Did you ever copy a manuscript written by Brother Ilfaylen's clerical assistant?"

Moldercay thought. He stroked his face, pursed his lips, pointed his chin one way and then the other. "I cannot say as I did, dear lady."

"It would have been very old. Illuminations may have been mentioned in it."

Moldercay looked blank but regretful.

Tessa stood up. "Think," she said, as much to herself as Moldercay. "It would have mentioned a journey, first by sea, then overland. Veizach would probably be named in it"—Tessa struggled—"Veizach, Rhaize. Bay'Zell."

Moldercay's chin came up. "Bay'Zell, you say?"

"Yes, yes. Ilfaylen and his assistant went on a journey to Veizach. On their way home they stayed in Bay'Zell."

"Come to think of it, I do remember reading something similar now. The scribe never mentioned Ilfaylen's name, though. He just wrote *my master,* or *my brother in God.*" Moldercay was now circling the kitchen, nodding to himself. "Some of the leaves were badly damaged and the colophon was unreadable—"

"Colophon?"

"The inscription page, where the scribe would have recorded the date and details of the manuscript, given it a title, and so forth. When the colophon was lost, so was I. I was reduced to copying blindly with no sense of what I wrote."

Feeling her chest beginning to ache, Tessa sat down. She didn't want to risk another attack like the one earlier. Not now. "So, you do recall the manuscript mentioned Bay'Zell?"

Moldercay took a deep breath and smiled. For a moment his short, bony body was transformed, and Tessa got a brief glimpse of what he might have looked like in his youth. "Oh yes. Bay'Zell. Franny loved me to tell her stories about faraway places. She liked to hear all the details of what people ate, how they lived, what they wore, and so on. She said that just because her body was stuck in one place, it didn't mean her mind had to be as well."

"Franny was the woman you left the brotherhood for?" Ravis said, asking a question man to man.

"Yes. I was quietly courting her all the years I spent copying in the cellar. Seeing how she loved to hear tales of distant places, I'd hunt out manuscripts that mentioned foreign cities and customs and recite the details back to her when we were alone." Moldercay smiled again, this time to himself. "Some women like to be wooed with gold trinkets and flowers. Not my Franny. She liked words."

"Did the manuscript mention Veizach?" Tessa was beginning to get frustrated. Ravis' hand was back on her arm, warning her to stay calm.

"I'm not sure," Moldercay said. "Parts of the manuscript were unreadable. Mostly I remember the details of Bay'Zell. The scribe's master was sick, if my recollections serve me, that's why they couldn't make the crossing back to Maribane. So while his master recovered his strength, the scribe went out and about in Bay'Zell, making notes on customs and habits, talking with the locals. Franny liked the journal because the scribe had an eye for women's fashions. He pronounced them scandalous, of course, but not before he'd described just how low cut their dresses—"

"Does it not strike you as odd," Ravis said, flicking his hand upward to silence Moldercay, "that with his master sick, the scribe went out and about every day in the city? Surely his first duty would be to look after his master?"

Moldercay shook his head. "I believe his master insisted he go out. Perhaps he was the sort of man who preferred to be alone in his illness."

Ravis made a soft, clicking sound with his tongue. "Perhaps."

"What about Ilfaylen's work in Veizach?" Tessa said, stepping in to fill the silence Ravis had caused. "Can you recall any mention of an illumination?"

Moldercay pulled on his lower lip. Boiling the bones had bleached his hands, and he looked as if he were wearing white gloves. "I believe the scribe did mention something about a pattern. He mentioned that his master was working hard day and night. Said he went through six bone styluses in a single day."

"Styluses. That meant he was using wax tablets, drafting out the details *before* he started work on the illumination." Tessa felt like grabbing Moldercay around the throat and forcing the information out of him. "What about the actual parchment itself? Can you remember anything about it? Its size, color. Anything. Think. *Think.*"

Hearing the change in Tessa's voice, Moldercay glanced nervously at Ravis.

Ravis shrugged. "Convent girls," he said.

Moldercay accepted this explanation with a solemn nod of his head. "Indeed." He walked over to the door and peered out into the early evening shadows. "Crust, don't let those bones dry out before I've had chance to rub them down. I'll be there in just a minute."

Thinking she had gone too far, Tessa went to apologize, but Moldercay chose that instant to swing around from the door. "You know," he said, "I think there was something about an illumination after all. Quite strange it was, really, now I come to think of it. I remember a page badly eaten by mold. I could only catch one word in half a dozen, but there was some kind of warning. Something about the scribe being . . ." Moldercay scratched his chin. "How did he put it now? Ah, yes. Bound to silence."

"Yes," Tessa said, excited. "Avaccus said that both Ilfaylen and his assistant swore an oath to Hierac, vowing never to speak of the designs on the pattern. Did the journal mention anything else?"

Moldercay shrugged. "Nothing that I can recall. He spoke a little about the vellum—its preparation and finishing."

Leaning forward in her chair, Tessa said, "Can you remember exactly what he wrote?"

"Just the usual things every scribe knows and takes for granted. How the vellum was bleached, scrubbed, painted, glazed, then pounced. Nothing remarkable."

"Was there anything else?"

"I don't think so." Moldercay began to clear away the bowls and plates. "The rest of the section was ruined by mold, and the next thing I remember mention of was the master's illness. The scribe believed his master first caught a chill on the day he completed his work, as his master complained of being cold and requested that a shawl be brought for his shoulders."

Tessa went to ask another question, but Moldercay stopped her.

"Please, my dear lady. There was no further mention of an illumination. I'm quite sure of that. The narrative skipped to Bay'Zell and then the passage home. Now, if you will please excuse me, I need to bathe the bones."

"But—" began Tessa.

"Come on, Tessa," Ravis said, cutting her off. "Moldercay has a job to do." He stood up. "Thank you for all your help, Moldercay. We'll show ourselves out."

"No, dear me. No. I can't have you doing that." Moldercay called for Crust. "Come and take these good people to the door."

He bowed to Tessa. "Good night, dear lady. My sister spoke most highly of you, you know. Said you reminded her of Nelly. I'm sorry I couldn't be of greater help."

"Thank you, Moldercay," Tessa replied. She was beginning to think she had pushed the bone keeper too hard. Avaccus had been right all along: there was no mention of Ilfaylen's illumination in the journal. There would be no mention of it anywhere. Which meant she had nothing to go on, and time was running out. "I'm sorry I was so . . . insistent. I don't know what came over me."

"Not to worry, my dear lady," said Moldercay.

"We all end up as bones in the end." Crust appeared in the doorway. His white apron was soaked through, and his hands were now bleached like Moldercay's. "Follow me, please."

Ravis and Tessa followed Crust from the kitchen. Just before Ravis stepped from the room, he turned to Moldercay and said, "You don't happen to recall where Ilfaylen and his scribe stayed while they were in Bay'Zell?"

Moldercay stopped in midstep, cloth and rubbing alcohol in hand. "Why, Castle Bess, I believe. King Hierac had just had the place built, and they stayed there with his blessing."

Tessa glared at Ravis, annoyed that after all the questions she had asked, he was the one who had finally uncovered something worthwhile.

Ravis smiled winningly, pretending not to notice Tessa's glance. "Thank you, Moldercay. You've been most helpful."

Crust guided them through the house in silence. Most of the tiny candles in the hallway had burned low. One or two had gone out. When Crust opened the door, wind and drizzle blew in Tessa's face. The idea of riding to Kilgrim turned her stomach. All she wanted to do was sleep. She was exhausted.

"Let's head back to the tavern," Ravis said as Crust closed the door behind them. "You're in no state to ride tonight."

Tessa wanted nothing more than to return to the tavern, wrap herself up in warm blankets, and fall asleep. It took all she had to shake her head. "No. We have to leave now. We've only got five full days. Even with a fast ship it'll take three to get to Bay'Zell."

Ravis looked at her without speaking. Tessa sent her last scrap of strength flashing into her eyes. She had responsibilities now. There was no running away.

After a long while Ravis nodded. "Very well," he said, turning to untie his horse's reins. "Let's get started. Camron will be expecting us in Bay'Zell."

THIRTY

he girl is still alive, sire." Ederius looked down at his hands. The middle and index fingers on his left had been bandaged above the knuckles with silk. Angeline couldn't tell if it had been done to protect against blisters or to cover ones that had already formed. He looked ill. Very ill. Yet Izgard seemed not to notice.

From her vantage point in the adjoining chamber, Angeline could see most of Izgard's quarters. She and Snowy had just been about to settle down for the night when she heard Ederius' voice filtering through the tent canvas. He had come to tell Izgard something, and from the tone of his voice, it was bad news.

"What else?" Izgard said, turning so his back was toward Angeline. "You haven't just come here to tell me that."

Angeline took a step nearer to the tent flap. Her own chamber was in darkness, but Izgard's was well lit. Lamp smoke floated through the slit in the canvas, making Angeline blink. Snowy was at her heels, legs bent, tail down, belly brushing the floor. He was stalking something, but Angeline wasn't sure what it was. It might have been the smoke.

"Easy, Snowy," she breathed. "No noise now."

Snowy pulled back his no-good head and frowned at his mistress.

Snowy insulted. Making no noise.

"Sire," said Ederius, still looking down at his hands, "my patterns make me uneasy. I fear the girl is a greater threat than we first thought. She carries a ring that is a match for the Coil."

"A match?" Izgard stepped forward. "What do you mean, a match?"

Ederius took a step back. "I have seen it, sire. It is cast from the same gold as the Coil and it mimics every twist and turn and barb."

Angeline didn't like the way Ederius sounded when he spoke. Surely his voice had once been a lot stronger than that? It was all the long days of traveling; that was it. Ever since the battle at Hook River, Izgard had made everyone ride from dawn to dusk each day. Long hours in the saddle, hasty camps, ill-prepared food, and little sleep were taking their toll on everyone. Angeline hated it. She wished with all her heart she had never left Sern Fortress. Izgard was heading for Bay'Zell, and judging from what she'd heard around the camp, there was going to be another terrible battle when he got there.

Frowning, Angeline turned her attention back to what was happening in the adjoining chamber. Ederius was speaking:

"I think they might try to destroy the Coil, sire."

"They? Who are *they*?"

"The girl and Ravis of Burano."

Izgard moved so quickly, Angeline saw him only as a blur. Swinging about, he sent his fist slamming into the camp table, setting charts rolling, papers jumping, and metal boxes full of pins and chalk jittering against the wood. "He is still with her? You told me he was gone. Said the girl had traveled to the abbey alone."

Ederius began to cough. Softly at first, but then as he tried to speak through the hail of coughing, spasms racked his chest, shaking his entire body. Spittle flew from his lips. A wet, frothy noise gurgled from his throat as he fought to control himself.

Angeline's first reaction was to go to him—he needed her. Yet as she put her hand on the edge of the canvas to push it back, Snowy growled: *Stay.*

Glancing from Snowy to Ederius to Izgard, Angeline hesitated. Her fingers brushed the canvas. Snowy's eyes narrowed. Angeline looked at the no-good dog a moment and then dropped her hand to her stomach. Snowy was right. Now wasn't a good time to annoy Izgard. Ever since Camron of Thorn had evacuated the town of Merin only hours before the Garizon army had planned to take it, Izgard had been as snappish as a hound on a hunt. Anything could set him off: a wrong word, an improper glance, an ill-timed intrusion into one of his private meetings.

On the other side of the tent flap, Ederius' coughing fit slowly began to subside. He held a white cloth to his face, and as his coughing ceased he folded it away.

Cupping her belly in her hand, Angeline breathed a sigh of relief. She had to learn to think before she acted. Ederius would not have welcomed her help—it would have meant trouble for both of them. He was just so ill, though, that was the problem, and no one else seemed to care.

Izgard was working him too hard. While the rest of the camp slept, Ederius would be at his desk, scribing through the night. Angeline knew because whenever morning sickness hit early, or hunger pangs stayed late, she'd peek out across the camp and check for Ederius' tent. Standing out amid the flickering yellow glow of watch fires and braziers would be the cool, steady burn of night oil. Ederius hadn't taken a full night's sleep in weeks.

"Drink it."

Angeline's attention was diverted by the sound of her husband's voice. She looked up in time to see Izgard handing Ederius a filled goblet. Angeline hoped it contained water, not wine. Wine was bad for people with coughs—everyone knew that. What Ederius really needed was her honey and almond-milk tea. Perhaps later she would send Gerta over with some.

Angeline's face crumpled in the darkness. Gerta wasn't here anymore. She was on her way across the mountains, guarded by two strange men who didn't care about her, sick and all alone. Angeline twisted her fingers into knots. Why couldn't she remember that one simple fact? Because she was stupid, that was why. She didn't think before she acted. Her brain was full of holes. Why, even a no-good dog like Snowy had more sense than she did.

"Now," Izgard said to Ederius. "Perhaps you would care to tell me where Ravis of Burano and the girl are?"

Angeline could no longer see Ederius, but she heard the sound of a cup being laid on the table, followed quickly by a muffled cough as the scribe cleared his throat. "I believe they are currently en route to Bay'Zell, sire. They should arrive a day ahead of us."

Izgard ran his hand across his cheek. "It fits. They will have arranged to meet Camron of Thorn there." Abruptly he turned to face the tent slit.

Angeline froze. Snowy bristled.

Izgard stared into the shadows behind the slit. Although he was staring directly at Angeline, right into the darkness surrounding her face, he seemed to be looking somewhere else entirely, somewhere beyond the room, the tent, the camp. His eyes dimmed.

After a moment he spoke: "All three want what is mine. Thorn would have my throne and my country, Burano would have my life, and the girl would have my crown. They cannot be allowed to continue. Bay'Zell must be taken, and swiftly. In three days' time the Barbed Coil turns five hundred years old, and I will have its power as my own."

Hearing Izgard's words, Angeline felt a cold weight form in her stomach. The skin on her hands and face stiffened, then cooled. It didn't feel like skin at all, more like tent canvas after a night of frost. At her heels, Snowy began to scratch at the mat beneath her feet.

"Ssh, now," Angeline mouthed, guessing that Snowy felt the same way she did: frightened, yet unable to express why. "It's all right."

Izgard chose that moment to spin around and face his scribe. His finger was up and pointing. "You and Gamberon were the ones who told me of its power. You both agreed I should take Bay'Zell five hundred years after its founding. Now you stand there and tell me you think some slip of a girl can take it from me. How can that be? You said the Barbed Coil could not be destroyed. Look what happened to Gamberon—he nearly died trying to crush it."

Stepping into Angeline's field of vision, Ederius spoke. His voice was still raw from coughing. "Sire, we know so little about the Coil. We know it is a powerful weapon of war, that Hierac feared losing it and commissioned an illumination to bind it to Garizon and its kings. We also know that it is inscribed with patterns that can alter a man's strength, his mind, even his body. Yet for the most part we use it blindly. I am not a great scholar like Gamberon. I need more time to—"

"Time." Izgard's jaw snapped as he spoke. "There *is* no time. In three days we arrive in Bay'Zell. Nothing can be allowed to interfere with its taking. Nothing. Sandor and his armies are of little consequence to me, Bay'Zell's defenses have been seen to. There is only one fortress in the entire city that stands a chance of holding out against me, and that fortress is Castle Bess. Garizon designed, Garizon built: it was shaped for foiling sieges. Now you tell me that Ravis of Burano and the girl who wants my crown are on their way there."

As he spoke, Izgard ran his hand along the tent pole, feeling for splinters or knots. Angeline knew her husband well enough by now to guess he was planning his next move. He liked to touch things when he was scheming.

Angeline suddenly wished she were in bed, fast asleep. She didn't want to hear what came next. Yet even as she sent her foot out behind her to check that the way back was clear, Izgard's head began to shake.

"We have no time for learning, my friend. I want them dead. All three of them. We will wait until they are together in Castle Bess and then destroy them. I will send out a troop of men tonight. They'll have the fastest horses in the camp, and orders to stop for neither man nor beast until they reach Bay'Zell. I hold the plans to Castle Bess. If the troop arrives in good time, there's a chance they can take the fortress by surprise. Thorn won't be expecting an attack so soon. Neither he nor Burano will guess we've sent a separate force ahead of the main army."

Izgard stepped toward Ederius. Angeline knew instinctively he would touch the scribe, and she was right. Reaching out with his hand, Izgard drew his index and middle fingers across Ederius' cheek. "And you, my friend," he said gently, almost lovingly, "will ensure they do not leave Castle Bess alive. I will send the men. You will send the Coil. Everything you have learned these past months must be drawn to defeat Burano and Thorn. Every pattern that can be used, must be used. Every creature that can be created from the raw flesh and bone of the troop must be sent to attack the fortress. We can take no chances. The Coil is mine, Garizon is mine, and revenge for past wrongdoings is long overdue."

Izgard's voice dropped low. His index finger burrowed into the scribe's cheek. "Burano had been on this earth twelve years too long. Because of him I no longer have a family to call my own, just a mindless child-wife and a sister long dead."

Although Izgard continued speaking, Angeline no longer listened. *A mindless child-wife.* She blinked, letting the words sink in. The world around her dimmed, growing colder and narrower like the walls of an underground tunnel. She felt trapped. Her bottom lip began to quiver. She was nothing to Izgard. Nothing. He had loved her once—he had said so on the day of their betrothment. Yet now he hated her.

Snowy, sensing a change in his mistress's mood, came and laid his head on her foot. Angeline knew she was supposed to look down and smile—as she normally would—but she didn't have the heart for it. She didn't feel like smiling. Father's words came out of nowhere to reprimand her: "That's what wide-eared girls get for listening at doors."

Angeline's chest hurt. The tunnel seemed to be closing in around her. Izgard hated her, Father was dead, Gerta had gone: she was completely alone.

Snowy picked that moment to issue a soft, doggy yawn. *Snowy here.*

Angeline nodded her head. She loved Snowy, but there was only so much a no-good dog could understand. Everything had changed. She no longer lived in a big, protected cocoon where nothing bad would ever happen to her because she was Izgard's wife and his queen. She lived in an armed camp, watched over by one man alone: her husband, who issued orders to kill people as easily as other men spoke of the weather—she had heard the truth of that tonight with her own wide ears. And now she knew what he really thought of her, it was easy to imagine other, more personal orders, on his lips.

Angeline felt a small, fluttering movement in her stomach. She thought it came from fear, but then as she waited it came again. It was her child growing inside. Her body was its protected cocoon, the only thing that kept it safe from the outside world.

Slowly Angeline began to back away from the tent slip, Snowy at her heels. Izgard continued to speak and touch and scheme, but she was no longer interested. Never again would she make the mistake of imagining Izgard loved her.

Without warning, Angeline's hand reached the ring from her bodice. She had so much, so much on her mind: something she had missed, some detail that would help her understand what

Tessa walked the decks of *The Mull*, designing patterns in her head. Every now and then she would stop by a masthead, a railing, or a flight of stairs, pull her ring out from under her bodice, and just stare at it. What had Ilfaylen painted on that parchment? How had he managed to bind the Barbed Coil? What designs had he used? What structures had he imposed? How did he know where to start and where to end?

Tessa sighed. For the eighth time in less than an hour, she tucked the ring back in its place. She had no answers. If only she had some idea of how Ilfaylen had carried out his task. Draw the problem, then solve it, Avaccus had said. Yet how could she draw it when she didn't even know what the problem looked like?

Feeling a telltale soreness in her back, Tessa headed for the nearest railing and leaned against it for support. Walking around the ship for a full afternoon had made her lungs ache.

She and Ravis had been on *The Mull* for two days. Tomorrow they would arrive in Bay'Zell. The journey so far had been a quiet one, and Tessa had used the time mostly to rest and rebuild her strength. *The Mull* was a fast ship, manned by efficient sailors dressed in sun-bleached linens who went about their work adjusting ropes and folding sails, never seeming to notice the dozens of passengers milling around the decks below them.

Tessa was glad to be left alone. She was getting better, but slowly. Things took her longer to do than before. She couldn't take a flight of stairs without resting halfway, and last night when she awoke in darkness, desperately needing to relieve herself, she had used the chamber pot in her cabin rather than take the short walk to the latrines. Ravis told her it would take weeks, even months, for her to recover her strength completely. Gritting her teeth, Tessa released her grip on the railings. She had no intention of letting it take that long.

Three days. That was all they had left. Izgard would arrive in Bay'Zell with his army, and the Barbed Coil would turn five hundred years old. Ravis was right: Izgard had planned it from the start.

Without conscious thought, Tessa pulled the ring from her bodice. She had to think. There must be something she had missed, some detail that could help her understand what she had to do. According to Avaccus, no copy of the illumination had ever been made; Ilfaylen had been searched every night to ensure that nothing was ever smuggled from the scriptorium. Even the parchment itself was checked for pinpricks. Yet Ilfaylen had obviously come to regret his work on the pattern. So why had he never tried to undo it? It made no sense. Tessa let the ring fall against her chest. She felt as if she were grasping at moths in the dark.

Choosing a path along the sunlit port side of the ship, Tessa began replaying Avaccus' words in her head, trying to recall everything he had said to her during the one day they'd spent together in the cave.

The smell of lemon oil and wax rose up from the sun-warmed deck, and all around her timbers creaked and strained as the ship rode wave after wave. On a bright, cloudless day like this, it was easy to believe other worlds and other places existed. The idea of ephemeras seemed somehow less shocking. Surely they were all ephemeras, each and every one of them. They lived and died and were gone. Perhaps they were reborn in another time and another place. Perhaps not. Tessa didn't know. One thing was certain though: just like ephemeras, people could make things change.

Tessa stopped in her tracks. *She* could make things change. Avaccus had hinted as much to her in the cave. *Trust yourself,* he had said. The words were close to his last. Turning about, Tessa headed back toward the main hatch. She needed to find Ravis.

Sailors moved high above her, shinnying up knotted ropes, leaping in and out of rigging nets, turning sails, and securing lines. As Tessa stepped from the shadow of a newly dropped sail, she spied Ravis emerging from belowdecks. Just as she was about to call his name, someone stopped to speak to him.

It was a woman in black, and for one awful moment Tessa thought it was Violante of Arazzo. Then the woman turned and Tessa got a clear view of her; she had neither Violante's height nor her fine chiseled features. Tessa let out a relieved breath. It was one of the passengers who had sailed over with them on *Tarrier*. The woman with the veil that only barely covered her eyebrows.

As Tessa looked on, the woman ran a hand over her veil and laughed. When Ravis laughed in response, she reached out and touched his arm. She was flirting with him! Heat rushing to her cheeks, Tessa dashed forward. She had stood by and let one woman lead Ravis away from her, and she wasn't about to let it happen again.

Ravis saw Tessa coming, but the veiled woman did not. She continued laughing in a way that caused her chest to rise and fall conspicuously, all the while sending her hands darting into the space that separated her from Ravis. Tessa didn't stop to think, she simply came to a halt alongside Ravis and very firmly put her arm through his.

"There you are," she said to him, not even sparing a glance for the veiled woman. "I've been looking for you since midday." Then, pretending to notice the veiled woman for the first time: "Oh, I'm sorry. Am I interrupting anything?"

The veiled woman regarded Tessa coolly. She was attractive in a well-groomed, expensive way. Her veil was made from fine lace embroidery, and it fluttered about her face as she spoke. "No, not at all. I was just inquiring as to when we might dock in Bay'Zell."

"Aah. You'll need to speak with the captain, then." Tessa edged a fraction nearer to Ravis. "I just passed him on the quarterdeck. If you hurry, there's a chance you can catch up with him before he retires for the night."

The woman pinched her lips together. Her face was heavily powdered, and specks of fine oyster-colored dust caught in her veil. "Well," she said, ignoring Tessa completely and speaking only to Ravis, "I'll be on my way, then. Good night, sir. I trust I'll see you again before the journey ends." Bowing with irritating slowness, she managed to reveal a great deal of cleavage before turning and walking away.

As soon as she was out of earshot, Ravis pulled himself free of Tessa, folded his arms over his chest, threw back his head, and laughed.

It was the most irritating sound Tessa had ever heard in her life. "Come on," she said sharply. "Don't just stand there laughing. Help me back to the cabin. I've spent the best part of the afternoon on deck." For some reason Tessa found herself blushing while she spoke.

Ravis stopped laughing, but his eyes didn't. Inclining his head in the direction the veiled woman had taken, he said, "That was, without a doubt, the most efficient dismissal I have ever had the pleasure of being witness to. Obviously where you come from women are taught to deal swiftly with their rivals. I dread to think what might have become of the poor woman if you'd actually caught her kissing me." He pretended to shudder. "Doubtless the deckhands would be mopping up the blood as we speak."

Tessa tried very hard to frown, but Ravis' eyes twinkled brightly, encouraging her to smile. "Just help me down the steps," she said as sternly as she could manage.

Bowing, Ravis came forward and took her arm. His kid leather gloves were as warm and smooth as skin. With no effort at all he shouldered half of her weight. "I was about to come looking for you," he said. "We need to talk about what we're going to do when we get to Bay'Zell."

Tessa nodded, glad of the change of subject. "I need time. I have to find out what Ilfaylen's original pattern looked like: what the main elements were, what designs he chose, what pigments he used. Otherwise I might as well sit down and paint a landscape in the dark. I need to have something to work from."

Reaching the bottom of the stairs, Ravis guided Tessa toward his cabin. "How much time do you need?"

Tessa shrugged. "Too much, probably. Emith might be able to help me, or perhaps there's something in Deveric's papers that might offer a clue. I don't know. If I hadn't let—" She shook her head, corrected herself. "If Avaccus were still alive, I could ask him how to draw patterns to gain knowledge, and actually search for Ilfaylen's illumination myself." Frustrated, she ran a hand over her face. "Given enough time, I can work things out on my own—I'm sure of it. That's what I was brought here for."

Tessa let herself be led into the warm, timber-scented darkness of Ravis' cabin. Unlike on *Tarrier*, here they had separate cabins. Ravis had insisted she get as much undisturbed rest as possible.

Striking a flint, Ravis lit an amber-colored candle and placed it on one of the crossbeams bracing the walls. Its golden light lit up a room that had been laid out with a soldier's sparseness and sense of order. Tessa recognized all the medicines Ravis gave her each day, arranged by size and type on a banded shelf above the bunk. Seeing them there like that, the only items on a shelf designed to hold much more, made Tessa feel sad, but she didn't know why.

Sitting on the bunk, she brought her hands together on her lap. Now that she had finally stopped moving, strength drained from her body, leaving her feeling shaky and overly conscious of the breath in her lungs. After looking at Ravis a moment, she said, "I think we are all ephemeras. You, me, Camron. All three of us were drawn to Bay'Zell. You and Camron were forced to stay in the city, I was pulled there from another place, and somehow we came together." Tessa felt for the hardness of her ring beneath her bodice. "I think it's because we can make things change."

Ravis regarded her carefully. "For twenty-one years I have been unable to change anyone or anything, even myself."

Tessa's hand hovered away from the ring and toward Ravis. She went to speak but caught herself. Twenty-one years. The skin of her scalp pulled tight. Deep inside her chest, close to her heart, a muscle ticked away like a clock. There was a pattern here.

"Twenty-one years ago?" she said. "That was when your father died?"

Ravis nodded.

"And seven years later your brother sent you off his land?"

"Land we fought side by side for." A trace of bitterness crept into his voice. "He told me I was a fighter and should go away and fight."

"Did anything happen to you"—Tessa made a quick calculation—"two years later? In summer?"

Ravis' whole body stilled. There was no other word for it: the muscles on his face hardened and set, his chest stopped rising and falling, letting the hollow dip in his throat collect shadows. Slowly his eyes darkened from brown to black. After what seemed like many minutes, he spoke. "My wife died two summers after Malray turned on me."

Tessa was disturbed by his bluntness. "I'm sorry. I—"

"Don't be sorry," he said, cutting her short. "Ask your questions, make your point; we haven't got time for the past."

Feeling the words like a physical blow, Tessa took a breath to steady herself. There was so much she didn't know or understand about Ravis. They were strangers, really. It was easy to forget that.

With Ravis' gaze pressuring her to move on, Tessa asked her final question. Only it wasn't really a question at all, as she had already guessed the answer. "Something happened five years after your wife's death, didn't it? In autumn? Something important?"

Ravis' tooth came down upon his scar. "I returned from the east in late autumn. The day I set foot on Drokho soil, Malray sent out his henchmen to kill me."

Tessa dropped her gaze to her hands. She couldn't look at him. The anger in his voice covered only so much. "Twenty-one years," she said softly, knowing it was better to speak than let the silence be. "Twenty-one years. Five patterns. Mine wasn't the only life Deveric manipulated. Yours was too."

"Meaning?"

"Meaning that both of us have been held back. You said it yourself—for twenty-one years you haven't been able to change anyone or anything. Nor have I." Tessa risked looking up. She was surprised to see interest on Ravis' face. "Up until now, until that day I met you in the alleyway, I was never able to be myself. Not properly. It was as if someone had a hand on my back and was directing every move I made."

Ravis stripped off his gloves and ran a hand through his hair. He looked tired, and for the first time Tessa wondered when and for how long he slept. He was always awake when she needed him.

"The dates on Deveric's patterns correspond to events in both our lives?" he asked.

"Yes. We're both caught up in something—a pattern, a plot. Fate."

"And you say we can make things change?"

Tessa nodded. "I believe that's why we're here now, together. And why Camron of Thorn waits for us in Bay'Zell."

"And what of you and me, Tessa McCamfrey? Can we change ourselves too?"

"We can try."

Ravis smiled then, slowly, allowing it time to reach his eyes. "You're very beautiful, you know."

"So was the woman with the veil."

"What woman? What veil?" Ravis was no longer smiling. He caught Tessa's gaze and held it. "I saw no one on the deck today, only you."

Tessa opened her arms and let Ravis come to her. He moved swiftly and silently, as if he had been waiting for such an invitation all along. Kneeling at the foot of the bed, he drew Tessa to his chest and held her tight. He didn't kiss her, just pressed her body to his as if she were something he needed to keep him warm, or safe, or both. Tessa held him. She ran a hand through his hair and down his cheek. Touching him seemed like an incredible luxury. She couldn't believe she had been granted the right to do it.

He smelled good, clean and fragrant and slightly foreign. The skin on his neck was rough, prickly, and Tessa rubbed her open palm against it, feeling as much as she could. Lying in his arms, pushed against his chest, touching his face and neck, she felt as if she were giving him something, yet she couldn't understand what.

Time passed, timbers creaked, the candle formed a stalactite of wax beneath the beam. Hands pressed into her shoulder and back, Ravis held Tessa fast against his chest. When finally their breaths drew shallow and their limbs cooled and the motion of the ship lulled them into a dreamy half sleep, they pulled apart.

Ravis caught Tessa by the shoulders and looked into her face. "You need to rest," he said. "I'll watch over you while you sleep."

Tessa shook her head. "No. Don't watch over me, come and lie alongside me instead." As she spoke, she moved back onto the bunk, bringing up her legs and making room for Ravis. "We both need to rest."

Ravis went to say something, then stopped himself. In silence he pulled off his boots and then moved across the cabin to the candle. As his fingers closed around the flame, Tessa looked at him one last time. His hair was damp with sweat, and his scar seemed almost white. The imprint of her body on his kid leather tunic was the last thing she saw before he snuffed out the light.

Tessa fell asleep the moment Ravis' body settled next to hers. She dreamed of patterns and other things: Moldercay and his charnel house, the woman with the embroidered veil, and the impression of her body on Ravis' kid leather tunic.

In the morning when she woke, she found Ravis still asleep beside her. Moving quietly so as not to wake him, Tessa rose from the bunk, smoothed down her skirts, brushed back her hair, and let herself out of the cabin. After stopping to relieve herself in the latrines, she made her way above deck.

Dawn had washed *The Mull* with silvery light. No one was about except an old seaman braiding a rope and a cabin boy waxing the deck. Tessa passed both without saying a word. When she reached the foredeck, she leaned over the railings, looked out across the prow, and searched for signs of land in the distance. After a moment or two, she spied a jagged line on the horizon. Bay'Zell. Seeing it, she felt the wall of muscle around her chest tighten. Her whole life had been leading to this.

As she watched the city grow larger, Tessa replayed her dreams in her head. After a while she turned from the railings and headed back belowdecks. Avaccus and Moldercay were wrong: Ilfaylen *had* made a copy of his illumination, and she knew how.

THIRTY-ONE

t took them three hours to disembark the ship. Armed guards searched *The Mull* from prow to stern. Local Bay'Zell militia lined the wharf, opening trunks, firing questions at passengers, frisking anyone they didn't like the look of.

Ravis was detained for an hour. The militia didn't like the look of him one bit. He was a foreigner, they said. He had one too many knives in his pack. He claimed to have been out of the city for only eighteen days, yet he had no outward-bound shipping documents to prove his claim. In the end Ravis had to send for a local sea captain to vouch for him. The man, a red-faced, eyebrowless fisherman named Pegruff, had not been quick in coming. Yet when he finally sauntered onto the wharf, arlo flask in hand, rope looped around his neck as if he'd come prepared for a hanging, it took him less than five minutes to secure Ravis' release. A few words, a knowing laugh, and the arlo flask passed from hand to hand was all it had taken for the militia to let Ravis go.

Ravis didn't thank Pegruff for the favor. He said the man had owed him and this now discharged the debt.

Pegruff didn't wait around long. After rubbing the rim of his flask against his sleeve to clean it, he handed the arlo to Tessa and said, "You two best watch yourselves from now on. Militia's as jumpy as mackerel in a net. They know Izgard's coming, and they think that by closing down the harbor, patrolling the streets, imposing curfews, and terrorizing every foreigner they come across, that somehow they can keep him at bay. Scared, they are. Though you'll never get a one to admit it."

Ravis nodded. He took the arlo flask from Tessa, drank,

then handed it back to Pegruff. "How long before Izgard arrives?"

"A day. Mebbe two."

"And the Sire?"

Pegruff spat on his flask. "Word on the street is he'll arrive half a day before Izgard."

"And word on the sea?"

"That he'll come a day too late." With that Pegruff took his leave. He asked no questions and offered no farewell, simply spit-polished his flask and walked away.

Ravis turned to Tessa. "Let's go and pick up Emith and his mother."

Tessa shook her head. "You won't be able to get Mother Emith out of her chair. She won't budge—even for Izgard."

"Then I'll hire a cart and pick her up, chair and all. For I tell you now, Emith won't agree to come with us without his mother."

Tessa nodded. Ravis was right. Bay'Zell was too dangerous a place at the moment. Izgard's army could be here any day now, and Emith would never leave his mother alone and afraid. She was all he had. Tessa picked up her pace. She couldn't wait to get back.

Walking quickly, but not so quickly as to attract the attention of the militia, Ravis and Tessa made their way across town. Bay'Zell was a different city from the one they had left eighteen days earlier. No longer brash, busy, and self-absorbed, it cowered like a child awaiting punishment. Shops were open, but only those that sold household items and dried goods had any wares. Fresh food was already in short supply, and when one unfortunate fruit seller wheeled his barrow into the street to set up shop, he was mobbed before he had chance to pin back the awnings on his stall. By the time the militia came in to break up the riot, the fruit seller had been robbed of all his wares. Peaches, plums, and other soft fruits had been stamped into mud at his feet.

Ravis guided Tessa away from the scene. "It's the militia's fault," he said. "I've seen it happen a dozen times before. Armed men on the streets can cause more panic than an entire invading army. Bay'Zell should have access to enough fresh food to live out a six-month siege, but now with people hoarding, most of it will go to waste. A man can grab as many freshly killed chickens as he can carry, but if he doesn't cook and eat them within two days, he'll end up throwing them away." Ravis squinted into the midday sun. "Especially at this time of year."

For the most part the streets of Bay'Zell were quiet. People looked out from half-shuttered windows, stood trading whispers in doorways, or walked alone in the middle of the road, wheeling carts or dragging bedding behind them.

Tessa didn't like any of it. She felt as if the entire city of Bay'Zell were condemned.

Her spirits picked up when they turned into a narrow, paved street. Looking ahead, spying the neat, blue-and-white facade of Mother Emith's house, Tessa swallowed hard. She felt as if she were coming home.

Despite Ravis' protests, she ran the last hundred paces. All her life she had been moving forward toward the ring; this was the first time she had come back.

In her mind, she could already see Mother Emith's face, see her chair and her table, hear her instructing Emith to tap another keg, *We have guests*. Tessa smiled a mad, happy smile. She had missed them both so much.

Catching Ravis' hand in hers, she dashed across the road toward the house. Ignoring the front door, she opened the side gate and let herself into the courtyard at the back. Everything was the same as normal: the hides soaking in lye, the kegs of arlo in the corner, the pile of pots and pans near the drain. Even the ash fire was burning. All the little details left Tessa feeling relieved. Nothing had changed.

Ignoring Ravis' plea for caution, she rapped firmly on the door. "Emith. It's me," she called. "Tessa. I'm back."

There was no reply at first. Ravis' hand crept to the hilt of his blade as they waited. Just as Tessa was about to knock a second time, the door swung open. Emith stood in the threshold, looking as neat and well groomed as ever.

His eyes were dead.

Tessa's heart stopped. All the heat left her face. "Emith." She meant to say more, but her voice failed her.

Emith smiled. "Yes, miss. It's good to have you back." He sounded like a dead thing. There was no inflection in his voice. Standing back from the doorway, he said, "Come in. I've just put a pot of tea on the hearth."

Ravis put a hand on Tessa's arm. She shook it off and followed Emith into the house. Every hair on her body prickled like a cold spike. Her stomach contracted in sharp, jabbing punches. As her eyes grew accustomed to the dim light of the kitchen, she had to bite the inside of her mouth to stop herself from retching.

The kitchen was just as she remembered. The hearth burned brightly and was loaded with pots, the kitchen table was scattered with cooking utensils and spices, and Mother Emith's stool was laid with her usual things: paring knife, silver scissors, embroidery bag, and spice boxes. There was even a plate of apples waiting to be peeled.

Mother Emith's chair was facing the outside wall, as it normally did in early afternoon, and when Tessa failed to see the back of the old lady's head peeking up from it, she shot a quick glance at Emith. He was looking down. Throat aching with dryness, Tessa took the few steps needed to bring her in front of Mother Emith's chair.

It was empty. She had known it from the moment she had entered the kitchen, the instant Emith had opened the door. His eyes had told her everything. She just hadn't wanted to believe them. Mother Emith was gone.

Turning back to face Emith, Tessa waited for him to look up. But he didn't. To look up meant seeing everything for what it was, and judging from the carefully tended appearance of the kitchen, he had spent several days avoiding just that. Everything was laid out as if his mother were still here.

Finally, slowly, the force of Tessa's stare drew his gaze. Looking up, he revealed eyes blank with pain. A muscle in his throat quivered. After a moment he began to shake his head. "She's gone, miss. I went to fetch lobster, and when I came back, she was gone." He made a small, helpless gesture with his hand. "They hurt her. Scared her."

Tessa felt herself swaying. "Who hurt her, Emith?"

"I don't know. They left a smell—like wounded animals."

Ravis hissed. Tessa grabbed the back of Mother Emith's chair for support. Izgard's harras. They had come looking for her.

Tessa closed her eyes. When she opened them a moment later she found herself staring straight into Emith's face. Some deep, deep part of him had gone. He looked lost. The world, which to him had always been filled with people who were either wholly good or just a bit misunderstood, was suddenly a place he no longer knew.

Tessa went to him. Knowing he was too timid for hugs, she slipped her arm through his and led him toward the hearth. There was an awkward moment at first when he shied away from her, but Tessa wouldn't let him go. She couldn't bear to think of what had happened, couldn't trust herself to speak, but at least she could hold him. And be held herself.

Camron stood high on the battlements of Castle Bess and waited. He was exhausted, but the idea of sleep seemed ludicrous to him. It was a luxury he didn't deserve.

As he looked out toward the west and the city of Bay'Zell, the sun dipped toward the horizon, creating layers of orange and purple light. Shadows lengthened, a breeze picked up, and the first of the night's stars twinkled to life. Camron took one deep breath and then another. He knew he should go downstairs to the great hall, see his men, issue orders, arrange defenses, listen to the latest intelligence on Izgard's position. But he couldn't bring himself to do any of it. Not yet.

It was the fault of Castle Bess.

He had thought he could just return and defend it. He hadn't counted on its memories: on the bloodstain on the stair, or the arrow nicks in the study door, or the sheer emptiness of its corridors. The place was darker than he remembered. And so quiet he could hear the past.

He couldn't bear to be in it. His father was everywhere, nowhere. Time stretched so that it took an eternity to pass through the guardroom, where a dozen men had died, then shrank to a pinhead whenever he stopped to think. Losing himself on a ghost of a memory, he would look up to see a nearby candle had burned down a full mark while he blinked.

They had arrived late the night before, so late it was daylight before the fires and ovens were lit. Water had been drawn from the well, supplies had been sent for, and all the horses had been brushed out and boxed. Most of the twenty men who had ridden with him from Hook River had slept throughout the day and were only now awakening. Camron didn't begrudge them rest. The past week had been hard on everyone.

Merin, Shale, and a score of other towns, villages, and hamlets along Izgard's path had been cleared. It was thankless work. There were no good sides to it, only bad. Loath to leave their homes, livestock, and fields, people were hostile to Camron's troop, somehow managing to blame them for Izgard's approach. The worst thing to Camron was that his men accepted the blame. They felt guilty about surviving a battle where so many of their comrades had died. Camron hadn't known how to deal with this, so he let his men be.

Truth was he didn't know how to deal with anything. Ever since the night his father died and Izgard of Garizon had crowned himself king, his beliefs had caved in one by one. He was sure of nothing anymore.

Turning about to face the darker sky of the east and then the southeast, Camron tugged a hand through his hair. His lips formed a grim smile. He remembered the day when he'd first met Ravis of Burano in Marcel of Vailing's wine cellar. Everything had been black and white then: his father was dead and someone had to pay, and Garizon was an enemy that needed to be crushed. Nothing was as simple as that anymore. His father had spent twenty-one years dreaming of the day his son would take the Garizon throne. Which meant that Garizon troops were no longer his enemies, they were his countrymen. Camron shook his head. He didn't know if he wanted any of it.

The only thing he did know was that another massacre like the ones at Mount Creed and Hook River had to be prevented at all costs. Both he and his father agreed on that. Finally.

Finding some unexpected comfort in that thought, Camron pushed himself off from the battlements and headed toward the iron gate that led to the interior of the fortress. He had things to do, defenses to prepare, and as he descended the granite steps of Castle Bess he prayed the ghosts would leave him alone long enough to get started.

Emith checked one last time that the back door was locked and then followed Tessa to the front of the house. It was dark now, and Tessa could barely see the cobbles beneath her feet. A quarter moon hung low in the sky, giving off a thin blade of yellow light. Even though it was not cold, every shutter on Emith's street was shut and bolted.

Ravis waited in the road with a filly and two ponies. He had slipped out an hour earlier, returning with horses, supplies, and various items Emith had requested for scribing. Catching sight of Emith and Tessa, he came forward and took the heavy bags from their hands. Within minutes everything was packed, strapped, and ready. They were on their way to Castle Bess.

It had been hard to talk in the house, so Tessa had said very little to Emith about her trip to the Anointed Isle. She had told him she needed his help to paint a pattern and that he should gather together all the parchment, pigments, and brushes he could find and prepare himself for a short journey. Emith seemed glad of something to do. It wasn't his way to ask questions, and he set about his tasks with quiet efficiency, pausing every now and then to run through lists in his head or recite the names of pigments he especially didn't want to forget.

When it came to choosing parchment, Tessa had asked that he bring only uterine vellum. She could not imagine Ilfaylen painting the pattern that bound the Barbed Coil on anything else. Emith had a dozen sheets of calfskin left over from his time with Deveric—they were a little stiff, but handling would soften them—and he placed these in a press to keep them flat during the ride out of Bay'Zell.

The city was quiet as they rode through it. Occasionally dark figures flitted in and out of the shadows, but no one besides their small party walked openly in the road.

"Militia's closed the gates," Ravis said, guiding his horse

away from a thick patch of shadow. Although he looked as calm as could be, Tessa could tell he was wary. His right hand rested on the hilt of his knife. "It won't do them any good, though. This city was never built to be defended at close range. Its walls are old and tumbled down. They have so many gaps and weaknesses that even a determined band of wandering minstrels could break their way through.

"The Sire should have got here a week earlier, manned all the old fortresses around the city, and forced Izgard to engage there, not in Bay'Zell itself. As it is now, the first thing Izgard will do when he gets here is move to take over the fortresses. There's a couple being defended by the militia, but Izgard will have them ousted in no time; most of them are Garizon built anyway, so his engineers will know them through and through." Ravis made a hard sound in his throat. "Bay'Zell is a sitting target."

Tessa glanced over at Emith, concerned about how Ravis' words would affect him. She was accustomed to Ravis and his cool military-type assessments of situations, but the place he had just dismissed as undefendable was Emith's home. Emith met Tessa's eyes and smiled weakly. After a moment he looked down.

Hearing Ravis gathering breath for another pronouncement, Tessa spoke to head him off. She didn't want Emith any more upset than he already was. "Castle Bess is the strongest fortress for miles, though, isn't it? Hierac built it to be his command post in Bay'Zell."

Ravis turned his head and looked at Tessa a moment. Nodding softly to her before he spoke, he said, "Yes. It's the finest fortress in the city. We'll be safe once we're there." Tessa knew he didn't believe what he said, but he sounded as if he did, and she was grateful for that.

"What do you know about transcribing manuscripts, Emith?" she said, changing the subject before Ravis had chance to broach another of his own. "Did the old scribes ever use any other methods besides pricking holes in the parchment to make copies?"

Emith moved alongside Tessa. Surprisingly, he rode well, and his pony seemed eager to his bidding. "Let me see, miss. . . . There's measuring and ruling, of course, and taking notes and rough sketches, but those two methods take more time and effort than simply pricking the underlying parchment and then using the pinpricks as a guide."

Tessa nodded. According to Avaccus, Ilfaylen had been searched every night for parchment and written notes—he hadn't even been allowed to take quill and ink to his chamber—so anything involving writing notes or sketching was out of the question. Briefly Tessa thought back to the woman on *The Mull*, recalling the way her face powder had caught in the elaborate embroidery of her veil. "What about pounce, Emith?" she asked. "Can it be used to transfer patterns?"

Emith made an interested noise and then thought for a minute. "Well, miss, I think perhaps a long time ago it was. I read about it once. In ancient times, well before the abbey on the Anointed Isle was built, even before the art of scribing was brought to the west by eastern mystics, scribes used to grind obsidian so finely that it could settle in the shallowest ridges left by the finest sablehair brushes."

Excited, Tessa nodded. "And they spread this onto the finished pattern?"

"Yes." Emith gave Tessa a curious look. "Once the pattern is covered with powder, the entire thing is shaken lightly to give the powder chance to settle into the depressions created by the paint. When that's done, a second sheet of parchment is prepared with casein, so the powder will adhere to it. This new parchment is laid over the original, pressed against it firmly for some minutes, and then removed. If done correctly, the original pattern is re-created in its entirety on the second sheet of parchment."

"Like Widow Furbish's embroidery pounces," Tessa said under her breath. Seeing Emith's puzzled look, she said, "It's how her embroidery patterns were copied. I upset a whole tray of them once and got covered in dark powder. I thought it was dust at the time." She shook her head. "The powder creates a negative impression on whatever is laid across it."

"Dust? Powder? What are you saying?" It was Ravis. Although he was now a good few paces ahead of her, his voice carried well, and Tessa realized he had been listening to everything she and Emith had said.

Tessa took a quick breath, then steadied herself in the

saddle. "I think Ilfaylen did make a copy of his pattern, and I think he used pounce to do it with."

Ravis made an noncommittal noise in his throat. He pulled on his reins, slowing his horse as they entered a dark courtyard closed in by high buildings. Taking his lead from Ravis' mare, Tessa's pony slowed without prompting.

"Remember the woman aboard *The Mull*?" Tessa said. "The one with the embroidered veil?"

Ravis turned and threw Tessa a smile. "No."

Tessa felt her cheeks heating up. She couldn't help but return his smile. "Well, there *was* a woman with a veil aboard *The Mull,* and she had face powder on her cheeks, and when she spoke it rubbed off on her veil. I didn't think much of it at the time, but later it got me thinking. It reminded me of that morning I met you on Parso Bridge when I was covered in powder. Widow Furbish used it to make copies of her embroidery patterns—there's no ink, measuring, writing, note taking or pinpricking involved. You just need powder and something to transfer the image on to."

"But didn't Avaccus say that Ilfaylen was searched every night? Surely Hierac's guards would have found any sheet of parchment he tried to conceal?"

Tessa glanced at Emith. He was looking puzzled, not really understanding what they were talking about, yet too polite to ask any questions. She would tell him everything about Avaccus and Ilfaylen later. To tell the full story now would only hurt him more: another person he had known and loved was dead. Wanting to touch him, yet knowing he would only shy away from her, Tessa patted his pony instead.

To Ravis she said, "What if Ilfaylen hadn't used parchment to make the copy? What if he had used something else? Something that even the guards wouldn't have given a passing glance to?"

"Such as?"

"Remember what Moldercay said about Ilfaylen? He said that the day the pattern was complete, Ilfaylen fell sick and asked for a shawl. What if he had used that shawl instead of parchment, transferring the powder image onto the fabric? It would work, wouldn't it, Emith?"

"Yes, miss," Emith said, a trace of eagerness creeping

into his voice, "providing the shawl had been prepared with casein first and was rolled and handled carefully afterward. A little of the detail might be lost, but the greater part of the pattern would surely be identifiable."

Tessa had to resist the urge to lean over and kiss him. "Yes, that's what I thought. Perhaps Ilfaylen asked for the shawl, wore it all day long, used it to take a copy of the pattern the moment the paint was dry, and then simply carried it out of the scriptorium when he was finished, claiming he was suddenly hot?"

"What about the pounce?" Ravis said, unconvinced. "How would he smuggle that in?"

Tessa was ready for this one. "It wouldn't have to be smuggled. It's fine black powder . . . Ilfaylen could have passed it off as pigment. All he needed was five minutes alone with the pattern to apply and shake down the powder, then take the copy. Even Avaccus said Ilfaylen was allowed a certain amount of privacy while he was scribing."

As she spoke, Tessa guided her pony up a series of low steps that led toward the city wall. Despite the cutting remarks Ravis had made about it earlier, Bay'Zell's outer wall looked tall and imposing enough to her. She didn't waste a minute worrying about how they were going to get through it, though. Ravis would either know the gatekeeper, be owed a debt by his son, or have some other acquaintance waiting to lead them to a secret gate. A smile began at the corner of her mouth. Ravis' way of handling things suddenly seemed very endearing to her.

"How can you be sure of any of this?" Ravis' voice got lower the nearer they drew to the wall. "Who's to say Ilfaylen's shawl wasn't just that—something to warm his bony old shoulders?"

Tessa made an impatient gesture with her hands. Details itched against her skin like ground glass. "Moldercay said something that started me thinking. At first I thought it was a mistake and just excused it, but it stayed in my mind. And the other night after you and I"—Tessa stopped herself, glanced at Emith—"finished talking on *The Mull,* it niggled away at me. I even dreamt about it. Moldercay said the vellum was bleached, scrubbed, painted, glazed, *then* pounced."

Emith looked up, understanding instantly what she said. "Pouncing is always done first to the vellum, miss, to prepare it to take the ink. If it was done after the pattern was painted and glazed, it would scrub the paint clean off."

"Yes," said Tessa. "That's it. I think Ilfaylen purposely dictated the list of vellum treatments to his scribe, making sure that pounce was itemized last. To anyone looking at the manuscript later, it would appear to be nothing more than a simple clerical error. Yet to those looking for a clue about the pattern itself, it would be a signpost in the dark. Ilfaylen even made sure that his assistant didn't have to lie about what was done. The scribe's account states nothing but the truth: the pattern *was* pounced last. It was dusted with fine powder"— Tessa sent a gentle smile Emith's way—"and, Emith, you were the one who told me that any finely ground powder is called a pounce."

Emith smiled back. "Yes, miss. I believe I did."

Seeing Emith smile made a lump form in Tessa's throat. He had lost so much, yet here he was, encouraging and helping her. She didn't deserve it.

"So," Ravis said, pulling the reins on his horse and bringing it to a halt, "assuming you're right and Ilfaylen did take some kind of copy of the pattern, what did he do then?"

"He traveled to Castle Bess, where he painted a proper copy from the outline on his shawl."

Ravis whistled. "You've thought of everything, haven't you?"

Tessa inclined her head. "I try to."

Inclining his own head in return, Ravis said, "Well, that would explain why Ilfaylen, sick and supposedly in need of care, sent his assistant into Bay'Zell every day to take notes. He didn't want the man knowing he was painting a second pattern."

Tessa nodded. "I think Ilfaylen made his entire illness up. Like you said, it gave him privacy, but it also gave him time. He knew he would never be able to paint a copy of the pattern on the Anointed Isle, so he gave himself an excuse to stay in Bay'Zell for a few extra days to complete it."

"While the original was still fresh in his mind, miss." Emith deftly pulled his own pony to a halt. "Working from an outline of a pattern is one thing, but unless you can recall the exact colors used in the original, you can expect to create an inexact copy at best."

Hearing Emith speak, Tessa was reminded of Avaccus' words: *"Emith is a modest man, you must not forget that. If it wasn't for his modesty, he would have become a brilliant scribe."* "Yes," she said out loud. "I hadn't thought of that."

Emith looked down. "You would have sooner or later, miss."

Ravis swung down from his horse, landing with a small thud on the hard earth surrounding the wall. "So, where do you think this pattern is now? Did Ilfaylen carry it back to the Anointed Isle? Did he send it to someone for safekeeping, or simply dig a hole and bury it?"

Following Ravis' lead, Tessa dismounted. Her legs betrayed her by buckling as she hit the ground. Cursing to herself, she worked quickly to lock her knees together before Ravis noticed. Taking a few light breaths to steady herself, she said, "I don't think Ilfaylen would have taken the pattern to the Anointed Isle. If it was found there, the holy fathers would have destroyed it. No. I think he put the pattern somewhere for safekeeping."

"Castle Bess?" Ravis took the pony's reins from her, managing to brush his hand against her cheek as he did so. Their eyes met for a moment, and Tessa knew her weakness had not gone unseen.

"Perhaps," she said, pulling away from him, conscious of Emith approaching her from behind. "If not, there may be some clue there, some record of Ilfaylen's comings and goings; what visitors he received, what orders he gave to the servants. Something."

Tessa felt another hand touch her shoulder from behind. It was Emith this time, pulling her cloak over her shoulders where it had fallen away during the ride. Could she conceal nothing from these two?

With two pairs of reins in hand, Ravis began to walk up the packed-earth incline to the wall. "Watch your footing," he warned. "There's all sorts of loose bricks and refuse ahead."

Tessa was glad to have both hands free. The wall blocked off the moonlight, making it difficult to see anything except the dull shine of the horse's tack and the handle of Ravis' knife. The air smelled of damp and decay, and as they drew nearer the wall, the ground dipped into a dank trench, giving Tessa the feeling that she was walking through a giant hollow left by an overturned stone.

A gap in the wall appeared ahead. At first Tessa thought it was just a narrow strip, but as she drew closer and her eyes grew more accustomed to the darkness, she realized an entire section of the wall was missing. Stone slabs formed jagged heaps to either side of the trench, and a sharp breeze cut through the opening in the wall. She noticed that the edges of the surrounding bricks were still sharp, the mortar barely discolored, and the exposed inner surface of the wall free of moss and damp.

Glancing over her shoulder, Tessa checked Emith's position. Satisfied that he wasn't close enough to overhear what she had to say, she touched Ravis' arm and whispered, "This isn't one of those tumbled-down weak points you mentioned earlier. The whole section's been newly dismantled—all the inside edges of the bricks are clean. I doubt if it's been like this since spring."

Even in the shadowy darkness close to the wall, Tessa clearly saw Ravis' tooth come down on his scar. "Quite the one for noticing details, aren't you?"

Tessa blinked. She was surprised by Ravis' sharpness, but then as she looked into his eyes, saw just how black they were, she began to understand. "You did this?"

Ravis shot a quick glance at Emith. Bringing his mouth close to Tessa's ear, he said, "Yes. I ordered this section and others like it to be destroyed." Before she could react, he took a breath and spoke again. "Never forget I am a mercenary, Tessa. I was in Izgard's pay for three years. My job was to do what was needed. When Izgard wanted extra troops to swell his numbers, I came to Bay'Zell to recruit men in his name. Later, when Izgard hinted at his plans to invade the city, I took the necessary steps to guarantee him ease of entry."

Tessa opened her mouth but found she couldn't speak. Unable to meet Ravis' eye any longer, she looked down at the angry red flesh of his scar.

Ravis laid a hand on her throat, forcing her to look up. "I

make no pretenses about what I do, I never have. A man pays me to do a job—any man—and I do it. There's no right or wrong for me, just orders and missions and gold." Seeing Emith approach with his pony, he released his grip and let Tessa go. "Never forget that."

Tessa made no move to step away. To her left, she was aware of Emith stopping to check his pony's bit. Bringing her hand up to touch her throat, she said to Ravis, "What else have you done in Bay'Zell on Izgard's behalf?"

Ravis shrugged. "A few things. I saw to it that all fortification and defense plans fell into Izgard's hands, ordered the key bridges to be weakened to the point where a direct hit with a missile will collapse them, encouraged drinking habits in those whose job it is to watch the city walls, and ensured that any armaments Bay'Zell has purchased in the past year have been of poor quality: the bow staves brittle, the arrows made of elm, not birch or ash." Ravis made a small gesture with his hand. "Would you like me to go on?"

Tessa shook her head. Emith was still tending his pony, and she got the impression he was doing so only because he did not want to disturb their conversation. Suddenly feeling tired, and not really understanding why Ravis was so intent on making her hear the worst about him, she inclined her head in the direction of Castle Bess. "So this is just another job to you? Another payment in gold?"

All Ravis' old bitterness stretched across his face in a smile. "I'm a born fighter, so I fight. This is just one battle more." He held Tessa's gaze for a moment, then turned and led the horses through the gap.

After a minute or so Tessa followed him. Just like earlier, when he had told Emith they would be safe in Castle Bess, she didn't believe what he said. It sounded like the truth, but it wasn't. Ravis just didn't know that yet.

In the salt marshes to the southeast of Castle Bess, where the ground was fed by a thousand narrow channels that ran from the sea at high tide, where sandpipers came each spring to feed on tiger moths and ghost crabs, and where nothing but salt grass and sandwort grew, forty men rode their horses at full gallop.

It was dark, but the terrain was flat and featureless, so they feared no damage to the horses. The horses themselves might have been skittish for other, more instinctive reasons, but snuffle caps dowsed in pine oil had been fitted around their nosebands, and the changing smell of their riders bothered them less than their shifting weight.

The riders gained mass as they rode. They gathered the night to them like blotting paper soaking up ink. Muscles swelled, skin stretched, bone thickened and compacted into plates. Teeth grew large in their mouths, tongues plumped, and jawbones reset themselves with a series of dull clicks. Blood ran from one man's nose. Clear liquid wept from another man's ear. All bodies shifted, fluid as shadows lengthening at sunset one moment, jarring as dogs tearing themselves from sacks the next.

Eyes dimmed. Colors drained from irises like wine from a glass. Blinking patterns changed. The glaze wetting the riders' corneas stung as it thickened and saltened. The saliva between their teeth smacked as they worked their jaws. Swallowing often, they tried to rid themselves of the excess.

The riders cumulated and densened. They *became*.

Thoughts and desires left them as soundlessly and unobtrusively as sweat evaporating from an upper lip. Their names fell away like shedding skin. If they were aware of anything, it was the golden warmth pulsing up from their bellies. If they retained memories, they were all of the womb.

Slowly, as their horses bore them west and northward, shape and meaning formed from the shifting pulp of thoughts, flesh, and bone. Gristle hardened. Purpose sparked. Eyes devoid of color borrowed a cast of purest gold.

The Barbed Coil sang to them. It shaped and created, fixing motive and mind-set and might. As the riders followed the tide channels to the gates of Castle Bess, they stopped being men and became *other* instead. They were creatures of the Coil now. And even as their smell and bulk finally spooked the horses, forcing them to abandon the creatures and proceed on foot, the Barbed Coil took them farther and

deeper. Its barbs shredded what was left of them and created
something new.

The horses screamed and reared and galloped back the
way they came. Ghost crabs scuttled back to their pools, and
tiger moths settled flat against rocks. The moon disappeared
behind a bank of cloud, yet it made no difference to the creatures of the Coil. Through their eyes the darkness looked like
the clear light of day.

THIRTY-TWO

And this scribe Ilfaylen stayed here, in Castle Bess?" Camron leaned forward in his chair as he waited for Tessa to reply.

"Yes," Tessa said. "According to Moldercay, Ilfaylen spent a week here while he recovered from his illness."

Camron made a soft sound and then stood. As he walked across the kitchen, light from the hearthstone caught his face, giving Ravis his first real chance to study him since they had arrived at Castle Bess.

Camron looked ten years older than when he'd seen him last. A scar ran down his cheek, and a second intercepted it along his jawline, creating a knot of white-and-yellow flesh. His skin was dark beneath his eyes and in the hollows of his cheeks. Lines had formed on his brow and alongside his mouth. His eyes were still bright, but it was a different type of brightness from before. The underlying core of arrogance had gone, and while Ravis couldn't tell what burned in its place, he decided that whatever it was gave Camron the look of a starved man.

Ravis wasted no time wondering how and why Camron had changed. War did all sorts of things to men.

Having reached the hearth, Camron turned and faced Tessa. The only sound in the room was the snapping of logs on the fire. The only light came from the flames. Tessa had just finished telling both Camron and Emith about her trip to the Anointed Isle. She spoke of her ring and its connection to the Barbed Coil, about what they were and where they had come from, and what the Coil had been forged to do. She told them how the Coil had been bound to the earth for centuries and how, two days from now, it would have been here for five hundred years. Both Emith and Camron drew breath at the mention of five hundred years. Like everyone else on the continent, they knew that bad things were always counted in fives.

Strangely, both men had accepted Tessa's explanation about other worlds and how they had shed from the first one like old skin. Perhaps they were tired, thought Ravis. Or perhaps, in their separate griefs, talk of other worlds, other places, and other lives gave them hope. Shrugging, Ravis turned his attention to his surroundings. Such speculation was not for him.

From the general tidiness of the kitchen, Ravis guessed that Camron and his men had been in Castle Bess perhaps a day or two at most. Soldiers set little store by neatness, and given half a chance they would have turned the room into a mess hall. Chicken bones would litter the floor, the pine refectory table would be scattered with herbs a fighting man could find no use for, and several days of sloppy eating would have drawn a summer fair's worth of flies.

In the corner of the kitchen, close to the inner courtyard door, lay several unopened crates and sacks of grain. Seeing them, Ravis nodded. Supplies had been brought in from the city. That was good.

"A famous scribe *did* stay here once," Camron said, breaking into Ravis' thoughts. "Many centuries ago, I think. As to whether his name was Ilfaylen or not, I couldn't tell you."

Tessa nodded slightly, gathering her hands into loose fists. "Do you have records that go back that far? Account ledgers? Diaries?"

Camron thought for a moment and then shook his head. "No. I don't think there's anything here dating back from that long ago. Certainly nothing written."

Frowning, Tessa sat back in her chair. Her hands were now fully formed fists, and from the look on her face Ravis could tell she was deep in thought. While her attention was elsewhere, he took the opportunity to check the rise and fall of her chest, assuring himself that her breathing had settled down following the ride.

The journey to Castle Bess had taken three hours. At first

Ravis had been worried for both Tessa and Emith, but seeing how well Emith handled his horse and how unaffected he was by the cold and the wind, Ravis had given all his attention to Tessa. Not wanting to let her know he was looking out for her, he had ridden most of the way at her flank, positioning his horse to act as a windbreaker, ready to steady and guide her pony as it picked its way through the sand dunes, sand grass, and rocks that overran the path to Castle Bess.

By the time they approached the castle, Tessa was slumped forward in the saddle, and Ravis could hear each breath she took. She appeared to improve once they arrived at the fortress, but Ravis still worried about her. He had no way of knowing what the next day would bring.

Ravis glanced at Camron. Soon he would need to talk with him alone. From the moment they had presented themselves at the castle's outer gate, Ravis could tell Camron had a limited number of men: the battlements weren't manned; it had taken minutes to raise the gate, not seconds, which meant that only one pair of hands was on the block; the entire north wing of the castle was unlit; and although their small party had been challenged twice—once at the main gate and then again as they crossed the outer courtyard—both times it had been by individual guards, not pairs. Ravis needed to find out just how many men there were, what weapons and specialties they had.

He also needed to know when Izgard and his army were likely to arrive in Bay'Zell.

All these thoughts he put to one side for the time being. Tessa had cautioned him earlier about speaking of such matters in front of Emith, and although holding his tongue wasn't the sort of thing Ravis normally did, he would do it this time. For Tessa.

As if aware she was in his thoughts, Tessa raised her head and looked at him. Her eyes were red from lack of sleep, her skin pale, yet Ravis thought she looked beautiful. She didn't have Violante of Arazzo's perfect features or glossy hair, but she had an irresistible softness to her cheeks that made him want to reach out and touch them.

Shaking his head at his own foolishness, Ravis said to

her, "You need to sleep." And then to Emith: "Both of you."

Tessa's head started shaking before Ravis had finished speaking. "I can't sleep. There's no time. I have to find out what Ilfaylen did with his copy of the pattern." She looked from Ravis to Camron. "I think the ring brought me to Bay'Zell because the answer is here, somewhere in this city, this fortress, or the surrounding area. We know Ilfaylen planted a marker in his assistant's journey book, so I think it's a fair assumption that he left other indicators either here in Bay'Zell or on the Anointed Isle. He wanted the copy to be found. Not in his lifetime, probably not even in his century or the next, but at some point in the future he hoped someone would come along, discover what the Barbed Coil was and what it did, and get rid of it. He planned on them reading his assistant's journey book and then heading south to Bay'Zell."

"According to Moldercay, the journey book was badly damaged," Ravis said, his hand ringing his empty cup. "What if it contained other markers that have been destroyed?"

Tessa jumped on his point in a way that made Ravis smile. "Yes," she said. "In all likelihood it did. But I don't think Ilfaylen would have left all his clues in one source. He was too meticulous a man for that. He must have realized there was a chance that his assistant's book would be lost or damaged." She leaned across the table. "A man who spent his days planning and painting minute patterns would surely have taken the time to think through the details of his plan."

Emith nodded while Tessa spoke. Of all of them sitting around the scarred pine table in the one-sided light from the fire, he was the palest and most withdrawn. He had not said a word while Tessa told her story, and although she had omitted the part about Avaccus' death, Ravis had a hunch that Emith already knew the truth. He was a quiet man, attentive to other people's feelings. And when Tessa skipped over the events in the cheese cave with a quick "Something happened and we had to leave," he would have noticed the forced smile on her face. Certainly he saw her shiver, as a moment later he was beside her, offering his cloak.

Clearing his throat with a polite cough before he spoke,

Emith said, "I think you're right, miss. I've known a fair few scribes in my time, and all of them spent more time planning than they did sleeping. They're nothing if not cautious men."

Tessa ran a hand along her temples. A thumb-sized burn could clearly be seen on her palm from the time she had worked against the harras in the Valley of Broken Stones. Ravis didn't like the look of it at all. He liked what it meant even less. Painting a pattern to free the Barbed Coil was going to be dangerous. Izgard and his scribe wouldn't just stand by and let Tessa unbind it. Ravis knew Izgard. He knew the Garizon king wouldn't be content with merely defending the Coil. He would strike down anyone who tried to take it.

"We could search the fortress," Tessa said. "There might be something hidden away."

Camron made a small gesture with his hand. "It would take us days to search Castle Bess from top to bottom. The cellars alone form an entire story belowground. And beneath them there's a maze of tunnels, cells, and natural caverns." He smiled—his first since he had met them in the courtyard. "As a boy I got lost down there once. It took my father half a day to find me."

"You have no men to spare." It wasn't a question, and once again Ravis realized how observant Tessa was. He wasn't the only one who had noticed Camron's lack of men.

Camron glanced at Ravis. Crossing to a high shelf, he pulled down a second bottle of berriac and cracked open the wax seal. Without a word he went around the table, filling everyone's cup. Watching him, Ravis realized that two months earlier Camron would never have dreamed of serving his guests with his own hand. He would have expected Tessa as a female or Emith as a lowly scribe's assistant to perform the task for him. Now he did it without a thought.

When all cups were full, Camron turned to Tessa. "Izgard could arrive here as early as tomorrow morning. If this pattern is as important as you say, then it must be found soon, before the fortress is overrun."

Camron sat down, adjusting his chair so he could face both Emith and Tessa. "Please understand me," he said, looking from face to face. "I don't mean to frighten either of you, but we have very little time. Castle Bess is the strongest fortress in northern Rhaize, but Izgard has the plans to it. He knows its weak points, and even if he didn't, he is coming here with such numbers that I doubt if we'll be able to hold him off for more than half a day. As things stand tonight, I could spare two men to accompany you from the castle and take you to safety. Not Bay'Zell—its days are numbered— but inland to Runzy. Once there you can move south or west. In the meantime I will search for the pattern myself, both in the city and here in the fortress, and the moment it's found I will bring it to you. I promise this on my father's name."

Ravis was struck by how much Camron of Thorn had changed. For someone about to defend a fortress with what Ravis guessed to be fewer than two dozen men, his offer was generous to say the least. Ravis chewed on his scar. For some reason he found himself thinking about what Tessa had said to him on *The Mull*, about how Deveric's patterns had held them back. Perhaps Camron had been held back too.

Shrugging off the thought, Ravis looked to Tessa, knowing she would turn down Camron's offer.

He wasn't disappointed. Placing her hand on Camron's arm, Tessa said, "I can't accept your offer. It's not a matter of personal choice. I have to do this. If I can't find the pattern tonight, then I'll try something else, think of something else. I have to stay here and see it through. Too much is at stake, too many lives have been lost. People have died because of me." She turned and looked at Emith. "A woman I loved is dead."

Emith gazed down at his hands. A muscle quivered in his throat. After a moment he spoke. "I can't go either, miss. I can't leave you here —Mother would never have allowed it. *Your job is to stay with Tessa; help her any way you can,* that's what she would have said. She loved you dearly, miss. Dearly."

A tear rolled down Tessa's cheek. She didn't reply.

Camron nodded. "If that is what you both want, then so be it. I'll mention the subject no more, except to say this. Until the moment that Izgard and his army appear on the horizon, my offer still stands: two of my men to take you to safety." He looked first at Emith and then Tessa. Seconds passed. Then, as a log splitting on the hearth caused the light to waver, all of them nodded as one.

Watching the three people at the opposite end of the table, knowing the value of what Camron offered, Ravis felt a stab of jealousy. He didn't want to become an outsider again. And even as the thought formed in his mind, another one dropped into place like a gift.

"Camron," he said, leaning forward into the space occupied by the three of them, "remember the night we met in Marcel's town house? When we talked about Deveric's illuminations and you said Marcel had let you take a look at them?"

"Yes? What about it?"

"Well, if I remember rightly, you mentioned Ilfaylen then. Not by name, but you said a scribe had stayed here once, and before he left he painted a pattern to show his gratitude to the staff. You said it hung in your father's study."

Tessa looked up.

Camron nodded. "Yes, I remember. But it's only a rough painting. There's nothing written on it."

"Can I see it?" Tessa's chair scraped against the stone flags.

"It's still in my father's study." Camron spoke the words as a warning. His face paled.

Guessing that he had not visited the room since the night of his father's death, Ravis said, "I'll get it for you—"

"No." Camron laid a fist on the table. "No one will enter that room except me."

Ravis stood. "Let me walk with you as far as the door."

Running his hand through his hair, Camron said, "I had not planned on returning there just yet." His voice was soft, distracted.

After a long moment Ravis crossed to Camron and offered him his hand. Camron clasped it briefly as he rose from the chair, and together they left the kitchen side by side.

Ederius coughed blood as he painted. Not much, a few specks. He kept a cloth close at hand, which he held to his mouth as needed. He never worried about anyone discovering it, as it looked to be just another of his pigment-spattered rags.

The blood had begun some days ago. At first it was nothing more than a pinking of his saliva, and he had managed to convince himself that it was a touch of stomach trouble or an acute soreness of the throat. Only now blood formed red streaks in his saliva, and if he coughed violently, it speckled his cloth. He was old, that was it. No longer capable of sustaining the pace Izgard had set since the battle at Hook River.

Even so, Ederius had started to notice that the worst instances of speckling happened while he was at his scribing desk, painting patterns, rather than sitting in the covered cart traveling from town to town.

Not liking the implications of this observation, Ederius turned his mind to the pattern in hand. His time was limited, as Izgard wanted him finished and ready to travel within the hour. The army would march through the four remaining hours of darkness, reaching the outskirts of Bay'Zell at dawn.

Ederius planned to rest during the journey. Izgard had recently ordered a camp bed to be laid in Ederius' cart and had taken to encouraging him to sleep while they were on the road. Ederius supposed he should be flattered by his king's attention, yet he knew the reason behind it, and it left him feeling numb.

Sighing, he dipped his quill into the sepia ink he had prepared specifically with Castle Bess in mind. Cuttlefish secretions for the fish that could be caught directly off its coast, topaz quartz for the minerals that shot through its granite heart, and vermilion for the blood that had been spilled within its walls. It was a fluid pigment, easy to work with, and Ederius preferred to apply it with pen, not brush.

The illumination was almost complete. The creatures had been created—though in truth he hardly knew what they were anymore—and they had arrived at the outer walls of the fortresses, unseen, unheard, and except for a colony of nesting terns that had fled to the night skies the moment they'd caught wind of the smell, undetected. Currently the creatures were stalking the battlements from the shadows surrounding the wall. Now all Ederius had to do was give them singleness of purpose so nothing would stop them until all inside were dead.

It was the simplest part of the pattern: a few lines danc-

ing around the creatures, binding them together so all felt
and acted the same, plus a little scoring with the sharp side of
the nib, ensuring the ink burned more deeply than any other
pigment on the page.

The Barbed Coil winked from its pedestal as Ederius finished the final design. It was becoming easier to work with
by the day. The terrible dark creatures it had called forth
tonight should have taken hours, even days, to create. Yet as
the Coil turned toward its five hundredth year, it had taken
merely an hour or two at most. Ederius felt less and less like
a scribe and more and more like an assistant. It was as if he
were no longer working with the crown, but *for* it. He felt his
hand was being pushed through each spiral, line, and curve.

Unaware he was shaking his head, Ederius stood free of
his desk. The illumination was complete. Marginalia had
been scripted in the blank parchment surrounding the pattern
to ensure its effects would continue long after the pigments
were dry—as long as needed for the Coil's creatures to do
their work.

Coughing a little into his cloth, Ederius stepped across
his tent and out into the night. He needed air and sounds and
smells. He needed to feel part of life.

As he stepped free of the tent ropes, he noticed a white
curl of smoke rising up from the ground close to the flap.
Peering down, he saw what it was: a bowl of steaming, milky
fluid. Straight away the smell told him it was honey and
almond-milk tea. Angeline. She must have heard him coughing and prepared her special remedy. Perhaps not wanting to
disturb him as he worked, or provoke her husband's anger,
she had left the bowl outside.

Ederius felt his eyes stinging. Kneeling by the little bowl,
he cupped its warmth in his hands and drew it to his chest.
He wanted to smile but couldn't. In his soul he knew Angeline's kindness was a gift he didn't deserve.

"I have twenty men in total. Five of the original longbowsmen you commissioned from Segwin the Ney, eight of my

own knights, and six of the men assigned to me by Balanon." Camron thought for a moment, smiled slightly, and then added, "And one guard sent to pull survivors from the field at battle's end."

Ravis nodded. It was worse than he thought. "What of Broc of Lomis?"

Arriving at a door splintered by crossbow heads, Camron came to a halt. Without turning to look at Ravis, he said, "Broc is dead. The harras slit his throat."

Ravis touched his heart. "I'm sorry. Broc was a brave man. A good fighter to have at one's side in battle."

Muscles to the side of Camron's neck worked for a moment, and Ravis thought he was about to speak, but instead his hand came down on the latch, releasing the locking mechanism and opening the door. He stepped across the threshold into the darkened room.

Ravis stayed where he was. Glancing down, he avoided looking into the darkness, but he could do nothing to avoid the smell. The room stank of blood. Ravis guessed it had not been cleaned following the deaths. How many weeks ago was that now? Nine? Ten? He kicked at the flagged floor with the toe of his boot, passing time.

Minutes passed. A soft sound came from inside the room. Something scraped against stone, and then Ravis heard Camron's footsteps padding toward the door. Camron emerged into the lighted hallway, looking like a ghost. His eyes were bloodshot, but there were no tears shining in the corners. He carried two things: a small painting the size of a roof tile pasted onto a wooden panel and a block of red sealing wax as big as a curled fist. Without saying a word, he handed the painting to Ravis and then turned and locked the study door.

Ravis wanted to say something to him, to offer what consolation he could, but anything he thought of didn't seem nearly enough. In the end he said, "Let's get back to the kitchen. I think we both need a drink."

Camron weighed the sealing wax in his hand. His eyes were the color of cooling metal. "Is there any way we can stop this war without bloodshed?"

Ravis shook his head. "I don't think so. People will die.

How many depends on several different things. This for one." He turned the painting to the light. "Can Tessa find what she is looking for? Is she capable of pulling it off?"

"Do you believe what she says?"

"Implicitly."

"Is it our only hope?"

Ravis ran his free hand over his scar. "Even if she succeeds in sending the Coil back to wherever it came from, it still leaves us with Izgard and his army to deal with. The field may be leveled, but it remains a field of war."

"And you and I?" Camron said, holding the block of wax so tightly, the heat of his hand molded the blood red edges. "What part do we play in this?"

"We stay here, defend the fortress, give Tessa the chance to do what she needs to, then escape as soon as we can. Once we're clear of Bay'Zell we'll have time and distance to plan our next move."

Camron shook his head. Relaxing his hold on the sealing wax, he said, "Remember when we first met in Marcel's town house and I swore to you I had no desire to take Izgard's place?" Ravis nodded. "I've learned many things since then, seen sights I wish I'd never seen. And I think the time has come for me to fight for the throne."

Ravis took a breath and held it in. Things had just become a whole lot more complicated. Camron could not fight with Rhaize forces against Garizon if he someday hoped to take the throne. The Garizon people would never forgive him.

Ravis met Camron's eye.

Then there were things that Camron of Thorn knew nothing about, other claimants to Izgard's throne. Like he himself. Izgard's brother-in-law, husband to his deceased sister, equal claimant to Izgard's wife, Angeline of Halmac, in the event of her husband's death.

Camron continued to watch Ravis, waiting for him to speak. Inside his mouth, Ravis' tooth found his scar. It felt like knotted rope. The past was coming to life all over again. This man before him was proposing they fight side by side for something they both had claims to. He was a good man, too. Just as Malray had been all those years ago.

Feeling an unexpected tightness in his chest, Ravis took

a few seconds to still himself. Why did things hurt more now than they had in the past? Nothing had changed. The facts remained the same.

Careful not to let his emotions color his voice, Ravis said, "Our only hope of seeing a fast end to this war is if Izgard is assassinated, and quickly. If we're lucky, his warlords will start fighting over who should take his place. If we're *very* lucky, they may even race each other back to Veizach in their eagerness to stake their claims."

"You said an assassination couldn't be done."

"Not by an outsider. No." Seeing disappointment on Camron's face, Ravis added, "After Tessa has completed her pattern, then perhaps we might find a way."

Camron looked down at the sealing wax, then up again at Ravis. His eyes were bright with need. "Will you help me take the throne?"

The tightness in Ravis' chest lifted. He felt as if he were seventeen years old again. After what seemed like a very long time he surprised himself by saying, "Yes."

Tessa didn't bother to wait for Camron to return with candles. She took the wooden panel and settled herself close to the hearth. In the blue-and-orange light of the ashwood-and-peat-packed fire, Ilfaylen's painting glowed like the skin on the back of her hand. It was signed with an *I* in the lower left margin, and it looked like no other pattern she had ever seen.

Straight away she knew it wasn't the copy she needed. The palette was limited, the parchment lower grade, and the design itself was oddly angular. The borders were typical enough—spirals and interlacing *XXX*s—but the main pattern area seemed to be a series of loosely connected geometric shapes. Squares, oblongs, ovals, and other more irregular shapes were outlined in a sepia-colored pigment, then filled in either with more sepia or one of a handful of other colors. Amber, a deep sea blue, a yellowy green, and a dull sandy red were the only other shades used in the design. All the pigments had been applied liberally, forming ridges and clots that could be felt with the hand.

"Five colors, miss," Emith said, coming to stand by her side. "Only five, and look what he managed to create with them." There was awe in his voice. "You're holding something painted by the great master himself five hundred years ago."

Tessa held the wooden panel toward him so he could take a better look. Five colors. Five hundred years. Surely it had to mean something?

"Light for the lady." Camron strode into the kitchen, carrying two great pewter candelabras. His mood had changed from earlier, not lightened exactly, but something close to it. He seemed more sure of himself now. As she looked on, he lit and placed candles in all of the separate holders, flooding the area around the hearth with a whiter, more serious light.

The colors on the illumination shifted with the change of light; geometric forms sharpened, and a score of minute details came into view. The pattern began to look less like a work of art and more like an architect's plan. The border consisted of all five colors threaded through each other in sequence. Directly above it, brushing against the main design, was a second, paler border consisting of spiky, loosely crossed *XXX*s. A date could now be seen on the opposite corner to the signature, but Tessa couldn't quite make out what it was, as one of the digits—either a 9 or a 0—was oddly misshapen.

Camron leaned over Tessa's shoulder to look at the painting. "I've never really looked at this before," he said. "It was just one of a dozen other things hanging in my father's study."

"Those *XXX*s look like plant forms, miss. Almost like reeds or grass."

Tessa nodded, instantly seeing the same thing as Emith.

A floorboard creaked to her left, and although she didn't look away from the pattern, Tessa was aware that Ravis had come to stand by her. His smell reminded her of the night they'd slept side by side on *The Mull,* and disguising the gesture as a sleepy stretch, she reached out with her free hand to touch him. His hand came up to meet hers, and for a brief moment their fingers locked.

"Does this mean anything to you?" she said to Camron,

returning her hand to the painting. "Spark any memories, resemble anything you know?" As she spoke, Tessa stroked her finger over an especially thick clot of blue pigment. Surely Ilfaylen could have done a better job of thinning his paints?

Camron shook his head, but slowly. "I'm not sure. There's something about it . . ."

Tessa circled the clot of pigment with her index finger.

"Miss," Emith said, "those XXXs remind me of the salt grass we passed on the way here."

"That shape there"—Camron hit the center of the board—"the square with the corners sliced off, is similar to the shape of the main hall. But it's not drawn to scale, and the other shapes surrounding the square don't match the adjoining rooms."

Tessa flicked at the clot of pigment with her fingernail. The lump broke off from the parchment and went skittering to the floor.

Emith caught his breath. The bones on Camron's wrist cracked as he leaned forward another degree. Ravis shifted his weight from foot to foot, causing his kid leather tunic to swish.

Lying within the crater of blue paint was a shock of pure gold.

A sharp thrill coursed down Tessa's spine. Blood pumped to her face. The hand that held the board shook, causing the illumination to shake along with it.

Emith stretched out a steadying hand. "It's an underpainting, miss. A marker."

"A marker, eh?" Ravis moved closer, touched the pinpoint of gold.

Tessa swallowed hard. She was having difficulty breathing and didn't want Ravis to know. After a moment she had collected enough breath to speak. Tilting the board toward Camron, she said, "Is this a plan of Castle Bess?"

"I'm not sure. I can't make any sense of it. I think I recognize one or two shapes, but that's all."

Scraping the last traces of pigment from the gold, Tessa studied the pattern. Everyone was quiet. The fire dimmed. A few moments passed and then she looked up, not at the three men forming a circle around her, but at the room they all stood in.

Details, she reminded herself. Details.

Fixing every angle of the kitchen in her mind, Tessa looked down again at the pattern. Her cheeks felt so hot, she was sure they must be glowing red. Her spine ached near the back of her lungs. Gaze skimming across the board, she tried to pick out the shape of the kitchen amid the dozens of forms incorporated in the design.

She found nothing. Her eye jumped from color to color, from shape to shape, unable to find a match. Frustrated, she banged the board against her knee.

"What's wrong, miss?"

Tessa waved her hand at Emith. "I thought I would be able to find the shape of the kitchen somewhere in the design, but it's not here." As she spoke, she flicked her fingernail over a second, less pronounced pigment clot. There was nothing but thinned sepia base paint beneath. She tried a handful more. Nothing. Which meant all the other clots and ridges were there purely to disguise the one holding the gold.

Emith made a polite *hmm*ing noise. While Tessa had been scraping pigment, he had been studying the pattern. "That one there"—Emith's hand hovered above the board, not daring to touch it—"looks like it might be the same shape as the kitchen, miss."

Tessa followed the line of Emith's hand. He was indicating a tiny oblong shape, no bigger than a baby's thumbnail. It matched the shape of the kitchen exactly, right down to the recess housing the hearth.

Reaching up, she planted a kiss on Emith's cheek. Of course! Why hadn't she thought of it sooner: nothing was drawn to scale. She had been looking for something large to match the size of the kitchen itself. Yet Ilfaylen knew he couldn't draw a true plan of the castle—it would only cause too much suspicion—he had to draw something that didn't look like a plan.

Emith, startled by the kiss, actually took a step back. "I could go and take a survey of all the other main rooms in the fortress," he said. "It might help us get some perspective."

Tessa wondered if he volunteered such a thing just to

avoid being kissed again. She shook her head. "No. It's not just a case of scale. It's perspective as well." Thinking for a moment, glancing from the large square Camron had pronounced as the main hall to the tiny shape representing the kitchen, she felt her scalp begin to itch. Yellowy green pigment had been used to color both. "What floor is the great hall on?" she asked Camron.

"The second floor, like the kitchen."

"And how many floors does the castle have in total?"

"Four counting the cellar."

Tessa checked the color of the oval shape surrounding the speck of gold pigment. "Didn't you say that beneath the cellar was a maze of old tunnels and caverns?"

"Yes, but—"

"Then that would count as five floors, wouldn't it?" Seeing the puzzled look on Camron's face, Tessa continued. "There's only five pigments used to color these shapes. What if each color represents a floor? The kitchen and the main hall are on this floor. Then this shape in blue here"—she tapped the oval containing the gold—"must be on a different level."

Camron put a hand on the board. "If you're right, then that would account for the fact that none of the shapes adjoining the great hall correspond to the actual rooms."

"Yes," Tessa said quickly, "because they represent rooms on different levels. See, there's an amber-colored room here, what looks to be a passageway just by it in sand red. Ilfaylen jumbled the whole thing up because he didn't want people to look at it and see a plan of Castle Bess. He wanted everyone to think it was just some abstract design." She could barely contain her excitement. The whereabouts of the copy had been hanging in full view of the castle and its occupants all along.

"What we have to find out, then," Ravis said, "is which color corresponds to which floor."

Camron nodded. "The sepia color is the ground floor. I recognize the shape of the inner bailey." He indicated a large circular shape. "And this"—his hand strayed to a long, sandy-colored oblong with many side branches—"looks like the great corridor that runs beneath the battlements. So that would place it as the top floor."

"Then we have amber and blue left." Tessa's gaze didn't leave the pattern as she spoke. "The cellar and the level that lies beneath it."

Emith coughed. "I may be mistaken, miss, but surely the blue color represents sea level."

Tessa smiled at Emith. He looked ready to flee if she made another attempt to kiss him. Turning to Camron, she said, "Are the cellars above or below sea level?"

"Above. To stop them flooding in extreme high tides."

"Then the tunnels and caverns below the cellar are at sea level?"

"Yes."

"Then that's where Ilfaylen hid the copy." Tessa stood. "Are there any oval-shaped rooms down there?" As she spoke, her eyes skimmed across the board, checking all the other shapes colored in blue. There were about seven in all, mostly long oblongs representing corridors.

"I'm not sure. One of the caverns beneath the east wing might be oval—"

Aaarrh!

As Camron said the word *oval* a scream ripped through the air. Everyone stood still. No one breathed. Camron and Ravis exchanged glances. A second scream sounded, and then a mighty bang shook the castle. Tessa felt the ground beneath her feet vibrate. Her skin prickled. Eight fingertips dug into the pattern.

"Harras," hissed Ravis, his hand stealing to his knife. "Tessa, Emith, take those candles and head down into the cellar."

Tessa opened her mouth to speak.

"*Now!*"

Another scream sounded. Cut off prematurely, it was replaced by a deep, rumbling noise. Camron's face paled visibly. He moved toward the door.

Emith looked to Tessa for guidance. She nodded. "Do as Ravis says. You take the candles. I'll take the bags."

"Water, miss." Emith's voice quivered. "I'll need water for the pigments."

Ravis cut across the kitchen, plucked a pitcher from a

shelf, and filled it with water from a bucket. He thrust it at Emith. "Here. Take it. Now *go*."

Tessa wanted to speak. She needed to tell Ravis that the Barbed Coil was capable of creating things far worse than the harras—whatever had chased her onto the causeway was darker and more massive than any harrar—yet Emith was already at the door, and the look on Ravis' face barred any kind of talk.

He drew his knife. "Camron, how do they make their way down to the cellar and the level beyond?"

Metal squealed in the distance as Camron turned to Tessa. "The stairway at the end of the corridor will lead you down into the cellar. Once there, follow the north wall until you can go no farther. Eventually you'll come to a flight of steps—only they're not really steps at all, more rough-hewn rocks. Take them and they'll lead you into the tunnels." He placed his hand on Tessa's shoulder. Even through the fabric of her dress she could feel how cold his flesh was. "It's very dark down there. You have to be careful. Some of the deeper passages might be waterlogged."

Tessa swallowed hard. All her previous excitement over working out the details of Ilfaylen's painting was gone. This wasn't some game, arranged so she could show off her new-found skill for reading patterns. This was real. Grabbing Emith's bags from the kitchen floor, she followed Camron and Emith out of the kitchen. Ravis brought up the rear.

As they came upon the staircase Camron had mentioned, Ravis leaned forward and whispered in Tessa's ear. "Stay down there until I come and get you. Take this—" He handed her a small pack. "There should be enough food and supplies here to keep you going for a few days."

Tessa was frightened by the tone of his voice. "Food and supplies?" Above her head, she was aware of footsteps pounding on stone. Someone called out an order. Looking ahead, she discovered Camron was no longer at the foot of the stairs. Something dropped in her stomach: she had lost her chance to wish him well.

Ravis ignored everything going on around them. He looked only at Tessa. "If the worst happens and the fortress is breached, I want you and Emith to stay in the level below the cellar for as long as you can. Don't venture up here for any reason. Do you understand?"

"But—"

Ravis put his hand on her lip. His scar was a white line cutting his mouth in two. His eyes were no longer dark. They were black. "I don't want to lose you," he said. "Stay down there and keep yourself safe."

Tessa looked at him a moment, then nodded. She couldn't speak.

"Good," Ravis murmured. "Now go."

THIRTY-THREE

Ravis ran toward the noise. Although he had never been in Castle Bess before tonight, he was familiar with its layout. Garizons built all their fortresses much the same.

In his mind he was counting men. Three screams meant three dead, maybe more. After switching his knife to his left hand, he drew his sword. In the distance he caught a glimpse of Camron running across the inner courtyard. His hair was dark with sweat. Ravis considered calling out for him to wait but pushed the idea aside. Camron would heed no one until he got to the gate.

Just as Ravis stepped onto the fine gravel of the courtyard, a low animal cry tore through the air. It sounded like a wolf, only deeper, colder. Every hair on the back of his neck stood upright. He had heard the harras cry out to each other in the Valley of Broken Stones. It was nothing like this. Swallowing great lungfuls of air, he cut across the courtyard, following Camron's footsteps to the gate.

The smell hit him less than a minute later. It made him gag. Once, many years before, he had been commissioned by a Terhas warlord to patrol the perimeter of his estate. One morning he had stumbled upon two men digging up a patch of earth. They were retrieving the bodies of two cattle thieves whom the warlord had posthumously pardoned. Dead and buried ten days, the bodies fell apart in the workers' hands as they raised them. Ravis still remembered the stench. The air smelled of it tonight. Of corrupted flesh, damp soil, and death.

Spitting to clean his mouth, Ravis approached the inner bailey. A handful of men were in the process of barring the gate. Camron was to the side, talking to a young man with dark hair. Two archers were positioned high in the east gate tower, firing at targets on the far side of the wall.

Ravis ran his fist across his scar. Things were worse than he thought. The outer bailey had been breached. Something had broken it down and was now in the main courtyard of Castle Bess.

The sound of the sea grew louder as they made their way to the second flight of stairs. Stone flags grew rougher, wetter. Many rocked as Tessa stepped on them, revealing damp undersides alive with crawling insects. It was very dark. Even with the two candelabras fully lit, they could see only a few paces ahead. Light hitting the granite walls was converted to a dull amber sheen that strained the eyes. From time to time odd pinpoints of light sparkled as if caught in the bevel of a jewel. Emith said it was the quartz in the stone.

Heavily laden with all of Emith's scribing equipment, Tessa struggled to put one foot in front of the other. The ceilings were so low, she was forced to walk with her back not quite straight, and her lungs ached with the strain.

Crates, chests, covered furnishings, beer barrels, stuffed and mounted animal heads, boards hung with rusting armaments, archery targets, and a variety of metal cages and clamps that might have been torture devices were all packed along the facing wall. A salty, moldy sea smell permeated everything, and as Tessa and Emith turned at the end of the corridor and headed down a flight of rough-hewn steps, it grew worse with every step.

One of the candles snuffed out, then another. Tessa and Emith exchanged glances. A thin breeze brushed past their cheeks. Tessa felt her toes getting wet. Dips in the steps had formed pools of water, and ancient-looking tide marks of white salt banded the surrounding walls at various heights.

"If the copy is down here like you say it is, miss," Emith said, "let's hope Brother Ilfaylen had the foresight to store it somewhere high."

It took several minutes to descend the steps. Emith offered many times to assist Tessa with the bags, but she held on to them stubbornly herself. All sorts of items jostled together with each step; painting boards rattled, pigment pots chimed, and mixing shells clicked together like crabs. Emith spilled a lot of water from his pitcher, but he maintained he didn't really need that much, "just a drop."

When finally they reached the end of the steps, Emith was the one who decided which direction they should take. "This way should lead us beneath the east wing," he said, picking a narrow tunnel that was barely wide enough for two people to stand in side by side.

Breath laboring heavily, Tessa followed him. Her mind was in two places: here with Emith on their way to find Ilfaylen's copy, and abovestairs with Ravis and Camron. Unconsciously she picked up her pace. Although she and Ravis were floors apart, they were working for the same end, and it suddenly seemed important that she find Ilfaylen's copy as soon as possible. Time was running out. Even if Ravis and Camron did succeed in defending the fortress against the harras—or whatever in God's name they were—Izgard and his armies might arrive straight after. Tessa felt her scalp tighten around her skull. Once that happened they were trapped.

"Miss, are you all right? You look pale." Emith held one of the candles up to her face.

"I'm fine. Really. We have to hurry." Even to her own ears her voice sounded unsteady, and Tessa glanced down, avoiding Emith's gaze.

The tunnel led steadily downward. Passageways branched off every few steps, and from time to time Tessa caught sight of cavelike chambers. Darting light from the candles revealed glimpses of high ceilings spiked with stalactites, cut stone walls built around great fists of natural rock, and pools of still water that seemed an unnatural shade of blue. Occasionally Emith would stop, pop his head into a chamber, and pronounce, "No. This one's not oval, miss." The echoes produced were maddening.

Abruptly the tunnel came to an end. Three ways presented themselves: two fairly wide tunnels marked with broad chisel strokes where stonemasons had chipped away at the rock, and a third, narrower opening that was little more than a fissure in the granite wall.

Emith moved toward the first of the wide tunnels. "This will take us under the greatest part of the east wing."

"No." Tessa spoke so sharply, Emith took a step back. "We go this way." She raised her arm in the direction of the slit in the rock. Something about its shape reminded her of the misshapen date on Ilfaylen's pattern.

Emith looked at her a moment, blinked, then stepped toward the slit, raising the candelabras as he did so to improve the light. Tessa was glad he didn't question her choice, as she hardly knew the reason behind it herself.

The fissure was a maw of jagged rock. As Tessa squeezed through, the sleeve of her dress snagged on a sharp edge. When she pulled her arm away, the fabric tore, sending echoes ripping through the cavern. Tessa cursed. She felt blood rolling down her arm. Forcing herself through to the other side, she was met by Emith shaking his head.

"No oval here, miss."

Tessa looked around. They were in a small, low-ceilinged chamber consisting entirely of natural rock. The ground was hard and uneven, and water had formed pools in the low points. Seams of crystal glittered around the walls.

"Is there a way through?" Tessa asked, rubbing the scrape on her arm.

Emith glanced quickly to his right. "Not really, miss."

Following his gaze, Tessa saw a small opening at the base of the cave wall. It looked barely large enough to squeeze a body through. When she looked up, Emith was shaking his head.

"Surely not, miss. Ilfaylen wasn't a young man. He wouldn't have tried to force himself through that."

Far in the distance an animal howled. Its cry cut through the cavern like a whiplash, killing all echoes stone dead.

Tessa's mouth went dry. Emith looked quickly to the ceiling, then down to his feet. Dropping the scribing bags, Tessa crossed the cavern. She was going through that opening come what may.

Emith ran after her. "Miss—"

"No, Emith." Tessa shook her head without looking round. "Camron said he was just a boy when he got lost down here— and what are young boys famous for?" She answered her own question. "Squeezing themselves through every nook and cranny in sight."

Rolling up her tattered sleeves more for effect than any practical consideration, Tessa knelt by the opening. She tried not to think about what sort of creature could produce a sound so piercing that it cut through layers of rock. Purposely being rough with her body to dispel such thoughts, she launched herself at the opening.

Rock grazed her cheek, then her jaw. Eyes closed, breath held, Tessa forced her shoulders and chest through the narrow fissure. Feeling cool air on her forehead, she opened her eyes. Everything was black. Bringing her arms forward, she felt for handholds to pull herself through to the other side. Her arm began bleeding again as it scraped against a rough edge. Sweat trickled into her eye. Feeling the beginnings of panic, Tessa kicked back with her feet, propelling her body forward.

Losing hair, dress fabric, and skin in the process, she managed to push herself through the split in the rock and into the adjoining cavern. As soon as her legs and feet were free, she called out to Emith, "Pass me a light."

Seconds later Emith's hand appeared in the gap, offering a single candle. Wiping sweat and rock dust from her face, Tessa took it from him. Swinging around, she then peered through the halo of light into the shadows and darkness beyond.

The cavern was massive. Salt and quartz crystals glittered from the floor and walls. Towering pillars of rock rose toward the ceiling like fossilized trees. Below them strangely shaped boulders lay in heaps, as smooth and flat as giant pebbles. The cavern floor was a snarl of warped and fissured stone, and salt and other mineral deposits formed pale rings of white, blue, green, and amber around a dozen shallow pools.

Holding the candle at arm's length, Tessa drew a slow semicircle of light before her. Eyes straining to see into the shadows concealing much of the far wall, she traced the outline of the cavern. At some point during the arc, the hair on her arm began to prickle.

She was in an oval-shaped chamber.

Tessa swallowed hard. Tears ached in her eyes. She felt a

great rush of emotion: fear for those defending the fortress, love for Ravis and Emith, and a deep aching grief for Mother Emith. Everything was true. Ephemeras, the Shedding, Il-faylen's illumination to bind the Barbed Coil. Everything.

"Miss," Emith called through the gap. "Are you all right? Please say something."

The worry in Emith's voice forced Tessa to take control of herself. Now wasn't the time to stand and wonder at how such things had come to be. She had to accept the truth and move on.

"I'm fine, Emith," she called, scanning the chamber for places likely to conceal a chest, sack, or manuscript press. "I'm in the oval chamber. The ground looks pretty treacher-ous—I'd stay where you are if I were you."

"No, miss. I can't let you look on your own. I'll just—"

"Please, Emith," Tessa cried, cutting him short, "stay where you are. Your shoulders are wider than mine—you might get trapped." As she spoke, she moved away from the gap, gingerly testing the rock beneath her feet. It held firm, and she shifted her weight forward, choosing a path to take her into the center of the cavern.

Stones and chips of rock rattled loose as she stepped around pools, over smooth-edged boulders, and beneath great columns of rock. Light from the candle revealed translucent, ear-shaped fungi growing in damp patches beneath boulders. Tessa didn't like the look of them one bit and changed her path whenever she spied any.

Scrambling from rock to rock, she became acutely aware that she was following in Ilfaylen's footsteps. Somehow he had managed to force himself through the gap and into this chamber. He must have crossed it in much the same way as she did: wary of his footing, anxious to disturb as little of the peace as possible. It was a fitting resting place for the only copy of the pattern that bound the Barbed Coil. The cavern had all the scale and stillness of a mausoleum.

Approaching the center of the chamber, Tessa lowered the candle to waist height and began peering into the shad-owed recesses beneath boulders and overhanging rocks. She felt certain the copy would be located somewhere close by—

the speck of gold had been painted dead center in the blue oval. Finding nothing but mineral deposits and more fungus, she switched her search higher to the stone columns that spanned the chamber from ground to ceiling.

Thick cords of rock twisting around each other created ridges of shadow, gaping hollows, and bolelike recesses in the stone. Fixing the candle in a pool of its own wax, Tessa began running her hands along the stone. It was cold and smooth, wet in parts where water trickled through gaps in the ceiling above. After finding nothing in the places she could reach, Tessa moved to the next column. Ilfaylen had obviously been a slight man—or he would never have been able to squeeze through the gap in the first place—so the copy probably wasn't concealed at too great a height. Tessa dismissed the idea that he may have climbed the stone—weight on any part of the structure could cause the entire thing to collapse.

The gray, amber-flecked stone of the second column was laced with fissures and cracks. The ground surrounding it consisted of loose boulders and fragments of rock that made Tessa nervous. As she circled the column looking for shadows marking recesses, she found it hard to keep her footing. Some of the fragments looked to have broken off from the column, and she wondered if her movements might cause others to fall. Glancing up toward the top of the column, she checked for any branches or swellings likely to break off. Spotting too many precarious-looking outcroppings for her liking, she took a step back.

As soon as her toe alighted on the boulder, it rocked. Tessa felt herself falling. Springing forward quickly to regain her balance, she grabbed hold of the column to steady herself. The portion of rock her hand fastened on to broke off instantly, sending her body tumbling into the column. Tessa's shoulder slammed into the stone. Something cracked. The entire column shuddered. Rock dust flew into her eyes. Chips of stone rained down from the column. The light went out. Then, as Tessa brought her hands over her head to protect herself from falling debris, a huge slab of rock crashed at her feet. Splitting on impact, it sent splinters of stone flying into the exposed side of her body.

Dust choked the air. Echoes ringed the cavern. In the distance, Tessa was aware of Emith calling her name.

Still. She kept herself very still, waiting for the echoes to subside and the cavern to return to normal. Her left arm and leg were bleeding, though she didn't feel much pain. The dust agitated her lungs and throat, making breathing difficult. Even though she knew the best thing to do was not to move until Emith came with the light, she decided to shift her body to the left, away from the dust flying out from the rock. Not being able to breathe fresh air reminded her too much of the night in the cheese cave.

Placing her left hand on the ground amid the jagged pieces of rock, she pushed her body round. Then, as she dragged her hand free of the dust, her fingers brushed against something that didn't feel like stone.

"Everyone get back while I pour the oil!" Ravis shouted over the clamor of splitting wood and thudding timbers. "Get back and stay back." Cloth-covered bit between his teeth, flint swinging in a pouch at his belt, and a full barrel of lamp oil wedged against his chest, he took the last remaining steps to the gatehouse.

Smoke choked the air—the creatures' doing, not theirs—and Ravis' eyes stung as he came to stand directly above the pile of dry kindling, furniture, floor rushes, and wall coverings that Camron and his men had just finished building. Paces in front of the gate, on the cleared gravel ground of the inner courtyard, the makeshift fire had been built with the intent of slowing down the enemy. Any second now Izgard's monsters would break through the gate. And it was high time they were given something to think about.

So they wanted to play with fire, eh? Ravis dug his knife into the top of the barrel, prying the boards apart. Well, let's see how fast they burn.

Balancing the barrel over the battlement wall, Ravis poured the lamp oil onto the firewood below. As he shook out the last few drops, the entire gatehouse shook. The gate itself rocked forward. Metal hinges screamed. The holding bar creaked like a ship at sea. Ravis threw the barrel the way of the lamp oil and then freed the flint from its pouch. He didn't take the wooden bit from his mouth. Not yet.

Swallowing a mouthful of naphtha-tainted saliva, Ravis glanced across the courtyard. The drawn bows of all four longbowsmen caught the light, the men themselves mere shadows behind the string. To either side of them, the eight remaining swordsmen waited, weapons unsheathed, shields up. Most wore either chainmail or breastplates. All had helmets. None wore full armor. With the bit in his mouth, Ravis couldn't smile, so he shook his head instead. Camron and his men had finally seen sense.

As if aware of the reason Ravis was shaking his head, Camron raised his hand in salute. Of all the men forming a loose semicircle around the fire and the gate, he was the most focused, standing forward a few paces ahead of his men, his knuckles white around the haft of his sword. He didn't want to fight his countrymen, yet he would do so, hoping to prevent a greater number of deaths later, when Izgard's army arrived in Bay'Zell. Ravis didn't know if such a thing were possible, yet he had no mind to dissuade Camron from his beliefs. He was just beginning to remember what it felt like to have some himself.

A tearing sound rose from behind the gate. Hearing it, Ravis took the bit from his mouth where the naphtha soaking the cloth had remained damp while he climbed the steps—held in his hand, it would have evaporated within seconds—and dropped it onto the floor while he lit the flint. As he struck the flintstone at arm's length from his body, a shot of cool air pushed past his face.

Crack!

Just as the flint sparked, something smacked into the gate. The holding beam exploded from its casing, snapping in two. The gatehouse and bailey shook. The gate caved, metal staves popping like dislocated bones as it fell. The air was filled with the sound of cracking and splintering wood.

Ravis grabbed the wall for support as he bent to pick up the wooden bit. Drier than seconds earlier, it ignited with a soft snap, bursting into white blue flames. Keeping his face well back, lest traces of naphtha around his mouth catch any wayward sparks, Ravis held the bit over the wall, holding back until the first creature emerged from the other side.

He didn't have long to wait. A fraction of a second later, a dark shadow blasted through what remained of the gate. Calling on the old gods—all five of them, the devil included—Ravis dropped the flaming bit onto the oil-primed fire below.

The moment the bit left his hand, he raced across the battlements, heading for the stairs. Even before his foot hit the first step, the fire took the spark. Less volatile than naphtha, the lamp oil ignited with a short gasp, spilling channels of hot yellow flames into the heart of the fire. Drapery and soft furnishings kindled instantly, creating a fierce wall of flame.

Something howled. Glancing down as he descended the steps, Ravis saw a creature thrashing through the flames. A second one followed, also alight. And farther back, in the shadows behind the gate, others moved forward.

Ravis ran a knuckle over his scar. What in God's name were they?

So dark they defied even the light from the fire, they sucked away at the very fabric of the night, consuming space and air and light. Massive, but liquid fast, they seemed the complete opposite of everything warmed by the sun. Ravis' mouth went dry. He tried to make out details, but somehow the creatures resisted scrutiny, like reflections cast on a rippling lake.

More creatures moved through the gate and into the flames. Some caught light, some didn't, yet the fire slowed none of them down.

As Ravis stepped onto the gravel of the courtyard, Camron shouted an order and the longbowsmen released their strings. Arrows shredded the air: gray flecks tunneling through the darkness, humming as they sped toward the gate. Ravis felt their breath on his skin. A wafer-thin second later, he heard them thudding into the meat of the creatures' chests.

Bone cracked. Punctured skin hissed. The creatures brayed and howled. None went down.

Hit full in the chest by broad-headed arrows shot from a longbow at a hundred paces, and not even one man fell.

Ravis licked the cold wire of his scar. As he watched, more creatures broke through the warped remains of the gate. Stamping through the flames, they dampened the fire with their bodies, making the area a fraction more passable for the creatures following after. Paying no heed to burns and arrow shots even though their flesh bled and seared, they advanced into the fortress.

Ravis drew his sword and knife simultaneously, making his way to Camron's side. It had been twenty-one years since he'd last fought with the odds stacked so firmly against him.

"No, miss. You open it." Emith pushed the leather pouch toward Tessa. "It's only right and fitting."

Tessa nodded once. Her throat felt so dry, it ached when she breathed. As she raised her hand toward the brown, age-wrinkled pouch, blood from a stray puncture wound rolled down her arm. Pausing to press her palm against the wound, she took a moment to pull herself together.

Everything had happened so fast: the column breaking up, the rock smashing to the ground, the darkness, fingers feeling the soft patina of old leather amid the debris of stone, then Emith making his way into the cavern to save her, bringing light for her eyes and water for her throat and rubbing alcohol for her wounds. Emith had been so gentle with her—just the way he used to be with his mother. Watching him bandaging the worst of her wounds, always mindful that he cause no further pain, Tessa realized he needed someone to take care of. He was that sort of man.

Together they had cleared the area around the column of rock chips and boulders and pulled the leather pouch from the dust. Tessa didn't know if the pouch had been lodged against the chunk of rock that had broken off or had been somewhere else within the column when the impact occurred and simply fallen out. It didn't matter. Ilfaylen's mark was stamped upon it, and from the minute she had seen the highly stylized *I* to right now, where she and Emith sat cross-legged in the small, low-ceilinged chamber adjacent to the oval cavern, everything else had been a blur.

Here, on the ground before her, was a leather portfolio that had once belonged to Ilfaylen.

"There, miss," Emith said, placing both candelabras on the ground before Tessa. "I've relit all the candles. It should be bright enough to paint by now."

Paint? Tessa swallowed. That was what the ring had brought her here to do: paint an illumination to free the Coil. Fingers rising automatically to her neck to check for the golden barbs, Tessa met and held Emith's gaze. "I'll need your help, Emith," she said. "I know so little."

Emith didn't hesitate. "Miss, the strength in my body, the wit in my hands, and the knowledge in my head is yours. I don't claim to be a great man with a great mind, but what skills I have managed to acquire in my time, as an assistant first to Brother Avaccus and then Master Deveric, I willingly offer to you." He smiled gently, his eyes very bright. "Mother would have stood for no less."

Tessa pressed her lips together, unable to smile or speak. First Ravis, now Emith. What had she done to deserve love from one man and complete loyalty from another?

Holding that question in her mind, she turned to the portfolio, cut the binding with the sharp-bladed lunular knife Emith carried in his pack, and pulled the covers apart.

Rock dust and leather dust wafted up from the crease. Smells five hundred years in the keeping rose along with the dust: sweat, the warm itchy scent of old leather, and the chemical bloom of dozens of pigments. Tessa smelled copper, arsenic, sulfates, ammonia, and many more. Hands trembling, heart beating hard in her chest, she pinned apart the covers and looked upon the contents of the pouch. A manuscript rested in a makeshift press of two beechwood boards held together by string. A letter folded in four, then sealed with a thumb of wax, rested on top of the press. Beneath the press was something that looked to be a length of wool or some other material, also folded and packed neatly. Flecks of dark powder sparkled within the weft of the fabric.

Tessa drew in a deep breath. To her side, Emith held as still as the stone that surrounded him. Flames from the candles flickered, creating an ever-changing sequence of light. Quartz glittered. The sound of the sea throbbed through the chamber like a pulse. Tessa picked up the letter and broke the seal. The script was sepia ink, the lettering sparse and readable.

Friend,

Do not despise me. There is no need to name the wrong that was done by my hand, we both know the nature of the act. I am an old man with many oaths broken: think not of the pride that drove me forward, think instead of the Faith that led me back.

Act swiftly upon the matter within. I swear it is as accurate a transcription as the One God gave me leave to make. Follow it well and it will lead you to the four places you need to be.

May your paints flow smoothly from your brush and your achievements begin and end within your heart.

I will be a long time awaiting forgiveness,

Ilfaylen

Tessa closed her eyes, a pressure pain ringing her forehead. She felt Emith take the letter from hand. Everything except the sea was silent as he read.

A minute or so later he spoke, his voice low and uneven. "Oh, miss. He had such a terrible burden to bear."

"I bear it now, Emith," Tessa said, surprised at the hardness of her voice. "Avaccus bore it too, keeping it to himself for so long that it turned his bones to lead." She shivered, remembering the old monk in the cave. She didn't want to end up the same way.

Reaching down, she freed the woolen wrap from beneath the press. Specks of black powder fell from it as Tessa brought it to her lap. Ilfaylen's shawl. As she handled the fabric even more powder fell away—the casein that had once bound the powder to the wool long since turned to dust. Stopping herself before the shawl was fully open, she handed it to

Emith to put to one side. She didn't want her first sight of the pattern to be some negative, colorless chart.

Emith handled the shawl as carefully as if it were spun glass. Taking his cue from Tessa, he opened it no farther. "You were right, miss," he said, laying it on the ground. "About everything: the copy, the pounce, the shawl."

Tessa shook her head, not wanting to hear any congratulations. She had done nothing except string a few details onto a single thread. Emith could have done the same if he had known all the facts.

Shrugging aside these thoughts, Tessa put her hand on the press. The beechwood boards were rough and cracked, and as soon as she cut the first length of string, they began to fall apart. Pulling off the remaining ties, she handled the wood carefully to avoid splinters and then opened the disintegrating press like a book. Coming face-to-face with a leaf of protective yellow parchment, she removed it and looked upon the pattern beneath.

Dust settled. Light from the candles ceased flickering. The sea grew as quiet as a lake. The air in the cave gathered into itself, becoming heavy and charged like before a storm. Tessa felt all these things as shadows on her back: they were inconsequential, curtains parting to reveal a stage. The only thing that mattered was the pattern itself.

Red, gold, and black were its primary colors. Lines of blood red pigment pumped minerals across the page. Flowing outward from the centerpiece to the side panels, they nourished the design like a mighty aorta, breathing life into every outlying line and curve. Gold was at the heart of the page. Gleaming on the outside edge of spirals, carrying messages from knot to knot, it drew the pattern together like a skeleton of spikes.

Black formed the shadows. Nothing was drawn without it; it underlined, undercut, and undermined everything. By turns it robbed the gold of its luster, then ran alongside scarlet threads, creating contrast. Forming deep hollows for spirals to fall into, then cutting fretwork and knotwork stone dead, black took as much as it gave. Maybe more.

Tessa's gaze darted from detail to detail. The pattern was beautiful, frightening, filled with power. Spirals were taut springs, lines hummed with tension ready to snap. Curves strained against their arcs, *XXX*s bulged like drawn bows, and borders seemed less like decoration, more like shackles, lashing the pattern to the page.

There was nothing of nature in it. No plant life, animal life, land, sea, or stars. The entire illumination had a deadness about it, an unnaturalness that showed itself in each buckling line and curve. It had all the glassy-eyed false luster of a preserved corpse.

Tessa shuddered. She felt out of her depth.

The pattern was an aberration. Looking at it, she knew in her heart what Ilfaylen must have known as he'd painted it. The work was not meant to exist. Grotesque, artificial, and constrained: it was begging to be undone.

Placing it on the ground before her, unable to tear her gaze from the design, Tessa spoke. "Start getting everything ready, Emith. Mix your pigments and prepare the vellum: we have a pattern to paint." The words were formal, stilted, but she forced herself to say them. She didn't want Emith to guess she was afraid.

"Yes, miss," Emith said, his voice small and filled with awe. "Should I match the pigments exactly? The red is mercury-based vermilion, the black looks to be carbon with jet."

"Yes," Tessa said. Then, "No. Whenever you can I want you to use vegetable and animal dyes, not minerals. This is a dead thing before me. I need to draw something with life."

Izgard flicked his wrist, and his lieutenant cried a halt. The order was immediately picked up by others down the line, propagating and amplifying until every man, horse, and pack animal had heard it. Slowly, gradually, over the course of a thousand paces, the dark, pounding mass of Garizon's army ground to a halt.

It wasn't dawn, not yet. But birds took flight, foxes found refuge, and the heat and motion of the horses thinned the dew. Mosquitoes still bit. Izgard saw blood on his lieutenant's neck and matching spots on his horse's flank. Izgard himself had not been bitten. Insects settled on him less and less these days. It was yet another gift of the Coil.

"Should we build a full camp, sire?" It was the lieutenant. Like every other man in the ranks, he already knew his orders, yet he would never presume to act upon them without direct confirmation from his king.

Izgard found himself warming to the man—even though his skin was pockmarked and uninviting to the touch. He nodded. "I want everything finished by dawn."

Turning to the horizon, Izgard searched out the yellow-and-black haze of Bay'Zell. He was not normally a man given to smiling, but his lips stretched pleasingly when he realized just how close he was to the greatest port city in the west. Seeing where Izgard's gaze was directed, the lieutenant dared to join his king in a smile.

Izgard did not begrudge the man the shared intimacy, though he saw fit to cut it short with further orders. "Set two squads to watch whilst the camp is made. And send a further two to patrol the borders when it's done. Our sons must be secure whilst they sleep." Let Bay'Zell stew for half a day, waiting for an attack. They had neither the manpower nor the balls to seize the offensive. While they sat and worried and waited for the Sire to save them, three of their key fortresses would be taken. One to the west, one to the north, and one to the east: Castle Bess. By the time the sun next set over the city of Bay'Zell, the full force of the Garizon army would be poised and ready to strike.

The lieutenant bowed his head. "Any further orders, sire?"

Izgard spun around. Scanning the ranks and columns of his army, he noticed a single line of covered carts rumbling to a halt near the rear. Seeing them, he felt a tremor of unease pulse down his spine. His two most precious possessions lay beneath the canvas of the second cart: his crown and his scribe.

Unable to shake off his disquiet, Izgard turned to the lieutenant and said, "See to it that the first tent erected is my scribe's. I want him ready and able to work within the hour."

THIRTY-FOUR

Pax, fall back to the door. Keep it clear until I sound the retreat." Camron spoke through a mouthful of blood. Kicked-up gravel shot against his left thigh and side. In the acrid, smoke-filled darkness, he could barely see Pax's face. Yet he heard all the eagerness in the young guard's voice.

"Aye, sir. I'm as good as there. Don't waste another man to watch my back." With that Pax was off, slipping through the crossfire of blades, claws, teeth, and gravel, heading for the main entrance to the keep.

Camron wished him luck. He needed it. Izgard's creatures had overrun the inner courtyard. Stamping down the fire with their bodies, they'd forced their way through the gate, impervious to arrows and flames. Even the harras had fallen under the strain of multiple arrow wounds, yet these creatures seemed to feed off their injuries and their own spilled blood.

Pain quickened them. Grunting or howling when they took a hit, they lashed out with taloned fists, sharp-boned elbows, and forearms as heavy and deadly as lead staves. All teeth, bone, muscle, and sinew, they pushed, clawed, and cleared themselves a path.

Every part of them was a weapon. Shoulders were battering rams sent barreling into doors, fists were clubs, claws were sharpened blades, and their dark open maws had all the jagged-tooth readiness of man-traps. They carried knives and shortswords, yet they used them with no finesse, merely hacking and cutting, never switching their grip to parry or block. When they lost their weapons to hand wounds or deflections, they used their claws and teeth instead.

Camron still wasn't sure how they had managed to break through the outer bailey—probably exploiting some weakness Izgard had discovered from studying the plans. That didn't worry him as much as the fact that the creatures themselves were obviously familiar with the layout of the fortress and were currently trying to block all retreats. They looked and fought like monsters, yet intelligence shone cold in their eyes, and a single will united them, making them think and act as one.

Bodies lay crushed underfoot. Camron couldn't bear to look at them. He knew he should keep track of how many had gone down, but he didn't have the heart for it. He had known these men for too long now. To count their corpses seemed a kind of betrayal.

"Start moving back."

Camron looked around at the sound of Ravis' voice. The mercenary was directly behind him, his body a black shadow except for the quick-moving silver of his sword. Camron was glad to see him.

"Pax is keeping the main entrance clear," he replied, his voice hoarse from shouting orders.

"Good." Ravis lunged at one of the creatures. "Then let's get the hell away from here." Glancing over his shoulder, he changed the grip on his sword, hefting it over his shoulder like a spear. "Seems there's just you and me left out here now; I think it's time we stopped playing fair." On the word *fair*, he aimed the sword directly at the nearest creature and flung it toward its chest.

Bone splintered with a sharp crack. The blade penetrated deep into the creature's chest, bringing forth a stream of dark, foul-smelling blood. Howling in rage, the creature stepped back. As it brought its claws up to pull out the blade, Camron felt a mighty yank on his arm. It was Ravis, dragging him back toward the keep.

"If I'd known you wanted to stay around and watch the show, I would have arranged to have dancing girls next." Even as he spoke, Ravis' eyes were scanning the area around the doorway, searching out the course of least resistance.

Realizing he was now the only one of them with a sword, Camron shook his arm free of Ravis' grip and began sweeping his blade in a defensive arc.

While the creature hit in the chest howled and stumbled,

clutching at his heart, others moved in to take his place. Feet crunching gravel, jaws smacking, eyes small and hard as flint, they spilled around their wounded ally like sea foam around a rock.

Ravis and Camron broke into a run. High above them in the keep, two longbowsmen took up position and began firing down on the first line of creatures. The arrows weren't enough to halt the advance, but those who had taken previous hits, or were scorched by the flames, slowed.

Camron felt a band of muscle relax in his chest. If the creatures could be slowed, they could also be killed.

The sound of swords clashing came from the darkness surrounding the door. Ravis flicked his knife from his left hand into his right. Camron brought his sword hand close to his waist. Relying on the archers to take care of the enemies behind their backs, both men turned their sights to those who waited at the door.

Pax, broadsword in one hand, lime wood shield in the other, was standing in the doorway, fighting off two creatures at once. Blood poured from a gash on his forehead and a second, lesser wound on his arm. Judging from the way his shield kept dropping, he was tiring fast.

"They're expecting us to keep them out," hissed Ravis to Camron. "I say let's force them *in* instead."

Camron barely acknowledged what he said. His mind was focused on reaching Pax. Sword up, he met the first of the beasts head-on. Anger drove his blade deep into the grizzled meat of the thing's shoulder. Sick of death, furious that another person he cared about was in danger, Camron fought with the blind, heedless frenzy of rage.

He hadn't wanted to fight again, yet there was no choice here. He couldn't stand by and see his home invaded and his men slain. His father had been right to condemn war—Camron had seen the truth of it for himself on the battlefield at Hook River—but that didn't mean all fighting was wrong.

This was right. It had to be.

Shaking off his doubts, Camron pushed the two creatures back behind the door. Jaws open, saliva frothing as they breathed, they sucked up the space in the hall. Their smell was sickening. Camron couldn't bear the thought of it in his lungs. Exhaling sharply, he lashed out with his sword, hardly caring if he sliced flesh, bone, or air. Izgard was the real monster here. What sort of leader would do this to his men?

Feeling the beginnings of a new type of anger, Camron stopped focusing on the creatures before him and started focusing on Izgard instead. How could that man call himself a king? How could he send his countrymen into battle in such a state? What became of their bodies later, when all the battles were won? Barely aware of what he was doing, Camron forced the creatures to defend themselves against him. Anger took him farther than any clever move; it raised his sword, placed blow after cutting blow, made him forget what it was to be afraid.

All along he had been trying to figure out what his father really wanted from him, yet here and now Camron started to realize the only thing that counted was what he wanted for himself. He couldn't rule a country because his father wished it. He had to feel it in his heart. And right now, fighting against a shadowed enemy that smelled as if it had been dragged from a grave, all he wanted to do was put an end to Izgard and his plans. The man should never have been allowed to take the crown.

Wood rumbled behind him. Glancing around, Camron saw Ravis barring the door. Pax's sword was in his hand. The young guard was nowhere to be seen, but a trail of blood leading down the stone steps to the granary meant he'd probably gotten away. Camron heaved a sigh of relief. There was just he, Ravis, and the two creatures in the hallway now. The bar across the door would hold—for a few minutes, at least.

Ravis came and took up position by Camron's side. Feeling the heat from his body, Camron realized he had no idea what it had taken for Ravis to close the door. Sweat poured from his neck and temples. Spots of blood spattered his face, yet it didn't look to be his own.

Smiling, Ravis began tearing into the nearest creature with his sword. "You did a good job pressing these devils back," he said to Camron between ragged breaths.

Despite everything, Camron found himself returning the smile. There was something showing in Ravis' face—a kind of mad, reckless joy—that was impossible to ignore. The man seemed to relish all the danger of the fight.

Working together, they isolated the first of the creatures. Already wounded many times, the beast was sluggish, dazed from loss of blood. Cornered, it lashed out ineffectively, roaring and spraying saliva, whipping its head from side to side. While Ravis watched his back and kept the second, more dangerous creature at bay, Camron moved in for the kill. Fear bubbled in his stomach, hot and black like boiling oil. Knowing he was either going to have to take the beast's head off or puncture its heart, Camron bided his time, feinting and badgering, waiting for the right moment to strike.

Then, as if Ravis somehow knew what Camron needed, he went on a rampage across the hall: smashing unlit lanterns, splintering wooden chests and doors, and sending displays of crossed weaponry crashing to the floor. Camron's creature looked up at the noise. With its guard down for half a second, Camron struck. Putting the strength of his entire body behind the blow, he sent his sword slicing downward, through shoulder bone, ribs, and heart.

The creature screamed. Chest convulsing, it fought all the way to the floor. Camron tried to remove his sword, but it was too deeply embedded in bone and wouldn't come out. Unable to bear the sight and smell of the dying beast, he turned away.

The second creature came straight at him.

Tired, shaking, and weaponless, Camron looked for Ravis. In the blink of an eye, the mercenary was there. Dipping to the floor for the briefest of moments, he picked up one of the weapons he had just dislodged from the wall and with a quick flip of his wrist sent it flying through the air toward Camron, haft first.

Catching the sword easily, Camron parried the creature until Ravis joined the fight, and together they battled side by side. Stronger and more alert than its dying companion, the creature fought with all the rage and desperation of a wounded animal. When Ravis disarmed it, it tore at them with its claws and teeth, springing forward, slashing their clothes and skin.

Behind his back, Camron was aware of more of its kind beating against the door. And somewhere high up in the fortress, the sound of further battle could be heard. Izgard's monsters had found another way in. Over in the far corner of the hallway, the dying creature's howls grew weaker and more human sounding, then eventually stopped. Stealing a moment to glance over his shoulder, Camron found himself looking into the face of a dead man, not a beast.

Strangely Camron grew more relaxed as he fought. Ravis was always there: behind his back, guarding his flank, stepping in front of him to deflect or ward off a blow. If Camron felt his sword arm dropping, Ravis noticed immediately and moved in to take the battle from him, holding the creature back until he had regained his strength. When Ravis himself took a bad blow to the neck, Camron stepped ahead of him, taking the brunt of the creature's fury until Ravis had recovered enough to rejoin the fight.

Camron came to rely on Ravis without question. It felt good to swing a blow knowing that in the crucial seconds when his arms were extended and his chest was wide open, the mercenary was there covering his weak spots.

Together they wore the beast down. Bit by bit, blow by blow, cut by cut, they weakened the creature, until it was so groggy from loss of blood that it began to make mistakes. That was when, without a word exchanged between them, Camron and Ravis moved apart, encouraging the creature to step into the open space in the center of the hallway, and then attacked it from both sides.

Camron lost count of how many blows it took to kill the thing. Exhausted, drenched with sweat, sick to his stomach with the smell and the gore, he kept stabbing the creature's flank until Ravis pulled him away.

"I think we can call this one dead," the mercenary said softly, putting his arm around Camron's shoulder. "That makes two down and only three dozen more to go."

Camron nodded. There was no breath in his body to speak. Unable to stop himself from shaking, he lifted his sword to his thigh and began to clean off the blood.

"Here," Ravis said, raising a hand toward Camron's weapon, "I'll do that for you."

Thinking it a strange offer to make, Camron glanced at Ravis. The mercenary was sporting a purple lump above his right eye and claw marks on his neck and cheeks. A mixture of sweat and blood ran from his nose in pink drops.

Ravis looked uncomfortable under the scrutiny. He shrugged. "I used to clean my brother's sword between battles. He said it brought him luck."

Seeing something he didn't understand in Ravis' eyes, Camron relinquished his grip on the weapon. "I want to thank you—"

Ravis cut him short. "Don't thank me. We're fighting for the same thing, you and I." After holding Camron's gaze for a moment, he began cleaning the sword.

Camron wanted to ask him what he meant, but before he had chance to frame the words, the entire hallway was rocked by something slamming into the door. Splinters shot from the wooden crossbars, hinges strained, and the creatures outside began braying like a pack of winter-starved wolves.

"Come on," Ravis said, handing back the spit-and-sweat-cleaned sword. "Let's get away from here while we can. These things can only be taken out one at a time—I say we go find ourselves another doorway and let a handful of the bastards through."

Camron smiled, glad in his heart Ravis was with him. The mercenary was a stranger, full of unknown motives and hidden emotions, yet in all his life he had never met anyone better suited to fighting at another's side.

Tessa painted. Belly down on the floor, vellum on a board before her, eyes squinting, wrist aching, she held her hand as steady as she could and copied a storm of scarlet spirals onto the parchment.

Glancing from her own pattern to Ilfaylen's, which lay propped against a rock to her left, Tessa worked on the detailed borders that would frame the main design. Instinctively she knew that copying Ilfaylen's pattern line for line wasn't right. She needed to do more than Ilfaylen, go further, deeper. Use his designs to gain access to the bindings and then blast them away with patterns of her own. Ilfaylen's copy was the map that would show her the way.

Aching all over, tired to the roots of her teeth, Tessa focused all her remaining strength into the design. To give less was unthinkable. This was what she had been brought here to do.

She just wished she were better prepared. There was so much she didn't know, so much she had to simply guess. Ilfaylen's illumination was subtle, sophisticated—she still hadn't worked it all out. If it hadn't been for Emith's quiet encouragement, she would have lost her way on the very first line.

Emith was everywhere, doing everything at once. If Tessa needed a clean brush, all she had to do was hold out her hand and he would place one into her palm. If a new pigment was called for, not only did Emith anticipate the exact color required down to the opacity and texture, but he also knew how much of the pigment was necessary and what brush size Tessa needed to apply it. If Tessa made a mistake and applied too much pigment to the vellum, Emith was there with his knife, scraping off the excess. If she painted too fast and her lines weren't as smooth and fluid as they should be, Emith would cough and urge her to rest.

Often, while Tessa painted one corner, Emith would quietly trace the exact same design on the opposite corner in leadpoint. Mirroring the pattern completely, he saved Tessa valuable time by providing a grid for her to paint over later when she was ready to work on that part.

Emith forced her to drink when she was thirsty, stretch her arms and legs before they became cramped, and chew on tiny clippings of rue leaf to head off eyestrain and headaches. There was nothing Tessa needed that Emith didn't think of first. If a candle grew too smoky, he cut away the offending wax and then relit the wick. When it grew cold, he put a shawl around Tessa's shoulders, and when a cool draft started blowing from the entrance, he blocked the opening with his pack. He even produced a small vial of almond oil from his tunic, which he rubbed into Tessa's wrists to soothe her aching joints.

Always he was there, in the periphery of Tessa's vision,

helping, advising, preparing pigments and glazes, shuffling around the cavern; by turns busy or thoughtful, never stopping to take a rest.

Although he never offered advice directly concerning the pattern, sometimes, when Tessa came to the end of a section and found herself at a loss for what to do next, Emith would hand her a shell filled with pigment and say, "Perhaps you should use this color now, miss. It might work well in that section over there."

He was always right. As soon as he spoke, Tessa realized immediately what had to be done next and chided herself for not seeing it sooner. Never interested in taking credit, Emith simply carried on with his work, silent until the next time his help was needed.

Part of Tessa was aware of all this, of all Emith was doing for her, of the flickering light in the cavern and the sound of the sea on the far side of the wall; but another, deeper part of her was gradually slipping away.

With the background painted and the borders and corner work fully fleshed, the pattern stopped being a simple sketch and became an illumination instead. The vellum Emith had brought was now soft, smooth, and pale as skin. With neither pores nor hair follicles to mar its surface, pigment glided over it like oil.

As Tessa put the last touches to the border, gaze darting constantly to Ilfaylen's pattern to check for details, she was aware of a shearing sensation passing along her body. Thinking it was another cool draft of air, she glanced over at Emith. He had his back to her and was busy mixing pigments as if nothing were amiss. Turning back to the pattern, Tessa continued painting. Pinpoints of pain began to pulse in her temples and her vision blurred, only to refocus sharper than before. She could now see depth between the layers of paint and dark flecks of impurities in the pigments as they dried.

Tiny tremors of tinnitus pattered in the bone behind her ears. Tessa felt things switching on her: the cavern appeared to flatten and dim, Emith's body took on the look of a shadow, light from the candles receded. And while everything else grew smaller and less substantial, the pattern expanded outward, becoming *more* than it was.

Tessa's first instinct was to pull back—she had spent her entire life avoiding the first telltale signs of tinnitus, and even now, after months of being in this world, the need to save herself from pain was strong. Yet she knew she had to continue. Upstairs, Ravis and Camron were fighting to give her time. Somewhere out in the night, Izgard and his army were preparing to conquer Bay'Zell, and deep within his camp the Barbed Coil ticked away like a clock. One day from now at midnight it would have been here for five hundred years.

Avaccus' words echoed in Tessa's head: *There is power in the number five. Ancient power custom shaped to be used by ancient things.*

Shivering, Tessa fought to keep her hand steady as she painted. She wished she were stronger, braver, more sure of herself. More like the old Tessa McCamfrey. Tessa's knuckles tightened around the paintbrush. She hadn't changed that much, had she?

Unsure of the answer, she clamped her jaws together, gritted her teeth, and drew a thick golden line on the page. Tinnitus thrummed against her temples, and all the aches and pains in her body flared as if they had been rubbed with salt. The gold pigment held the light long after it dried. Tessa caught the faintest whiff of an odor that had no place in the cavern: the rich wet-earth scent of decay.

Tessa was aware of herself splitting. The clearheaded part of her that kept an eye to the pattern, kept the brushstrokes in line, and took things from Emith as needed stayed the same. But another, less detached part ran with the pigments down into the vellum. Colors brightened. The air grew warmer, thicker, wetter. Sounds, noises, and sensations beckoned from the other side. Tessa thought she heard Ravis shout an order and then Camron hiss a curse. Something warm ran down her cheek, yet when she raised a hand to wipe it away, her skin felt perfectly dry.

Things crowded close: the high-pitched grind of tinnitus; sounds of fighting, animals howling, and footsteps on a wooden stair; smells of blood, sea salt, pigments, and smoke; and pain from every cut and bruise she'd ever had.

Tessa wanted it to stop. She was under attack from all sides; her skin crawled with sensations, her head throbbed with noise. Taking a deep breath as if she were preparing to thrust her head underwater, she braced herself and pushed her way through.

Through the paint, through the vellum, through the clamor of sights, smells, and sounds, through to the other side.

Darkness. Tessa opened her eyes in darkness so complete, it was hard to believe she was alive. Everything was gone.

Dimly she was aware of another part of herself far in the distance, painting furiously away at a pattern. The image faded rapidly, like a dream upon waking, and soon all Tessa could conceive of was the dark.

She was nothing in it. Nothing.

If her body was with her, she could neither see nor feel it. If she took breaths to sustain herself, they came and went with nothing to show.

Isolated, rapidly losing perspective, Tessa tried to make her way through. All the nights she had ever slept through were nothing compared to this. There was no weight, no direction, no right or wrong way; the only marker she had was herself. All she could do was move in the direction she perceived as forward. Only every way was forward, and every turn led her back.

Time passed. Blackness folded around Tessa, leaving nothing for her thoughts to fasten on to. All sense of purpose drained away. Light was a dead memory. Warmth was something beyond hope. Feeling the first flutters of panic, she tried to recall the reason she was here. She had something to do . . . something to work against . . .

Shaking herself, Tessa fumbled in the dark. The only thing she could remember was her name.

Tessa McCamfrey.

And the fact that she possessed a ring.

As soon as the word *ring* formed in her thoughts, she felt something pull against her neck. Warm, sharp, heavy for its size, the ring slipped into the darkness as discreetly as a letter pushed under a locked door. Aware of her body now, Tessa raised her hand toward it, and for the first time since the day she'd found it, she put on the golden band.

Instantly the darkness changed. It grew edges and depth and began to stretch ahead like a road. The pain of wearing the ring was like a slap in the face. Tessa remembered everything, became aware of what was happening on the other side of the vellum.

She saw herself, nose pressed close to the pattern, about to begin work on the first of four knotwork panels. The corresponding panels on Ilfaylen's illumination dominated his design. Intricate, thickly twined cords of gold, black, and scarlet wound around each other to form a hard spine of knots. Even after many glances, all four panels appeared the same. Looking at them now, though—seeing them through eyes that were, and at the same time *weren't,* her own— Tessa saw that each panel was minutely different. It wasn't as much that their contents differed, more the tension running through them. All four knots strained in different ways.

Tessa rubbed the barbs on the ring, thinking. What was it Ilfaylen had said about his illumination? *Follow it well and it will lead you to the four places you need to be.*

Four panels straining as if they held something down between them . . . Tessa dug her thumb into a barb. That was it! Each panel represented one of the Barbed Coil's bindings. Her job was to re-create the four bindings, then break them one by one. *Paint the problem, then solve it,* Avaccus had said.

The other, faraway Tessa took up her lead stick and began outlining the first knot. Emith was close by, cleaning gold paint from one of the brushes. He seemed pleased.

Turning away, leaving part of herself to work on the pattern, Tessa took her first step down the darkened road. Now that she knew what she had to do, it was time to search for the strength to do it. Painting was only half of the job.

The ring led the way. Pulling Tessa along by the finger, it guided her through the darkness and into another place. A vacuum rush filled her ears. Something sucked her in. Black tendrils, heavy as lead splinters, brushed along her skin. Black filaments filled her eyes, nose, mouth. Mercury-slow lightning carved her image in the air. Panic seized Tessa for one terrible moment, and then a memory came to her like a gift.

She had been here once before—for the briefest of instances when she'd traveled from her own world to the world of the Barbed Coil. She was in the cracks and folds between time and space. The place ephemeras slipped in and out of, the place where Avaccus said the Shedding began.

Like sand settling in still water, the black filaments cleared from her eyes. Things became known to her. Other worlds, other places, other times, other lives. Other ephemeras, their purposes so subtle that she could never hope to fully understand them, glistened before her like raindrops on glass. Waiting. Tessa recognized one of them from her own world. Yes, she thought as she passed it, that too had slipped away.

Pain, suffering, joy, love, and hate were all there in the refuse of the Shedding. Tessa felt the quiet push of other people's emotions. There was power to them: the kind of power generated when a river suddenly switches course in midstream. Emotions were all changes of mind and heart.

And with that thought in her mind, Tessa left the place. The truths it harbored were too vast, the secrets it kept too revealing. It was a place of utterness. A crammed void. Tessa didn't want to know and understand it. Like an ephemera, she was just passing through.

Turning away from Shedding and all the knowledge and confidences it held, Tessa stepped onto the darkened road and let the ring lead her back.

Moving through degrees of darkness, back toward the cavern and the pattern and the shadow of herself she'd left behind, Tessa became aware of all the noises and troubles around her. Her wrist throbbed, her back ached. Fumes from the pigments stung her eyes. Far above her, separated by layers of black space, Camron and Ravis fought for their lives. Tessa heard their straining breaths, tasted fear on their tongues, felt sweat and blood roll across their faces. She experienced what they did. And surprisingly, among all the panic and fear, there were instances of joy.

Ravis fought with a heart full of memories. Camron fought with a mind gradually clearing of doubt. They protected each other like brothers: battling side by side, watching each other's backs, sensitive to each other's injuries and weaknesses. As Tessa looked on, she got a sense of something growing between them, a closeness built on spilled blood, shared danger, and growing trust. Both men were hungry for it.

Tessa's throat began to ache. Something rolled down her cheek. Thinking it was another ghost sensation, she ignored it.

As she came back to her body and reaffirmed her grip on her brush, Ravis looked at her. His gaze cut through all the layers and space between them. He knew she was with him. For a quarter second, perhaps less, they were together. Nothing was said, no messages were passed, yet when Tessa turned back to the pattern, she found the beginnings of a new kind of strength.

There was power here, among Ravis, Camron, and herself, and as Tessa began applying paint to the first knotwork panel, she drew on it, shared in it, and gave out all of her own.

Ravis felt Tessa leave him. There for less than an instant, she brushed against his mind, then left. Ravis couldn't decide if she had taken something from him or given something back. He just knew he felt blessed. Tessa was alive and well and had come to no harm.

"Hey! Aren't you supposed to be helping me with this?" Camron put his foot on the massive granite block he had been struggling to move. "Who's stopping to watch the show this time?"

Ravis raised his hands in an admission of guilt. Truth was, from the moment he had first become aware of Tessa's presence, he wasn't sure what he had been doing. Another of the creatures lay dead at his feet, and his sword was wet and dripping blood. Glancing down the steps to the floor below, he saw a dozen more of the things breaking through the barricade of chests, bookcases, stone statues, and doors ripped from their hinges that he and Camron had built minutes earlier. The beasts tore through the barrier as if it were made of tinderwood.

Ravis and Camron stood on the second floor of the keep, at the top of the stairs, in the great gallery that lay open to the floor below. So far they had barely managed to stay ahead of the creatures and slaughtered less than a handful. Ravis' entire body was shaking—with exhaustion, fear, excitement, he didn't know. Probably all three. Camron stood to his right, sweat soaking his undershirt and plastering his hair to his head. Ravis took a quick survey of Camron's wounds, checking that none of the bloodstains on his undershirt and britches had gotten bigger. Satisfied, he came and stood by Camron's side. Together they pushed, kicked, and dragged the stone block to the edge of the stairs.

Weighing more than a good-size millstone, it was dislodged from its position at the foot of the gallery's main window, where it had been placed as a window seat or lookout step. Wet blood helped the block slide along the floor.

Once it was in place, resting on the brink of the top step, they waited for the first of the creatures to break through the barricade and move forward onto the stairs. As they looked on, one creature smashed its shoulder into the last stack of chairs and chests, toppling it over and freeing the way to the staircase. Jaws snapping in triumph, it shot forward. Others came behind it. The air was filled with the sound of their hard, frothing breaths.

Ravis and Camron didn't move. By unspoken agreement, they waited until the stairway drummed with footsteps and the first creature's head was level with the top step. Kicking out at the exact same instant, Ravis and Camron sent the granite block toppling down the stairs.

Slamming into the first creature's chest, it sent its body flying out and down. The creatures behind tried to move out of the way; some succeeded, but most were hit by the block or the falling creature as they crashed from step to step. Bodies bounced down after them; the cracking of skulls and bones was almost indistinguishable from the cracking and splintering of wood.

Camron turned to Ravis and held out his hand. "Eight down," he said, "Less than three dozen to go."

Ravis grinned. He took the offered hand and gripped it hard. "Let's go and find the others." Spinning around, he moved away from the stairs.

"Ravis." Camron halted him. "Do you feel it too?"

"Feel what?"

Camron shrugged. "I'm not sure. It's as if what we are doing is important. It means something."

Feeling his old harrar wound throb against his ribs,

Ravis nodded. Camron was right. By fighting here, together, they weren't just buying Tessa time. They were feeding her strength as well. Unable to find the right words to explain how he felt, Ravis said, "You and I have to keep fighting—that's all I know." It was more than that, a lot more, but Camron seemed to accept what he said.

"Let's go and fight then." Camron glanced down the stairs. Some of the creatures were already recovering, pulling themselves off the floor, their bodies jagged with broken bones. "Those aren't the only creatures in the keep. Others have broken through around the rear."

Ravis nodded, and together the two men made their way across the main hall and through to the gallery beyond. The sound of fighting grew louder with every step. There was no clashing of metal, no ringing of blades, just the dull thud of flesh meeting flesh, high screams, ragged breaths, and cracking floorboards. As they approached a curved doorway, the noise became deafening. Blood spilled from under the door.

Ravis drew his sword. He knew he should be afraid of what he and Camron would find on the other side, but a part of him was eager to face it. It was like fighting for his father's estate all over again. They were being attacked on all sides, the odds were against them, they never knew what they'd be called upon to deal with next. Ravis glanced at Camron. And by his side was a man he was learning to trust.

A wet-throated scream set the door timbers vibrating. Something smashed against a wall. Glass shattered. Camron drew back his foot, ready to kick down the door.

Ravis placed his hand on Camron's arm. "Before we go in there I want to tell you something."

"What?" Camron barked out the word. He was impatient to get to the other side.

"You're not the only one with a claim on Garizon." Ravis increased his pressure on Camron's arm, holding him while he looked into his eyes. "I was married to Izgard's sister. She died without leaving a will."

Camron drew a breath. His eyes shifted color from gray to slate. Cords of muscle strained in his neck. "Why tell me this now?"

Ravis ran a tooth across his scar. He wasn't sure of the answer himself. It had something to do with Tessa, yet there was more to it than that. "I want you to know you can trust me."

Seconds passed. Something massive moved on the other side of the door, causing the stone flags beneath their feet to vibrate. Ignoring the noises filtering through the wood, Camron looked at Ravis without blinking. Finally he said, "Then we are together in this. As brothers."

Hearing Camron's words, something deep in Ravis' chest shifted into place. His eyes stung, so he closed them. When he was ready, he opened them again. Finding himself staring into Camron's face, he nodded once. There was nothing further to be said.

"Right," Ravis cried, turning away. "Let's kick this door down on the count of three. One, two, three—"

Bursting into the archers' gallery, they were met by the sight of blood-sprayed walls, broken swords, and mauled limbs. A creature charged straight at them, claws smeared with tissue from whatever man it had slaughtered last. Behind it came something darker, larger, colder. Walls shook as it moved.

Ravis fought. He fought until blisters burst in his sword hand, until the muscles in his shoulders sizzled with white-hot pain and every part of him was covered in blood. Through it all, through the terror and the pain and the killing, he never lost sight of Camron of Thorn. The man was seldom far from his side.

"Quickly, Ederius. Quickly." Izgard leaned forward over the desk. "I need to know what is happening in Castle Bess."

Ederius managed to nod as he coughed. It took him longer than usual to control the attack, and after it was over the cloth he held to his mouth was speckled with blood. He folded it quickly away. Outside, the sounds of hammering, construction, and rolling carts could be heard as the camp was built around the one tent standing: his own.

"I will work as swiftly as I can, sire," Ederius said, binding the calluses on his painting hand with silk. "Though the gathelocs should have done their work by now."

Izgard exhaled, spraying Ederius' cheek with a fine, milk-colored mist. "Take no chances, scribe. Paint."

Ederius did as he was told, dipping his brush into pigment and letting the first mercury-rich drops bruise the vellum. He had hoped his king would leave him to work on his own, but Izgard pulled up a stool and brought his elbow to rest on the scribing desk, settling down to watch the pattern emerge on the page.

"ome here this minute, Snowy," cried Angeline, too tired to chase after him any longer. The no-good dog had found grasshoppers in the grass and was jumping around like a mad thing, gnashing his teeth, pouncing, bristling, and barking as loudly as he could. Not all the grasshoppers he barked at were actual grasshoppers, though. Some of them were plain old leaves. Snowy didn't seem to care either way. Anything that moved—and was a great deal smaller than him—was fair game.

Snowy here. Snowy here.

Snowy came tearing up to Angeline, tail wagging furiously, tongue out and lolling from side to side. Angeline wanted to be angry at him for running away from the cart before her tent was ready, and making her chase around the campground in the dreary light of dawn, but Snowy looked so funny and happy and just plain doggy that she couldn't even bring herself to frown. What else could you expect from a no-good dog? Besides, it was rather exciting to be out and about so early, watching all the goings-on in the campground.

Spying Ederius' tent in the middle of all the mayhem of carpentry, staves, poles, and piles of folded canvas that would soon become the camp, Angeline found herself wondering about the honey and almond-milk tea she had left for the scribe the previous night. Had he found it? Had he drunk it? Had it made his cough go away? Keeping a tight hold on her hood, lest the wind blow it back and reveal her hair to the surrounding workmen, Angeline made her way toward the tent. She knew Izgard would be angry if he found out about the visit, but more and more these days she cared less and less about her husband and what he might think.

Snowy chased a few more grasshoppers just to prove that he could, then followed along at her heels.

Approaching the tent, Angeline listened out for any signs of activity inside. Sounds of coughing shook the canvas. Not liking the thought of Ederius being sick and all alone, Angeline pushed her way into the tent. Then froze.

Izgard was there, back facing toward the slit, sitting close to Ederius, the Barbed Coil on a pedestal before him.

"Control yourself," Izgard said to Ederius, who was coughing into a cloth. "Finish what you have started."

Snowy growled.

"Ssh," Angeline hissed, letting the tent slit fall closed behind her. If Izgard noticed her entrance, he was too preoccupied to care. His fingers dug into the back of Ederius' chair. The side of his face that was visible to Angeline was lit up by golden light from the crown. A line around his mouth hardened as Ederius continued to cough.

Recognizing the first signs of anger in her husband, Angeline *willed* Ederius to stop. She didn't want him coming to harm.

The scribe rocked back and forth in his chair, his shoulders shaking and his throat pumping out hard, hacking coughs. Angeline hated to hear them and scrunched her face up very tight. At her heels, Snowy was so quiet and well behaved that Angeline wondered if he was actually asleep, eyes open. A few seconds later, Ederius finally brought his coughing under control. Folding away his handcloth, he picked up his brush and continued painting. Breathing a great sigh of relief, Angeline bent and petted Snowy.

"Now," Izgard said very softly to his scribe, "tell me what you saw in the pattern that made you afraid."

Ederius shook his head. When he spoke his voice was so low and weak, it made Angeline's throat ache. "Sire, something is wrong. The girl is painting a pattern. I can feel her knitting pigments around the Coil. She is trying to undo its bindings."

Izgard punched his fist into the back of Ederius' chair, splitting the cross timber in two. "Go after her. Destroy her. Burn the skin off her hands, her arms, her face."

Angeline shivered. Snowy fastened his teeth on to the hem of her skirt, then tugged on it sharply, pulling Angeline back toward the slit.

Let's go. Let's go.

Angeline snatched her skirt away, leaving Snowy snapping air. Snowy was right: they *should* go. But Ederius was very ill and Izgard was very angry, and she wasn't a little girl any longer. And she wasn't going to run away.

Tessa felt her body changing. Close to completing work on the first knotwork panel, she drew shallow breaths and her heartbeat slowed. Sweat stopped trickling down her back and along her neck. Her eyes and mouth grew dry, and her senses retracted, leaving her aware of little but the paintbrush in her hand.

Her body was filling like a waterskin, growing heavier and denser and slower. It became increasingly harder for her to push pigment across the page. Somewhere high above her, Camron and Ravis battled for their lives. Surrounded by a dozen thrashing creatures, they fought with a singleness of purpose that allowed nothing to come between them except their blades. To break them up would have been more difficult than to slaughter them both at once. Tessa felt the power of them; her body gathered it up and stored it, converting it to something else.

As she joined the final two lines on the page, she was aware of a strange taste in her mouth. The ring, which was still on her finger, tightened around her bone. Tessa felt only pressure from the barbs, no pain. Before her, the finished panel hummed with all the tension of a coiled spring. A perfect copy of a copy, ink still wet.

"Emith, I need your knife." The words fell from her mouth like stones. She noticed blood running down her finger from where the ring had broken her skin. "And a clean brush."

Emith was quick to do her bidding, handing her the finest sable brush he possessed. All the time she had been painting, he had been matching pigments. Using only vegetable or animal dyes, he had re-created every color in Ilfaylen's palette. Now, though, Tessa wanted none of them.

She was going to break the first binding with her blood.

Ilfaylen's copy was as dead as stone. Its colors were mineral bright, its vellum had the yellow-and-blue cast of a cadaver. To break the Barbed Coil's bindings, Tessa knew she had to give them life.

Raising a hand that felt heavy as lead, she turned the knife handle until the blade was facing down. As she leaned over the pattern, the ring dug farther and farther into her flesh, itching away at her bone. Blood rolled down her hand and onto her wrist. Still, there was no pain. A slow, thick shudder passed down Tessa's spine. Her body didn't feel like her own anymore.

Swallowing hard, she brought the blade over the panel. Eyes searching out the main thread that bound the knot, she fought the desire to let her arm drop to the floor. She wished she could be sure of what she was doing.

The panel consisted of one large, many-coiled knot, and although several colors meandered through the design, one single black thread held all the tension.

Tessa took the knife and began scoring along the line. When the line weaved through threads of red and gold, Tessa severed them with her blade; when it twisted itself into tight, snaking curves, she slashed along each minuscule fold, pinning them one by one. Like a surgeon preparing to operate, she opened up the panel, drawing back the skin and exposing the raw muscle beneath. The vellum was still in the process of absorbing the wet pigment, and as Tessa's blade traced along the line, it drove the blackness farther and deeper into the vellum. Yet at dead center, where the tip of the blade scored deepest, a thin furrow of pigment was scraped away.

The taste in Tessa's mouth sharpened. Her entire body seemed to condense. Everything—blood, senses, moisture, ligament, and bone—shrank inward like a curling fist. When she breathed, she sucked up more than air. Pigment fumes, fibers, and chalk from the scored vellum raced down her throat and into her chest.

Tessa felt the Barbed Coil. Straining against its bindings

like a god on a leash, it glittered with complete and utter coldness.

It knew nothing of good and evil. It knew only of war.

Blind, powerful, older than both worlds Tessa had walked on, the Coil was a force unto itself. One purpose drove it. One thing fed it. One image alone was reflected in its gold.

Tessa's heart contracted, shifting downward in her chest. A dry, tight sickness shook her to the core.

The Barbed Coil had to go.

Nothing, *nothing* it had done so far, no wars, butchery, bloodshed, or invasions, came even close to all it could do. It could take a world and destroy it.

With a hand too heavy to shake, Tessa picked up the sable brush and dipped its tip into the blood running around the ring. As fast as falling rock, she brought the tip down onto the page, letting her blood flow into the naked furrow within the black.

Everything that had been stored inside her body came out: all the power, love, and brotherhood she had pulled from Camron and Ravis; all the grief she felt over losing Mother Emith and the guilt she bore for failing to save Avaccus' life; all the anger she held toward Deveric and his patterns. And every bit of frustration, pain, and loneliness her tinnitus had ever forced her to bear.

Blood blazing with emotion, Tessa gave the pattern life.

Vellum crackled. Black pigment hissed. Tessa drove her blood into the page, working it into the heart of the pattern; going against every line, curve, and convention Ilfaylen had used to bind the knot. Hot, furious power flowed through her body. Spurting out with her blood, lashing downward with the brush, it tunneled through the parchment like a terrible, fast-moving worm.

Something snapped.

A noise, like an arrow shot, whipped through the air. The cavern shook, sending stones and rock dust spraying from the walls. The air buzzed, ringing in Tessa's ears like a thousand tiny bells. Pressure blasted along her body, then everything stopped.

The first binding was cut. The Barbed Coil was coming unloose.

"Miss! Get back!"

Disoriented, it took Tessa a moment to respond to the sound of Emith's voice. Whipping her head around, she saw Emith standing at the entrance to the chamber. Something was trying to force its way in. Tessa saw an arm thick with muscle and then a claw. A dull thud sounded, and chips of rock fell to the floor by Emith's feet. A hairline crack appeared in the wall directly above the entrance. Whatever was on the outside was too large to fit through the opening and was smashing its way in. Inhaling sharply, Tessa got a whiff of the smell. She recognized it immediately. The stench of the creature in the abbey.

"Miss! Get to the back of the cave. *NOW!*"

Tessa jumped at the command. It was the first time she had ever heard Emith raise his voice. With her last scrap of strength, she edged backward.

The entrance wall shook. Chunks of rock fell away. A great laboring breath sounded as the creature forced its shoulder through the gap. Seeing its seared and bloody flesh, Tessa let out a small cry. The creature was massive, distorted, not human at all. Even as she looked on, it struck out at Emith, ripping its claws along his chest.

"Emith! Come away."

Emith shook his head. Red lines bloomed across his tunic. "No, miss. It has to be stopped."

As Emith spoke the creature blasted the wall with the full force of its body. The cavern shuddered. Tessa's teeth banged together. A huge slab of stone crashed to the floor like a closing gate.

Tessa tried to scramble to her feet. Emith needed help.

"Stay where you are," Emith cried, rifling through the contents of his pack. "It's not going to hurt you. I won't let it."

With that he wheeled around and threw something at the creature's body. It was dark and fluid, and it took Tessa a moment to realize it was ink. The black liquid coated the creature's arm and shoulder, acid falling onto flesh that was already burned. The creature let out a high, piercing cry. Emith snatched the lunular knife from the floor where Tessa had dropped it and began stabbing the creature's arm and shoulder. Tessa looked on closemouthed as Emith flung himself at the creature, striking out time and time again with reckless frenzy, oblivious of the damage he was doing to his own body by driving himself toward the rocks. Tears gathered in his eyes. His lips moved back and forth, and he began murmuring words that Tessa couldn't hear.

Watching him, seeing how his knife hit rock as many times as it hit flesh and his entire body shook with a kind of furious fear, Tessa realized that Emith was no longer in the cavern. He was back in his mother's kitchen, fighting to save someone who could never be saved.

When the creature began to back away, Emith pushed forward, continuing the onslaught. Sobs shook his chest as he fought. Sticking its upper torso dozens of times with his knife, Emith forced the creature back through the entrance and into the tunnel beyond. Tessa thought that would be enough, but it wasn't. Emith followed after.

No longer able to see what was happening, Tessa listened to the sound of feet slapping against stone and the soft gasp of breath. Sobs and animal cries soon blended into one. The entrance wall shuddered from time to time, and drafts of air caused by the moving bodies wafted through the entrance, making the candles flicker. After what seemed like a very long time there was silence. Minutes passed. Tessa strained to hear something, *anything*. Then Emith appeared in the entrance. He held the knife out before him. The blade was bent and misshapen from being driven into stone. Dark blood coated Emith's face, his hands, and his knife. Great strips of fabric had been torn from his tunic, and his hair was ashy with rock dust.

"It won't hurt you now, miss," he said, his voice soft, almost bemused. "I promise."

Tessa dropped her head into her hands. Her shoulders began to shake.

"Miss, please don't cry. It will be all right." Emith rushed across the cavern and knelt by her side. "I'm sorry if I frightened you."

Tessa couldn't speak. How could she say that of all the things she had gone through, nothing disturbed her more than the sight of Emith holding the bloody knife?

"Here, miss." Emith handed Tessa a scrap of cloth. Although he tried to hide it, Tessa felt his hands trembling. "You mustn't let what happened upset you."

Bringing her head up, she said, "I'm sorry, Emith. For everything."

Emith smiled weakly and patted her arm. "It's all right, miss. Really it is."

Tessa noticed that the blade of his knife was now free of blood. Somehow, in the seconds she had spent looking down, Emith had found the time to wipe it clean. It was just like him to clear up a mess straight away. This small observation had a calming effect upon her, and after a while she let Emith guide her back to the pattern and the pigments.

Taking the bent and jagged blade from Emith, she began scoring the vellum. Once again her body built up strength as she worked. When she was ready to use the paintbrush, the ring drew more blood from her finger and she dipped the tip into the fattest red bead and sent it down to the panel, to the center of the knot.

The moment Tessa's blood came in contact with the page, a wave of heat blasted her hand. A pair of wolf eyes winked at her through the vellum. Tessa jerked back. Pain ripped along her arm and up toward her face. She smelled burned flesh. Emith screamed at her to put down the brush, but she didn't want to let go. Someone had to pay for what had happened here tonight. Emith should never have been forced into a situation where he had to stab and kill someone. He wasn't that sort of man. He was kind and gentle and always thought the best of everyone. Now his mother was gone and his life had changed, and someone lay dead by his hand. None of it should have happened. None of it. This wasn't Emith's fight. This was hers. Setting her mouth into a hard line, Tessa went hunting for the wolf in the vellum.

Ederius screamed. His palm flew open and he lost his grip on his brush. A tremor, less pronounced than the one half an hour earlier, shook the tent and the ground it stood on. Automatically Angeline looked to the Barbed Coil. When the first tremor had occurred, the crown seemed to waver, like something seen through the heat of a fire. This time the gold dimmed. The reflections it gave off darkened, and for a moment Angeline thought she saw something monstrous reflected there. When she focused her gaze it was gone.

"Here," Izgard cried, thrusting the paintbrush into Ederius' hand. "Paint! Stop her!"

Ederius nursed his palm. Even from where Angeline stood, she could see the burned meat of his flesh. "Sire," Ederius said, his breath racing, "I cannot—"

Izgard slammed his fist into the back of the chair. Already split into two pieces, the wood fractured and broke apart. Splinters whistled into Ederius' flesh. "Stop her! Stop her! *STOP HER!*"

Angeline stepped back. Snowy stepped right along with her, cowering in the folds of her skirt.

Ederius began to cough. His eyes watered and his skin grew waxy, and his entire upper body began to shake. Blood dotted his robe where splinters had pierced his skin. Angeline winced as he closed his burned palm around the paintbrush. Surely he wasn't going to carry on? But he did. Fighting the spasms gripping his chest, Ederius dipped the brush into the nearest of his pots and drew pigment onto the page.

Angeline clutched the fabric of her skirt. How could Izgard make him work when he was sick?

The scribe's coughing grew worse as he painted, and with his free hand he held a cloth to his mouth to catch spittle. The lines he drew were thick and heavy-handed. When a hail of coughing pumped from his throat, paint pooled on the parchment.

Izgard punched his finger into the spill, then thrust the paint-wettened tip into Ederius' face. "What do you call this?" he said, snatching the cloth from Ederius' mouth. "Take control of yourself. *PAINT!*"

Ederius tried, but Izgard's fury only upset him further and he leaned over the desk, his shoulders shuddering. Angeline twisted the fabric of her skirt. If only Izgard would give him a minute to recover. Seeing Ederius laboring for breath only made Izgard angrier, though, and he pounded the desk with his fist. Spittle flew from Ederius' mouth onto the parchment. Only it couldn't be spittle, because it wasn't clear. It was red . . . with blood.

Seeing what it was, Izgard screamed at Ederius to stop coughing.

Angeline let out a tiny cry. She took a step forward.

Snowy growled: *Stay.*

Ederius' face was turning blue. More blood sprayed from his mouth. He couldn't stop coughing.

Unable to bear it any longer, Angeline rushed over to the desk. Her arm came up and her hand bunched to a fist, and before she knew it, she smashed Izgard in the jaw. *"Stop it!"* she cried. "Leave him alone."

Izgard whipped back his head. Blood trickled from the corner of his mouth, and he wiped it away with his fist. His eyes were etched with gold.

Seeing them, seeing what was and wasn't behind them, Angeline stopped breathing. Her stomach collapsed downward into soft folds. Behind her, she was aware of Snowy making anxious, yelping noises from the area close to the slit.

Let's go. Let's go.

Angeline turned. Even before her skirt started moving to catch up with her body, something exploded against her spine. Joints cracked. The world flashed red and white. Pain streaked across her ribs and back. Stumbling forward, she tried to get away. A shadow fell across her face, a thick breath was sucked in, and then Izgard's fist found her mouth.

Angeline's teeth smashed together. Her bottom lip split, spilling out blood. The room began to spin. Suddenly she didn't know which way was up or down. Toppling sideways, she brought up her hands to protect her belly as she fell.

Please, she thought as she landed badly on her shoulder and hip. Please don't hurt my baby.

In the background, Ederius' coughing grew weaker and more wet sounding. As Angeline struggled onto her stomach, she risked glancing over at the desk. Through vision blurred by tears and punches, she saw Ederius' body sliding to the floor.

Somewhere in the distance, Snowy howled frantically.

Let's go. Let's go.

"I'll teach you to strike me."

Angeline barely had time to work out what Izgard said before pain tore through the back of her skull. Out of the corner of her eye, she saw Izgard pulling something back: it was one of the cracked boards from the back of the chair. It has blood on it, she thought, preferring to look at the board rather than the dark blankness on Izgard's face.

He wasn't going to stop until she was dead.

The board came down again and again, on her shoulders and arms and her ribs. Angeline tasted blood. Dots of light shot before her eyes. Warm wetness ran along her shoulder, pooling in the pit of her arm. The world around her began to fade. Then the board came up one more time, at an angle to catch the soft flesh at her side. Seeing it, Angeline froze. She tried to mouth a prayer, but her words wouldn't come. The board blurred as it came toward her, displaced air that cooled her face.

Tiny paws raced across the chamber. A low, vicious growl sounded, and then something white streaked through the air, heading straight for Izgard's arm. Angeline saw teeth and dog fur and raised hackles.

"Snowy," she cried, tongue heavy with blood. *"Stop!"*

Fur bristling, tail down, eyes bright with purpose, Snowy locked his jaw onto Izgard's arm. Paws kicking air, the little dog shook his head furiously from side to side, teeth sinking deep into king flesh, blood welling over pink-and-black gums.

Izgard dropped the board in midswing. Crying out in anger, he whipped his arm back, trying to shake Snowy off. Frothing at the mouth, Snowy wouldn't let go.

Angeline screamed and screamed for Snowy to come away. Pain was everywhere in her body, but it meant nothing. Only Snowy counted.

Moving back toward the desk, Izgard lashed his arm back and forth, but Snowy's grip held firm. Jaw fixed in place, teeth grinding bone, Snowy lowered his tail.

Snowy here. Snowy here.

Izgard spat out a curse. His face was purple with rage.

Blood welled over his forearm as his body thrashed air. Glancing ahead, he drew back his arm and sent it smashing into the side of Ederius' desk.

Angeline murmured, *"No."*

Snowy's body shot forward, slamming into the wood, back first. A short cry sounded. Bones cracked—lots of tiny ones—Snowy's jaw sprang apart, and his body thudded to the floor. A second passed. The no-good dog made no move to get up. The right side of his skull was strangely flat, and fluid began to leak from his ear.

Close by, Ederius lay motionless.

"Snowy?" Angeline asked. "Ederius?"

Neither answered.

Izgard brought his hand to his chest, rubbing at the tooth-serrated flesh. His eyes were on the Barbed Coil. The crown seemed somehow *less* than it was. It looked almost weightless. Izgard scooped it up in his arms and, without sparing a glance for Angeline, stormed out of the tent.

Angeline let her head slump to the floor. She wanted to close her eyes, but wetness kept getting in the way. The tent was quiet. "Snowy?" she called to fill the silence. "Snowy?"

Knowing no answer would come, yet powerless to stop herself from hoping, Angeline cupped her belly with both hands. And waited . . . and waited . . . and waited. Still Snowy didn't move. After a long while, she shook her head. Such a silly, disobedient, reckless, fearless, no-good dog. And she loved him so much, it tore at her heart.

Struggling to her feet, feeling so much pain in so many places that she found herself oddly detached from it all, Angeline made her way toward the desk. Broken bones slowed her down but did not stop her. First she went to Ederius, laying her hand over his mouth to check for air. There was none, so she closed his eyes and folded his hands across his chest and told him she was sorry many times. His face looked very beautiful, and it seemed to Angeline that he looked younger than he ever had before. Worry no longer creased his brow. She would have liked to lay a kiss on his cheek, but her lip was still bleeding and she didn't think it was right to stain his skin. Ederius had always been so tidy about himself.

Turning away from the scribe's body, Angeline took a breath to steady herself, then looked at Snowy.

The no-good dog looked asleep. Angeline took him in her arms and held him to her chest. He didn't feel like Snowy anymore, more like a pillow stuffed with bones, but she held him all the same. He was warm and his gums were still wet, and a torn-off bit of grasshopper was lodged between his paws. No, Angeline corrected herself, pulling away the fleck of green stuff. It wasn't a grasshopper at all. Just a leaf.

Smiling gently, Angeline put down the little dog. It was hard to pull away. Rising to her feet, she cupped her belly with both hands, trying to fill the emptiness left by Snowy. It didn't go. It *wouldn't* go. It would be with her always.

Biting down on her broken lip, trying to be as strong as Father had taught her, Angeline made her way to the opposite side of the desk.

THIRTY-SIX

Blood drying beneath Ravis' tunic reeked. Something stung his left eye. A blister on his sword hand leaked pus onto the handle of his ax. It made his grip surer. Half a dozen paces ahead of him, Camron traced a line in blood.

They were on the battlements, at the top of the keep, standing beneath the blue-gray sky of a new dawn. One more of the creatures lay dead—his skull cleaved in two by Camron's ax. Camron drew its blood across the flags with the toe of his boot. Ravis knew it would have been *his* blood on the flags if it hadn't been for the quickness of Camron's hand. Cornered, unweaponed, out of breath, space, and time, Ravis saw the blade coming that would tear through his side. He saw his own reflection in the metal. Then Camron, whom he had left searching for weapons on the stairs, was there, burying his ax deep into the creature's skull, stopping the blow in midstrike.

Ravis glanced at Camron. His face was a patchwork of claw marks, bruises, lumps, and scabs. Half his left eyebrow had been torn away, and the eye beneath was leaking blood. Catching Ravis looking at him, Camron gestured toward the line he was drawing. "Standing around doing nothing again, Burano."

Ravis grinned. It hurt quite a bit of his face to do so and reopened at least two scabbed-up wounds, but it was worth it. Camron of Thorn was worth it.

Beneath the ripping of the wind and the crashing of the sea, a third, more insistent sound could be heard: footsteps rising from below. The last of the creatures were coming.

Camron stepped onto Ravis' side of the line and came to stand beside him. Both men weighed their axes across their chests. Ravis didn't know how many of Izgard's creatures were left—after the first dozen slaughtered he stopped keeping count. He didn't know what weapons they would carry or what state they would be in. He just knew that it felt good to be here, with a woman worth fighting for many floors below him and a man worth fighting with an arm's length from his side.

This was all he wanted.

Chewing on his scar, watching the line Camron had drawn across the battlements dry and turn brown in the warm, salty air, Ravis wondered if Malray had been right all along. Perhaps he could never be more than a fighter.

Suddenly that didn't seem like such a bad thing. Maybe, when all this was over, he would send a letter to Malray. Maybe he would ask for a truce.

At that instant, the battlement gate burst open and Izgard's creatures charged onto the roof, pushing the last traces of the night before them. Maws bristling with teeth, snouts notched with bone, they siphoned off the fresh air of the sea and replaced it with a stench all their own.

Ravis and Camron exchanged a glance. They waited until the creatures crossed the line of blood and then came out to meet them.

Tessa drew the last line of blood on the fourth panel. Closing her eyes, she tensed her muscles and waited to feel the impact of the unloosing.

Nothing. The overhead rock creaked once and a small amount of dust tumbled to the floor. The ground didn't shake, the air remained still, there was no sense of anything changing.

Tessa's chin fell to her chest. Glancing at Emith, she said, "I don't understand. All four bindings are broken. Ilfaylen said in his letter that there were four places I needed to be—and I've been to them, yet the Barbed Coil is still here. I can feel it."

Emith made a thinking noise. "Did you do everything the same, miss? Perhaps you ran out of strength."

Tessa shook her head. Power was all around her. It fed the air in the cave. Wherever Camron and Ravis were, whatever they were doing, what emotions they were feeling, were so strong that Tessa could feel them weighing upon her shoulders like a thick winter coat. There was a new source of power, too. Another person—farther away, but still close—changing, fighting, becoming someone else. Tessa's body gathered strength from all three.

But for what? The final binding had been broken. Her work *should* be done.

Tired, frustrated, the burns on her palm jabbing away at her nerves like hot needles, Tessa went to pull off the ring. She couldn't stop her hands from shaking, though, and when she tugged at the gold, the barbs dug deeper into her skin. Fresh blood welled around the base of her finger. She beat her hand against the cavern floor. The ring wouldn't give.

"Miss, come away. Rest for five minutes." Emith tugged at her arm. "Let me bandage those burns."

Tessa's scalp itched. She barely heard the last thing Emith said.

Five minutes.

Five.

Avaccus' words echoed in her ear: *There is power in the number five. Ancient power custom shaped to be used by ancient things.*

Tessa felt as if she were hearing them for the first time. Her pulse quickened. Leaning forward, she looked over Ilfaylen's copy. The scribe believed he had bound the Barbed Coil four times. What if the *entire* pattern itself formed a fifth binding and Ilfaylen hadn't known it?

Throwing back her head, Tessa closed her eyes, took a long deep breath, and counted to five. She had no choice but to carry on. "I need some new pigments, Emith, and a clean brush." As she spoke, she was aware of her voice dragging over the words. She was exhausted. She couldn't remember the last time she had slept. "I'm going to paint another panel. In the center."

"Are you sure it's safe, miss?"

"Whoever was trying to stop me is gone." Tessa shuddered. "Dead."

Emith bit back a small cry. "I'll get the pigments ready."

Tessa waited. She felt her body growing heavier and slower, filling up with strength. Like a magnet attracting metal filings, the ring pulled it in, fastening the power to Tessa's bones, preparing her for the work she had to do. *Paired ephemeras*, Avaccus had said. *The ring is a sister piece to the Barbed Coil and is working through you to free it.* Feeling the base of her finger pulsing, and the barbs scratching away at her bone, Tessa knew he was right. Izgard's scribe had seen the truth of it, too. Her own anger had carried her only so far; the ring had done the rest.

"Here, miss." Emith held out two shells filled with black and gold pigment. "I've made them nice and thin so they'll be easy to work with."

Tessa took the shells from Emith. Seeing him now, she found it hard to believe he had killed the creature only two hours earlier. The blood on his cheeks and beneath his fingernails had gone. The tears in his tunic had either been pinned, patched, or pasted, and the rock dust had been combed from his hair. Yet even though he looked neat and composed, his hands still trembled as he passed Tessa the shells.

The skin on her own hands was taut, burned. Her stomach felt heavy and jagged, like a split stone. Crouching before the pattern, she groped for the image of the Barbed Coil. It came to her immediately, blinding like a glance into the sun. The paintbrush felt awkward in her hand, but despite the burns and the fear and the heaviness, she didn't lose her grip.

The first dot of pigment on the page set the cavern floor rumbling. A band of cool air unsettled the dust. Light from the candles brightened. The crashing of the sea grew louder, more insistent. It sounded like a beating heart.

Drawing power from many sources, eyes darting constantly to Ilfaylen's copy for guidance, Tessa painted. There *was* ancient power in the number five, she could feel it massing in the bones behind her wrist.

Marcel of Vailing always slept well and deeply. When the city of Bay'Zell shook, causing his town house to tremble and his

bed to rock, it only sent him further to sleep. He dreamed he
was lying inside a giant purse swinging from a rich man's
belt. He did not wake. Upstairs, one of his glass-topped
lanterns—still burning due to an oversight by his ravishing
but absentminded maid—fell to the ground and smashed.
Still he did not wake. Nor did he wake when oil-hot flames
spilled over his desk, setting his latest set of figures—a little
chart designed to show his most valued clients that enemy
occupation needn't necessarily have an adverse affect on
their investments—ablaze. Similarly, when flames spread to
the curtains and walls, and the entire top floor filled with
smoke, Marcel continued to sleep like a baby. The rich man's
purse was so very, *very* cozy.

It was only when smoke started pouring beneath his bedchamber door, and flames from the floor above began to tear
through the ceiling, that Marcel finally stirred. And by that
time it was too late.

Black clouds rolled across the sky, turning the thin light of
dawn into night. The earth rumbled, causing partially constructed tents and corrals to collapse. Izgard heard camp
workmen calling to each other, shouting warnings and curses,
speculating over the cause. All agreed it was a bad omen.

The air stank of sulfur. The darkness itself seemed to be
tinged with a yellow cast. Izgard didn't like it. He moved farther from the camp, the Barbed Coil pressed close to his
chest. Men and lords approached him, but he sent them all
away. He couldn't bear to look at them. To meet their eyes for
even half a moment meant shifting his gaze from the Coil.

The barbs drew less and less blood as he walked. The
pain they inflicted became duller and less substantial. And
then there was no pain at all.

Izgard fell to his knees, clutching at his crown. The
Barbed Coil felt as light as a shadow. Its gold edges dimmed
as he watched. Its long, gleaming coils stopped reflecting the
outside world and began reflecting something inside instead.
Something dark and unavoidable, like death.

Thunder crashed down from the sky. The earth Izgard

knelt on buckled and thrashed. Grasshoppers and grassflies took flight. A sound, like the howl of a wild animal trapped belowground in a tunnel or a well, broke through the darkening air.

The Barbed Coil winked once, then slipped away.

"No!" screamed Izgard, tearing at the emptiness it left behind. *"NO!"*

Angeline took the pins from her hair and shook out her golden locks. She undid the ties on her cloak and let it fall to the ground as she walked. Soldiers stared at her. Workmen called to her. One lord offered to accompany her back to her tent. She shook them all off. Perhaps they thought she had been beaten witless by her husband or gripped by sudden madness. She didn't care.

It wasn't hard to walk, not really. One arm and perhaps a rib or two were broken. Other pains in her head and jaw and back bothered her, but she knew Father would have considered it cowardly if his daughter had given in to pain. So she didn't. She hadn't even changed her dress from earlier, but she had cleaned away as much of the blood as she could reach. The water she bathed in turned red rather quickly, and she had avoided looking at it after a while.

The flask she held kept her hands warm as she walked. The lid was on extra tight to keep in the heat of the drink. Angeline wondered why she felt so cold, as the air surrounding her was stuffy and humid, like before a summer storm. She shrugged. Perhaps it was the steel in her Halmac bones.

She walked through the long grass out of the camp. She didn't think of anything as she hiked over banks of crumbling white stone and fields of yellow grain. Thinking only made her weak.

After a while she spotted him, lying facedown in the shade of a beech tree. The Barbed Coil had left him—she knew that even before she got close enough to see. His shoulders were shaking, and odd sounds—not quite words—escaped from his throat. He was covered by many different types of blood, and his fingernails were caked in dirt.

He looked up as she approached. "Angeline?" His voice was soft, distracted. She had brought the sun with her, and he squinted as he looked into her face. "It's gone."

Angeline nodded. "I know."

"Ederius?"

"He is dead."

Izgard closed his eyes. "God forgive me."

Angeline knelt at his side. His eyes were clear now, and it hurt her to look into them.

Raising a hand to her cheek, he said, "My beautiful Angeline. My angel. What have I done?"

His touch was gentle. Angeline felt her body respond to it against her will. She fought herself. "I have brought you something, my lord," she said, indicating the flask. "Some of my special honey and almond-milk tea. I always made it for Father when he was unwell." As she spoke, she took the stopper from the flask, allowing the aroma of honey and almonds to fill the space between them. "I've even brought a cup."

Izgard stroked her cheek, then her hair, as she poured the drink. Tears glistened in his eyes. "Ederius," he said softly. And then: "Did he feel much pain?"

Angeline did not answer. She tried to stop her throat from aching but couldn't. She offered him the filled cup. "My lord," she said.

He looked into her eyes. "Will you not join me in this?"

Everything that was inside Angeline wavered. Breath caught in her throat. Sweat formed like dew on the palm of her outstretched hand. She couldn't think of Snowy and Ederius—the pain was too new, it hurt too much—so she thought of her baby instead. Her free hand came to rest on her belly, and from somewhere she found the strength to meet his eye. "Perhaps I will take a sip later, my lord. Your need is greater than mine."

Izgard hesitated.

"Do you not trust your own wife, my lord?" Angeline asked, holding the cup steady. "I prepared it myself."

After what seemed a very long time, Izgard held out his hand. Their fingers touched for a moment, and then he brought the cup to his lips. He never took his eyes from her as he drank. Angeline held his gaze all the way. Inside her heart was pounding, and a terrible sickness churned away in her stomach, but outwardly she remained calm. For Snowy. For Ederius. For the baby.

When he had finished drinking, Izgard settled himself back in the grass. He yawned.

"Rest now," Angeline said. "I will watch over you while you sleep."

Izgard nodded. He closed his eyes and within minutes he was asleep.

After listening to the rhythm of his breaths for a while, Angeline struggled to her feet. It was time to go. She didn't know how long Ederius' white arsenic pigment would take to work, and she couldn't bear the thought of hearing Izgard cry out in pain. Picking the flask from the grass, careful to get none of the milky fluid on her skin, she replaced the stopper, tucked the flask under her belt, and then turned and walked away.

Through grass fields and into the beech forest, through the forest and onto the salt marshes, through expanding bands of sunlight and warming air, she walked until she could go no farther, until the edges of her broken bones pierced her skin, until the bruise on her jaw swelled up so much that she could no longer open her mouth to breathe, and until the memory of holding Snowy's lifeless body in her arms finally went away. Collapsing amid ghost crabs, tiger moths, and sandwort, on a stretch of salt white soil, Angeline drew her aching body into a ball and settled down to rest. She couldn't go any farther, couldn't think anymore, couldn't decide if what she had done was wrong or right.

Closing her eyes, drifting off into the welcoming darkness, she imagined herself back at Castle Halmac with Father and Snowy, sitting close around the fire, safe and sound. She wished with all her heart she were back there. Gerta was right. No good had ever come to a lady while she was *out-side*.

avis made his way down through the keep. Bodies littered every step and passageway, and he passed none by without checking for signs of life. Pax helped him carry the few who were still breathing. Together they moved the injured men into the kitchen, placing them close to the fire and wrapping them in blankets, seeing that each man got water or brandy, or both. Quickly Ravis showed Pax how to stanch wounds. He wanted to go and find Tessa, check that she and Emith were unharmed, yet somehow there was always one more task to do. Wounds had to be cleaned and wouldn't wait; embedded claws and teeth needed to be picked out by hand; alcohol had to be splashed onto raw tissue, blood vessels cauterized, and skin stitched. Pain had to be eased. These were his men, his troop. They had fought long and hard against all odds, and he couldn't turn his back and leave them.

His own pain was nothing. His tongue and gums had been split, a portion of his cheek had been sliced away, and knife and claw wounds crossed his shoulders and arms. Strange, but the only thing he felt was the scar on his lip. It throbbed against his jaw like a toothache. Thinking perhaps the old wound had been reopened, Ravis brought his hand to his mouth. The knotted scar tissue was dry and unbroken.

"Ravis. Go to Tessa. I'll take care of the men now." It was Camron, appearing in the kitchen doorway. Ravis had left him on the battlements after they'd finished off the last of the creatures. Camron had asked for time alone, so Ravis had gone on ahead.

"Sit, Camron. Let me see to that cut above your eye."

Camron shook his head. "It's nothing." He smiled. "Far better to spend the time on yourself. You look awful."

Ravis smiled back. "That makes two of us, then."

Against Ravis' will, memories of the last fight flashed through his mind. Claws slashing, jaws clicking as they opened wide to tear flesh, and then the sickening crunch of compacted bone as ax heads severed spines. Ravis shuddered. He could hardly believe that he and Camron had made it through.

"Ravis. Go. Find Tessa."

Looking up into Camron's face, Ravis felt a muscle knot in his chest. He wanted to say something to Camron, to hold him there, by the door, and stop time moving forward past this point. They would never be this close again.

After a long moment Ravis conceded to time, nodded once, and left. Camron would take good care of the men. He would not have done once, but now he would.

It was easy to follow Tessa and Emith's trail down through the cellar and into the caverns below. Neither of them had given any thought to concealing their tracks. This struck Ravis as endearing at first, then he spied spots of dark blood upon the rock beneath his feet. Increasing his pace, he raced along the pathway, calling Tessa's name. Sweat was pouring into the gash on his cheek when he finally came upon one of the creatures lying flat on plain of rock, dead. Its legs and lower torso were burned black from walking through the fire set at the gate. Broken arrow shafts jutted from its back and side, sword wounds bit deep into its neck. Still, that wasn't what had killed it. Not quite. Hundreds of small knife cuts over its chest, neck, arms, and flank were what had finally finished it off.

Ravis crouched by the body for a closer look. Some small part of the thing's features had reverted back to what they once were, and he could see the man lying beneath the misshapen bone and swollen gums. His eyes were open, and they were no longer cast with gold. They were brown.

"Ravis."

Ravis looked up to see Tessa emerging from an opening in the rock wall. A clean bandage concealed a wound on her right hand, and the underside of her chin appeared to be burned. She was shaking slightly, leaning against the rock for support. A moment later Emith appeared behind her, and straight away Ravis knew that he had been the one to kill the creature, not Tessa. Something in his eyes had changed.

Quickly Ravis tore away what remained of his sleeve and

placed it over the creature's face. He didn't want Emith seeing it as a man. Better to let him believe he had killed a monster instead.

"You are both all right? Tessa? Emith?" Ravis looked from one to the other as he rose. Each nodded in turn. "And the Barbed Coil?"

"Gone."

Ravis closed his eyes. When he opened them again Tessa was beside him, touching his cheek. He opened up his arms and let her come to him, stroking her hair, feeling the warmth of her body against his. He held her only for a moment, conscious of Emith's presence and not wanting to embarrass him or shut him out.

"Come," Ravis said, touching Tessa one last time as he let her go. "Let's go upstairs."

"I'll just get my paints together." Emith began to move away.

"Leave them, Emith. I'll come down and get them for you later."

"But the brushes need to be—"

Tessa put her hand on Emith's arm. "Let's go upstairs for now. We'll worry about cleaning everything later."

Emith made a small gesture with his hand. "Yes, miss."

Ravis stood in front of the creature's body as Emith and Tessa walked past. Exhaustion was beginning to set in, and he felt his feet dragging as he followed the path up toward the cellar. By the time they climbed the last of the cellar steps and emerged once more into the main body of the keep, pain had begun to cloud his vision. The gash on his cheek stung fiercely. His sword arm ached, and the scar on his lip continued to burn away at the nerve beneath.

Camron sat in the kitchen, close to the fire. Wounded men lay asleep or resting in a loose circle around the hearth. Dead men lay on the opposite side of the room, near the door. Pax was nowhere to be seen.

"He's gone to take a look at Izgard's camp," Camron offered, unasked. "I told him not to draw too close."

Ravis nodded. He pulled out chairs for Tessa and Emith, while Camron brought over a pewter flask filled with brandy. No one, not even Emith, bothered with cups, and all drank from the flask. Seeing Tessa wince as her wounded hand closed around the metal, Ravis fought the desire to go to her and hold her tight. There would be time for that later. For now . . . Ravis' finger trailed along his scar. For now he needed time to think.

He left Tessa and Emith in the kitchen, telling them he was going back to collect Emith's things. Truth was, he didn't know where he was going. Taking a path at random, he found himself in the great gallery. The place smelled of death. Spills of dark blood had run into the mortar cracks between stone flags, into worn depressions on steps, and down along the slanting stonework surrounding the great hearth, where it had collected in a pool around an island of firewood.

Ravis shifted his gaze away from the blood, only to find himself looking at bodies instead. Half a dozen creatures lay scattered around the room, some lying at the foot of the staircase, others close to the tumbled barricade of doors and chairs. Broken bones pierced their skin, arrows jutted from their shoulders and chests. Some had terrible burns on their hands and faces, and others had great chunks of flesh hacked clean away by greatswords. All had slit throats.

Seeing the deep gashes stretching from one side of their jaws to the other, Ravis realized that Camron had done something he had not thought to do himself. He had given these men peace. While he himself had run down to the cellar in search of Tessa and Emith, Camron had moved among the creatures, ensuring that all were dead. From the fresh blood spilled from some arteries, Ravis could tell that one or two had still been alive when Camron came upon them.

Sobered, Ravis took a deep breath and lowered his aching body to the ground. Camron had thought to put an end to the creatures' suffering.

To him they were his countrymen.

After a long, long while, Ravis stood. As he had promised, he went back to collect Emith's scribing equipment. Forcing his body through a slim fissure in the rock wall, Ravis found himself in a small cavern scattered with inks, pens, pigments, and sheets of vellum. Ilfaylen's illumination lay atop a wooden support board in the center of a cleared space. The vellum had been torn in parts, and what might have been a beautiful pattern was ruined by streaks of blood and thumb-prints. Without looking at it closely, Ravis picked it up, held it over the lit candle he had brought with him to light the way, and set it alight. It released the smell of sulfur as it burned. Within seconds it was gone, leaving behind nothing but a band of yellowish smoke and a handful of ashes.

Tired and hurting all over, Ravis gathered Emith's belongings into a sack. As he packed away the last items, his hand came to rest upon a single sheet of unmarked vellum. Glancing to his side, he saw a quill pen cast amid the debris of pigment shells, pigment-stained rags, and broken brushes. He picked it up, turned it in his hand. A minute passed, and then he bit down upon his scar and reached back inside of Emith's pack, looking for a container of ink.

Settling down into the space that hours earlier Tessa had occupied, Ravis wrote a letter. To his brother. It wasn't easy; sometimes he couldn't find the right words, and other times the cut on his cheek stung so much, he couldn't think. Yet he wrote it, and by the time he was finished the burn had left his lip.

I ask for nothing from you, it read, *except that you remember the past. All of it, the good as well as the bad, and the love that was there before the hate. . . .*

Ravis tucked the folded vellum into his tunic, then made his way upstairs.

Pax met him by the door. "The Garizon camp is in chaos," he said. "Izgard is dead."

Ravis nodded. "Any sign of his warlords?"

"I'm not sure. I watched as a whole troop mounted their horses and rode east."

"They've started scrambling for power already," Ravis said. "It won't be long before others follow suit. The Sire and his army should be able to send back those who are left."

"I'm going to ride out and take a look myself." Camron entered the kitchen via the courtyard door. His wounds had been bandaged, and he was wearing a clean tunic. Ravis noticed he favored his left leg as he walked.

"Keep yourself safe," Ravis said to him. "If you're not back within a couple of hours, I'll come looking."

Camron acknowledged the caution with a grin. "You

forget who you're talking to, Burano. I know a thing or two about the land around here." With that he left, slipping out into the courtyard and the bright morning beyond. Seconds later Pax followed him, claiming his own horse needed brushing down, and a moment after that Emith picked up his bags and went the same way, mumbling about fresh water for his brushes and fresh air for himself, and finally Ravis and Tessa were alone.

Ravis came to Tessa and held her close. Touching her soft, pigment-flecked hair and her hot, scorched cheeks seemed like a blessing he didn't deserve. He couldn't let her go. So they stayed together, holding each other, until Camron rode back into the courtyard hours later, safe and excited, calling for everyone to join him outside in the warm light of day.

EPILOGUE

The birch, oak, and chestnut woods of Runzy were beautiful to walk through in the dimming light of a breeze-driven day in midautumn. Leaves crunched beneath Tessa's feet and swirled along with her cloak. Some even got caught in her hair. As she made her way back to the manor house, she found herself feeling for her ring: something about the gold leaves reminded her of ephemeras. Perhaps it was the fact that next time she came here they would be gone.

The ring felt warm and heavy in her hand. Its barbs flashed as they emerged from the darkness of her bodice. Satisfied that all was as it should be, Tessa tucked the ring back into place and moved on.

Emerging from the woods to the cleared area surrounding Camron's manor house, she spied Camron and Ravis on the steps. Ravis spotted her instantly and waved. Tessa felt her heart jump a little as she returned the gesture. She had so much to be grateful for. Walking suddenly seemed too slow, and she burst into a run, hoisting her long skirts around her knees and making for the manor house as fast as she could.

Camron grinned as she approached. Ravis flat-out laughed. Doubtless she was breaking all sorts of rules of conduct by running in the company of men. Not caring one whit about that, Tessa came and sat by Ravis' side. He made a space for her and hugged her close, then whispered something soft in her ear. Blushing, she jabbed him in the ribs. Really! How could the sight of bare knees have that effect on anyone?

All sorts of papers and charts were laid out on the step between Ravis and Camron. Tessa glimpsed inventories, bills of sale, and maps of Garizon and its borders. Seeing where her gaze rested, Ravis said, "We'll be heading into Garizon before the first snow blocks the passes."

Tessa nodded. She'd known this was coming. After Izgard died from the shock of losing the Barbed Coil, the war had turned inward. The Garizon forces had broken up and returned home. The death of their king, the loss of the Coil, and the bad omen of the earthquake had been nothing compared to the havoc wrought by Izgard's warlords. Fighting among themselves over who would take the king's place, they had raced back to Garizon, each determined to be first to claim the throne. Many bloody battles had been fought since. Thousands of Garizon soldiers were dead.

"We have to do this, Tessa," Camron said, his gray eyes shifting colors as he spoke. "We can't let Garizons go on killing each other."

"Izgard is dead," Tessa said. "Isn't that enough?"

"No. Not anymore." Camron ran a hand through his hair. "It stopped being about revenge for me a long time ago. It's about people now. My people."

Tessa leaned forward and put her hand on Camron's arm. She could hardly believe this was the same man she had met all those months ago in a wine cellar in Bay'Zell. He had changed so much—all of them had, but perhaps he most of all. "Does this mean you're going to try to take the throne?"

Camron shifted his gaze to Ravis. There was a question in his eyes. The two men looked at each for a long time, and Tessa knew that to them, she was no longer there.

Ravis' scar was white in the failing light. His eyes were inky, unreadable. After many minutes he spoke. "I am a fighter, Camron. My brother told me that a long time ago, and whether it was true at the time or whether it became so later doesn't matter anymore. I'm not a man to rule and watch over land. I have all I want here"—Ravis found and pressed Tessa's hand—"and here. . . ." He patted the scabbard containing his knife. "And I will fight with you, at your side, because you are a brother to me, not because I expect to share in your rewards."

Camron looked down. Heavy breaths pumped through his chest, and it was a while before he could control them enough to speak. "If you wanted this—if you wanted to bring peace and rebuild Garizon in your own name—I would stand by you."

"I know." Ravis created silence for those two words to rest in, then said, "But you will do a better job of it than I. You think of Garizons as your own countrymen. I never will. I have no wish for the throne."

The breeze picked up, strewing golden leaves over the steps. Camron caught one in his hand. Closing his fist around it, he stood. "I never knew what it was to fight for myself, for something I believed in, until that night I fought at your side in Castle Bess." Opening his palm, he let the crushed leaf fall to the ground and held out his hand for Ravis to take. "I owe you more than I can ever repay."

Ravis rose and gripped Camron's hand. "There are no debts between brothers."

Camron held Ravis' gaze. He went to say something, then stopped himself, simply nodding once instead. With a short wave of his hand, he turned and made his way back to the house. Ravis watched him go.

Tessa took a deep breath and settled down to wait until Ravis was ready to speak. Surprisingly, it wasn't long.

"I received a message from Malray today," he said, his voice soft, almost puzzled. "He's here. In Runzy."

"He wants to see you?"

"Yes. Violante persuaded him to meet with me. She spoke with him in Mizerico. Told him I was a fool. And that while he was busy plotting some new way to kill me, I had actually spoken up to save him."

"I don't understand."

Ravis made a small gesture with his hands. "I hardly understand it myself. Violante and I spoke so little about Malray. I thought—" He shook his head. "I thought I'd made my feelings clear."

"Perhaps you did." Tessa met Ravis' gaze, and after a moment he looked away. "Is Violante here, with Malray?"

"No. She's in Rhiga. Malray says in his message that she's caught the eye of the Liege's son and is busy being wooed."

Tessa tried not to let the relief show on her face. Just the memory of Violante of Arazzo was enough to make her feel plain and disheveled. Absently she smoothed down her dress. "So will you see him?"

"Yes. Soon." Ravis glanced up at the darkening sky. "Tonight."

"How can you be sure it's safe? It might be a trap."

Ravis leaned forward. "He's willing to come here, Tessa. Unarmed and alone. Remember what you said on *The Mull*? About how Deveric has been interfering with our lives for twenty-one years? Well, it's over now. This could be a new start for all of us: Camron, you . . . me." Something shone in Ravis' eyes as he spoke, and Tessa reached over and kissed his cheek. Scar tissue brushed against her lips.

"Do you still want a portion of Burano land?"

Ravis shook his head. "No. It was never about the estate. I would have fought for anything just to be at Malray's side." He made a small gesture toward the woods. "Autumn leaves, even."

A strong breeze rustled the leaves underfoot. Tessa stood and tugged Ravis up. "Come on. Let's go inside. It's getting dark."

Hand in hand they entered the house. Warm light from the candles surrounded them, and warmth from the fire made their cheeks glow. Emith came dashing over to greet them, a wax tablet in his hand.

"I think I've found something, miss," he said, holding out the tablet to catch the light. "This pattern here, the one with the double row of knotwork, looks similar to the one you were working on just before you broke the first binding in the cavern."

Tessa nodded. "Where did you copy it from?"

"Master Deveric's last painting, miss, the one that drew you to the ring. The pattern's repeated several times: in the border and around the central medallion." As he spoke, he helped Tessa off with her cloak. "It just might be the one."

Tessa took the panel from him and looked at it more closely. A string of S-shaped knots had been etched into the green-black wax. Frowning, she brushed flakes of excess wax from the surface. For the past few weeks she and Emith had been working to find a pattern that would enable her to get in touch with her family back home. She didn't want to go back, but she wanted to let her parents know she was safe. And she needed to say good-bye.

"I've already traced it out in hardpoint, miss. So all you'll have to do is paint."

Tessa smiled. There were times when she thought that killing the creature in Castle Bess had changed Emith, yet it was hard to pin down how. Sometimes he stayed in his room for hours at a time, mixing pigments and binding boars hair onto brushes. Other times he didn't act like himself at all. Last week he had told Pax to stop returning from town with his horse lathered and overworked. Tessa smiled at the memory. Pax hadn't known what to say—though he had gone easy on his horse ever since.

"Have you two got your bags packed?" Ravis was busy building up the fire. "Pax will be wanting an early start in the morning."

Tessa nodded. She and Emith were going back to Bay'Zell. She had decided to spend her time there until Ravis returned from Garizon, and Emith had plans to turn part of his mother's house into a small school and teach local children how to read and write. He didn't say it, but Tessa suspected that one day he hoped to come across a child who was talented enough to be trained as a master scribe, so he could pass on all the knowledge he had gained from Avaccus and Deveric. Tessa hoped very much that such a child would come along. Emith had a lot more to give.

"I'll just see to the last of my things," Emith said, shaking down Tessa's cloak and draping it over a chair close to the fire. "Miss Gerta promised to help me pack the food for the journey. She says that bread should always be wrapped in waxed linen to stop it from turning stale."

Tessa and Ravis exchanged a glance. The old Garizon maid had been in Runzy for less than a month, yet Emith had already taken it upon himself to care for her. She was blind in one eye and her body jerked and trembled as she moved. Watching them together made Tessa's throat ache. Every time Emith opened a door for Gerta or brought her a shawl or a hot drink to warm her blood, it was like watching him with his mother all over again. He was the kind of man who needed someone to care for—nothing had changed that.

Gerta and her mistress were planning on staying in Runzy until it was safe for them to return home to Garizon, so tonight was Emith's last chance to look after the old maid before he left. Tessa's smile was sad as she watched Emith deciding whether to return to his chamber or cross the entry hall to the kitchen. After a little anxious brow furrowing, he took the path to the kitchen: Gerta's domain.

Ravis came to stand by Tessa. "You be sure to keep yourself safe in Bay'Zell," he said, taking the wax tablet from her hand and placing it on a chair. "I don't want anything happening to my wife while I'm away."

Tessa didn't reply. She slipped her arm through his. After all these months she still found it hard to believe she could touch him whenever she wanted. She loved him very much.

Ravis put his palm flat upon her arm, holding it against him. "Come on," he said, moving toward the double doors that led into the great hall. "Let's go and catch up with Camron."

"Hold on a minute!" Both Tessa and Ravis turned at the sound of Pax's voice. The young guard dashed from the kitchen, nearly bumping headlong into Emith, who was heading the opposite way. Pax was carrying a jug of wine that sloshed liquid over his tunic as he moved. A handful of pewter goblets were tucked under his belt. Grinning from ear to ear, he stopped, extracted two goblets from his belt, and poured wine for Ravis and Tessa. Handing Tessa a cup, he tilted his head in the direction of the double doors. "I wouldn't go in there just yet."

"Why not?" Tessa asked.

"Because Camron is in there, asking a certain young lady to marry him."

Tessa glanced at Ravis. "Do you think she'll say yes?"

"Well, according to Bay'Zell law she's his anyway. Anything that washes up on the beaches and sand marshes surrounding Castle Bess belongs to the landholder. Camron found her, he holds the land, so legally she's already his." Smiling, Ravis pushed against the door. "Let's go and find out what the lady herself says, though."

Grinning all the way, Tessa and Pax followed Ravis through to the great hall.

Angeline of Halmac and Camron of Thorn were standing

at the far side of the room, looking out at the courtyard beyond. They were holding hands but pulled quickly apart as soon as they realized they were no longer alone. Seeing Angeline by the window, her face lit up by the setting sun, Tessa marveled at how quickly she had recovered from her injuries. Tessa still remembered the terrible state she was in when Camron brought her back to Castle Bess. She was barely alive, her lips cracked and dry, her body limp and broken. Numerous bones in her ribs and fingers were cracked, and deep gashes marked her shoulders, neck, and back. She was horribly bruised. Although Angeline had fought with all her strength to keep the baby she had been carrying, she lost it two weeks later. The physicians were cautiously optimistic of her chances for having more.

All of them had cared for her. Emith, Ravis, Tessa herself, Pax, and most of all Camron. It was hard not to love her. She was gentle and sweet natured and strangely tough when it came to bearing pain. No one questioned her about how she had come to collapse on the sand marshes that day—Camron wouldn't allow it. Right from the start, right from the very first night he'd stayed awake by her bedside, seeing her through the worst of the pain, he had been fiercely protective of her. He was like a young boy who had found a stray puppy: he would let other people care for her, as long as everyone knew she was his.

They had not spent a day apart in weeks. Tessa had watched their closeness grow. Sometimes, just for fleeting instances when Angeline looked into the flames of a roaring fire, or heard a door slammed shut by the wind or voices raised in anger, Tessa saw a glimpse of something dark and afraid in her eyes. There would be a moment when Angeline's entire body stiffened, then Camron would be beside her, touching her hand, brushing a stray curl from her face, making whatever scared her go away.

"Does no one knock in this place?" Camron asked, eyes twinkling as he turned to greet them. Seeing Pax loaded down with wine jug and goblets, he beckoned him forward. "Come and pour Angeline a cup of wine, Pax, before we lose whatever's left to your tunic."

Tessa noticed Camron's fingers retwining around Angeline's as he spoke. When Pax had poured wine for everyone, Camron leaned toward Angeline and said softly, "Tell them."

Angeline glanced nervously at Camron, then cleared her throat. A long moment passed while everyone waited to hear what she would say. Looking down at the floor, she worked to control a muscle quivering in her throat. Finally she spoke, her voice shy and halting. "I want to thank all of you for taking care of me these past months. All of you. You've been so good to me. I don't deserve it. I feel as if I've been given a second chance." She hesitated, glanced again at Camron, who smiled back at her with such gentleness that Tessa felt a lump form in her throat.

Angeline took a gulp of air and let the rest of her words out in a great rush. "What I actually mean to say is Camron and I are getting married, tonight, before he goes away."

After that everyone in the manor seemed to find their way to the hall. Gerta came and passed out food. Her bad eye was covered by a patch and she couldn't judge distances too well, but Emith was more than happy to help her carry heavy trays loaded with ham and drumsticks and lay bowls of fruit and cheese on tables of her choice. Pax called in the entire troop and spent the good part of an hour devising a series of festive toasts, each one more elaborate than the last. Servants bustled, filling glasses and removing empty trays. One man started singing, and someone else began plucking on a fiddle. Through it all Camron never left Angeline's side. He was very gentle with her, giving her plenty of time and space to speak for herself.

Tessa ate and drank and danced. Like everyone else, she couldn't stop grinning. It was only when she had drained her third cup of berriac that she noticed Ravis was nowhere to be seen. Feeling a small pulse of unease beat in her temples, she set her cup on the nearest table and worked her way across the room.

The entry hall was empty, and the fire was burning low from lack of care. After stopping to pick up her cloak, Tessa approached the outside door. Sounds of merriment from the great hall made it difficult to hear anything outside except the wind. Gently, so as to make no noise, she lifted the latch and pulled open the door.

It was full dark now, and Tessa's eyes needed a minute to adjust. A sharp gust of wind made her blink. She headed down the steps and into the courtyard. All the shutters had been closed, and only thin strips of light escaped from the house. Somewhere ahead a horse snuffled and shook out its mane. Tessa heard the metal fastenings on its bridle jingle. Focusing on the sound, she made out the form of a sleek stallion. Its shanks shone an oily black color in the darkness. Looking past the horse to the stable wall, she saw two figures standing close.

She recognized Ravis straight away. His dark hair was pulled back from his face and his hands were ungloved. The man he was speaking with matched him in height and coloring but was more heavily set. The two men seemed to be involved in a heated discussion, as their jaws worked furiously up and down as they spoke. The stranger made mercury-quick gestures with his hands. The same sorts of gestures that Tessa had seen Ravis make a thousand times.

Tessa's heart thumped in her chest.

It was Malray. Here.

Grabbing the edges of her cloak against the wind, Tessa risked taking a few steps forward. The horse smelled her and stamped its feet. Neither man noticed. Ravis was talking; his right hand moving up from the knife at his waist to his lip. Abruptly Malray shook his head. Tessa heard Ravis raise his voice, caught a brief snatch of a sentence, where the words *father* and *brother* were said. Malray took a step back. His hand fell to his side, and for a fraction of an instant Tessa thought he was about to draw a weapon. The wind died off. Then something happened. The space separating the two men seemed to contract. Both men tensed for a fraction of a second, then somehow they came together. Tessa couldn't tell who was the first to step forward or the first to open his arms. She just saw them fall toward each other, saw their shoulders shaking and the fierce intensity of their first contact. She heard them draw ragged, hungry breaths.

After too brief a moment they pulled apart. Even from where she stood, Tessa saw tears shining in Ravis' eyes. Both men edged back into their own separate spaces.

Tessa turned away. She had intruded upon them long enough.

As she took her first step toward the door, she became aware of something pulling against her neck. The surrounding shadows thickened. A breath of cool air fluttered across her cheek. Gray noises ground against her eardrums, working their way through tissue and bones until they formed a wedge of darkness, like a blind spot, inside her head. Tessa lost seconds. She was aware of nothing except a brief skimming motion, light as a thief's touch, above her collarbone. The stench of sulfur brought her back, banishing the noises and darkness as quickly as they came. Immediately, she brought her hand to her chest.

It was gone.

The ring was gone. The ribbon that held it was hot to the touch, and tiny fibers bristled along its length. Looking at it, Tessa shook her head. Even though she had known for many months that one day the ring would disappear, she hadn't thought it would happen so soon. It seemed so sudden. So final. It felt like the end.

No, Tessa thought, ripping the ribbon from her neck. It wasn't the end at all. It was just another beginning. Crushing the empty ribbon in her fist, she went to wait for Ravis in the hall.

Tessa raised them. She had impaled upon them Tony enough.

As she took her first step toward the door, she became aware of something pulling against his neck. The something, the small everthislsame. A bunch of cool air fluttered across the sheets. She forced herself toward her confusion, working as the memory brought years, and sounds until they formed a window of darkness, like a blind spot, inside her head. Tessa few seconds. She was aware of nothing except a brief shimmering mouth, high in a mist's touch, above her collarbone. The step in at sailor brought her back, hand and the words and darkness as quickly as they came, laminatingly she brought her hand to her chest.

It was gone.

The ruts was gone. The ribbon that held it was not to the touch, and they others trailed along its length. Looking at it Tessa wondered how it was chill? She had labored for many months that one day the rope would disappear, she sought it flowing it would disappear with it, leaving it stranded or emblem. So. chain, it still in life, the sun.

No, Tessa thought, typing the ribbon from her neck. It wasn't the end of it all, it was just another beginning. Chasing the fringe ribbon to her fist, she went to wait for it to grow limp fist.

More J. V. Jones!

Here is an excerpt from
the new epic fantasy adventure by J. V. Jones
A CAVERN OF BLACK ICE
Sword of Shadows
Book 1
On sale March 1999 from Warner Aspect

In Mask Fortress, the Lord Commander's foundling
daughter is haunted by nightmares of ice; in the
Blackhail clanhold, two brothers find their kins-
men slaughtered by swords that draw no blood; at
a remote farm, a hardened warrior leaves
his family to follow a raven's summons . . .

And soon, in a deadly wilderness where nature
and the gods have no mercy, Ash March and Raif
Sevrance must face a harsh challenge, as J. V.
Jones takes readers to the stark beauty, cruel peril,
and incredible magic of the northernmost reaches
of The Known Lands.

Chapter 9

THE DHOONESEAT

Vaylo Bludd spat at his dog. He would have preferred to spit at his second son, but he didn't. The dog, a hunter and wolf mix with a neck as wide as a door, bared its teeth and snarled at his master. Other dogs leashed behind it made low growling noises in the back of their throats. The wad of black curd spat by Vaylo Bludd landed on the first dog's foreleg, and the dog chewed at its own fur and skin to get it off. Vaylo didn't smile, but he was pleased. That one definitely owed more to the wolf.

"So, son," he said, still looking at the dog. "What would *you* have me do next, seems you ill like the plans made by your father?"

Vaylo Bludd's second son, Pengo Bludd, grunted. He was standing too close to the fire and his already red face now glowed like something baked in an oven. His spiked hammer trailed on the floor behind him like a dog on a leash. "We must attack Blackhail while the win is still upon us. If we sit on our arses now we miss our chance to take the Clanholds in a single strike."

Sitting back on the great stone Dhooneseat that formed the center of the mightiest and best-fortified roundhouse in the Clanholds, Vaylo Bludd considered spitting again. With no black curd in his mouth, he worked up a dose of saliva by jabbing his teeth against his tongue. Stone Gods! But his teeth ached! One of these days he was going to find a man to pull them out. Find a man then kill him.

Vaylo Bludd swallowed the spit. He took a moment to look at his second son. Pengo Bludd had not shaved back his hairline in days and a bristling band of hair framed his face. The longer hair at the back, with its braids and twists, was similarly ill tended. Bits of goose down and hay were caught in the matted strands. Vaylo Bludd made a hard sound in his throat. Legitimate offspring were born to complacency and arrogance. You wouldn't see such sloth on a bastard!

"Son," he said, his voice as low as a dog growl, "I have lorded this clan for thirty-five years—a good five of that before you were born. Now I dare say you'd think it boastful of me to point out just how far Bludd has come under my lording, but I say I don't care. I am clan chief. Me, the Dog Lord. Not you, Lord Of Nothing But What I Choose To Give You."

Pengo's eyes narrowed. The hand that held his leather hammer-loop cracked as it curled to a fist. "We have Dhoone. We can have Blackhail as well. The Hailsmen—"

Vaylo Bludd kicked out at the wolf dog, making it jump back and yowl. "The Hailsmen will be expecting us to attack. They'll have that roundhouse of theirs sealed as tight as a virgin's arse the minute we break their borders. Hailsmen aren't fools. They won't be found slacking like Dhoones."

"But—"

"*Enough!*" The Dog Lord stood. All the dogs leashed to the rat hooks skittered back. "What advantages we had here will not be easily got again. They come with a price, as such things do. And it will be for me to say when and if we use such means again. We have Dhoone. Make use of it. Go, take Drybone and as many of those useless brothers of yours as you can muster afore noon, and ride out to the Gnash border and secure it. All the Dhoonesmen that rode away are likely there, and if an attack is going to come then it will more than likely start at Gnash." Vaylo smiled, showing black aching teeth. "While you're out there mayhap you can claim what land you see fit for your steading. I heard it said once that a chief should always house his sons on his borders."

Pengo Bludd snarled. Tugging on his hammer-loop, he raised his hammer from the floor and weighed its limewood handle across his chest. The spiked hammer-head bristled like a basket of knives. Eyes the same color as his father's burned coldly like the blue inner-tongue of flames. Without a word he turned on his heel, his braids and twists swinging out from his skull as he moved.

When he reached the chamber door, Vaylo stopped him with one word. "Son."

"What?" Pengo did not turn around.

"Send the bairns to me afore you leave."

Pengo Bludd snapped his head, then continued his journey from the door. He slammed it with all his might behind him.

The Dog Lord took a long breath when he was gone. The dogs, all five of them including the wolf dog, were quiet. After a moment Vaylo bent down on one knee and beckoned them as near as their various leashes would allow. He tousled them and slapped their bellies and test-ed their speed by grabbing their tails. They snarled and snapped and nipped him, wetting his hands and wrists with their frothy saliva. They were good dogs, all of them.

Unlike most hunters and sled dogs whose fangs were

filed to stop them chewing through leashes and ruining pelts by tearing at game, Vaylo's own dogs still had fangs of full length and sharpness. They could rip out a man's throat on his say. None of them had names. Vaylo had long ago stopped keeping track of all the names of those around him. A man with seven sons, who all had wives and inlaws and children of their own, soon gave up keeping tally on what people were called. What they *were* was the only thing that counted.

Feeling separate pangs of pain in each of his remaining seventeen teeth, the Dog Lord stood. Bones in his knees cracked as they dealt with his weight. The Dhooneseat, carved from a single slab of bluestone as tall as a horse, beckoned him back. Vaylo moved away from it, picking a plain oakwood stool close to the hearth. He was too old for stone thrones and too wary of growing used to them. A bastard learned early that he always had to be ready to give up his place.

Glancing toward the door that his second son had slammed moments earlier, Vaylo frowned. That was the problem with all of his sons: none of them knew what it was to give up their place to another. They knew only the politics of take.

Behind his back, Vaylo could hear the dogs scrapping amongst themselves. He heard the wolf dog's low distinctive growl and he knew without turning to look that the dog was being attacked by the others because of the favor its master had showed it. Vaylo made no move to interfere. Such was the way of life.

So, he thought, stretching out his legs before the fire as he looked around the room, *this is the great Dhoone roundhouse.* Men calling themselves kings had lived here once. Now there were only chiefs.

A smile spread across Vaylo Bludd's face as he remembered the last time he was here. He had not been invited that time either. Thirty-six years ago it was now, in the dead of night whilst Airy Dhoone, the clan chief at the time, and his sixty best men were away. Vaylo slapped his thigh. That bloody guidestone had been murder to move! Old Ockish Bull had ended up with a hernia as big as a fist! And of the other four dozen clansmen who had helped pull it free from the guidehouse, only two were able to move the next day, and none could mount their horses for a week.

Vaylo chuckled. The whole operation had been without a doubt the most misguided, ill-planned, fool-stupid thing fifty grown men had ever conspired to do. They never did get the guidestone further than Blue Dhoone Lake. It was still there today; at the bottom of the copper-tinted lake, resting amid the silt and the sandstone, sunk within three hundred paces of the Dhoonehouse itself.

No one but the fifty knew that, of course. When they returned to the Bludd roundhouse twenty days later, all swore blind that the collection of rocks they arrived with, pulled by a team of mules in a war cart, was none other than the broken-down guidestone itself. Not some quarry-purchased rubble and a bucket of ground glass. And it *had* made such an excellent outhouse . . .

Vaylo Bludd leaned forward on his stool. Those were the days! Jaw was all that counted. Jaw had taken him, a bastard son with only half a name and enemies for brothers, to the chiefship he held today. Take, he had. But it wasn't an assuming, born-to-expect-it kind of take. It was take hard learned and hard won. He hadn't gone to his father for a hand out. Gullit Bludd had said but a handful of words to his bastard son from the moment he acknowledged him as his own. And a good half of them were curses.

Knocking.

The Dog Lord looked to the door. He had been too long alone and his mind had got thinking, and that was never what a Bluddsman was about.

"Enter."

Expecting his second son's children who had arrived from the Bludd roundhouse this morning, Vaylo's gaze was focused halfway down the door when it opened. A man's waist met his eye. Seeing the long white robe and smooth, almost womanish hands, the Dog Lord let out a long hard sigh. If you dealt with the devil, his helpers always arrived soon enough.

"Sarga Veys. When did you get here?"

A tall man with a sallow complexion and womanish eyes entered the room. Although dressed in the plain white robe of a cleric, Sarga Veys was no man of god. "In my own small way, Lord Bludd, I have been here all along."

Vaylo hated the man's high voice and the overly fine shape of his lips. He hated being called Lord Bludd too. He was nothing but the Dog Lord, and both he and his enemies knew it. Suddenly angry, he cried, "Close the door behind you, man!"

Sarga Veys was quick to do his bidding, moving in the loose-jointed way of a man possessing little physical strength. The dogs growled behind his back. Sarga Veys didn't like the dogs, and when he was finished with the door, he moved as far away from them as possible. When he spoke, a tremor that may have been fear, yet Vaylo Bludd suspected was anger, showed itself in his voice. "I see you're making yourself at home, Lord Bludd. The Dhooneseat quite suits you."

A small nod on Sarga Veys' part led the Dog Lord's gaze to the foot of the Dhooneseat, where a thin strip of leather lay on the stone. Vaylo's eyes narrowed. Such a tiny thing, a bit of leather fallen from his braids, yet the devil's helper had picked up on it straightaway. Not for the first time, Vaylo reminded himself to be cautious of this man.

"So," he said, hands patting his belt for his pouch of black curd. "You've been within the Clanholds all along. Tell me, did you stay in the safe refuge of a stovehouse? Or did your master want you closer for the show?"

"I don't think," Sarga Veys said, color rising to his cheeks, "that where I stay is any business of yours."

The dogs found much to dislike in Sarga Veys' tone of voice. Snarling and snapping, they tested their leashes in his direction. The wolf dog began worrying at its tether.

Sarga Veys' mouth shrank. His violet eyes darkened.

"Dogs!" called Vaylo Bludd. "Quiet!"

The dogs became silent immediately, dropping their heads and tails and slumping down onto the cut-stone floor.

The Dog Lord watched Sarga Veys closely. Wondered, for a brief moment, if he hadn't seen the man's throat working along with his violet eyes. That was another thing to remember about devil's helpers: no matter how weak they looked they were seldom defenseless. Sarga Veys was a magic user, Vaylo was sure of it.

"Did you ride here alone, or with a sept?"

"I head a sept as always."

Head? Vaylo doubted that. Protected by one, more like it. Seven fully trained, fighting-fit swordsmen would hardly allow a man like Sarga Veys to lead them. Hard campaigners couldn't stand his type.

"I shall be riding south to meet my master after I've left here." Sarga Veys seemed more at ease now the dogs were quiet. He took a moment to smooth back his fine hair. "I shall tell him, of course, of your great success. Assure him that everything went smoothly, and report that you are well on your way to becoming Lord of the Clans." Sarga Veys smiled, showing small white, but ever so slightly inward slanting, teeth. "My master will be pleased. He has done his part. Now it's up to you to do—"

Vaylo Bludd spat out the wad of black curd he'd been chewing, silencing Sarga Veys as effectively as his dogs. "Your master wasn't the one who planned the raid and took the risks. He didn't cut through the darkness and smoke not knowing what each new step would bring him. His blade wasn't bloodied. His sons weren't risked. His balls weren't froze with the waiting."

"Thanks to my master," Sarga Veys said, his voice dropping a tone lower, "your blades weren't as bloodied as they might have been."

Crack!

The Dog Lord smashed his foot down on the hearth stool, breaking its carved legs like sticks. Across the hearthwell, the dogs shrank back against the wall. Sarga Veys flinched. A muscle in his throat quivered.

"Try any of your foul magics upon me," Vaylo cried, "and as the dogs are my witness you will not leave this roundhouse alive."

Hearing their name spoken, the dogs thrashed their muzzles and snarled, spraying the surrounding stone with drops of urine.

Unable to take a further step back as his heels were

already pushing against the door, Sarga Veys pinched in his lips. "Yes. I see now why they call you the Dog Lord."

Vaylo nodded. "That's me." With the side of his foot, he shoved the broken stool away.

"Well Lord of Dogs, or whatever else you choose to call yourself, you took my master's help quick enough when it suited you. I don't believe your anger caused you to break any stools then. Yet now you stand here at the very hearth he helped you win, issuing physical threats to his envoy in the manner of some common stovehouse brawler." Sarga Veys stepped forward. "Well let me tell you—"

Vaylo cut him short with a fierce shake of his head. "Tell me what you came to say. Then begone. Your voice grates on my dogs. If your master has brought a message, speak it. If he has named a price then name it." As he spoke, Vaylo watched Sarga Veys' face. It wasn't right that a man have violet eyes.

Sarga Veys made a small shrugging motion. He brought his facial features under control, yet it took him a long moment to do so. When he spoke there was still a residue of anger in his voice. "Very well. I bring you no message from my master. When the deal was struck he asked for nothing in return, and continues to do so now. As he said at the time, he wishes only to see the Clanholds under a single firm leadership, and he believes that you are the man to do it. I cannot say when and if he will offer his help again. He is a man with many claims upon his time and resources. I do know, however, that he will be watching your progress with interest. I should imagine he would be quite upset if after all the trouble he has taken, you find the Dhooneseat as comfortable as a padded cot and decide to bed down upon it. There are many clanholds yet to be taken. "

The Dog Lord sucked on his aching teeth. Glancing around the old Dhoone chief's chamber with its huge blue sandstone hearth, its comfortable animal hide rugs and wall coverings, and its smoky isinglass windows, he thought hard upon Sarga Veys' words. They weren't truthful, Vaylo was sure of that, yet there *was* truth in them.

"I have plans of my own for Clan Blackhail and the rest," he said. "And will move upon them in my own good time. I must secure the Dhoonehold first."

A quick smile flitted across Sarga Veys' face. "But of course. My master places great store in your judgment."

Frowning, the Dog Lord crossed toward the door. He had the satisfaction of seeing Sarga Veys shrink away from him, but the pleasure was only fleeting. He really didn't like the man at all. Veys was dangerous. He had a temper better suited to a man with the muscle to use it.

"You'll be on your way now," Vaylo said, reaching for the door. "Be sure to tell your master that the message you came expressly *not* to deliver was heard well and good."

Sarga Veys inclined his head. As he did so, Vaylo realized that the skin on the man's face wasn't as smooth and hairless as he had first thought, just razored with an expert hand.

"I shall tell my master you find the Dhooneseat to your liking," Veys said. "And that you have . . . how should I put it? . . . *longterm* plans to take the Hailhold as well."

Vaylo Bludd came close to hitting Veys then. His face flushed and his fist curled and the bones in his jaw and neck cracked all at once. Smashing the heel of his hand down upon the door handle, he fractured the oak lintel beneath. "Leave!" he cried. "Take your sly half-truths and your mincing halfman ways and get your bony, well-shaved arse off my land."

Sarga Veys' violet eyes darkened to the color of midnight. His face twisted and hardened.

"You," he said, his voice rising higher as he lost control of it, "should watch that dog-muzzle mouth of yours. You're not talking to one of your animal-skinned clansmen now. I came here as a visitor and envoy, and at very least should receive due respect." Stepping over the threshold into the corridor beyond, Sarga Veys turned and faced Vaylo Bludd one last time. "I wouldn't get too comfortable on the Dhooneseat if I were you, Dog Lord. One day you just might turn around and find it gone."

With that Sarga Veys clutched at the sides of his robe, lifting the fabric clear of his ankles, and stalked away.

The Dog Lord watched him go. After a length of time he let out a heavy breath and closed the door. The last thing to remember about devil's helpers was that they were often more trouble than the devil himself.

Crossing over to his dogs, Vaylo slapped his thigh. "What do you think, eh?" he murmured, bending down to rub throats and cuff ears. "What do you make of the halfman Sarga Veys?"

The dogs yelped and growled, tussling for attention and nipping his fingers. Only the wolf dog stood his distance. Sitting close to the wall, its massive shoulders twitching in readiness, it watched the door with orange eyes.

"You're right, my beauty," Vaylo said to it. "The Halfman has told me nothing I don't already know: only fools and children never watch their backs."

"Granda! Granda!" Tiny feet pattered against stone

and then the door burst open once more. "Granda!" Two small children appeared in the doorway, smiling, giggling and shrieking loudly.

The Dog Lord thrust out his arms toward his grand-children. "Come and give your old Granda a hug and help him with these uppity dogs."

The dogs managed something close to a collective groan as the two children raced across the room to Vaylo Bludd. The eldest child, a bright beauty with the dark skin and dark eyes of her mother, giggled madly as she hugged her grandfather with two arms and pestered the huge pony-sized dogs with her feet.

The dogs knew better than to growl at Vaylo Bludd's grandchildren, and allowed themselves to be vigorously petted, teased and called by ignoble names. The children called the wolf dog Fluff! And he answered to it! It was the funniest thing Vaylo Bludd had ever witnessed, and it never failed to make him laugh out loud. He loved only two things in life: his grandchildren and his dogs, and when he had both together in one room he was as con-tent as a man could be. Within a month he would have all his grandchildren here, in the Dhoonehouse safe and sound, where he and and his dogs could watch over them.

As he tousled the hair of the youngest grandchild, a fine black-haired boy who Vaylo secretly thought looked much like himself, Sarga Veys' words preyed upon his mind. *One day you just might turn around and find it gone.*

Vaylo glanced around the chief's chamber, his eye picking out the details of defense: the glint of spiked gratings blocking the chimney flue, the iron clamps punched into the stonework around the windows, and the pullstone lying flat against the wall beside the door;

all emblazoned with the Bloody Blue Thistle of Dhoone. Would his grandchildren be safe here? It was the finest roundhouse ever built, ten times more defendable than the Bluddhouse, yet it was the only thing the Dog Lord had ever taken without jaw. There was shame in that, and Vaylo knew it; the Stone Gods would rather a man win an oatfield with blood and fury, than take a continent with tricks and schemes.

Seventeen teeth ached with a fierce splitting pain as for the first time in his life Vaylo Bludd found himself wondering if he had done the right thing.